THE SOUND IN SILENCE

USA TODAY BESTSELLING AUTHOR

M.L. PHILPITT

The Sound in Silence (Fractured Ever Afters #5)
Copyright © 2023 by M.L. Philpitt

This is a work of fiction. Names, characters, organizations, places, events, and incidents are products of the author's imagination or used fictitiously. Any resemblance to actual events, locations, persons living or dead are entirely coincidental.

Warning: This book contains mature content. Reader discretion is advised.

Cover Designer: Cat Imb, TRC Designs
Editing and Proofreading: Rebecca Barney, Fairest Reviews Editing Services
Formatting: M.L. Philpitt

AUTHOR'S NOTE

The Sound in Silence is book 5 of The Fractured Ever Afters series. This reads as a standalone but for complete background on the characters' lives, you can start with book 1, The Hunt in Elusion which tells the story of Ariella's sister, Della.

Timeline: This book begins when, in the Freedom of Captivity, Flynn and Nico argue in front of Erico. Therefore, this is right before Nico was made Boss and Erico referring to him as an underboss in the beginning is not an error.

This book has content some people may find triggering. You can read the content warning list on the last page.

This book uses Canadian spelling. This means words will have U's in them, "re", or double LL's. (colour vs color, centre vs center, signalling vs signaling, etc.) These are not typos.

For those who struggle to see the light in the dark.
Who find getting out of bed impossible some days.
Who prefer to remain invisible in a world full of chaos.

You are seen.
You are valid.
You are allowed to not be okay all the time.

Sometimes the greatest strength is allowing another to
see your struggles.

— ERICO ROSSI

1

ERICO

Some people come into our lives and change it, even before we realize what they're doing.

That's what Aurora Corsetti is doing to mine. Altering the course of my life in ways I couldn't even begin to predict before today.

Entering Nico Corsetti's office, I'm met with a tense silence as he leads me inside. An air of agitation rolls off him, making the room more stifling, but it's a familiar sensation. Comforting, even, which makes me more curious about the pending conversation, even before we've begun. The few times I've met Nico in the past, he's concealed his emotions, so this tension is unlike him.

When Nico, underboss of Montreal's mob, invited my parents and me to his engagement party, it was a prime opportunity for me to meet his sister, Aurora, who'll be my future fiancée. An arrangement I would only be completing for the benefit of the *Famiglia*. Us meeting for the first time with the distraction of an engagement party seemed less contrived.

Aurora is every bit as classically beautiful as photos showed her to be. She arrived at the party with her head high, which was admirable considering the obvious anxiety radiating from her. When she requested we avoid a swarm of guests, it was nearly laughable because if she couldn't handle her brother's party, she would fail at being my wife.

Her need for 'air' or whatever fucking excuse she gave before running off was met by deaf ears. If it was a game, I had no desire to play. As I later explained, when she was in the hospital after being drugged, our union was a wise move for both families. Other than a few pointless vows, the exchange of rings, and a marriage certificate, I couldn't care less.

My role as underboss keeps me busy, and I'm weeks away from moving into Father's role of Boss. After I wed, he'll be stepping down and handing over complete control of the *Famiglia*, which makes the requirement for an heir more pressing. Getting married is simply the first step in ensuring the organization's leadership continues under our bloodline.

"You can take a seat." Nico gestures to the chairs in front of his ornate, oak desk. It reminds me of mine, with the carvings on the side. At least my future brother-in-law has good taste.

Months ago, he proposed a union between me and his sister to mend past feuds, started long before either of us were born, when his father and their organization's current head, Lorenzo, slaughtered my uncle. On the day of my uncle's wedding to Caterina Bellini—now Caterina Corsetti being Lorenzo's wife—control of the organization shifted to his brother, my father, and soon, me.

Nico claimed it's time to look forward and not at the past, and I agreed to the idea of combining our families. Having no immediate female relatives to wed him or his brother, since our initial conversation happened before he married his wife, Della, it came down to myself and his sister.

So at the party when Aurora took off, I excused myself under the guise of searching for her, which appeased my parents. But instead of turning the way she had, I went left down the hallway and strolled through the Corsetti mansion, thinking about how different it looks from my own, especially after recent renovations.

With the engagement to Aurora planned, my parents moved out of our mansion in the Hamptons, so she and I could make that our home. It'd be more Aurora's than mine though, since she'd be living there, while I stayed in my Manhattan condo, as I typically do since it's close to work, and would only visit on weekends. Nonetheless, the mansion I've called home my entire life is too stifling and old-fashioned for the updated Hamptons beach-style homes now there, so I had it redone. Walls replaced with massive windows, letting in natural daylight and the oceanfront view. New fixtures, fresh white paint, and the bathrooms and kitchens refitted with finer building materials.

"Drink?" Nico offers, gesturing to his sidebar. He certainly needs one, I think, to ease his tenseness.

"Please." I force a smile, granting him a look of ease. Within minutes, I have a glass of liquor in my hand, and I sip it, appreciative of the bourbon's smooth, rich texture.

Nico finally takes his chair, the leather cracking loudly in the silent room. Everything seems louder in silence...especially people.

One woman in particular.

As if the universe wanted me to think about *her*, a large man bursts through Nico's office at that precise second, agitation radiating off him in waves as he explodes at his boss. Nico looks appalled, but I excuse them to talk, amused by the show, even while my head blocks out their conversation, using the few moments to think about a silent woman that has been plaguing my mind for weeks.

Never would I have believed Aurora's need for escape would have led me to *her*. When I walked the seemingly empty hallways, I found one that wasn't.

She stood at the very end, gazing at an abstract painting of mute browns, tans, and white. Its boringness instantly made me want to gouge out my eyes, but thankfully, the woman gained my attention instead.

There was a lot I noticed about her, but the most striking feature was her deep, burnt hair. So bright against the dreary walls, and even more unique against the swarm of blondes and brunettes in attendance. It hung in soft waves, over the back of a jade green dress, which made everything about her seem even more vibrant. The dress was the second thing to capture my attention. A slim gown, curving around hips that demanded to be held, and greeting the floor with her barely-there sways. It was simple and not elaborate, unlike Aurora's gown, which was obviously chosen to make a statement.

It was there that Aurora's absence changed how I'll forever look at the colour green.

It was also there that I realized, twice already, I was comparing this stranger to my future fiancée, all without even seeing her face.

She heard me approach, based on the stiffening of her back. Shockingly, she turned to face me too, and I recall my steps faltering, my heart literally skipping a beat with my stolen breath. Captured by a soft, round face, speckled with the lightest of freckles, a slightly upturned nose and full lips. But her eyes. Those are what I still see in my dreams, weeks later. It was those fucking eyes I got lost in, and was unable to stop gazing at, even later that night, when I learned who exactly she is to the Corsettis. Sapphire blue eyes that widened slightly with my approach, and when I spoke, I expected some acknowledgement within them. Some flicker of unease or curiosity.

But instead, she gave me nothing but silence.

Still, I stood in the silence that dulled the throbbing in my head caused by the party. When I commented on the painting, she gave no response.

It was a strange encounter, lasting about ten minutes, before she returned to the party. Trying to process our interaction, I remained behind for a few extra minutes, and when I also went back, she was nowhere in the crowd. Later at dinner, she was seated by the head of the table, beside Della, and met my gaze for the briefest of seconds before shyly looking away. She never glanced my way again. I knew this for a fact because I couldn't stop looking, even when my mother explained she's Della's sister.

"Sorry about that." Nico's voice pulls me from my memories, right as the distant sound of office doors slamming shut make their way to us. "He's normally not like that."

"It's fine." Whatever to move this conversation along so he can finally explain why I'm here.

Nico requested support with a potential war he was facing, which I almost denied since we're not technically allies yet. It seemed like more of a bother for my soldiers. But with the engagement to Aurora only weeks away, being here might move the engagement along quicker and get it over with sooner, so I chose to come.

"Seems you have your hands full here."

Nico chuckles, but it's not a sound of ease. He's on edge—nervous, which tells me I should be too. For a second, I empathize. It's not a simple task, having to step into the footsteps left by one's father, and we both share that burden.

"You have no idea," he replies, sipping from his own glass. "It's related to what I want to speak with you about actually."

"Oh?" I sit straighter. My movement draws attention to the comforting weight of my Glock strapped to my side. A weapon the Corsettis haven't apprehended out of mutual respect and trust. After all, within three weeks, I'll be this man's brother-in-law.

"First, thank you for making the trip from New York so quickly to aid us. Your support would have been tremendous, but we didn't foresee circumstances turning out how they had. Regardless, your willingness to help is appreciated."

"Of course. That's what family is for, right?" I answer carefully, my grip tightening around my glass.

"Exactly." He pauses, his stare hardening. "Which is what makes this next part so difficult—"

I rest my drink on the edge of his desk, preparing for the news. No one enjoys hearing 'difficult' news, but in this line of work, Nico could possibly be announcing deceit. This feels too close to what Father warned me about. He doesn't approve of this agreement and claims the Corsettis shouldn't be trusted.

"Aurora's return into the family has been...different than what we believed it'd be. She's complicated and didn't take to being Lorenzo Corsetti's daughter well."

What is he saying?

"She's chosen her own path and it's one I can't compete with. Believe me, I've tried."

"Speak plainly, Corsetti," I demand, all the guise of niceties disappearing with impatience. "What are you not saying?"

"That my sister refuses to wed you."

Recalling the woman I met with in the hospital wasn't the same girl I was introduced to at his engagement party, so this isn't all that surprising. There was a new desperation in her, which she didn't bother hiding. Hell, even when we met for the second time at his wedding, she didn't mask her hatred for the circumstances. Something changed in her during the week between his engagement party and his wedding.

"When has that ever stopped a union?" It's a well-known fact that women in mobs don't always get their way, but backroom deals have already been made; therefore, it'd entice a war to break them.

"Because I'm backing her decision," he replies with a firm finality that proves Father's presumptions were correct.

"Think hard about your decision, Corsetti." My warning is blatant. *Decide wisely or we'll have to react appropriately.* "This is twice your family will have fucked us over."

"We're not breaking off the engagement," he continues, his tone leaving little room for argument, if I wasn't already verbally toe-to-toe with the man. "I'm proposing an amendment."

"Intriguing," I reply honestly, my temper de-escalating into unease. Given Aurora is the only Corsetti female, an amendment would be...My mind searches for another family member of equal value but comes up empty. Unless there's long-lost daughters Lorenzo and Caterina have been hiding, whoever Nico offers will be an insult after Aurora.

While Nico blows out a long breath and manages another sip of his drink, I study his body language for leftover nerves—shaking hands, a tight grip—but find none.

"My sister-in-law, Ariella Lambert. You wouldn't know her."

I do know her.

After the engagement party, it was her, not Aurora, who starred in my dreams. I know her—know *of* her—but before now, I didn't have a name to put with her alluring face. *Ariella.* A unique name for the silent, mysterious woman who made me, for the first time ever, feel like I was drowning. Lost for words, unable to breathe, trying to solve the puzzle that is her.

But remembering why she's being mentioned, I end up with numerous questions. "Your sister-in-law, Corsetti? That's pretty cold, even for me. She never asked to become a part of your family when you married Della."

"She volunteered."

Volunteered? The beautiful woman who hadn't spoken a word *volunteered* to be married off. Suddenly, I long to learn more because who would agree to such an engagement? It's one thing for a woman born into this lifestyle to smile and march down the aisle because it's their duty, but it's another for an outsider to willingly do it.

What are they playing at?

"I understand she's not as valuable as my—"

"She's fine," I interrupt, his brows lifting in response to my quick agreement. A protectiveness regarding his pending insult has me biting my own tongue, tapering down the sudden, strange emotion. "Surprised her sister would allow this."

He huffs a snort, his gaze drifting to the door, presumably imaging his wife somewhere beyond it. "They had a few choice words. Della's pissed, yeah, but if Ariella's offering, I accepted in order not to wreck what we've been building between the organizations."

Meaning he didn't want a war he couldn't win.

"Of all the women I thought I'd be offering to you, she was at the bottom of my list. If you don't accept, then—"

I cut him off again. "She's fine. I accept."

He jerks. "Just like that?"

No.

Yes.

Father will be pissed I'm not arguing, but the mystery surrounding Ariella distracted my mind for days after the engagement party. After I finally managed to get her out of my head, Nico's wedding brought all those thoughts back when I watched her walk down the aisle. When I should have been observing the ceremony, I was instead preoccupied by studying her standing up there as Della's maid-of-honour.

Everyone else at that wedding seemed happy for the couple, but Ariella didn't. Her mouth was in a near permanent flat line, but there was no sign of dislike or hostility toward the groom. During their vows, she managed a small smile, and at the reception, she was again smiling with Della. I don't believe it was the couple, but something certainly lowered her mood, and not knowing what—so I could fix it—drove me mad. My parents pushing me toward Aurora to dance saved me from going to Ariella.

"Not just like that," I reply. "I have questions, but to answer yours: a future boss's sister-in-law is still a good match." Others might not think so—Father especially—but she still aligns us with the Corsettis. "If she's volunteered, it'd be insulting to deny her. Agreeing to marry a stranger, move away from her home and to a new country, to be a *Famiglia* wife, is..." I trail off, suddenly reluctant to share my thoughts. *Resilient. Commendable. Enthralling.*

"Yeah," he agrees with a slight smirk. With every passing second, his stress seems to be decreasing. "There's things you should know about her, though. Facts that might change your mind."

Doubtful. Once again, I'm struck with appreciation for Nico because if he believes what he's about to tell me would change my mind, it's admirable not to be hiding it.

"Ariella and Della have had a difficult past, but Ariella more than her sister."

I move to the edge of my chair, dreading his next words, but also anxious.

"Two years ago, Ariella and their mother were in a car accident. Their mother was killed."

Fuck.

"Losing her mother, or the accident itself—something in that event changed Ariella. Now, she only verbally speaks to her sister. She was diagnosed with trauma-induced selective mutism."

That explains why she wouldn't talk to me at the engagement party. It wasn't her being shy, rude, or averse. She *couldn't.*

She lost her mother and her voice in one go. A burning spreads through my body, but I can't identify it. Even glancing at the door behind me, imagining her somewhere beyond it, has me shifting in the chair, needing this conversation to end soon so I can find her.

"So you can see why this adds a challenge?"

It doesn't.

Perhaps it should but I don't care. We'll get through it.

Father will kill me. With me taking his position soon, she'll be a Boss's wife. How will she perform the social duties expected if she's unable to talk?

But she's the very woman who's intrigued me for weeks now. Plagued my mind, my senses, my everything. To deny her offer, to turn away from his proposal, makes me sick to consider.

"She's spent the past few years in a medical centre, which is where their stepfather shoved her after the accident. Recently, she's moved in here so she's still adjusting. My family's doctor has her file, but she's refusing any form of further treatment." He holds up his hands, palms out, like he's defending his own actions. "Ultimately, it's her choice what she does so I haven't pushed. Nor do I know the details of the conversations she and the doctor have had."

"It's fine. I'll get her set up with the *Famiglia* doctor."

"You're okay with this?" he checks, gripping his cup a bit

tighter than before. Like the final offer to still turn away is making him apprehensive again.

"The agreement stands, Corsetti."

He tips his head a fraction in acknowledgement, takes a swig of his drink, and when it lowers back down, two fingers lift to gesture toward me. "You have questions. Go ahead and ask them."

"Not for you. For her. I want to see her."

2

ARIELLA

Being a shadow is great.

It's what I've always been, and what I continue to be. What I appreciate, even. No one looks twice at a shadow when it's blending into the background. Opposite of all the attention Della once received. She's the eldest, smart and beautiful. When we were younger, guys were quickly sucked into her vortex. Back then, I wasn't salty about it because there were times where the thought of having to share so much of myself with another person made me ill.

Which is why there's a benefit to being shoved into the backdrop and ignored.

It's easier to exist in the dark than shine in the light.

The amusing part, in high school, Della despised the attention, and was fine being single and focused on her school work and friendships. Yet, between the two of us, she was the first to be wed. I mean, considering the past few years, it makes complete sense, which is why I'm pleased for my sister.

But it's ironic. Because while she didn't want the attention from guys, I did. To a point. I dreamed of going off to university, meeting my happily-ever-after, starting a life together, and having kids eventually. I fantasized about discovering myself.

In some ways, I suppose, the dream of emerging from the ocean of a lifetime of disappointment to discovering the surface and what life on land has to offer is still tempting.

Moving into the Corsetti mansion after Della got married to the mafia family's second-in-command made my life better and worse. Being away from the medical centre and home with Della is great, but it also brought me into the Corsetti family's fold and all their drama.

With the return of Nico's sister, Aurora, much of the attention has been on her, allowing me to hide again. Able to stick to the background unless Della drags me out or Nico's mother, Caterina, insists on 'getting to know me better.' By now, she must realize I'm not interesting, not like Della. I don't leap in front of bullets to save her son. I simply *exist*.

When they do leave me be, I wallow in bed when the darkness becomes too overpowering, or when exiting the bedroom assigned to me gets too overwhelming to consider.

The very bedroom I'm currently sitting in, staring at the space that's never quite felt like mine. Depending how Nico's current conversation goes, this might not be my room for much longer.

Sending Nico the message I had surprised everyone, including myself. Aurora created a problem by falling in love with her bodyguard, and I solved it by volunteering for an arranged marriage, to the man Aurora was supposed to marry.

Why? Who knows. A method to feel something perhaps. To get away from Della, because as pleasant as it is to be with her again, she's suffocating. While I'm content to remain in my bedroom, lights off, and concentrate on breathing and remaining semi-sane, she's trying to drag me into her light.

It's not wanted, or required.

Maybe it's a way to find the happily-ever-after I always dreamed of, and watched, in a single accident, get robbed from me? Locked beneath Nico and Della's protection, I'll never meet anyone. And really, who'd want to get to know the traumatized, mute woman? This way, getting into an arranged marriage means shackling myself to a man.

Fuck, I'm pathetic.

According to Nico, Erico Rossi, the underboss to the New York *Famiglia*, is as ruthless as they come. Earlier today, Nico brought me into his office for a serious conversation and explained what my offer truly means. Moving to New York, becoming a wife, and requiring to survive in a world I wasn't born into, but rather, forced into. First by Mom's marriage to Stefano De Falco and then by Della, when she willingly stuck around. I suppose, by me too when I agreed to live here. But was there truly a choice?

Perhaps volunteering to wed Erico Rossi my way of thanking the Corsettis for saving my sister and me from a worser fate? One Mom found herself paying. Everyone here has been kind since we moved in, and they've been understanding of my limitations. I'd miss them by leaving.

But I'm drowning.

Della believes my life will worsen amongst the *Famiglia*. Maybe, but maybe not. Perhaps they're the land I've been seeking.

Erico and I initially met by accident. Hiding during Della's engagement party, from the noise and bustle of the guests, he found me studying a painting. I'd snuck away because watching my sister celebrate becoming a wife got too overwhelming. She looked flawless striding through the ballroom on Nico's arm. Her head was held high, she donned a dress that was made for her, and while terrified of messing up in front of others, she made it through.

I was proud of her, but it also reminded me of everything I don't and will never have.

The first time I met Nico, when he visited me in the medical centre for information about our stepfather, I recognized the good in him, despite the criminal life he controls. Even then, his care for my sister shone, but at their engagement party, it was stifling. No man would look at me like he does her, not with my current difficulties. Her sunlight was bursting from her, making the shadows of my darkness even blacker. Consuming me until I slipped out undetected.

When I heard his soft steps approaching me in the hallway I hid in; I knew it was a guy because the oncoming sound didn't have the same pierce of a woman's heel. I assumed Nico, searching for me at my sister's request, but instead, it was the very man I saw being introduced to Aurora.

Erico Rossi from the New York mob family who was slated to be her fiancé.

He was every bit classically handsome up close as he was afar. Night-black hair that was styled neatly, but it only made me curious what it looked like free and unruly. Eyes so dark that stared at me with a burning question in his gaze.

Who are you?

I'd heard it as though he spoke aloud. He stopped beside me and introduced himself. Asked my name, how I was enjoying the party, and if I was okay.

If I was *okay.*

No stranger has ever asked me such a thing, not unless they came donning a lab coat and stethoscope too. For the first time ever, I was silent, stunned, in a manner having nothing to do with my mutism.

When I didn't respond to any of his questions, he never gave up asking more. I didn't even try to talk because there would be no payoff. Within minutes, Erico would return to

Aurora's side and I'd return to being the strange woman in the background.

After a while, he accepted my silence, and for the first time since arriving into the Corsetti's mansion, I *breathed*. Like my mind was an absolute blank slate. Stressors from the past, worries of the present, fears of the future—they all melted away in exchange for absolutely nothing.

Was it that single meeting that had me volunteering to wed him? If so, I'm even more pathetic because that tiny interaction meant so little to him, considering he didn't look at me twice for the rest of the night. His attention, rightly so, returned to his would-be fiancée. The second time I saw him was at Della's wedding. He was a guest and I was the maid-of-honour; that's all. Two people co-existing in one room and nothing more.

The door opens, pulling me from all my musings as Nico fills the doorway. His flat mouth and grim expression make my stomach drop in disappointment. Of course, Erico denied the offer. He nearly had the Corsetti princess, so why would he want the mute sister-in-law? It was a fantasy waiting to happen. A fairy tale I stupidly swept myself into, the same way every storybook princess seems to get themselves closer to the prince, only to have him yanked away.

"He agreed to the union but wishes to speak with you first."

He agreed?

I slide from the bed, my legs wobbling with every step toward the doorway. The large decorative mirror resting against the far wall makes me flinch at my own experience. Both times Erico has seen me, I've been done up for the celebrations, making my current appearance more striking—and not in a pleasant way. Hair that I'm pretty sure I haven't washed in over three days is drawn in a messy, crooked ponytail, and I'm wearing yoga pants and a tank I only remembered to change out this morning.

Well, he should know what he's getting, I suppose.

At the doorway, I pause, staring up at Nico. Other than Della, he's the only one here who's heard my voice, but it was only a single time. With every repeated attempt, the usual tightness chokes me.

Dr. Shappo, the Corsettis' doctor, theorized my trauma is linked to trust, explaining why Della continues to be my safe person. But when Nico showed up at the medical centre that day, searching for ways to save her, my mind granted me use of my voice. Let me trust Nico enough *for* Della.

I force a smile to rid Nico of his pinched expression as he murmurs, "Ariella, I can still end this. The situation isn't your burden to bear, and while you're doing a huge service, I feel guilty."

Making my silent statement known, I step by him and into the hallway, heading for the staircase that'll take me to the main floor and his office. He falls into step beside me, his hands shoved in his front pockets, his shoulders slouched lower than I've ever seen.

"I'm serious. I'll alter the terms and can send him away, but once you meet with him, I'm not sure anything I say will change his mind."

For once, it feels nice to have another person broadcasting their own worries, especially someone so naturally guarded. Halfway down the stairs, I lay my hand on his arm, reassuring him of my decision once again.

He doesn't smile, or really acknowledge me at all. Instead, he's silent as he leads me toward his office. At the doorway, he points to the wall beside it. "I'll be right here if you need me."

I wave him off and open his door, stepping right inside before any sort of emotion other than minor confidence has a chance to creep up. Especially since there's a few others threatening to tear me down: trepidation, self-hatred, doubt, sadness. Name it, I'm feeling it.

I shut the door with my back, my hands weaving together behind me as I stare at the figure across the room. The man perched on the edge of Nico's desk isn't the same friendly face from the party. This time, I think I'm truly seeing New York's underboss. Flat expression, drawn features as he leans against the rich, wooden desk, his legs crossed at the ankle and his arms loose by his side, with his hands perched on the desktop for balance. He's an image of ease, with chilling features that imply everything but relaxation.

His voice only amplifies the emotion. "Come here, Ariella."

The command forces my feet forward. Bowing to men has always left a sour taste in my mouth. Perhaps it explains why Mom's marriage to Stefano made me sick from the moment she announced the engagement. Witnessing his alpha-dog treatment of her was horrible.

But instinct says this isn't the time to be defiant. Not unless I'm turning around and taking up Nico's offer to escape this.

Erico's sharp gaze stalks me, his eyes raking up and down my form. Starting from the mess atop my head, over my bare shoulders, my stomach, and toward my legs. No doubt, questioning his sanity for agreeing to this match. It's okay because I'm doing the same, wondering how I'll *live* with this man.

The same way you do here. In your room, alone, with your head buried in the blankets.

Ah, the voice. My dark voice that visits me constantly. There's comfort in being reminded it's there. Without it, I'd definitely be lost in this interaction.

My spine tingles with an awareness I despise, and my hands curl by side. I feel suffocated. Like I shouldn't be enjoying it, but even with his flat expression, he's making me intrigued.

Interested in seeing how the version of him I first met translates into the present.

In the same breath, I shove the feeling away. Of course, my stupid mind is interested in him, the same way it was from our very first meeting. But this is a wedding of convenience for us both. I'm a stand-in for the Corsetti princess. He'd never be interested in me beyond completing his duty.

When there's about three feet of space left between us, I stop, straightening my back, my chin lifting half an inch to hide my apprehension. The corner of his mouth twitches at whatever's in his head as he continues appraising me. Understandable, considering this marriage is essentially him buying me.

You had to get a man to purchase *you for someone to be interested.*

Sometimes, I hate my brain for being correct, even in its depreciating, grim thoughts.

His head tilts and his hands lift from the desk's surface to instead cross his arms over his chest. His expression remains impassive, which I assume is a positive thing. I think. Do I hope so?

"Hello again, Ariella."

Oh, goodness, is his voice somehow deeper than it was the first time we met?

I bob my head in greeting, hoping Nico explained my limitations, or he's about to get quite the surprise.

"Seems we're about to get to know one another very well."

My mouth presses into a small smile, in response.

"Right." He doesn't seem surprised by my lack of response. If anything, I think I catch disappointment flick through his gaze before he suddenly asks, "Are you a virgin?"

For a second, the abrupt question throws me, but then I recall where I am. Who I'm with. With a straight spine, I shake my head. Lost that to an old high school boyfriend when I was eighteen.

The reminder of such a time is a pang to my heart. Not toward Evan, the guy I dated. Not even sure what happened to him after high school. But more, for the simpler time. A time when I laughed with my friends, composed music regularly, and looked forward to all life had to offer. A time where I dreamed of getting a music degree and becoming a teacher. Of meeting a nice man, and eventually having my own family.

Funny how a single person can alter the course of one's life so badly. If Mom had never met Stefano...

Erico grunts, bringing my focus back to him and the conversation. "Well, I guess that's to be expected."

Is it?

"Are you on birth control?"

I nod. Mom brought me to the doctor right around the time Evan and I began dating. Said she would rather me be safe than sorry. I never stopped taking the pills because I've gotten used to the other benefits.

"Get off it."

I open my mouth, an argument pending, if only I can get my voice to work, but then I remember what my offer of marriage truly means. *I* basically decided this, and Nico re-explained as much.

Heirs.

A notion both exciting and terrifying. Wanting kids is one thing, when I also desired the life that went along with it. Meeting someone, getting married, and then, as our lives permit, starting the family with the man who *chose* me. Getting children in this kind of relationship means our children won't witness their parents in love.

But this might be the only way you ever have children.

Might? Try: this is the only way.

Besides, producing heirs on command is better than nothing, right?

"Ariella?"

Right. He's waiting for a response, while my inner voices are battling back and forth over a decision I can't even make for myself.

I nod.

"You understand why, don't you?" His voice softens, reminding me of the man I met in the hallway.

Another nod.

He stares for a long ten seconds, in which I count each one, never feeling more scrutinized than this second. An experiment he finally decides to examine closer when he pushes off Nico's desk and takes the three strides toward me, standing closer than he was even the night of the party.

Warmth from his body emits and for once, I'm not completely against another person standing so close. He smells good, like something I can't quite place. It's musky and sweet, an odd combination that suits him.

His hand comes into my vision and every instinct demands I shy away. But after today, he'll be allowed to touch me in any way he deems because of the choice *I* made. It's that reminder keeping me still.

He tips my chin up with a single finger, his strength overpowering my will. I'm forced to look into his dark eyes rather than his chest as his thumb strokes gently over my skin. I melt. His calloused thumb feels *right,* even though I convince myself it's only because no one's touched me intimately in many years.

This is fake. You're a stand-in for the real thing.

"Nico claims you volunteered for this arrangement. Is that true?"

Even in his grip, my nod feels weak.
"There was no coercion on his part then?"
No, I mouth, with a slight head shake.
"So what made you of all people volunteer to marry me?"

3
ERICO

There's no room for oversight in my position. Everything is black and white. Roles understood. Performances expected.

Witnessing my parents' relationship gave me the outline of what mine will be. Two people who co-exist, eventually have a child to continue the bloodline, and that's all. There's normality in this kind of connection. The lack of deep feelings mean the *Famiglia* will always come first. A future I expected to put into motion with Aurora, who, after meeting her at the engagement party, I knew would be the ideal woman for my needs. Having no interest in her, we could very easily recreate what my parents have. Emotionless, each of us playing our part. We'd live separately, save for the occasional visit home.

The unexpected variable was *her*.

The redhead that makes my head want to explode and my hands to explore. The silent woman—traumatized, according to Nico—with zero stake in mob politics. Yet, here we are, discussing our union, leaving me tongue-tied and without words as I planned on outlining her future. My thumb strokes her cheek, fascinated as her skin grows a deeper shade with her blush.

She shrugs to respond to my question about why she volunteered herself. A part of me feels cautious, as to why *her*. What game is going on that I'm unaware of? While the other part of me is simply curious as to why she did this. What's in her mind that led to this?

"You have so little stake in your sister's new family, so I was surprised when Nico said you were making this sacrifice." Another shrug in response and I finally drop my hands back to my sides, releasing the skin I could very well grow addicted to touching. "All right then. My position keeps me busy, which I assume you're aware of. This means, you'll be on your own frequently. I'll be living in the city, at my Manhattan condo, and you'll be staying at the Rossi mansion in the Hamptons. A bodyguard will be assigned to you for protection. Understand?"

She nods, her expression blank and devoid of what's in her head. Surely as I recite facts, regret must be creeping up? This can't be the life she desires.

"Eventually, I will need an heir and we will work through that. I'm sure you understand, Ariella, you and I will not be like your sister and Nico."

Romance is too much work. A relationship is simply unfathomable to consider when working in New York's crime district. Relationships demand equality and sharing stories with one's partner, but any woman who's privy to what I do, knows better to ask, and anyone who isn't, shouldn't be knowing.

Again, she bobs her head, her expression remaining unbothered. While her agreement is positive for my needs, it pains me to see her falling so easily, so quickly into it. No fight, no spark... it almost doesn't match the gentle flame buried in her azure eyes.

"One more thing: your medical needs. We'll get your file

transferred to the *Famiglia* doctor and any support, any therapy, can be decided between you and him."

For once, she actually does something. She reaches into her pocket and pulls out a phone, her fingers rapidly flying over the screen before she turns it toward me to read what she typed out.

NO MORE COUNSELLING. I'M OVER PEOPLE
TRYING TO FIX ME. PLEASE.

I smile. Maybe it's her tenacity; the clear determination in her plea. Even if I don't know what she sounds like, I can almost predict the way she'd verbally say that. Throaty and smooth, with a final plea tacked on almost like she didn't want to add it at all.

"Sure thing, Ariella."

Before she has the chance to put away her phone, I yank it from her hands, holding it away so she knows not to bother fighting me for it. I scroll through her apps until finding her contacts and add a new entry with my name and number before giving it back.

"If you need to contact me between now and the wedding, you now have my number to do so. Anytime. Call or text." It's doubtful she will.

The corners of her mouth pull up into a slight grin that seems entirely forced, and I vow right then and there, one day, I'll work for a genuine smile. Not sure why I want it, but I do.

"Do you have any questions?"

An expectant head shake that makes her red hair fly. A stream of sunlight from the window behind us catches on the colour, highlighting her face, making her look younger.

"How old are you?" I demand, suddenly aware of the unknown fact.

Her left hand raises with two fingers held up and her right with one. Twenty-one.

Christ. "Ten years younger than me." A few years past high school, a sister wrapped up in mob life, a mother deceased from a car accident, and soon to be shackled to a man a decade older than her when she's hardly experienced life. This isn't different than marrying Aurora, who's the same age as Ariella, but it feels like *more.* Like a tightness in my chest from the guilt is telling me it's different. Aurora was bred into this life. With Ariella, I sympathize.

"Well," I break my stare with her and manage to walk around her, heading for the door, "I'll speak with Nico about finalizing a few details, including a date, and then..." I stop, tongue dabbing at my dry lips. I don't recall the last time someone's made me feel as uncertain as I do now. Not nervous, but still a sense like I'm about to trip. "Then I suppose I'll see you at the wedding."

I take a step but not toward the door, in the direction I was initially headed. Instead, it's back toward her. I'm close enough to catch the flicker of emotion—of heartbreak—before it's gone. So quick I believe I imagined it as I finally turn away.

My father pinches the bridge of his nose, seething from where he's seated inside one of our clubs. Since Father is days away from retirement, he's been wrapping things up slowly and going from business to business—both legal and the underground ones—and finalizing anything he has his hand in.

"Do you realize the severity in what you have done, Erico? The Corsettis refuse to give you Aurora, so you agree to wed a *no name.*"

That's precisely what I did, but a surge of protectiveness brings my fist down onto the desk's surface, jolting him enough until he drops his hand from his face. "Don't speak about her like that."

Father's eyes narrow, the warning of a man who's slaughtered hundreds. In that moment, I'm pleased to have no brother because if he had another option, I get the sense, it'd be him and not me taking over. "We had the ideal candidate and you choose a *mute* instead. We have no idea her upbringing, her family, if she's even pure or not. How do we know she isn't hiding a child somewhere?"

Every question Father throws my way has my teeth grinding, but I don't argue his points because they're valid considerations, even if they're none I'm entertaining. Not when *she*—the fucking siren—the *sirena*—who's been invading my mind since the first glance will be mine. At least with my ring on her finger and her tucked in my home, I'll get so much of her, my mind will finally be freed.

But Father's days away from stepping down, as per our agreement that with my marriage, I'd also be taking over as *Famiglia* Boss. So, keeping a calm voice, I explain, "She's Nico Corsetti's sister-in-law. We wanted to align with them, and Ariella will still accomplish that."

Father wipes at his forehead before dropping his weight onto the chair's backing. "Months ago, when you announced the deal you and Corsetti struck, I had my doubts. When Caterina Corsetti was supposed to marry your uncle, the Corsettis stole her from us. I never wanted to fix the instability between the two organizations, but you insisted, and I respected your choice. With you running things soon, can't fault you for wanting a clean slate with our northern competitors. But *this*," he pauses, the weight of his word filling the room, "this was a stupid decision."

Pressing my hands into his desk, I lean forward. "If you still trust me to be Boss, then you'll trust this decision. This is a win because whether it be Aurora or Ariella who stands with me at the end of the aisle, we're still aligned with Nico. As for everything else you mentioned, she has no secret children."

Father's lips press together as he takes a long moment to consider my words before finally grunting. "I fucking knew the Corsettis would pull something. That's why I insisted to Lorenzo we move your wedding up, and yet, only weeks away, and they've *still* managed to fuck it up. No matter because while you were in Canada, I was working on a secondary option for you, and with this news you've brought back, it's a good thing I did."

I straighten as he reaches into his desk drawer and pulls out an image, tossing it toward me. It's of a woman, sexy and with a grin that says she's aware of her own looks. Confident, staring right into the camera, her dark eyes promising danger. Long black hair tumbles around her shoulders and melds with the off-shoulder black gown.

"She is?" I flick the photo back toward my father, uninterested in why he has a picture of a stranger.

"A potential wife."

"In a week, I'll have a wife." That was the deal made with Nico. A quick engagement; enough time for Ariella to say goodbye to her sister and for me to get things prepared here. The counter-agreement was that the ceremony would happen in his home, and not here. "Don't need her."

He takes the picture back, studying the woman as though she's an item for sale. "I entertained your agreement with Nico, but given today's events, this woman could be a more suitable candidate. Her name is Vanessa Volkov."

"Volkov," I repeat, my blood instantly icing over. "Of *the* Volkovs? The Russian Bratva. Father, what did you do?"

"Nothing yet," he replies, and instantly, my blood pressure drops a few degrees. "But we can very easily. The Corsettis ruined a connection they want—need—more than us. And don't claim otherwise, because at first sign of trouble, they requested *your* help. Well, we could better benefit having the Bratva on our side. They have weapons I've been dying to get my hands on, son." My father leans forward, his dark eyes brighter and more excited than normal. "Ursin Volkov has already agreed to entertain the concept of an offer. If we make one, and he accepts, Erico, you'd be king of a motherfucking empire. No one in the world would dare oppose us."

The Bratva makes the *Famiglia* look like a joke and even I have to admit that. Two days ago, I might have taken this offer. A dangerous, precarious one, but Vanessa over Aurora *would* be more beneficial, and I trust Father's decisions, even when I've doubted him in the past. All he's ever done in his time as Boss was make the *Famiglia* an organization I'd be proud to lead, and with the Bratva connections...

But that was before a fucking siren with red hair flashed her eyes at me.

The image on his desk evaporates, the woman being swapped out with Ariella. Instead of black hair, I see red. Instead of a dark gown, I'm seeing a jade one.

"I've already agreed to the arrangement. If I turn around and deny Ariella, the Corsettis have full rights to attack."

Father stabs his finger into Vanessa's picture. "If we gain the Bratva, then war will be worth it. We'll have them on our side and can wipe out the Corsettis for good. We'd claim control of Montreal too at that point."

So much power. So much control. It's tempting. Like a ripe apple, waiting to be bit, but I've made my decision. To even consider taking the stranger in the image as my bride makes my stomach churn. To witness the disappointment on Ariella's face when she learns her offer was declined after being accepted. Not when I still have so much to uncover about the woman.

"I said no, Father." Finality rings in my tone. "But we can still marry Vanessa to someone else in the *Famiglia*. Caladin is single." Just the way my cousin enjoys it for his own personal reasons. "I'm marrying Ariella Lambert, as agreed upon with both her and Nico Corsetti in a week. The ceremony will be held in their house, in Montreal, if you and Mother would like to join me."

Father scoffs. "That's it then? I offer you the world and you opt for a mute woman who won't be able to provide what you need."

"Stop," I demand, biting the inside of my mouth until I taste blood, to prevent from saying what I *really* want to. "She'll be fine."

Father laughs, throwing his head back. "Fuck, Erico, please tell me you're not pussy-whipped already. The *Famiglia* will demand your complete attention. You know this."

"And they have it. But just because she's not a Corsetti by blood doesn't mean you have the right to insult her. She'll still be my wife." I pause before admitting, "Father, she *volunteered* to this."

"And?" He rolls his head in a half-shrug. "That's a power play move on her part. After seeing her sister with a mob boss, maybe she wants her own."

Maybe, but the little I know of Ariella tells me that isn't it. I don't *know* why she agreed to the wedding, but I doubt it's for power.

"Or not. Maybe she's simply loyal as fuck, and we could benefit from having that on our side."

Father's eyes roll and he reluctantly re-places the image of Vanessa back into the drawer. "Loyal or stupid. Something feels off about this, Erico."

"Then I'll figure it out," I promise. After the wedding.

He levels his stare. "If you're certain about your decision, you'll be the one telling your mother the wedding she's in the thick of planning for you and Aurora needs to be cancelled."

He tosses his head back because we both know how that conversation will go.

After an annoying meeting with my mother, a meeting with Ariella's future bodyguard, and then a phone call with the mansion's housekeeper, I head from my condo down to the private garage for only Caladin and me, since he lives on the level beneath me. Instead of bed, which is the only place I should be headed after the gruelling day of flying from Montreal to New York, I slide into the front seat of my favourite car, my custom-painted matte black Porsche 918 Spyder.

There's nothing better than the feel of the leather wheel, the rumble of speed as the thin tires fly me over the cement and down the connecting roads, the pure power as everything around me blurs while I speed toward Brooklyn.

Father would kill me if he knew my extra-curricular activities.

Watch me care.

4
ARIELLA

When I was a little girl, I dreamed of this.

Well, not *this* exactly.

I imagined standing in front of a mirror with Della by my side and our mother on my other as they fussed over me. I'd be wearing a large, white wedding dress with a long train. They'd hand me the bouquet of red roses before walking me out to my chosen groom.

Instead, I get the bleaker, modified version of that dream, but really, after the disappointment that my life has become the past few years, this outcome is almost expectant.

Della's arms weave around my shoulders, hugging me from behind. In our reflection, her eyes dim, matching her frown. "Smile, Ariella. Please. A single smile so I'm able to let you go today."

For her, anything. My lips curl up and I search for something cheery to cling to, to force happiness into my heart. "You chose well," I compliment, gesturing to the white dress I'm donned in.

Nico and Erico had agreed to a small ceremony, which I'm

thankful about, though annoyed neither asked me what I wanted. Either way, my decisions would have been the same, so at least Erico and I are on the same page. My plan was to wear whatever semi-decent thing I found in my closet, but at Della's insistence, I found myself dress shopping. She was the one fighting the hardest to get me out of the union, but she begrudgingly accepted it and has instead tried to make me content in any miniscule way she can.

Is happiness even in the cards for me? Truly.

Dress shopping provided a sense of normality I appreciated. Even Aurora accompanied us, showering me with constant apologies. She's the one who refused to wed Erico and she's taking all the blame on my offer, even if it's misplaced.

The dress Della picked out is lovely. A soft, white silk going to my knees and leaving my shoulders bare. My hair's been left down and loose, and my makeup simple. Today's a formality and nothing more.

Della releases me after a final peck on the cheek. "Well, I should go downstairs and let everyone know you're ready. Come down whenever, although I recommend sooner rather than later or else Erico might come hunting for you."

Unlikely.

Either way, I wave as she exits my bedroom and leaves me alone for the last time.

I study the room that's been home for a short time. Since Erico's insisting on leaving for New York right away, I'm already packed and my bags were brought down earlier, returning this room to being the guest room it once was.

When I leave the room, it's with a tug on my heart. This will be the final time I walk from this doorway, walk the halls, descend the staircase. By tonight, it'll be a different staircase, different hallways, and another bedroom doorway.

By the time I reach downstairs, it'll be the beginning of the end. Of nothing. Of losing any meagre chance I *might* have once had for a natural happy ever after as I chase my designed one.

Erico arrived over an hour ago, but I haven't seen him yet. Della said his parents didn't join him, which makes me both terrified and pleased. Terrified because if not today, there will come a time I'll have to meet them. But pleased, I won't have to interact with them quite yet. His cousin, a man no one here has met before, came too.

At the base of the stairs, I study the house, knowing it's one more hallway until the ballroom, where everyone waits. The very room that began all of this. The space Della's engagement party was held in and what initiated Erico and me meeting.

A short walk. A few dozen steps and I'm right there. The arched entranceway showing the makeshift aisle the people in attendance created.

My eyes go to the end. To *who's* at the end.

When Della walked down the aisle, Nico's entire focus was on her. His love for her, his weakness apparent. No one in attendance could question their feelings for one another.

That's nothing like the look Erico is giving me.

Appreciation, sure, as his gaze travels the length of me. He settles on my hair for a beat longer than the rest, and I long to touch it, to shield it from his probing examination.

Checking out his purchase.

Instead, I study the people in attendance as they form an aisle, urging me from one end to my fiancé's side. Rozelyn and Flynn are closest to me. Flynn only watches on and Rozelyn manages a half-smile before glancing at her feet, the relationship between her and everyone else still strained. Beside them, Rosen bobs his head and Aurora's guilt is unhidden. A pinched expression as she mouths, *I'm sorry*, for what's likely the millionth time.

To my right is Caterina and Lorenzo. Lorenzo tips his head in respect as I pass, but it's Caterina's tight expression that holds my attention. Similar to that of her daughter, she glances away from me toward Erico, her glare apparent. Beside them, Rafael's usual smirk is watered down, and Isabelle, who I barely know, simply observes.

Closest to the front is Nico, and he's who gains much of my attention. His head dip is even deeper than Lorenzo's, his expression a mixture of the respect of his parents and the apology of his sister.

Della's at the front, beside the minister, standing as my only bridesmaid and one of the witnesses. She's not hiding her sour expression at all, and for a moment, I feel like laughing, if only my face muscles were working still.

To the right of the minister and Erico is another man. His dark hair is messy, like he's just rolled out of bed. He's expressionless, almost bored, rocking lightly on his feet. That must be Erico's cousin that Della had mentioned.

And finally, I look at the reason behind this entire façade. Erico's gaze still remains flat, but I search for something. Appreciation, guilt—any emotion indicating who I'm about to wed.

I'm by his side much too soon, and take my place between Erico and Della, each representing a time in my life—the past and the future. Giving my back to Della is like literally turning away from my past, but we both know that's exactly what's happening. I'll no longer be Ariella Lambert, the quiet daughter, the silent sister, the shadow. I'll be dragged from my darkness to be Ariella—

My thoughts cut off. Even saying it in my head is unsettling. Ariella Rossi.

In mere minutes, *that* will be my new identity. Wife. American.

I'll no longer be able to exist in the background because I'll be to Erico what Della is to Nico. A mob boss's wife.

My thoughts create a tornado of emotion inside me that I can't breathe through, or escape. My standard gloom is always present and never evading, but it's matched with a feeling of...of concern for my future?

A gentle touch breaks through the thoughts. Erico's fingers brush the back of my hand as his head tilts a fraction in question. His brows follow, and I curse myself for allowing my walls to lower and emotions to spill out for anyone to see.

They're my protection. They're how I was able to go undetected at the medical centre. How I've hid my diagnosis for years from my own sister and the very inquisitive crime family we've moved in with.

"Are we ready to begin?" the minister asks. I nod, and so does Erico. "Very well then."

Thankfully, his speech goes quickly and then it's a matter of the vows. I've written no personal ones and I doubt Erico has either, so the minister goes through the standard vows until it's time for the *I do's*.

That's when I stop breathing.

Erico speaks first, his hands finding mine with those two powerful words. He's likely ensuring I can't escape, but he's also grounding me. Keeping me present through everything he promises me.

Fake, empty promises said for the minister's sake and not mine.

Della reaches forward to hand me a simple, gold band. It's heavy, likely expensive, and I slide it onto the fourth finger of his left hand.

Then it's my turn and the minister repeats himself.

I do, I mouth.

Erico takes my left hand and slides a diamond ring on my

finger, which I lose my breath at. A single large diamond in the centre of a thin, gold band. On either side, smaller emerald jewels.

It's beautiful.

But then I remember who this ring was supposed to go to. No doubt, Erico bought it because it reminded him of Aurora's green eyes. Drawing my hand away, I ignore the weight of his ownership and let it hang by my side and away from view.

The minister has no issue with the fact I hadn't said the words aloud, which tells me someone here warned him of my troubles. He nods with a gentle smile and then seals our agreements with the last officiating statement: "You may now kiss the bride."

Kiss. I hadn't thought about this part.

Idiot, he's marrying you to eventually breed you. Not for your stellar personality.

Erico's hand goes to my hip as he steadies me. He pauses, his eyes searching mine, although I'm not sure what for. Seeking permission? Already gave that the moment I agreed to the union.

This has to happen...so I lift onto my toes because even in the heels, I'm still shorter than him. My hands land on his arms, the rich material of his suit like silk. It's then I realize, the last time I kissed someone was...*Fuck, I don't even remember.* That's how long it's been.

His other hand cups my face the same way he had inside Nico's office last week. With his hold, I'm trapped. He brings me closer and lowers his head.

For some reason, I imagined a chaste, cold peck. An unfeeling kiss to seal the unfeeling marriage about unfold.

That's not what I get at all.

Erico's lips press firmly against mine, soft and melding all at the same time. Almost with a vicious roughness, but I wouldn't refer to this kiss as rough by any means. More like, impactful. Telling. Possessive.

I kiss him back.

The tightly strung nerves in my arms, shoulders, and back decompress with every pass of his lips. My fingers curl in his jacket, not as a way to keep him steady, but more so to avoid me touching him. My lips open a fraction, testing, and I feel the gentle touch of his tongue once before he pulls back.

His dark eyes seem even blacker, the colour expanding most of his eye. He's breathing heavy but I'm...

...I'm *breathing*. Genuine air for what feels like the first time in years.

The minister pronounces us husband and wife, and while those terms should be my focus, they're not. Instead, my mind is too busy reliving that kiss. The way, for even a moment, I stopped thinking about everything else. Stopped feeling anything other than his mouth on mine. Stopped hating myself for just a fucking minute.

Maybe this won't be so bad.

The minister gestures toward a small table a few feet away that I hadn't noticed earlier. He directs Erico and I to sign our names, and without thinking twice, knowing at this point, it's too late to turn back, I etch my signature on the line. Della and Erico's cousin sign as witnesses and then it's done.

A marriage certificate. A wedding officiated. A ring of ownership.

A new name: Ariella Rossi.

5

ERICO

Leaving the Corsetti household was an event that took longer than expected, so by the time the Rossi private plane lifts from the airfield, only a stretch away from where the Corsetti's plane is parked, the sun is nearly set, which means we're technically running late.

Ariella takes the couch across from me and Caladin and pulls her legs up, curling into a ball as she stares at the ground. She doesn't hide her emotions now, or perhaps she's thinking about the goodbye she shared with her sister.

Which was partly the reason leaving had taken so long, but since I was robbing this woman of her entire life—the country she's grown up in, the city she's lived in, her newfound family, and the only remaining survivor of her original one—I wasn't going to rush her out the door.

Besides, the look Della continued to throw my way was a threat alone. *Do not rush this or I'll have your balls.*

Della refused to let Ariella go, but it was Ariella who broke contact. She has less reservations coming with me, which only makes me want to know her reasoning more. Whatever's in her head allowed her to go with less emotional turmoil than I expected.

All the Corsetti women took turns hugging her goodbye while the men spoke with Caladin and me. Nico had a few comments about her protection and well-being but each one of them was cautious to not overstep. Everyone there knows, no matter what they all feel about her now, she's not their concern.

She's *mine*.

I glance at the gold band on my finger, marking me as hers too. A piece of metal I knew I'd eventually wear. Hell, by the end of this month, one way or the other.

I have a fucking wife. Ariella Rossi sounds more right in my head than it should for a marriage that means nothing to me.

When the stewardess from the other end of the plane makes a noise moving around a tray, Ariella jumps. She's barely looked at me since leaving her home. A drive that was prickling with disdain and discomfort as she stared out the window, sitting the farthest from me and my cousin.

Caladin shares a look with me before his attention reverts to his phone. He's barely spoken since we initially arrived to the Corsetti mansion, but I know my cousin well enough to see he's bristling with energy, his unspoken statements about to burst.

With a heavy sigh, I gesture to the back of the plane, to the single, small doorway, and tell her, "There's a room back there if you'd like a nap. Flight's slightly under two hours."

For a moment, it's like she hasn't heard me, but then she rises to her feet and shuffles past us and toward the back of the plane. She enters the small room and shuts the door without looking back.

Once she's gone, Caladin swaps couches from beside me to the one she occupied, grinning. "Well, cuz, your life's about to be interesting."

"Interesting is one way to put it," I murmur, still staring at the door.

"She's barely looked at you since the *I do's*."

"Yeah," I agree, recalling the ceremony. Through it, I couldn't stop thinking about my bride. Wondering what her dreams were and how badly marrying me would shatter them. She looked away from the ring fast enough, which I hate to admit was a punch to the gut after I spent all week getting the perfect one custom made. The emeralds beside the classic diamond remind me of the dress she wore when we met.

"Still leaving tonight?"

"Shh. And yes." I haven't told Ariella yet because I'm uncertain if she'll be pleased or not.

We won't have a traditional wedding night, even if our kiss made me second-guess my decision on the matter. It was a kiss I expected to be stiff and cold, but instead, she kissed me back. I swear, something in her turned on because I saw a tiny light as I pulled away. As quick as it was there, though, it was snuffed out. In that second, I made her another silent vow.

To turn that light back on.

If she was so responsive over a kiss, what would she be like in my bed, on her back? No—riding me. Witnessing her take charge of our pleasure; the speed, the depth, the intensity. The image of Ariella bouncing on my cock, her wild hair free, bombards my mind. It's only my cousin's voice that keeps me present before I accidentally go begin our honeymoon in the plane's tiny room.

"Well, I wish you luck on that. Who knows what the heads are gonna demand of you this time."

"You may as well sit in on it too. Fly down with me."

He groans again. "Or I could not, and not subject myself to spending more time with them than I have to. Better things to do than review paperwork."

My brow arches. "Like continuing to fuck your way through New York?"

He shrugs. "You're off the market now, so someone's gotta take charge. Besides, you're leaving your new wife all alone on her wedding night..." He trails off, his salacious grin earning his death—even if I know he's only fucking with me.

My leg darts out and kicks his shin. Between the two of us, he'd win hand-to-hand simply because the guy spends half his life in a gym and the other half in an underground fighting ring. But my kick is sufficient to make my point.

It does based on his chuckle. "Already possessive over her? That didn't take long."

"Whatever," I scoff. "It's not possession when I already own her ass." I lift my left hand, wiggling my ring finger with my point.

"Say that a bit louder, why don't you. She might not have heard you."

My gaze darts to the bedroom, wondering if she's awake or not. Lying there and listening in on this conversation, or if she's unable to hear us over the engine noise.

Caladin's laughter fades when he catches where I'm looking. "Serious talk. You sure about this?"

"Too late now. Paper's signed and everything. Ariella ensures a partnership with the Corsettis. Any attack now means we have our northern partners. You saw them today; she's adored by the entire family. They'll fiercely protect her, Della most of all, and Della has sway over Nico, so they'll never back down from helping us if it means her potential safety. Contrary to my father's beliefs, Ariella's a wise move."

A chess piece. That's all she is to me.

Caladin nods slowly as I speak, digesting everything. "Hm, yeah, I agree. What's her story though? The mutism thing is a bit...interesting."

"None of your business." The last thing I plan on doing is discussing her traumas with him, especially while she's within earshot.

Caladin only chuckles again and glances out the window to his right. "Whatever, cuz. You do you."

When the plane lands under two hours later, I stand to retrieve Ariella from the back. The door hasn't opened the entire flight, and I assume she's fallen asleep.

Caladin walks the opposite way. "I'll ensure her bags get unloaded and will meet you in the car."

Inside the small bedroom, I find her curled up on her side, the blanket pulled over her entire body.

"Ariella."

Nothing.

I gently tug the blanket from her shoulder, revealing her face first, and then the rest of her body. She must feel the difference in air temperature, but if she does, she shows no sign. Strands of her hair lie over her face and I flick them off, revealing what she fell asleep hiding.

Dried teardrops stain her cheeks. Not many, which tells me she didn't cry for long, but still, the sight of them makes my own throat tighten with emotion in a way I've *never* felt before.

I've never felt protective over a woman whatsoever, but despite the situation surrounding our new relationship, I want to keep Ariella safe, for reasons more than the surname she now bears. I want to ensure she doesn't cry again, especially when we both entered the union with eyes wide open.

My finger strokes over her cheek once, then twice, and finally her lashes flutter. Her mouth parts in a small yawn and she stretches. The movement makes her breasts rise from the simple dress she wore for the ceremony. The white is beautiful and in many ways made her red hair bolder, like the green silk had.

"We've arrived."

She blinks up at me, first with a furrowed brow and then with widening eyes, as though forgetting and then remembering all in the same flash of where she is, why she's here, and who I am to her.

Stretching my hand out, I offer her the support to sit, and then eventually stand. She's slow coming up, her arms bending to stretch with her movements. A sleepy but almost genuine smile finds me and I commit it to memory, wondering if this is what she'll look like every morning.

"Come on." I lead her from the plane's bedroom and past the couches, and by the pilot who dips his head in acknowledgment. "Careful on the steps."

The sun's plunged low in the sky, making it dark with a slight glow. The airfield is lit up with the tall lights fixed around so I have faith she won't fall, but still, my pace is slower than normal, ensuring I'm there to catch her tumble if she missteps.

The door to the black town car is already open, and my driver, Matthew, stands beside it. Presuming Caladin is already seated and her bags already stowed in the trunk, I gesture for her to enter first. She does after the slightest hesitation, her gaze skirting the empty field. I wonder if she's thinking about the fact she's no longer in Montreal. Or if she's regretting this now. I wonder everything that's in her head.

And hate that I care.

Caladin's tucked in the farthest corner, head buried in his phone, having claimed the bench behind the driver's seat. Ariella presses herself against the left side of the car, leaving ample space for me.

"Want to be dropped off at the condo?" I offer, my less-than-subtle hint saying my cousin won't be coming home with us.

Caladin smirks without looking up from his phone. "That'll work, sure."

Ariella shows no interest in the hour-long drive from our private airfield in New Jersey to Manhattan. Perhaps growing up in a chaotic city too, she's used to the bustle, the traffic, the honking, and the crowds dangerously walking into traffic in their rush. If it differs at all from Montreal's chaos or if it's quite similar, her expression gives no indication as she keeps a stoic stare out the window and ignores us. I want to ask her if she's ever left Canada before, but don't. Like a deer, I could spook her and then I'll be back at ground zero.

Besides, my wondering needs to end. No more caring about the woman who's merely an accessory. It's all Aurora would have been to me; therefore, it's what Ariella and I *will* be.

When the car finally stops in front of the *Famiglia*-owned condo building Caladin and I both live in, I get out of the vehicle to allow Caladin by. Ariella remains inside, pressing far to the other side.

"Not coming up?" He gestures toward the upper floors.

I shake my head. "She'll be staying at the family mansion. Makes more sense. It's safer and she'll like it more."

In a lower voice, he whisper-yells, "And maintains the distance between you two. Be honest."

I only nod. He slaps me on the arm and heads toward the glass entrance doors, equipped with a doorman, who greets him as he strides inside.

Once seated again, I command Matthew to drive us to the mansion, and Ariella stiffens but doesn't face me.

It makes for a long three-hour drive through the city's traffic and out toward the Hamptons, passing numerous smaller towns on our way. All beautiful and picturesque in their own way. They manage to keep Ariella's attention, as her hands fiddle with the edge of her phone case, composing a rhythmic sound that fills the car. A sound I find oddly soothing.

Once we enter the Hamptons, the houses get more spaced out. Each one large, each one with a huge amount of property. Grass on one side, the ocean waterfront on the other. The Rossi mansion is at the very end, owning a massive stretch of the island, right on the edge of the water.

As we approach, Ariella's expression finally breaks into amazement, making me smile. At least, she'll enjoy her new home. There's a bit of pride that she enjoys where I'm locking her inside. Through any window of the newly-renovated mansion, she's likely to see the ocean so hopefully, she enjoys water.

I could ask her, but her tiny gasp fills the silence, as we drive up the long driveway and around the circular water fountain maintained in the centre of the roundabout. The sound tells me she's mentally present.

"Welcome to your new home."

6

ARIELLA

My first immediate thought is to deny his claim because this isn't my home.

But then my inner voice reminds me, *It is since the moment you sent that text to Nico.*

My second thought is how much nicer Erico's mansion is compared to Nico's. The Corsetti mansion is beautiful in an old-fashioned, dark brick, castle-y kind of way, but Erico's home is downright gorgeous in its modernity. Cut lines, glass windows making up many walls, and yet, I can't make anything out through the windows, telling me they're one-way. And likely bulletproof too, given its occupants.

"It was recently redone," Erico states, gesturing out the car window. "It used to look similar to the Corsetti mansion, a style my parents really enjoyed, but I like to be able to see the ocean easily."

An oceanfront property? Once we hit the sign advertising this as being the Hamptons, it's no different than most of the other houses we've passed. Yet, I don't taper my glee with another dream coming true: to live by the water. It's an expen-

47

sive one I long realized I'd never have. The fantasy of writing music in a large room overlooking the ocean often kept my mind busy.

You have that now. But you shoved yourself onto a man who already owned that life. This isn't an accomplishment.

Any of the excitement making my chest lighter moments ago evaporates in a blink.

Erico climbs out of the back seat and stretches his hand for me to take. I ignore it, instead standing on my own, staring around the wide-open space. The massive property with neatly trimmed grass and the salty scent of the water *right* there. It's visible over the land, against the skyline of the house. Just a couple inches of dark blue, but still, present.

Erico gestures toward the front entrance. "Come. You'll get a tour tomorrow."

Tomorrow. Right. It's our wedding night.

Fuck.

That's the traditional activity, right? Erico put his ring on my finger and now he gets to fuck his vows into me. Consummate the marriage and begin impregnating me.

Based on the sealing kiss of our wedding vows and his overall demeanor, I suspect he fucks well. So many years have passed since the last time I've had sex that I'm sure I'm all dried up now. Hell, his kiss today was the first moment of intimacy in a while. Perhaps that's why it felt so good; it was simply my body reacting to cravings finally being met.

But this feels wrong, and my feet are grounded to the driveway. Having sex tonight crosses something off on his wedding checklist, rather than him wanting it—craving *me*.

Does that matter? That little voice slips into the cracks of my true feelings with that consideration.

After a second, Erico shoots me an annoyed look and

returns to my side, taking my wrist to tug me. His hand feels the same as the ring circling my finger—entrapping and permanent.

He only releases me once we're inside the building, when he pulls me to a stop in front of two people who couldn't be more different from one another. One an elderly, stout woman. Her dark hair is done up in a tight bun and her light blue, summer dress falls nearly to her ankles. She immediately throws me a welcoming smile that eases some of the tightness inside my chest.

Beside her is—I blink. *Holy hotness.* A guy—a man. He doesn't look much older than me, but he's standing pin straight, dressed in a black suit, his hands behind his back, his legs slightly spread. Based on his demeanor, and my knowledge of the Corsetti household, I suspect he's a guard. He watches me, and dare I say it, an appreciation courses through his blue eyes. His blond hair is tucked behind his ears, perfectly groomed.

I look from him to my new husband, whose intense gaze bores into me. The stranger and him are nearly complete opposites as well. While Erico is dark, the stranger is light. Both might be dressed in a suit, but they wear them differently. Erico emits an angry vibe while friendliness radiates from the stranger.

Being mute means observing people, becoming familiar with people's tells, their attitudes, their vibes, all based on their stance, expression, and projection of self.

Erico clears his throat and gestures to the woman. "This is Carlotta. She's my housekeeper and can give you a tour of the grounds tomorrow. Any questions about the house, she'll be able to assist."

Why not you?

Idiot, because he's already stated what life will be like. Two separate lives fused beneath one, miserable household and the vows that bind us.

"Pleasure to meet you." Carlotta smiles warmly.

"And this is Sebastian." Erico motions to the suited stranger, whose grin expands with the introduction. "I've assigned him to be your bodyguard. He will be around the mansion when you are here, will drive you anywhere you wish to go, and will accompany you to those places. I'm sure you've pieced together that my role comes with enemies, so Sebastian will ensure none of them get near you."

"Happy to be of service, ma'am," Sebastian says, his hand stretching toward mine to shake.

Not a fan of *ma'am* as a moniker, but we'll get to that another time. I take his hand, which is so much larger than mine, in a quick shake. When Erico makes a noise, I drop it, his warmth quickly evaporating away, and I instead nod a final greeting.

"For now," Erico cuts in, "I'll show you to our room."

Our room. At least, he's not forcing me to sleep separate from him. That counts for something, right? With his body beside me, my head and heart can be tricked into thinking this is a normal marriage.

Erico leads me toward the twin staircases that curve up the side of the wall to the upstairs level. We take the right side, but my gaze wanders the higher up we ascend.

Wow. The second floor has two halves with a single hallway-bridge connecting them. I glace to our right, toward where a set of double doors hide the rest of the mansion, and then to the left, where I catch the sight of a large bed through the doorway.

Instead of focusing on that though, the height of the second floor allows me to see the massive floor-to-ceiling windows that begin on the floor beneath us and stretch to the very top of the mansion. A huge wall of light pours in, but what mostly catches my attention is the body of water through it.

Breathtaking.

"Ariella." Erico's firm command breaks my stare as he's standing in the doorway to what I presume is the bedroom. He gestures for me to enter first, so I do, marvelling at the same kind of window in it.

When Nico showed me the bedroom I'd be living in, my mind was blown over its beauty. It was larger than any room I've had before, with a lovely view of the grounds outside, and the forest in the distance.

But this...this is ethereal. Double, no *triple,* what I had at Nico's. An apartment on its own. To my right, a sitting area with high back chairs that seem more expensive than the rent I once fought to contribute to. My eyes sweep over them toward the main attraction: the king-sized bed made up of an emerald green bedspread. The bed's wooden posts are dark, stretching high to the vaulted ceiling, where a black canopy acts as a covering.

I've always wanted a canopied bed.

Ironic.

Tearing my gaze away, I inspect the massive space that could fit easily another handful of king-sized beds. The wall across from the bed boasts an electric fireplace and a flatscreen. To the right of the fireplace is two doors, and I wander toward them, peeking inside. A bathroom in one, probably about the size of mine at the Corsetti's, and a closet in the other. Women's clothes hang on one side of the closet, shelves of shoes that probably aren't even my size.

Bought for Aurora most likely.

With that grim thought, I study the opposite side of the closet, lined mainly with dark clothing. Suits and workout gear seem to be the focus, but one thing's obvious: it's men's clothing.

When Erico said we wouldn't be a regular couple, I believed we'd have separate bedrooms. I don't know how I feel about this. Conflicted, mainly, since some part of me is pleased to have this shared space, a place we can attempt to ever be more. But another part of me wishes for my own room, so I can bury my head and be miserable whenever the realization that I've subjected myself to a loveless marriage gets too much.

In a single statement, Erico tosses that entire conflict away. "Most of the time, you'll have this room to yourself. Remember, I mentioned that during the week, I'll be staying at my condo. Being in the city is more convenient for work."

Right. Guess there's no reason for the emotional conflict. There's nothing to feel bad about. No choice. Pretending this is a regular marriage is useless when he won't even be living here during the week. He'll be the stranger who comes home on weekends, fucks his heir into me, and then leaves to do whatever he needs to. I'll be a convenience factor.

Before the self-deprecating thoughts grow again, I turn away to study the far wall. Like my room in the Corsetti mansion, this one too is made up of windows. Dark green curtains are pulled back to reveal the ocean beyond. Water fills the view, and I imagine falling asleep to this. Much better than the forest I once stared at. Gentle waves slosh to the side of the land, kissing the edge, before dipping back down.

Suddenly, Erico speaks but not to me. A murmured short conversation I don't turn around for, and then they're gone, based on Erico's silence.

Then the door shuts and my spine prickles with complete awareness.

Why does this feel like a death march?

I *chose* this and now I have to live with it. Live in unhappiness that I'm not this man's first choice, or even second. Survive through the pain that this will be the only romance I'll ever see, and without him, I wouldn't have any other options.

Sex will be an act. A task that begins tonight to produce his heir. Without feeling and emotion, without either of us actually caring for one another. The beginning to the next chapter of my lonely life.

What did I do?

Erico's footsteps bring him deeper into the room and my eyes flash to the windows. With the setting sun, the windows reveal enough of a reflection, I'm able to watch him come up behind me—not that I need to observe when I feel the sweep of his eyes over my back. With the dress my sister picked, the backing is low so when he sees me roll my shoulders, trying to rid myself of the ticklish sensation, he witnesses my feeble attempt.

He comes up behind me, his heat making my head swim. Or is that nerves? His hand lifts, and he drags a finger down the centre of my spine until reaching the dress's edge. This is where he unzips me, I'm sure. Will he lay me down on that huge bed or will it be done right here, standing?

His touch disappears and—

Thump.

"Your bag."

My attention flies toward my feet, where, sure enough, my single bag of everything I own has been dropped. It only holds my focus for a brief second because the sound of Erico's steps moving farther away steals it.

He walks right to the bedroom doors and just when I expect he'll lock it—lock us in for the night—he instead opens them, pausing in the threshold.

"I have to go down to Vegas for a bit. Might be two nights,

could be a week. Not sure what's happening until I arrive. I can text you, if you'd like."

He's leaving? *Now?* Why does my throat end up in my stomach when this reprieve should be everything I want?

I glance at the bed. A symbol for what should have happened but is now the dividing line between us.

I should feel only contentment, but instead, I'm perplexed with myself.

My mouth opens, and right when I think I *might* actually be able to talk, the voice inside my mind creeps into my consciousness again.

Fear—

Death—

Silence—

It's better to be silent and not witness what you've lost.

The bag at my feet has my phone and it'd be so easy to retrieve it and text him my question, but I don't because my body doesn't allow movement. All I can do is observe as Erico presses his lips together and nods, seemingly accepting the fact I won't respond in any non-verbal method either.

"Make yourself at home. Go anywhere. Do anything, Ariella. Please don't coop yourself up in this room. Before your bag was brought up, I had someone program Sebastian and Carlotta's cell numbers into your phone so you can easily get a hold of them, or simply for conversation. They are both aware you will not speak with them and all my men have been instructed to give you space. Provided they obey, the only soldier you should be seeing over the next few days is Sebastian." He stops, his gaze skirting the room and then finding me. His mouth opens. Shuts. Opens. Finally: "I'm headed right back to the plane. Have a good night, Ariella."

Then he's gone and the door is shut behind him.

He said not to coop myself up in here, but in that motion—

the door shutting with his absence—it feels like *he* has. A single pane of wood blocks me from him—from his escape. From this marriage.

Erico's obviously following the declaration he made the other day and I respect that. This will be the simplest, most non-obligatory arranged marriage ever.

Yet, the blackness creeps over me. Over my vision, my mind...my heart, making me gutted. Hollow and alone.

More alone than normal.

Why did I volunteer for this? I don't know—to find *someone* in this shitty life Mom dragged me and Della into. Maybe I thought Erico could be that person. Maybe that's why as much as having sex out of obligation isn't appealing, a small part of me hoped that tonight could have been the beginning of more.

My legs give out right as I make it to the window, and with my back against the pane, I slide to the floor, drawing my knees up.

I'm so stupid.

Tears form, the burning sensation so familiar, being they're a regular occurrence. I'm the only woman in history crying about the freedom associated with an arranged marriage; yet, they continue to fall.

Because even when I force a man down the aisle, he wants nothing to do with me. Yesterday, in between Della's last-minute ditch effort to change my mind, Caterina cut in with advice that still rings in my ears.

"Once, my sister told me to make Enzo into the prince I wanted. Do that with Erico. This arranged marriage isn't the end. It can be happy."

Her advice lodged uselessly in my heart. Useless because Erico already made his stance known.

Still...maybe I want some happiness in this darkness. The

shadows followed me since I was fourteen, always struggling to feel joyful. When my sister was cheery, mine was fake. For her, for Mom, and eventually, for everyone else. Stefano, Rozelyn, and Yasmine, when meeting them. The medical staff at the centre. The Corsettis when they took me in. Most likely assume that keeping my head down is a trauma response, but reality is, it's my mind struggling to remain present and not to succumb.

No one will choose me. Not even my own husband.

The ring gets warm around my finger, as though the memory of earlier today finally returns. I curl my hand into a fist, feeling the gold and the weight of the jewels. A ring not even meant for me...

Scoffing, I rip it from my finger and toss it to my right, into the room's corner. The overhead light catches on the diamond at the exact angle I'm taunted by the gleam, but I don't care.

Erico doesn't care. As long as I act like his wife outside these walls, the rest doesn't matter. I've willingly chained myself to a man who'll never give me a happy ending.

Masochism much. I did this to myself, and this is the price I'll pay.

At least being away from Della, with an ocean around you and music to compose will keep you from following the dejection into the darkness forever.

With a heavy sigh, I wipe the tears away and reach for my bag, rooting around until finding my cell phone. A few messages sit waiting, all from Della. Demands to contact her as soon as I can. Questions about the flight, about the mansion, and mainly about Erico's treatment.

What treatment? Does leaving count?

I swipe them all away and open my messaging app regardless, finding the thread I've yet to delete even knowing I should. If Della or even Nico knew about who I've been trying to reach, they'd be pissed.

I begin typing:

> Hey. You won't respond because you haven't to all the other messages I've sent, but stuff's changed in the past few days. I'm married. I volunteered for this, to take the place of Aurora Corsetti in her engagement to Erico Rossi from New York. Stupid, right? This is me letting you know, and I'd love to get your opinion on how dumb I am. When I should be running away from this lifestyle, I did exactly as Della did and married right into it. I miss you. I hope you're safe and okay, and again, I know you won't respond. You probably don't even have your phone anymore. But I continue to message on the slim chance one day you'll answer. Anyway…yeah.

That one gets delivered and it'll remain unread, as did the previous dozen. Scrolling up, I reread everything I've typed over the past few weeks. The check-ins. The updates about progress within Corsetti's household. The begging and pleading.

My thumb strokes over the top of my screen, right where her name is.

YASMINE DE FALCO.

7
ERICO

Contrary to what I said to Ariella, I don't leave the mansion right away. First, I check in with Carlotta to give a few instructions over the kinds of food Ariella enjoys, which I'm only aware of because Nico gained a report from Della at my request.

Then I head to my office for a private conversation with Sebastian. I won't be here for long, so I don't bother getting comfortable, and instead perch on the edge of my desk as he enters, stress tightening his face.

Sebastian has been inducted into the *Famiglia* for three years now and has proven himself to be a proficient, useful soldier. Meaning, he obeys orders really fucking easily. At twenty-five, I chose him thinking it might be nice for Ariella to have someone closer to her age, to ease her into her life here, but based on the appreciation in her gaze earlier when I introduced them, I'm second-guessing my choice.

"Sir," he greets, stopping halfway through the room. His hands fuse behind his back.

"Thanks for coming." I keep my voice smooth and eased.

"I'll be heading to Vegas right away. Not sure how long I'll be gone. It's for the quarterly meeting, but you've heard how these go. Once there, more shit gets brought up and the next thing I know, days will pass." If I didn't enjoy them so much, I'd despise attending. They're a pain, a task, but there's a sign of strength in them. A symbol of my control. "While I'm gone, ensure Ariella leaves her room."

According to Nico, she's a quiet woman who enjoyed hiding often in her room. In his house, I can understand why she would, but despite mine being new to her, she'll be alone for the next few days; therefore, there's little excuse for her to hide. I *want* her to emerge and become familiar with the property because it'll only save her future pain.

"Got it."

"And you will inform me when she does."

He nods again, his throat moving with his hard swallow. Perhaps, in that motion, he's hiding his true feelings about my request. Not that my own are any different. There is no plausible reason for wanting to know what she does in her day. Maybe it's guilt, but something nags at me to *want* to know.

There's also no reason I put her in my room. With my wedding to Aurora approaching at the end of the month, I had a suite across the house set aside. The very room I initially was going to re-assign to Ariella, but the moment she walked down the aisle toward me was the moment I changed my mind. Once again, there's no exact reasoning behind my actions besides a blatant desire to see her in my bed, my silk sheets hugging her body.

With the moment re-imbedding into my mind, the rest of the ceremony does too. Today felt fucking *real*. The dress she was in made a statement: that despite walking into a loveless marriage, she created something realistic. Her family made her an aisle for her to walk down.

A part of her wanted what happened today. The same part that led her to volunteer for it.

When I wasn't gazing at her, I was studying Nico and Lorenzo, seeking some sign that this was a ploy on their part, but found only guilt on both men's faces. It made me feel better about accepting her offer and declining Father's. Lorenzo stared at Ariella with respect and Nico a mix of respect and guilt, and when he slid to me, wariness. No one in that room wanted the wedding...except Ariella.

Her reasoning is elusive. Confusing, since all she's done tonight is look at me like I'd eat her alive. The second we entered my bedroom, she kept staring at the bed, and it's obvious where her mind was.

It was where mine had gone too. On the activities that happen between a man and wife on their wedding night.

What I couldn't figure out is if it was fear or longing she felt. There was a flicker of disappointment in her eyes when I announced leaving for Vegas, but it cleared for relief.

I'm puzzled over her confusing emotions and in my role, that is bad. Reading people is simple. Necessary too. But my elusive wife is confounding.

Which makes her dangerous.

"Sir, are you okay?"

I blink, coming back to the present, to my office with Sebastian. See, dangerous. Just thinking about her distracts me.

"Yeah, I'm fine. Let me know what she fills her days with."

"Do you want her to be aware of my presence or remain hidden?"

I hesitate, once again re-living the look in her eyes when she met him. Not that I believe Sebastian will act upon anything, even if I saw the same appreciation reflected in his. He knows better because he's aware of the consequences. But still, I don't like this doubt.

What do you expect of her? A loveless marriage and for her to take no lover in all these years?

My jaw clamps with the thought. No. No, I hadn't thought that far ahead. With Aurora, my plan was to impregnate her as soon as possible and then free her. But I doubt that's an option with Ariella. She's too...too gentle. Too wary and jumping on her—literally—would make me a villain in her eyes. More than I likely already am.

For some reason, I don't want that.

"Yes," I finally respond, my back teeth grinding together, fully aware my agreement to his two-optioned question answers nothing. "Don't be too obvious but you don't have to hide. Given what I so far know of her, I think the more she gets to know you, the more amicable she'll be to having you around. The less she'll fear you."

At some point, she might even enjoy his company more than my own.

"But when you're around, remember whose ring she's wearing, Sebastian. Whose surname she bears."

"Sir?" His brows dip, and mine even rise, half-surprised he's going to pretend I didn't notice earlier. That's simply insulting.

"I trust you, Sebastian, and it's why you were chosen for the task, but if your eyes stray, I will be the final thing you'll ever see." I pause, letting the threat hang. Waiting for his stuttered agreement until dismissing him.

He's a good kid so I have little doubt he'll obey, but the reminder for us both makes *me* feel better about leaving the city. He's young, and sometimes youth equals stupidity, and stupidity needs behavioural reminders.

Only when he's exited my office do I move as well, gathering my phone and checking last-minute emails on my laptop. The latest reply from the private tech company I hired to complete a deep dive background check on Ariella's family told me it'd be twenty-four hours until they had a response. According to the email, it's been nearing thirty hours and no response. So I shoot them a less-than-friendly prompt and shut the computer again. They're hunting for facts I could ask Ariella directly for, but something tells me I need to be better equipped when dealing with her.

Finally finished and ready to go, I exit my office and take the long hallway decorated in paintings of the beach until pausing in the foyer, my gaze sliding up the wall and toward the bedroom doors she's locked behind.

I wonder if she's gotten undressed and showered by now. If she's becoming familiar with my space, and making it hers too. A notion that should irritate me, but instead brings a smile to my face. Despite everything, I don't want her to hate it here or else it'll make for a very agonizing marriage.

I turn away and head back outside where Matthew is still waiting by the car, as I instructed him earlier to do. Once we're both seated and he's pulling away, the temptation to glance at the house behind me grows with every turn of the wheels, but I stare forward.

Distance will be a good thing. Ariella deserves happiness, and that's not me. Not a husband who won't have the time of day for her. Who doesn't *want* to have the time of day for her. Leaving her behind right away is ideal; it sets the expectations of what's to come and what not to expect from me.

So why does it feel so fucking wrong?

～

Vegas. Sin City.

A place filled with tourists who eagerly throw away their hard-earned money on the slim chance of winning big. The saying *the house always wins* is very true. *I* always win. Not them. Once in a while, a lucky fucker, usually by random chance, will strike a huge win, to ensure our casinos continue to promise prosperity. But it's only ever just enough cash to lure customers to continue gambling on that one percent chance while we rob them of their money.

The *Famiglia* has expanded in recent years, giving us a foothold into some of the southern states, including Vegas. Given the profitable city between the casinos, hotels, clubs, bars, and strip joints that both locals and visitors travel in for, it was an easy takeover and one that's grown our legal holdings exponentially. While the underground scene in Vegas is still strong, the drugs still desired, it's those legal businesses that make Vegas worth our time.

Since the party city is enjoyed by all, it's become the base of so many *Famiglia* meetings, where all the capos from the organization come together and report on profits and dealings to me and Father. Now, only me.

A car waits for me right off the tarmac. The driver doesn't need any direction before taking me toward the same condo complex I always stay at when I'm visiting. We own properties all over the country, in all the cities we frequent, for this very purpose.

When he pulls into the underground parking lot, the time on my phone reads five in the morning. I flew half the night, and my nap on the plane did little to settle my racing thoughts. Since New York is three hours ahead of Vegas, it's already eight in the morning, which means Ariella could be waking soon, if she hasn't already.

Despite the lack of notifications informing me so, I open my messenger app, tapping on a conversation between Sebastian and me, staring at it for a couple seconds, impatiently waiting for the bubbles, indicating he's typing and letting me know she's up.

But there's nothing. Maybe her head is as full as mine was for the entirety of my flight, and she's hiding from her new reality. Either way, when she wakes, if she's not already, it'll be her first official day as an underboss's wife. She'll have new responsibilities. Things I was prepared to shove at Aurora right away, but am hesitating with Ariella. The concept of forcing her into anything sickens me.

I exit the car and head straight for the elevator, typing in the code that'll lift me straight to the private penthouse suite, without stopping at any other floor, regardless if another tenant requests the elevator. Inside, I lean against the deep, wood panelling, exhaustion pulling my eyes down.

Thankfully, Vegas is a quiet city in the morning, and my meeting is this evening. After the day and night I've had, my head needs to be focused, which means sleep is my entire plan for the first half of today.

The second my feet pass the threshold of the penthouse, my phone rings. I hate the little leap my stomach does, hoping to either see Ariella or Sebastian's name—who'll only call in regards to my wife—but the sensation immediately quells at spotting *Mother* on my screen.

My thumb hovers over the red button to end the ringing, but knowing her, she'll continue incessantly until I pick up. So I do, not hiding my dislike with an exaggerated sigh. "What?"

"Good morning to you too, son."

"What?"

"You're cranky. It's a disagreeable look on you. One would think your wife isn't pleasing you well enough."

I shut my eyes, focusing on the breath running through my body before I say what I truly want to. Even though, this is simply my mother. Bitchy, and the first to tear someone down. It's why she managed to keep pace with Father all these years.

"I'm not having this conversation with you." Every word is

a punch as I stride through the condo, heading down the hall to the bedroom. The sooner I sleep, the less painful conversations like this will feel.

"Yes, well, sorry to be a burden," she says in the most non-apologetic way a person can manage, "but you are. You were married yesterday."

I glance at the ring on my left hand, a constant reminder. "I'm aware," I reply dryly.

"Don't be smart with me, Erico. I mean, you were married yesterday and I haven't met your wife yet."

That pulls me to a stop in the doorway of the ensuite bathroom, glancing at the phone like I haven't heard her correctly. "The key word in your sentence was yesterday. Did you expect me to drag her from Montreal straight to you?"

"Yes, actually."

Oh, for the love of— I pinch the bridge of my nose, focusing on breathing again. "Well, too bad. Even I'm not that much of an asshole. The woman gave up everything she knew."

"Well, now she'll be running the *Famiglia* alongside you, so I'm not entirely sure it was a chore to do so. She knew what she was agreeing to."

For the first time since answering this call, Mother has stated something I partially agree with. Ariella did walk into this eyes wide open, but it also doesn't mean I was dragging her to my parents first thing.

"You were invited," I remind her. "You could have come to Montreal with Caladin and me and met her then."

"Could have, but I had a nail appointment and your father was busy. We planned for a wedding at the end of the month. You can't expect everyone to drop everything simply because you decided to swap brides as well as the dates."

Always busy. A nail appointment was more important than her son's wedding, but I'm not surprised by this. Just annoyed as I drop the phone to the counter and wash my face, tapping the speakerphone button so this unfortunate conversation can continue.

"Is there a purpose for your call, Mother?" I grit, hands wringing the facecloth imagining it something else entirely. Something I can use to shut her up.

"Yes, there is, actually. As I was saying, since we haven't met her yet, nor has the entire *Famiglia*, your wife will be throwing a party. An introduction for her to the heads and their wives, as well as any of our partners. It'll be a sign that you have your wife, and she's capable of throwing a decent event." Mother pauses, her next question icier than anything she's said thus far. "She can do that at least, can't she?"

Pushing away from the counter, I grab my phone. "You want Ariella to throw her own event to welcome her into the *Famiglia* and that's when you and Father will meet her. You truly think that's best?" Although, a party will mean numerous people for Mother to stress about, which means she can't spend all her time stressing out Ariella. I suppose, there's a win in there somewhere.

"Yes."

"I'll talk with her."

"Erico—"

"Stop," I cut her off. "Just stop. Look, I'm fucking exhausted. You know I'm in Vegas for the next while. I will discuss it with my wife when I'm home because she barely knows her way around my mansion, let alone hosting a party."

There's silence and knowing Mother, there's a million insults she's presently biting her tongue on. Thankfully, she goes with none of them and instead, in a sour tone, mumbles, "Fine. But there was another reason I called you. Your father wishes to speak with you."

Oh, good fucking hell, the pain doesn't end. As the phone

shuffles in the background, I kick off my shoes and strip my coat, tossing it onto a nearby settee until I hear a deeper voice replace the shrill of my mother's.

"Erico."

"Good morning, Father." Just speaking with him has my body tensing.

"I won't be joining you for the meeting, but I will be there after."

"Okay." It's not the first I've ran it alone but usually he skips informing me.

"Despite our disagreement the other day over Ariella, I did say a year ago, that with your marriage, I'd be handing you the *Famiglia* as well. Even though that wasn't supposed to happen until the end of the month, I think now's the time, son. Time for you to be Boss."

Boss. Fucking hell. Every thought of Ariella, the conversation with Mother, even my exhaustion as I drop onto the bed is gone. Wiped away by only excitement. Pride. No fear, no nerves. Father's trained me well.

"Th-thank you," I manage after a moment. Father did say after I was wed, but my father also changes his mind so often, I'd have no doubt he wasn't ready for retirement quite yet.

"It's time," he repeats.

"Thank you," I say again, having nothing else to. Nothing else that formulates in my head anyway.

"Do the meeting," he continues, "and I'll be there after. With all the heads already in Vegas, I felt it easiest to do it now."

"Makes sense."

"Good job, son. I'll see you soon." *Click.*

I drop the phone on the bed, staring blankly at the wall in front of me. It's happening. Soon, I'll be in control. I'll be in the exact position my father always trained me to be—his role. Boss.

In the aloneness of the penthouse, I smile. Genuinely smile.

Years of fighting, of training, of practicing weapons led to this. The deals, the meetings, the kills, all to get here.

When my phone vibrates against the comforter, I'm not even bothered by it this time.

SEBASTIAN

She's awake. Just went down for breakfast.

Day one of being an underboss's wife will be also her final day as such. By tomorrow, she'll be a Boss's.

Instead of answering Sebastian's text, I open another thread and type in her name.

ME:

Good morning, Ariella.

The word beneath my message goes from *delivered* to *read* and an eagerness I've never felt before courses through me. Along with a curiosity, to see how she'll respond. It'll be in her message I can attempt to decipher how much she despises me.

In the meantime, I finish undressing, keeping one eye on the screen, waiting for her reply to slip into place. After two minutes, she still hasn't sent one.

ME

Sleep well?

I climb beneath the blankets after prompting her, settling into the bed. Instantly, sleepiness wants to pull me under but the urge for her response keeps me awake.

After another minute, there's still no reply.

ME

Hope the room was to your liking. Enjoy your day.

Still fucking nothing...

I return to Sebastian's message and furiously type out a response.

ME

> Does she have her phone on her?

SEBASTIAN

> Yes. She's staring at it too.

I know that because of the damn read receipts her phone is sending me. I flip back to the other conversation.

ME

> Stop being childish and ignoring me. I know you're on your phone.

That ought to do it.

One minute...

Two...

If this meeting wasn't so important and pre-scheduled, I'd fly right back home and—

Do what? I don't have a reasonable answer for myself, but I'd...I'd show her all the reasons she's not allowed to ignore me.

Another minute and she's obviously not going to respond at this point. My finger hovers over her name to call her, but then decide otherwise, reminding myself the uselessness in it. So what if she's ignoring me? Couples who don't care about one another don't send *good morning* messages to one another. She's reminding me of my own decisions.

So before my exhaustion drives me to make stupid choices, I connect my phone to the charging cord, shut off the lamp, and bury myself in the bed. Right before passing out, the image of red hair and feisty eyes fills my head and it's with those colours, I allow the blackness to steal me.

8

ARIELLA

Witnessing Aurora's return to her family was a shitshow, not that I'd react differently if I was in her place. At first, she hid in her bedroom to avoid her family, and while the thought to do the same crosses my mind when I open my eyes, my grumbling stomach coupled with the fact that Erico isn't present convinces me to leave the bed.

But everything feels different. The room I stand in the middle of—not mine. The bathroom I use, noting how all my preferred soaps and items are already stocked, isn't mine. Touching *anything* feels like I'm invading a stranger's space.

Essentially, I suppose, I am.

A stranger with a claim on me.

Day one of being a wife to a man I barely know. Who barely knows me. What do I do with myself? At Nico's, I was allowed to do whatever, but with the ongoing drama my sister wrapped herself into, it was easy to hide away when I wasn't with her. Curled up in bed with my notebook and continuing writing music, an old hobby I only recently started up again.

Sometimes though, when the darkness grew, it made leaving my bedroom impossible. It'd require Della coming to my door and urging me out, completely unaware of why she had to do it. But some mornings, lying with the comforter covering my entire body, staring at only the shade the blanket provided, was alleviating for the deprecating thoughts repeating on a loop in my head.

None of those accompanied me today.

Despite the unknowns of my life, after finishing in the bathroom, I head right for the massive windows, yanking open the heavy drapes until the sight of the ocean is enough to convince myself of being content.

My wet hair gets wrapped up in a bun because I don't have the energy to care enough to dry it. Similarly, I find leggings and a tank top from *my* bag and avoid all the expensive clothing Erico stocked.

Every step through the mansion is strange. Quiet, like my body is uncertain if I'll get in trouble for being here. This isn't *my* home so every step feels dangerous almost.

I retrace the path Erico took me on yesterday, over the connected balcony and down the sweeping, wide staircase until I'm by the front door again, glancing through the mansion, searching for the kitchen.

Beyond me, by the back of the house, it opens into a huge sitting area with the floor-to-ceiling windows I can see from upstairs. Through them, the world. It taunts me because somewhere out there is my sister, my old life, the city I grew up in, all so far away. Montreal is where I was born, raised, went to school...lived with Mom.

Where I lost Mom. Now, not even in the same country, it feels like I'm further away than ever from her.

I never even got the chance to visit her gravesite.

Della gave me a picture of it, of course, but shortly after the accident, Stefano had me sent away. By the time Mom's final resting place was all set up, I was forgotten. Della begged Stefano for the medical centre to let me out on a day trip to visit, but the asshole refused.

Once moving in with Della and the Corsettis, we meant to. But between her wedding, Aurora's return, and the battle with Stefano, I never got the chance.

As I stare at the ocean outdoors, I wonder if I ever will.

Mom would love this place. She, like me, had an affinity for water.

Blinking away the sudden formation of tears, I look away from the doorway, from New York and the world beyond the glass, and toward the rest of the sitting area I've stumbled upon. Low, white couches, high back chairs by the fireplace stretch into one wall, glass tables, and the opposite wall, a huge fish tank.

That, I wander closer to. Bright, colourful, tropical fish swim around. A few of them, which I can't help but smile at. To have tropical fish requires specific equipment—pricey equipment. I know because as a child, Mom bought me a goldfish in place of me wanting a Blue Angelfish, since it was all she could afford.

I study each fish, taking in their bold colours when the familiar and desired yellow and blue catches my eye. What are the fucking chances he owns a Blue Angelfish, the very fish I always dreamed of having? Apparently, pretty good, since here one is.

"Morning, Mrs. Rossi."

I jump, but in more than just surprise at the voice suddenly appearing. Also, from that name. It's the first time someone's referred to me by my married name.

I don't like it. They should never use it again.

With a stiff back, I look away from the fish tank and to the stout woman Erico introduced to me yesterday. Carlotta, the housekeeper. She's smiling, obviously trying to ease the tension. It's not her fault I despise my new name, so I try to force my lips to move into responding. Instead, I think a grimace is the best I manage.

"You must be hungry. I'll show you to the kitchen, if you'd like. Make you some breakfast."

I nod because that's precisely where I was hoping to find. She turns with a small hand wave for me to follow, so I do, walking down a short, white hallway connecting the sitting area to a large kitchen, filled with shiny stainless-steel appliances.

"You like fish?" she asks suddenly, glancing over her shoulder.

I nod.

"Erico too. Even as a young boy, he was always bugging his parents to buy him some. When he was six, he even tried for a pet shark. That request was vetoed." She chuckles fondly and switches on the tap, washing her hands.

I hate that he and I have that in common. Not wanting a pet shark, but our appreciation of water creatures.

Carlotta continues sharing pleasant childhood memories of Erico, like this is supposed to make me feel something for the man. "As if he didn't get the hint, he then asked for a dolphin when he was ten."

I snort, once again, pushing pleasant thoughts of him away. His likes and dislikes shouldn't matter to me.

"You can sit." She nods to the high chairs pushed into the granite island.

I'm still hovering in the doorway, cautious to place myself in all this...this light. The kitchen is so white, it nearly reflects the massive dump of sunlight coming in from the half-wall of windows, including a door obviously leading to the back of the house.

While lovely, it makes me miss the Corsetti mansion. As much as the design of this place is prettier, the darkness and more traditional style of Nico's house meant it was easier to blend in with the shadows.

"Alternatively, the dining room is right through there, if you'd like to have your meal there instead." She gestures to a doorway opposite of me. Through it, I catch sight of a long table. Too formal.

I point to the counter, hoping she understands my meaning. *I'll eat here.*

She smiles and her dress makes a swishing noise as she heads for the very wide fridge behind her. "What would you like to eat? We have traditional breakfast foods—cereal, fruit, bagels, and the sort. I can also whip you up some homemade waffles."

Waffles. Things are already seeming a bit better by the prospect. I nod eagerly in agreement, causing her to laugh and head for another large cupboard, where she begins pulling out ingredients for batter.

"Got it. Waffles it is. Coming right up."

As she busies herself, I finally claim the chair closest to the door and watch her work. Looking from the kind housekeeper to the windows to my right, to the outdoors. Out there, I'd have an uninterrupted view of the body of water, and I make it my goal to go out there soon.

When I hear another set of footsteps come up behind me, I curve my back, hunch my shoulders and lower my head, aiming to hide from the newcomer.

Of course, the greeting of, "Mrs. Rossi," indicates I've failed.

The bodyguard from last night, Sebastian, steps up beside the counter, resting his hands lazily on the edge. His youthful charm is infectious, and I smile tightly to be polite.

"Good morning."

I manage a small wave in return.

"After you eat, I can take you around the mansion and grounds, if you'd like," he offers, to which I nod my agreement. If I'm not living my life locked in a bedroom, it'd be smart to know my way around.

My phone vibrates at the same time Sebastian moves away, and based on his steps, he wanders back to the doorway. Maybe even out of the kitchen entirely, but I don't check. I pull out my phone, assuming it's Della—who I'm surprised *hasn't* messaged again yet—but my mood takes an even deeper plummet at the name flashing over my screen.

ERICO

Good morning, Ariella.

Scowling, I lay the phone to the side, screen down, and focus on Carlotta silently working. She's heating the waffle maker presently while rapidly stirring the batter. I focus on the noise of her task, but still, it doesn't block the phone's next buzz.

ERICO

Sleep well?

If I answer, maybe he'll stop bothering me. After all, he's taking the time out of his busy schedule to check on his new wife, but all I hear in my head is his declaration of how this marriage will go, and the last thing I want—need—is hope. To start clinging to a concept that'll never happen. There's little point in these niceties if his plan is to ignore me afterwards.

There's a lot I've dealt with and a lot I'm willing to take on, to put my head down and ignore. But the specific experience I *refuse* to live through is any emotional back and forth.

Not wanting me—fine. Typical. Used to it.

Acting like he cares to ignore me another time—even my own misery has that limitation.

> ERICO
>
> Hope the room was to your liking. Enjoy your day.

That sounds very final, and I close my phone, aiming to ignore it for good.

"Two more minutes," Carlotta suddenly murmurs, pulling a plate from the cupboard over her head. She digs out maple syrup, which I sincerely hope is the authentic Canadian stuff and not some cheap knockoff. Living with Nico and his family was when I *truly* experienced the best quality maple syrup, rather than the low-cost stuff from my childhood. When Carlotta rests the bottle on the counter, I catch the label, and breathe, thankful for this place being stocked well.

Another vibration from my phone and a longer message fills the screen, irritation filling every word.

> ERICO
>
> Stop being childish and ignoring me. I know you're on your phone.

Only one way he would. I glance behind me, toward where Sebastian last was. I don't see him, but I'm sure he's watching me. As polite as he might be, he ultimately works for my husband, which means every little move I make can be reported back.

But Erico's message is yet another reminder. *This* is the true Erico. Maybe I am being childish, but what does he care? I almost message him that too before opting to flip over my cell and make my point very obvious through actions.

Carlotta slides a plate over with two homemade, fluffy waffles stacked on top of one another, a pile of whip cream, and a drizzle of maple syrup that makes everything instantly better. The pile is framed by sliced strawberries. When did I last eat? Yesterday morning? Under the watchful eyes of both Della and Aurora.

The moment I stick a fork into the pile, Carlotta says, "Enjoy, Mrs. Rossi. I have a few things to do but message if you need anything." She walks by me before I can comment on her using that moniker. People must stop doing that.

Eating becomes awkward then, as I sit in a kitchen I've never been to before ten minutes ago, in a house that's supposedly mine now. Not a house bought with my partner of choice. Rather, one I forced myself onto, who already declared where and how the household would run.

The food becomes stale in my throat, flavour dissipating for disappointment.

Fuck. The car accident did a lot to my brain apparently. Made me lose it entirely.

As I finish eating, steps return to the kitchen. They're louder than Carlotta's, telling me they're likely Sebastian. Sure enough, he stops by the counter, his hands coming to rest on top. I focus on those hands, inches away from my own. My eyes travel the length of his arm, which is clothed in a leather jacket, and finally up to his handsome face. He has a boyish charm.

"Mrs. Rossi." He tips his head. "Carlotta's food is delicious, isn't it?"

Without responding to that question, I bring my phone closer, swiping away the messaging app last open in favour of the notepad app I use so frequently now. Being mute isn't without its challenges, and I'd do anything to *not* be. But every time I try to speak, I get choked up again. The final words I spoke to Mom arise in my head and clog my throat, making it impossible to speak through. Sometimes, I don't bother even trying.

I used to write on whiteboards and notebooks in the medical centre, but once Nico got me out, he and Della bought me a cell, and it's been more convenient to talk over text messages or through the notepad app.

PLEASE STOP CALLING ME MRS. ROSSI. MY
NAME IS ARIELLA.

His dark eyes study my screen before flicking toward me. "It is your name though. But if you insist, then Ariella is it."

Thank you, I mouth and his attention falls right to my lips. My skin heats—I hadn't meant to do that. But instead of interest, he seems curious. His head tips slightly to the side, his eyes narrowing on my mouth and then dropping to my hands.

"Do you know sign language?"

I do because the speech and language pathologist at the medical centre taught me. While the doctors and psychologists were focused on my trauma healing, mental health, and speaking again, other professions came in to give me alternate solutions. Learning American Sign Language was one of them, except then I realized how utterly useless it is when no one in my life knows it.

Besides, away from the medical centre, I slipped right into the background. The Corsettis have too much going on and I wouldn't be a bother to ask them to learn a whole new language just for me. Even asking Della felt like I'd burden her. Besides, I got the sense, it'd reactivate her determination to "fix" me, and I'd rather not deal with that. So sign language became yet another skill I have but never use.

I nod, now curious why Sebastian is asking.

He pushes off the counter, lifting his hands into the air. Throwing a crooked smile, he murmurs, "Don't make fun if I'm no good." Then his hands move up to his forehead by his ear, and swoops out.

Hi.

In sign language.

My mouth gapes open. Sebastian knows sign language. Or at least enough to greet me.

His hand rests on his chest and he lightly taps it.

My.

His index and middle fingers on both hands come together, and he taps them against one another in an X sign, facing down.

Name.

And then he spells out every letter of his name with the correct corresponding sign. Mostly, correct anyway. Some rickety, some close enough I understand.

At the end of it, I only have one question, which I sign back to him. *How do you know sign language?*

He watches intently, his brows dipping, then chuckles, slightly nervous. "Sorry, understanding is more challenging for me. Could you do that again but slower?" When I do, he answers, "Oh, my seven-year-old nephew was born deaf, so a lot of my family took the time to learn it."

That's sweet. Slowly and so he can catch it, I sign, *Is that why you were chosen to guard me?*

He shakes his head. "Mr. Rossi isn't aware of my nephew. No one here is. I don't talk about them much. It was a happy coincidence, but I figured I'd let you know in case it's easier, or better, for you if you'd like to sign instead. Can't promise I won't need your help sometimes, but it's another option. Up to you, of course, Mrs. Ro—Ariella."

Thank you, I reply with my hands.

Maybe, just maybe, it won't be so terrible here.

9

ERICO

Exhaustion keeps me passed out until late morning. Even then, by the time I get up right before noon, it doesn't feel like enough sleep. My eyes are still heavy, my body weighted. It was the most restless sleep I've had in a long time.

No matter, since I'm only in Vegas for a couple of days, I shouldn't be switching my sleep schedule up too much. When I reach for my phone, there's a few texts waiting, but the latest being from Sebastian gains all my attention.

SEBASTIAN

> Started a tour of the mansion. It started raining into the afternoon so she didn't get to see the property or backyard yet. Tomorrow maybe. She wanted to go back to your room to rest.

Somehow, I don't believe she's simply resting, but the fact she's left the room at all, on only her first day of her new life, is enough. It speaks a little to her tenaciousness, which for some fucking reason, appeases me.

Instead of responding, I toss my phone to the side and get ready for the day. I dress quickly and head down to the car waiting for me.

Responding only answers the eagerness within me, rather than ignoring the feeling of needing to know about my wife. The facts I am aware of isn't enough. I already feel, deep down, if it was Aurora in Ariella's place, the details her family would have provided me would have been sufficient. But what Nico passed along about Ariella isn't enough.

Which brings me to an email that was delivered while I was asleep. From the few men I've had running background checks on her. I want to know *everything*, right down to the hospital her mother birthed her inside.

As I'm driven to one of the *Famiglia* bars that's been chosen for the quarterly meeting, I read over the details they've so far found, my stomach clenching with the first fact. The anniversary of her mother's death is in a week. Fuck.

Instantly, I'm at a loss. If Ariella's upset that day—and rightly so—I won't know how to console her. Now that I think about it, I've *never* soothed someone about a death. Plus, she may not want my support, being that I'm practically a stranger to her. Worse, because by the time the anniversary comes around, I'll have only been back home with her for a matter of days, if that.

Fucking Christ.

I keep reading, the second line becoming just as intriguing as the first.

Her birthday is tomorrow. It'll make the eleven-year age gap between us ten, being that she'll turn twenty-two.

Fuck Corsetti for not letting me know this. Or perhaps, he wasn't aware either. Della certainly does though, which means she kept that information from her husband, in turn keeping it from me.

By the time I enter the empty bar, only a few of the *Famiglia* capos already arriving, I head for a booth in the back, signalling to the bartenders who're setting up for the day to bring me something strong. A few of the heads glance at me from their places around the room, one even standing as though to approach, but the glare I shoot every one of them keeps them away.

In truth, it's not their fault I'm annoyed, immediately feeling the tightness winding my form, frustration clamping my jaw shut.

I won't be home for her birthday. Distance aside, that's an asshole move on my part.

Can I fly home and back in time tomorrow? Would that even be wise to show up in New York, only for the afternoon and...do what? Take her out for a proper celebration? There's so little I know about Ariella, I'm not even sure *what* she'd enjoy doing.

The mantra of *fuck* continues to roll through my head as some idiotic soul takes the seat across from me. Clearly, the look I gave the room upon entering wasn't enough so I lift my eyes, scanning past the glass of alcohol that was delivered while I was lost in thought, and onto the man across from me.

My father's inquiring eyes drill right back, his mouth flat as his arms come to rest over the tabletop. He shouldn't be here until tomorrow for the leadership change, since he opted to skip the meeting.

"What a surprise." I tip my drink toward him in greeting but leave my tone unimpressed. He always taught me that one's tone has more of an impact than words. Instead of outwardly stating my displeasure, to make it known through *how* I say it and the behaviours that go along with it.

He reclines against the booth, sliding one arm along the

back, which tells me he's calm. Unresponsive to my annoyance because whyever he's here, he feels he's in the right.

"Business in the area," is all he replies with as two fingers lift from the back of the booth's bench. It's a signal to the bar, and within a minute, the waitress is bringing over another glass of liquor for him. It's clear—his favourite gin. Everyone in his employ is aware of his preferred drink, so there's no fumbling over inquiring what he'd like.

Once the waitress is gone again, I shoot him another unimpressed stare, leaning back in the booth as well. "What business? I'd know about any business you're conducting here. The only reason you should be in Vegas is for the quarterly meeting later today, which you've already declined attending, and tomorrow."

Father's head dips to the side, a slow smirk spreading over his mouth, which he quickly hides with a sip from his glass. "Still not coming to the meeting, no. I have a different one."

My eyes narrow because he's being shifty right now. Sketchy actions imply sketchy results. "What meeting are you having that I'm not privy to? If it affects the *Famiglia,* I should be aware."

His lips press together in fake-thoughtfulness. Fake because Father never considers anything for as long as he's now pretending to. "You will. In time."

Before I can make my next argument, he stands from the booth and abandons his half-empty drink, and strides right out the front door. He obviously, somehow, knew I was here and whatever game he just played was to let me know the dice has been rolled.

Not that I don't trust my father...but I don't completely trust him either. A paradox, yes, but that's been our entire relationship, especially in the past year or so. With more command being handed to me, he's changed from the man I knew growing up.

Did you ever really know him though?

I suppose not. A lot of my childhood was spent with Carlotta parenting me. Mother was always here or there—parties, spa days, shopping—while Father stayed away from the mansion more than he was there. If not travelling for work, he was passed out in his numerous offices or a condo apartment, preferring to sleep and live where the organization needed him most rather than be a parent.

So whatever Father's doing now, he believes it's for the best, but not informing me doesn't sit well either.

There was a single vow I made to myself growing up. That I might not be having a typical marriage with Ariella, but our children, my heirs, they *will* know me. I *will* drive the near three hours home each day and spend evenings with them, whether that's training, swimming, or visiting a park. They'll have what I never did—a father.

The fact I'm sitting in Vegas, almost three thousand miles away from my wife and all the ability to begin creating those children, is not lost on me.

My gaze is stuck on the door Father left out of, debating to follow him or not. I still have hours until the meeting begins, which would give me the time to trail him and see what he's up to. If only to settle the churning in my stomach and the instinct that something is majorly wrong.

Making my decision to follow, I swallow the final chug of my drink and abandon my glass, rebuttoning my suit's coat as I stand and head toward the door.

A body steps in front of me, and I'm about to curse whichever brainless staff dared block my way when their outfit registers. Certainly not waitstaff, nor one of the heads, who are all men. Instead, a striking white dress, way too tiny for casual day-to-day use anywhere outside of Sin City. It's made even more striking due to the bold waterfall of black hair, with fanned bangs framing her face. A deep red is painted on her lips, curling upwards and pulling my attention to devious, deep blue eyes. In turn, she's also studying me.

Hands with fingernails long as they are sharp come up to rub my forearm. Every nerve demands I shove her away, but I know this woman. And it's her surname protecting her from me injuring her pretty little face, and what the consequences would be if I did.

But that doesn't stop the millions of other thoughts in my head. The realization that last name or not, she's my enemy. An enemy on *my* territory demands action. But then she'll throw one tantrum to her daddy and I'll be dealing with the fallout, which is why, for now, I clench my fists, reining myself in until I know what the fuck a Russian is doing on my property.

Vanessa Volkov.

"Mr. Rossi." A head tilt in greeting and the attempt at a soft tone, which doesn't work. I shoulder her hand away, but when she glances at the space I've subtly created, she only smirks and says, "You're even more handsome than the photos show." A strong Russian accent makes her voice a purring rumble, throaty, and almost annoying.

What does Ariella's voice sound like? Throaty, soft-spoken, cheery—so many options.

"Miss Volkov," I return the greeting, attempting to keep my mood in check until determining why the princess of the Bratva is *here* on American soil, in *my* club. If she's here, then her father, the Bratva's leader, Ursin Volkov, must be slinking around nearby. "What an unlikely surprise."

She laughs, throwing her head back, which seems entirely too fake and grates my nerves. "If you were to speak with your father, it's actually not so unlikely."

My eyes flash behind her, to the door Father left out of, and our entire conversation hits me. The meeting he avoided telling me about is *this*. Vanessa's presence is my secondary concern, next to the fact that the head of the Bratva is somewhere in my city, making deals with my father. A deal that could be positive for the *Famiglia*, given how powerful the Bratva is, but they're almost *too* powerful. They're an organization I'm pleased not to work with, because doing so only puts us closer to them, and nothing good can come from that. Sometimes the price of power is too great to pay.

Father, what the hell are you playing at?

She steps forward and runs a hand up my chest, pausing right over my heart. "Come now, Erico, don't ignore me."

Every word from her mouth flicks at my nerves until I grab her thin, breakable wrist between two fingers, and jerk her away. My fingers add an extra pinch, a warning, which based on how quickly her smirk slides away for surprise, works. At least she's smart enough to recognize when the game's up.

"Never refer to me by my first name. It's Mr. Rossi to you. Get out of my sight. Run back to your father."

When I move to step around her, she follows, blocking my path again, her early seduction swapped for pure focus. "*Mr. Rossi*, we have things to discuss while our fathers chat about the future."

The future. Of fucking course. Father was insistent for me to wed her versus Ariella. I thought after the conversation he and I had, the topic would be dropped—but clearly not. Which means, I need to find him and break whatever deals he believes he's making.

My arm sweeps out and I force her to the side, only barely remembering to not push her too roughly. "Get out of my way, Miss Volkov. If you've forgotten, I'm married."

She opens her mouth to argue, but a stream of men burst

through the bar's entrance, saving me from her response. My capos from all over the country file in, nodding toward me. If they notice Vanessa and who she is from afar, no one comments as they head to the door by the entrance and walk downstairs to the basement, where it's set up for these large meetings.

I glance at my phone, noting the time, which explains why everyone's suddenly arriving. Fuck. I'm torn between finding my father with Vanessa's unwilling help, and doing my actual job.

The last person to enter heads toward me rather than the staircase. He's dressed in a rumpled suit, which knowing him, was probably yanked out of a laundry basket minutes ago. He shoves his dark bangs from his eyes, which narrow in on the woman at my side.

"Leave, Miss Volkov. You have five minutes."

And then I walk toward Caladin, meeting him halfway. His gaze remains over my shoulder, his finger coming up to point. "Is that..."

"Yes." I knock his hand down to his side and grab his shoulder, spinning him with me as my stride doesn't break. "Just walk. Don't speak to her. I'll explain later." By the basement's stairs, I glance back to see Vanessa heading toward the front door, an extra bob in her steps that make me roll my eyes. But I ask my cousin, "Why are you here? Thought you wanted to sit out."

"I did." He sighs deeply, dramatically. "But your father showed up at my condo earlier this morning and dragged me with him. Said he'd be handing over leadership in the days coming, since all the heads are here. Which means," he spreads his hands, "here I am with nothing better to do. Which, also, by the way, do you know how uncomfortable it is to sit with your father on a plane all afternoon? I'd rather have my balls cut off than do that again."

I chuckle and shove my cousin down the darkened steps, only lit by a single light. He and Father always had a strange, tense relationship, regardless that Caladin has lived with us since he was ten. His own parents, my aunt and uncle, were both killed in a shooting gone wrong at one of the *Famiglia* businesses when he was a kid, so my parents took him in. We grew up together like brothers, one room away from each other, until he was eighteen and decided to move out. Mother paid him less attention then she paid me, and although Caladin trained with Father and me, there's always been a disconnect between them.

We make it to the bottom of the stairs, where half the men are already sitting in a circle, waiting patiently for me to begin.

I straighten my suit jacket and walk for the head of the table, Caladin remaining behind me, even as I sit. Leaning against the wall by my shoulder, where he'll be for the rest of our lives. It became obvious years ago, while he'd be right for the underboss position once I move up, he's more my Consigliere than anything. I need his advice, his support, and he enjoys the freedom of the role.

Right before calling the meeting to a start, my phone lights up with a message.

SEBASTIAN

She won't come out of her room. She's been in there since this morning when the rain began. It's nearly seven but she refuses to eat.

10

ARIELLA

Rain pounds heavy against the bedroom's windows. Furious, turbulent, and aligned to the exact beat of my heart. The sky is a dim, welcoming grey, exactly like my emotions. Outside is chilly, precisely like my internal temperature, no matter how tight of a ball I've curled myself into.

Other people despise the rain for bringing their mood down and ruining plans, but I love it. I love how the obscurity gives me a chance to hide. No one says, "Come outside, it's beautiful," when it's pouring, which means not having to invent an excuse.

From beneath the blanket, I observe the vicious rain mingling with the massive body of water surrounding the property. It's been pouring since this morning, and according to the weather app on my phone, it'll continue into the night and tomorrow, which means the tour Sebastian began will be postponed for a while.

It's probably for the best though. The tour I got of the

mansion only made me sadder. I kept thinking about what Mom would tell me as a teenager.

Mom flicks hair off my forehead before pressing a kiss there. "I'm sorry, Ari. I know you wanted to go on the class trip."

"It's okay," I reply through a dry throat. It doesn't feel like it is, but I get it, so there's little point in showing Mom I'm upset when she's already aware I am. "No biggie."

Her smile informs me she sees right through my lie. "One day, I want the best for you, honey. I want you to grow up and make a good life for yourself. To live in a big, beautiful house and never struggle for money."

If only she saw me now. I did it. I managed to get into a big, beautiful house—my third by now. But not in the ways she or I planned. *I* did nothing to earn the mansion.

That was hit number one on my mood this morning.

The second was the ocean I continued to watch through the wall of windows. Mom loved the ocean too. As a kid, she'd frequently take me and Della to the Lachine Canal—which isn't the prettiest, by any means—but it was water. After walking Old Montreal because she adored the cobblestone roads, we'd sit on the grass by the Canal.

Della and I made her dreams a reality. We found better lives. The caveat being it took marriage and criminals to do it.

In a way, Mom made her dream come true as well. When she got with Stefano and we moved into his mansion, although it was half the size of this place and the Corsetti mansion, it was still larger than we'd ever seen before. Despite the hell and pain Stefano dragged everyone in my life into, I'm thankful for one reason: Mom smiled so much by his side.

It's fucked up to despise and yet be grateful toward the man who killed her, but for a while, she loved him. It was enough for us all, even if I hated him from the second we were introduced.

"Della, Ariella, this is the man who's been occupying so many of my evenings. Stefano, meet my girls."

The man has a rat-like face that has me questioning Mom's interest in him. His personality must be fantastic because when he smiles, it churns my stomach.

"Nice to meet you both." He reaches a hand out for Della, and then me, and I return his shake, unable to look away from his toothy smile. Charming, in some ways, and Mom's basically swooning by his side, but his gaze darkens, studying Della and me.

Almost like he's judging us, but not in a mean way. More like, deciding if we're suitable or not.

I don't like the way my heart thumps faster, my senses picking up a disconcerting sensation, as he releases me and turns back to Mom.

But this place...this isn't the dream she once wanted for me. This is a gilded cage. A place I willingly chose too—that's the kicker.

Moving in with Della into the Corsetti mansion never felt permanent. Almost like, deep down, I *knew* it'd be temporary. It was a stepping stone in life. But as Sebastian showed me around the mansion, *this* feels like forever. There were different considerations as I took in everything, reminding myself that this is now home, even when it doesn't feel like it.

I told him that too, through sign language. His response: "Yet. It'll happen, I'm sure. After all, it is only your first day here."

When the sky shifted into grey and the rain burst from the clouds, it was a sign. By then, I already felt the familiar—and this time, welcoming—darkness consume my mood. Like a switch, my positive emotions flicked off, taking all of me with it, until the only thing I desired was to hide.

The rain gave me that excuse since Sebastian was unable to

show me outside. Hours later, I'm still buried beneath the blanket, breathing through the misery, the sudden low feeling—the depression I've been surviving with—managing—since I was fourteen. At sixteen, I was diagnosed. But only Mom knows, and my secret died with her. We never told Della because I asked Mom not to. As teenagers, I didn't want her perception of me to change, and as adults, I've become a burden on her, so admitting what I spend so much time hiding feels wrong.

The doctor leaves the room so Mom and I can process the news together.

The diagnosis of clinical depression.

"It makes sense," I conclude after a few minutes. "I feel like so much of me makes sense now."

Mom approaches my chair and leans down to take me into a tight hug. Her hair, blonde like Della's, fills my nose with her fruity scent. It's comforting and grounding for my emotions.

"It changes nothing, honey. Nothing at all. You're perfect, and I love you. We'll talk with the doctors for any strategies they feel might help stabilize your mood, but only if you want. We came for answers, and if you're happy just knowing, then you're strong enough to manage this challenge." She releases me to face me once more, her palm stroking hair away from the side of my face. "Ari, you're strong. Knowing changes little. Now you better understand yourself. You don't need to decide anything right now."

My eyes burn from tears shed hours ago when the emotions mounted, growing so impossibly heavy. When my chest felt like it'd cave in. When breathing was a difficult task.

In the hours passing, Sebastian's come to my room twice, asking if I need anything, and Carlotta on rotation every hour, offering food. After the first four checks, I managed to text her to leave me alone, so she'd stop feeling obligated. Her reply was that she left a tray outside the door anyway. That was hours ago but I haven't gotten up for it.

Food seems so far away from what my body needs.

Throughout the day, Della's called twice and messaged a whole lot. Aurora too, and one from Nico. A missed call from Caterina, only a few minutes ago. I'm moments away from switching off my cell, even if every single message almost made me smile. They *care* enough to check on me. Della, I expected, but not the rest of them.

When you don't respond, they'll assume all is well and will stop caring. Then you'll be alone again.

True. But for now, I still can't answer. Can't pretend to be okay.

Nothing from Erico. I wonder if he's aware I've been in our room all day. I wonder if he cares. At what point will Erico discard a half-starved, depressed wife? It's easy to hide from Della, but to spend a lifetime with Erico doing so is something else. If he's gone often, it's doable.

When in this marriage farce will Erico realize he doesn't want someone with depression? The simple thought should be enough to force me from bed, but all it does is bury me deeper.

I don't *want* to be like this. But I don't know how to be what he'll need.

When my phone vibrates again, I slide it closer to me to see the screen. Guessing who's messaging has been a game of mine throughout the day.

Della.

But it's not her.

ERICO

Are you okay?

Like a fucking transport truck, his simple question slams right into my heart. A sick form of pleasure has me hugging my phone to my chest. He's asking. He knows. Probably from Sebastian's reports, but considering he's the same man who took off right away, he's still finding it in his undoubtedly busy day to check on me.

His is the first message I debate responding to but my screen is consumed by an incoming call.

His call.

Fuck.

I can't answer. Can't talk to this near-stranger, not with how I'm feeling.

Every ring has me more and more tempted to answer, so ending it sooner is better. I tap the hang-up button, ending his call, rather than letting it go to voicemail.

A text immediately follows.

> **ERICO**
>
> Why are you not answering me?

I stare at the phone until more bubbles pop up.

> **ERICO**
>
> Why won't you leave the room?

Because. I wish I had an ending to that. An exact purpose behind my *because*...but I don't.

> **ERICO**
>
> I swear to fuck, Ariella, answer me before I fly home and drag you from that room myself.

I shut my eyes. He doesn't get it—he probably never will either. But coming home, all for him to return to Vegas when he's hauled me from bed, isn't what I desire. I wish I knew what I *want.*

Love. Genuine love. What he's doing isn't from a place of care. It's obligation.

Rolling onto my back, I take the phone with me, fingers

over the keypad, readying to respond before he makes good on his threat.

ME

> I'm fine. Just tired. New life and all that can be exhausting.

The text's status immediately switches, telling me he's read it, and with every passing second, my heart beats a bit faster for his response.

But he doesn't respond. After a while, I drop the phone to the bed and roll until I'm facing away from the windows—away from my phone. My eyes shut and I feign sleep for myself, convincing my body to rest, even if it's much too early.

Just when it's about to work, my phone vibrates again, and I hate how fast I retrieve it.

ERICO

I don't believe you. Eat.

Why, so I don't starve to death and you're left with nothing?
Tempting to message that to him, but I don't.

After abandoning my phone, I roll over again, and right before I shut my eyes for good, I remember exactly which day it is.

In a mere few hours, I'll be twenty-two.

Waking up the next morning, I hope to feel better. I don't.

The gloom clings, even as I finally drag myself from bed and toward the bathroom. It's a win when I climb into the shower and wash up. A win when I dress in clean clothes.

In one way, I suppose I am doing better.

Must come with age. Wisdom and all that shit. Happy birthday to me.

But I'm not. I stare at the bed, feeling the most absolute longing to return to it. The rain continues, which means all I'll be doing today is occupying myself. My one and only hobby—music—can be done from right in this room. No point in sitting downstairs, where Sebastian and Carlotta are.

But if you go down, you'll be pretending to be human again.

Sometimes, my inner voice is too good to me. It's so correct.

When I return to the bed to retrieve my phone, there's a few messages already waiting. Many from Della wishing me a happy birthday, which I make a note to actually respond to later. To do what I've always done and pretend for her. She has enough to worry about without adding my mental health to her pile.

The next is from my husband. I wonder what time it is in Vegas, and what he's been doing all night. He's in a party city, two days after his wedding. How much is he celebrating right now?

How many women has he fucked for our honeymoon?

That makes me grow cold, to the point when my finger taps his message, it's impossible not to feel a blatant anger about an accusation I have no proof of.

ERICO

Please eat today.

No promises, buddy. He's not ordering me from a place of care. More so his heir maker doesn't die before he could impregnate me.

I shut the app and tuck my phone in my back pocket as I wander from the bed and toward the massive window. I fell asleep with the curtains open so they're already drawn, and for a moment, I just zone out, watching the water and rain battle for control.

God, what I wouldn't do to be in there right now. To swim away from everything.

You did this, my voice reminds me.

I did. An act I'm regretting with every passing hour.

A knock on the door pulls my attention away, and for a moment, I go still, wondering if Erico did indeed come home, like he threatened to.

That would mean he cares. He doesn't care.

"Mrs. Rossi." *Sebastian.* "Ariella, if you'll come out, there's a surprise for you from Mr. Rossi. It was just delivered."

That has me walking toward the door. Not pleasure, but a curiosity driving me forward. When was the last time I was surprised? When Mom introduced her new boyfriend to Della and me. When Nico Corsetti visited me at the medical centre.

But when was the last time *I* was surprised? When someone surprised *me* with an item?

Never.

I think the answer is...never.

What could Erico possibly get me that's a surprise? A new fancy car—don't want one. More clothes—based on the closet, I have enough. Jewellery—I'm not even wearing my wedding ring, which is still in the room's corner from where I tossed it.

I open the door to find Sebastian raising his fist, presumably to knock again. Surprise flashes over his face and his arm jerks back to his side. "Oh, Ariella, good. Just got off the phone with the boss. He sent you something. Come, I'll show you the way."

He walks down the hall without checking I'm following, but I do. Fuck Erico for using curiosity to tug away the black shade coating my form. Not entirely sure how I feel about that.

Sebastian leads me over the bridge and down to the main floor. He turns left toward the entranceway and the connected hallway we toured yesterday. We pass the small library, which is half the size of the Corsettis', and toward another room by the end of the hall, which is completely empty. Huge but empty. When asking about it, Sebastian shrugged. Called it an extra space that's sometimes used for parties and left it at that.

It's that door he opens.

The large room is still quite empty. White, painted walls, and a massive window, showing the side of the house and a bit of the ocean. If I was Erico, I'd make this room my office, so I could observe the water while working.

The difference from present to what I saw yesterday is the black piano tucked against the far side, facing the window.

Holy fuck.

I step into the room without another thought. The door shuts behind me and a quick glance finds Sebastian has left me alone to check out my surprise.

But how did Erico know? Is this Della's doing?

Composing music is one thing, but my love for the piano runs deep. As a child, I started composing and singing songs, and performed in talent shows throughout elementary school. Mom always praised me for my singing voice, and the older I got, the more other people did too. I never craved fame or to make a career from it, but it was a calming hobby. Made me feel joy. Writing a song, composing the tune with the piano, and singing the lyrics made the blackness fade into a pale grey. In high school, I often borrowed the music classroom but once graduating, I lost all access to pianos until Stefano came into our lives. He owned one I'd often use.

Post-accident, I stopped composing all together. The hobby reminded me too much of what I'd lost—Mom, my voice, my individuality. It was Yasmine, during her visits, that convinced me to get back to it. She saw my notebook one day and, with permission, began flipping through it. Having someone read my private thoughts; the notebook acting as my journal for so long felt weird. There was no logical explanation for allowing her to read it.

In some ways, I'm pleased I did. She suggested I start by composing again, even if I wasn't comfortable enough singing yet, even to myself. I did, and continued to right until moving in with Della.

When my mood was light enough, I'd compose. I even wrote something to sing at her wedding, hoping *that* would be the thing to wake my voice up. Ignore everyone else and perform for her...but it didn't pan out that way.

I haven't written since the wedding.

No point. Even writing for myself is losing meaning as things continue to change around me.

But Erico purchased me the very tool meant to bring me back.

I wander toward it, tempted by the shiny, black coating, which I can't help but drag a finger over, feeling its smooth exterior. The brand name of Bösendorfer tells me he researched and found one of the best brands on the market.

I don't know what to think. Somehow he *knew*...The same man who blatantly stated we'd lead different lives, live in different homes, who ran off the moment he got his wedding ring on my finger, is the same person who learned something authentic about me. His gift could have very easily been thoughtless materialistic items, like jewels, rather than something he believed I'd sincerely enjoy.

He was correct.

This is a game, Ariella. He's trying to lure you in. Make you feel like you're content to be a domesticated housewife he can visit when he feels like it.

My inner voice might be correct...

But for now, I lift the lid to the ivory keys, pausing when I find an envelope with my name etched on it. I pick it up and slide out the letter, reading every word as my confusion deepens.

Ariella,
Happy birthday. I'm sorry for my absence, but I wanted you to have this in my stead.
Erico.

The letter falls onto the keys, my brain numbing, still unable to formulate a proper word for what he's doing.

Instead, I cry. Tears, the same I've been crying for nearly a day now, continue to slide down my face, but instead of sadness and despair, I'm *lost*. Not happy—can't be that. But not unhappy either. Lost. Confused.

Confounded with how to feel about this. It's like he's buying me...but he's buying me with such a lovely gift, I can't help but accept his purchasing of me.

Instead, I sit, slumped, staring at the piano, tears dripping down my cheeks.

So fucking confused as I stare at the piano, my fingers aching to touch it, to play music. To go retrieve my notebook and perform the songs already written. To revise old ones and make them better.

Why did he do this? Why does he taunt me with niceties?

My phone rings, the screen flashing with the FaceTime app.

Fuck. He's calling me. Do I ignore him? That'd be a bitch move, considering what he's done here. But my cheeks are warm from crying, and though I wipe them away, it'll be impossible to hide the red rimming my eyes. Ideally, he won't pay attention.

I tap the button to answer his call and Erico's face fills my screen. I prop my phone up on the piano keys and manage a small wave in greeting as I try to decipher the room he's in. Its bright, white walls. I think he's leaning against a headboard. A hotel room?

His greeting smile immediately shifts into a frown, his head tilting to the right. "Why are you crying?"

Damn it. I shrug, pressing my lips together to stop another wave of his fake caring.

His eyes narrow, obviously seeing through my lie, but thankfully, he switches topics. "Happy birthday, Ariella."

How did you know?

How did you know when my birthday is?

How did you know what hobbies I have?

Slowly so he can catch it, I mouth, *Thank you. How did you know?*

Erico smirks, giving me a look full of sin that heats my insides. "You have no faith if you think I wouldn't have had your background looked into. Of course, I know your birthday. As for your hobbies, I had my driver search your backpack yesterday before bringing it up. He saw the notebook and sent me pictures of it to look over. The lyrics and the matching music notes you assigned to each one. All your scribbles as you changed and modified them. And the little messages you wrote yourself about how you'd perform these on a piano."

No apology for searching my personal items. I should be angry he's so invasively checking into my life—especially when he could simply *ask* me. *Talk* to me—but instead I merely smile, way too pleased and appreciative to be annoyed for long.

"Why didn't you tell me it was your birthday?" he asks, his tone colder than before. Almost like he's annoyed.

Because you wouldn't care. Because it doesn't matter. That was in my head though.

To respond to his question, I shrug, hoping my eyes convey my thoughts.

"We're married, Ariella," he reminds me, as if I could forget the entire reason I'm in the U.S.. "It means we tell each other facts about ourselves. Mine is two days before Halloween, by the way." He pauses, the angle of the phone changing with his movement. It puts some of his chest into view. He's in a white button-up shirt, the top two buttons undone. "I'll admit, I know nothing about pianos, but I was reassured that one is a top brand. If you want something else, I can make it happen."

My head shakes rapidly to deny his latest offer, and then I lift both hands with my thumbs up, enticing a deep chuckle from him that causes my own insides to flip in pleasure.

"Got it," he says lightly. "Glad you approve then." He pauses again, his amusement melting away for a serious expression once more. "One day, I hope you allow me to hear you play."

Allow. Such a simple word for a man who doesn't require me to give any permission.

Was I wrong about him?

"I've heard you haven't left your room for an entire day. Why?" he goes on.

Fucking Sebastian. I shrug.

His lips pinch. "There are consequences for lying to me."

Nico warned me of the consequences when he was still trying to convince me to change my mind about my offer. Said the *Famiglia* is a big deal; that they won't hesitate to remind a woman of her role. Which goes against every bone, every fibre of my being, not to let another man dominate me.

Nothing, I mouth and shake my head slowly. Because what's wrong doesn't have words. Feeling alone in a life he's already stated would get more lonely means nothing is wrong. Not to him anyway.

Again, he seems like he doesn't believe me but instead moves on. "Fine. I didn't call to fight with you. I wanted to see you and nothing more. Wish you a happy birthday. Ensure you're okay since you're worrying Carlotta and Sebastian."

But not you.

"For now, I have to return to business and should be home in a couple more days."

I nod because his words leave no room for argument, but once again, I don't know what I want. The gift to lure me from my room isn't it, but the genuineness in this conversation might be. That he *wanted* to wish me a happy birthday. He didn't have to get me a gift at all. He certainly didn't have to call—no, video call—at that.

Okay, I mouth, but don't hang up.

Neither does he.

He watches me, his eyes bouncing around his screen. No doubt, questioning his sanity for agreeing to take me as his wife. A woman he literally bribed to get out of the bedroom.

The thought snaps like a rubber band in my head. My birthday provided him the means to get me out of bed. A bribe and a way to keep me silent for longer.

Maybe my beliefs are wildly incorrect. Maybe they're not. At this point, I can't tell what's reality and what's my mind going into its dark but welcoming crevices.

Either way, I wave goodbye because that's what he expects. I use my right hand to hide my ringless left one, thankful he hasn't noticed I'm not wearing it. Or he has, and he simply doesn't care. Somehow, that thought makes it worse.

He can return to his day and I'll hide behind my walls until I must emerge, pretend to be his wife, and then get to disappear again.

"Have a nice day, Ariella."

The screen goes black.

Grief hits me. I don't cry, but my body certainly wants to.

Not sure why at this point, but something about the abandonment right there on the technology shatters me. Breaks me. My mood both lifting and lowering. The depression becoming unreasonable, but my mind can't make sense of what's reasonable anymore.

I lower my phone to the bench beside me and clear the way for my fingers to stroke the keys again. I press down on the centre one, a low *ding* filling the empty room around me.

Tears fall again, no longer able to be kept at bay.

I cry because I'm sad about Mom.

I cry because I'm no longer with Della.

I cry because I've gotten a husband, like I dreamed of.

I cry because I shackled myself to a man who wants little to do with me.

Another finger presses down onto another key. And then another. Not making any music per se but causing sounds regardless. Sounds my ears have long missed.

Sounds that make me feel...dare I say it?

Happy.

Makes the tears slowly dry up, as my gaze locks on the phone by my side. If I understood my husband's intentions, it'd be better, but taking off to Vegas right away, gave me no chance to figure him out. He still remains the handsome man I ran into at Della's engagement party, and watched from across a dance floor at the wedding reception.

Every sound clears away the misery bit by bit. I'm not ungrateful, and I hope he doesn't think so.

Just confused.

Over his actions.

Over my emotions.

Over what in my brain decided *this* situation was best.

11

ERICO

I toss the phone onto the bed and stand, quickly striding into the bathroom and away from that stupid piece of technology. It taunts me with availability and ability—being a method to contact my wife, even when I really shouldn't be bothering. It'll cause her to end up with unrealistic expectations of me. Of *us*.

But when I learned about her birthday, even I couldn't be that much of an ass. Some deep instinct knew she'd like a piano. After I was sent the pictures of her notebook, I poured over her lyrics. The pain in her chosen words. Being musically challenged and unable to understand the notes she was assigning to some of them, I can't even pretend to imagine what her songs would sound like, but a curiosity certainly struck me.

Then I was supposed to have it delivered, and Sebastian show it to her, and that was it. Never a phone call. Certainly not a video call when I realized a regular call requiring the use of voice wouldn't be enough.

But when her face filled my screen, every fight I've been having with myself vanished. Fuck, she's beautiful. There's misery in her eyes—deeply wedged—but it began fading over the course of our call.

I scowl at my cell phone as I finish readying for the day, and have to slide it into my pocket. Vegas never starts their days early, so it'll be hours until the city is bustling. Hell, it should have been hours more until I was up too, considering, according to the time on my phone, I only went to bed four hours ago after the meeting ran late, and the afterparty ran later.

Father never appeared at the meeting, and through every casual conversation with a head, I was one more minute away from finding his ass and determining answers. But the party after the meeting is tradition. With all the heads together, they enjoy making it worth their time, and for all Caladin's bitching about being present, he continued to slide drinks my way, somehow understanding what I needed.

The alcohol never got me drunk though, when thoughts of my new wife home alone was sobering enough. I feel like an asshole—guilty even when the emotion has no place here. I shouldn't *be* guilty about following my own rules. About maintaining the necessary distance so I can continue leading the *Famiglia* without stress or concern of another person's feelings.

But the alcohol didn't stop my planning, or me scouring the pictures of her songs again. Or emailing my staff until someone got me the contact information for a music store in New York.

The look on her face made everything worth it.

And got her out of her room. Hopefully by now, she's eating too.

I exit the condo, placing all thoughts of Ariella into a box in the back of my head as I continue to focus on why I'm in Vegas at all. She can't distract me when I have stuff to deal with.

The meeting yesterday was productive, even if I was only half-listening. If it wasn't for Caladin's frequent jabs in my side, I might have zoned out completely. The *Famiglia* has had a lot of progress in recent months, which meant plenty of updates. A few distant relatives praised me for bridging the connection between us and the Corsetti family, while others grumbled. The consensus is split over abandoning a decades-old hatred of Lorenzo Corsetti or letting it go entirely and moving forward for the benefit of the organization. Either opinion, no one commented on my bride switch, which was wise of them.

Once in the elevator, I text Caladin, who's also staying in one of the condo apartments in this building, to meet me at the car in the underground parking lot. Knowing him, he'll be a few minutes as he drags his ass to get ready.

Sure enough, twenty minutes later, the elevator doors open and my rumpled cousin strides out and into the open back door of the town car.

He settles into the seat across from me, his mouth open in a wide yawn, his eyes still lined with sleep. "Do you not fuckin' sleep anymore? I have a headache from hell."

"Called a hangover. Next time, don't get drunk." I tap the car's roof, signalling to the driver we're ready to go.

"Whatever. Why're we up so early?"

"You know every time my father or I are here, we prefer to stop into our Vegas locations directly, regardless if documentation is checking out. Since I'm up and it's still before noon, which means half the city is still passed out, we can get a start on it."

"Believe me," his eyes narrow into slits, "I'm aware half the city is passed out still and I'm insanely fuckin' jealous to not be one of them. But why do *we* have to get a start on it?"

"Because with me becoming Boss tonight and you also sliding into a new role, we need to ensure we're a united front, even now. Consider this a prime opportunity to show people why you'll be by my side."

His arms cross over his chest as he slumps deeper into the

seat. "Fine. But if you want any sort of conversation out of me, we need to make a coffee stop."

~

Once Caladin's slurping noisily on his coffee, we begin our trek to the nearest address I provided the driver earlier. He's two sips in when somehow the drink of life begins its work and wakes him up.

"So. You end up finding the perfect gift for Ariella?"

I glance up from my own cup. "How did you know I was looking?"

He rolls his eyes. "All last night, it's all you spoke about. Going back and forth between options. Kept talking about your guilt."

Fuck. "Did I admit what I was guilty about?"

My asshole cousin drags out the suspense for longer by taking another sip of his drink, grinning around his cup because he fully knows what he's doing. "'Bout leaving her so soon after the wedding," he finally answers. "I mean, you *did* stay for a few hours, right? Consummate the marriage and all that."

Any other family member would have gotten an immediate lie, but the guy who's like a brother to me, who's the only one to ever earn all my truths instead watches me shift in my seat as I admit, "No."

His mouth falls open. "Well, fuck, no wonder the guilt. I wouldn't be surprised if she threw that gift at you the moment you finally walk through the door. You realize, if anyone in the organization learned you didn't consummate, it'd reflect badly on you?"

I level my stare with him. "Quite aware, thanks, which means shut your mouth."

He shakes his head once, throwing an unimpressed look my way. "Just sayin', it's not what I expected from you."

"You know I don't have time to love a woman. It's not how I'm built. She'd take away from the *Famiglia*."

He rolls his eyes again. "Since when does sex equal love?"

"Besides," I skip over his last question, "she's not like that. I won't do that to her. Her background isn't...typical. She's not from this world, so I can safely assume a lot of the regular traditions will be put aside."

For a beat, Caladin only stares. He takes another sip and glances out the window, scanning the passing malls. "Now that's interesting," he finally murmurs, his eyes coming back to me, staring at me with a serious expression I see so infrequently from him. "Very interesting, cuz."

Way into the evening, close to midnight, everyone re-gathers at the meeting place, but instead of me at the head of the table, Father is.

Father, who strode in minutes ago without glancing my way. Fucker avoided me—and everyone else for that matter. Every call to him, or request for my men to be on the lookout, he's slid by us all until he was ready to be seen. Which means, I still didn't get to ask him about the Bratva's presence in Vegas.

For now, something more important is about to happen. Something bigger than him and me and our arguments over the organization's future.

The change of leadership. It's above him, me, and our visions. It's *for* the *Famiglia*.

"When Gia announced I'd be granted a son, I dreamed of this moment," Father begins, scanning the room of gathered men. "For anyone with a son, you know what it's like—the knowledge that he'll be taking over for you. Following in your carefully laid footsteps and utilizing every minute of training you've put him through. There's a pride in doing so, which I've witnessed multiple instances in my time as Boss, always envisioning the day I'd experience that pride too. When I made Erico my underboss, it was the beginning of that feeling." He stands, this time looking toward me, where I'm on his right side. His eyes glisten, and for once, not with malice. He's correct in that there was only ever a single time I've seen his current expression, and that's was during my first promotion. "When he took over as underboss, it was only a matter of time before we came here. Once, I believed I'd remain your loyal Boss until the end of my days, serving right up until death claims me, but after recent months, I have complete confidence the future of the *Famiglia* is no longer with me, but with my son."

He glances at me again, and I feel my chest expand with breath—with new life. *My* new life as it's dangled inches from me. Minutes away from becoming a reality.

Then he scans the room, addressing everyone here. "Thank you all for coming to watch this momentous moment in our history. All our leadership under one roof to witness this makes me proud to have your trust. Your knowledge that handing over the *Famiglia* to my son is for the best. He's a man I know will lead you all right, with a new bride by his side, and eventually an heir."

His bitterness is buried beneath the pride he speaks of, but I catch a slight wind of it. His disapproving of Ariella blatantly stated for the room, if anyone here can figure out his tells.

Father turns his body, facing me now, his hands pressing together as though he was praying. I bow my head, my hand over my heart, waiting for his next words.

"Erico Rossi, underboss of the *Famiglia*, I now entrust the organization in your capable hands. From this day forward, you will be Boss. Do you agree to uphold the *Famiglia*, to ensure their prosperity, and to *always* place the organization before anything else?"

Those words, I've never heard before, but now my life makes sense. All Father's done was place the organization before anything else, including Mother. Me as well, to a point, because I was a part of his job. Training me for this moment, so the typical relationship a father and son might have, that was never us.

This is all I've ever prepared for. The reason I told Ariella her rough reality. I'm *not* a typical man. I'm a Made Man. One vow away from being Boss. The *Famiglia* already owned my life and loyalty, but now they own *me*. Everything I am will be for them.

And nothing will get in the way.

"I agree."

Father grins as I dip my head lower, the weight of my vow settling on my back as he waits for me to finish the ceremony with the final words that'll seal everything.

"Per la Famiglia." The Italian slogan flows from my lips as easily as the day I learned it.

The room breaks out in cheers, everyone repeating the slogan in a mutual chorus, but around Father and me, it feels like a silent bubble instead. Everything around us is muted, allowing me to hear his murmurs.

"Good job, son." His hand rests heavy on my shoulder, making a statement, even as he leans closer. "I'll expect you to remember that vow, Erico. Do not disappointment me. Continue making me proud, and not feeling like this will be the biggest error on my part." When he straightens, that pride from earlier is gone, replaced by an evil gleam in his eyes.

Our stare holds until Caladin whoops and jumps between us, his arm hooking around my neck as he steers me away and toward the staircase, where most of the other men have already gone, ready to celebrate the leadership change in the empty bar, which has been closed for the night for this purpose.

"Looked like you needed saving there," he mutters in my ear.

I'm swarmed by the others when we make it upstairs, people slapping me on my back, my shoulders, even my head, until they guarantee I'll wake up with both a headache and bruises.

Questions about who'll be my underboss arises, which I shrug off, because I truthfully don't know. Many assume it'll be Caladin, but I announce he'll be my Consigliere instead, based on his skillset and how we work together. It does present a problem for me, having to pick someone who I trust enough, but it'll be another day's concern.

Eventually, I make it back to Caladin, who's leaning against the bar, a beer bottle in his hand. He raises it up to greet me while also sliding a shot my way. The bar is littered with them, the two bartenders continuously pouring and lining them up for people to take.

"This mean I gotta respect you now and all that?" He smirks.

I shove my shoulder into his, jostling his half-empty beer. "Like you ever have before."

"I don't want the underboss job," he states, his tone flat and serious.

"I don't want you to have it. You know what I need of you. Besides, I'll pick whatever random family member I feel a decent relationship with, and it'll only be temporary until my own son is old enough to take the position."

A son...Always a fact, a requirement in my life, but for the first time ever, it hits me exactly why I need one. To be *this*. To do what I just did. To become an underboss and eventually, my new position.

Caladin's punch pulls me back to the present. He grins as he takes a chug from his bottle. "Just got thinking about children, didn't you? More reason to get home to your wife, no?" His brow lifts, challenging me to argue the fact.

Requiring an heir changes little right now. Ariella's so new to this world, to *me*, I don't want to shove motherhood at her yet. If she's hardly leaving her room after an entire day, what would another role do to her? It's not exactly a healthy option at the moment.

I shut my eyes, blocking out the fact I'm already breaking my own vows by placing her happiness before the *Famiglia*. If Father knew where my thoughts were, he'd be beating on me.

Sebastian messaged me once today and reported Ariella spent the majority of the day using her piano. I hate how pleased that made me.

As though thinking about him sent him some imaginary vibe, he texts again.

SEBASTIAN

She's in your room for the night. Also, congrats, Boss.

Clearly, the news already got spread to the organization-wide call out, informing all the soldiers of the change in leadership.

ME

Thanks.

I glance up from my phone to the rowdy crowd again, spotting my father right before he ascends a back staircase, leading to the offices above us. Pushing away from the bar, I barely throw a goodbye toward Caladin before I'm slipping through the crowd to follow.

I catch up right as he's taking a seat behind the desk, and based on his expression as he spots me in the doorway, he's unsurprised I followed. His hands fold over his stomach as he rocks back, leveling his stare with mine.

"You should be celebrating your promotion with the men. Consider yourself lucky I wish to retire because that role shouldn't be yours until I die. Especially with your recent decision-making."

His indirect insult rolls right off me as I step deeper into the office and slam the door shut to ensure no nosy fucker overhears. "Why'd you do it then? Why promote me if you felt I wasn't up to standards?"

"I have my own reasons," he replies in a non-answer. This is typical of Father though.

It doesn't matter when the demand for other facts are greater. "Are you really retiring when you're having secret meetings with Ursin Volkov?"

He grins but doesn't reply.

I head to the side of the desk, standing beside him rather than behind it, which forces him to spin to better see me. It's a power move, which we're both aware of. As of an hour ago, this desk became *mine* and standing on the other side places him at an advantage.

"Vanessa Volkov bombarding me here yesterday changes nothing, Father. I'm already married."

"I'm well aware of that, son," he says dryly. "Vanessa simply accompanied her father on his trip to Vegas and then wished to remain behind yesterday to congratulate you on your nuptials."

Except that conversation didn't happen at all. Bracing a fist on the desk and one on the back of his chair, I lean closer, towering over him. "Don't lie, Father. I've never even *seen*

Vanessa until the photo you showed me the other day. Very doubtful she'd congratulate a couple she's never met. Tell me why you're having meetings with the Russian Bratva. You claim *I* make stupid decisions, but you're allowing them on American soil!"

My insult seemingly glides over his thinning hair, and I don't get a response. Even a flicker of emotion as his gaze remains steady and undisturbed as he replies, "I'm working on a business deal."

A deal with the Bratva is precarious and can end one of two ways. One of which, being our death. No one here would risk dealing with them because such a high-level agreement would come from the top. From me. Which means, I need to at least be aware of what hell my father's about to drag this organization through.

"What. Is. The. Deal?" Each word is punched, strained behind gritted teeth.

"You will see soon enough."

My fist tightens on the desk, seconds away from ending up in his face if he doesn't answer directly. "Perhaps you're right, Father. Maybe you stepped down much too early because in case you've forgotten the past hour, you gave up your rights to hide shit from me. *I'm* Boss now."

In a burst, he jumps to his feet, his palms shoving into my chest, creating a force of distance between us. "Son, first lesson to leadership: if you want to play the game, play it fucking right. You've been Boss for two-point-five seconds. Those men," he gestures to the door and the bar beyond, "are much more loyal to me than you. I have *years* on you, boy, so be fucking careful how you talk to me."

"The capos maybe, but not the soldiers." I cross my arms, lifting my chin as I stare down at my aging father. "And firepower is tougher than a bunch of old assholes arguing."

Father tips his head, almost like agreeing with me and then abruptly switches the topic. "How's your marriage?"

Even the thought of Ariella passing through my father's head makes me cold. "None of your business."

"You can't hide your mute bride away forever, you know. It's like your mother said. She has to meet everyone eventually."

"I know," I bite out. "I've had other focuses, in case you've forgotten."

We end up in a stand-off, and previous experiences with him already deem he won't let up until he believes he's won. So I walk away without glancing behind me.

"Go retire, Father, and if your insane plans with the Bratva involve double crossing me, you're fucking done. I'll prove exactly how effective all your training is."

12
ARIELLA

The piano changes a lot.

It clears the dim clouds that were devouring me and gives me something to do for the remainder of the day. At some point, I retrieved my notebook, despising how tainted it now felt, knowing Erico had read my private emotions, displayed through song. Even Della has never seen the book in its entirety.

But I spent the whole day testing out one of my original songs, trialling all the notes I theorized would work over the years. Carlotta eventually delivered food to my new music room, which I ate, and I made further plans with Sebastian to finish our tour tomorrow.

Even the dark, little voice managed to remain quieter than usual. Except, I know it's only a matter of time before something triggers it back.

I also finally respond to my sister's messages, telling her thanks and that I'd call her tomorrow.

By the time I retire to my new room, I feel *okay*. Okay as I can be, but that was Erico's plan after all. Drag me from this room with the temptation of something better.

I spend an extra long time in the shower, noting how it's even more grand than the one I had in the Corsetti mansion. The whole bathroom seems larger, the tile a shade of blue rather than plain white.

I've been comparing this place to Nico's house a lot today, and in every way, Erico's surpasses it.

I slide into the centre of the bed, noting how much space is around me. A king-sized mattress compared to my queen at Nico's, but there, I slept alone. The space beside my body taunts me. It knows here, I'll eventually be sharing this spot.

Not sure how I feel about it.

Vvvvv.

My phone vibrates against the bedside table and I retrieve it, wondering who'd possibly be calling me this time of night.

Erico.

Through a video call again.

I could ignore it and claim I was already asleep if he asks. Or I could respond and what—talk?

What do I want?

I rest the phone down and lean away, but as fast as I avoid the device, I'm snatching it up again, tapping the answer button before the call dies and I lose this chance.

Erico fills my screen, and I catch his shoulders lowering. Relief that I picked up?

"Twice in one day," he murmurs. "I'd hoped you were still awake."

Why? I emphasize my lip movements with a head tilt so he catches the question.

"Because I wanted to see you."

A pleasurable shiver runs through me and my hand tightens on the blanket's edge, out of sight from the screen.

"You're in bed," he states.

I nod.

"Is it comfortable? To your liking?"

I nod again, unsure why he's asking these exact questions.

"I heard you played the piano most of the day today. This pleases me, Ariella."

I'd be annoyed at Sebastian doing his job again if it wasn't for Erico's final words. Something about the way his lips melded over the term *pleases* and my name makes my insides tighten in desire.

If only there's paper around because I want to use my own words rather than a head gesture to admit my true feelings about the gift. So I hold up my finger, indicating to him to give me a moment, and switch to the messaging app.

ME

> I really love it. Thank you. It was exactly
> what I needed today.

As soon as I send that, I swipe back to the call, watching in time as his eyes flick to the top of his screen, presumably reading my text which has just been delivered.

"It's my pleasure, Ariella. I hope you're able to find some of your old self with your new life here."

Because that's the girl he met. Not this depressed version of you.

Aw, damn, the voice is back. Fuck. Right when I thought I'd be in the clear for the night.

Smiling through the grim thought, I nod slowly, indicating I want that too. With the piano, it just might work.

"Well, I also wanted to call and let you know of some changes in my life. In *our* lives actually. I've been promoted to the *Famiglia* Boss."

My smile freezes, my eyes flicking over to the corner of the room as my brain digests his news. If he's Boss, I'm no longer an underboss's wife. I think—assume—the pressure of my role just grew. Became significant, as I'll be looked at to produce the next heir.

A well-known fact I was prepared for when I volunteered. Hell, I *want* to give him his heir because then I'll get to be a mother. But suddenly, it's not on our timeline. It's on whatever the organization demands of him because soon, they'll want the future locked in.

"Ariella?"

Right.

Congrats, I mouth through a tight smile.

"Thanks," he replies. "The heads of all my branches are probably still celebrating. Taking advantage of the free booze and all that, but I called it quits about an hour ago." He angles the phone until I can see the edge of the bed. "Long day. Tomorrow will be longer. I have a few more things to do in Vegas before I return." He pauses, rolling his lips together. "And Ariella, I *do* want to return to you soon."

So he can begin his heir-making program.

Despite my inner voice being probably correct, I push out a smile for him.

"Anyway, I wanted to let you know. And..." He looks away. "And to see you again, that's all."

My stomach knots, the hand around the blanket's edge even tighter as we both fall silent, unsure of what to tell the other, while disturbed with his final words. For him, I'll assume, because they're not in line with his distancing plan, and for me, because I don't know how to feel.

I don't want to end up *hoping.*

So much of my life, I've hoped all to lose it. Hope for a good life, all for Mom to die. Hope for safety, all for our stepfather to wreck that. Hope for a happy ending, all to end up forcing myself upon a man who required a wife—whether that was me or another woman.

"Have a good sleep, Ariella," Erico finally murmurs. "And happy birthday once again. I'll be seeing you soon."

The screen flashes black, leaving me uncertain if his latest statement was a threat or a promise.

Right after breakfast the next day, I head to the bedroom for absolute privacy when I call Della.

"Finally!" she answers on the first ring. "Fuck, can you *not* leave me in so much suspense? It's been two days since I had to say goodbye to you, and while I know we've gone for longer without seeing or talking—" she's referring to when Stefano had me locked away, "—it's still weird, you know. Guess I've gotten used to you being around."

For the first time in days, I use my voice. When no matter the fuckery of my mind, which prevents me from being normal, Della always manages to break through the trauma. The knowledge that *she's* safe. Safer than anyone I know. Besides me, the only other living proof of our mother still on this earth.

"I missed you too, Della."

"Nico's been telling me not to stress, but that's all I've been doing since you left. God, Ariella, to not have you here reminds me of when—"

"It's fine," I cut her off before she can mention our dead stepfather's name. "I'm fine."

"Are you?"

Not completely. "Today feels good." *Walls back up.* The same way as I've hidden my true emotions for months away from her probing.

"Today," she repeats, a deep skepticism lining her tone. "But not yesterday?"

I shrug, despite knowing she can't see me. "Not really."

"It's hard not to have Mom here, right, on your birthday?" she incorrectly assumes.

"Yeah," I agree regardless.

"Happy birthday—belated now, I guess. Twenty-two."

"Thanks."

Five seconds of silence pass before my sister groans. "Ari, elephant in the room much. Tell me what it's been like in New York, with Erico. Reassure me so I don't fly down there and kick his ass. *Please* tell me he did something for your birthday."

Skipping past all her other questions, which require putting words to my emotions, I answer her last one. "He bought me a piano."

"Fuck," she breathes. "Seriously? That's amazing. Guess he's not so bad, after all, eh?"

"It's fine," I say immediately, utilizing my typical reassurance. *I'm fine* never means a person is fine. But then, knowing this is *Della*, my sister, who, despite my ongoing determination to hide every truth from her—to protect her in ways only a sister can, despite her being the eldest sibling—I stop lying. I *want* to admit this. To be reassured by another person on this level. Fuck, to seek guidance from her even. "I don't know how he is, Della, because I don't know him at all. When we arrived to his house in the Hamptons, he dropped me off and took off for a Vegas trip."

"Fucker," she curses. "Like, I get he has responsibilities in his role as an underboss, but that's a dick move." She pauses. "But, then also, he wasn't supposed to get married until the end of the month so this probably threw off his plans a bit."

She's reminding me of everything I'm not and how I'm not

wanted. I disturbed his plans when the wedding happened three weeks earlier than he planned for.

Della's always more logical than me. In some ways, she's also more emotional, so despite her logical statement, if I know her, she'll follow up with some cursing—

"But then, he could have cancelled his stuff," she rambles on. "A man who cares would have."

That's the thing. Erico doesn't care.

"Or fuck, kept the original wedding date and solved all of this. Then you'd still be here for a few more weeks and he could have gone gallivanting in Vegas all he likes."

"Della," I whisper, aiming to break her tirade before she says more shit I won't like. "Stop. It doesn't matter anyway."

She's silent, her anger radiating through the phone, indicating her disagreement. "Fine." I can picture her sulking. "When's he coming back?"

"Dunno. Last night, he mentioned it'd be soon."

"Last night?"

"Yeah..." Suddenly, I don't want to admit this next part. Like it almost feels too personal to share. But I do. "He called me, to inform me be was promoted to Boss. And then yesterday morning, he called to wish me a happy birthday."

"That's...nice. Still not liking this whole set-up, though."

"Too late now." And that's not even telling her he plans on living apart from me.

"Yeah, well...ugh! Why'd you volunteer again?"

So I can feel less alone. So I can make a family for myself, only to realize I'm an unwanted task he's only treating well, the same one would feed a pet.

My entire mood shifts and the urgency to get off the phone builds. Especially since Sebastian offered to finish the tour today and it's bright, sunny, and hot out, I don't want my mood to drive me to bury my head in the pillows again and not leave this room.

"Someone's at my door, Della," I lie, "Gotta go." Before she says goodbye, I jab the red hang-up button, dropping the desvice and striding away from it.

Della gets to live her perfect life with a husband who adores her. Who wants to spend his entire life making her wishes come true. With Nico, she'll always have a voice.

With Erico, I never will.

The irony isn't lost on me.

Before my mood shifts anymore, I exit the bedroom without retrieving my phone, heading right for the kitchen, which is where Sebastian said he'd meet with me after my call with Della.

He glances up from his cup as I enter, his light eyes growing even brighter. He's like a hyper puppy and his grin is infectious, making mine too impossible to hide. "Good chat with your sister?"

Testing him, since he enjoys the practice, I sign to him, *Yes, thank you for waiting. Ready if you are.*

Since I moved slow enough, he seems to catch most of it, nodding as my hands return to my side. "If you asked if I'm ready, it's a yes. If you asked anything else, well, it's still a yes and I hope I won't get in trouble for agreeing to it."

My responding laughter is more of a huff as he gestures toward the back door for me to take the lead. I'm excited as I open it and step onto a stone path. One of those paths where the round stones are imbedded overtop the grass and not in a straight line, making the walk odder than it needs to be.

But it's not the path that has my attention *at all*. It's the Olympic-sized pool it leads to.

Oh my god. My steps quicken, flip-flops struggling to keep pace as I rush down the path for a better look at the massive pool, easily taking up a third of the space behind the house. The water is clear, a light turquoise as it reflects the sky above. It's surrounded by a cement border, wide enough for the dozen or so lounge chairs scattered around, each one with a small table between them.

If the pool wasn't enough, it's the view. Since the Rossi property sits on the edge of the land, only a few feet away from the cement is the clear fence, ensuring that people don't accidentally end up falling off the cliff and into the ocean.

But me, I walk right up to that fence, pressing into the glass, secretly hoping my weight will break it. Anything to get me closer to the vast ocean filling every inch of my sight. With the day's heat, lack of breeze, and bright sun, the water is calm. Only a few ripples over the smooth surface as I stare out into it.

Sebastian comes up beside me, resting his forearms on the railing. My attention actually moves from the water to him, to his rolled-up sleeves of his black shirt, studying the red poppy tattoo etched on his arm. I want to ask about it.

"Beautiful view, right?"

I nod, attention returning to it, and then to the pool behind us. I can definitely imagine swimming here all day, staring at the ocean around it. Studying water while in water sounds pretty damn fantastic. Then to go inside, eat whatever delicious meal Carlotta whips up, and spend the evening with the piano. Yeah. Until Erico remembers he has a wife back home, I can pretend to be living a fantastic life. If anything, I won't be pretending one day. When my idiotic brain realizes the love I was chasing will never happen, I'll have all this empty happiness to occupy me.

At least my cage is pretty.

I push away from the fence and head for the poolside, kicking off one flip-flop once I reach the cement. Testing the water, I dip my toe in, the silkiness of bliss coating my foot until I can't help but moan.

Fuck, I've missed swimming.

Swimming and music. Both activities that Erico's returned to me.

I turn to find Sebastian where I've left him and lift my hands into a signing motion. *Going to get changed.* And then I take off, into the house, without checking to ensure he understood me. He'll figure it out.

13
ERICO

Caladin's sprawled on the couch in my condo, mindlessly flicking at the back of the leather. "You're fucking serious? What is your father *doing*? He's gonna get us all killed."

"I know, I know." My hands rub my face. For the majority of the day, I've been trying to have my father tracked, to see where precisely he's hiding our Bratva friends. "I'd like to go home. Business is done here. But it feels unfinished when I know that...that *eel* is slithering in my city."

He barks out a laughter. "Eel. Seriously? That's the best you can come up with." He shakes his head a few times, but returns to the serious version of him I need. "It's fucked when I can't find them in the same damn city."

It is. Caladin's the best tracker in the *Famiglia*. If someone needs to be found, I ask him. He'll always retrieve them. He's been holed up in one of the back offices of a casino here, scouring the city's footage when we pulled it from all the major roads.

"Unless the Volkovs already left," Caladin suggests. "We could very well be searching for literally nothing."

"Maybe. But that doesn't answer where my father's hiding. He hasn't taken the jet back home, which means he's still in the city. If he's here, I bet they are too."

"Why's your father such an ass? He really sucks at taking no for an answer. I mean, throwing Vanessa at you…"

Caladin always speaks direct, and more often than not, I'm thankful for it. I lift the glass in my left hand in a toast, silently agreeing with him before I down it in one go and stand. I begin toward the bar, but instead, rest the glass on the nearest flat surface and head for the door. Something about the way the sun shone right against the wood paneling of the bar flashed another image through my mind. An image of another room, much grander than this one.

Caladin scrambles to get to his feet, rushing after me. "Where to now, Boss?"

I throw a look over my shoulder right as I exit the condo and hit the button for the elevator. "Must you call me that?"

He shrugs one shoulder. "It *is* your position now."

"Doesn't feel like it," I grumble as the elevator shows up. "Not when my fucking father is still trying to maintain control of shit."

As the elevator descends, Caladin realizes he still has no idea my plans. "Where we going?"

"Palms Casino. Just remembered, we own the Empathy Suite." The place costs one hundred thousand dollars per night. Easy money maker for rich motherfuckers who have nothing better to spend their wealth on.

"And?"

"And, whatever my father is up to, he's trying to make nice with the Bratva. Which means putting them up at the most elite place we have access to."

The best thing about being me is that staff always hands over information without hesitation. The moment we entered the Palms Casino lobby, the pale faces of the reception staff told me all I needed to know. And then one, unsuspecting soul revealed the rest the moment Caladin and me approached.

"Sir, you've just missed your father."

I throw a *aha* expression to my right, where Caladin's leaning against the counter, rolling his eyes at me. "Was he with people?"

"A large man and a woman. Young. Long black hair."

"Ursin and Vanessa," I summarize to my cousin before demanding, "They say anything before they went?"

The boy nods rapidly, until his long bangs cover his face. "Your father said they're checking out. He's finished with your room." He shifts, glancing to the computer in front of him and back. "Um, were you also looking to use it? A cleaning crew can get up there immediately."

"Don't bother." I shove away from the desk and spin on my heel, tipping my head for Caladin to follow. "At least, I was right. I'll call the Vegas airport. The Volkovs either arrived by their plane, or they took commercial, so I wouldn't know they were in the city." If Father gave their flight team approval to land on Rossi territory by his jet, he risked me learning about their presence before he was ready for me to.

I'm barely past the hotel lobby when my phone rings, the Rossi pilot's name flashing over the screen. *This can't be fucking good...*

"Erico here."

"Sir, I just saw your father."

I was fucking right. I dive toward the corner of the lobby, lowering my phone but upping the volume so Caladin can hear too. But leave it off speakerphone, so the pilot's voice doesn't travel too far.

"Where?"

"Airfield. I thought he was going to ask me to return him to New York but minutes after he arrived, another plane showed up. Plain black. He and two others boarded it and flew off."

"Young woman, older man?"

"Yes."

"Thank you." I hang up and tuck the phone away, staring at my cousin until something makes sense in all this. "He's gone, and that plane better be taking the three of them to Russia and not New York. Fuck, Cal."

He taps my shoulder. "Look, now you know where they've gone. They're no longer in Vegas, but you know who still is? You. Man, you need to go home to your wife before she thinks you completely despise her." With a gentle shove, he angles me toward the hotel's doors. "Let's go back to New York and keep an eye out for your father. I'll get men on it, ensuring a black plane makes no appearance anywhere in the state."

"Thanks." Because my cousin's right. As much as a part of me wants to remain in Vegas and avoid Ariella, I can't. With the meeting and leadership exchange done, and Father and his Bratva drama also presently flying away, there's no reason to be here. "If he's headed to Russia, then I want to know why."

"Easy way to figure it out. Call your mother in a day or so. Ask her if he's around."

I scowl. "But that means speaking to her."

～

Once boarded on the plane an hour later, I text Ariella informing her I'm on my way.

After a few minutes, no answer.

I then call, minutes before takeoff, while I still can.

No answer.

"The fuck."

"Say that louder," Caladin chimes, extra annoyingly. "Didn't hear you well enough."

"Not talking to you."

"Right." He grins, kicking one leg over the other. "Because you're trying to call your wife. Oh, how the tides have changed."

"It's not like that," I deny. It's not. But after talking with her twice yesterday, and mentioning last night that I'd be home soon, I simply wish to inform her that *soon* is now.

But still no answer...

I bring up another conversation.

ME

Is Ariella around her phone?

Sebastian always responds right away, but after a full tense two minutes, when he still doesn't, a cold hand grasps my dead heart.

"Fuck."

"What is it?"

"Sebastian's not answering. Neither is Ariella. Something's wrong."

"*Or* she just got tired of waiting for her honeymoon and found someone who'll give it to her. Literally. Sebastian's young, man. No doubt, they've been fawning over one another."

The glare I shoot my cousin promises death. Neither would

do that, aware of the consequences. Especially Sebastian, since I'd have complete right to order his death. To exact it myself.

Right as a tenseness like I've never felt clenches around my nerves, the pilot pokes his head from the cockpit. "All ready to go, sir, if you are?"

"Yes," I manage through a tight throat, ignoring Caladin's smirk. "Please. Go. Let's return to New York."

Where I'll get to figure out the exact reason my wife is fucking ignoring me.

And then I'll show her all the reasons she's never to pull this shit again.

14

Once I return to the pool, the misery I felt during my conversation with Della is completely gone. Gone and swept away by the water. Apparently, I'm a simple being with simple needs if a single inground, outdoor pool changed my day's outlook.

The early afternoon sun beats down on the pool, meaning I've chosen the hottest time of the day to be out here, but all bets were off when Sebastian showed me literal paradise.

Thinking about my bodyguard draws my attention to the fact he's no longer out here. I pause by the cement's edge, taking a quick sweep of the pool area, along with the massive grassy stretch of land to the side, not spotting him anywhere.

Oh well.

I steal the lounge chair closest to the pool's edge and kick my flipflops off. Without testing the water again, I plunge in, taking an immediate dive, my body slicing neatly through the water, wetting every single part of me like some awakening bath. It's there, I sigh, more content since the second I hugged Della goodbye and followed Erico out to his car.

The water's warm from the sun. If it was chilly, I likely wouldn't care anyway. Dipping my head, I bask in the chlorine-filled water, my long hair becoming weightless beneath the surface.

Even after years of not swimming, instincts return, keeping me buoyant as I first complete a circle of the massive pool, and then end up on my back, eyes shut against the sun's gleam.

As I bob, sound of steps approach, so I spin until I'm facing the opposite way and angle my head back, blocking the sun with a hand. Sebastian returns with a towel in one hand and a water bottle in the other.

From my back, I swim toward him, only realizing the closer I get, how much of me is on display. Parts of my body even Erico hasn't seen. The triangle top and string bottoms doesn't hide much, but it was the only swimsuit I found in that massive closet. The plain black is exactly what I would have personally chosen for myself, and I wonder if it was Erico himself who chose it or one of his staff.

Sebastian drops the towel onto the chair by my shoes, and then the water bottle, after holding it up to me. "Stay hydrated."

Then he lowers to the lounge chair beside mine, one leg on either side, his elbows resting on his knees to keep him upright. The heat is much too cruel for the rolled-up black shirt and cargo pants he's wearing but somehow, he makes it work. When he was inside, he must have gotten his sunglasses because he lowers them from his head to his eyes, giving him such a dangerous guise to his appearance, I physically feel it in my core.

I finish my swim on my stomach, hiding my chest beneath the water until I get closer to the edge and lift my hands from the pool. *Thanks,* I sign to him.

He replies, "No problem."

Closer, I catch how his skin is reddening from the heat

already. Considering how he's dressed, I wouldn't mind company in the pool. I wonder if he's allowed to. After all, how much is Erico allowed to complain when he basically forced this guy to hang out with me? We may as well both take advantage of it.

Can you come in and swim with me? I sign, but based on the lowering of his brows, it was much too fast. I repeat, slower this time, but he only shakes his head, his expression pinching in embarrassment.

"Still didn't catch that, sorry."

This time, I go very simple and point to him and then the water. Twice until he understands.

"Can I swim with you?" When I nod, he adds, "I can't, no. But it's okay, Ariella. If it's company you're looking for, I'll be here." He gestures to the chair he's on.

After witnessing the drama between Aurora and her once-personal bodyguard, I guess I get why he needs to maintain the distance.

I complete another pass of the pool before returning to the edge closest to him. I go for water, but then end up in a one-sided conversation about his nephew, in which my signed responses become more and more complicated, simply to challenge him.

For easily an hour, we talk back and forth. Me, signing, and Sebastian switching between vocals and hand gestures, depending the length of his sentences. I've alternated between the water and sitting on the pool's edge to give my body a break from the chlorine.

After I asked about his nephew, he asks me about my own family, even if there's not much to say. He tells me about his induction and training into the *Famiglia* and how his father was a guard, his grandfather, and so on. His family has a long history with Erico's, but nonetheless, he's enjoying his life now. He asks me about my music and the piano, and once again, I keep those details to a minimum. I don't invite him to listen, even though the thought crosses my mind because not only does that disrupt the tentative non-friendship boundary between us, I'm reminded of what Erico said to me.

"One day, I hope to hear you play."

Dare I think it, Sebastian's gaze remains unwavering. Even through his sunglasses, I feel him watching me every time I take a lap around the pool, and I'm not sure how to feel about it. Sebastian's cute in a puppy dog way, and I love being able to speak with him in a less awkward method than texting or writing notes, and his easy friendship is an added bonus.

After another dip around the pool, Sebastian offers to retrieve food, and I nearly agree if it wasn't for the abrupt shade that powers its way around the side of the house and toward us. The shade isn't from clouds that suddenly turn grey, or my mood becoming depressed.

Erico's large steps brings him around the mansion to the poolside, where he's staring us both down. Sebastian scrambles to stand, leaving the relaxed state he's slowly found himself in over the passing hours. I, meanwhile, slip right beneath the water and tread a few feet away from the edge, keeping one uncertain eye on my husband as fury rolls off him in thick, pointless waves.

Whatever he's about to say to me, it better be with kindness only.

At the pool's edge, he's staring down at me. Bearing, is more like it. His eyes unblinking, his mouth flat, jaw tight until, after a long minute, he *does* blink. Then his gaze slides to the left toward Sebastian and he jerks his head. "Leave us."

Sebastian quickly steps around the lounge chairs, but before he's gone entirely, I lift my hand, palm toward him, fold my fingers down, and then lift them open again in the sign language representation for *goodbye*. Sebastian nods, telling me he understood. Just because Erico's decided to be a dick doesn't mean he can't get a proper acknowledgment.

Our exchange doesn't go unnoticed as Erico's breaths come out in stinted pants, sharp gaze flicking between me and Sebastian's retreating back, like he's determining which fight to have first.

With a sugary smile, I swim away, floating on my back and creating enough distance between us so when he yells, it can be from afar. So what if I've been friendly with Sebastian? It's better than hiding in the bedroom all day, right. Besides, Erico already said he might be gone often, especially now as Boss, so being on good terms with the staff, who'll be around me constantly, is smart.

By the time I complete a circle around the pool, Erico has removed his suit jacket, his shoes and socks, his Rolex, and his phone, placing them all on the seat Sebastian last occupied, almost like trying to make a claim on it too.

Then he walks to the edge of the pool, right by the stone steps.

And down them, ankles in the water.

And another step, continuing until the water's up to his hip, and then his chest.

He's insane.

Quick, powerful strides take him to my side, and even paddling can't get me away fast enough. One second he was by the pool's edge and the next, I'm being pinned to the wall, his arms framing my body, keeping me captive.

His wet clothing clings to his form, his white button-down shirt making the planes of his chest more prominent. Beneath the shirt, made transparent by the water, I spot a few dark tattoos. Water droplets cling to his face from his quick shark-like swim to my side, and he's barely panting, telling me he's also spent a lot of time in this pool and is a proficient swimmer, considering he did this all with clothing that got weighed down by water.

"What are you doing?" he bites out, his wet lips brushing against one another in a way my insides appreciate all too much. Even as my mind is still catching up to the fact that Erico has returned without warning from Vegas.

My eyes flick around the pool, my answer obvious.

"Sebastian never informed me you were out here."

Wow, there's making sure I'm not hiding in a room and then there's this.

"In fact, he never answered the text I sent him. Neither did you." He sent me a message? Must have done so before I abandoned my phone on the bed. "But now, I see why I was ignored by the two people who shouldn't be."

Do you? My brow lifts a fraction in question.

One of his arms leaves the wall at my side and a single finger drags over my neck. Other than the kiss sealing our vows, this is the one and only time he's touched me and I hate how good it feels. Hate the way my desperate body aches to cling to the sensation, to ensure it continues. He patches something inside me, though. Something that was lonely before thirty seconds ago. But then also *causes* that same loneliness because my mind and body know, this is fleeting. It'll always be momentary with him. Everything will have a role—a purpose behind it. He'll touch me to impregnant me. He'll touch me in public when he has to show a partnership. But that's it.

Even if the look in his dark eyes claims something else.

His finger slides down my neck, chasing water droplets dripping from my hair and onto my chest. His touch pauses right at the edge of the bikini top, and I curse my breathing for stopping. For the falter in my heart that I have little doubt he feels.

"Because when you dress like this, how can he resist looking?" He fingers the string around my neck. "Of all the fucking swimsuits stocked in your closet, you choose this one?"

There's more? I put on the first one I found. Definitely would have worn a more modest one had I saw the others.

"I rushed back from Vegas to see you. The video chats got tiresome when seeing the real version of you was a possibility. The one I can touch." His thumb slides over the curve of my breast, his eyes pinning me to the spot. *"Sirena,"* he murmurs, and I don't need to understand Italian to comprehend what he's calling me. *"La mia sirena mortale.* My deadly siren, luring out the killer inside me if other men continue to gaze at your body how Sebastian was checking you out."

Well, you don't want it. If I could talk, that's precisely what I would say. I try to tell him that too. For my wet lips to part and to speak the words, but metal on metal fills my ears instead, a scream accompanying it, and I remain silent. Again. For my safety.

His other hand slips into the water so I'm no longer caged in. But I am now, in other ways. By the way his hand splays across my hip, fingers wrapping around me. His other traces the edge of my bikini, not touching, just tempting. So opposite of the man I knew days ago.

Do you know him at all though?

"You seem to forget, Ariella, you're *my* wife. Just because I go out of town, doesn't mean others get to move into my place."

So that's what this is. A damn power trip. Erico felt his little caged pet was seeking comfort elsewhere and can't handle the challenge.

I fucking hate the insinuation though, and shove my hands

into his chest while pushing off the wall, trying to use my strength to dive through the water and escape. If I succeed, my death look tells him as much too.

But I don't because he doesn't budge. My strength nothing to his own. The hand enticing ungodly feelings over my chest slides upwards to the column of my throat. He doesn't linger for long, his thumb and forefinger gripping the side of my jaw as he angles my face to wherever he wants me.

Another show. Proof that I'm merely his doll, his plaything. The wife he'll keep by his side that no one else can touch.

Yet, I can't move, and not because of his physical hold, but rather the hold he has on my emotions. The confusion I'm feeling toward his own anger and annoyance, while feeling also an appreciation I *should* despise.

"You're very difficult for me to figure out, *quello silenzioso*. It's maddening. Your eyes say you hate me, but your body claims otherwise. Which tells me, it may not be hate you feel but a need for protection. Feeling like you should be protecting yourself from me?"

I roll my eyes, saying *Are you serious?* in the only method I can at the moment.

"If I explored your body, I could prove it to you."

Beneath his hold, I manage to lift my chin a fraction. Not sure if I'm daring to call his bluff or for him to release me. Either option wouldn't be what I crave though. Whatever's in his head isn't pleasant, it's control. And that's not what I want our marriage to be.

"Do you want me to explore?"

Yes. I shake my head in denial because it won't mean anything.

"Very well then. You're in charge, Ariella."

Am I? Somehow, that isn't the sense I've been getting from him. Not every time we've been in the same room, and especially not how my conversation with Nico suggested he'd be. Nico made it sound like if, on my wedding night, I didn't lie on my back and spread my legs willingly, Erico could force me. Nico claimed the *Famiglia's* morals are different. Rape doesn't exist between a couple, and it was a fact he shared with absolute bitterness and apology. I accepted it and told myself Erico was kind when I met him, and I'd cling to that memory on our wedding night.

Of course, nothing of this marriage has gone how I expected it to.

Erico releases my hip and neck simultaneously and instead cups my face, holding me almost tenderly. "Happy birthday, Ariella, for real this time. Telling you over video chat or in a note accompanying the piano isn't the real thing. I'm pleased to hear about all your piano usage."

Fuck, what's he doing? Luring me in with kindness only to shove me away in my corner again.

It's perfect, I mouth, giving him my honesty. At least, we can be amicable, right?

His eyes flick to my mouth and even though moments ago, he said it's in my control, I wonder if he'll kiss me. I wonder if I *want* him to kiss me. A replay of our wedding kiss under the guise of this marriage.

I don't want him to.

I'm unsure what I desire.

I don't want him to kiss me because his hot and cold personality is annoying. He talks of separate lives, but he comes storming in here when it's convenient for him.

I turn my head away, my hair creating a wall between us, and in the last second before my eyes flicker shut, I spot his disappointment.

"You know sign language." Not a question but a fact spoken with bitterness.

I nod and he says nothing more as his hands slide from my face down to the sides of my neck, my shoulders, and toward my arms, almost like he's tracing me. Like he can't get enough of touching me. I shiver when his hands travel the length of my arm, his fingers weaving between mine, and I remember the exact item I'm missing when I feel his own brush against my bare finger.

Ripping my hand from the water, he stares where we're linked together.

"Ariella, where the fuck is your ring?"

15

ERICO

Possessiveness over a woman—over anything, really—isn't my game. Requires too much energy. Unless it's directly endangering the *Famiglia*, I don't care for it.

But fuck. Already, arriving home, I was tense because by the time the flight landed, hours had passed since messaging Ariella and Sebastian and neither had a good excuse for ignoring my texts. My nerves were frayed and I arrived home antsy and on edge, immediately searching out my wife, all for Carlotta to direct me outside.

Instead of going through my house, I purposely went around the building to practice calming down before I lost it on a woman who, I knew deep down, didn't deserve my wrath over a text. My soldier, now he'd be a different story, but I'd be dealing with him later.

That was the plan anyway. Take the long way, calm down, and reappear in Ariella's life as *not* an asshole. Then I witnessed how they were talking, the way he was looking at her, her body language, and mentally, I lost it. Years of my father's training in control prevented me from murdering my soldier right then and there in front of her.

It was discipline and unease I even had that passing thought that prevented me from spending the rest of my afternoon disposing of a body. Possessiveness over something I own is natural, but less so, if I don't care for them. Besides the promise of the *Famiglia*'s future, deep down, I shouldn't care about Ariella. *Don't* care about her.

So why did my jaw clench, and my stomach knot, witnessing her smile back at him? Carefree and easy and unlike anything I've received from her in our video calls. The short chats I didn't realize, until seeing her in the pool, I was clinging to so desperately, knowing they were something only her and me shared. That even when gone, she agreed to meet with me.

And then, when I directed him away, and she spoke to him with her hands, purposely using the language both know I don't comprehend to share their final, secret message had me seeing red. Worse, because he nodded back. He *understood*.

Fucking sign language.

How does he know sign language?

They've been talking in a code I don't understand. They have a connection while I'm left on the sidelines.

And I don't know how to feel about that, other than my body's reaction—knotted and tense with flashes of death coursing through my mind—telling me I feel *something* about this. Something not positive either...

Death would be too kind for the young soldier who gazed at her like she was his sun. A fucking *sirena*. Meant to lure men in with her striking hair, inquisitive eyes, and flawless body. She did precisely that when I met her at Nico's party, and Sebastian's fallen into her trap, putting us all where we presently are.

Initially, I planned on only dropping in to see her and by tonight, I'd be back in my Manhattan condo until the next time

I felt like visiting. When I felt it suitable to reconnect with her in person, but now leaving seems impossible. Not only because she'll be alone with Sebastian again, but gazing down at her...I don't *want* to.

I entered the pool with the intention of showing her exactly what it means to be my wife. What I'm allowed to *take*, until I got close to her and the reminder of who I am. What I won't be to her had me pausing. The thought of traumatizing her further, in different ways, has me sick to my fucking stomach so I had to cool that unwelcome possessive feeling that had me craving to claim her. To bend her over the edge of the pool and slam deep inside her cunt, using what I had already purchased. What is rightfully *mine*. What, after dealing with my father and Vegas, I *need*.

Catching her without her goddamn ring on only shoots another wave of fury through my bones. It's the only emotion I've felt since arriving home, and it's getting tiresome, but she makes it impossible to not be angry. We both agreed to this union, but at first chance, she discards the symbol of our connection.

Fuck. That.

Logically, she could have simply removed it for swimming, but it's the dead look in her eyes suggesting otherwise.

Hauling her away from the pool's siding, I drag her toward the stairs, wrenching her along with me. As I rise from the water, it pours off me in a heavy downfall, slashing against the cement and soaking it instantly. Climbing into the pool nearly fully dressed may not have been my finest moment, but it was a necessity to prove a point.

With the last shred of my sanity, I head for the lounge chairs and release her only to wrap her in the towel. I tell myself it's to ensure she doesn't drip water everywhere, but really, it's to ensure she's warm in the air-conditioned mansion.

"Go." I gesture toward the back door after retrieving my phone, watch, and wallet from where I've discarded them on one of the lounge chairs. "Lead me to wherever you hid your fucking ring."

If she threw it in the ocean behind us, I'll murder something. Not her—never her. But something. Some*one*.

She passes me, her spine stiff, and heads right through the mansion's back entrance, passing Carlotta cleaning the kitchen. A quick sweep of the immediate area finds it scarce of Sebastian, so at least he's still clinging to some instinct.

Ariella heads down the stretch of the house, into the front foyer, and immediately up the stairs. Her steps are mechanical and stiff and she never glances behind her, to check if I'm following. As we approach our bedroom, some of my nerves unwind. If it's in here, it's safe.

Inside the room, I scan the unmade bed, and for some reason, it brings a smile to my face, knowing that's where she's been sleeping. It's a fleeting smile though, since the second she heads for the room's far corner, it's gone. She crouches, presumably retrieving her ring.

It meant so little, she tossed it away like garbage.

I should be pissed, except I'm not. Instead, there's another emotion I feel so infrequently, but I'm...sad.

She returns to my side, the jewellery pinched between two fingers, and I snatch it from her, taking her left hand in the same movement and jamming it onto her fourth finger.

"This stays here from now on. I see it gone again, and I'll solder it to your hand. Don't test me."

With a pinched expression, she rips her hand away and turns toward the bed, partially climbing on it as she reaches for something in the centre. Her position stretches out her body, water abandoning her swimsuit to instead cling to the bedspread. When she stands, she's holding her phone.

Which explains why my text messages and calls went unanswered. I likely sent them after she began swimming. I can't be pissed about that any longer. Sebastian still has shit to answer for though.

Without looking at me, she types on it, and my phone pings almost instantly.

> **ARIELLA**
>
> Awfully angry and possessive of a man who wants nothing to do with me and this marriage.

Is that what this is about? I wouldn't have wed her if I didn't want the marriage.

I'm about to answer when another message comes through.

> **ARIELLA**
>
> I wasn't the wife you were supposed to have, and I get it. Your role demands other things. Like you said, we'll get you an heir, and that'll be it. Therefore, inside the house, if we're not going to act like a couple, what's the point?

My mouth runs dry with no response while she regurgitates what I already said to her. Of course, she's questioning my willingness, because I've stated as such. I should walk away and use this. Let the understanding of our marriage truly set in for us both. Officially begin it now, since leaving right after the ceremony was confusing on all levels.

I *should* do all of that, but instead, my mouth opens, and the words that pour from me aren't the ones I should be saying. "The point is that *we* are married, Ariella. You took the vows. You accepted the ring."

She sets her jaw as her fingers fly over her phone.

ARIELLA

A ring you bought for another woman.

That's what she thinks?

You didn't exactly suggest otherwise at any point. Fuck.

Ariella stares at me for a beat, a yearning bringing her teeth over her bottom lip. A full minute passes before she blinks, accepting, and turns toward the closet, obviously giving up on me. She manages a step before something flashing in my head throws my arm to the side. It loops her waist and tugs her right to my side with an addictive, little gasp from her. A hint of her voice, and with that, I crave more. Her body presses against mine, my arm keeping her waist to me, my height making it so I'm looking down on her.

"I bought this ring for *you*, not Aurora. Hers wasn't purchased yet." In truth, I was avoiding it. "This," I snatch her hand, bringing it between us, "was hand-picked by me because the emeralds are the exact shade of the dress you were wearing when we met. The moment I saw this one, I imagined it on only your hand. No one else's." When some of the tenseness in her shoulders deflates, when I feel like I'm winning, I add softly, "I'm not the villain you're making me out to be, Ariella, but if it takes you time to realize that, then so be it."

Her mouth is right there, and like the pool, I want to kiss her. To lay her on the bed and grant her the wedding night she deserves. To spread her legs and explore everywhere, to peel down her swimsuit and discover the heat between her thighs. I want to see if she prefers to be dominated or to dominate.

Because that'll tell me how right or wrong we are for one another. How mechanical and forced producing an heir will be, or, with time, we can come to enjoy one another.

I shouldn't even care about that—any of that. I meant what I initially told her and there's no suitable reason I'd be considering otherwise. I should release her. Back away. Leave this bedroom and be done with this. Leave this house entirely and return to the city. We can go forward as friends until the day I need to begin producing the *Famiglia's* future. So many shoulds, and I don't do any of them.

I hold her. Stare at her. Spot the glimmer of hope reignite in her eyes.

Fuck.

I can't do this with her. *To* her. Meet her expectations all to rip them away from her when I won't be who she desires. My parents, for all their drama, have an amicable relationship. Romance-less, based on what I've witnessed, but not hatred.

That's what I need to duplicate here. Ariella must comprehend it's not okay to go without her ring, and it's less okay to despise me. But we can be friends. Comfortable companions throughout our lives together. Never romantic in the way she's hoping for us to be, all based on that little shine in her depths.

Another chill of protectiveness runs through me, but it's strikingly different than before, when I arrived to see her in the backyard with Sebastian. That was driven by stupid jealousy; this is to keep her safe. Being protective over Ariella means no harm will come to her—not even from me.

So I release her and back away two steps, turning my head to avoid witnessing the emotions pass over her expression. I head for the closet, quickly undressing and changing into dry clothes.

Once I'm refreshed, I return, finding her standing exactly where I've left her. "Change and come downstairs for food. I'm hungry."

I exit the bedroom, without looking toward her, and head to the kitchen, requesting Carlotta to whip something up quickly. While she works, I head toward my office and text the only soldier who'd be hanging around the mansion.

Sebastian's standing in my doorway within minutes, and

shuts the door when I gesture him closer. He stands straight on the other side of my desk, his expression flashing in nerves before smoothing entirely, and I respect that. He's trying to hide his emotions.

Getting straight to the point, I start. "Your family has been working with mine for generations. You're a good kid, Sebastian, and I chose you for this task out of respect for your father and grandfather. I also hoped, with your age, you'd be less intimidating to my wife."

"Yes, sir," is all he wisely replies with, his throat moving with his swallow.

"You know sign language." It's a statement.

His head bobs in a jerky nod. "My kid nephew was born deaf. It's a skill my entire family learned to communicate with him."

One apparently Ariella knows too. A fact the Corsettis should have mentioned.

"Was it difficult to learn?"

Sebastian shrugs a shoulder, some of his tenseness already easing as he realizes I'm not reprimanding him. In truth, I brought him in here without a concrete plan. He needs a reminder of his place, but can I deny her a connection to someone else?

Yes. I could.

"Not really," he answers. "Depends how good you are at learning stuff like that, I guess. I began with the letters and basic words, and then slowly built up. Like anything, it requires time and practice." He pauses, glancing over his shoulder and then continues, like whatever he was thinking about reaffirmed his choice to add, "Mrs. Rossi's been helping me actually. Given how infrequently I see my cousin, my sign language is rusty, but talking with her has been helping."

"Hm." I stand and he paces back a step, his eyes widening as

I wander to the side of my desk, propping my hip there with my arms crossing over my chest. "Don't see this as a negative thing, Sebastian, but I will be reassigning you. You'll return to your old duties with one slight alteration."

Another jerky nod, a gulp, and a flash of disappointment, telling me I've made the right decision. "Okay, sir. What's the alteration?"

"You will be teaching me sign language."

16

ARIELLA

Ten minutes after Erico's left me to change into dry clothing, I head downstairs. I've tossed on jean shorts and a plain tee, and tied my wet hair up in a bun, dressing almost as simple as the tank and joggers I was wearing when he agreed to wed me.

On my hand, the heavy ass sign of ownership.

Because the giant bed, the closet with both our items, and this damn house isn't a proficient enough method to flaunt ownership, he just *had* to add the ring to it.

I'm being silly. Maybe. After all, marriage equals a wedding ring, and I know that. Della gazes at hers, almost dreamily, immediately causing my own jealousy to flare. More than anything, I crave the sign of partnership—not ownership. Being chosen by a man.

My stomach feels hollow, and not because of hunger. The irony in how our lives turned out is still a bitter taste in my mouth.

Erico's parting words flit through my mind.

"I bought that ring for you, *not Aurora...the emeralds are the*

exact shade of the dress you were wearing when we met...I'm not the villain you're making me out to be..."

I *am* making him out to be a villain but only because he started it. He designed our life based on his own wants, and so be it. For a minute, when he was holding me, it seemed like something had already changed...but no. Reality crashed down and he released me, not only physically, but the faint wishing I was losing myself to.

Our bed is more inviting than ever. To bury myself into it and not come out for the rest of the day because as much as swimming made my mood light, Erico's return sucked it all away. Even as I walk back downstairs, my limbs lack energy, compelling me in one direction only—to the bed.

But before the master of the house drags me downstairs, because I suspect that's what would happen, I obey his earlier command. At the bottom of the steps, I pass Sebastian, who barely spares me a glance before disappearing out the front entrance.

Not even a wave to the person he's spent all morning talking to? If I wasn't already feeling my energy and mood drain, that knocked it down another peg.

Before Erico finds further reason to bitch, I head toward the kitchen, only for Carlotta to immediately redirect me to the attached dining room. A place Sebastian showed me in the tour, but there's yet to be a reason to use it.

At one end of the ten-person table, there's Erico, an iPad in one hand and a mug of coffee in the other. The entire stretch of the table has been cleared, except for the opposite end, where a serving plate, glass of water, and fork and knife wait.

"Sit, Ariella. Join me." A command given without even looking up from his tablet.

I see how it is. I all but march my way to the far end and sit, staring at him. All this and for what? I could be eating lunch at the kitchen island, how I have been since he dropped me off. Or, better yet, poolside, per the original plan before Erico decided to reclaim his position as lord of my cage.

Nico warned me to keep my temper in check, not that he'd ever seen me upset before, but cautioned me still. Behind closed doors, the Rossi family could potentially be worse than they publicly display, and Nico was determined to make me realize how precarious my place would be.

Slumping into my seat, I sit in silence. For once, affliction aside, while waiting for something to happen. Is this his attempt at displaying power? Drag me from the pool and force me to sit through lunch with him, all while he ignores me.

I don't realize I'm gripping the edge of my seat until Carlotta's footsteps break my glare. She heads to my side first, resting a glass of iced tea in front of me—a drink she's learned I enjoy—and then a fresh chicken Caesar salad. Crispy lettuce, the ideal number of croutons, freshly shaved parmesan, all mixed with a creamy salad dressing, making my mouth water nearly immediately.

I smile at her to say thanks before she walks to Erico's end of the table. For her, he glances away from the iPad, murmurs something I don't catch, and then she leaves us alone. The second she's gone, he returns to the device and begins eating, all without looking away from the tablet. My sigh is small, more of a disappointed huff, as I stab the lettuce with my fork. I hoped Erico inviting me down here was for a reason, but no. I'm simply an object for him to control.

A fact I'm already well aware of, but don't need the reminder. Knowing and experiencing it is different.

While delicious, the salad tastes almost bland. That's what happens when the dreary clouds consume me, though. The room's air feels neither warm nor cool. The food is both tasty and bland.

Walls. Right, my walls. My mask. How I managed for months around Della. She never suspected, even before the accident. It feels harder now—more challenging to *want* to put my mask back on, but while Erico doesn't even look at me, doesn't inquire about my meal, the difficulty is becoming less and less. Hiding my mood changes for the rest of our lives *should* be impossible, but if this is how my life will go—being ignored—then no, it'll be all too simple. Especially when he runs off to his city apartment and leaves me here alone, in this mansion.

Mask is on, walls are up, and I finish the remainder of my salad, sip some of the iced tea, and drop my fork onto the plate with a purposeful clang to announce I'm done.

Nothing. Not even a blink as he too scoops his final bite into his mouth.

Got it. Message received. Time to go die in bed.

I stand, shoving my chair away with annoyed huff, and walk toward the doorway. At first, I believe he'll let me go, but then he talks in a low voice, pulling me to a pause.

"When I am present, you will join me for every meal. We will get to know one another before I introduce you to your role. This is a kindness to you, so be grateful. Given my recent promotion, I might be in and out for the next while. And you just got more valuable to my enemies. You will never leave these grounds without a bodyguard. I will not have you risk your life."

Because then who else would give you your heir?

Getting to know one another...is that what this farce was?

Thoughts course through my head until all I manage is a jerky nod before escaping out the dining room, past the kitchen, and toward the sitting room with the brightly coloured tropical fish. I'm exactly like them. Trapped in a small space, circling the glass until they go insane.

The windows all around me, the ocean beyond, this is my tank.

My deep sigh could probably be heard by Erico if he cared to listen.

Every fibre of my being longs to lie in bed for the remainder of the day, or until he drags me from it for supper, whichever comes first, but I don't. Instead, I head back outside to the backyard, letting the warm, summer air wash over me. Ideally, it'd replace my earlier mood, but seems the weight is much too heavy. The darkness too grim to see through.

With Erico returned, my mask will never come off again. It's slipped in the past few days while I've been mostly alone, but Erico isn't allowed to witness that vulnerability.

I pass the tempting pool, but the image of him caging me has tainted the activity for today, so with a scowl, I walk toward the edge of the land, where the glass fence keeps me safe, and kneel on the ground, pushing myself as close to the barrier as possible. Below me, gentle waves rock against the land.

So fucking tempting to immerse myself within that water. To leap in and allow it to take me to new places. Maybe somewhere I'll find genuine happiness.

I never would, of course, but would Erico care? Would he search for my body beneath the waves?

Probably not. You're replaceable.

The wind picks up, the sun sets, and my body grows numb with the evening chill, but still I remain. It's a pleasant sensation, and when Carlotta retrieves me for dinner, casting worried looks every step, I ignore her.

She leads me into the dining room where Erico already

waits before backing away, leaving us alone. Without a word, I slink to my seat at the far end of the long table.

His dark gaze lifts from his wine glass as he stalks my steps. "You sat outside all day, and into the evening. Not the wisest or safest, Ariella."

Reprimanding me? You can't care that much if you never checked on me.

I shrug.

Carlotta returns with two plates of pasta, and I couldn't have asked for tastier meal. Pasta is my weakness; the carbs no concern, given its deliciousness. I dig right in, spinning the fork until I have what's probably an unhealthy amount of pasta on the utensil. Which I shove right into my mouth, all beneath Erico's amused gaze.

"Enjoy pasta, huh? That's something you haven't mentioned."

There's a lot I haven't mentioned to you.

"Be sure to serve that on the dinner menu at the next party."

Excuse me?

A fact provided by numerous sources pre-marriage, but it was easily ignorable when Erico left for Vegas. A dinner party involves people from his life. People who'll undoubtedly want to pay respects to their boss's wife.

To me.

The pasta suddenly holds no flavour.

"My mother's expecting it soon, but I've told her, we'd discuss it. Until you're settled, there's no rush."

Settled. Not comfortable. Like a brand-new puppy brought to the home. Unsure of where to go and how to act, but with time, trained to be calm and *settled* until the owner deems them fine to be around others.

My responding smile is tight, more lips clamped together.

After this, I'm escaping to bed. It's late enough to call it a day. I've human-ed enough.

When I go to bed, then what happens? This will be the first night Erico and I sleep in the same bed. Given his promotion, will he already begin trying for an heir? Based on earlier, though, he did say it'd be in my control. Maybe he'll head back to the city and will save us both.

Erico cuts into my train of wayward thoughts. "After dinner, I have a meeting. Don't wait up because I may be late to bed."

I nod, because what else is there to do? At the very least, he answers my curiosity. Ideally, sleep will have already claimed me by the time he comes to bed. It's strange for a man who claims to want to lead separate lives to also want to share a bedroom when there's other rooms in this massive place.

Appearances? Who's the show exactly for? Not his staff, considering they'd be paid to keep quiet.

After my final bite of pasta, I manage a deep, calming breath, though it does little for my mood. I dismiss myself by standing and don't look toward him. Erico doesn't speak, and I slip from the dining room.

17
ERICO

Ariella escapes the dining room, leaving me with a sudden urge to chase her. I'm smart enough not to entertain my desires and remain seated, hand clenching my fork for something to focus my strength on that *isn't* spreading her legs on our bed, licking my dessert from her cunt.

The moment I taste her cunt will be the moment I lose control completely, which is why I can't. How easy would it be to become obsessed with her? To be so would be unhealthy and distracting.

Already, by staying here and not heading back to the city is a horrible idea that invites further issues.

Growing up, I didn't have the same loving parents as those others my age did. Caladin's parents, before their deaths, were so utterly in love with one another and it always amazed me how the two brothers—my father and Caladin's—could enter their unions with completely different stances. Once, despising how Mother and Father basically ignored one another, I vowed to use my aunt and uncle as an example for my future marriage instead. But that was when I was an optimistic teenager. The longer my training, the more I realized what being my father truly meant for the *Famiglia,* and the better I understood his stance on marriage. Loving Mother would have distracted him. He gained my utter respect for doing what he needed to.

That's the stance I'm following. Falling deeper into the *Famiglia* means doing right by them. Now more than ever.

Already, she'd have a target on her back if any of my enemies learned I was married. Simply being my wife puts her in danger, but if I loved her...if they knew I had a weakness...we'd both be fucked. And that's *her* death, but if she cared for me and I died; if a stray gunshot made her a widow, I'd leave this earth by shattering her heart and soul. Even I'm not that selfish.

Focus. That's how to be a proficient Boss.

When Aurora Corsetti's hand in marriage was offered, given her strange upbringing away from her family, she seemed like an easy option. She'd be independent and perhaps happy to be left alone, given it was how she was raised. She'd be the ideal mafia wife.

With Ariella, that's not the case. Perhaps because I met her while engaged to someone else, I *allowed* myself to be intrigued. To let the façade slip out of unbridled interest. Then finding myself wed to the very woman who sparked the intrigue, I was doomed before this began.

It takes Carlotta entering the dining room to clear away our empty dishes to break my stare with the doorway. After thanking her for the delicious meal, I go to my office for my meeting with Sebastian. Learning sign language is counterintuitive; finding a new communication strategy for the woman I require distance from isn't wise.

Still, when I spot the young soldier leaning beside my office door, I welcome him inside, ordering him to sit instead of going away.

Sebastian perches on the edge of his chair as he watches me take my own seat. He's obviously still tense from earlier, uncertain, but he'll realize in time, teaching me to speak to her in alternative means is enough of an apology from him.

"Teach me the basics. We'll go from there."

"The alphabet will be good. When in doubt, you could spell what you want to say."

"Proceed then."

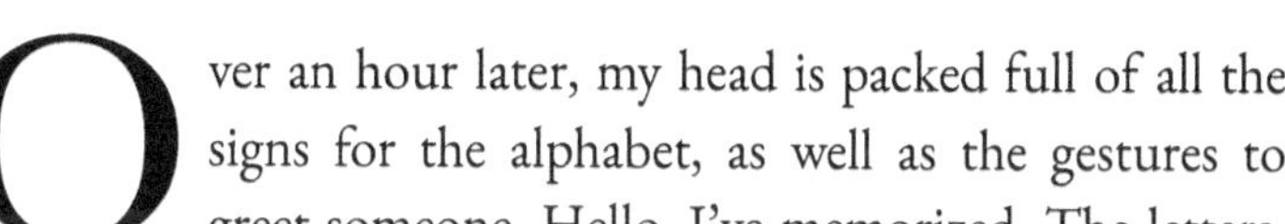

Over an hour later, my head is packed full of all the signs for the alphabet, as well as the gestures to greet someone. Hello, I've memorized. The letters, maybe half of them.

"Thank you, Sebastian. I'll text you when I have time for another lesson."

"Sounds good." Sebastian leaves my office unscathed, his steps quickening by the door. He's a patient teacher, and in another life, one where he didn't induct himself into the crime, territory battles, and weapon and drug deals, he'd be a good school teacher. He's also a damn good solider from a great and loyal line of men, so I'd never offer him an out. Not that I think he'd take it.

Alone again, I pick up my phone, glancing over the text message received only moments ago.

CALADIN

10pm. Rio's bored and he's betting 10k on this.

Racing is the second-best feeling in the world and when I can, I drive in every event, every bet. Rio's races aren't as often anymore since he nearly got caught and thrown in jail, so he's scared to attract the law's attention again. He won't because when I learned of his arrest, one phone call got him free, and the police are aware not to touch him again. Rio always brings in the best drivers, creating races with the highest stakes, and I can't have my only form of entertainment locked away. Once, I debated bringing Rio in, making him my staff, meaning the *Famiglia* would get a cut of the profits, but I actually enjoy participating in something *not* in my control.

I've won almost every race too.

The offer is extremely tempting since it's been a while since Rio hosted a race. Ten thousand dollars is chump change compared to the Rossi fortune, but nonetheless, useful and easy cash.

ME

I'll be there.

I type it, but don't send the text. Ariella is likely asleep by now and wouldn't notice me gone and yet, my thumb is hovering over the send button before backspacing and replacing it with different words:

ME

Pass.

Still tired from travel.

The races are held on a few different roads—one in Brooklyn, some in Queens—and all are far away from here. After the race, it'd be quicker to return to my condo rather than the hours-long drive back here, which is a benefit, but still...

Knowing Caladin, he'll question me since I almost never turn down the offer of a race, and though a part of me desperately needs the exhilaration, the escape driving that fast brings, my lie remains as I exit my office and head to my bedroom where my sleeping wife is.

Christ.

She doesn't know this, and never will, but Ariella's the first woman to be in my bed. First woman other than my mother and staff to even be in this house. Previous hookups are not brought here because I enjoy my privacy and won't risk a stranger in my space—whether that's here or my condo. Having a woman be aware of where I live, or even internal facts such as my love for tropical fish, can be risky. People can do insane shit with basic facts, and in my role, one can never be too careful.

My wife will own many firsts.

The bedroom doors tap gently as they shut, and I realize I have no idea if she's a light sleeper and the subtle noise woke her up. She hasn't moved, but she could be faking. I tread to the closet, stripping as I go.

The closet's light casts a strip over the carpeted floor and right onto her. She's sleeping on her side, one arm tucked beneath the pillow while the other is against her chest. She'd look so peaceful, if not for the slight furrow to her brow, the tightness in her jaw. Whatever's in her head, it's preventing her body from completely relaxing. Nonetheless, she's breathing evenly, the blanket rising and falling in gentle movements. She's on the very edge of the bed, almost like pushing herself farthest away from my side.

After slipping on pyjama pants, so she doesn't find me naked, I go to the bathroom to quickly wash up, making a mental note to shower in the morning, and then walk toward the bed.

But not my side. Not right away.

I go to hers, inspecting that dip in her brow that I touch. Her skin is smooth and for once, her guard is down, so I can't help myself but trying to ease her. When she shifts, I yank my hand away, and return to my side of the bed.

My side. Before days ago, this entire bed was mine, and now there's sides.

Once I'm beneath the blankets, the space between us feels even greater. Emotional, mental, and physical.

This is good.

But not what I want.

I lie down facing her, wondering if she's felt me slip into bed. Probably not because she's still *on* the bed. Somehow, I get the sense if she knew, she'd suddenly find the floor to be a better place to rest.

Right when I close my eyes, Ariella whimpers. She lets out a pained moan that has me reaching for her. Her head rolls back and forth on the pillow, the dip between her eyes growing more prominent. Her mouth moves, her eyelids fluttering.

Nightmare?

Is this what the last few nights have been like? What her *life* has been like? Restless sleeper or nightmares from her traumatic accident?

I reach for her again, when her mouth parts, her sound freezing me.

"Mom!"

A sob, a scream, a thrashing, and then like the accident: sudden silence.

Sleep takes her under again.

I don't move. I *can't* move.

She spoke.

Well, screamed.

But I heard her voice. Throaty but also soft. Packed of a fear I want to protect her from. To help her talk again without the heavy emotion dragging her down.

She mumbles incoherently and shifts, rolling until her face

is shoved into the pillow, a position I'd normally smirk at, but my insides are still numb because there's nothing amusing in her display of fear.

It was great enough to break through her other fears, the ones the trauma's created. The ones preventing her from speaking with anyone but her sister.

Ariella's mutism was a fact I was prepared to live with when I agreed to marry her. A challenge we'd overcome together, and learning sign language is one step in that direction—albeit an unseen step at the time.

But it's now more. There's something deeper there I wish to help her unfold, to *heal* her from her struggles, so she doesn't have another nightmare ever again.

Do I mention this in the morning?

No, I decide. I won't because I get the sense, she'd hide from me even more, simply to prevent me from witnessing her nightmares. Or she'd attempt to move out of our room. And do I really want to mention that she's likely reliving the moment she lost her mother?

Based on the intel my men discovered, we're days away from the anniversary of her mother's death, reminding me to reach out to Nico. For Ariella's sake, I doubt he'll deny my request to return to Montreal, so she can be with her sister on the day.

Once Ariella's silent, I return to lying on my back, staring at the white ceiling until sleep decides to come. It never does, and after a few more minutes, another whimper bursts through the silence.

Fuck this.

Despite everything I said earlier, my actions come from a place of wanting to care for her. When's the last time anyone actually held her, told her it'd be okay, and let her cry it out? Has she had a solid cry in the near three years since the accident?

I want to be that for you.

Want and need are very different things, though. More so, what *she* wants. People are typically easy to read, but Ariella, fuck, I can't piece her together.

Looping my arm around her waist, I pull her to my bare chest, tightening my hold so she can't go anywhere. She won't know about this, not if I wake before her, which is likely since I'm an early riser.

She whimpers again and tries to pull away. A weak attempt only lasting the blink of an eye before she sighs and settles.

It's there, late at night, holding my new wife for the first time, I realize what I refuse to act on.

I'm too intrigued by her to completely ignore her.

18

ARIELLA

I went to bed alone, and when I wake, I'm still alone. Based on the dip in the mattress, Erico had come to bed at one point, but after a quick pat, the sheets are cool, which tells me he's been gone for a while.

Likely woke to avoid you.

It's that low thought making getting out of bed arduous, but if I don't, Erico will wonder, and if he looks close enough, he might see what others don't.

So I go through the motions. Get out of bed, shower, tie my wet hair up, and dress in the first thing my hands touch—jean shorts and a simple blouse—before slipping downstairs, keeping my steps as quiet as possible. No one's around, which feels odd, but the silence is pleasant, as is not having staff wait on me.

After pouring a mug of coffee, I walk the length of the house toward the music room. It's too early for a swim, and music's my only other option in this large place. At no time do I see Erico, but it's not all that surprising, even if a stupid part of me was wishing to.

He's probably gone by now. Returned to the city for work and his condo, far away from me.

As expected, the large room is empty, with only my piano tucked in the corner. There's nowhere to rest my mug, other than the floor because I don't want to risk staining the piano, but perhaps I'll ask for a small table.

When I reach the piano, there's a coaster on top, and with a silly smile, I rest my mug on it. Someone foresaw this issue. Carlotta is extremely likely, but somehow, I feel it was Erico, playing his games again.

Once the coffee's in its new place, I lift the bench's lid, having found it to be a storage space, ideal for keeping my notebook in. At first, I nearly didn't, since it's the book I've clung to for so long, the pages only I've read, and having it in here means it's vulnerable to others' eyes. But if I'm to live out my life here, I can't keep my possessions in a tiny bag I guard forever.

My heart slows with ease when I retrieve it unharmed and open to the last page I was working on, trialling a few new notes and rewriting lyrics as I've whispered them to myself.

Hours pass, or that's what it feels like, when the door opens and my back prickles with the knowledge of who's intruded.

So he hasn't returned to the city.

"Heard you skipped breakfast, and now it's lunch. You must be hungry."

Shrugging, I don't turn around. Maybe I am, but eating doesn't hold any appeal.

He crosses the room, his shoes making soft taps, which sound closer as he approaches. My breath aligns to each one, giving my mind a place to focus as he comes up behind me.

Then his hand sweeps over my bare neck and I don't know what to do. How to react.

It's a gentle touch, but almost possessive too.

I'm torn between shutting my eyes and enjoying the sensation and pushing him away, protecting myself through this inevitable heartbreak.

"You play beautifully. The tune carries out of the room, and I'll be honest, I remained in the hallway, listening for a few minutes before entering."

Because he knew I'd stop playing once he entered. Deceptive...but sweet, I suppose.

No one's heard me play before and I feel like he deserves to be told that. Why? Not sure. A final thank you for the gift? I reach for my phone, which is beside my now-empty mug and type on it.

YOU'RE THE FIRST TO EVER HEAR ME PLAY
PIANO.

He reads over my shoulder. "Besides Della?"

WE DIDN'T HAVE A PIANO WHEN I LIVED WITH
HER OR GROWING UP. I TAUGHT MYSELF IN
HIGH SCHOOL IN THE MUSIC CLASSROOM
AFTER SCHOOL. MAYBE THE MUSIC TEACHER
OVERHEARD, BUT THAT'S ALL.

"I'm honoured." His touch sweeps where my hair and neck meet again. "Come eat, and then return."

Since he's not being an ass today, I'll entertain his niceties. When I shut the piano's lid, he backs away, giving me the space to stand. Turning, I see him for the first time today. He's dressed more casually—casual for him at least. Slacks and his normal shiny shoes, a button-up shirt that's rolled at the sleeves, portraying muscular arms that I think I'd enjoy around me. His hair isn't as styled, like he rolled from bed and never bothered fixing it. It makes him look younger, more boyish...cuter.

I hold up my phone with a message I quickly type before I can stop myself:

YOU'RE HERE.

He smirks. "As opposed to where?"

YOUR CONDO. YOUR WORK. NOT HERE.

He glances away quickly, licking at his lips. Nerves? "Yeah, I...I think I'll stay here for a while. Work from my office."

My heart thumps erratically. While I can't assume, I am, assuming the reason behind his ongoing presence. Me. Why he's not taking off might be something he'll never admit, and I should *want* him to go and leave me in peace, but this means something. Right?

He leads me from the room, but to the backyard instead of the dining room. The sun's shining bright, reflecting over the pool and into my eyes, so I shield my face with my hand.

By the poolside, a small table has been set up with two covered plates. I tip my head in question as he leads me to the chair facing the lake.

"You seem to enjoy the outdoors and we only have a couple months until it's cold, I figure why not soak up as much sunlight as we can. Besides, I'd like to get to know my wife better."

Since when?

He takes his own seat across from me and I search his expression for his duplicity. I'd prefer it was there, only to quell the confusion in me.

I rest my phone on the table, opening the messenger app to be prepared for any reply I must give. Not sure what the man possibly wants to know, but I pretend to care about his interest with my mask firmly on, my smile fake and pleasant, practiced from my days with the Corsettis.

"When did you realize you enjoyed music?"

And so, it begins.

After lunch and twenty questions, my smile became less fake and practiced and more real. More authentic, even while red flags were being erected in my mind.

Why is he being nice all of sudden?

What does he want?

Is this some sort of mating ritual? Ease me before he breeds me. Then he can be finished with his job, and we can both move on.

Erico's asked me all the questions people in long-term relationships should know about their partners. He not-so-subtly skipped over my post-high school years, when Stefano came into our lives, and of Mom and the accident.

He was patient while I responded by text. If he got annoyed, then he wore his own mask and hid the emotion well. Even Della gets irritated sometimes because my murmured short sentences are less than what she grew up receiving. When Nico visited me at the medical centre to ask about Della, he was so agitated while I wrote my responses on a whiteboard, it was nearly amusing. Lorenzo Corsetti never spared me much time, and Caterina, if she was annoyed, did manage to keep her mask on as well.

Half of lunch was spent watching every curve of his face, of his eyes, which often reveal what a voice won't, the skin around them for any crinkle and indication of annoyance, of his mouth, watching for any tick.

Nothing. Patient as ever.

I didn't like how it made me feel.

Comfortable.

Every time I feel comfortable, something bad happens.

Moving into Stefano De Falco's home was something I fought Mom over, but slowly—*very slowly*—I became eased. And then the accident occurred.

The medical centre was where my depression felt the worst, when my only visitors were Della and Yasmine. But my conversations with my stepsister were always at a minimum because she shouldn't have been there. They were almost downright uncomfortable meetings for us both. By the time I accepted the centre, I was yanked from it and forced to, yet again, conform to new standards within the Corsetti household.

So it's bound to happen soon. Erico's kindness will come with a price I'm not equipped to pay.

He leads me back to the music room, and with a parting smile, leaves me alone again to head back down the same hallway, toward his office. Confusion swirls over if lunch did what he wanted.

Or did it do what I needed?

19
ERICO

After a pleasant lunch and returning Ariella to her music room, I regretfully head for my office. I'd rather watch her play, but business is stacking up in the days I was away in Vegas. Father dumped a lot on me—probably to see me either rise to the occasion or fail.

My intrigue with my wife is truly an unwanted distraction. The moniker I once called her floats through my mind: *Sirena*. She really is a fucking siren, right down to her fondness for swimming, her adoration of water, her dream of owning tropical fish, and her musical talents—some of those facts uncovered in my many questions during our meal.

Tropical fucking fish. As a child, I begged Mother for them after she denied all my other requests for aquatic creatures, which as an adult, I see why she had. In a household with staff, ownership meant not having to actually care for them, so she agreed. Years later, I continue to keep tropical fish, always replacing when I lose one.

Now, I wouldn't get rid of them for the world, making my wife's dreams come true even unknowingly.

My phone vibrates for the millionth time today. Every time Ariella was texting me a response, three more from other people also arrived. Soldiers, my mother, Caladin. All with varying degrees of business, so when I'm back at my desk, I have enough of a distraction to keep me away from Ariella and her music for hours.

First: Caladin's messages, since they're simplest.

CALADIN

> Dude, you gotta come back to the races. Some big names in town. Rio's looking for you, man, because some huge challenges. They're determined to beat you. Get out of your wife's pussy and come. 10pm for the next three nights are lined up. I've already told them you'd be here so don't be a letdown.

Caladin is correct in that I should return to my hobbies, a reminder of my life before Ariella. If my lessons with Sebastian end earlier, then yeah, I can make these, even with the three-hour drive toward the city for these. Three hours there, three hours back, plus the time spent racing. Fuck, that's the entire evening and well into the middle of the night by the time I return.

Or you can just stay at your condo.
Unlikely.

ME

> Count me in.

CALADIN

> Reread my message. You didn't have a choice.

Chuckling, I close that message thread and open the one I have with my mother. She's texted and called all day, leaving voicemails each time I denied the call. As much as this conversation is the last thing I wish to have, she's easier to deal with over voice than arguing over text. So I tap her name and initiate the return-call.

"What?" I demand the moment she picks up the phone.

"That's not a respectful way to speak with your mother. I never raised you like this."

You barely raised me at all.

Rather than fight about the past, I lower my tone to replace annoyance with fake pleasure. "Apologies, Mother. There's a lot going on. What can I help you with?"

"Did you not read my texts?" Her voice hikes higher, indicating she's about to go off. "Or listen to the *many* voicemails I left you?"

Pinching the bridge of my nose, I stare at the time in the corner of my laptop's screen, deciding this call will be limited to five minutes. Another four and half to go, and counting.

"I'd be here all afternoon when I have better things to do, so no, I did not."

She sighs heavily as if I've demanded she sell all her designer shoes. "Or you can be a better businessman. And son."

"Or I can hang up and continue my job by talking with the actual businessmen I'm presently dealing with. What. Do. You. Want, Mother?"

Another heavy sigh, only this time she answers, "Dredging up the last thing we talked about: it's been days, Erico. Time for Ariella to make her debut to the organization. I'll even assist Ariella plan it."

"She needs nothing from you," I shoot back instantly. "Besides, I've already mentioned to Father, she needs more time to settle." I use the opening to not only change topics, but to solve a mystery. "Where did Father fly off to?" The Bratva's jet never landed in New York, which means he went elsewhere with them.

She completely ignores my question about Father's location. "This is why marrying that nobody was not wise, Erico. Even if she did link us to the Corsettis. Sometimes, the price isn't worth the outcome. If your father—"

"Stop," I cut her off, a burst of anger over her latest statement taking over. "My mother or not, *never* talk about my wife like that."

"Erico," she murmurs in her usual placating tone, "I simply meant, she's not exactly who we had in mind for you."

"Father wouldn't have made me Boss if he didn't trust in my abilities. The same goes for my wife's. You know better than anyone how it is. Your entire status in the *Famiglia* was due to Father's role. You *are* him. Ariella is *me. With* me. On my side, so fucking deal with it."

Another beat of silence and a low sigh. One I was likely not supposed to hear. When she talks again, her tone is more paced. "Like I was saying, you know the consequences of not hosting something for the organization soon. People need to meet your wife, Erico. She's their new *Famiglia* queen." Words spit with a tinge of bitterness. "You know I'm right."

My thumb and forefinger pinch my nose tighter because she fucking is. With our wedding being nearly a week ago, and planning a party would still take days, this shouldn't be held off much longer, out of respect for the *Famiglia's* traditionalists. It'd be viewed as disrespectful not to host them soon.

But can I do this to Ariella already? Presumably the Corsettis warned her what being my wife would involve, but still...

"Pick a venue. Send me the date, time, and address. We'll be there."

"Uh, son, I think you missed the point. *Ariella* must plan this."

"You'll get your party, Mother, but do you really think a

bunch of old fuckers will honestly care, or even distinguish, who put it together? Until she's more settled, I'm not forcing anything on her. This is my final word on the matter."

"Fine," Mother bites out. "Whatever, I'll do it better anyway. Tell your wife we need to plan a girl's outing eventually. I'd like to meet my daughter-in-law properly. I'm sure you don't have a problem with that." Her tone declares *I dare you to say otherwise.*

"Whenever she's ready. Goodbye, Mother."

Click.

With a groan, I rub both hands down my face, willing my head to erase that conversation. Before my next task, I pour a drink from the bottle of alcohol I keep stocked in here, taking a heady sip.

Moving on to more important things, I dial Nico Corsetti's number.

He answers on the first ring. "Corsetti."

"Nico," I greet, utilizing his first name instead.

"Erico. You're not who I expected."

"Sorry to disappoint."

"Funny. Heard congratulations are in order for the new *Famiglia* Boss. The news travelled quickly to us."

"I had no doubts of that, but thank you. And on yours as well." Days after my wedding to Ariella, Lorenzo handed over control to Nico, according to our intel.

"What has you calling today, when I'm sure you're very busy?"

Another sip of my drink before responding. "Ariella."

"Is she okay?" he asks with a bit more alertness than before. My flash of annoyance is quickly quelled since it goes to show how many people care for her well-being; a fact I'm curious if she's aware of.

"She's well. Settling. She's found some hobbies around the

mansion to keep her busy. She's the purpose of my call but not the focus, per se." I pause, bringing up my calendar on my laptop, noting the date two days after my three back-to-back races. "You must be aware the anniversary of Ariella and Della's mother is approaching."

"I am. Della and I will be taking a trip to the cemetery where she's buried." He pauses, his next statement said with bite. "Their dickhead of a stepfather never brought them to visit."

If he's taking Della there, then the stage is set. "Well, that's why I'm calling. I'm seeking permission to enter your territory, on that afternoon, so she may pay her respects. I'll bring a single soldier with me, and no weapons but my personal one—you understand."

"Considering Della's been hinting at having her sister come up, absolutely. It'll be good for the two of them to have each other. If all goes well, I'd say we make it an annual standing agreement."

This right here is the reason Corsetti over Volkov is preferred. Nico's much simpler to deal with. There's more humanity in his own dark heart, which softens for his wife. A weakness to anyone who wishes to do him harm, but given who my own wife now is, it makes him valuable to me. The power the Russians control isn't worth the nuisance to gain it.

"We'll tentatively set that plan," I agree, "and we'll be there in a few days."

"I'll have my driver pick you up on the airfield. I'll text you my pilot's information and yours can set the trip up with him and our airfield. See you then, Rossi."

"Goodbye, Corsetti."

A much more productive phone call than the one with my mother.

Downing the rest of my drink, I consider the rest of my

tasks. Contracts Father started but never finished, that I now need to handle.

Shit to keep me busy and away from my wife.

~

Dinner is the same as lunch, only spent in the dining room. Unable to help myself, I continue to bombard her with questions, and am pleasantly surprised when she starts asking more of her own.

Afterwards, she gets ready for a swim while I retreat back to work. Except instead of sitting at my desk, I'm too busy observing her from my office windows, hating with every fibre of my being how fucking impossible it's becoming to *not* watch her.

When the sun dips into the ocean, I'm about to demand she come inside, but then she wisely grabs her towel and leaves the pool. She wraps her body in the towel, covering her tiny, wet bikini that held way too much of my focus. Today's swimsuit was a pale blue.

Once she's inside the house, I get prepared to leave for the long drive to my race. According to Carlotta, Ariella heads to bed early each night. Which is strange because it's not like she's a super early morning riser, so it's curious how much she sleeps. No matter because it means she won't be up to inquire about my absence.

At dinner, she texted, asking about my own hobbies, which I semi-lied about and claimed I enjoy running. I *do*, as it's my preferred form of cardio, and something I complete every morning, but certainly not a hobby. Admitting I race to a woman who lost her mother in an accident feels insensitive.

Before exiting the mansion, I text Jack Scuttle, a fifty-year-old married man and Ariella's new bodyguard, requesting he remain in the house until I return. He's who I should have chosen as her guard from the beginning.

When I spot his car pull up to the front of the mansion, I throw him a quick wave and speed off in my McLaren 360. At the end of the road, I message Caladin, informing him I'm on my way with an estimated time of arrival.

The leather wheel beneath my grip feels smoother with the promise of what's coming. My shifting is smooth, effortless, as my speedometer climbs.

Every sense in my body attunes to the vehicle.

It's a thrill like nothing else in life.

It's adrenaline fuelling parts of me hidden from the rest of the world.

It's a high no drug compares to.

I think I'd like to share it with Ariella one day.

20

ARIELLA

Three days pass and with every minute, my confusion over Erico's actions grows.

The first day—the one after he dragged me outside for lunch and began this weird routine of twenty questions—he had a couch added to the music room. Padded, beige, and tucked across the opposite wall.

The second day, there was an entire sitting area. More chairs, and another couch added, along with a table.

The third day, a large desk pushed against another wall. This one had a note taped to it. An explanation, which didn't help clear *anything* up.

So you have a place to write your music.

The other furniture never came with such a note, but I learned why that first day. When hours after I found the couch, Erico entered the music room and sat on it. Propped one leg up over the other and merely challenged me with a lift of his brow when I glared.

Every day after that, he's come in.

Three days of him watching. Three days of silence. He doesn't talk or do anything when he's with me.

Three days of growing confidence because each day, after watching me play for hours, his only words come right as he's leaving, and it's always with the same statement: *'You play beautifully. I'd love to hear you sing one day.'*

We spend every meal together. Sometimes talking—him speaking, me texting—and sometimes not. He seems to set the atmosphere, which has me more and more frustrated, wondering if he's waiting for me to take charge one day.

He mentioned a party that his mother is hosting in our stead. A party *we're* supposed to put on, but apparently, he made it her task. I smiled and nodded when he told me because, while not stated, I understood what he actually did for me. Party planning is one of my tasks, as the Boss's wife, but he protected me this time. *This time.* Eventually, this moment will catch up with me.

Our days are relatively positive. Friendly. In the evening, when I swim, he locks himself in his office. But then at nighttime, he leaves the property.

Night one, I believed it was for business. He's a Boss of a mafia family after all, and even I'm aware that most of the underground sketchy deals occur at nighttime, away from prying eyes and under the cover of darkness. He leaves early in the evening because despite his claim to be working from his office, it's a long drive into the city. I assumed he wouldn't be back that night, but he crawled into bed around three in the morning, long after I passed out.

Night two, more business dealings. Same departure and arrival time.

Night three was when the darkness creeped into my thoughts. After two and a half days of feeling decent, with a stable mood that hasn't been taunting me with the temptation to hide in bed all day, it hit me. After he left the third night, it wiped away any progress I've been gaining. The pestering inner monster slithered in and snatched my heart again, my thoughts, and planted the negative ones.

Perhaps he's cheating. Took a mistress. You're not doing your job as his wife so of course he went elsewhere, to someone who will give him what he needs.

God, I tried to ignore the voice. Bury it beneath the deep-rooted feeling that I don't believe Erico would do that.

But it always has a counterargument. *He left it in your control. It's been a week and you've done nothing with him. He's gotten tired of waiting.*

Still, I push on. Pretend it's not bothering me. Convince myself, he's doing his job. But every evening, it's the exact same pattern, the same timings. Every night, when I go to bed and he comes into the bedroom to change from his suit to more casual clothing.

Every time, I try remain awake, staring at the time ticking away on my phone. But he's gone so long, I end up falling asleep. Which is probably best since my heart couldn't handle observing him sneak in during the middle of the night.

There's numerous reasons for his actions, and I know this, but the nagging, evil voice decides otherwise.

On my back in the pool, sunglasses on, I stare at the sun, seeking answers within the glaring rays. Nico blatantly warned me of this, having no precise insight into how the *Famiglia* manages relationships. He said this organization was as traditional as they come and keeping a mistress isn't unheard of.

That's what's crushing me. What makes me almost want to turn onto my stomach and drink in the chlorine until I become part of the pool water. It's one thing to give up my chance of finding a man who *chooses* to be with me, who wants me and the life we'll create and the children we'll have. I volunteered that chance away and accepted a man I'd hoped to find a shred of happiness with. But my silly heart hoped he wouldn't resort to *that*.

If he is...I don't know what I'll do. Living with it seems so impossible. Sickening.

What I *do* know, is I won't waste my life not knowing. Three days has sucked, but I won't spend a lifetime wondering, worrying, *pretending*. No. If he is, he'll admit it to my face so I can work through my emotional consequences.

Being mute, people stopped remembering who I am and who I was; all they see is the silent woman they deem to be 'quiet' due to the diagnosis. With all the changes in the last two years, this had been my armour against others, but before, I wasn't quiet *at all*. If someone pissed me off, they knew it. If I had an issue, I was vocal about it.

While I may be unable to speak to Erico with my voice, we *will* talk. It's a silent promise I make to myself and the sun above. And to him, where he watches me from his office window. He does so often, but I pretend not to notice. I refuse to live with the wonder, the fear, the heartbreak. More so, I refuse to blame him for something he might not be doing. Miscommunication and misunderstanding are not for me.

And now's as good of a time as any. Rolling to my stomach, I paddle to the pool's stairs to exit, just as a shadow encompasses the cement.

I pause, halfway out of the water, and glance up at the stranger. A soldier, I presume, based on the similar clothing to Sebastian's, and even that I've witnessed the Corsetti soldiers wearing. His beard is speckled with white, as is his dark hair. He stands poised, arms behind his back, his expression flat, almost scary.

"Apologies for intruding, Mrs. Rossi, but Mr. Rossi

mentioned you're out here and I wanted to introduce myself before we begin our travels tomorrow."

Tomorrow? What's happening tomorrow?

"My name is Jack Scuttle. I've been assigned as your bodyguard in place of Sebastian."

Sebastian's absence became obvious after day one. I texted him, only for him to ignore me. I did the same on day two and was ignored again. It wasn't hard to piece together who's at fault, and when I demanded an answer from Erico one supper, he skipped over answering.

It's pissed me off because speaking with Sebastian had been fun. Natural not to have to use my phone to communicate. Easier, and just someone to help break up my monotonous days. After the drama with Aurora, I understand the boundaries between soldiers and us, but all I wanted was a friend in this new world and he was an easy contender.

I look up at the man, at Jack, as I finish climbing out of the pool. His eyes remain on my face, respectfully, and even retrieves my towel. If I hadn't already guessed it, Jack's avoidance indicates the precise reason Erico sent Sebastian away, his response the day he found Sebastian and I talking also being further evidence.

Answers. I need fucking answers. Because *if* he took a mistress and I can't even have *a fucking male friend...*

With a final forced smile toward Jack, in which I aim to be polite because my sudden rage isn't at him, I ignore the offered towel and walk right into the house. Carlotta's vacuuming, and for a second, I feel bad to be making a mess, but at this point, I'm committed. Besides, she can blame Erico for my actions.

My wet feet slapping against the marble flooring echoes through the mansion, so perhaps he'll hear me coming. If not, he's certainly about to *hear* me in other ways.

I don't knock, don't wait for permission. Just throw open

his office door, while cursing the fact my phone is outside and I have no actual way to yell at him.

By instinct, my mouth opens and—

Crash!

Metal scraping against metal.

Tires squealing.

Fucking Christ, not now.

My mouth snaps shut, my mutism a fucking curse. How can I act how I used to without speech?

"Ariella. A pleasant surprise." Erico shuts his laptop and pushes his chair back as though about to stand, completely ignoring the obvious rage I dredged in with me. His eyes flick down my body, pausing first on my breasts, and then between my legs. Lustful looks won't halt this conversation, even though they do make my core clench. "You're dripping water everywhere. Where's your towel?"

His phone is beside his laptop, so I gesture toward it, basically demanding him to unlock and hand it over. He opens a note app and slides the phone over his desk, toward me.

WHERE DO YOU GO AT NIGHT?

He reads upside down before I get the chance to spin the phone, and his mouth presses together. He shifts in his desk chair, and that's when the darkness returns. When my stomach sinks and any progress I feel we *might* have had evaporates.

"I didn't want to tell you."

I'm fucking correct...

TELL ME RIGHT NOW.

His dark eyes flick from the phone to me, unusually stormy. Like *he's* upset with *me*. "You asked for this. No one, besides Caladin, is aware, so keep this between us. It's a hobby the *Famiglia's* leader shouldn't be participating in, given it's not exactly what the organization would deem as a noble death in their name."

Dangers...something he shouldn't be doing. I think I assumed wrong.

"I street race."

Street race. I repeat the words in my head twice until they make more sense. He races...cars?

"You're confused."

I'm confused because I was wrong, I think.

Erico tilts his head and gestures for me to come around the desk, but I remain firm where I am. "You're confused because you assumed something else, correct? Something that had you storming in here, dripping water everywhere and soaking my carpet. What was it?"

Fuck. I hadn't considered how to handle this part. Hadn't figured out how to handle being wrong.

I wander closer. Not sure why. I tell myself it's so I can soak a larger area of his carpet.

With his phone in hand, I type another message:

I WASN'T SURE. YOU CAME HOME IN THE
MIDDLE OF THE NIGHT FOR THE PAST FEW
DAYS. YOU SHOWER RIGHT AWAY. I ASSUMED.

"You were awake?" Then he shakes his head and reaches for me. His large hand binds my wrists, and with a quick jerk, I'm standing in front of him, my hips against the edge of his desk. Water drips from me onto his pants, which he ignores. "When I come home, I shower right away because of the environment and people I'm around. A lot of exhaust from the engines, people smoking all sorts of shit, and not exactly the cleanest areas of the city. I wash it all off before I get into bed."

That makes sense and now, I'm a greater idiot.

"The late timing is because it's a few hours to the city, but I return because I want to." His hand tightens around my wrist.

"What was it you were assuming, wife? What, in that lovely head of yours, did you think I was doing?"

I don't want to say. He could get mad.

When I don't respond, Erico drops my wrist and with both hands, cups my waist, dragging me over his lap instead. A small squeak comes from me, as my legs naturally hug his hips until I'm in a crouching position over him. My bikini wets his clothing, and droplets from my hair slide down my back and onto his hands. Our chests are inches apart, the tense air we're each breathing, the same.

Holy shit.

Erico takes the phone between two fingers and reangles my hand until it's between us as he repeats, "What were you assuming?"

He's going to hate this, but I type:

I THOUGHT YOU WERE CHEATING. THAT YOU
HAD A MISTRESS.

Erico flinches the second he reads my message, but his expression remains impassive and without anger. His eyes shut, and he inhales deeply, before focusing on me again. He speaks in a low, measured tone. "I understand why you'd think that, but that's not me. I won't do that to you, I promise."

Empty words? I guess time will tell. I'd like to believe him this instance, but time changes shit. Personalities shift. Promises break. Villains emerge.

He strokes a hand down my back, fiddling with the ends of my soaked hair. "I'll admit, I'm now disappointed in myself."

With my nail, I find the place right over his heart and draw a question mark, hoping he catches my action and understands the question. It shouldn't be so easy to touch him, but I suppose, when one imagines this man beneath them late at night, dreams and hopes become vivid.

"Because I don't know how to *be* a husband, Ariella. I vowed not to create the kind of marriage my parents have, but as I spent more and more time with my father...well," he shrugs, his crooked grin making him seem years younger, "I understood the appeal. But then you fucking ran head-first into my life and shit changed. *I* changed. What I desired changed."

With his phone, I type:

BUT YOU DIDN'T WANT A WIFE. YOU DON'T
WANT ME.

"Yes to the first, no to the second. I didn't want a wife, you're right. What I told you in Nico's office was supposed to be the truth, but every day with you is making it impossible to stick to that plan because I *want you*. You intrigue me and you have since the moment we met. I'm sorry I didn't give you that impression. Like I said, my own ideals shattered with our marriage and I've been determined to fight against that change. But then there's times, I can't help myself. Watching you preform the piano every day for the hour I permit myself when I have other tasks I should be doing doesn't matter. Or sharing every meal with you. Working from home rather than the clubs. Living here rather than my condo. I'm *trying*, Ariella, but I need you to teach me how to be who you need."

Oh. What happens when an airplane crashes into a brick wall?

The wall doesn't make it.

Yeah.

Chip, chip, chip goes some of the bricks that make up my wall.

Am I good enough then? Has the little voice been wrong this entire time?

Impossible. That voice has always kept me safe.

I write to him:

WHY DID YOU NEVER SAY ANYTHING ABOUT
RACING?

He crooks another grin and his eyes rake down my form. "Do I need to spell it out? My wife stopped talking after a traumatizing car accident and she's mad I didn't tell her I race?"

When he puts it like that...I snort, trying to stifle the laughter that emerges as a strange huffing-giggling sound. My gaze flicks to the windows behind him, taking time to compose myself, but returns sooner than meant to, when his large hand cups my cheek, warm and so fucking inviting.

"There she is," he murmurs. "That right there. Fucking gorgeous, *la mia sirena*. I long to make you laugh again, Ariella. To never stop making you laugh."

Is he trying to tell me he wants me to be happy? That's all I've ever desired too.

WHY THE DISTANCE BETWEEN US THEN? YOU
DON'T TOUCH ME.

At this point, why not ask everything?

This time, his dark eyes become near-black with his dead expression. He plucks his phone from me and tosses it onto the desk behind us Then his arm bands around my waist and I'm yanked even closer to his chest, until I'm breathless, until there's no space between my breasts and his chest, when I can see the different shades of brown flecks in his eyes.

My hands have nowhere to go, and like he's aware, he grabs my wrists and places both my hands over his chest. His heart thumps gently beneath my right one, while my own heart feels like it's going to vibrate from my body.

"Do you not remember me saying I wouldn't do anything until you tell me to. The last thing I want is to freak you out. I'm a patient man, so whenever you're ready, I will be too."

The frown pulling down my lips serves as my next, silent question, which he somehow reads.

"Disappointed? You wanted me to bring you in here after only a day and fuck you on my desk? Against the window? Take you like a common whore with no penance for your own feelings?"

At least you'd be touching me. I glance at the phone on his desk behind us, longing to have my voice back.

His hands come down heavy onto my thighs and he presses me onto him. Over his cock. Over his—*Oh my god.* My eyes fly to his, my mouth parting in surprise. It's one thing for a man to say it, but it's another for him to prove it.

He's getting hard beneath me, from only me kneeling over him. With my hips in his hands, he rocks me slowly, and I swear he's growing harder. While my core clenches around nothing, my breaths become more tainted with lust.

"Don't think I don't crave you, *sirena*. I do. Every damn night, I lie beside you, hoping that eventually, I'll be granted the honour to taste you. From the moment I agreed to keep you as mine, I vowed not to hurt you further than you've already been. I refuse to be yet another villain in your backstory, but I also don't want to be your hero. I want to witness *you* rise up and save yourself."

I don't know how to save myself.

<h1 style="text-align:center">21</h1>

ERICO

Before this marriage, I wasn't entirely sure I had a heart.

Torturing men, listening to their screams and pleas for life, for breath, for even a break in the pain before continuing—none of that ever made me bat an eye.

But Ariella does. My words, the ones encouraging her to control her own fate, came from somewhere, and I'm pretty sure it's the beating organ beneath her palm.

My heart.

I've never been so fucking grateful for it until now, when her eyes get misty and those lips part in surprise. Her breath hikes and the perfect breasts stop rising altogether. Surprised for sure, but the look in her eyes tells me it's a good astonishment. One she's pleased about.

After she stormed in here, looking like the water goddess I didn't realize I needed, everything I've said to her has been the truth. I don't know *how* to be a husband.

When her hand curls into my shirt, right over my heart, her nails scraping the skin there, I'm almost sure she'd only need to do it a single time before finding the sensitive organ. So before she does, I lay the rest of me out for her.

"You think I don't want you when you became my every fantasy today? You strode in here, no care that you were dripping water everywhere, all to yell at me. Truth is, I *admire* you." My hand slides up her bare back, her skin so fucking soft, until I finger the ends of her wet hair. "You have fire that you hide from others, and I noticed it the moment we met at Nico's party, but now I wonder, how many people have gotten the privilege of experiencing it? Because it's a shame if they haven't, and I'm considering myself the luckiest motherfucker on the planet to have.

"I knew you were something that day, and then learning you *volunteered* for this marriage just about broke me, Ariella. Mafia wives *become* strong by their husband's side out of obligation, but when you came to me, you already were. The suspicions you had"—suspicions that not only gutted me but proves I need to do better—"other women may have brushed aside. Ignored it because they believed it was the proper thing to do." God knows my mother had. "But you didn't give two fucks. You strode in here and demanded the truth." My hand on her hip tightens, holding her until there's no space between us. Her heat drags over my cock, my pants wet from her swimsuit, but if she keeps looking at me how she is, they'll be wet for a whole other reason. "I appreciate that about you. You dominated the room, commanded the truth, and didn't hide your true feelings."

Emotion builds in her eyes, making them somehow larger, but before it overwhelms her, I need her to know the rest of what I want from her. Of what we could *be*.

"I want you to be in control because I get the sense you haven't had enough of that. First with your stepfather controlling things, and then your sister bringing you into the Corsettis' lives. And then when I brought you here, but not again. *You* control me. *You* decide what we do."

Her gaze drops to my lips and instantly, I feel like a winner. This isn't what I expected when she strode in here: to have her nearly naked in this scrap of a bikini and on the verge of riding my dick, but I certainly refuse to end this now. Not when the craving to push my laptop off my desk so I can lay her back on it and strip the clothing from her body before finally consummating this marriage grows impossibly strong.

But I mean what I told her.

Stroking my thumbs over her cheekbones, I bring her face closer, meeting her halfway. When I speak, our lips are so close, mine tingle with desire.

"Tell me to kiss you. Grant me at least this, Ariella."

Between my hands, her head rocks lightly, and if that wasn't enough, she mouths, *Yes*, as her eyes flutter shut and for the first time since our wedding ceremony, I kiss my wife.

I kiss her, but I want her to claim control. To test her and see how far she'll go. That fire in her gaze, the one threatening to explode, merely needs a spark, and I want this to be it.

My lips move over hers, my tongue tracing her mouth until she opens for me. But the second our tongues meet, *mia sirena* comes to life. She rises up on her knees as my hands fall away from her face and clamp her hips, pinning her over my lap. She cups my cheeks, angling her face, and with that single move, I discover the real version she's been burying.

She lets out a breathy moan, making my cock jerk beneath us. I long to lay her on my desk and explore her body. First her neck, to discover if it's sensitive, then her breasts, and finally the heat between her legs. I'll kiss her there until she grants me permission to taste the rest of her.

But this is all in her control, and finding a woman who

enjoys dominating seems so fucking impossible in my role. They all think they need to be submissive to me, not understanding that in the bedroom sometimes, it's nice to let go.

When she pulls back and ends the kiss with a look I think is almost regrettable, I realize how much I don't want her to leave this room yet. When she goes, will there be a new understanding between us in which we *try* to make this a proper marriage or will my shitty lack of knowledge take over and throw Ariella back into doubting my desires?

With strength of pure will, I remove my hands from her body, and wrap them over the top of my chair, fingers digging into the fine leather to steady me.

"I won't touch you until you tell me to, but I want you to explore. I want you to do what *you* want. Command me how you will. You feel me between your legs, and I bet if I were to check, I'd find you soaking."

Her instant blush tells me I'm correct.

"Which means you're needy, and I want you to take what your body desires without the worry of me touching you."

She smiles, and all her previous concerns seem to melt away. I'm no longer staring at the woman I've married, rather the person she used to be, before life brought her down. The woman she's meant to become again, and it's then, I make a silent vow to her.

You will be who you want to be again, Ariella. I'll ensure that much.

Her hands slide from my face to my collarbone where she steadies herself as she rotates her hips, and despite the two layers of clothing between us, I pretend there's none. That my freed cock is sliding between her bare pussy before she takes me into her body.

Hair falls into her face and I long to push it away, but my

grip on the leather doesn't allow me to. She's staring down, between our bodies, with an almost curious expression as she rocks her hips. And again. And again until I hear it. Her gentle moan.

"Let me hear you. Don't hide from me."

Her head tilts up until she meets my eyes again and with a wicked grin, she rocks faster. Her fingers work at my shirt, and the moment she uncovers my chest, her hands explore freely. My chair feels very fragile suddenly. We've only just begun and I want to tear it in half to touch her.

I *want* to beg her for permission too, but not yet. First, she'll come like this. That's my single desire for us—to see her become so free and trusting, the orgasm sweeps her.

Does she scream or try to hold it in with a low moan? Does her body go stiff, her muscles uncooperative, or does she ride it out? Reactions I long to discover for myself.

As if it wasn't torture enough, she finishes unbuttoning my shirt all the way to the bottom before lingering around the waistband of my pants. If she undoes my zipper and touches my cock, I'm a fucking goner.

Instead—and thankfully? Regretfully?—her touch is limited to my chest, her hands sliding up and down my stomach, my abs, my chest, while her legs tighten around me. My cock demands more, to feel her orgasm directly.

And it's a fucking sight to behold. She gasps, having brought herself to the edge, and with a look that's almost panicked, almost surprised, she hauls her chest to mine. Her triangle-covered breasts allow me to feel her hard nipples as she steals my mouth again.

My hands grip the seat tighter. Rather it than her because I'm seconds away from breaking my own deal. Her thrusts increase, her whimpers lost in our kiss as her tongue fights mine, a battle for domination she's winning.

"Come, Ariella," I murmur. "Let me see you come."

Not a screamer, but her loud moan, mingled with a kiss immediately plants itself in my head. I'll never stop reliving this second, especially if it's the only moment of us like this.

She pulls back, slyly grinning, which I'm grateful to see. There's no hesitation or regret in her expression as she comes fully down from her orgasm.

My cock isn't pleased with us. It strains beneath her, craving her heat. Her wetness right fucking *there*, separated by my slacks and her bikini bottoms, which hardly constitutes as clothing.

If she were another woman, I'd fuck her right now. Take her on my desk. But lust will not destroy the progress made today. Even if I'm a greedy fucker and my next words come from a place of masochism.

"You're gorgeous. This will live in my head for a long time coming. But I need one more thing from you. Touch yourself. Let me *see* the evidence of what we did."

Her blush returns, but she obeys me, even when, for a second, I doubted she would. She slides her hands between us, into her bikini bottoms, and I curse the science of angles because I'm unable to watch as she strokes herself. She lifts her hand, her middle and index finger gleaming.

"Fuck." And fuck *me* for asking this of her. If fucking my wife wasn't already a dream, I now want to taste her. Want *her* to instruct me to taste her. I'm not sure we're there yet though. My mouth is dry, but I crave the hint of what I hope will eventually occur. It'd be so easy to lean forward and take her fingers in my mouth, but even in this, she's in control.

"Let me taste you, *sirena*, please."

It's been a long time since I've pleaded with a woman. Usually, it's them begging me for release because they think it's what I crave. That because I dominate in life, I need to in the bedroom as well. But they're wrong and finding a woman who understands is challenging.

"Just one taste, so I know. So I have something to dream about until you let me between your legs." *If* she does.

Her eyes narrow playfully and I swear, this woman's making me a mind reader because I can almost hear her denial.

"Ariella, you're going to make me lose my mind." My hands tighten around the chair, the leather squeaking, proving my point.

Her eyes flick to the side in what I think is debate. Minx. But then she brings her fingers toward me and the second she's in reaching distance, I take her tips between my lips, sucking deeply, tasting her delicious, sweet flavour.

Fuck.

I release the chair and in one, quick movement, have her in my arms as I walk her to the desk, placing her on top for another heated kiss. Her legs wind around my waist, her confidence remaining. She grasps the edges of my shirt until I break the kiss.

She reaches for my phone, quickly types on it, and shows me her question.

WHAT HAPPENED TO ME BEING IN CONTROL?

I glance from the screen to her, finding eyes sparkling with mischief and a crooked grin, so I know she's not upset.

With my thumb against her bottom lip, unable to stop touching now that I have in the first place, I reply, "Once I tasted your cunt, I had to see you on my desk just once. Kissing you was the safest option. Believe me," I reaffirm, "if today hasn't proved I *do* want you, *sirena*, then I'm fucking up more and more as your husband."

Her gaze flicks to my cock tenting my pants, finally accepting the proof before typing another question.

I'LL ADMIT, I'M VERY SURPRISED IN WHAT WE
DID. AREN'T YOU MAFIA MEN ALL BIG AND BAD
AND DOMINANT?

Yet again, she's not avoiding conversation and hiding her curiosity, and I really fucking appreciate that.

"In life, in my role, I take charge. I relish control, enjoy commanding others to do my bidding. In the bedroom, occasionally. But more often what I crave most, is to hand over control to someone else. To *you*." I cup her cheek, tipping her head back so no part of her expression is hidden from me. "I enjoy both roles, but you...from the beginning, I sensed you also relishing the power. Once freed from the bounds keeping you down, you'd shine, and trust me, you have today."

She bites her bottom lip, and I rub my thumb over it again, trying to free it from her teeth. She spends a long time writing on my phone before revealing her message.

BEFORE THE ACCIDENT, WHEN I WAS A
NORMAL GIRL, I HATED WHEN MY EX-
BOYFRIEND TRIED TO PIN ME TO THE BED.
HE'D WRAP HIS HAND AROUND MY NECK, TRY
TO TELL ME TO "TAKE HIM," TO "ENJOY IT."
WHEN I TRIED TO BE ON TOP, HE ALWAYS
FLIPPED US OVER, TOLD ME HE WAS IN
CHARGE. AFTER HIM, I ASSUMED NO GUYS
LIKED ME BEING IN CONTROL SO I STOPPED
TRYING AND DID WHATEVER THEY WANTED.

She might not realize it, but she just sentenced a man to death. With a mental note, my men will scour her past until finding the fucker who made her feel less. Even back then, she wasn't her true self—wasn't *able* to be herself.

That changes now.

I don't realize I'm seething until she touches my arm, her head tilting in question. My jaw unlocks, and I tuck away the revenge for now, focusing on only her.

"That's the difference between a *kid* and a *man*. A kid thinks they need to be in control of their partner. A man knows what he wants, but more importantly, he understands his part-ner's desires, and interactions become what *both* need."

Beneath my thumb, her lips fall open, and I tease the edge of her mouth, imagining how she'd look with my cock there instead. One day, hopefully. If she sucks as well as she kisses, my control will be less than nothing.

"For now, we need to get you hydrated."

Without further warning, I scoop her up. She gasps lightly, scrambling in my hold until her arms lock around my neck, her legs at my side. My hand selfishly holds her ass to keep her steady as I ensure she has my phone until we find hers.

I walk her straight down the hallway, past her music room, which I've slowly been outfitting for her needs, by the main sitting area with the huge wall of windows and fish tank, and into the kitchen. It's empty, thankfully, because after our experience, I'm not ready to share Ariella with anyone else.

I plop her onto the island counter, hearing her hiss as the cool temperature touches her bare skin. I fill a glass with cold, filtered water from the fridge and hand it to her.

With a small smile, she sips, barely swallowing any of the water before she's typing her next message on my phone.

> THERE WAS TWO THINGS I WENT INTO YOUR
> OFFICE TO TALK ABOUT. TO YELL AT YOU
> ABOUT THE SUPPOSED MISTRESS AND ABOUT
> JACK.

Jack Scuttle who is happily married and loyal as hell to his wife.

> WHY DID YOU FIRE SEBASTIAN?

A question not asked with curiosity but with an anger I relish in seeing. Spark. Match. Light. And...flames.

"I didn't. He's been reassigned. He's a damn good soldier, and I'm not losing him."

She pouts, which would look cute if it wasn't for the antagonism blasting through slitted eyes. Fingers typing faster than before, she writes:

HE WAS BECOMING MY FRIEND. HE KNOWS
SIGN LANGUAGE. IT FELT NICE TO TALK
WITHOUT PAPER OR PHONES.

Which is the exact reason I'm working with him, but until I can hold a semi-decent conversation, I'm not admitting it to her.

"Your bodyguard shouldn't be your friend. He was looking at you in ways I didn't enjoy, *wife*." I step between her legs, caging her in with my arms. She doesn't bend backwards though, doesn't play into my strength, but rather leans closer with her own before typing her long response.

IT WASN'T LIKE THAT AND YOU KNOW IT. I
WOULDN'T DO THAT. HE WAS FRIENDLY WHILE
YOU LEFT ME ALONE IN THIS LARGE HOUSE
WITH NOTHING TO DO. HE'S THE ONE WHO
SHOWED ME AROUND, GAVE ME COMPANY,
MADE ME FEEL LESS ALONE. THEN I LEARNED
HE KNEW SIGN LANGUAGE AND IT WAS TOO
PERFECT. YOU HANDED ME A FRIEND WHICH
YOU'VE NOW REPLACED AND I DON'T LIKE
THAT.

Christ, she really knows how to stick it to a man. In that long message, my mind changes two different times. First, to obey her wishes and grant Sebastian to be by her side again, and then to keep the change I've put in place.

"Abandoning you the first day is a regret I'll live with for the rest of our lives," I admit. "But I'm not changing my mind on this."

She frowns, causing my chest to split.

"But," I start with a sigh, "you'll likely see him around the mansion. At events and such when we need guards. For you, I'll ensure he'll always be assigned those tasks so you'll have opportunities to see him."

She returns to the phone, beaming, with a final message:

WHAT WAS JACK TALKING ABOUT WHEN HE
MENTIONED TRAVELLING WITH US
TOMORROW?

202

ARIELLA

I'm going home.

Well, I suppose I'm *leaving* home—my new home. And heading toward my old one—the one I've known my entire life. Where Mom and Della and my childhood memories reside.

I don't know what's home anymore. What is and isn't, but what I do, is I get to see my sister again.

The moment Montreal's skyline comes into view, sitting becomes nearly impossible, if it wasn't already, considering I managed the entire flight with Erico pretending not to be watching me. But I felt him continuously glancing from his laptop to me.

Random games on my phone kept me entertained for the flight, and I wrote a bit in my music journal, which I brought with me. Knowing the day laid out in front of me—the day I haven't allowed myself to process yet—I may need a space to write about loss.

The pilot's voice comes over the small speaker, announcing

we're landing within minutes, as the plane takes a sharp swoop and angles itself down to the ground.

"You'll be okay."

Erico's statement drags my attention from the windows toward him, watching as he shuts his laptop and tucks it to the side. There wasn't a question in it; no, "are you okay?" Just a blatant fact, like he knows I will be.

He can't know for certain though. Not when even *I* don't.

After yesterday, Erico's been looking at me a lot more often, and if he was anyone else, I'd think it creepy. We didn't kiss again after his office, or touch in any way, but the memory of his mouth against mine, of riding his hard body, filled my mind, my dreams, making sleep nearly impossible. A few times, I debated rolling into him, kissing him, exploring his body and granting him the permission to touch me, but I ended the fantasy before it began when the uncertainty took hold again.

Still, no regrets storming into his office yesterday. What do they say about relationships? Open communication is best. Guess that's a fact.

When I finally passed out, I was woken only hours later by the most vivid dream I've had all week. This wasn't a surprise though, and even without Erico mentioning the trip to Montreal, I'd still recall precisely what day it is, based on the dream alone. Every year, like clockwork, it infiltrates my mind. In the days and weeks leading up to the anniversary, it's flashes. But the night before, it's *everything*. Every heartbreaking second, every hellish moment of that traumatizing experience.

I hate it.

Hate Mom.

Hate myself.

Hate Stefano.

But appreciate Erico more than words can say because my heart was nearly ripped open when he revealed gaining permission from Nico to take me to Mom's gravesite. Something I'd never done yet; something, I didn't even do when living with Della, but Erico's making it possible.

The plane takes another sharp turn and angles its nose up as it descends to the ground, landing with a thud and speeding to a slowing roll and eventually a stop altogether. Through the window at Erico's back, I spot us parking beside the Corsetti plane, which is indicative by the plain white body and single black stripe on the wing.

Jack, who was seated toward the front of the plane, stands and assists the pilot in opening the door. Erico offers me his hand, which I give him, using his strength more than I thought I'd need to get me up.

He wraps an arm around my waist and hauls me to the open door, where the late morning sun is streaming through. I'm thankful for yesterday for an entire other reason now. How would today go with my walls still strongly erected, without letting him support me?

Erico walks down the metal steps first, his fingers still linked with mine as I officially re-enter my home city as an *other*. The rules are different. I'm technically wed to an ex-enemy of the city's crime lord. There's protocols in place that even I must follow. The first being, getting into the car Nico sent for us, as he is now in control of how I go about my own city.

Once my feet touch the tarmac, Erico releases me. Immediately, I reach for him, but he steps out of the way just as a body barrels into me, staggering me back two steps as I fight for balance. Blonde hair fills my mouth as my older sister yanks me into a tight hug.

"*God*, you have no idea how much I miss you, Ariella. Life isn't the same without you around."

Except she doesn't need me. She's found a new family. Nico's parents respect her, and Aurora can be a replacement sister, plus she has one of our ex-stepsisters, Rozelyn, here. Even Rafael, Nico's younger brother, can be another sibling to her. He has the younger brother annoying energy vibe, so it works.

Della releases me from her hug to study my face in her usual manner with her eyes sliding into slits. Not sure what—if—she spots anything, but it has her quickly throwing a glare toward Erico, who's standing beside Nico and a black town car. Probably the same one I've driven in numerous times.

She whispers, "Are you okay?"

"Yes." I think...better than okay. At least, I'm getting there.

"You better be telling me the truth. If he's doing *anything* you don't like, let me know. I'll get Nico on it."

With a meaningful look involving a sad smile, I remind her, "You know as well as I do, that's not how this works. Erico could be beating me to near-death every night and Nico's hands would be tied."

The example was meant to be the extreme, and her cheeks go paler than normal. "Maybe so, but I'd send him to war over you, Ariella, and you know I fucking would."

She would, which is the issue. "He's treating me well, Della. Don't worry."

The next look she gives is for Erico rather than me. A warning one as we approach him and Nico.

Nico tips his head toward me. "Mrs. Rossi, I hope you're enjoying your new home."

Della reacts the same time I do—with a small squeak. It's the reminder I'm no longer his sister-in-law. Well, I'm not *only* his sister-in-law now; I'm the wife of an ally.

I smile my greeting, which he accepts, stepping aside to gesture for Della and I to climb into the car. As I follow my sister into the vehicle, Nico points for Jack to sit up front with the driver. In the car, Della takes my hand into both of hers and angles herself into me, purposely keeping the men away. Based on the look she gives Erico after he sits beside Nico, she's still blaming him for taking me away.

Patting the back of her hand, I shake my head, silently telling her to stop being mean. *It's fine,* I mouth to her right as the car starts moving.

We leave the airfield and drive straight into the city. The trip is silent. Della leaning into me while the men work on their phones. With every building, every vehicle, every highway exit we pass, the reality of this trip becomes more obvious. Less ignorable. I'm not visiting my sister. We're visiting our mother. Our *dead* mother.

Hold it in, hold it in, hold it in.

I don't know how I'll manage.

When the driver pulls in front of the cemetery, my first thought is how lovely it is. The late summer breeze knocks through the trees surrounding the block's worth of property. The grey stones in the middle of the wrought-iron fence seem fitting, like it's appropriate they have such a pretty piece of land to call home. At least Stefano did this much—gave Mom a decent resting place.

Nico gets out of the car first, followed by Erico. Della releases me to exit behind them, and then it's my turn.

I feel stuck.

Weighted.

Grey clouds creep up, despite the hot sun beaming through the windows, flashing onto the black sundress I found in our closet. Almost like Erico had it purchased for this day specifically, like he somehow knew.

Erico's face appears in the car's opening, his hand stretching toward me. He says nothing. Doesn't ask me to exit the vehicle. Doesn't reassure me in anyway. But he's *here,* and that's what I need.

He knows it too.

Somehow. Reading me. All my walls being more and more fragile with every passing moment with this man.

I lay my palm in his and allow him to take me from the vehicle's safety and toward facing the pain buried within the pretty cemetery. The rocky ground of the surrounding patch of grass digs into the foam of my Toms shoes, the pain echoing the one in my heart.

He drops my hand but not before whispering in my ear, "Sometimes even the strongest of us need a little help now and again."

Della steps between us in a not-so-subtle way to loop her arm through mine then leads me down the cement path. Erico mentioned Nico sourcing the exact gravesite where Mom's buried and must have provided Della the directions because she walks us right toward it without hesitation.

Right down the stone path with gravestones on either side of us. All those dead people, with families still out there. Or maybe not, as we pass one with a 1762 date on it. Perhaps their family line died off, perhaps not. So many stories within this property and Mom's become yet another one.

Della stops and pulls me down a particular row, passing stones of every size until reaching the final one. Small, grey, newer than some of the others. Only a couple years old. The inscription drops me to the ground, my bare knees slamming into the cool, trimmed grass.

Valerie Lambert

1978—2020

Beloved wife & mother

Memories immediately bombard me.

I scream.

The same kind of scream from that day. The warning, the fear, the anger of not being listened to. The same scream I later released when I awoke in the hospital, confused, frazzled, with the final word I'd spoken to her echoing in my head, taunting me with its evil sorrow.

She didn't listen to me then, so what was the point in talking at all? People only pay attention to what they want to. If Mom had, then she'd be alive.

I fall forward, onto my hands, gripping the grass at the base of the stone—*her* stone. It's not right she even has a stone. That this is what her life became. Her two orphaned daughters—because our birth father may as well have died, for all we know—sobbing at her fucking gravesite because she married the wrong man.

Della's arms come around me as I scream and sob and let it all go into the grass. As I release the torturing pain, the endless rage, and the shattered grief into the ground. The grass, the dirt, and the roots beneath me carry my silent message toward the urn of Mom's ashes.

Am I even still screaming? I have no idea anymore. Nothing makes a difference.

It didn't then.

Mom getting a call to head to the library, where she occasionally volunteers, is strange, since they typically work around her schedule and not the other way around. Mom being Mom agreed regardless since she had no other plans.

Then her driver wasn't available. Her driver is always available. He was hired by Stefano for her. It makes no sense he'd be elsewhere.

Which is how I find myself seated inside the passenger seat of one of Stefano's smaller, spare cars. How many does one person need? This is number three, I think.

"Something about today feels off, Mom," I tell her, eyes cutting to the side where she's driving.

My mother shrugs and smiles, too caught up in bliss to look deeper beneath the surface. Since the moment Stefano came into our lives, the dark clouds that often consume me have been more present. Less ignorable. Everything good comes to an end and I'm waiting for this to as well.

I've been living with depression for years at this point, but every side-eye Stefano shoots my way, or bitchy comment from Yasmine or Rozelyn, his two daughters, makes the black hole a few feet deeper, demanding I jump in and hide myself from them.

"You worry too much, honey." Reaching over and effectively ending this conversation, she twists the knob and turns up the volume of the 80s music blasting through the speakers. It makes my head hurt.

After another block, the feeling doesn't go away. Above us, a grey cloud covers the sun—like a warning. Mom slows the vehicle down at a red light before stopping it altogether and she drags her fingers along the wheel, awaiting the green. Since marrying Stefano, she hasn't driven herself anywhere, so maybe she's simply missed the freedom. That's what I try to convince myself of anyway.

Glancing away from her, I rest my head on the backrest and I stare out the side window as a car is coming to a stop behind us.

But instead of slowing, it's maintaining its speed. It's coming too close for a safe stop. I don't know how to drive, but even I can distinguish that. It's basic math.

"Mom." I reach over, turning the music down. "Mom, I think someone's about to hit us."

Closer…The vehicle is white. A van. I can't make out the driver due to the angles. Still not slowing…

"Mom!"

"Ariella, you're being sil—"

Crash!

Metal scraping against metal.

Tires squealing.

Mom screaming.

Control robbed.
Our car being shoved into oncoming traffic—
Honking. So many honks…
Crash!
"Mom!"
The last spark are her eyes. Blue like mine and Della's.
An apology within them.
A final message: I love you.
The flash of headlights beyond her shoulder. When they turn off, her eyes shut, and my body slams forward, head smashing against the front dash.
And then…it's over.

23
ERICO

Her scream is what I'll hear in my dreams every night until my soul exits this world.

Guttural, tortured—a yell—a howl—a plea from a girl to her mother.

Ariella drops forward, sobbing into the grass at their mother's gravestone as Della hugs her from the side.

I step forward, needing to hold her myself, to care for her, but am quickly blocked by Nico's arm. Without looking away from the sisters, he shakes his head and murmurs, "Leave them. They need this. They deserve to be alone."

At first, I snarl and am about to shove him away, but then, when after a long minute she lifts herself from the grass and falls into her sister's arms, I realize he's right.

"Believe me, this is extremely difficult for me to watch too. I'd like nothing more than to go hold Della and reassure her she's okay, but for now, there's someone else she needs more, and I can accept that." Dropping his arm, he tips his head to the side. "Come, let's walk and leave them be."

I hesitate, glancing back to ensure Jack and Nico's driver are still standing by the cemetery's entrance. Satisfied no one's getting by them, I follow Nico, shoving my hands inside my slacks after a final look to Ariella.

"Originally, we mentioned an annual trip on the anniversary," Nico starts, "but if there's a time she really needs to visit, when the grief is hitting harder, just message. Let's be honest, both of them lost a mother that day, but Ariella was affected most."

"You're not half-bad, Corsetti, despite what my father says about you." At the very least, he cares so much for his family, including his extended family.

He chuckles. "Yes, I'm sure your father's descriptions of me are colourful. Either way, I'm pleased that we've found this common ground."

I glance toward Ariella and Della—the common ground they've each become for two past enemies. "I agree."

Nico follows my gaze and smirks, slapping his hand on my shoulder. "It's the Lambert way. Those women wrap a man around their finger like no tomorrow. Can I assume, all is going well between you two?"

"Yes," I answer carefully, unwilling to offer any details about Ariella and my relationship. When he doesn't probe, I use the opening to ask what's been nagging me the entire trip up here. "When we first met about Ariella, you mentioned the accident that took their mother from them. Said it was their stepfather; the same man you called for my assistance on."

Nico makes a noise, indicating he's listening and waiting for my point.

"I doubt De Falco would have been driving the vehicle himself. Who caused the accident?"

Nico stops walking entirely, scanning the trees around us before returning his attention to me. "After meeting Della, I had Rafael, my brother, look into it. The accident was deemed precisely that, but I felt there was more to it. Despite the research, nothing concrete was dug up. De Falco's recent confession confirmed what we all suspected. Other recent events had us learning that he was using a group of mercenaries to do his dirty work. While the ones we found are all dead, I can forward you everything we have on them and the files about the accident, as well as Rafael's number, since he had more dealings with the group's leader than I did. Maybe you can dig something else up because you're correct. De Falco only ordered the hit, which means someone else was driving that vehicle. Since their mother was the only victim in the accident, the fucker must have escaped."

"Appreciate it." I step, encouraging us to walk again.

He follows. "If he's alive and you find him, I'd be grateful for a piece of him."

"He's mine. All fucking mine, Corsetti. For her."

"Hm." His tone is light, amused, but I'm not laughing whatsoever. "I'll get you the information then." Even as he speaks, he roots for his phone to shoot off a text, likely to his brother.

We reach the end of the stone path and the other end of the cemetery, so we turn around, slowly walking back the way we came.

"Enamoured with her?" He nods toward the sisters, like I couldn't decipher who he's asking about.

I shrug. Not his business.

"Less pissed about the switch in brides then?"

"I was never angry," I counter. "Besides, shit works out like this for a reason. How's Aurora?"

"Happy with her chosen man."

"Good."

Eventually, we get near enough to make out both Ariella and Della talking. I wonder if they're talking to one another or their mother. Despite the day, I'm selfish enough to be jealous of her family for getting to hear her voice.

Like Nico is thinking the same, he asks, "She talk to you yet?"

"No."

"You sound a little bitter." He's chuckling again, sharpening the annoyance in my nerves with every sound. If he was anyone else, I'd have my gun drawn to shut him up. "It'll happen," he continues. "She's gone through a lot, but I'm sure in time, she'll open up. Today's bound to earn some brownie points."

Nodding, I agree, but *brownie points* isn't what I want. Using her mother's death and this visit isn't a tool to bring us closer together.

Once we near the row they're in, we stop walking, remaining on the path. The sun's high in the sky, taunting the sisters with its life, its warmth. We'll stay here until dusk, nighttime, midnight, for all I care. However long Ariella needs.

After a few more minutes, Ariella reaches into the bosom of her dress and pulls out a rolled-up piece of paper. She unwraps it, shows her sister, and then refolds it before sinking her fingers into the base of their mother's headstone. She scrapes a tiny pile out, uncaring as the dirt wedges itself beneath her nails, and creates a small hole, no larger than a chipmunk would need to bury an acorn. The paper flutters into the hole before Ariella pushes her dirt pile overtop and presses her body's weight down, ensuring the dirt remains packed tightly before lifting to her feet, Della beside her.

Nico takes a step, assuming they're done, but stops when the sisters don't move. They link hands and continue staring at the stone. Becoming statues exactly like so many around us.

It's another few minutes before they turn away. Della throws herself right into Nico's arms while Ariella stops in front of me, her gaze locked on her dirt-stained fingertips, fiddling with them.

My arms ache to hold her, embrace her like Della and Nico are, and prove she can rely on me for the emotional moments. I reach for her the same time she does me. Her arms wrap my chest, her head resting over my heart. Her face is stained with tears, which she rubs into my shirt. Minutes pass and her hold grows tighter and tighter.

I love that she wanted my support, though. That she trusts me enough to at the very least hold her, care for her during the tough moments. I rub up and down her back, easing her with every method possible. For as long as she needs.

Over her head, I catch Della observing from Nico's arms. He's murmuring something in her ear that she's slowly nodding to.

"Whenever you need to visit her, you let me know, okay? I'll make it happen with Nico."

After another moment, she lifts her head from my chest, revealing fresh tears. I wipe them away with my thumb, as she manages a soft smile.

Thanks, she mouths before pulling out of my hold entirely and returning to her sister's side. They link hands and begin walking from the cemetery, Nico and me following close behind.

Nico offers to host us for dinner, but Ariella shakes her head, denying his request, so we head back to the airfield. After a long goodbye with Della, she climbs the stairs into our plane, her shoulders lower than earlier. I wait until she's inside the plane before shaking hands with Nico.

"Thanks for this."

"Thank you," he replies, releasing me so I can go.

Della blocks my next step. Her gaze darts to the plane's windows and back, her teeth sawing on her bottom lip. "Give her time. She'll be okay. She admitted reliving the entire accident when she saw the grave."

"Got it." *To relive such a thing.* "Did she describe what happened?" How horrible was it for her to re-experience that?

Della shakes her head. "It's one thing we never spoke about, even years ago, and honestly," her expression pinches before she blinks into the sun above, "I don't want to know."

After a final goodbye, I take the metal steps two at a time. Jack follows behind and begins assisting the pilot for takeoff, while I seek out my wife, who isn't on the couches. The door to the small bedroom at the back is shut, and without knocking, I enter, finding her curled tightly in the centre of the bed. Her eyes are clamped shut.

Sitting on the edge, I stroke the back of one of her hands. Her eyes open, finding me instantly. "You'll get through this, Ariella, even if it feels like you won't. You have in the past, and you will this time because you're so fucking strong."

She nods but I wonder how much she actually heard me. Giving her hand a final pet, I stand to leave her when her hand darts out for mine, delicate fingers wrapping my wrist. The metal of her ring grounds me, lowering me back to her side.

Stay. Please, she mouths, and shifts to make room.

Like I could deny her anything. I slip into the bed beside her, barely in position before she's rolling over and burying her head in my chest. Another day, I'd relish holding her like this, but this feels different.

Because the moment I wrap my arm around her waist, she grasps my shirt and sobs burst from her heart again.

"Cry it out, Ariella. I have you. Thank you for trusting me enough to be this vulnerable."

24
ARIELLA

The next day, my emotional walls erect again.

Grief is a funny thing and I've gone months without being sad about Mom. Without her being more than a passing thought. Yesterday was *hard*. Almost as hard as when I first woke in the hospital to find Della clutching my hand before delivering the heart-shattering news. Nothing made sense then, and I relived it all yesterday.

Mom's entire life has been subjected to a cemetery for the remainder of her time on Earth.

Growing up, life wasn't the easiest. Mom worked two jobs to ensure Della and I were cared for and had what we needed to get by. After Della graduated from high school, she also got a full-time job, to contribute to the household. Then Mom met Stefano, and while she's never admitted it, I believe his money was some of the appeal.

Do I think she truly loved him? Yes. Mom was very strong-minded, so marrying a man she didn't care for isn't something she would do. But knowing the man she was coming to like would also prevent her from crying over past-due bills at one in the morning might have been a driving force behind the speed of their relationship.

Unwittingly, Della and I followed in her footsteps. Each of us wed to the head of a mafia family. Each of us with new paths, that somehow, I feel Mom would be proud of.

Which is why, after I cried out every drop of liquid in my body yesterday, my grief slipped into the corners of my mind once more, and by the time I open my eyes the day after, waking alone in bed, I feel *okay*.

Erico's already gone for the day, but he warned me he would be. Said he had to run into the city for a few things and would return in the late afternoon. Even through my tears, I smiled when he told me. It felt *normal* for a husband to have these conversations with his wife. We might not be the meet-cute I once dreamed of, or even the happily-ever-after, but we're headed in the right direction, I think.

Dressing for breakfast, I laugh to myself. I feel fucking *good*. After yesterday, and even the day before, my depression has faded. Not gone—never gone. This diagnosis is stuck with me, and I it. Any little deep emotion will bring it to surface, but for now, I'm more confident. Happy. *Right*.

Not like I'm a burden. Not like Erico's only here to fuck me, impregnate me, and abandon me to this empty life.

"You're happy today," Carlotta greets me when I all but skip into the kitchen. She takes in my pale, pink sundress with a grin. "You look good too—not that you don't always. I just assumed, after yesterday—I'm sorry, Mrs. Rossi. Coffee?"

I nod and take my seat at the island as she prepares the mug. She assumed I'd be locked away in bed after yesterday. I debated it too. So easy to let myself get sucked beneath the wave of emotions and forget about life. But I *want* to write and play my music today. I *want* to spend time with my husband later — while he's still interested.

The thing I *don't* want to do is attend the party his mother's throwing tonight. Erico insisted on getting her to move it to next week, considering our day yesterday, but I waved the offer off. Mom wouldn't want me to live in darkness my entire life. She'd want me to embrace this party and prove to the entire *Famiglia* I'm a force to be reckoned with. So it's with her in my memory, I mentally prepare for tonight.

Even if that feels damn near impossible.

I take the mug from Carlotta and after a wave goodbye, head for my music room. There, I find another addition to the room—a huge decorative rug in the centre that takes up much of the floor. The carpet is a deep emerald green, and in the centre, a black outline of a mermaid. A siren. *Sirena.*

Funny man.

Careful to skirt the edges of it, not wanting to accidentally spill coffee on the beautiful design, I head for my piano.

Hours later, the door opens, and while I immediately know who's entering, my fingers don't break their pace with the piano's keys. Being only a few notes from the song's end, he'll have to wait. My ears perk, listening for his steps, which I expect to be directed toward the couches, but instead, they're growing louder as he approaches.

"Bella, mia sirena."

His fingers sweep aside my hair, brushing along the base of my neck as the song comes to a lulling close, my fingers sliding from the piano keys to turn around and face him, smiling.

His dark hair is more messy than usual, a contrast to his neatly-pressed suit. For once, in my dress, we match.

The light feeling from earlier returns like a force in my stomach. At some point, he's bound to realize he's fucked up in wanting to treat this as an actual marriage and he'll break my spirit when he pushes me away again. Because everything good in life always comes to an end, so until then, I'll capitalize on this.

His thumb strokes my cheek, right by my mouth and I turn into his touch, a low, contented moan working up my throat. "Fuck, Ariella, a man can get used to a greeting like this."

Except a better greeting would be for your wife to speak to you. To ask how work was.

No, stop! The negative voice will not win this time.

He bends, dropping to his knees in front of me, which puts his face in line with mine. My only warning: "Stop me now if you don't want this."

I lean forward the same time he does to meet his kiss. His hands come around my back and he hauls me closer to the edge of the seat, fitting himself between my legs as he cups the back of my neck. It's then I realize our positioning. My clothing. My legs that are spread open.

Touch me. I think I'm ready for this—for him. For how much? Not sure. But for more than faraway stares and cautious looks.

I grab strands of his hair by his neck, kissing him back as roughly as he's kissing me. He makes a sound of appreciation, his interest of my domination emerging.

Dominant. Never would have coined that to myself, but it makes complete sense.

His noises encourage me, makes me feel like I'm doing this correctly. I take one of his hands and rest it over my right breast.

Erico breaks the kiss, a question flickering in his dark, smoky eyes, even as his hand flexes around my mound of flesh. A low moan threatens to come forth, my nipple budding beneath my thinly padded bra.

"Giving me permission to touch, *sirena*? If you are, you'll have to tell me when to stop because I have a fucking craving for my wife that needs to be satiated."

For *me*.

Controlling his wrist, I drag his hand down my chest, my stomach, toward my hips while my legs slide farther apart. A silent instruction for him to touch.

"Let me taste you, Ariella. The other day has me dying for more."

Does he mean—here? The floor, or that brand new carpet, or the couch?

Either way, I nod, and gift him my control with a simple arch of my back. His other hand comes down on my thigh, large and warm, as he caresses up and down my leg, inching closer to my core with each pass.

Until suddenly, he grips me beneath my ass and stands, lifting me with him. A surprised noise spurts from my lips as he carries me to the side of the piano and rests me on the cool, smooth surface before moving the mug and coaster to the floor.

"You're still in charge. You don't like something, end it with two taps to the back of my head."

The back of his—?

His hands drag up my legs again until his fingers hook in my panties, and he pulls them off before tossing them to the side. His eyes remain locked on mine the entire time, testing, pleading for me to not end this.

I don't think I could if I wanted to.

After the other night, after the dream, I incorrectly began second-guessing us. Perhaps he was finished with me. Maybe he missed being in control. So many doubts that were clearly me being me. He's not ending this. He wants it. Me. *Us.*

He smooths his hand over the piano top by my hip. "You know, when I purchased this, a fantasy to take you on the surface came to life."

His fingers trail over my thigh and toward my centre. He pauses there, eyes on mine, before sliding two fingers through my wet slit. My body opens for him, my legs falling wide, as my silent cry fills the room.

"Wet already and I've barely touched you. This is how I know this marriage is meant to be. We're made for one another, *sirena*."

I'd like to believe that statement, even if he's only saying it from a place of passion.

With my heels digging into the hard surface, I lift my hips and arch my back, chasing his touch, pushing his fingers over my clit. With an arched brow, I challenge him.

Touch me how we both want you to.

"So good at giving commands," he croons. "You know exactly what you crave, like a perfect, little queen." His hand stops, his index finger poised at my opening and my breathing stalls, seconds away from rocking my hips and taking him into my body myself. "*My* fucking queen, Ariella. All mine."

With that statement, his finger sinks inside me, curling and immediately finding the place I'm most sensitive. He strokes the spot roughly, somehow *knowing* what I enjoy. Not to be treated like a princess, not in this, but rather, a queen. My head thumps back onto the piano, unable to watch any longer as pleasure tightens my eyes together, my mind focusing on only one thing: the spark igniting within me.

His finger slips out only to add another, stretching me slightly as he re-enters. My cry isn't silent this time, my moan low, and I punch the top of the piano as my orgasm very quickly rises to the top, unable to be tapered after so many years of being untouched.

"Command me, Ariella. What do you need from me?"

Everything.

But his previous words about tasting me echoes in my head

again, so I reach my hand into his hair, snagging a clump of his hair as I urge his face between my thighs.

"That's exactly what I was hoping for."

His head lowers beneath my strength, not that I think he needs further encouragement, and his tongue swipes up my centre before nipping my clit between his teeth. He bites down lightly at the same time his fingers pulse against the spot inside me again.

And that's it for me.

I chase the instant high, heels digging into the piano as I rock on his tongue, fucking his fingers in and out of my pussy roughly. He doesn't stop me, doesn't pin me down, just allows me the control to feel my orgasm how I need to. My hand presses as heavy as I can onto the back of his head, ensuring he doesn't think to abandon me now of all times.

When the pulsing inside my core slows, and my breathing evens out, my hand sliding limp from his hair, he lifts his head, but not before gently biting the inside of my thigh. "Hottest fucking thing in my life." His fingers gently pull from me and he reaches up with his other hand, flicking off stray strands of my hair from my face. "How will I ever be able to stop touching you, *sirena*?"

You don't, that's how.

Once my hair is off my face, his hand drops to the edge of my dress, to tug it down, baring my nipples one by one. Cool air greets them, making them tighter than they already were.

"These deserve to be worshipped and I'm glad to be the one who gets to." He lightly tugs on each nipple, my core pulsating in tandem with his touch before sucking them each in his mouth. His teeth scrape the sensitive skin of both before kissing his way down my body, right back to my core.

My legs fall open again and his hands press down, holding me steady at the precise second his mouth covers me. Without his fingers accompanying his licks, this feels different. Less pressure and more easing, almost. His tongue drags slowly over my core, teasing my clit, my opening, but that won't do. I grip his hair again, reclaiming control of his movements as I slowly rock my hips, creating a pace I'll orgasm to.

He chuckles darkly, right into my pussy, the sound embedding into the deepest parts of me right before his tongue chases it. He fucks me with it, like he had with his fingers, and his eyes flash up, meeting mine. This is the memory that'll live forever, seeing his tongue inside me, his hands massaging my flesh, and his eyes begging me to become his in another way.

A second orgasm hits me like a freight train. But more so, it's very...*wet.*

Oh, my god, I'm not...

But I can't stop it. With a moan and a final thrust, liquid gushes from my pulsing pussy, wetter than I've ever been, creating a mess I genuinely didn't know I'd be capable of. I've *never* orgasmed like that before.

Erico's licks turn to slurps as he cleans me, and my body slumps onto the piano, muscles limp and useless. But then a deep-sated curiosity to witness the mess I've created has me lifting my head, studying between my legs. It's all over my piano, and him. He's completely soaked with *me.*

While I'm downright mortified, Erico wipes the back of his mouth with his sleeve and chuckles. "I take back my earlier statement. *That* was the fucking hottest thing."

I gesture to the space between me and the piano, the mess, hoping he understands the urgency.

He does but a strange look enters his eyes and he lowers his arm slowly, almost in awe. "You've never squirted before, have you?" When I shake my head, he curses. "I can see why this would be alarming to you then. Well, let me ease you—" He reaches for my hips, somehow managing to lift me over most of the mess and off the piano. Once on my feet, he cups my face, staring into my eyes until I believe his next statement. "You are a goddamn dream come true, Ariella. A dream I didn't even know I had. Now come," he drops his hands to take mine, "let's get you cleaned up."

I follow him out of the room, but a quick peek back at the piano has me yanking on his arm to pull him to a stop. That's twice now I've come and I still haven't seen him undressed. Felt him between my legs, sure, but not beyond that.

Stealing my hand from his, I quickly grab my phone from its location on the piano bench, shooting him a text as I walk back to his side.

ME

What about you?

He smirks, looking up from his phone after reading the text. "Believe me, that *was* for me."

25

ERICO

Caladin drops his feet from my desk after I basically shove them off. He'd come here earlier this evening, figuring the drive from here to the country club is closer and with the news he had to share, it was simpler. For him anyway, as that's what he's claiming.

The event's at a country club owned by the *Famiglia*, one of our legal businesses purchased at the demand of my mother. She claims the beachfront property is the ideal location for celebrations such as tonight, and since most of the guests are flying in from other parts of the country anyway, she's not concerned with a convenient location.

"Anything on Evan Brown?" Ariella's ex-boyfriend's name is laughably simplistic. Like his parents despised him. It was easy enough to find her school records, her graduating class, and from there, anyone she had previous ongoing conversations with.

Caladin rolls his eyes. "Yeah but not until you explain why I had guys searching for him. He was her *high school* boyfriend. Dude, that was how many years ago? Obsessive much."

I level my glare at him. "Just answer my question."

"Answer mine." After a long stare from us both, he rolls his eyes again and concedes. "Whatever. Yeah, we found him, but he won't be any help to you. In the couple years after high school, he was picked up for dealing a couple times. No charges really stuck for too long. Seemed a lot of community service or week-long stints in jail. One day, neighbour called something in, and he was found OD'd in his bed. Guy's dead."

"Well, isn't that a shame." In truth, I'd have enjoyed doing him in myself, but if he's no longer breathing, then that's good enough for me. Saves me from taking time away from Ariella to kill his unfit ass.

"Gonna now admit what he did to warrant you hunting him?"

"When they were dating, he hurt her in a manner of speaking. Wasn't great with her." It's one thing to not appreciate a woman's dominate nature, like he obviously hadn't with Ariella, but it's another to force her to the bed by her throat and take it how *he* wants.

"Well, shit." Caladin whistles. "I take it all back then. I get why you wanted him found then."

Glancing at the time on my phone, Ariella's bound to be nearly ready, so I lead him from my office and down the hallway toward the entranceway to wait for her.

My cousin skips behind me. "Hey, nice job on the races, by the way. Three back-to-back wins. Damn, I bet two out three on you, but all three!"

I sharply turn so the dick almost runs into me. "You bet I'd only win twice? Asshole. You deserve that loss."

My voice must have carried to upstairs because a flash of colour enters my peripheral vision and there she is, standing at the top, making Caladin's comment matter less. So much, he's no longer a thought on my mind.

Nothing is a thought on my mind. Nothing but the vision walking toward me.

Donned in a slim, shimmering, purple dress that catches in the overhead crystal's lighting, it garners all my attention. It's held up by two thin straps that lay on each shoulder, and the top is cut into a V, highlighting the slight swell of her breasts, alongside the diamond necklace. The dress falls right to the floor, the peep of silver heels preventing it from dragging on the ground. Her hair is up off her neck in an elegant bun. I wonder if she did that herself and where she learned to do it. Earlier, I offered to hire a hairdresser to come to the house, but she waved me off.

The closer she gets, the deeper her blush, but she *must* realize she has no reason to be self-conscious. Not when she's a fucking vision. And the reason behind my private shopper's raise.

A firm slap to my back tries to interrupt my unyielding stare. Death itself wouldn't make me look away from Ariella though.

"Dude, tongue back in your mouth. You're drooling. Quite unattractive for someone of your old age of thirty-one." When I'm about to shove my cousin through the door, he shoulders me aside and dramatically drops into a bow as Ariella lands on the bottom stop. "Mrs. Rossi, you get prettier every time we meet."

She smirks but her eyes find me, which makes my cousin's antics less irritating.

Caladin notices too and with a dramatic pout, he straightens. "Fine, fine, I got the hint. Meet you two in the car."

"Back seat," I holler after him. He replies with a loud laugh

Once the door's shut and Ariella and I are alone, I'm able to fully appreciate her. Unabashed and without a pesky voice over my shoulder.

"God, Ariella." I reach for her, my arm finding an easy home around her waist. "I'm seconds away from calling my mother and telling her to cancel this stupid party. What I wouldn't give for a repeat of this morning with you in this gown."

Eating her out on the piano is another memory I'll re-live. Every new experience with her replacing the last. Even when I had her spread like a meal, she silently took what she wanted, what she needed, and the release her body gifted me was proof of what we can be.

Ariella shakes her head and types on her phone. She grips it like a lifeline, which I suppose it might exactly be that tonight. She's not leaving my side though.

My own pings with her message.

ARIELLA

We can't because it'll cause drama. You've shielded me well but we both know what this marriage means to your role. I must step up at some point.

Once, I'd be pleased by that message, but I'm finding myself disappointed she's becoming stronger and more confident. Not because I wish to *not* see her rise up as my queen, but rather, I'm becoming selfish where she's concerned and want to keep her all to myself.

Reaching for her, unable to stop touching, I curl a loose tendril of hair around her ear. "I hate that you're right. Plus, my mother will bitch to the end of eternity and no one wants that. Rain check, I suppose."

Looping her arm through mine, I lead her to the passenger side of the car. Once she's seated and buckled in, I join her and Caladin in the car, and we head to a night I'd rather do without.

The moment we're off my property, Caladin leans forward,

putting his face between our seats. "So. Yeah. Thanks for letting me tag along on date night."

"Put your seat belt on," I command, unamused.

Completely ignoring me, he utters to Ariella, "He's no fun. All day, the bastard has me running around on an errand and *this* is the thanks I get! Whatever. I'll cab it home."

"Trust me," I say dryly, "the means in which you get home later isn't even a blip on my mind." Especially for mentioning an errand that Ariella certainly doesn't need to know about.

The moment she picks up her phone, I know her text is for me, so when the screen on the car's dash flashes with a message, thanks to the Bluetooth connection, we all get to read it.

> ARIELLA
>
> Don't be mean. We can at least drive him home.

"Ha!" Caladin slaps my shoulder. "What she said. I like her, Erico. When you eventually force me down the aisle for whatever random alliance you decide to utilize me for, make sure the bride will be as pretty and as amusing as this one." Then he turns his charming smile right to my wife, who meets it with her own.

Caladin's not a threat and I know he's only pulling this shit to get a rise out of me. So I should ignore it, but damn, he makes it impossible.

Thankfully, since the venue is so close, we quickly arrive. The rustic-style club is lit up with streamers of fairy lights going from pole to pole, wrapping the roof, and illuminating the dark area.

A red carpet is laid out...because Mother. It's a hint of how flashy she's made this event be. Father always appreciated her willingness to be the perfect mafia wife, but glancing at my own, I'm learning there's numerous definitions of the word *perfect*.

I park by the valet's stall and he opens Ariella's door, assisting her out. Caladin and I both get out, simultaneously buttoning our suits' coats up.

Before I manage a step toward Ariella, Caladin's arm blocks my way. "Jesus, man, I didn't realize until witnessing you tonight. You're downright obsessed with your wife. You're falling for her, aren't you?"

"Shut up," is my mumbled reply as I push him away and join Ariella, after handing my keys off to the valet.

Caladin, still laughing, strides up the red carpet and through the double doors, giving us a peek of the chaos inside. Taking Ariella's arm into mine, I pose us to look how everyone in there expects us to. A partnership. A Boss and his queen.

"Ready?"

She nods. But in her mind, I think she's shaking her head no.

"Sooner this starts, the sooner we get home. Think we'll need a long, hot shower after this."

The moment we enter the building's lobby, Mother is on us immediately, her pin straight hair as sharp as her delicate nerves and cat-like nails that jab in my direction. "You're late by five minutes. Bad form considering all your men have come out for this. Some even travelling—"

Ignoring her, I pull Ariella through the next set of doors and the noise of chatter from hundreds of guests help tune my mother out. The party is the lesser of two evils at this point.

Guests turn, some tipping heads respectfully, others murmuring to one another. All their attention lands on the woman at my side. Most with curious stares, others even managing gentle smiles. That's good. Cools my blood, knowing I won't be fighting my own men on her behalf tonight.

The old-style country club with dark wooden beams running through the ceiling gives this place a cabin vibe. Each beam is strung with fairy lights, which is very typical of my mother's design preferences. At the far end, a long table that stretches the room is home to more food than we can all possibly eat, complete with a giant ass five-tiered cake at one end. A fucking wedding cake.

My mother's trying to make a point.

If this night already didn't suck, it certainly does now when a body breaks from the crowd, heading toward us. The very someone who magically disappeared on a plane and hasn't been heard of since.

Father approaches, his snake-like smile flicking between Ariella and me. "We need to have a quick meeting. Leave Ariella here."

Leave my wife alone in the lion's den? Not likely. But fuck, if I need to speak with him. To demand what the fuck he's up to with the Volkovs.

Even as Father tugs on my free arm, I shove him away, not being subtle for our guests. "Your meeting can wait until I at least have her settled."

With a sneer, Father brushes his hand down his suit jacket before gesturing into the crowd. As if knowing, the couple people lingering there shift aside, baring the way for another man to approach. He grins too toothily, as though he's already won a game only he's playing.

"You see, son. Waiting isn't an option."

Ursin fucking Volkov.

26

ARIELLA

Erico turns us immediately away from his father, his eyes scanning the massive crowd. This reminds me a lot of Della's engagement party, when people whose names she'll spend years trying to remember descended, all wanting to speak with Nico Corsetti's future bride.

Hundreds of curious faces stare at me with varying degrees of interest. They remain back, likely awaiting Erico's permission to approach, which honestly, I hope he'll never give. By his side, I'm safe. With them...I can't say for certain.

Walls up. Mask on.

Learning to hide my depression from people has taught me to use the same skill for the other, unwanted emotions, like the anxiety presently making me cold. Causing my nails to dig into Erico's sleeve as a silent plea for him to not leave my side.

"Where the fuck did Caladin go?" he mutters, doing a visual sweep of the venue. "Him, I trust leaving you with."

I want to make my fears known to him, but with the crowd still observing us so closely, they'll pounce. And that's not including the very large mountain of a man standing beside

Erico's father, who's watching us with a chilling look in his depthless eyes.

A thin, cool arm snakes mine and an even icier voice says, "Go with your father, Erico. It's time I officially meet my daughter-in-law."

Fuck. Having seen Gia Rossi at Della's party, I avoided her even then. Luckily, I had no reason to approach the three Rossis and remained in the shadows when I wasn't by Della's side. And minutes ago, with our arrival, Erico moved us past her so quickly, I didn't get a good enough look at my mother-in-law.

She's tall, reaching a foot over my shoulder, though I suspect her heels have something to do with that. Her face is packed with too much makeup for my liking, her eyeshadow a bright contrast to the plain, white dress she wears. It's long, reminding me of a wedding dress. Her hair, the exact dark shade as Erico's, is pin straight down her back.

Cold eyes study me while I'm doing the same to her, and at the end of her examination, she smiles too widely. It's fake. Being practiced in feigning emotions, it's easier to spot when someone else does it too. So I shoot her back an identical smile, and wonder if she sees through me as well.

We're trapped between both his parents, leaving Erico with little option. I manage a reassuring look his way, which based on the furrow in his brows, he doesn't believe at all. Still, with a final scan of my face, he follows his father and the other man through the crowd, which parts for them.

Once they're gone, leaving me alone with Gia and a room full of strangers, his mother gets right to it. "Lovely dress," she comments, reaching out to pinch at the skirt. "A little bold for my liking, but we all have our own preferences, don't you agree? I prefer muted tones, especially for such events. But you'll learn."

Insults tossed into a compliment. Got it.

I throw her back another sugary smile and scan the room, searching for Caladin again. Erico's cousin is amusing, and I'd much prefer him to Gia's company.

You're being silly. This is Erico's mother. You're stuck with her for the rest of your life.

Gia pats my hand in a way that seems affectionate to outsiders but against my numb skin, it feels like a warning. "Erico will be back soon. Come on. Let's get the introductions underway. Everyone's dying to meet you."

Before I can fully take in her words, she's pulling me into the crowd, stopping at a couple, and then a group, and then another, doing all the talking while I remain silent. I don't even bother with my phone to type responses, letting Gia take the lead. Besides, even if I wanted to add in my own reply, at the speed Gia yanks me around, it'd be impossible to do so. She never hesitates in mentioning my mutism, and now I get Erico's aversion to his mother. Bitch.

Her standard greeting: *"Hello [whoever she's dragged me to]. This is Ariella, Erico's new wife and the newest member to the Famiglia. Already, she's taken on such a burden. I should note, if she doesn't respond, it's because she's mute. Bye now. Enjoy the party!"*

Again: bitch.

Thankfully, that message is met with a few different responses, mainly from the other wives. Some icy looks, but a lot of easing smiles, and even an attempt to talk directly to me before Gia's yanking me away from the kindness. Some of them even prove to not be half-bad when they glare at Gia but smile at me. Probably a lot of women here in similar circumstances, and we're all just playing this game.

Every time we take a pass through the room, I scan for Erico. He's bound to be back soon. How long could this random meeting possibly be?

Gia eventually leads me toward tables of food and drinks. Without looking toward the staff, she holds out a hand and a waiter, comprehending her silent demand, places a champagne flute into it. She first offers it to me, but I shake my head, earning only a narrowed glare in response. At this point in the night though, haven't I've done enough?

"Very well. We don't know how well you handle your liquor yet anyway, and the last thing Erico needs is for you to embarrass him in front of his business partners."

Embarrass him after one champagne flute? Whatever.

Maintaining her glare, I hold out my hand to make a point, and the wide-eyed server slips a glass into my hand too. I despise champagne, learned that at Della's party, ironically enough. But the tiny sip I allow between barely parted lips is worth the look on her face.

Chin tilting a fraction, nose in the air, she steps around me. "Well, Ariella, this is where I leave you. Erico's bound to return shortly. It was lovely to formally meet you. We need to get together soon for lunch."

Sounds horrible. I lift my glass a few inches in a mini toast, telling her *sounds great* with the action.

When she finally walks away, her heels much too loud for my liking, I hand the flute right back to the server. He takes it with a knowing smirk and rests it in the bin of other discarded glasses.

Gia's barely gone a full minute when someone new approaches. Erico *really* needs to return now so we can finish this thing together and get the fuck out of here. The scent of flowers bombards my nose, like someone bottled a garden and doused her body with it.

The woman stops beside me, her head tilted in a way, so she's looking down on me, despite her only being a few inches taller. Wavy black hair mingles with her dark dress. Her examination of me ends with her arms crossing over her chest, accentuating her curves, which almost look too fake. Her nose hikes like she's smelled something unpleasant, all while she grins. Not forced, but rather, malicious.

I despise her already.

Erico, where are you?

"Hello. Lovely to meet you. After hearing so much about you, I feel like I practically know you by now."

Based on her tone, it's not lovely at all, but more noticeable is the thick, Russian accent.

I force a smile in greeting, looking behind her for escape. She inches to the side, putting herself back in my view.

"It's quite amazing Erico even married you. Mousy. Don't see the attraction at all."

A mix of insults and self-depreciating agreements run through my head, resulting in me just gaping instead, unsure how to respond or act. Still knowing, I need escape though.

"Ah, sorry, I should introduce myself." Her hand comes out toward me, but I don't return the shake, only earning a chillier glare from her. "My name is Vanessa Volkov. From the Bratva."

Another mafia family, I think? If she believes her name will mean something to me, she's sorely mistaken me for someone who knows what the fuck they're doing.

Another step to the right, another fake smile. Anything to end this odd conversation, but then she continues, her voice like nails on a chalkboard, and it has nothing to do with the loud accent. "Oh, but I skipped over who I *should* be. I'm the woman Erico was supposed to marry."

Those words make me pause because who *is* this woman? I am very aware of who Erico was supposed to marry instead of me. Hell, I lived with her. Was present when Aurora learned of her eventual engagement, and then watched the union go up in flames when she chose her bodyguard, Rosen, instead. Or was

Erico engaged to this woman even before the agreement for Aurora's hand?

Nico would have mentioned that to me...right? And according to Della, the deal for Aurora's hand was struck a year before she was even returned home. Erico wouldn't have made such a deal if he was already engaged.

She's lying.

"At least, I'll be by his side one day," she continues in a sing-song voice before abruptly gasping, her hands flying to cover her mouth. It doesn't hide her evil grin because she knows precisely what she's done. "Shit. Excuse me. I hadn't meant to speak out of turn. Well," she lowers her hands, her malicious smirk expanding slowly, "now that—what's the saying? Now that the cat's out of the bag? Yeah, that. At least you're aware of your future. Of being tossed aside. Where do you think your husband is right now? He's working out a deal with my father."

Lies. Fucking lies. That's not who Erico is. Not what he'd do to me.

For once in my damn life, I hate that my voice is broken. I *hate* that I can't fight for myself, so all I do is walk away. Teeth smashed together, right back into the crowd, praying anyone will begin talking to me, to save me. Caladin's the preferred option, but right now, I'll even take Gia's bitchiness over what I just experienced.

I open my mouth, practicing what I would tell this Vanessa woman if I could, pretending I'm able to fight for myself when—

Crash!

Metal scraping against metal.

Tires squealing.

Vanessa follows, shoving aside a couple until her hand clamps down on my shoulder and she's spinning me around, leaning much too close for my liking. "Pathetic, *Mrs. Rossi.*

Enjoy the name while you can because you won't have it for long."

Snarling, I shove her off me, earning a shocked gasp. People nearby murmur, but I don't care. Rage pulses behind my palms. I'm so sick of people assuming everything about me simply because my voice is broken.

My voice is broken.

I'm not.

I turn away again.

"Ariella, you must admit, I'm the better option for him. After all, you can't even *speak* to—"

Smack!

My hand burns, the sound of skin on skin bringing the entire party to a silent screech. Everyone who wasn't already watching the action is now. Gia appears, her mouth open, eyes narrowed on me rather than Vanessa.

Breathing heavy, I glance at my reddened hand and then to the matching shape on Vanessa's cheek. *I hit her*. Holy fuck, I don't even remember turning back around, but I had. Wrath controlled my actions, shutting her lies up, and taking control of me.

"What the fuck is going? Move!" Erico's voice cuts through the crowd and he and two other large men appear at the edge of the crowd. His father, whose looking between Vanessa and me, and presumably her father, if her earlier words are even half-true. He heads to Vanessa's side, removing her palm from where she's covering her injury, his own cheeks flushing as red as I've made her skin.

Erico *was* talking to Vanessa's father...

No. This isn't what it looks like. I heard the conversation when we arrived. Erico's father was the one who dragged him away. He never wanted to go.

Erico immediately comes to my side and cups my cheek

before checking over my sore hand. His eyes search mine for an explanation. "Are you okay?"

I nod. Emotionally sore, but the pain in my hand is so worth shutting Vanessa up.

Watching Erico become Boss is a shift I see with my own eyes. His care and kindness melts away, leaving his dark eyes as lifeless as the day I met with him in Nico's office. His expression is deadly, empty. He drops my hand and gives me his back, one arm slightly angled to shield me. Protecting me even now.

"Get the fuck out," he commands to Vanessa's father in an icy tone.

The man steps in front of his daughter, recreating a similar position Erico is to me. "Excuse me? Your wife owes my daughter an apology. She *slapped* her. Abused her! What kind of *Famiglia* respect is this?"

"Respect," Erico repeats with a tone I've never heard from him before—and hope to never again. "You dare come onto *my* property and talk about fucking respect? I said it back there," he gestures in the direction they came from, "and I'll say it again. Go home to Russia and get out of the States. You are trespassing because you were not invited by me. I don't care what promises my father made you, but you are not welcome until *I* say you are. You want a war, Volkov?"

Erico's father steps forward, trying to diffuse the situation, but based on his stance, it's clear whose side he's talking. Not his son's. "Erico, we've talked about this. I don't think this," his gaze darts around the room, "is the best place for this conversation."

Erico doesn't spare his father a glance. His hand goes for his holster and he unclips his gun, angling it at Vanessa's father who doesn't bat an eye, even with a deadly weapon trained on him. The crowd backs up a few steps while Erico's father lifts his hands, gesturing for Erico to lower the gun.

"There's already a war," Vanessa's father warns. "One of yours hit *my* daughter."

"Ursin, we're both aware who enticed my wife to hit Vanessa. The next time your bitch of a daughter even *looks* in my wife's direction, I'll kill her myself. Do not test me."

Vanessa's face flashes white, making the red mark on her cheek even bolder. She grasps at her father's back at the same time he—Ursin, Erico referred to him as—pulls out his own gun. Before he cocks it, Erico's father once again steps between the men, only this time, faces Ursin. They share a few mumbled words, which Erico doesn't allow them to finish.

"Volkov, ten seconds. I'm not playing. You were not invited to my country, so get out. If you need a reminder of where you are: you're in a room packed full of men who'll kill you and your daughter at my command. Get out of my city. Get out of my country within the hour. If you don't, we *will* fire first."

Ursin shoots one final scathing glare Erico's way before grasping Vanessa's wrist and pulling her through the crowd. People move for them to pass, their attention stalking them. Erico's also staring in the direction they go, and only when they exit the building, does he gesture to unnamed figures in the room. Soldiers step forward from the party's edges, somehow remaining subtly in the background this entire time. One of them is Sebastian, who meets my surprised gaze before focusing on Erico's orders.

"Follow them to the airport. Make sure they get out of this country within the hour. Call me if they linger."

The trail of four men follow the Volkovs.

With them gone, I suck in air. So does everyone else, I think, even though the room is still tense. Electrified. I touch Erico's back, hoping to gain his attention again, to calm him down, but beneath his suit, all I feel is his seething, deep breaths. He lowers his gun and tucks it back into the holster, so that's progress.

His father steps forward, gesturing to the crowd of onlookers. "Well, now that that's been—"

"We're leaving."

Erico reaches for me and tucks an arm around me. I curl into him, breathing in his scent. Two weeks ago, I never would have believed Erico Rossi would be my safety net. When I assumed he'd drown me in this life, he's been the one keeping my head above the waves.

Gia joins her husband, scanning the room, her expression almost nervous. "Son, what—what are you doing? That was an unfortunate mishap, but you don't need to leave over it."

He stops in his tracks, turning slowly to his parents. "The *only* thing protecting your asses right now is the blood we share. You don't think I'm smart enough to see through the bullshit charade that was? You invited them here when I've made my stance explicitly clear. Mother agrees to keep Ariella company the moment we arrive so you, Father, can pull me into some backdoor meeting. Then *conveniently* Vanessa finds her way to my wife's side."

Gia scans the crowd again and speaks low, even though everyone in the room is so attuned to the family drama laid out in front of them, they probably still hear her. "Erico, enough. We'll discuss this later."

"Yeah," he agrees, surprising me, "we will discuss this later. Another day, another month, another fucking year. For now, we're done." He grasps my hand, but instead of pulling me toward the door, he faces the crowd. "Thank you all for coming. This is my wife, Ariella. She's your queen and you'll all fucking treat her as such. If you don't, hopefully today is a display of what will happen."

And then we're gone, outside in another breath, and he immediately gestures to the valet who rushes to the side of the building to retrieve his car.

The moment we're alone, Erico cups my face, smashing his lips to mine in a rough, possessive kiss I'm all too happy to accept. *If* there were any leftover doubts from Vanessa's words, his mouth removes them.

"God, Ariella. Do I even want to know how that happened?"

Probably not. But what's most relieving is that he didn't immediately ask for the story inside. He took my side and asked questions later.

Like an equal partnership.

I lift my phone between us and shoot him a text, mentioning all the things Vanessa said to me. For the first time, Erico glares at the phone, as though annoyed I'm unable to use my voice.

When his dings, he quickly reads my message, cursing, and glares down the dark road. "Fucking bitch. I'll hunt her down so she can pay for every single thing she said."

Don't. I shake my head, holding onto his lapel just as his car arrives. The valet hands over the keys and Erico helps me into the car. The short drive goes quicker than our trip here, and glancing at the speedometer proves why. Not a terrifying speed, but certainly an energy to get us home quicker.

He abandons the car in front of the house and helps me out, his hand stroking over the one I slapped Vanessa with. "Sore?"

I shake my head. Not anymore.

"Let's get you inside and into bed."

27
ERICO

Once Ariella showers and is in bed, she stares expectantly at me because I mentioned on the drive home I'd provide an explanation of what happened tonight. She deserves it, and I want to give it.

This night, while suspected would be shitty, turned out so much worse. Now I'm on the verge of war with the Bratva and at odds with my snake of a father.

I take a seat on the edge of the bed, leaning on the post and start. "A few days before our wedding, my father came to me with a different proposition. One that would have us aligned with the Russian Bratva by marrying Vanessa Volkov. Father never completely liked my deal with the Corsettis, so when Nico offered you in Aurora's stead, he saw this as the Corsettis getting away with treachery, now twice in one lifetime."

Her expression lowers and I can all but see the thoughts racing in her head. The self-doubts returning.

"I denied him right then and there. Said I'd honour the deal Nico and I made originally, and then the revised one with you."

Why? she mouths.

"For the same reason I agreed to wed you, Ariella. From the moment we met, I was intrigued. As I've said in the past, I couldn't deny your offer and already made up my mind—we both did. What my father proposed could be profitable for the *Famiglia*, but I wanted you instead."

Her ocean-coloured eyes soften, melting away some of those doubts.

"He was adamant though. Determined to gain the Bratva. After we married, I figured he'd drop it considering—" I lift my left hand, using my thumb to spin my wedding band, finishing my sentence with the action. "Tonight was a complete surprise. The moment I saw Ursin approach, I knew it wasn't over. Rather than argue in front of everyone, I figured it'd be safer to hear them out." Little did I know how wrong I was. "Fuck, Ariella, I'm sorry."

She shakes her head, her brows dipping. Her mouth opens and shuts twice before she retrieves her phone.

ARIELLA

What happened wasn't your fault.

It was, but I won't waste time arguing.

"Vanessa wouldn't have approached you if I was there, so it was. In the back room, her father tried to convince me to divorce you and wed her. After denying both him and my father a few times, I was determined to return to your side, but the moment I entered, the loudest sound echoed through the room, silencing everyone else." Despite everything, I chuckle, recalling the confusion, and the utter pride when I realized it was her, hand red from standing up for herself. "Everything that bitch told you was a lie to tear you down. I'm not marrying her."

ARIELLA

You're not mad I hit someone?

My laugh isn't contained. I abandon my phone and walk around the bed, taking her face between my palms. My obsession with touching her has grown to unhealthy lengths, but the more we're around one another, the less I care about the distance I once craved.

"Mad? *Sirena,* I'm far from fucking mad. I'm proud you defended yourself. If I'm mad at anyone, it's myself, my parents, and the Volkovs. Not you." The one positive in this: the *Famiglia* wives now know not to fuck with her. "You slapped the Bratva's daughter without hesitation. You're a hundred times the woman she is. With every fibre of my being, I pledge there is *nothing* the Volkovs will offer me that'll have me choosing her over you. I'm too addicted to you to release you."

I release her face because even with all that said, an energy thrums through me and I know the precise way to release it. The look in her eyes offers one way, but I won't be gentle tonight, or even submissive. I need to hurt someone and it certainly won't be in this bed.

Before doubt creeps into her gaze again, I kiss her forehead, gently stroking her wet hair away from her face. "I need to deal with a few things. Make sure my father's not planning an uprising as we speak, and to ensure the Volkovs left the city. I'll be back way later, okay? Get some sleep."

Whatever's in her head gets masked and she covers my hand with her own, nodding once. But before I pull away entirely, her hand snakes behind my neck and she pulls me in for a kiss.

The moment her tongue strokes over mine, I feel myself losing it. Restraint. Rationality. The need to climb over her, pin her down, and fuck her into the mattress grows stronger, and my *sirena* of a wife knows it too. She reclines onto the pillows, taking me with her, tempting my control. Before it's gone entirely, I manage to pin her wrists to her side, preventing her from further touching me as I break our kiss and glance meaningfully at my hold, so she comprehends my next statement better.

"I hate denying you but I'm not what you need. I'll demand control and that's not something I want for you right now."

She bites her bottom lip but nods, agreeing. Not arguing the fact that what I give *could* be what she needs—because we both know it'd be a repeat of previous experiences for her. That alone, her recognition, brings a smile to my face.

I release her wrists and straighten, turning away from the lure of her siren call.

ME

Gym. Join if you want, or don't. I need to release my energy somehow and right now, a fight is really fucking appealing.

CALADIN

But I have a sure thing in my bed.

ME

Then don't come.

CALADIN

But the practice will be good for me. It's been weeks since I've had a fight scheduled. Can't let my body slip.

ME

So come. You're pissing me off. Also, I have another job for you.

CALADIN

You don't stop, do you?

ME

Not when it comes to my wife. Where the fuck were you at the party?

CALADIN

Hiding. Looking for ways to sneak out. Wish
I stayed closer. Could have kept the snakes
away from her. Sorry.

ME

Yeah, me too.

CALADIN

I'll be the first to admit I never expected her
to do THAT. Admirable. Firecracker beneath
the silence, huh?

ME

You're the second because I'm the first. But
yes, she's stronger than she lets on.

I assume you're on your way over? I'm
pulling up to the gym. Considering you've
been talking with me instead of enjoying
your "sure thing," she can't be that great.

CALADIN

I'm leaving. Fucker.

After a drive faster than I'd risk with Ariella in the car, I park in front of the *Famiglia* gym in Brooklyn. It's an old warehouse that was converted into a space for us years ago, only a half block away from the one we use to torture enemies in.

I exit my car, which had anyone else owned, would be attractive for thieves in this area of the city, but this is *Famiglia* property and New Yorkers know better than to even glance at this stretch of land.

I head inside to change into shorts and a workout tee I leave here for this occasion and head to the far corner, with the blue mats, to begin stretching and warming up. Sending slow punches to the hanging punching bags, bouncing on the balls of my feet to prepare for my scrap with Caladin.

Within thirty minutes, the doors open and my cousin walks in, grinning in the infectious way he does. Fucker loves this shit. While I race, he's one of the top fighters in our underground rings. When he's not doing his job, his free time is at this gym, constantly training and working out.

He's already changed and after tossing his metal water bottle to the side of the mats, he steps up, jerking his chin toward me. "Shouldn't you be off caring for your wife?"

My fists slam a final time into the punching bag, my breaths coming heavier with my warm-up when I speak. "Fighting you means not hunting the Russians." Which would be a battle I wouldn't win without proper preparation.

"Got it."

"Warm-up?"

He scoffs. "As if. *You* will be the warm-up."

He's likely correct. We're evenly matched in terms of bulk, but he fights a lot more than me. He's always preferred the physical over the weapons that I usually revert to. When we spar, I have him pinned first maybe only two percent of the time. He wins the rest. It doesn't bother me though.

Knowing his tells and his moves, I swoop in, reaching for his legs. Caladin fights a lot of people who make the obvious choice of where to attack first, so he shouldn't be expecting me to follow one of his own moves.

He goes high, while I go low, as expected, and a shoulder into his gut has breath whooshing out of him. Throwing my bulk at him, I knock us both to the ground, my arm reaching for his neck.

He evades me and rolls to his feet, walking back two steps and surveying me as I'm slower to straighten. "What has you in a fighting mood?" he asks between slow pants.

I circle the mat, studying his form, debating how best to attack this time. "My parents pissed me off. They're pulling so much shit in hopes I'll divorce Ariella and send her back to Montreal to get with the Volkov girl."

Caladin curses and drops his arms for a second. This is usually how our fights go though. One punch, one hit, and it leads into a whole conversation. "Your parents are dicks. No offence."

With his arms lowered, it's clearly a tactic because once I'm in range, he throws a leg up, roundhouse kicking me in the side. I stumble before righting myself, throwing myself onto him again but narrowly missing him. My trajectory takes me down to the ground and before I right myself, a shoe's pressing heavy into my back.

"I win."

Reaching behind me, I yank at his ankle, but he sees it coming and skips to avoid the grab. But his quick steps make him unsteady and he nearly trips over me. It does what I need though, and with a roll and a swipe of my arm, I trip him.

He lands beside me, panting, the fight momentarily paused as we both catch our breaths. After another moment, he sits up, legs crooked, palms positioned in the mat to keep him upright as he studies me.

"What do the Volkovs have that your father wants so badly?"

"Beats me." I wipe drops of sweat off my forehead with the edge of my shirt. "Power. Weapons."

"Personally, I think you made the right decision. For one, the Bratva's known for backstabbing and I doubt being married to the Boss's daughter would protect you for long. They're ruthless, so as fast as you're saying *I do* to her, Ursin's getting stabbed in the back and replaced by someone else, in which case, all your dealing might be for nothing. Smarter to have the Canadian connection since they're closer. More useful. That's not even comparing the two women."

I also push into a sitting position, curious of his thoughts on this topic. "Yeah?"

"Yeah. I mean, never met Vanessa, but I've seen pictures. Pleased your father isn't trying to use me for the connection. I'd be insulted if I cared. She just *looks* like a bitch."

"She is." Thinking about what she did to Ariella today, I recount what my wife told me she said.

"I take it back then. Triple bitch. Good on Ariella for standing up for herself like that. In front of the heads too. They'll all see now, you and her are the real deal."

The real deal. The corner of my mouth pulls into a smirk at the concept.

He catches it, of course, and reaches over to shove a hand into my shoulder. "Except, thought you didn't want the real deal."

"I didn't. But she's...I don't know, man. Different."

"Didn't know that was possible."

"Me either." I lift my gaze, focusing on my cousin so he sees my true feelings. "You know better than anyone what I planned for my marriage, but something about her never fit that mold. No matter how much I tried to make it a thing in the beginning, I just...couldn't."

"My point exactly, cuz. With Vanessa, you wouldn't have these struggles. The fact you are with Ariella says she's best for you."

His statement would almost be emotional if I didn't know better. After Caladin lost his parents when he was ten, he blamed them both for orphaning him. Their love for one another was the reason they were together, and he thinks love is dangerous. It made for amusing conversations when we were dumb teens and aware of what our futures would entail: marriage. He doesn't want love because it's a danger, and I don't for how distracting the emotion can be.

"Getting all emotional on me now," I tease.

He shoves into me again, scoffing. "Whatever. Says the guy obsessing over his wife." He pushes to his feet in a single, swift movement and reaches a hand down for me. "Come on. We're not done. Still gotta kick your ass."

28

ARIELLA

Floating on my back in the pool, I reflect on Erico and me. Based on the way he kissed me after the party gone wrong, I was so certain we'd sleep together, but then he pulled away to do his job.

The old me would have fallen into self-deprecating hatred, believing I wasn't enough for him, so I'm proud I didn't. The look in his eyes said he wasn't my Erico, so he's right. Whatever demons were in his head, they were robbing me of my husband, so having sex wouldn't be everything we *could* be.

That was two days ago and since then, it seems like I've hardly seen him besides the time I spend in my music room, when he still takes his breaks to observe, kissing me every chance he gets.

Each night since, he comes to bed very late but seems calm when he does. He always starts out on his side of the bed, but at some time in the night, I end up in his arms, which I don't mind. He's very warm and holds me tightly. He feels like every-thing I've ever dreamed of finally coming to life.

Maybe the white-picket fence dream is coming true. We

haven't spoken about it lately, but he'll need heirs in time. Step one: *be* with him, but if progress continues how it's been, then perhaps our child and me won't only be an accessory for him. I want to hope we'll be a family. A true family. One I've spent years dreaming about having.

My phone ringing has me rushing from one end of the pool to the other. Water pours off me as I climb out and I quickly wipe my hands on the towel before answering the call, catching Della's name on the screen.

"Hey," she starts immediately. "Haven't heard from you in days, since you left Montreal. How's things?"

"Good. Great." I take a seat on the edge of the pool, dangling my legs into the water as I stare at the glistening ocean around us. The late afternoon sun shines over the calm water.

"Great?" she echoes. "That's...promising."

I shrug though she can't see me. "I don't know, Della. I've been feeling good."

"A certain mafia boss has something to do with that, I assume."

"Yeah. He's just...he's more than I thought I'd get. What I always hoped for."

"You mean the man and life that you used to dream about?" Of course she remembers because when she was trying to talk me out of the union, it was the point she continued to utilize. "That's good though. Not everyone in this life sucks, and I'm glad you're finding happiness. He seemed boring when I met him at the engagement party, but then, he was also with his parents and there to meet Aurora. Seems like you're stealing his heart."

"I wouldn't go that far."

Prickles dance up and down my spine, forcing my gaze away, and to the house behind me. Movement in one of the windows catches my eye and I spot him approaching the window, leaning against the nearest wall to watch me from his office. I smile, even though I'm not sure he can see it from his distance and turn back to face the pool again.

Della makes a noise. "Well. I'm glad things are good. He's not making you uncomfortable at all?"

"Not even close."

"Anything else going on?"

There's been quite a few instances where I've lied to my sister, and I find myself doing it again. Telling her I slapped another person makes for an interesting topic, but then she'll ask why, she'll get defensive because that's who Della is, and that'll all mean telling her about the Volkovs. Which isn't her business.

Not her business. Shit.

Technically, we're on different sides, even if it'll never feel like that. Even if there's an alliance between our husbands, it doesn't mean the Corsettis get to know all of the *Famiglia's* secrets and vice versa.

"Nope," I lie. "Settling more and more in, I guess. You?"

Della gets chatty for a few minutes about herself, her work in one of Nico's clubs, and spending more time with Aurora lately. Jealousy burns through me, but as quick as it's there, it's gone. It makes sense they're getting closer to one another. I wonder if Erico has any female relatives around my age. Given the outcome of the party, I didn't exactly get the chance to meet everyone. Before the accident, having a social life was never my priority, but my sister often provided what I needed. Now, besides Erico, I'm alone.

Once she hangs up, I slip back into the pool. We're still a few hours away from supper, and I'd like to spend at least another one of those in the water.

Not even ten minutes later, the mansion's back door slams shut. Even though I can't see him from where I'm floating on my back, my body thrums with every step he takes. It knows what my eyes haven't looked at yet.

I roll in the water, catching as he drops into a lounge chair, my mouth slipping open as quick as he moves. No suit. Shorts. No shirt. Sunglasses covering his eyes. My mouth waters, my core clenches. He's dressed so casually and looks fucking good.

Dress like that more often.

With one leg on either side of the chair, he reclines back. His head tilts up to the sky, but I still feel his gaze on me. He hasn't said anything, so I continue swimming. Maybe he'll join me. Other than the first day, I've never spotted him in the pool.

I do another few laps on my back. Backstrokes up and down the large pool while he merely observes. Every time I near his end, I feel his eyes on my bare skin. I picked the bikini I had on purpose. Silver and smaller than the rest, for this purpose. After the pool, I was going to visit his office. Based on previous conversations, I think he's waiting for me to make a move.

And I'm ready.

I dreamed of it last night. Of teasing him to the brink, he'll lose his mind. I woke up with a wetness between my legs that made me pleased he was already gone.

So after my final lap, I climb out of the pool. His gaze stalks my every step by him and toward my lounge chair where I pick up my towel to wipe my face, and then grab the water bottle to hydrate.

"How is it, your bikinis get tinier and tinier? Not sure if I owe my shopper a raise or to fire her."

Smirking, I drop the bottle back to the chair and walk to the end of his. He repositions his legs on top, somehow knowing my exact plan as I throw one leg over each of his and lower to his lap. Without asking, I grab his sunglasses and toss them onto the chair beside us, so I can see his eyes.

"You're getting my clothes wet."

I plan to do a lot more than that.

My hands stroke up his bare chest until reaching his neck. I pause there and lean forward, taking his mouth in a heated kiss. He grips my hips, but the moment I feel his touch, I shake my head and replace them by his sides.

"Not allowed to touch, am I?" A single brow hikes.

Head shake.

"You really know how to torment a man."

Nod.

"Fuck, Ariella."

I smirk and kiss him again. He kisses me back, his tongue battling for dominance. The chair squeaks beneath his touch and I assume he's grasping onto it. Then I roll my hips, the same I had in his office that one time. Between my legs, his cock grows.

Without breaking pace, I lean away and reach behind my neck, undoing the string on my bikini top. When marrying Erico, I never thought I'd rediscover any of the confidence I once had—years ago—but this is all him. *He* gives me this strength to put aside everything else.

The bikini top falls forward and his hands shift from the chair to my thighs, curling around my flesh, nearly to the brink of pain.

I'm causing this. *I'm* making him desire me.

I yank on both strings on my hips until my bikini bottoms drop open, baring my pussy to his gaze. His *hungry* gaze.

"*Cazza. Bellissimo.*"

Words unfamiliar to me but based on the reverence in his tone, I think I appreciate them.

"*Sarai la mia morte.*"

Again. I tilt my head, needing him to translate.

"*Sirena*, you will be my death. I don't think I've wanted a woman as much as I do you."

His simple statement, whether truthful or not, pushes aside the darkness that constantly encourages me to go beneath the waves. I won't allow it to consume me today. I'll win. I'll be who *I* want to be.

"Ariella, as much as I'd love to fuck you right here and now, I really want you in our bed."

I nod, glancing around the backyard. With his role, anyone can stumble out here, something I didn't really consider when I started stripping. In one swoop, he has me in his arms, one beneath my ass, the other around my back. He turns for the door as he take my mouth again, his kiss tasting a bit different than the others.

Tinged with hope.

We somehow make it to the bedroom without falling, and he drops me immediately on the bed. I bounce to a stop and pull him overtop me. He follows, his fingers crawling up my stomach until I remove his hand, pinning it to the bed. Then I push him to the side, until he's on his back and I'm climbing overtop him, my pussy sliding against his bare skin.

He clasps my hips, but as fast as he grabs me, I stop him with a smirk and a playful shake of my head before pinning his wrists to the pillow beside his head.

Leave those there, I mouth.

He fists the pillow case as I lean down to kiss him, rocking my body against him until I feel his erection beneath me. It's incredibly erotic for him to still be wearing shorts while I'm naked over him.

He hisses, his grip tightening, and my eyes flick up. A wariness builds that he'll move them, that he won't want me like this, that he'll take over. And then his hands move an inch before stopping again and I freeze, watching him.

"I'm yours to control, Ariella. If you want me to leave my hands here, I will, I promise." He pauses, his tongue dabbing the corner of his lip. "I have an idea that you don't have to agree to, but I think it'll help us both."

This is it, idiot. You ruined a good thing. You—

Stop!

The voices must stop.

I slide off him, nodding for him to go ahead. He stands from the bed and disappears into the closet, rifling around for only a moment before returning, a black rope hanging from his hand.

No. My right hand curls around my opposite wrist. Being quiet doesn't mean I'm completely innocent, and while I've never been tied up before, there's a reason for it.

He spots my instant guard and rapidly shakes his head. "Fuck, no, Ariella. This isn't for you. I told you, I wouldn't do anything to you that you don't want."

He did. But I suppose fears and instinct arise regardless.

He approaches the bed again and pulls my arms from one another, until he's also sliding me from the bed. He hands me the rope. It's softer than I would have assumed.

"We don't have to," he repeats. "I promise I'll control myself, but I want *you* to completely enjoy this, and constantly checking if I'm moving or not might take you out of the experience. Having more control might give you a bit more comfort. I'm yours, Ariella, however you need me."

I'm yours. That's what's repeated in my head over and over as I nod, glancing around the room, annoyed I've left my phone outside.

Reading me, he understands immediately what I need, and reaches into the back pocket of his shorts for his phone. There's no password anymore and unlocks immediately, almost like he removed the code for this purpose.

I try not to focus on that.

YOU ONCE SAID YOU ENJOY GIVING UP
CONTROL IN THE BEDROOM BUT I NEVER
WOULD HAVE THOUGHT BEING RESTRAINED IS
YOUR THING.

I expect him to smirk, to tease me for asking, but he merely tips my chin up to better see my face. "Honest truth: it's been a long time since someone has, but it's enjoyable. I *want* you to be free to explore me however you wish to. I'm laying myself in your hands. Tell me what to do, *la mia sirena*."

He doesn't give me a chance to instruct him though—or maybe he simply doesn't give me time to doubt myself because he kisses me again, his hands resting low on my hips.

It's not rope he handed me. It's a continuation of what I had outside.

Courage.

Strength.

Confidence.

The ability to not only finally have sex with my husband, but to be desired. To be trusted to the point, he'll be bound up. If anyone told me six months ago, I'd be wed to a mob boss and minutes away from tying him to *our* bed, I would have laughed in their face and wrote them a song about silly dreams.

He trusts me. If there's a single lesson from all this, it's that.

With this, my trust for him also builds. At this point, I wonder how much of me *doesn't* trust him. And it's with Dr. Shappo's theory that my trust for people is linked to my trauma, I break his kiss and open my mouth to talk.

Crash!

Metal scraping against metal.

Tires squealing.

Fuck. Why did I think it'd be different this time?

Speak, dammit.

Nothing. Air.

Maybe I'm forcing it.

I want this, though. To trust him with my voice and hope he won't destroy that part of me.

Erico's brows meld together and he smooths a thumb down my cheek. "You okay? What's in your head?"

Nothing, I mouth, responding only to his second question. Nothing and everything.

"Don't force it." His thumb drags over my bottom lip. "Not for me. If it never happens, so be it. I'm happy with you either way."

If there was an element of my mask still on my face, it's now gone. Fallen off. Shattered once it hit the ground.

"We also don't have to do this if you're not ready either. There's no rush."

There's not, but I can do this. I *want* to. I'm the one who began this outside, and it's that courage I grasp onto again, gripping it as tightly as I do the rope. I step back and gesture for him to remove what little clothing he's wearing.

Without hesitation, he does, stripping his shorts until his cock bobs free. A part of him I've felt between my legs but never imagined being so...so fucking perfect. The last man I've seen was my high school boyfriend and, with Erico in front of me, I realize he was so far from being a *man*, it's not even funny.

I tilt my head toward the bed, waiting while he stretches in the centre. My thighs clench. My core tightens around nothing —just the promise of what'll be there. With the rope in my hand, I rest it on the bed first, mentally trying to calculate how I'll do this.

"There's four pieces there," Erico cuts into my concerns. "Wrap each around the bedposts and then my wrists and ankles and make a knot we'll be able to untie later."

I nod, following his instructions and manage to do one foot after a moment of struggle. The rope is almost silky, probably for the user's protection, but it doesn't cooperate at first. With

Erico's gentle suggestions and his patience for remaining still, I get both ankles tied before kneeling on the bed to do his wrists.

They seem more intimate since my chest is so close to his face as I lean over him. But now practiced, tying his arms go quicker. Right before moving away, Erico snags one of my nipples between his teeth. My body instantly reacts, a moan and a giggle working through me, but I slide away from him before he takes completely over.

His cheeky grin follows me off the bed before he tests his restraints, finding him bound tightly and stuck.

"Seems I'm yours, *sirena*."

I'm starting to believe that, yeah.

29

ERICO

If Ariella seducing me outside wasn't the sexiest thing I've ever experienced, this is. Having her grind on my lap and strip her bikini will easily make its way into my top ten experiences with her, but I think I'm minutes away from number one.

I've spent two days distancing myself from her out of fear I'll rush her. Every passing second, there's a mounting need to consume her. But now there's a desire to watch her consume *me*. Ariella taking control outside was a beautiful fucking thing.

She seems awkward and unsure of herself, but given that she's risen to every challenge, I suspect she will this time too. Me being tied up is as much for her as it is me, and it has little to do with control and domination. Me placing my trust in her pretty, little hands will help her discover her own courage and self-assurance.

But in case she needs further encouragement, I murmur, "Ariella, you choose the pace. Explore how you want to."

She blinks, as though wakening from a trance I almost lost her in. With a small shake of her head, her damp hair clinging to her shoulders, she climbs on the bed and kneels between my legs. I watch her, curious, anticipating where she'll begin when her nails scrape up the insides of my thighs.

My cock becomes harder beneath her gaze, and the moment her hands brush my underside, I'm a goner. Thirty-one fucking years old and I feel like an inexperienced teenager after one brief touch, about to come right fucking then.

She slides a hand around my shaft, slowly stroking me until my teeth sink into my bottom lip and I'm thankful as ever for the ropes keeping me down.

Still, I need to praise her, to reaffirm her actions. "I've never known a woman's hands to be so perfect. *God*, your touch is fucking bliss."

She pauses, casting a doubtful look at me.

"Ariella, I'm fucking serious. Keep it up and we won't have long."

With a rough jerk of her hair, she orders me not to rush my orgasm. That gaze is so fucking expressive, and like it's unlocked something—her confidence—she grins again and tightens her hold on me. One hand strokes the base of my cock, the other petting my head, her thumb circling the sensitive spot, making me groan. She strokes me for another minute before climbing overtop me, placing her wet pussy right against my length.

"God, *sirena*, yes."

She's so fucking warm. Wet. What I wouldn't give to be able to touch her right now...but the knowledge I'll soon be getting to watch her guide me into her also makes up for it.

But instead of heat encompassing my cock, I'm robbed of the promise. Instead, she rocks her cunt against me.

"Ariella."

She shushes me with a hand over my mouth. Even tied, it'd be easy to buck her hand off me, but I've given her this control, and I crave to see how she manages it.

Just like outside, just like the day in my office, she rides my cock. Her wetness ensures there's no friction, which makes breathing fucking impossible. Makes everything but feeling *her* impossible.

"Fucking tease. My beautiful, beautiful tease."

How anyone could mistake this girl for being shy now seems impossible.

Her pace slowly picks up, as does her breathing, quickly becoming shallow, her nails digging into my abs. Her head falls forward, focused, and the grin she once wore is now almost pained, driven with desire, with the craving to come.

My cock demands domination. Demands she untie me so I can throw her onto the mattress and fuck her hard, while the other half of me only wants this—to witness her lose her mind. To finally see her take control of her own life.

She rides me until she's quivering, her legs clamping my waist. Until she moans and the rush of her desire slips from her pussy and soaks my cock, suggesting how drenched she is inside.

Her breaths shallow out, her shoulders lowering as she meets my gaze with a wicked smile. One promising more. One promising happiness. One promising confidence. And that's the fucking sexiest thing in the world. Ariella shining through her own darkness.

"Bellissima." Beautiful. Too tame a word for what's really in my head. "The vision of you this instance will be with me until the day I die."

A striking fact because they're not words said in the moment. They're the fucking truth. And the fact of the matter is exactly that: being aware I'll likely go before my wife. I'll likely eventually fuck up, will be taken out by a bullet when my luck runs out, when the crime life catches up. She'd be a mafia widow, able to move on from my death and find someone outside the entrapment of our marriage.

But now…now that my wife is Ariella, I fucking refuse to let her manage that grief. To allow her to move on. Death will have a motherfucking war on his hands if he thinks to come for me.

Ariella's hands glide up my chest, breaking my thoughts. Her nails scrape over my nipples until cupping my neck as she leans closer. Her wet pussy rubs against my abs while she kisses me slowly, seductively.

Her quiet moan makes me want to break these ropes. To touch her. But I refuse to be like that asshole from her past and force something on her she won't like.

"I'm fucking dying to get my hands on you."

She grins, shaking her head as she inches back down my body again, placing her pussy against my cock. She lifts onto her knees and in one hand, my length.

God, I want to touch her. Just to hold her hips. Not to control anything, but to help her.

But she doesn't need my help. Pauses there, taking only my head into her entrance. I'm not inside her, but the feeling of needing to weep if she doesn't lower herself becomes stronger every second she doesn't.

"You okay?" I manage to ask. There's no fear present in her expression but still, I have the urge to be certain. "We don't have to do this."

Every fibre of my being silently begs for her not to end this. I'll respect it if she's not ready, but will also require a cold shower if so.

She shakes her head and then lowers herself another inch, her mouth falling open as my cock stretches her tight pussy. My gaze is torn between wanting to watch her face and wanting to watch her pussy stretch to accommodate my size.

"You're doing good, baby. Get yourself nice and wet for me. You need to lubricate my cock to accept you."

She nods, and her free hand, the one not holding me,

strokes down the front of her body and—*Fuck.* Two fingers rub at her swollen clit.

My fucking Christ.

She gets herself wetter, even though after her orgasm, she's plenty fine, but I won't end this experience for anything in the world. My arms lurch against the restraints, demanding to touch her, to help her with that pretty clit of hers.

She inches onto me again, my head disappearing inside her pussy and that steals every bit of my attention. She sinks another inch, hissing again.

"Give yourself time."

She obeys, pausing, her eyes shut tight. After a moment, another inch, and my body is so fucking confused how to react. Either lose myself to the bliss or witness her take the rest of me. Ecstasy wins and my eyes clamp shut.

Then she taps on my cheek, and my eyes peel open. She crooks a finger toward her and then makes a sign with two fingers to my eyes, and then lines them up with hers.

Eyes on me, she commands.

With her making the choice for me, I return to watching her take my cock. She looks so fucking perfect, I'd freeze us in this moment if I could.

She releases me and sinks the rest of the way, lifting once and plunging down again. Her cry, feminine, husky, and a hint of her voice, mingles with my groan, both of us stuck in the moment.

And then she rocks herself, lifting onto her knees.

"Shit, fuck, Ariella. Wait." My jaw clamps, my eyes shutting despite her earlier order.

Focus. Don't come. Don't fucking come. My arms yank on the bindings, seconds away from breaking the headboard to get freed.

She squeezes me so perfectly, it takes repeating the phrase

three times along with a few steady, deep breaths, to ensure I don't. That and the fact she actually listened when I said stop and froze overtop me. When I open my eyes and spot the downtrodden expression, I realize why.

Goddamn, the sight of her heartbreak ruins me.

"Out of your head. Whatever you're thinking, isn't it. You feel so fucking perfect, Ariella, and I've been dying to have you. If you don't give me a second, I'll come way too soon."

Her lips purse, considering my words, but as fast as she does, it's gone for the wicked siren to return and she winks. Lifting on her knees, my cock glides out of her halfway, and she sinks down. Three times she does that and three times I curse. My fists are so tight, my bitten down nails imbed into my skin.

I warned her. I fucking *warned* her, but it's there. Tightness runs through my balls, my abs, through my every nerve igniting my orgasm. This is almost embarrassing. I can't come before she does again—this isn't how I imagined this playing out. Ariella deserves to be dripping with desire, limp and wrung out from the numerous orgasms she has before I come.

"Fuck, Ariella. Fuck, fuck—"

She lifts onto her knees, my cock slipping completely out of her. The room's air mingles with my cock, wet from her desire, but it's not cooling at all. Rather, it heats me more. Draws attention to her absence.

She grins, her tongue dabbing at the corner of her lips as she sinks back onto me. I hit the deepest parts of her and she moans, her hands dancing up her stomach until reaching her breasts, and she's pinching her nipples.

My orgasm returns quickly, and while I don't warn her this time, she knows. Probably in my expression, probably in the way I'm yanking on her ropes, maybe even in my growl.

"Goddamn. Wife, you better fucking enjoy this while you can because when I'm free, I'll—"

My threat cuts off when her cunt takes me again. Blinding pleasure fills my vision; white consumes me. I'm coming whether she likes it or not—whether *I* want to right now or not.

Her pussy tightens, pulsing as her low moan fills my ears. It entices my own, which won't be robbed again. With a final lurch into her, I come, filling her cunt with cum.

The moment her movements slow, she falls onto my chest and reaches up to undo my wrists, and then behind her for my ankles. Somehow, being her submissive was the best and worst thing ever. Worst because not touching her was torture.

I sit up and drag her on top of my lap. Anywhere our skin touches is melded together, not a fraction of space between us. Her hand lands over my rapidly beating heart, and I cover it with my own.

"It takes a lot of trust for me to allow myself to be tied up in another's presence." I brush damp strands from her face, hugging her tighter. "But I didn't even have to debate that with you."

I trust my wife.

I think I more than trust her if I'm being honest with myself.

30

ARIELLA

Is this what happiness feels like?

There's not even a hint of the darkness. All of it has been consumed by the bright light glowing within me. For once, my head isn't weighed down by the immensity of unending wondering. Isn't stressed about the ever-fraying snipping of my fragile nerves.

Well, there is one thing that's poking at the back of my head: good things frequently end, but with how I'm feeling this second, the world could blow up and I'd refuse to move.

Erico hugs me tighter, burying his face in my neck. He inhales, and for some reason, I find this really sexy. I wrap my arms around his neck, just holding him.

Feeling cared for.

Truly cared for and by someone who isn't my blood.

His hands drift down by back and cups my ass, his fingers creeping close to my centre, making me squirm. As his fingers graze my wet core, his cum still dripping from me, I shiver. As he demanded, I stopped taking birth control right before the wedding, but I haven't been tracking my cycle.

Did today do something?

Do I *want* it to do something?

Children have always been a part of my life's plans. Children *now*, when Erico and I are finally in a better place, might be too soon. I'm selfish and want it to only be us for a while longer.

He fingers the cum dripping from my core, lightly rubbing my swollen clit. "You feel fucking amazing, Ariella. Watching you take control of my pleasure was everything I could have imagined and more."

I smile. He was correct in that sex with him, like *that*, was much more enjoyable than any instance in the past, although I'm certain there were a lot of other factors that had gone into it.

Lost in my head, I barely notice when Erico shifts to the end of the bed and takes me with him. He stands and grabs his cell phone before walking us to the bathroom. First, he retrieves a towel and rests it on the counter before setting me on top of it, hands me his phone, and then heads for the large tub on the other side of the room.

After he starts the water and tests the temperature, I write him a message:

SHOULDN'T I BE THE ONE TAKING CARE OF
YOU? YOU WERE THE ONE IN ROPES.

He gives me an incredulous look before taking my face in his hands. He seems to enjoy holding my face. Not that I mind whatsoever. "You're all mine, *sirena*. Mine to care for."

All mine. His tone sews that promise right into my heart. Into my emotions where I'll never not be able to relive them.

I smile. A genuine fucking smile.

"After a hot bath to ease your muscles, I plan on feeding you." He lowers one hand to my hip, his fingers splaying along the insides, brushing along my pussy. "And then I'll be eating dessert. Poolside, dining table, our bed, your piano—you pick a spot. I'm eating, one way or the other."

My cheeks flush.

He grins, and it looks entirely youthful and fun, it's easy to forget who this man truly is to everyone outside this bathroom. The look only lasts for a moment though, as he taps my inner thigh.

"Sore?"

A bit. I nod. It's been way too many years since I've had sex, and he's not exactly small by any measurement. The last time I orgasmed before him, had brought myself to completion, has been…I can't recall. Having the desire to bring myself pleasure has been rarely present, considering the darkness so often prevents me from getting out of bed. Tasks like eating are sometimes a chore I only complete to ensure my mask stays upright; anything extra is simply useless, time consuming, and energy sucking.

Instead of frowning or even grinning, his expression turns almost deadly…cold. Cold with a possessiveness in his gaze that eases me. "Good. I want to be all you feel."

Well, damn. Can't argue with that.

With a look I think is reluctance, Erico returns to the tub, switches off the water after a quick additional test, and comes back to my side. He lifts me from the counter and carries me right into the tub, stepping in first and adjusting me as he sits. He takes the phone I'm still holding and rests it on the small table to the opposite side of the tub. Still in reach, but now I can lower my arms beneath the water.

Erico has found the perfect temperature that immediately works at my muscles. My head falls back against his chest, my arms limp over his legs. My knees, which were upright, fall open against the tub's sides. When Erico rubs my shoulders, I groan, thinking how death could come now and I'd die happily.

"Good?"

"Mm." Hopefully my noise suffices to do what I need it to, and based on his chuckle, it does.

His hands work down my arms, lightly massaging every part of me. He reaches my thighs and does the same until I'm unable to hold them up at all and they stretch alongside his.

"Sleep if you want." His hands brush my hair to one shoulder, keeping the other side bare for his lips, which he trails up and down my neck. "I got you, Ariella."

You do.

So I do exactly as he commands and shut my eyes, not meaning to sleep, but between his touch, the hot water, and the orgasms minutes ago, I drift.

When the water cools, I'm woken by Erico lifting me from the tub. After wrapping a towel around me, holding me in his opposite arm, he notices me blinking awake.

"You slept for about a half hour," he tells me before carrying me to the bed.

He's still naked and dripping water everywhere but doesn't seem bothered by this. Once laying me on the bed, he disappears again and returns wrapped with a towel around his waist. He hands me his phone which he also retrieved, giving me a voice to reply.

Thank you, I mouth and gesture to the bathroom, indicating the bath.

"You're—" But then he stops, his brows melding together. His lips roll together and with an expression of complete determination, his right hand comes up to his chin and downwards in an arc. At the same time, he mouths, *You're welcome*, but his words don't matter. Because I understood the action.

He used sign language.

Before I allow myself to think on it too long, because it's quite possible he only knows that single sign, he makes more motions: *I've...been...learning.*

Awkward gestures, spaced out as he struggles to remember the correct actions. But he manages. He's signing...

With a crooked smirk, he explains, "Sebastian's been teaching me. Not an easy skill. That's where I've been spending a lot of my evenings. I'm trying, Ariella. You might need to give me time to get it right."

He *is* trying. Not only is he trying; he's *been* trying for a while.

My heart burns, the truth fighting to be freed. To be said.

I think...I think I—

Stop. I can't allow myself to open up *that* much. Not now, not yet. It'll come crashing down if I think it.

I'm torn between needing to get off this bed and go to him, to replying back in ASL, or letting shock keep me down. He gives me no choice by coming around the bed and leaning down for a heated kiss. It doesn't last as long as I'd like before he's dragging me to the closet.

"I'm hungry for dinner. Besides, sooner we eat, the sooner I have dessert."

After dinner was cooked, Erico sent Carlotta away for the night because the moment we were both done eating, he came to my end of the table and dropped to his knees, spread my legs, and buried his head in my pussy, bare because he demanded I not wear anything beneath the short, blue sundress.

When he stands after giving me two orgasms back-to-back, his mouth is wet from me, and all it does is make me want him again. Will there be a time I ever get enough of him?

Erico helps me stand, my legs wobbling when I follow him back to the kitchen. He takes both our dishes, rinses them, and puts them in the dishwasher before pulling me outside to the pool.

There, I collect my phone, noticing a text message from Della she sent hours ago, and my abandoned swimsuit. He snatches that, fingering the strings.

"The moment you left the pool, I was a damn goner. You knew it in your every step, didn't you?"

I grin.

With the setting sun casting a beautiful orange glow over the property, I take his hand and pull him to the edge, leaning on the glass fence to gaze at the ocean.

My favourite sight, I sign to him, and he seems to catch every word, nodding the entire time.

"It is beautiful," he agrees. "I'm thankful so many generations ago when my family claimed this as Rossi property, they chose this spot for the mansion. The house they had built was so boring. Too many walls. Reminds me of the Corsetti place. I had this redone recently," he signals behind us, "to replace the walls with windows. Lets the light in, and the view of the ocean is always around me."

My stomach knots with how he unknowingly built a house his future wife would adore.

"But I have to disagree on your statement of this being a favourite sight," he continues. "Once, maybe. But now I'm torn between you in your bikinis, you playing your piano, and you coming on my face, my cock. Just the sight of your orgasm will stay with me forever."

Forever. Such a long time. It's everything I've wanted from this marriage. Hell, this is *more* than I believed I'd get.

Maybe you are good enough. For once, the dark thoughts are positive.

Testing the strength of those thoughts, I inch closer. Without hesitation, Erico wraps an arm around my waist and pulls me into him. We look like a movie moment, together, staring at nature as the setting sun glows in our eyes. It'd be bothersome if I didn't love it so much.

There's so much I don't know about my husband. So much I only know minimal details of. Such as those races he attends. I can't picture the mafia boss beside me doing something as reckless as racing cars.

Crash!

Metal scraping against metal.

Tires squealing.

I shake it off, returning to the present. That wouldn't happen with Erico in the driver's seat. He seems like someone who's confident enough. But I also imagine him controlling his car, his glee of a race win, the adrenaline of the rush, the speed in which he flies.

Question, I sign after a moment.

Erico's hold on me tightens as he brings his arm closer to his other to reply, *Yes?*

When's your next race? I peek up at him, waiting for his response.

"Sorry, *sirena,* I missed all of that. Don't recognize those words. I think you started with *when?*"

With my phone, I type the question again.

"Tomorrow night."

I WANT TO COME.

I angle the phone so he can see and I know the second he reads it, when he jerks away, shaking his head. "No."

I cross my arms and mouth, *Why?*

"Why?" he repeats, tone incredulous like I've asked the most ridiculous thing ever. "You're asking me *why* you, after experiencing a horrible vehicle accident, aren't authorized to come with me to a damn race?"

Yes, I reply with my hands, even though I know he was being sarcastic in his question.

He shakes his head—more of a rough jerk. "You think I would risk you like that?"

YOU WON'T HURT ME. I'M SURE YOU'RE A
GOOD DRIVER

I message and show him my phone.

"And if something happens? There's a reason my parents would lose their fucking minds if they learned I do this, and have been for a few years. It's dangerous. One flash, one hit, and done."

I hike my brow. I'm more than aware of what occurs in accidents.

He paces away, growling, his hands dragging through his hair. He's not winning this though.

ME

Please, Erico. I'm trying to learn more about my husband. Trying to be a good wife. I want to see your interests.

He takes his phone from his pocket, to read his most recent text. Instead of turning around to talk, he messages back.

ERICO

You being aware of them is enough.

ME

Not for me.

I walk toward him, resting my palm against his back. *Please,* I say in my head. My lips even form the words. Sound doesn't follow, but I wish it did. I wish I could be better—try harder to speak with him.

He turns abruptly, his hands clamping on my upper arms so tight, I nearly drop my phone in surprise. "Fine," he says in a tone implying it's not at all. "The races are quick. It's a thrill and a payout from the betting pot. I've never had a near-miss and I won't this time either."

The facts he lists seem to be more for himself than me.

"Tomorrow. Nine-thirty, be ready." His gaze drops to my bare thighs peeking beneath the sundress. "Not a dress. Pants. Now, excuse me. I have a lesson with Sebastian."

He walks away, shaking his head.

A therapist at the medical centre once encouraged systematic desensitization. It was with her support, getting back into a car as a passenger was doable. It's how I know tomorrow night will be fine. No lights, no traffic, and more importantly, no evil stepfather. Just Erico and me, and a quick drive.

It'll be fun. I'll consider this another stage in the desensitization process.

31
ERICO

I must be out of my fucking mind.

Racing has never scared me. I'm in control, I win. My cars are made for this. It's an easy and thrilling time. At one of my last races, ironically, I did imagine Ariella in my passenger seat—for a brief second before I remembered all the reasons it wouldn't happen.

Guilt's a bitch. Our three-hour drive to Brooklyn, where the race is being held, will be at speeds faster than the legal posted limit, as a test. If she can't manage that, we head home. If she can, then I'll be ten percent more comfortable with what's about to occur.

I park my McLaren by the front of the house while waiting for her to finish getting ready. If she obeys and puts on what I've laid out on the bed, then she'll be exiting the house in baggy jeans and one of my hoodies. Where we're going, I want her covered.

The sky above, though nighttime, grows darker. Grey clouds overshadowing the moon, threatening rain the weather app warned me about minutes ago. All day, it's been clear skies, but obviously, the weather's decided now to be a dick. I've raced in rain before, but it's never ideal, and with Ariella in the car, it's even less so. The roads get slicker, the stakes higher.

I lean against the hood to wait her out and call Caladin, in the meantime, to update him. He'll be there tonight, as he frequently is, making the deals and amping up the betting.

"Hey!" A loud thumping in the background slowly fades. Presumably, he's turning down his music. "Running home to change and then heading over. You on the road? You're not exactly in the city, so if you want to make the time, better get on it."

"Home. Waiting for Ariella to finish getting ready."

Silence. *Cough.* "What? She's coming?"

"She insisted." Much to my chagrin.

"The silent woman insisted?" he asks with doubt.

I chuckle, thinking of her tenacity. "You'd be surprised how expressive she is."

"You're okay with it? Given her past—"

"You think I want to?" I interrupt harshly. "You know what's there. Who's there. The kinds of people attending these things. Focusing on the race is one thing, but having her around all those dirty fuckers will be a whole extra task. But she has this damn hold on me, cuz, I can't help but grant her this, even though I also want to keep her here, locked away for safety." Still an option... "She won't leave my side, and everyone will know better than to fuck with her. I won't hesitate to put a bullet in an asshole's skull if he looks at her wrong."

"Plus, I'll be there."

"Yeah," I agree, though I have no intention of requiring his support. "It's a one-time thing. She thinks she can handle this, and you know what, maybe she can. Maybe we're all too careful with her. She knows herself, her past. She's smart, Caladin. She wouldn't have asked for this if she didn't think she was ready."

"Whipped," he comments with amusement. "Fine, whatever. Just get here soon. The sky's getting dark, but as long as the rain stays away for another few hours, we're good. Anyway, I just got home from the gym. See you two soon."

Click. And right on time because then the mansion's front door opens and Ariella bounds down the stairs, coming to a stop right in front of me where I'm perched on my hood.

"Fucking Christ, you're going to get me killed."

In a less-than-shocking turnout, she ignored my suggested outfit completely and is instead wearing a white dress. High on the thigh, and a scooped neck, her arms bare. Between it, and her hair in gentle waves around her, she's a contrast to the darkness, which I suppose is a positive thing. Her lips are a bright red, matching her hair, her eyes shadowed with dark makeup. Her feet are encased in black ballet flats.

She looks so damn innocent. Delicious.

And if it wasn't for the mischievous look in her eyes, I'd believe she *is* innocent.

I push off the hood to bring her between my legs. "My god, did you *not* see the clothes I laid out for you?"

She rolls her eyes and brings her phone between us, types, and then turns so the screen faces me.

> DO I LOOK LIKE SOMEONE WHO'LL BE TOLD
> WHAT TO WEAR?

"You will if you don't want people to die." She tilts her head, so I add, "When we arrive, you stick to my side. No exceptions. The moment you attempt to stray, I'll throw your ass in this car and we're coming home. Where we're going, there's criminals, and I won't take a chance with you." Even if they know not to fuck with me.

Slowly, a smirk stretches her red lips. She's adorable in a sexy way and I admire her as she signs something, which means it's a simple statement. All day, she's been talking more and more with her hands, sticking to easy sentences, which I'm grateful of, and I've been replying when I can. Even when I'm wrong, the smile she gives me for every attempt is worth a thousand failures.

You're suddenly possessive.

"I was always possessive." I line her hips up with mine, my hands fingering the edge of her dress. "I now have a reason to show it." Shoving away from the car entirely, I walk her to the passenger seat and hold open the door.

Once we're both inside, my hand rests on her thigh. With her position, her dress has ridden up, and now, I don't care about the outfit she's chosen. In fact, I love it. My fingers dig into her thighs, instructing her to remain still.

It's with one hand, I take us down the road and off our property at a speed that would get me pulled over by the cops, if it isn't for the recognizable plates on this car.

The near-three-hour drive back into the city is long and has me wondering if I should bring her to my condo sometime. It'd be much more convenient to have her closer to my work than way out here, but then she'd lose the pool and her music room, which occupies so much of her days, so as quick as the idea comes, I shove it away.

Besides, the drive goes a bit quicker than normal at my speed, and I continue to shoot more questions her way, picking apart everything I've yet to know about her. The questions are only a short blip of the trip; most of it's in silence, giving me a chance to think and focus on the road.

My hand on her thigh is two-fold: for my own selfish pleasures, but to also feel for any stiffening in her body or sudden changes. She handles the drive well, and I catch her even smiling a few times.

While I ignore how fucking *right* this is. Once, when I was an idealistic child, I pictured whoever I'd find myself shackled to also enjoying my own hobbies. Back then, they were much safer. Back then was before I realized how exhausting a marriage could be and chased the kind my parents had. But this...this is right, and though many instincts demand I turn around and return Ariella to our bed, safe inside the mansion where I can stick a hundred guards at the door, there's a selfish eagerness to have her with me.

Once we make it to the city, I weave between traffic and listen for any changes in her breathing, but she remains calm and seemingly unaffected. Gazing out the window like we're going for a casual, leisurely Sunday drive rather than speeding through a city at eleven at night, until finally reaching the long Brooklyn road often used for racing. Cops enjoy breaking the races up but once they notice plates, they leave us alone.

I slow as we approach, warning her yet again, "Stay close. Caladin will be here too. He's the only other person allowed near you."

At the start of the next road, I'm halted by a thick crowd. They mingle, shouting with beer bottles lifted in the air. The smell of cigarettes and weed sneak through the car's filters. At the sight of my car, a few turn, screaming unknown, drunken statements.

I park beside the only other car here. A Subaru WRX that, based on the number of add-on lights strung to the outside of the car, the owner spends more time making it look good than managing what's beneath the hood.

Easy win.

Easier because I recognize the vehicle. Which means, I know

who I'm racing even before Caladin breaks through the crowds to report my contender.

"Stay in the car," I order. "Just for a second." The crowd here isn't known for being stellar people.

Caladin cuts me off before I can reach her side, a hand coming up to block my way. "Hey," he lowers his voice to a murmur I barely hear over the crowd, "while we're alone. I looked into the accident like you asked. Corsetti gave me access to Stefano De Falco's phone records. I didn't think he'd be dumb enough to contact the driver directly, and I was right. One number came up the most, and the owner went by the name Gage. Same mercenary that Rafael Corsetti warned me about. Said he was the leader of some gang, but he and his brother killed all their men. Anyway, so I had Gage's phone records pulled, looking into everyone he's ever called, seeing who's alive and dead. Two are still alive. And one...one's credit card records showed on the date of the accident, he booked a car rental. So I had the rental place's systems hacked." Caladin pauses, rolling his lips together as his eyes dart to Ariella who, shockingly, remained in the car. "He rented out a white van on that day. Not sure how he got out of the manslaughter charge, but it doesn't matter anymore because we found him, man. We're tracking him, and Corsetti's hunting his ass as I speak. We'll have him soon."

And this is why Caladin is my best tracker. No one else would have been able to put all that together *and* find him. His news might be the second-best thing to happen to me this week, next to fucking my wife.

I slap him on the arm as I continue to Ariella's side. "Thanks. We'll talk more later. Let me know when you get him."

Keeping myself at an angle, I let Ariella out of the car, readjusting her dress after she stands before the slithering fuckers around us see anything. But first, I back her into the car, crowding her.

"Kiss for good luck?"

Smiling, she gives me a kiss so heated, my cock demands bending her over the car right this instance.

"What do I get if I win?"

Her eyes flick between us, staring meaningfully at my waist. Her look can mean numerous things but as long as it ends with both of us naked, I don't give a fuck. She lifts her hands between us and signs slowly. I think I make the sentence out correctly, and if I do, then there's no way in hell I'm losing this race, but still, I verify.

"I win and you'll tie me up?"

She nods, smirking.

"And if I lose?"

Nothing, she replies with her hands.

Grinning, I pull her away from the car so I can shut the door, while still using my body to block her from everyone.

"Custom says I talk to my opponent. Share a few words. More bets will be made. Give the crowd a show I don't actually care for, and then we begin. And once again, *sirena*, stay fucking close." I squeeze her hand, emphasizing my next words. "I'm not releasing you so don't bother trying."

She nods again, this time her expression serious, and sticks tight to my arm, her other hand even coming down on top of mine. It comforts me, her touch. Provides a strength I didn't realize I was missing.

Caladin takes her in, and whistles low. "My, oh my, Mrs. Rossi, you look like an absolute doll. Remind me to send whoever designed that dress a raise because it's well-deserved." Casting a wink my way, the asshole adds, "If Erico isn't giving you what you want, come find me."

Throwing more weight into my step, I shove my shoulder into his as I pass him, shutting him up with an *oof* but still, he only chortles, completely aware of the pointless jealousy he's provoking in me.

The sky cracks, lightning threatening to crash down. For now, it backs my annoyance for my cousin.

Despite Caladin's joke, he takes up Ariella's left side, winking at her before his expression shifts into one that's serious and deadly. The one that says not to piss him off. The trio of us walk toward the crowd as a large fucker shoves through it.

Blake Anders.

"Anders," I greet, wiping the shit-eating grin off his face. Every time we race, I win, so I don't know why he bothers.

His eyes dive to the woman clinging to my arm and rakes her body in a way too slow and leisurely for my liking. One more second and he'll lose his eyes, and then he'll definitely lose the race. "Who's she? Tell me she's the loser's prize. Because if so, I won't even bother turning on my car. You can have this one if I get her."

Ariella presses close to me and while every word from his disgusting mouth has me wanting to murder him, I'm glad she comprehends why I don't want her wandering freely.

"This is the *Famiglia's* newest queen and if you don't show some fucking respect, Anders, you deal with me. You might be a gang's ringleader, but I rule the fucking country. This is *my* city. *My* drugs you're dealing. Don't forget that."

His eyes narrow into slits that do nothing for me. This is his game. He lords over his own minions so much, he forgets his place sometimes. Racing him is always good because it's a reminder of where he belongs in the hierarchy. The bottom.

"Right." His voice grates, his arms crossing over his chest like he's aiming to make a statement. "Word did spread, yeah, that you gained a new whore by your side. Surprised you haven't killed her yet. She seems a little gentle for you, Rossi."

"He's trying to get beneath your skin," Caladin murmurs. "Don't let him. In fact—" He cuts himself off as he strides toward the observing crowd, his arms rising, his voice booming with unclear words. Either way, he gains the crowd's attention and after the show, money starts flying. Words and threats, curses and dares, all about the race. For good measure, he slaps Anders' shoulder, knocking him back into the crowd of admirers.

With him gone for the moment, Ariella looks at me, her eyes a bit wider. Good. So she sees that life with me isn't all mansions and swimming pools.

Having her here, a bright flash of white amongst so much black and leather, makes me want to bundle her up and return home, to her safe bubble, where none of this exists. Yet at the same time, I want to release her hand and watch her claim her place in the underground's throne as the *Famiglia*'s queen. I'm a crime lord and she's a crime lord's wife, and with the chance, I bet she'd fucking excel at dealing with even a fraction of what I do.

She reaches up and cups my face, bringing me down to her height where she lays a claiming kiss. Those of the crowd still paying us attention observes—observes her own claim on me.

"Give Caladin a few minutes. He's amping up the crowd after that showdown. A bunch of bullshit, but people's cash will flow quicker now. Then we'll start."

I do what I always do, and linger by the edges. Normally people avoid coming too close because they know better. Sometimes women will try to approach, only to be sent away with a gesture. There's no one in this crowd I'd let near my cock, even in my pre-marriage days.

When the cheers increase, I know Caladin's nearly finished.

He pushes back through, winking as the crowd disperses to the edges of the city road, on the cement to make room for Anders and me. There's a white stop line a few feet away, always used as the starting line.

"Pot's bigger," Caladin announces, skipping back to our sides. "More than normal are betting against you. They think she'll," he nods to Ariella, "distract you. Then the other half are motivated by the show."

"That's precisely what'll happen." Ariella *is* a distraction but not for the reasons they think. I'll lose the race, money be damned, before I lose her to her traumatic memories that racing could dredge up. But if she's okay, then I'll win the race and won't stop driving until we're back home and I'm buried between her legs.

"Good luck, not that you need it." He heads nearby for his bike, where he's about to drive the stretch of the race toward the finish line. The crowd often splits themselves between watching the pre-race and watching the ending—catching the winner. Caladin places himself at both ends for the bets.

Anders breaks through the crowd, his arms spread to make himself bigger. "Last chance, baby. Climb in my car and experience a winner."

A growl works its way up my throat, alongside a comment, if it wasn't for Ariella pulling from my arm. First, I reach for her, but then she passes him with a haughty look and climbs right back into our car.

Ignoring him, I get in too. Anders drives his vehicle to the starting line where a woman stands, gripping a white flag. He leans out his window to talk with her, which means I only have a moment.

Once I'm situated and my car's on, I cup Ariella's face, ensuring she sees the seriousness sketched onto mine. "One sign of distress and I stop the car and we go home. I hate that you're making me do this."

She smiles and brings her hands up, making a sign I've learned only two nights ago, and even mouths along. *I'm fine.*

Searching her eyes, I seek the lie. And find none.

"I know you are. Well then," I release her, putting the car into drive so I can move it to the starting line, "buckle up."

32
ARIELLA

Erico's concern for my well-being might be the element of a relationship I've always craved, but his worries are pointless. Speed didn't cause Mom's death; a villain did. An evil stepfather who used her, me, and my sister for his own gains. He paid someone to ram us into traffic. The accident occurred from a standstill.

That's not what's happening today. Erico racing a guy won't bring flashbacks.

I think. I hope.

Either way, his concern, the look in his eyes, only makes me love him more.

Wait...

As Erico brings the car in line with his opponent's, I feel like I'm being removed from the moment. Here but not *here*. Physically present, but not mentally. My mind is drifting, to the past, present, and future. To every moment with Erico I've experienced and every moment still to come.

I think I've felt it for a while but never put words to it. Never wanted to until I *knew*. Until I felt safe enough not to have this happiness yanked from me. Marrying Erico was my way to find a smidge of happiness in this mafia lifestyle I was dragged into, but at the same time, I never would have believed we'd become *this*. A duo.

"Ready?" His question brings me back.

The engine revs. Erico glances out my window, toward his opponent, who's grinning and revving his own engine.

My husband doesn't even look like the mafia boss I've come to know. He's carefree, almost younger. Right down to his ripped jeans and Henley. An outfit that made me drool upon leaving the mansion. Erico in a suit—sexy. Erico casual—mouth-watering. In a way, he reminds me of when he came out to the pool in only shorts yesterday. That ended well, and ideally, tonight will too.

A woman stands between the vehicles and she lifts the flag, stealing my attention. I've seen enough movies to know what this means.

Erico stares straight down the dark road. Despite being in the city, most of the streetlights are off, which makes me wonder if this is set-up as such. Strange, but perhaps it's to hide the race. I would have thought these were done on back roads, but what do I know?

Erico reaches for my hand and places it overtop the shifter before covering it with his own. His fingers flex over the shifter, over me, including me in his experience. His eyes narrow on the road and even his mouth flattens, every ounce of his focus on the race.

The sky crackles again, only this time, instead of the threat of rain like all the previous cracks, the cars are slammed with large, heavy raindrops. The wipers automatically switch on to clean the windshield, and none of the observers seem to care about getting drenched. Guess when their money's on the line, water doesn't scare them.

"Fuck," he mutters, and I know why. While it's summer with hot temperatures, the rain won't be icy, but can still result in worsening visibility.

The woman, now a blurred image through the front window, lowers the flag.

I'm shoved back into my seat with the speed the car takes off at. Erico moves the gearshift quickly, effortlessly, my hand in his control. The road around us blurs, becoming black. There's nothing describable around me. As fast as rain pounds at the car, it's sliding off the sides, speed rendering the wipers useless.

This feels fucking amazing.

I laugh.

This is why he does this. This sensation of flight, of freedom, it's ethereal.

I don't stop laughing.

Erico glances over, his expression wondering if I've lost my mind. The look doesn't last long because he focuses again, his hand tightening around mine. "We'll win together, *la mia sirena.*"

We'll win. Inclusion. A simple but powerful thing.

I glance out my window, searching for his opponent through the heavy downpour. The front of the other car is in line with Erico's back passenger side, which means we're winning if our speed maintains.

He hadn't said how long the race goes for, but I never want it to end.

We pass a cluster of buildings at the same time his opponent falls back. So far back, he's behind us. Erico likely sees him in his rearview mirror, but I watch through the side mirror. It hadn't felt like our speed increased, but maybe it did. We're winning.

The headlights get closer, the other car speeding up. But he's behind us. Not trying to go around us.

Erico, look in your mirror. It's in my head, my words on the tip of my tongue. He looks too close, like he's about to hit us—

"Mom..." *I reach over, turning the music down.* "Mom, I think someone's about to hit us."

Closer...The vehicle is white. A van. I can't make out the driver due to the angles. Still not slowing...

"Mom!" —

He's still not moving over. I focus through the headlights, catching the guy's grin at the precise second everything in my head clears.

When my trust for Erico emerges, and the fear for his life consumes me. For *our* lives. For something to ruin, to end, all the goodness we've been experiencing, and I can't allow that.

An engine revving.

Crash!

Metal scraping against metal.

Tires squealing.

Erico's car jerks, like it's been bumped.

Metal scraping against metal.

Mom screaming—No!

New memories replace the other ones. New fears.

Everything in my head shatters with the next flash of headlights.

When the car—

"ERICO!"

He immediately swerves to the left, narrowly avoiding the hit from his opponent at the precise second the other car slams forward and disappears down the road. Was it all a ploy to win and I just caused Erico the race?

No. I feel it in my gut. It was too similar.

Erico downshifts, breaks, and swivels the car onto the sidewalk, the wet cement gliding against the car's thin, sports tires. It takes us to the grassy stretch lining the road. For a moment, we're tilted, and then flat, parked in the centre of the grass.

Between heavy breaths, both of us trying to make sense of what just occurred, Erico lurches from the car, coming around to my side and yanks me from it. I'm in his arms, perched on the hot hood of the car, his head buried in my neck. We're soaked instantly, the water washing away our near-deaths. It gives energy, drenching us with *life*.

"Holy fuck," I breathe. "I think he tried to..."

I'm talking.

I laugh. A bit maniacal, disbelieving. I'm *laughing. Oh, my god, I've spoken to him*. I did what I've been dreaming of for days. The walls around my heart crumbled enough to allow him inside, the trust I've been feeling for a while now becoming obvious.

The fear of losing him.

Everything came to a full circle. Yelling my mother's name was the last word I spoke when I was "normal." Yelling Erico's name is what allowed me to open up to him.

Both in similar circumstances.

He cups my face in both hands, his eyes searching my face, like he's seeing me for the first time. Maybe he is. Maybe he's uncovered a piece of the old me. The rain dousing us changes nothing; he doesn't blink as water drips from his lashes.

"Ariella, your voice...You saved us, baby."

"I-I spoke." It's getting easier now. "He tried to—I spoke. I didn't think, Erico, I just reacted. All I could think about was him crashing into us. I had to warn you."

"You warned me," he repeats, disbelief making his voice a half pitch higher.

I stare over his shoulder, in the direction his opponent disappeared to. Whatever happened hadn't ended the same way my first accident did. I'm alive.

We're alive.

I shouted and no one died. I warned him and *saved* us.

I didn't lose him.

I didn't lose myself to the darkness.

I *found* myself.

My giggles shift into tears and the next thing I know is I'm pulling his face to mine. Or he's pulling me to him. Not sure which, but our lips meet like the storm above us. Desperate and hungry, full of control and drive, each of us fighting for dominance.

I'll never admit it to him, but that was scary. Not in the way he believes though. I *did* have a flashback, but the speed had nothing to do with it.

My hands push up his soaked shirt, hands petting over the wet, smooth skin beneath. I want him like this. I want him *now*. Maybe it's a shock response. Maybe it's lust. Maybe it's my body reacting to the storm overhead.

All I know is he feels the same way.

"Ariella, I gotta feel you."

"Take me." My voice sounds strange, unused. Even to me. Even when alone, I stopped talking to myself. Stopped singing. Became a shadow because it was easier that way.

Perhaps I've discovered another piece of my husband, or maybe it was what happened, but Erico's demeanor switches. He yanks me off the car's hood, spins me around, and with his palm to the back of my neck, shoves me down. My panties are shoved to my knees with his free hand, and a finger swipes through my core.

Moaning, I spread my legs as wide as my panties allow for. The heavy rain feels heated, though it might be the warm car beneath me. It soaks my back and makes my ass cold and wet the second Erico flips my dress up.

He undoes his jeans, lines his hard cock up, and plunges

inside with a single thrust. Filled to the brim, the pleasure immediately robbing me of breath, my nails scrape uselessly against the wet metal of his car. The storm above, the thunder crashes, matched to my breaths and his thrusts.

"Fuck, that was close. Never again." *Thrust.* "After today, I'm locking you inside our bedroom. I refuse to lose you."

In his statement, I hear, *I love you.*

"Erico." I groan, his thrusts getting punishing. On the verge of painful but this man would never physically hurt me.

"Say my name, *sirena*. Grant another one of my dreams, I beg of you."

"Erico." I'll say it again and again and again. And when my core clenches, when the orgasm sweeps roughly through me and I bow my back, fighting to get closer, for him to be deeper inside me. To be what the storm is. All-encompassing, energizing, and renewing. "Erico, I'm coming."

He bends over my back, changing the angle entirely, and I cry into the car's hood, my head unable to be held up any longer. His mouth traces the curve of my ear as he thrusts a final time, growling when my pussy tightens around him.

"Feel me. Let me hear you. No one's coming near you again, Ariella, I fucking promise."

The orgasm slams into me, my cries mingled into the heavy rainfall. My insides are filled with his heat before he slumps onto my back, his pants in my ear.

"I can't believe that happened."

"Which part?" He positions himself upright again, and my core is emptied when he pulls from my body.

"Every part." I haven't had two seconds to process it, being swept up in the chaos of the moment.

For one, I spoke. My voice worked again. Without hesitation, and even afterwards. When Erico slides my panties up my legs and lowers my dress, I stare at him. After tonight, I can't return to being silent. Trauma memories aside, he's made new, better ones in my head, and they're what I'll focus on.

And then, two, the fact we were almost ran off the road by his opponent.

Lastly, being bent over the hood of his car and fucked roughly.

He follows my gaze to the hood, only rather than the appreciation and admiration I'm feeling, his mouth slips open. His hand rubs the back of his mouth, his eyes saying something else. "Fuck. I pinned you down. Fuck!" His hands shift to his hair. He turns around, his back tense. Worry emits from every part of him and I'm taken back to when I recounted previous sexual experiences and it all dawns on me.

"Hey." I reach for him, shaking my head, pulling on his arm until he faces me again. "Don't you dare apologize. That was exactly what I wanted. What I needed."

Still looking doubtful, he asks, "You better not be lying. You're not hurt or..." He trails off, but I can imagine the numerous endings to his question.

"No. No, I guess...I don't know. It's different with you. Maybe with you, I enjoy both the control and submission."

He yanks me against his chest again, his lips smashing into mine. Rain flavours the kiss and I pull at his clothing again, wanting to do it all over.

"As long as you never lie to me. Always tell me the truth so I know. I can't fix shit if I don't know."

The sound of a motorcycle interrupts my response, and through the rain, Caladin appears. He parks his bike at the edge of the road and hops off, running toward us, his feet slipping over the grass.

"Holy fuck, what the hell happened? Are you two okay?" His eyes dart between us and I wonder if he can tell. "Anders finished the race, took the money, and sped away like his ass was on fire. The fact you lost is one thing but you would have been right behind him. I waited a whole five minutes before coming to find you."

It was only five minutes.

"Find him," Erico commands, his tone colder and harsher than minutes ago. "He tried to drive us off the road and I want to know why."

Caladin jerks back, clearly surprised. "What the hell would he do that for? You've raced him twice in the past and he's never pulled that kind of shit."

"Exactly. Find him. He'll be answering for it."

Caladin nods and takes a single step back, first checking, "You two okay, though? No injuries."

"We're fine."

We're better than fine, in my opinion.

Caladin accepts Erico's response and hops back on his bike, turning around and zooming back the way he came.

Once alone again, Erico leads me to the passenger seat. Instantly, the leather seat is soaked from my clothing. Erico takes his spot too and starts the car, driving it slowly over the grass, the cement, and the road. The low car's bumper thumps with the movements, making me wince with the fact it's likely getting scraped up.

"Well, that was fun. Your next race, I'd like to do that again, but maybe let me see you win."

He shoots me a scathing look, not amused with my teasing.

33
ERICO

For the remainder of the night, my selfishness keeps me in bed with Ariella. The urge to hunt Blake Anders is nearly as strong as the desire to hear her cry out my name over and over.

Maybe it's shock, but I don't think I've processed that, after all this time, she's trusts me enough to talk to me. Having no idea exactly how trauma works, I accepted I never would. Maybe she needed to manage the loss more—I don't know. Della was the only lucky one of us, understandably so, and I accepted that I'd be clinging to the single word she shouted in her dreams.

When she yelled my name in the car, pure instincts had me checking every angle around us, spotting Anders tailgating me, and swerving to safety in less than a blink of an eye. I despise myself for being so focused on the road and getting us through the storm, I hadn't noticed what he was doing.

But that was it, I assumed. My name as a warning, and I'd get nothing further, but then she laughed and continued to talk. Screamed my name as she came on my cock, while bent over my car, a fantasy I hadn't realized I had until that moment.

Being home is different. I think. Again, no idea how mental health diagnoses work so I've spent the night terrified, that was it. A trauma response to an almost-accident based on a previous one and she'd return to being silent.

Therefore, with Caladin hunting Anders, I've been selfish and had her coming over and over, if only to hear my name from her lips as many times as her body was physically able to gift me.

I started out dominating her, stealing four orgasms back-to-back, but ended with me on my back and begging for my own release. This woman is fucking perfect. Once given her power back, she's happy to share it again. Exactly like I need, like I want.

So pulling from her in the morning is shitty, but I was woken with a message from Caladin, stating he's caught Anders with support from some of our men. That was an hour ago, but I ignored my job for this.

Watching Ariella wake up in my second home.

Given that we were drenched last night, I took her to my condo instead of driving all the way back to the Hamptons. There's nothing here; my apartment kept very basic and boring, but it was a safe place for the night. Besides, it's thrilling to bring my wife to yet another one of my homes, another place she's the only woman to be in here, other than the housekeeper occasionally cleaning.

Ariella stretches, her back arching and pushing her breasts into the side of my body. A sleepy smile graces her face as she blinks her eyes slowly open, finding me.

"Morning." *Please verbally reply.* I've become addicted to her voice and not hearing it again is unfathomable.

"Good morning."

She's still here. I don't know why, or how, or if this is how it'll be with everyone, but a part of me doesn't care. In fact, I'd love nothing more to be one of the few she'll speak to.

I can't tell her everything in my head, so I show her, by rolling her over and kissing her. Our tongues tangle, our legs melding together. My cock wakes up, nestling with her heat.

But then my phone's vibrations cut through the air and I curse. She laughs, tapping the back of my shoulder until I lift off her. "Stop ignoring your job. You're the Boss, in case you've forgotten. Go do your things. Sounds like you're needed."

I roll off her but not before bringing my finger down to her core. "I am needed. To make my wife come."

"And your wife needs to have her insides left alone for a day. You've put them to work last night." She sits up, groaning, her hand resting on her stomach. "And apparently my abs too."

"Good. Means you'll feel me for the rest of the day. Speaking of," I glance at the time, "since I'm gone for the day, and this place doesn't have anything for you, I've asked Jack to come for you in an hour. He'll drive you to the mansion. Then later this afternoon, the *Famiglia*'s doctor is stopping by to check on you."

I texted him when I woke earlier. Speaking again is one thing, but the fact her mind switched tells me she needs support more than I can provide.

With that announcement, I disappear into the attached closet, much smaller than my mansion's, and return dressed in a suit to find her pouting.

"Erico, I'm fine."

"Neither of us have medical degrees, so I agree to disagree until a professional reassures us." I approach the bed, dropping a quick kiss on her lips. "Caladin needs me. Shower, dress. Jack will text you in about an hour. I'll see you back at home later."

Caladin's propped against the shut door of the warehouse, picking at his nails mindlessly with a knife. At my approach, he kicks off it. "Make this quick or else we're gonna need to start putting these fuckers somewhere else. Because by tomorrow, we'll have her mother's murderer." He grins. "Yeah, Corsetti called. Said our intel and coordinates checked out. I'm taking men up North to the border to get him tomorrow morning."

"Perfect. For now," I roll up my sleeves and snatch the blade from his grip, "we get answers about last night."

He follows me into the dimly lit warehouse, where Anders is chained. Caladin shifted the trajectory of the chains so rather than him bolted to the floor, his arms are lifted over his head, a bandana shoved into his mouth. His eyes widen upon my entry and he stumbles back a step, his arms yanking on the chains as he tries to balance on his toes.

"He was buggin' the fuck out of me," Caladin comments. "Kept screaming bullshit so I shut him up."

I approach and whatever he's trying to say gets louder, his shouting muffled by the cloth in his mouth. I jerk it around his neck and he sucks in three gulps of air. "Rossi—Mr. Rossi, I swear, I was coerced!"

Somehow, I knew it wouldn't be long until he squealed. He boasts a big game for the races, but he's certainly no mercenary. Not a criminal in that sense, which makes gaining answers more pressing.

I angle the blade until it's pointing over his heart; a threat he won't misunderstand. Fear will have him spewing everything, believing it'll save his soul. "Talk. Everything you know. *Now.*"

He bobs his head in an almost animated way. "I was paid. Five thousand dollars showed up on my doorstep yesterday morning with a note to smash into you. Said once the job was done, I'd get another five."

Fuck. Someone out there wants me dead then. With the speed involved in these races, whoever set this up, is aware that being shoved off the road makes death a high likelihood. The car would lose control, the buildings easy to crash into, the car flippable.

Cocking a brow, I ask, "You obeyed the directionless order when you could have brought this to me and saved your life?"

His skin pales and his eyes dart from both Caladin and me then back. He jerks in the chains, angling himself away from the knife, and tears fill his eyes. He's a pathetic, blubbering mess. "Man, you know any animosity I feel toward ya is just for the races. Friendly competition and all. I don't want you dead!"

"Yet you listened to the command."

"Have you met *you* people? If I didn't listen to the order, I'd be dead too!"

Maybe. Or the greedy fucker wanted an easy payday and didn't use his measly brain to think admitting the note and cash to me would have given him an even better payout. "How'd that work out for you?" With the knife, I spin it, gesturing to the warehouse. "You still ended up here."

He jerks in the chains again, trying to skitter back, only for the metal to pin him to the spot. "Dude, let me go. I'll give you the money, the note. I'll hand it all over. Just let me fuckin' go." His tone drops to a plea, his pathetic tone nearly laughable.

"My wife was in the car," I state with a deadly, flat tone. He's not getting out of here—truth or otherwise—for the dangers he put her in. "There are no second chances, Anders." I take two steps, coming within a foot of him.

"Man," he sobs, jerking roughly again. His legs kick out, trying to hit me, but getting nowhere. "Dude, let me go. I'm sorry. You're both alive so it worked out."

"We wouldn't be if you succeeded. If *she* didn't warn me. I'm sorry, Anders," I say although my tone implies no empathy —nor do I feel it at all, "but to try to take her from me is an act against the *Famiglia* and no one survives such a betrayal."

With a single thrust, I jam it into his heart. The skin squelches, his eyes widen before the light fades, and his body drops, slumping and jangling the chains. I release the knife's hilt, leaving it inside his body, and wipe my hands on my pants after the cleanest death I've probably ever bestowed. He's lucky.

"Didn't drag that out at all," Caladin murmurs, his lips pursing. "Didn't want to take his offer up on getting the note? See if we can track whoever's after you by handwriting."

"Send someone to his apartment. Idiot probably left it lying around. Find his phone. Figure out everyone he's been in contact with. It's not a coincidence this happened last night of all times."

Caladin's already tapping at his phone, sending out orders. "You think they're after Ariella."

"Not sure. Timing's weird. But no one knew she'd be with me. No one but you, and I know you're not behind it."

He shakes his head. "I'd die for you and her before I ordered your deaths. This is weird."

Yeah, I mentally agree, instead ordering, "Get a cleaning crew in here. Dispose of him. Have the place prepared for our next guest."

Caladin follows me out of the warehouse, his eyes narrowed and studying me. "No one's safe from your *protect Ariella* rampage, are they? Means I should probably stay on her good side to not piss you off."

"Do that." I shut the warehouse door behind us, locking in the scent of death and betrayal, tainted with greed. "There's one positive thing that came out from last night."

"Fucking your wife against the car?" Caladin laughs. "You two were so damn obvious."

"There's that, but she spoke to me. Inside, when I said she warned me, she actually *warned* me."

Humour slips off his face, his mouth forming an O. "Your mute wife is *speaking* now?"

"I don't know how it works, but at least to me, yeah." Just saying it out loud, hearing her voice in my head, causes me to smile. And has my cousin punching his fist to my arm, chuckling.

"Well, good for you, man. Good for *her*, I guess. I'm getting this isn't any small feat."

"No." For her or me. Whatever the reason she was able to speak, it was the acclimation of trust, of...something. Of *us* and it's a gift I'll cherish every day.

He shakes his head and backs up, nearing the building again. "Well, I'll wait here until people arrive to remove Anders' body. Then I'm taking a couple to the border with me, if you'd like to join. Or," he waggles his brows suggestively, "too busy wrapped up in your wife's voice?"

"Work, actually. I have to drive to a few of the clubs to complete some rounds. Haven't been to any of our locations in a while. Besides, it keeps me away from the house for now, while Doc checks on Ariella."

"Gotcha."

I drive off, without looking into the rear-view mirror. Without looking back at that man's corpse.

Killing a man wasn't the most striking part of my day so far. Learning that someone wants me or Ariella dead—or both—is.

34
ARIELLA

"Hey," I greet as soon my sister answers the phone. Seated by the fish tank, watching the multi-coloured creatures go around and around, I'm waiting for Erico's family doctor to arrive. Entirely unnecessary, but at this point, I'm so used to every variety of professional, what's another one to add to my roster?

"Hey!" she replies, her voice almost tinging with a question. "You called *me*...and you sound well."

"I feel good." Better than in a long time. The darkness hasn't creeped up at all today.

Yet.

Stupid annoying, inner voice. It's entirely incorrect. The nice feeling *will* stick.

"That's...great." She chuckles. "So Erico's treating you better than the beginning?"

"Yeah, that's actually what I called about." I pause, my thoughts formulating into statements that'll make sense for us both. "Della, I managed to *talk* to him."

Silence.

Three seconds pass.

Ten seconds.

"Della?"

"That's...wow. Not what I was expecting you to say. So, like...you...like...what?" For once, my articulate sister is so tongue-tied, I laugh.

"I really don't know. Every time I tried to in the past, my throat gets clogged. Like I can't force it out. The memory of—"

Crash!

Metal scraping against metal.

Tires squealing.

"Anyway," I continue, without losing myself down that train of thought, "it was different this time."

"This time," she repeats, still in that questioning tone. "What made *this* time so different?"

If I admit everything, Della's protectiveness will return and she'll freak out that I joined him for the race. Admitting *why* and what got me to speak would mean telling the rest.

I go with a partial truth: "I don't know how it works, or what was in my head. I called his name, and then...kept going. That was yesterday. Late last night, I guess. This morning, I woke almost convinced I dreamed the entire thing." I pause, thinking over my next words, my excitement for them not tapered down. "I'm able to talk to my husband. I *want* to talk to him."

After all that, she only replies with two words. Words that are already facts to me. "You're happy."

The sun smashes through the final dimness.

"I am."

"You care for him. I've never heard you sound like this." Her tone is edged, concerned almost.

"I do. I think. You sound weird, Della."

"I'm just—I'm happy for you." With a lower voice, she

continues, "When you volunteered and we fought, remember how I kept reminding you of the whole nine-yards thing you always dreamed of? The husband, the kids, the house. But your counter-argument was that due to Mom's choices, our futures changed too drastically for you to live that once-possible life. Despite everything, it's working out."

We're no love match like you and Nico, but yeah, we're getting there.

"He's trying. More now than the beginning. At first, he didn't want a relationship, but it's not like that anymore. In this fucked-up world that we found ourselves in, Della, we made something of it. Mom would have wanted this for us, I think. You found love in an unlikely place, but Nico would burn the world to keep you safe. And I—" I stop. Admitting I care for Erico is one thing, but the rest seems too soon.

I almost expect her to push me, but my sister only makes an appreciative noise right as a knock sounds through the entrance of the house. Carlotta rushes from upstairs and somehow, manages to get her aging body to the front door all before I even stand from the couch.

"Gotta go," I mumble into the phone's speaker. "Meeting." Then I hang up as the door opens and Carlotta is waving the visitor inside.

The *Famiglia* doctor looks nothing like the Corsettis'. While the Corsettis' is an older man with a receding hairline and a grandfatherly smile, Erico's is probably about twenty years younger, fit, with all his hair. Blond with a spattering of dark strands.

He shakes Carlotta's hand with a charming smile and then approaches me, his arm stretching. I take it, open my mouth in greeting—

Crash!

Metal scraping against metal.

Tires squealing.

Hm. Maybe Dr. Shappo was right. Maybe it's a trust thing. A comfort thing. And Erico's made his way inside my very tight circle.

When my mouth clamps shut, he simply smiles and gestures toward the couches behind us. "Please, don't strain yourself trying to talk. Dr. Shappo from Montreal forwarded your file to me and I've read it over, even into your time at the medical centre. SLP, psychiatrist, psychologist, GP; they really threw everyone at you, huh?"

I nod once in agreement, uncertain how to respond. The doctor drops in the chair across from me and roots through his leather bag before retrieving a notebook. He rips a sheet of paper from it and hands me a pen.

"To reply, if you'd like. My name is Dr. Rancott. I've been with the *Famiglia* for quite a long time, and have been looking forward to meeting the newest Mrs. Rossi."

Right away, I scribble my name onto the paper and jab my nail into it, shooting him a meaningful look that means *refer to me as this.*

He smiles, the skin around his eyes wrinkling slightly. "Of course, Ariella. Well, Mr. Rossi mentioned you're not interested in further counselling, which, after reading, I suppose I under-stand. Tired of it all?"

I nod.

"I did have a phone call the other day with Dr. Shappo though, and he mentioned his theories about why your sister is the only one you feel comfortable enough to speak with. Did he ever mention this to you?" When I nod, he asks, "And how do you feel about it?"

I shrug, not really wanting to delve into theories, but do agree, now more than ever, with the previous doctor.

"Fair enough. Well, I've come to check up on you after

yesterday, and to introduce myself, in case down the road, you do wish for extra services. Then I won't be a stranger to you. Mr. Rossi didn't share many details, other than you were nearly hit by a vehicle."

He didn't tell the stranger that I spoke to him. I don't know why, but it makes me feel better. If the doctor knew, he'd be interested in why Erico's added to the list alongside my sister.

I scribble on the paper.

I'm fine. Erico avoided the hit

Once he reads it, the distracted look in his eyes indicates something else. He won't say it though. He won't point out the similarities between yesterday and the accident that began all this. There's more similarities than Dr. Rancott's even aware of.

He flips through his notebook, murmuring, "There's a few things I'd like to check out, and to draw some blood."

Why? I mouth. Needles and me, we're not enemies, but if I can avoid giving blood, that would be great.

"Because it seems like it's been a few years since your last blood test, according to your file, and it's standard procedure for the *Famiglia*. Especially the mother of our future Boss."

Right. Sometimes, being wrapped up in Erico and swimming and my music, I forget the real reason I'm here. To be a wife—to host parties and create Erico's heir.

Seeing no other way, I lay the paper off to the side and shuffle toward the edge of the couch, indicating for him to begin. He reaches in his bag for gloves and comes closer with a vial.

A few minutes later, he's pulling a needle from my arm, my hiss loud in the otherwise silent room. He's probed my muscles and nerves and asked me a million questions about my cycle, which I've managed to answer most of them.

Irregular periods—even on the birth control pill, my cycle was only less sporadic than when not on it.

Hot flashes—since puberty. I've come to assume they were a part of my period, when I do have one.

He's collected two vials of blood and caps them both off, wrapping them in a cloth which he places in his bag.

"Two because I'll be running quite a few tests. Otherwise, everything else looks good." He undoes the torniquet around my upper arm and dabs the small dot of red the needle left behind. "Band-Aid?"

I shake my head.

He drops a business card on the couch beside me. "Mr. Rossi has my number, but if you need or want to get a hold of me directly, call or text any time of the day." He gathers his things and tips his head. "If that is all, goodbye and have a nice day. It was lovely to meet the *Famiglia*'s newest member."

The moment he walks away, Carlotta appears from down the hallway, as though she was waiting nearby. She lets Dr. Rancott out and then offers, "Lunch? Build your sugars back up?"

Erico hasn't been in contact all day, reminding me a lot of how marriage was at first. Sitting in the music room seems lonelier now than before. Without Erico's visit, I'm playing for only myself and it's more boring than it should be.

The last page in my notebook has a particular song I've poured endless hours into, writing it for Della and Nico's wedding. It was supposed to be my gift to them because it was something Della and I grew up dreaming about, even when she adamantly refused to ever be married at all.

I didn't sing it though. Didn't even play it. The days leading up to the wedding, the dark clouds got grimmer and the realization of how stupid I am crashed down. Playing a song for my sister in front of all those people after the wedding planner spent days sourcing the best DJ. All those people watching. Judging. Singing was out, especially when I couldn't even sing for myself.

Even before my interest in piano, I sang often. Everything and anything. Any little tune in a store, if I didn't know the words, and sometimes, I'd invent the lyrics. After the accident, everything musical went away.

All the music notes in my life faded. Life isn't a musical, so there was little point.

Considering singing, even when no one was around, was impossible. The single time I attempted, late at night, alone in my room, I couldn't. My self-hating, dark hole was so deep, it felt impossible to drag myself out of.

'Maybe you're unable to sing to yourself because you lost faith in yourself. You feel like, after your mother's death, there's nothing else, but you're wrong, Ariella. There's you.'

Those words became her parting ones because Yasmine stood up, gave me a one-armed hug, and left my room of the medical centre.

Ironically, that became her final visit. Unknown to either of us at the time, because weeks later, everything with her father went down.

If I could learn to sing for myself again, perhaps I could sing for Erico.

I think he'd appreciate it. Maybe even *like* it.

It's something I could work toward. To sing for not only him, not only me, but *us*.

My phone vibrates, moving it an inch over the piano top, and I grab it quickly, heart hammering with hope it's Erico's deep, possessive rumble I'll hear on the other end. Instead, the screen flashes with Dr. Rancott's name. After he visited this morning, I imputed his number so I'd never lose it.

"Mrs. Rossi—Ariella, it's Dr. Rancott," he greets the second I answer. "I'm sorry to be calling you so soon, but I had a rush order put on a few tests this morning, on your blood-work, and I received some distressing results."

Ice freezes my nerves. Dread becomes everything I focus on, clinging to the kind doctor's concerned tone.

Then he talks again, but my nerves are already ice. Which means, the only thing left is for them to shatter into thousands of pieces. Of sharp shards meant to stab, to protect myself from harm. But even wanting to do so is impossible when, in his next few statements, I lose everything.

Not only myself.

"Ariella...one of the tests was to check your follicle-stimu-lating hormone levels. They're high. Higher than I've ever seen."

He's speaking literal science and I'm not following along, but I *know*. Without the definition, he's already admitting something's wrong with me. With my *hormones*. Hormones indicate a few things in a woman's body, but the most prevalent—

I crumble. In the centre of the music room, with nothing to hold me up, my shaking knees drop me to the ground, right on top of the siren carpet.

"FSH is associated with women's eggs production," he continues hammering the life-changing news into my head. Like an ice pick—jab, jab, jab—in you go; sharp and meant to break apart ice until there's nothing remaining. "The higher the trace of the hormone indicates a woman's fertility chances. Matching your levels alongside some of the answers you provided about your cycle..."

I can't listen.

My mask isn't up. The emotions not hidden. Not here, while I'm alone. When the darkness can consume me in ways greater than it's ever been before. Not only consume, but *destroy*.

And for once, I want it to. Desperately plead with the darkness to devour me whole, so I don't have to live any longer.

This isn't...this can't be happening. Not now.

Everything good always ends. Right on time. Right when everything is *right* in my life.

"Mrs. Rossi, this *isn't* over. I will have more tests ran until we get more concrete responses, but right now, based on your levels...Ariella, there's a very low likelihood of conception. Your body doesn't have enough of the hormone to produce eggs and—"

I hang up.

The phone slips through my hand and crashes to the floor.

The floor in which I drop into a ball, my forehead to the carpet.

The doctor says it's not over, but it is. This reminds me of when I woke the morning after the accident, tried to speak, only to be bombarded with flashbacks and memories. That was when my stupid, useless brain stopped sending speech signals to my mouth.

Except this time, it's not my speech. It's not even my brain. It's my *body* betraying me in the worst fucking way possible.

A part of me is broken.

Another part of me is broken.

You're a joke. Good things don't happen to people like you. You'll never be good enough for Erico.

There's the voices again, but this time, they're so correct, it makes me sick.

I'm not enough.

I'll never *be* enough.

I'm broken.

Useless.

My arms wrap around my middle—my useless stomach. A stomach that'll never stretch with a growing baby. The only other fucking thing I wanted in this world. A man to love me and a child I create.

Why is life so damn cruel? Was the accident, losing my mother, *and* my voice not enough?

I scream into the floor.

Pain. Agony.

Blackness. The darkness can consume me. At least, it's better than reality. Reality brings heartbreak.

I cry until the pain fades.

In other words...

...I don't stop crying.

35
ERICO

"We have him. Bringing him to the warehouse now," Caladin reports through my cell's speaker. "Two for two. Anyone else I'm hunting in your wife's name? Tell me now before I get comfortable on my couch."

"Smartass. I'm finishing up shit and then I'll be over."

The moment I hang up, my phone rings again, my family's doctor's name flashing on the screen. He messaged earlier to inform me he met with Ariella, who'd been brought back to the mansion hours ago, but for him to be calling snakes a chill down my spine that will only thaw when he says what he needs to.

"What?" I bark with a bit more edge than I mean to. But my tone can't help the discerning feeling of this moment.

"Sir." His low voice is unlike him. Dr. Rancott is a very direct man, and is probably one of the few fuckers who shows no visible fear toward me. The shakiness in his tone, in that single greeting, the news can't be positive.

And there's only one person he'd be phoning about after today.

"Sir, I put in for a few rush tests on Mrs. Rossi's bloodwork, and some of the tests came back. A lot look fine, except one thing. You should know—and I've already phoned her—but there's extremely high levels of follicle-stimulating hormone appearing in her blood—"

"Get to it," I grit, the pen in my other hand seconds away from being snapped in half. Not even from impatience, but with the fact that the moment he mentioned the term *hormones*, my heart stilled. "Skip the science talk."

"Sir," I almost hear the gulp in his voice, "her body can't produce eggs. She won't conceive. She won't be able to give you an heir."

"She knows?"

"Yes."

I hang up, throwing my phone to the desk as the conversation replays in my head.

"She won't conceive."

"She won't conceive."

"She won't conceive."

Fuck.

"She won't be able to give you an heir."

She knows. Which means he phoned her. Which means she's home dealing with these emotions alone. I wish I could know which emotions those were too. I couldn't even pretend to understand her feelings.

Fuck, I don't even know what *I'm* feeling.

Rage.

Blistering rage, burning every nerve in my body, every shred of sanity I've clung to my entire life. Killing, fighting, racing, dealing—all the adrenaline-induced activities I've thrived in, but none of them are even close to the sensation igniting me at this moment.

But it has nothing to do with the possibility of being without an heir.

It's because *she's* the one affected by this.

I'm up and out of my chair, phone in hand, shoving out of the bar's back room I was using as an office for a day in between my visitations, within a second.

And then I'm home, with no recollection of the hours-long drive. I abandon my car in front of the mansion, engine running, and bolt inside, nearly bowling over Carlotta who lingers nearby.

She gestures toward her music room, so it's the direction I rush in, her holler propelling me forward. "She's been in there for hours, sobbing. She won't let me in."

When I'm within distance to her music room, her cry guts me. If there was any shred of my being still held together, she destroys it.

I shove open the door, spotting her in the centre of the carpet, curled up with her head forward. Her hair's a waterfall around her body and for the first time ever, I despise those red strands because they're protecting her from me.

I'm across the room within a second, dropping to my knees and tugging her into my arms. She shoulders against me at first, but then realizes who's grabbing her and she practically crawls into my lap. Limp, her eyes red and dry from her tears. She's quivering, and I tighten my arms, trying to quell the shakes.

"Ariella."

No response. Not even sure she's heard me.

I reposition her until she's cradled in my arms and stand, keeping her against my chest, head in my shoulder, and carry her from the room and through the house, not releasing her until we're both seated in the centre of our bed.

"Ariella, I'm so fucking sorry, but I refuse to accept this. I'll hire a dozen more doctors to continue testing, if I must. This isn't over."

Still no response, but I'm not expecting one. Her gaze has remained open and empty, desolate as she zones out staring at the bed.

After a long moment, her ragged breath blows over my arm, easing me. At least, she's trying. "It is," she whispers in a tone more broken than anyone I've ever heard use. "Because this all makes sense."

"How does this make sense?" I stroke her face, clearing the strands of hair away.

"Because everything good in my life ends, so it was only time we did too."

We're not over. The thought flitted in my head sometime between Dr. Rancott's call and when I took Ariella into my arms. Unions within the mafia are to ensure the bloodline continues, and as a Rossi, it's of the utmost importance. My entire purpose for agreeing to a marriage at all—Ariella, Aurora, Vanessa, or anyone else—is for an heir.

But Ariella became much more than that.

I won't let her go. A million tests can have the same outcome, and I refuse to release her. Ariella's mine for better or fucking worse. Everything else can be figured out later.

"I'm not letting you go," I tell her. "I don't care what one doctor claims."

"Yeah," she replies, her tone filled with doubt. "And when multiple tell you the same thing?"

"Still won't matter." I grip her the back of her neck, forcing her to look in my direction. "Ariella, there are other ways."

"Your family—"

"Fuck my family." For the first time ever, I mean it too. Mother and Father will lose their fucking minds, but I don't care. The *Famiglia* will see this as a betrayal...but I don't care. The organization I've spent my entire life breathing for is secondary to the tiny woman in my arms.

Ariella pushes against my arm, trying to sit up, so I help her since it's the most sign of life I've seen from her since arriving home. Her expression is still desolate, staring at the bed rather than me.

"You know what the funniest part in *all* this is?"

There's nothing funny about it, but I wait for her explanation.

"Growing up, my plan was always to have the fairy-tale ending. Not sure why or where that dream even came from, but all I knew, is getting a good job, meeting someone to fall in love with, eventually marry, buy a house, and begin a family was it for me. Then Mom met Stefano, and within years, all my possibilities were ripped away. Interesting how someone else's relationship can deem that, but it was their marriage that led to her eventual death. The accident that took *me* from me.

"And then my life ended. I was shoved into a medical centre, only ever visited by two people. The random day Nico dropped in, I sensed changes unfolding. He offered me an out, to be free with Della again, so obviously I took it. But then they got together, and at that point," she shrugs to herself, "I already lost the future I dreamed of, so I remained with the Corsettis. Mom's marriage brought us into mob life, and Della's relationship kept us there. Besides," she snorts lightly, "what was the point in leaving? I didn't believe I could have the life I once dreamed of, and who'd want me anyway? Mute, unable to function normally. Pretty pathetic."

My hands curl by my sides, ready to counter every single one of those points. If only she'd look in a damn mirror because I craved her the moment I met her at Corsetti's engagement party.

Her eyes lift slowly to mine. "You want to know why I *truly* volunteered to marry you? Other than the fact that I'm downright pitiful and pushed myself onto you. I was seeking some sort of semblance of my dreams. I never deluded myself into believing you'd love me. Marriage to you isn't what it'd be for me, but it's okay." She scoffs. "Makes me a masochist, I guess. Marrying you would also give me the children I wanted. If the past version of me ever looked into the future, she'd see this. At least from the outside, I could pretend to have achieved my dreams."

Gutted. It's a sickening feeling—*fact*—to be helpless. I can't *do* anything to help her through this. There's no one I can hurt who'll fix this. Just endless doctors to provide hope.

"Ariella—"

"But now, it's fucking over, Erico. It's *over*." Her gaze finds me again but there's no more sadness. Not for the moment. She's moved through that stage of grief. No, there's a brokenness instead. Acceptance mingled with misery mixed with anger. "You need an heir, and I can't provide one." I'm about to counter, but she continues, her voice firmer than before, "You know what the *worst fucking part* of *all* this is? I fucking fell in love with you. I *love you* and when I'm able to finally say it, it means nothing."

She loves me.

I've never wanted a woman's love. Never *felt* a woman's love. Even my own mother's love was distanced. A mother's love, sure, but once I reached ten-years-old, I spent more time with my father than her, allowing her to return to her pre-child life of shopping, alcohol, and parties without concerns. Despite wanting a sibling, I never got one because I'm certain they only had sex to create me, and once my mother was pregnant with a boy, they accomplished the goal of their marriage.

That's precisely what I expected mine to be like. I never expected to gain my wife's love.

But *Ariella's* love, I crave like fucking air. I've been grasping at it for days now, unaware that's what I was even reaching for. Perhaps I have since the beginning, since the moment she volunteered for this union, and I was able to see the silent woman from the party wasn't *her*. It wasn't her entire personality, despite the façade she dressed herself up in. There's more to her and I found myself wanting to uncover it. Longed to taste it for my own.

Longed for *her*.

A stray tear drips down her cheek.

I've fucked up again. After everything she disclosed, my response is lodged in my throat behind guilt. The guilt that it was my own doctor who brought this all to light, guilt I'll also never be what she wanted. She craved normal. To fall in love.

Guilt because this changes nothing.

When she shifts, and her hair blocks her face, I bring her closer, first pushing her hair away. I don't kiss her, not yet, just cup her face and stare into her eyes, searching through the layers of pain to the woman I've discovered to be my everything.

"Ariella, you won't be changing my mind. We'll get every single fertility test we can ran, and even if they all return with undesirable results, we *will* do whatever we need to. You will get your child, and if not from science, we'll fucking adopt."

"Your family—"

"Doesn't matter. *Sirena*, I'll entice an internal war with the *Famiglia* to keep you. You're not going anywhere. What we've learned today doesn't change how I feel about you."

Amidst the misery, a small flame ignites in her eyes. A spark. It's present and now it must continue to be fanned, to ensure it blazes and doesn't dim.

"How do you feel?" she whispers, resting her hand over my heart.

I lay mine overtop, ensuring she feels my next words. "I don't know what love is, Ariella. My parents sucked at conveying it. But if love exists, it's what I feel for you." My hand presses into hers harder, trying to imprint her touch onto my skin so I never have to be without it. "I'm obsessed with you and have been since the beginning. I fell in love with you before you spoke to me, but giving me your voice, *sirena*, that was a gift I'll never be able to repay."

The spark grows brighter.

But when I'm about to kiss her, it dissolves. Like a lighter being snapped shut.

She falls against my chest, her hands covering her face, hiding from me.

And cries. Sobs.

Apologies, *I love you*s, begging for hope, negative statements about herself, mentions of guilt—everything and anything.

She's rolling through every grief stage within minutes of one another. Back and forth. Years of hopes and dreams being confused with reality. I reply to nothing she mumbles, whether the truth or a lie. She has to feel every emotion bombarding her, so I hold her through them all, rubbing her back, petting her hair, gripping onto her so she knows.

That no matter what happened today, I fucking love her.

And I'll burn the world down to keep her.

My family included.

36

ARIELLA

Darkness.

Misery.

Amongst the pain, there is a light continuing to break through. A support like none I've had in the past. A person that held me for all the hours passing. One? All night? Time goes differently when you're crying.

At some point, I'm sure I passed out because I recall him undressing me, and then there was a pillow beneath my head.

Through the ongoing tears, the wave after wave of breathtaking despair, I heard him. *Heard* all his reassurances. Swallowed them like a fucking pill, like medicine to heal my wounded soul. I love him more for them, but it doesn't change the fact of what we learned.

I might be unable to conceive.

Science, adoption, all the options he's listed are fine, but they're not the same as growing the child myself. Not the same as learning all my dreams are being ripped from me one at a time.

Processing, I am not.

Eventually, Erico presses his lips to my forehead, but the time is unknown. I can't check because my eyes refuse to open, sealed shut with dried tears and exhaustion. He lingers, inhaling, and I don't know why, but it brings a smile to my face.

His fingers remain on my hand until he's gone entirely. He must shut the curtains because the light behind my lids dim even further. After he goes, sleep tries to drag me under. Exhaustion has me craving the bliss of nothingness, but it never comes. Only hovers while my racing thoughts are ongoing.

Maybe I eventually doze, or I don't, but my phone's ringer cuts through the silence.

My sister's name flashes on the screen, providing me every reason to *not* answer it. But if I'm correct in my assumption, then she won't stop until I shut the phone off. My fingers slide over the two buttons that'll bring up the power option...but instead, I swipe, answering the call.

Maybe for once, I don't want to wear my mask. Don't have the strength to lift it to my face and bury the truth any longer. Erico's seen and is acceptive of me so far, so why wouldn't my sister?

"Why did your husband call mine, who texted me, to call you?" is her flurry of questions.

The device is heavy, my weakened muscles unable to hold it to my face. I stick it on speakerphone and drop the phone to the bed.

"Also, I'm in the car with Aurora, and you're on speaker, but I could call later, if you'd like. Nico messaged minutes ago, and he sounded sketchy, so I didn't want to wait."

Another smidge of light. Aurora's presence doesn't matter. My sister's energy, while overwhelming, is secondary to the feelings. The words that slip out during my next breath, whispered so minutely, but impactful on my soul, so uncaring that someone other than my sister can overhear.

Like saying them aloud, to someone outside my marriage, makes them more *real*.

"I can't have kids."

Silence.

I sense them glancing at one another, can practically see Della leaning forward.

"What are you talking about, Ariella?"

"They ran a test. My body can't produce eggs. I won't conceive."

Are the words truly being said aloud, or only in my head? Admitting the impossible, but then again, my mood also tumbles backwards, to the time before Erico found me on the floor. Numbness creeps up, wrapping around my throat. If I speak so matter-of-factly, maybe my own brain will soon accept them.

Della makes a soft noise. "Ariella...no. No. That's always what you dreamed of."

I know.

"Is Erico aware?" Then she scoffs, answering her own question, "I'm dumb. Of course he does, considering he's the one who spoke with Nico. What did he say?"

Silence. This time for me. Everyone on this phone call knows the reality of this situation. It's almost fitting in a cruel way that Aurora's listening in. Ironic since it should have been her conceiving the *Famiglia* heir.

"He claims it doesn't matter. That he cares for me. That he'll get more doctors and more tests ran until we get a more desirable response. He says no matter the outcome, we'll have a child one way or the other."

"That's a better response than I thought he'd give, to be honest. This is positive...even if it's not exactly what you're looking for. If he's willing to work with you, then maybe I didn't give him enough credit."

"I love him," I admit without another thought. "I don't know how or why, but he broke down my barriers, and I do. I *can't* lose him, Della. I've lost so much I care for. He can't be yet another person."

"He won't be. I'll have his balls if he does." There's shuffling in the background and then, "Hang on. I'm hunting down Nico. We'll be there in a few hours."

Here. No. On another man's territory. Then my sister will see me in all my miserable glory.

"Don't, it's fine, Della. Besides, the moment of my vows, we ended up on separate sides."

"I know," she replies regretfully. "But I feel so lost right now. What can I do to help?"

Get me a better functioning system.

Another voice comes through the speakers. Softer, packed with empathy. "Ariella, it's Aurora." *Knew that.* "Look, you mentioned it being your egg production, which means for now, you can still *carry* a child." She pauses. "I'm sorry, I suck at this. I'm just trying to say, there is a positive here. Be with Erico. Let him support you. If you need to talk, call us. You know we love you."

What she's suggesting makes sense, but hope is difficult when one's mood already deems things are hope*less*.

"Ariella?" my sister calls when I haven't responded in a while.

I hang up and bury my head in my pillow.

Let the darkness consume me.

The bits of light seeping through—I need to grasp them. I know I do.

But for now, I hug my stomach and cry in the silence of the room. I sob until sleep swallows me whole.

37
ERICO

All night, I held her with only one goal: being there for her. Holding her through the agony, but every minute of that night that passed, every sob, every hiccup, festered my own rage until remaining still became nearly impossible. I still did, *for her*, but the longer I tapered the killing streak, the more I comprehended my true feelings toward her.

And the more pain I wanted to inflict.

Alongside the sickening realization that there is nothing and no one in this world I can cut deep enough, punch hard enough, that'll change Ariella's medical results. But it would give me a place to release the pent-up emotions that embedded into my heart throughout the night.

By the time morning arrives, she finally passes out, so I detangle myself from her with a quick kiss to the forehead, my hand lingering on her skin, revelling how smooth her skin is. I hate how early I have to leave her, having to drive into the city, but ideally, she'll sleep all day.

After calling Nico and demanding he get Della to phone her sister, Caladin meets me at the warehouse without questioning why the sudden urgency to be here. He dismisses the soldier he posted on guard duty with a nod of his head. While they share a few words, I pass right by them both and stalk inside the dim warehouse, the scent of dried blood and fresh piss greeting me.

Caladin jogs to catch up. "Whoa, good morning. Hello. Anything? Do I not deserve a greeting after retrieving the fucker?"

No one's screams will alter Ariella's outcome, but the fucker Caladin's speaking about deserves death for taking something from her. So for now, he'll do.

The man in question is in chains, bolted to the floor. He's glaring at me from behind the dirty, red bandana shoved into his mouth. He remains still, not fighting the chains, unlike so many of the other unfortunate souls who find themselves in here.

File on him states he's a mercenary, wanted in numerous countries for various crimes. He knows what's happening, what to expect, which is why there's still not even a single flash of dread when I rip the bandana from his mouth.

"What'd I do to you? Who'd I kill?"

His cockiness will make his death even more thrilling.

"Two years ago, you were driving a white panel van. Your orders were to slam another car into oncoming traffic."

His gaze lowers, eyes moving back and forth like he's searching through memories. Then a slow grin spreads over his mouth. "Oh, yeah. That was a decent payday."

"Yeah." I tilt my head, feigning consideration. "I hope that payday was worth making an enemy of the *Famiglia*."

His eyes dart over my form, to Caladin hovering behind me, and then the warehouse, and finally, his distress reveals itself. "Wait. *Famiglia*. What the fuck am I doing in the U.S.?"

"The accident you caused killed a woman. Changed the

lives of two other women when they lost their mother. One of those women is my wife."

With every word, realization hits him, and he finally starts fighting. For his life, a greater understanding of why he's here. The chains rattle and he backs up as far as he's able to. I don't approach though, simply remain rigid where I am.

"Wait, you know how it is, man. It was two years ago! I was *paid*. Take out the fucker who hired me for the job. I'll tell you his name, if you let me go."

I smile, but not one that indicates pleasure with any of his words, and even release a light chuckle, informing him precisely how unamused I am by his begging because there's nothing this asshole can offer me, I'm not already aware of. "Gage Roche hired you under the command of Stefano De Falco." His mouth drops open. "The Corsettis killed both of them. But you...you're *mine*."

"It was two years ago!" He returns to his earlier argument, his pointless fighting continues as he wrenches his entire body into the chains. "Look, she's still alive, isn't she?"

"You must enjoy pain," Caladin mutters from behind me.

If he does, then he's about to have a damn buffet. I walk by him, heading toward the farthest wall where a metal table is. Numerous torture options, tools and knives, wait to be chosen.

But as I stand there, inspecting every single death-delivering, pain-inflicting weapon, I see Ariella in my head again. Not her smiling, or swimming in her sexy bikinis, or even playing her piano. No, instead it's the tears that consumed her all night. Her sobs, which shattered my own control, awakening a part of me that requires a blood debt. The slightest bit of feeling to be worthy of helping her through her own pain.

I *need* this man to feel an ounce of what she does. Losing her mother, her voice, her life all in one hit. The pain she's surviving through now though...that's something else. It's her strength that reassures me she'll make it through.

So I turn away from the table and instead, shed my coat. The fucker doesn't deserve knives or bats, or any tool. It'll be my fists that take him out. The absolute pleasure of using him like a punching bag, to release the monster within.

"Unchain him."

The man's expression brightens, but it's pointless. This isn't an escape. It's an execution.

Caladin steps forward, looking at me like I've lost my mind. And maybe I have. "Erico—"

"Unchain him," I repeat. "Trust me, he won't escape."

My captive's happy expression falters in a blink, and he scans the warehouse again, licking at dried, chapped lips. He's seeking an escape and locks onto the door far behind me, but he won't even make it three steps toward his fatal attempt.

Caladin obeys me, digging out a key from his pocket, while still shooting me confused glances. The moment the man is completely freed, he takes off toward the door.

Big mistake.

I lunge.

~

A slow clap fills the now-silent warehouse, the skin-on-skin sound echoing through the building. It seems somehow louder and quieter than the screams, the squealing of blood, the breaking of bones that's otherwise been the music.

Straightening, I watch my cousin approach, appreciation and surprise filling his expression, while my breath catches up from the workout.

"Erico, what the fuck was that about?"

With his foot, he nudges the body on the ground, which is growing as cold as the cement floor. There's nothing distinguishable about him anymore. A face smashed in, body parts cut and strewn around us. The scent of blood and death fill my nose, but I breathe it all in.

And feel fucking fantastic.

Thinking he could escape and proving to him how he couldn't was exactly what I needed to feel *something*. He managed to fight back pretty decently and got a hit to my ribs, and one to my cheek, which is now sore. But his hits only alleviated my urge to make him pay. For her, for Della, for their mother, the fucker's dead. Everyone involved in their pain is gone.

"Um," my cousin's loud voice breaks my thoughts, "I ask again: what the fuck was that? I've never seen you so psychotic. I mean, when you asked for him to be released, I assumed you lost your fuckin' mind, which after witnessing this bloodshed, I think is exactly the case." He pauses, studying my blood-soaked shirt, which is cold and sticky against my chest. "Erico, you completely lost your shit in a way I've never seen. What's going on?"

"He killed their mother." First instinct says to hide the truth for as long as possible, to not let this get out to the rest of the *Famiglia*.

"Yeah, but that was..." He trails off, glancing at the lump of flesh between us. "It was something, Erico. Quite the show. Clearly, something's on your mind."

Caladin's not only family, but he's my most trusted, and really, I don't *want* to hide this from him.

"What I'm about to tell you needs to stay between you and me."

His sharp gaze narrows, and he straightens, as though aware what he'll be hearing isn't light.

"Doc checked her blood. She's unlikely to conceive."

His mouth falls open. "Um. Wow. Okay. Not what I was expecting."

With the single fact out, the rest of my emotions pour out. Right here, in a blood-stained warehouse, with a mangled corpse between us, I admit everything to my cousin, my chest growing lighter with every single syllable.

"I'll get every fucking test available ran. Hire every doctor. Get second, third, fiftieth opinions before giving it up." My breath becomes harsher, the next truth painful in ways knives and violence can't match. "Caladin, she fucking *wants* kids. You know what she told me last night, in between tears and speaking in a tone so fucking calm, it was nearly deadly? Since childhood, all she's wanted was the happy life. Grow up, meet a guy, get married, pop out some kids."

"And she got you," he jokes lightly, trying his usual thing of easing tension. Except it's not a laughing matter because he's correct.

"Yeah. She volunteered herself, searching for the happy ending she craves, knowing that with this life, children would be a guarantee."

He sighs, his dark eyes filled with regret. "Fuck. I'm sorry, man."

Finally, I lift my head, meeting his gaze so he realizes the meaning behind my words. "You know as well as I do, I didn't expect to enjoy my wife. Caring for her wasn't supposed to happen, but it's what has. You didn't see her face. This shattered her, and it fucking *kills* me, that no matter how many alternatives I offer, it won't change the news she received.

"But there's still hope, right?"

I called Dr. Rancott on the drive in, begging for every test he can muster, demanding he hire every specialist in the world.

And asked for the gritty truth: the likelihood of his results being incorrect.

"Very little," was his response. I hung up after that. It was the best I could do before turning the car around and hunting him instead.

"Yeah," I tell my cousin, a partial lie. "Yeah, there's some hope."

"You know, if she really can't—"

My hand slices the air, silencing him. "Nothing, Caladin. What I told you today stays between us. No one else can now." Even if he's correct, there will be a time, others will have to be made aware. "I won't lose her. I won't let her go," I admit, my tone losing some of the edge.

He nods slowly, rolling his lips together. "If any of them," —He doesn't define *them*, nor does he need to— "learned this, they'd view it as a betrayal. That you're choosing your wife over the *Famiglia*. And the fact of the matter is, you could very well be. Honestly, I never would have thought there'd come a day you did put someone above the organization." He pauses, approaching by a single step. "But you got it, I'll keep my mouth shut. All I know is, it sucks this is happening, but there's no one more able to shoulder the pain than her." He slaps me on my arm as he passes, heading for the door. "I wish you luck with my entire fuckin' heart, man, and if you need to talk, you know where to find me." I trail him to the door, working up some way to thank him when he speaks again, this time, lighter and more like the Caladin I'm familiar with. "But the next time you need to release some anger, come find me and we'll spar."

I whistle. "Death wish. You'd spar after watching what I did?" I tip my head toward the warehouse, indicating the death there.

He laughs and shakes his head, all but shoving me toward

my car. "Go home, clean up, and be there for her. I'll get him taken care of."

My feet press firmly into the dirt for a second. "Any word on who paid Anders?"

Caladin frowns. "No, and it's weird. No note in the apartment. Couldn't even find the cash. His phone was gone too. No trace."

"Keep searching."

~

She's in the same spot I left her, lying on her side, facing the window. The blanket's pulled up to her hip, but then I hear her voice, and stop in the doorway.

"—maybe because I'm not actually face-to-face with you, I can. If this even counts since you're not going to listen to these messages, are you? Why am I'm bothering anymore? If anyone will find you, it'll be your sister. I miss you, though. Something's happened...something heartbreaking, and while everyone here is giving me hope, it's not the same, you know?"

My hand slides form the doorknob, heart hammering faster, if only to keep it working and not to shatter with her despondent tone.

"They're showing me the light but it's so difficult to drag myself from the darkness. To *want* to. It's only been a day since I received the news, but damn, this hurts. It feels like everything good in my life will be ripped from me soon and I have no control to stop it. Again. Erico made a lot of my negative thoughts go away, but they're returning stronger."

Negative thoughts?

"Getting out of bed seems impossible. Even thinking of my music or swimming isn't doing it. The news might have put me into this mode, but I think my brain's what's keeping me here."

Her brain?

"Anyway," she sighs, "this is my verbal diary, I guess, and before your phone kicks me off, bye."

She sighs again and I count to ten before entering, so she doesn't realize I was lingering outside the door. When I finally enter, she hears me immediately and peeks over her shoulder. For a beat, her misery burns away into surprise as she sits up.

"W-what happened to you?"

I debated showering in a guest room, but the moment I arrived at the mansion, seeing her was my every focus, so the plan to hide my blood-caked clothing didn't remain.

"Not my blood," I reply and head for the bathroom. The shirt isn't salvageable, so I toss it right in the trash, alongside my pants, and then enter the shower.

Beneath the hot spay, I wash all the blood from my skin. It tinges the water as it's sucked down the drain. Standing there, I reflect on every interaction with Ariella, right from the beginning when I left her here alone and Sebastian reported her not getting out of bed for those days after.

Her mood's ability to flick on and off.

The subtle self-hating comments.

Oh.

Sometimes it's easy to forget who my husband actually is when he only allows me to see the non-criminal side of him. But watching him stride through the bedroom, stripping his blood-soaked clothing on his way to our bathroom made my insides clench with desire, my stomach flutter.

Am I really this fucked up already? Or is this some trauma response to the misery? My body's way of searching for something positive.

Erico's presence has made me sit up, which is further than I've gotten in hours on my own. After my call with Della, I dragged myself to use the bathroom, but that was the last time I moved. My stomach feels hollow, but I'm not hungry. My eyes sore, but I don't want to sleep.

I don't know what I want.

A few minutes later, Erico returns to find me chewing on my lip, a towel around his waist. Instead of his usual heated grins, his brow's dipped low, his eyes shadowed with concern. I vow when he returns from dressing, I'll fix my expression to seem more okay.

Based on the look he gives me when he comes back, dressed in a pair of low hanging shorts, I don't succeed.

Without pause, he strides to the edge of the bed and scoops me in his arms. Tossing my phone on my lap, he walks me from the bedroom.

I don't know what he's doing, but I'll never tire of his hold. Especially now, since it might have an expiration date. He claims otherwise, but when push comes to shove, he'll choose the organization over me, and I can't even despise him for that.

Silly, pathetic fool in love I am.

"What are we doing?"

"You're eating. Because the fact I have no idea the last time you did scares me."

He descends the staircase, and with every step away from the bedroom, more of that lightness continues to peek through. I ruin it by asking the very question I've been wondering since he left this morning.

Resting my hand on his heart, I ask, "I'm sorry. Are you mad?"

He takes so long to reply that old worries creep up. *Of course, he is. You're no good to him anymore. Useless. Always second best. You shouldn't be his wife.*

Finally at the bottom of the stairs, he replies, "Yeah. Extremely mad."

See? You're no good for—

"But not at you." His hold tightens, his gaze capturing mine. "Never you, Ariella, and don't you fucking think it. I'm mad *for* you. Pissed you'll have to experience this doubt, these feelings. Of everyone in the world, this isn't fair."

In the kitchen, he deposits me on the counter and turns for the fridge. He begins pulling out a bunch of food—eggs, meats, cheeses, vegetables—and I realize *he's* going to cook. My mafia boss husband is working in the kitchen, of all places, and it seems laughable.

Only an hour after he killed someone. Presuming that's what the blood came from.

"Omelet?" he offers, already retrieving a pan, which begs the question how much choice I have in this.

Unable to talk through the cotton in my throat, my hands come up in a *Yes* sign.

He gives me his back as he begins preparing the vegetables and cheese to be mixed in with the eggs. He works in silence, while I mentally practice phrasing a question about his bloodied clothing.

But he talks before I manage to. "Once, any betrayal toward the *Famiglia* could be the only thing to trigger my rage. Traitors have no place in this world and my role means protecting the *Famiglia*, and doing what's right by them." The knife sounds so much louder when it clangs against the smooth countertop, and he focuses on me. "But the rage I've been living with since I found you on the carpet yesterday is like no level I've felt before. I *hate* you're going through this, and not because I need a son. The future of the *Famiglia* isn't even a consideration over your happiness."

And then, like he hasn't just shattered my heart in every right way, he picks up the knife and finishes slicing the onion. My eyes prick with tears, but it's not from the onion's juices emitting into the air.

"I hate that you have to go through it with me," I mumble. "You have no idea how much I want to be normal. To not have to live through test after test. For once in my life, I just want simplicity."

His grip tightens, his slices quickening, and I realize I should stop talking before he accidentally injures himself with the knife.

"So, you cook, huh?" I state, shifting the conversation as he heats up a pan.

"You are normal, Ariella. Don't believe otherwise."

Back on that then. He begins pouring the egg mixture into the pan, the sizzling sound filling the room, and I'm thankful I don't need to respond.

He remains silent as he finishes cooking. He makes one large omelette, flipping it flawlessly until sliding it onto a plate. He brings over a fork and hands me the plate but doesn't remove me from the counter. The scent of fresh food activates my hunger and my stomach knots in pain, the first bite feeling so much tastier than usual.

He watches me take that first bite, observing almost clinically until nodding. "Good."

I take another two delicious bites, once again thankful to have him. Not only for cooking, but for making me eat. From experience, it's unlikely I would have done it myself.

"When did you realize you had depression?"

He asks it so offhandedly as he wipes the counter, I almost question if I heard him clearly. He drops the cloth and spins, positioning his arms behind him so he grips the edge of the counter, where he leans between them. A position of ease, if it wasn't for his tight hold, the veins in his arms popping.

How does he know? My mask should be up. He shouldn't have noticed. When he came back, I sat up, I spoke, I acted human enough he shouldn't have seen through it.

Oh, who am I kidding? Was the mask on entirely, or did it slip from my face and I allowed it to? For the first time ever, I *let* someone see the truth I've always hid.

"When I was sixteen," I murmur, swallowing my latest bite. It now tastes like dust and is unappetizing, so I rest the plate off to the side, my hands fisting together on my lap. "Mom knew, obviously. To this day, Della doesn't. Hid the diagnosis from her so she couldn't fuss over me because that's who she is. How did *you* figure it out?" And when? How much time has passed in which he allowed me to keep my blissful secret a lie?

"Whoever you left the message for, I overheard in the hallway."

No apology for listening in on a conversation that wasn't his business. No break in eye contact. I shouldn't expect anything less though.

I also shouldn't have left that message for Yasmine. I don't know why I did. It's only ever been texts, but in the silence of my room, my voice worked. The emotions overtaking everything else my brain struggles with and I *needed* to talk. Maybe to inform her, maybe to use the call as a diary. Either way, I reflect on what I said to her; what would have been indicative for him.

But then he answers my curiosity: "You spoke about a light and darkness that you struggled to bring yourself from, and negative thoughts that you were combating. Said getting out of bed seems impossible, which is why I carried you down myself. Swimming and music aren't appealing to you right now. You blamed your brain." He pushes off the counter and steps between my spread legs, his large hands sliding up my thighs until he's holding my hips. "And then I thought about how Nico told me you were a quiet woman who preferred to remain in her room, and how you didn't leave the room here for the first few days."

"Is that weird though? Considering I was shoved into a new place."

"Maybe if you didn't turn away all offers of food and ignore Sebastian." He quirks a smile. "Subtle, but the hints are there."

I cry. Without warning, sobs break down any self-control. My hands cover my face at the same time he pulls me into his chest, my legs hugging his hips. I lower my hands to press my face against his bare shoulder instead, using his warmth to melt the tears.

"Pathetic, huh," I mumble. "You talk about your admiration for my strength but all I do is cry. Cry and hide away in the darkness."

His hand cups the back of my hair, stroking the strands. "Pathetic you are not. Sometimes the greatest strength is allowing another to see your struggles."

"My weaknesses, you mean." I pull back to look him in the face.

"Depression isn't a weakness, *sirena*. Nothing about you is weak. I'm simply the lucky one who gets to see the real you."

Yes, the *real* me. If everything else about me wasn't about to drive him away, then this surely will.

He cups my face and shatters the dark thoughts with a simple kiss. Simple, but powerful, and when he leans away, there's a heat in his eyes I want to burn in.

Want to, but can't. Even thinking about being intimate with him shuts my mind down. The mood is too great, too heavy right now to think about anything further. So I hug him instead, linking my ankles together behind his back and bury my head into his neck, and let him hold me, comfort me.

Heal me.

We stay like that for an unknown length of time before he releases me with a gentle smile and reaches for the plate I abandoned. "You will finish eating," he commands, "and then we're spending the day together."

After all that, he thinks I'll function enough?

"In bed, by the pool, wherever you want." He cups my cheek. "But I'll be there for every tear, Ariella."

"Don't you have to work?"

He only shrugs.

"So you're on suicide watch?" It's a joke, despite the

unamusing nature of the subject, but then I realize he might think I'm serious, so I backtrack, "Wait. No, that's not...I don't —won't."

He smirks as I stumble over my words and taps the tip of my nose with his finger. "I'm on *sirena* watch. We'll just call it that." He backs away from my hold and returns to cleaning the counter as I pick up the fork again and shovel the now-cold egg into my mouth and reflect on what happened.

Erico's gained every reason this week to kick me out, despite his assurances he wouldn't. And still, it hasn't happened.

Because he's good for you. He's right.

When I finish eating, he silently takes the plate and loads the dishwasher at the other end. He works in silence, until I break it, the earlier questions I had returning because he never answered them.

"Who'd you kill?" It's almost laughable to ask such a thing so casually. "Don't hide it from me. You were covered in blood. That was clearly a slaughter."

He shuts the dishwasher before responding, staring at me with a near-troubled expression, his brows low, lips pinched. "Slaughter is the correct term. Let's just say, I released a lot of my anger this morning. He was dying one way or the other, but became my project for self-care."

Self-care is one term I wouldn't think to use in this situation. "But who was it?"

With a sigh indicating he doesn't want to admit it, he replies, "The driver of the white van that caused your accident."

My expression falters, my mind blanks.

Or does it.

Crash!

Metal scraping against metal.

Tires squealing.

That singular moment. Calling for Mom when I saw the

van approaching—I knew there was a man in the driver's seat, obviously, but when I woke in a hospital bed, Della crying by my side, with a larger headache and bruises than I ever believed a body could function through, the driver became the least of my worries.

But somehow, a man who'd come into my life *two years post-accident* dealt with it.

"H-how—"

"The Corsettis were very willing to share the information they had. Gage Roche and Stefano De Falco might not be here any longer, but leads don't die, and Caladin is *very* good at tracking. Within days, Caladin found him, and with Nico's support, he was captured and handed over to us. He's no longer breathing, Ariella. For *you*. For what you lost, for your mother, for your sister. For the ways your life changed because of a single hit. And believe me, I didn't go gentle on him."

Based on the state of his clothing, I'd say not.

Other women would run from the red flags. Me? I hop off the counter and right into his arms. His arm bands around my waist, gripping me as tightly as I hold his neck.

"Thank you."

Thank you for taking away another person in the nightmare.

Thank you for being here with me.

Thank you for being more than I ever wanted.

Thank you for loving me.

Even if he hasn't said the words, he doesn't need to. I feel them. In his actions, in his words, in his kiss.

"Always, *sirena*."

And *that*, I do believe.

39
ERICO

CALADIN
You guys still alive?

ME
Dumbass.

CALADIN
Hey, don't judge the person who's been sitting in on all your meetings. This isn't my job, so you're welcome.

ME
Don't test me. Anyone else would get a punch for the snarky comment. You're lucky you're you.

CALADIN
Pfft. You wouldn't survive without me by your side.

ME
Keep pissing me off and we'll test that theory.

CALADIN

Ha! Big words coming from a man cooped
up in his home for, what, three days now?

How is she?

Surviving.

It has been three days, but it's only felt like one. We talked a lot in that time. Sometimes in bed, most times on the lounge chairs by the pool. I preferred outside because the sun and sight of the property gave her something to look at rather than the darkness beneath the blankets.

She identified what the depression feels like for her—the shadows and darkness, as she referred to it, but indicated grey levels. The stages she feels her mood dropping in before she reaches complete blackness.

Either way, she's agreed to inform me if something triggers her. In truth, I don't know how to help her, but I want to. Want to know so I can try. When I told her that, she said my presence has been helping her.

I don't think I've ever grinned so fucking wide.

CALADIN

Hello?

ME

She's better today. She's managing.

Over the days, I tried to avoid the topic of fertility unless she brought it up, despite it being such a prevalent subject, what triggered her darkness. She never did, so I didn't mention anything. In the silence though, I thought about every route, have been sending emails back and forth with the doctor, who's apologized over and over. As much as I wish I could find it in my black heart to hurt him for delivering the news, it's not his fault. There is no fault to place anywhere. Just shitty facts we must live with.

CALADIN

So you're back at work now?

ME

Reviewing the contract from your meeting the other day.

A contract for a new weapon's dealer. One who's promising an arsenal that'll rival even the Russians. Maybe then, it'll shut my father up.

CALADIN

I'm free then?

ME

Yes. Thank you.

Yesterday, Ariella expressed interest in getting up on her own. So she dressed in a bikini that had my blood heating and I joined her for a swim. It was for only twenty minutes, but it felt nice.

And she accepted my kiss—accepted *all* of my kisses over the days. I kissed her until I couldn't any longer, until I risked ripping the swimsuit from her and bending her over the pool's edge. An activity I vow to do soon, when she's ready. She apologized, but I waved her away. If her mood brings her to a place where eating is a struggle, I certainly don't want her feeling pressured to have sex.

Today, she awoke and told me she'd be using her piano for the morning. Wanted to get back to playing. Said she's only a light grey now. As much as I craved watching her perform, still eagerly awaiting to hear her sing, I took the chance to get work done.

As soon as I set my phone to the side, finished with my

conversation with Caladin, my office doors burst open. The start of a smile graces my face because other than Carlotta, who doesn't come in here, and a couple guards stationed around for protection, Ariella's the only other person in the house. But the person who enters lowers my countenance faster than I ever believed it could drop.

"What the fuck do you want, Father?"

He strides through the office, in a suit looking two inches too short for him on the arms. His face is red, which means he's annoyed. His usual guise whenever he'd bitch at me when I was a kid, when I didn't listen to his instructions well enough.

"Is it true?"

"Is what true?"

"Your useless wife is infertile?"

And now, doc's just earned his death. Clearly, he's forgotten my parents are no longer in charge. I push to my feet, suspecting this is a conversation better had standing.

"Don't call her useless, and she's not infertile. It was one test."

He cocks his head to the side, his smirk mocking me. "You're in denial."

"It changes nothing." Except in his eyes, it does, but I'm ready to fight him on this.

His expression cools a fraction, his hands tapping impatiently on the back of the chair he's standing by. "Sticking to your agreement with the Corsettis, even after they denied you Aurora, is admirable. But the shtick is up. Send her home. Get the marriage annulled. Nico can't argue this because of the outcome. Perhaps he should have done his due diligence, considering her unknown heritage, but we should have too." He shrugs, like he's speaking about breeding farm animals. "Marrying in your position is to ensure the lineage, and he's aware of this. The *Famiglia* is relying on you for its future heir, and I'm sorry, but Ariella cannot do that for you."

What I hate most about my father in this precise moment, is he's correct. The old me—the pre-Ariella version—would have agreed without a second thought and sent her packing. A wife unable to conceive an heir is a betrayal to the *Famiglia*. Nico would have to take her back or risk a war, since he sent someone who'd be deemed as "ineffective."

But I'm not that person any longer and every word I told Ariella about our future was the damn truth.

"Why didn't you ever fall in love with Mother?"

He blinks, taken aback. "Excuse me. Is this really your largest concern right now?"

I stare.

"Fine." Shaking his head, he answers, "It's just not how it is. Your mother has some lovely qualities that have remained—thankfully—since the moment I married her, but love is a useless emotion in this world. Maintaining a normal relationship, on top of my job, is exhausting. Running the organization is a priority, exactly as I've taught you. Where is this coming from?"

I stare. It's in my silence he should discover his answer.

He huffs a single chuckle. "Son, I'm sorry, but it's over. This is why you don't fall in love with your wife. Now, you feel like you're stuck, but I will make this extremely clear: get rid of her. Divorce her. She will not give you the son you require. This is the time to connect with the Volkovs."

I've never punched my father before, not even in training. When sparring, he's always had his men fight me, which as a kid, I hated. I wanted Father to train *with* me, rather than observe like I'm the science experiment he was putting together.

Perhaps, that's exactly what I've been. If his father raised him one way, he's done the same with me. Without emotion.

The *Famiglia* being his entire focus. Father lived and breathed the organization. Looking back, had he and my mother ever actually spent an evening beneath one roof with me, longer than the odd forced dinner and holidays?

It was those very ideals he shoved into my head—that his father gave him, and probably so on—which I entered marriage with. It was what Ariella and I were supposed to have.

But she changed everything.

"We'll have a child," I grit, my hands curling by my side, a punch to his face seconds away from happening. "I'll get a son, even if we fucking adopt."

"Adopt?" His face flushes a deeper red, and then white with shock. "No. That is taking this entire thing too far." He slams his hand down on my desk, his old desk, in a way meant to be threatening. "*No!* Bringing in your no-name wife was insult enough on the Rossi lineage, but you will not further taint our bloodlines by adopting a nameless orphan."

I'm around my desk in an instance, my expression the only warning of what's coming. My hand fists in his shirt, right around the neck, and the buttons strain. Good. I hope they break.

He pants, his hands coming up to push me off, but lack of time in the field and his age plays against him and I'm stronger. Not that he ever paid me enough attention to realize that.

"Erico—"

"Leave. Before I ensure you don't leave here at all."

He gapes, his feet stumbling to keep up with the pace I've set. "I'm your father—"

"Are you?" I interrupt, a cruel smile taking over. "Blood doesn't make a family. It simply forces us to acknowledge one another in this fucked-up world. The second I was born, you didn't care for me or Mother. Your job was done—*I* was that task. But I'm changing things. Ariella isn't going anywhere, and the future of the *Famiglia* rests in *my* hands."

I thrust him through the open doorway, releasing him with a rough shove.

My father sneers and straightens his button-down shirt before pacing backwards, his head moving in a slow, almost saddened shake. "I tried to reason with you, Erico. Just remember that."

The door to the music room opens and I smile. Erico mentioned only an hour ago, he'd be busy for most of the day, but I'm pleased he's stopping in earlier than planned. My fingers continue over the piano's keys without breaking, continuing to play until he speaks or the song ends, whichever comes first.

"Wow, you have some talent in you, after all."

Not Erico. My fingers stop pressing the keys, my final note more of a blend of sounds than anything decipherable. A female voice, one semi-familiar, and when I give her my attention, I see why.

Gia Rossi fills the doorway, her hands coming up in a slow clap. An action maybe polite if done by others but seems more ill-intended than anything, based on the slight hike in her nose, the flat line of her mouth.

I stand from the piano, not sure how to act. Gia didn't make a great initial impression on me, but she's still Erico's mother, which means I need to play nice for him and for the *Famiglia.*

She stops clapping as she halts in the centre of the room, standing right on my siren carpet. "Did you write that?" She sounds genuinely curious.

I nod, forcing my mouth into a slight upturned smile for sake of manners.

"Are there lyrics too?"

Another nod.

"None you'll sing," she concludes, any bit of kindness gone in that single assumption. Her hands lower, resting in front of her stomach, calling my attention to her pressed, dark pantsuit. "That's unfortunate."

I stare, first at her and then the door. If Erico's mother is here, his father probably is too. Which means playing the polite daughter-in-law for the time. Perhaps the party was a one-off and from here on out, we'll have a civil relationship.

Even if the churning in my stomach and the chill down my spine, say otherwise.

"My husband is meeting with Erico, so I thought I'd find you and apologize for the party. I'll admit I was out of line."

Surprise flutters through me, making my mouth dryer. Okay. This is a step in the correct direction. I force a smile, one tighter than I'd like it to be, but a start.

"My son is tenacious, and marrying you is a sign of that. I couldn't see it at first, so I am sorry."

There's almost an insult woven in that, but at this point, I'm learning it's simply Gia's personality. She's rough, bitchy, and nothing will change that. Brushing aside her snide comments would be best, so I accept the apology with a tip of my head.

"Right then, would you like to get a drink?" She gestures toward the doorway. "I can certainly use some coffee."

Following her for a drink sounds like something I don't want to do, but her offer is a band-aid. She's *trying*. In the beginning, Erico mentioned me having to teach him how to be a better husband. Given Gia's a boy mother, maybe she's unfamiliar with the whole daughter thing.

I nod and step toward her. She turns and falls into step beside me. Her thin hand awkwardly comes up and she holds my shoulder, pausing my walk.

"You're a lovely girl, Ariella. Very beautiful and I can see why my son is smitten with you. This hair—" She pinches a few strands between two fingers, staring at the colour in the afternoon sun streaming through the window. "Such a lovely shade. It'd take a lot of dye to get mine to this point. You and Erico would have made such beautiful children."

Her statement is a knife to the heart; a reminder of what we won't have. This isn't her bitchiness. This is downright cruel.

I wrench my head away, ripping my hair from her hold, even though my scalp slightly burns.

"And that's why I'm sorry, Ariella, but this is for the *Famiglia*."

For the—

And then there's a syringe in her hand. She yanks my hair again, and my arms try to block her, but she maneuvers between them, and then there's a sharp stab in my neck. I still fight. I push away from her, throwing myself in the direction of the door.

Erico...I need Erico.

My vision blurs, the doorway no longer identifiable other than a giant black hole. The angle changes at the same time my knees burn. Am I on the floor?

What is...?

Sleep takes me.

～

The rumble beneath me slowly draws me from sleep. I blink open my heavy lids and stare at leather. Leather and light, and even warmth as the sun beats through the car windows and blankets my form, contradicting the chill consuming my nerves.

What the fuck? Gia *drugged* me.

Even thinking it has my head thumping lightly, the signs of a headache downright annoying. I groan, pressing my hand to my forehead, hoping the pressure eases the thump as I push into a sitting position, to orient myself. A mound of hair falls in my face, and I move it aside, scanning my surroundings.

A car. The outside is houses and a waterfront, so I don't think we're very far from the mansion.

Directly across from me are two people. Gia smirks before her gaze shifts out the window, as though not having any more time for me. By her side, Erico's father stares, a hardened look in his eyes.

The moment I focus on him, he speaks. "If someone had told me a regular woman from Montreal would destroy my family, I would have laughed in their face. But that's what is happening, Ariella, and what needs to stop."

His words barely register before the car takes a sharp turn. My balance rocks, my palms keeping me upright. Still dizzy from them drugging me, still trying to make sense of how I'd gotten from my music room to a vehicle.

"Luckily," his drawl continues, "my son agreed. We all know he requires an equal woman by his side, and you're not it."

Of course, I'm not. I've never been good enough for him.

I shake my head of the thoughts. Of the old worries returning once again.

Erico agreed. Why wouldn't he?

No! He wouldn't do this.

No. I don't believe their lies. It's all *lies*. Erico has said and proved otherwise. All they're trying to do is create confusion. The old me would have latched onto their words, and they would have formulated all sorts of self-doubt, but no more.

No more. I have to get out of here.

The car's driving too quickly, promising death even if I were able to leap from it. My mouth opens. *Where are we?* I try to ask, only for nothing to come out. *Come on, brain! If you're going to begin functioning, now's the time to.*

Gia faces me, her red lipstick forming a bold circle as she fake-pouts. "Still can't talk, hm? Such a shame. It's unfortunate that low-life street racer didn't succeed in wiping you out." She pauses, glancing at her husband. "It's amusing Erico thought we were never aware of what our own son was up to. Street racing. A nasty habit that can end so horribly, so quickly."

You could have killed your son too. They were so desperate to get rid of me...I'd be more shocked at the revelation if my head wasn't still so fuzzy.

"Perfect timing," Erico's father announces.

I follow the trajectory of his gaze, catching the road we're turning onto. Lined with trees, a massive cement ground, and the ocean beyond. A single, white plane is in the centre of it.

Shit.

Gia smiles at the same time the realization hits. They're sending me away. To Montreal? Or somewhere Erico won't find me?

Maybe he orchestrated this.

No! He didn't. He didn't and he wouldn't. He has no idea where I am—no idea how to find me.

The car jerks to a stop a little ways away from the plane. I scan the airfield, seeking escape. If I run, how far will I make it before Erico's parents track me down?

The plane's stairs lower and a man appears, followed by two huge guys dressed in cargo pants and leather coats. Guards, presumably, which makes the other man very important. He descends the steps and I glance at the Rossis, who haven't moved. No one does while he approaches the vehicle and I try to make out the man's features. The eel-like grin, the dark hair, pale skin looking like a corpse himself.

I recognize him. Ursin Volkov from the Russian Bratva. The man who caused all the drama with Erico at our party.

Fuck.

Gia chimes, "You're taking a trip, Ariella, and you won't be returning. Our son will be able to move on from you in peace."

41
ERICO

Ariella isn't in the music room, so I head down the hallway, past the kitchen and toward the doors leading to the pool. I've been tucked away a lot longer than I meant to, so she probably got tired of playing and moved onto swimming.

As suspected, she's reclined on a lounge chair outside, facing away from the door. A large, wide-brimmed sunhat I've never seen her wear is perched on her head, her long red hair swept up beneath it, keeping her neck bare.

I stop walking. In all the times I've known her, Ariella's *never* worn a hat. Said she prefers her hair free, exactly like her free-spirit.

The closer I approach, the more the red flags rise up the pole.

Something's wrong. It's in the slope of her neck, the curve of her shoulders, her skin paler than normal. And the fact that she's lounging rather than swimming. Ariella's very rarely outside of the water.

My gun's in my hand in the next second, the barrel pressing

against the hat of the woman I know to *not* be my wife. The click as it's prepared to shoot seems louder amidst the quiet outdoors, over the thrumming of my beating heart.

"Why are you in my home?" The gun jabs into the back of her head. "Up."

The woman lifts two pale, slender arms, her palms out in submission. As she stands, she grabs the hat, and lifts it from her head, tossing it onto the lounge chair she abandons. Her wavy hair tumbles down to her waist, black as midnight.

Even before she faces me, I *know* in my gut who'll be staring back at me. The malicious curve of her mouth, the hardened eyes, the pursing of her lips as she drops her hands to her side and cocks her hip slightly.

Vanessa Volkov.

I readjust the gun until the barrel is directed right at her forehead. "I'll ask you again: why are you in my home?"

She shrugs slowly and grins, an almost dramatic flair to her paced movements. "Figured I'd check my future mansion out. Quite like the pool."

"Ten seconds before the bullet finds your brain, Vanessa. Talk."

She rolls her eyes. "Words, Erico. All words. You wouldn't harm me and risk a war with the Bratva. We both know you'd lose."

"You think I fucking care?" I seethe, every word out of her bitchy mouth enticing my mood to go darker and darker. "Where is my wife, Vanessa?"

"You're looking at her. Well, your future wife, anyway."

My finger tightens, even though I know I won't kill her. Not yet. Not while she's clutching onto the facts I require. "How did you get in my home?"

"Right through the front door. Walked in with your parents

after they disposed of your guys. Your wife's bodyguard is knocked out on the front step."

My arm falters, my hold weakening. Of fucking course, it was my parents. Father's visit wasn't only to convince me to end my marriage; it was a set up. When I didn't agree, they enacted whatever bullshit plan they created and left Vanessa here. For what precise purpose, I will learn.

I lower the gun only for my hand to snap out and clench the bitch's throat. For now, she's valuable because she knows where Ariella is. Vanessa gasps, which I cut off with a tight pinch of my thumb and forefinger, dragging her nearer until she's uncomfortably close to my chest but able to see the threat of death in my gaze if she plans on double-crossing me.

"You have three fucking seconds to tell me where my wife is or I will strangle you until you're a corpse at my feet." My fingers flex with my threat.

"F-fine." She gasps, her long, red nails scratching pointlessly at my hand. She can mark me up all she wants because they're doing no harm to my skin. "M-my father."

I release her with a rough jerk, and she gasps life back into her. Bent over, breathing through her mouth, her hands cupping her throat. She finally glances up, glaring, but with her obviously still alive, I clench her arm and propel her into the direction of the garage.

"We're going on a drive and you *will* take me to her. You mislead me, you're dead."

She stumbles, and without fight, answers, "Nearby airport in Southampton. My father has a plane there. Your parents paid off the owner so no one alerted your men of our arrival."

"Why?"

"To remove her from your life."

Her unspoken words are what really hits. *They're going to kill her.* I drag Vanessa straight to the garage, punching my thumb into the reader. The whirl of the door opening has never felt so slow, and impatience gnaws at me, energy bouncing on the tips of my toes until the door's opened enough I'm able to shove us both inside and in the direction of the nearest car.

"Get in. Shut up."

She does without a fight, her glare her only weapon as she rubs her arm. There's no battle in her, and I wonder exactly how much training Ursin Volkov spent on his daughter. None obviously, deciding to use only her body to get ahead.

The moment I'm off the property, pressing the gas to take me to unimaginable speeds, I dial Caladin, his "Hey!" connecting over the Bluetooth and emitting through my car.

"Southampton airfield. Now. Bring men. Whoever's with you."

There's noise in the background and a door being slammed shut. "Um, okay. What's going on?"

"My parents kidnapped Ariella and left Vanessa in her place. They're taking her to the plane. Volkov is here."

"Shit!" More shuffling, voices, and another door. "Okay, fuck, coming. Leaving one of the clubs now. I have three with me. We'll be there as soon as we can."

"Make it faster." *Click.*

"You really should reconsider," Vanessa mutters the moment I hang up. "When your parents learned of your wife's deficiencies, they were only too happy to call up my father and renegotiate."

If I didn't possibly need her, now that I know where to go, provided she isn't lying, I'd get rid of her. But with Ariella's life in Ursin's firm grip, I'm not taking any chances. Leaving Vanessa with me was the single stupidest thing he could have done. Assuming they'd expect to be gone with her by the time I found Vanessa, and clearly, they're delusional if they believed that'd change anything.

"You're one more word away from losing your tongue, Volkov."

"Whatever. You're making a mistake."

"My wife isn't a mistake."

I press the gas harder, knowing if cops spot me speeding, they'll look the other way. Either the car itself or the licence plate will remind them, I own this city. I'm still ten minutes away though and it's nine minutes and fifty-nine seconds too long for my liking.

Finally, fucking *finally*, I make it to the edge of the airfield, spotting the single plane parked in the centre, my parents' car a couple metres away.

"Fuck." If only I had more weapons...If I play this right, my single gun will do.

I stop the car feet away from my parents and am out, by the passenger side, instantly. Vanessa throws herself from the car, screeching as she tries to take off in the direction of the plane, but she doesn't make it three steps before she's in my grip. One arm clenched around her neck, I yank until her back's to my front, my gun jammed into her forehead.

A few feet away, my parents stand, my mother's eyes darting between me and Vanessa while my father simply frowns. A fucking *frown* is all his heartless ass manages as I've ruined his plans. A couple feet from them, Ursin fucking Volkov, flanked by two guards, their own guns angled toward me.

In a hold identical to the one I have his daughter in, Ariella stares, her eyes wide but flashing with relief. The gun positioned at her head means I need to play this really fucking smart. I'm one against a small army, but they have me pinned by my weakness. By *her*.

I keep my eyes on her as I approach, reassuring her while I speak to Ursin directly and ignore my traitorous parents. "Simple trade, Volkov. My wife for your daughter."

Instead of Ursin, it's Father who speaks. He approaches, one foot in front of the other, his hands lifting to show he has no weapon. He's staring at me like I'm unhinged, which maybe I am. Maybe having my heart ripped from my chest and a gun shoved against her forehead has me seconds away from sparking a war. Vanessa or Ursin, one of them *will* die, but I have my preference.

"Erico, consider what the Volkovs can do for us. An heir, for one."

I ignore him, not bothering to grant him an ounce of my attention. Not looking away from my wife, whose eyes dart around the area, seeking escape.

I'm coming, sirena. I've got you.

"Keep my daughter," Ursin says, shrugging. "I have who I want. She's who'll bring you to your knees. You can't tell me if I rid the world of this common whore, you'd turn away my daughter then." He jabs the gun into Ariella's head harder, making her whimper, and red tinges the edges of my view.

"The second you move an inch, Volkov, your daughter's dead. Think this through."

He scoffs, the sound of a man with entirely too much confidence. He jerks his head, indicating the guys at his side who remain steady and focused. "Three against one, Rossi. *You* should think this through."

The odds might not be in my favour, but it doesn't stop me from planning. Caladin showing up now would be really fucking convenient because with my parents hovering nearby *and* the cause of this shitshow, they're no help.

Ursin steps toward the plane's stairs, dragging Ariella with him, so I move too, shoving Vanessa forward. She hisses, and the two men approach.

"Let us leave, Rossi, and we'll make the *Famiglia* more powerful than you could ever dream of. Let me take your pretty, little wife and you can keep my daughter." The eel of a man drags his nose up the column of Ariella's neck. "By tonight, she'll no longer be your concern. By tonight, she'll be a body thrown in an incinerator. One of many that get dumped in the Russian northern mountains." His eyes flick to me, his smile malicious. "Think her blood will be as bold as this hair of hers?"

Ariella's jaw clenches and she tries to turn her head farther away from him. She jerks in his hold, but he has her too tight. I want to tell her not to fight, to keep still, so he doesn't hurt her, but I refuse to suggest my little warrior stops fighting her battles.

Her eyes flash to me, narrowing, and somewhere between that look and her next blink, *la mia sirena* steals back her control.

Causing chaos to break out.

42

ARIELLA

Erico doesn't have a chance against three guns. His parents are unlikely to help—assholes that they are. Which leaves me and him against the rest. Meaning, only him, because I'm useless in Ursin's hold.

Useless but not helpless.

Warning Mom that the van was going to hit us, and her doing nothing about it, was a moment where I *tried*. Tried to be the hero, only to be ignored.

When Mom was dating Stefano, I made my concerns known. Something felt off about him and his entire family situation, the secrecy surrounding his home, but she ignored me.

Della insisted on following our stepfather's commands, all to keep me well and safe, and every time I told her not to, that we'd survive together, it fell on deaf ears.

Every single time I've tried to speak, there was only silence.

I want to make noise.

I don't want to be silent and useless.

Erico married *me*. Learned to love *me*. Claims *I'm* the *Famiglia* queen he needs by his side.

Time to prove it to him.

Time to prove to *everyone* that I might not be able to talk, but I'm fucking loud.

There is a sound in silence and it sounds precisely like this moment.

The moment where Ursin and Erico go back and forth with their demands and threats. When Ursin jams the gun's barrel into me harder, ensuring a headache tomorrow, all while his men approach Erico. Ursin has the advantage, and Vanessa and I are literally in the same exact position, being used as leverage.

No more.

My squirming was a test to determine how much freedom I have. Arms—none. Legs—plenty. And despite the grip on my neck, I can still use my head.

In a blast of movement I only warn Erico about with the narrowing of my eyes, I lift my foot and kick it as high as I can, aiming for Ursin's dick. At the same time, I lean forward and slam backwards, ramming the back of my head into his face.

The *crunch* tells me I've succeeded.

His hold loosens enough that I rip from it and drop to a crouch, everything a flurry of darkness and movement.

A gun shot sounds over the airfield.

Silence.

Sickening silence and the worst sensation begins creeping up until it's Ursin behind me who drops, a hole straight through his skull. Vanessa's agonizing screech bellows when Erico releases her to fight.

Ursin's guards surge forward, ready to avenge their leader, but Erico shifts the trajectory of his gun toward the first, and then the other, and they both stumble dead.

Silence again. Finished so quickly once *I* fought by my husband's side.

Then interrupted by tires squealing as another car comes zooming forward, parking beside Erico's.

I tense, crouched by the plane's staircase, watching the scene as Caladin's loud, booming laugh comes from the new car. "Goddamn it, we're too late."

Erico pays his cousin no attention, reaching immediately for Vanessa, who's since crouched by a vehicle to hide. He yanks her to her feet and growls. "You will get in your fucking plane and return to Russia. I *ever* see you in *Famiglia* territory again, I won't hesitate to shoot. Go home and tell the Bratva that if they want a war, I'm ready. I'll take them down one at a fucking time, but they will *never* go near what's mine."

She bobs her head in a jerky nod. He releases her with a shove, in the direction of the plane, and she all but runs toward the stairs. She passes me without a second look as I rush the opposite way and head for Erico, right as Caladin comes up to my other side. The men he brought with him linger by the car, seeing no apparent threat.

Vanessa trips going up the metal steps and pauses at the top, her gaze finding her father's corpse, and for a moment, I pity her. It's difficult to lose a parent, even if she deserves no empathy from me.

Her expression hardens and she becomes the woman I met at the party again. Her gaze lifts to Erico, her words a shout from the distance. "The Bratva *will* retaliate, Rossi. You've just begun a war you won't win."

She turns and disappears in the plane, and another man appears, lifting the stairs. The Volkov pilot presumably, who hid during the fight.

The moment the plane's doors shut, I crave Erico's arms. Even when his parents claimed *he* was the one sending me away, he saved me. Erico hugs me briefly but quickly releases me, only his fingers dragging over the back of my hand in acknowledgment before he approaches his parents waiting nearby.

Caladin whispers, "You okay?" and I nod, throwing him a smile of gratitude.

"Erico—" Erico's father immediately starts only to be cut off by him.

"Leave."

"Excuse me?"

Erico points off into the distance. "I will call a pilot. You will go home and get whatever you need. By midnight, you both will leave this country."

His mother steps forward, crying, "Erico, we were only—"

"Silence!" Death's sounded kinder than Erico's tone. "There is nothing you will say to save you from my wrath. My *own parents* tried to get rid of my wife!"

His father explodes, almost shoving Gia aside. "Erico, you will drag the *Famiglia* down with your obsession with that girl. We were trying to do what's best for you. The Bratva is—was best for us. Power, strength, bloodlines. They had it all and you threw it away for *her*."

I barely see his arm lift, but Erico slams his fist right into his father's face, knocking him to the side and into his mother. Caladin snickers, but I don't know what to think anymore, what to do.

"One more word out of your mouth, and I won't hold back."

Rubbing at his jaw, his father spits. "You're making a huge mistake. The heads of the family will turn on you and you will have an internal war. Do you really want that after fucking with the Bratva?"

"Then maybe it's time for the *Famiglia* to enter a new chapter. Maybe it's time for the old capos to be cleaned out."

Gia steps in front of her husband, once again, crying in a

whining tone, "Erico, you're our son. We're your parents and you can't—"

"Parents?" He barks a single laugh, no humour whatsoever. "No, you're not. Was I ever your son? *Really* your child. I was a product of sex, created as an heir, trained to be Boss. You both showed me no love. I was your *task* and nothing more."

"You're an embarrassment," his father spits, and right when I think Erico's about to attack again, he simply points to their vehicle.

"You're done. Leave. You step foot in the States again, even our shared blood will not save you. Retire far away from here and I never want to see either of your faces again."

He turns away from them, giving them his back, heading straight for me. I glance over his shoulder, watching as his parents climb back into the car that brought me here, but the last thing I catch is his mother's saddened expression before Erico consumes me.

His hands grab my cheeks, his mouth descending on mine with more passion than ever. He walks me backwards two feet, pressing me into the hood of his car. His tongue finds mine, consuming, devouring.

I let him.

Somewhere behind us, Caladin mutters, "Way to make a guy feel single. I'll help clean up."

"Fuck," Erico drops his forehead to mine and all I breathe is *him*, "a million fears went through my head when I found Vanessa in the backyard instead of you. I died a few deaths. Never again."

"Thank you," I say simply, cupping his cheek. "Thank you for coming for me."

"Always," he replies, his tone guttural. With a single swoop of his arm, he's lifting me by my ass and lowering me on the hood of his car, stepping between my legs, getting as close as possible. "I'm sorry the people who birthed me are monsters. I'm so fucking sorry for what they've done today. If there's one positive, though, I hope you see now, when I claim I'm never letting you go, I mean it." Somehow, he manages to bring me closer to him, no space between our bodies now. His lips stroke gently over mine as he repeats, "I'm never letting you go, *sirena*."

A beautiful threat.

"Good. I'm so glad it was you I shackled myself to."

It's meant as a joke, but he's completely serious when he replies, "Me too, Ariella. Me fucking too." He kisses me again and this time, my core clenches, my body bending backwards, pushing my breasts into his chest. He's sparking a craving that even the death and violence of the day hasn't quelled. "I never meant to fall in love with my wife, *sirena*, but you taught me how. I love you, Ariella."

My heart soars, his declaration wiping away every ounce of darkness inside me. Every previous instance since the second he placed his ring on my finger. "That's the first time you've said those words to me."

With a downturned expression, he shakes his head. "Remember a while ago, I told you I needed to be taught how to be a husband? This is a prime example because I've loved you for a while now. I'm just a moron who's never told you."

"But you're my moron, so it's okay," I tease, pressing my hand over his heart, feeling the gentle thumping—*my* thumping. The heart that now beats for me. "Besides, I've felt your love and that's all that matters. Actions speak louder than words, haven't you heard?"

"Not until I met you. From the very first time I met you, hiding in the Corsetti wing, you've proved how loud silence can be." His eyes search mine, the same way he had that night. "*Sirena*, from then on, I was so taken with your silence, not understanding why at the time. Your eyes. This striking damn hair. It was a struggle to give Aurora an ounce of my attention through dinner when you were all I wanted to stare at. When I returned to New York, you continued to plague my mind, and I hated myself for it. You were the sister of Nico's wife, related to my own would-be wife through marriage, and I had no right to think of you in any manner other than civil politeness. But *fuck*, I couldn't stop myself." His lips trail the corner of my mouth, his smile imprinting on mine. "Couldn't help being obsessed with you. When Nico told me you volunteered for the union, I was thrilled because the redheaded *sirena* invading my mind for weeks would be all mine."

After his speech, after my heart's been ripped to shreds and taped back together, I tell him two words only: "All yours."

He kisses me again and I lean against the hood, fond memories of this very car in the middle of a rainstorm. Logically, I know this isn't the place, but fuck, I want it to be.

"Hey, lovebirds!" Clearly, Caladin thinks otherwise. "Maybe *don't* fuck ten feet away from dead bodies. Just a crazy idea."

Erico lifts his head to peek over his shoulder, toward his cousin. "Maybe *don't* cut into other people's business. Just a crazy idea." To me, he whispers, "He's right. We should go home. Clean you up. Because then I plan on dirtying you up."

43
ERICO

I carry her straight into the bathroom when we get home, depositing her first on the counter, and then switching on the shower so the water heats up. She allows me to strip her clothing, and I brush along her bottom lip, ending her smirk, before removing her pants.

"You laugh, but I'm gaining immense pleasure from this."

"From undressing me?"

"From taking care of you."

Once she's naked, I study her body, paying special attention to her neck in the bright bathroom lighting. She claims to be fine, but I must see it for myself, to ease the protective instincts threatening more death, if she isn't. There's no bruises, no swelling, besides a tiny dot from where she was drugged, so she seems fine enough until I invite the doctor here tomorrow.

Besides, he'll be explaining how the fuck my parents learned of her fertility results.

For now, I walk her straight into the glass-walled shower. Water crashes down on her, making her hair a deep red, and she laughs. "I also think you enjoy carrying me."

"All part of taking care of you. But for now—" I lower her to her feet, and once she's steady, grab soap and a loofah and begin washing, "turn around."

She does and I slowly wash her back, dropping to my knees in front of her as I wipe over the globes of her ass, her legs, her feet. She groans, her head falling back. Sex and freedom in her every motion, and it's a beautiful sight.

"Turn."

She obeys, placing that pretty pussy right in line with my face. I'll return to that soon, but first, I wash her front, over her stomach, chest, and breasts.

"Never thought I'd enjoy the sight of a man on his knees for me." Her wicked as sin grin promises so much more.

"Yeah?"

She strokes her fingers down the side of my face, tenderly, and praises, "Mhm. You look really good down there. I could get used to it."

Abandoning the loofah, I trail my fingers up the back of her legs and lift my face back to her pussy, so when I speak, my breath blows over her cunt. "Then I say, get used to it, and tell me how I can serve my wife from my knees."

She stills in hesitation, but after a single breath, the air in the shower changes. Electrified with her power. With a control I don't think she even realizes she has.

But fuck, this woman has *every* ounce of domination over me.

Her fingers drag down my cheek toward my jaw and she grasps a firm hold, tipping my head up to look at her, and my cock immediately jumps to attention. She's everything like this and I will be whatever she needs. Her thumb drags over my bottom lip and *fuck me*. She bends, pressing a single kiss to my lips. It's our most chaste kiss, and yet, I'm on the edge of panting for more.

"You missed a spot when you were washing me."

"Oh yeah?" I retrieve the loofah. "Where's that, wife?"

"My pussy."

She lifts her left leg and drapes it over my shoulder, placing her pretty cunt inches from my mouth. She never said how to clean her, but I drop the loofah in exchange for massaging her inner thighs until she rewards me with a moan.

"Good boy," she murmurs her praise, testing the statement with a whisper. "That feels really nice, but I'm still aching. Clean me with your mouth, Erico. Lick my pussy until I come on your face."

Gladly. Her commands, spoken with sex, will be addictive.

With both my thumbs, I part her pussy lips, baring that little ball of nerves that's about to make her lose her mind. I blow on her clit first, then flick my tongue against it, then blow again until she groans. Fingers weave in my hair and then she presses weight onto my head, shoving me right into her pussy.

"I said *lick*. Don't tease."

"Your wish is my command, *sirena*."

Keeping her parted with my thumbs, I lick, flicking my tongue back and forth over her core, and then covering her with my mouth, fucking my tongue inside her heat. Her hold on my hair becomes painful and she controls my movements, pushing her hips against my face. Riding herself to her orgasm.

She quickly comes, drenching my face in ways the shower is failing to. Her cry is one that'll reverberate in this room until the next one she gives me. And for our entire lives.

I was so damned close to losing her today. Not again.

Panting, she yanks on my hair until I detach from her. My lips are soaked and I meet her eyes. Her heated smile as she cups my cheeks makes my erection throb.

"So good at that."

"How else can I serve you, wife?"

"Take me to our bed and fuck me."

She doesn't need to ask again. I stand and she drops her leg from my shoulder, reaching behind to switch off the shower. I lift her in my arms and walk us both out the bathroom and toward the bed. Water darkens the thick carpet and I couldn't care less.

I drop her onto the bed, stepping between her legs, but she moves instantly, rolling to her knees and off the bed. She points to where she was just lying with her teeth scraping over her bottom lip.

"I wasn't done with you. On your back."

I obey her but not before flicking her nipple with my thumb as I pass, watching as the tight bud gets harder, her lips pressing together to hide how much she enjoys it. It's fun to witness her control slip bit by bit.

Once I'm on my back, she climbs over me and rubs her wet pussy against my cock. Her hands link with mine, positioning them by my head and pinning me down.

"You look so sexy like this, Ariella."

"And you look so perfect, submitting to me like this."

"Only to you."

The next rock of her hips has my cock inside her tight heat. She squeezes my cock head and then the shaft as she lowers herself inch by inch, her breaths coming deeper. She moves up and down, wetting me before taking me entirely inside her.

"God, you feel so good buried inside me." She groans, her head tipping back, her control slipping again.

I grip her hip with one hand and urge her to lean back with my other as she moves. It puts her core at a different angle, my cock brushing the most sensitive part of her.

"And you feel fucking fantastic, wife."

Through her breathy moans, she smiles, meeting my eyes as her head rolls to her chest. Her hand balances on my abs. "I ever tell you, I love being referred to as that? When you say it, it feels *right*."

"Because we are right, Ariella. Two sides of a seashell that have found one another."

"Perfect for one another in every way," she agrees, sinking down on me at the same time I thrust. "I love you, Erico, but now, fuck me. I command you to."

"Gladly."

As much as I enjoy her on top, I flip us over, sinking even deeper. My arms hook beneath her legs and I spread them, keeping her as helpless as she makes me feel as I hammer inside her cunt.

"H-hey..." she protests through pants, "I was...on top."

"Believe me, you're still in control, *sirena*." I lower my head, taking her mouth as I kiss her into her next orgasm, swallowing it with every thrust of my cock. And I swear, her hand reaches inside my chest and fists my heart.

Steals it for herself.

Her pussy tightens around me, and fuck, I want to follow her down, but instead, I look to her, seeking instruction as she pants, wiping hair from her face. Her playful, knowing grin tells me she sees what I'm looking for, and her legs lift, hooking around my waist.

"Be my good husband and fill me with your cum. Ensure every inch of my body knows you're its master."

I pinch her chin, staring into her eyes. "No, baby. From the very first second you batted your fucking eyes at me, you've been my master. You control me in ways no one else can or ever will. Therefore, I will do nothing but continue obeying you."

With her permission, my thrusts quicken. I grasp her hands, looping my fingers into hers as I hold them to the side, simply *holding* her hands as I ride her. As her back arches and sweat drips from her neck. I chase the drop with my tongue. Heat builds, the pressure becomes pleasurable, my orgasm approaching.

"I'm going to come," I warn her.

"Do it, Erico. Now."

My next thrust is my last as a blinding pleasure consumes me.

Consumes *us*.

The very way *la mia sirena* did to me all those months ago.

44

ARIELLA

Erico flits around the bedroom, dressing, while I observe from bed, leaning against the pillows. Both my legs are drawn up, arms draped over my knees, sheet covering only to my waist.

He's preparing to drop by a few clubs to...do whatever his job consists of. So much I don't know of his life. So much I *need* to know if I'm going to do this right.

Especially since you can't provide an heir.

My inner critic, for once, isn't malicious, but truthful. The *Famiglia* needs to see me as still valuable to the organization, even if my main task won't happen—possibly happen.

"I want to come with you."

Erico pauses, his fingers looping one button through his suit jacket's top hole. "Excuse me?"

"I want to come," I repeat, angling to my knees to shuffle toward the end of the bed. "The heads might have met me at the party, but I think it's only fair your staff and soldiers do too. If you're visiting your clubs and such, let me come. Please."

He approaches the bed, his expression flat and deadly,

reminding me so much of what he looked like facing Ursin on the airfield. A *no* is undoubtedly about to follow, but then he grasps my right ankle and pulls me toward the edge of the bed, stepping between my thighs. He cups my face and hauls me to his lips, pressing a kiss that ignites my entire being.

"Fuck, how did you even come into my life?"

"I forced myself upon you, if you've forgotten."

He shakes his head, skating a hand down my bare back, cupping my ass, his fingers dangerously close to my sated core. "No, you never forced. You just knew what I needed before I did. Get dressed." He releases me with a tap to my ass, stepping out of my way. "Yes, you're fucking coming with me. I'd be honoured to have you there."

With a gleeful whoop, I head for the closet, rifling out a dress that'll be appropriate for today. It's a light teal, a similar colour to the dress Erico met me in, with cap sleeves and a modest neckline.

When I return to the bedroom, he's leaning against the bedpost, staring at his phone, but looks up at my entry, his eyes becoming a molten brown. "Damn, you're gorgeous." He follows me into the bathroom, leaning on that doorway instead, as I finish getting ready. "You know," he starts conversationally, "Mother never did this. I guess Father never wanted her to, or she didn't ask. Not sure. But the soldiers only knew *of* her, unless they were tasked with guarding her. You might be the first *Famiglia* queen to want to meet all the men."

I freeze, brush halfway down my hair. "So, how many people are we going to piss off when I go?"

He comes up behind me, taking the brush from my hand and finishing my hair for me. "Who, the heads Caladin and I are still debating replacing? Who cares. If they say anything, it gives me the ammo to get rid of them. Like I told my parents, it's time for a new era. You're it. I bet you my soldiers will gain mass respect for you after today. There's a major difference between protecting someone because they want to and because they have to."

Well, that makes this seem better. I meet his eyes in the mirror, pressing my lips together before addressing a major subject matter hovering in the background in the two days since the near-kidnapping. I reported to him what they told me, that they were behind the near car accident too. He didn't seem overly surprised and called off the investigation he had going.

"Have you heard from them?"

He steps back since I'm done and leads me from our room. "Not directly. They're in the Bahamas. All our planes are outfitted with trackers; plus, I had their pilot email me whenever they landed. I've had men travel there to keep an eye on them; temporarily, until I'm satisfied that they're settled and won't do shit."

I touch his arm, feeling a bit guilty for what happened. "I'm sorry you lost your parents because of me."

He throws a sad look my way. "I never truly had parents."

Hours later, we return and I might have experienced the most stressful, anxiety-inducing, *best* time ever. Even if my fingers ache from all the rapid typing on my phone to respond to any questions.

Erico took me to two underground casinos, eight bars, and four nightclubs. I met all the staff in each one—waitresses, bartenders, dancers, whoever—and met many of Erico's soldiers stationed at each one.

Even got to see Sebastian again. Turns out, he visited his kid nephew over the weekend and had an extra-long conversation with his newly-practiced ASL skills.

My favourite bar was the last one we dropped into, when Erico had a conversation with the bartenders, and one of the waitresses pulled me aside.

"Hope I'm not overstepping, Mrs. Rossi, but thank you for making this trip. You know, in all the years Erico's father owned this place, we never once met Gia one-on-one, unless she came in for a drink."

That made me smile. In fact, a lot of the day made me smile to the point, my mouth now hurts.

Erico shoves me right up against the door once we're inside, and grasps the dress, yanking it over my head. He yanks down my panties next, and the mansion's temperature makes little bumps rise against my skin.

"Wh-what are—"

Then he drops to the floor, spreads my legs, and spears me with his tongue. After a long, languid lick, he pulls back to respond.

"You, my fucking wife, have had me hard all day watching every one of my men turn to absolute puddles with your introduction. How different would my life be if you weren't the one who walked down that aisle to me?"

"Sweet, but that doesn't answer what you're doing." My hand sweeps his hair back, fingers slowly dragging through the dark strands.

"What's it look like?" Fire ignites in his depths. "I'm worshipping at the altar of my queen."

He buries his head between my legs and certainly worships me until I'm screaming his name over and over.

∾

The next day by the pool, I send off my final message to Yasmine. There's a lack of control in clinging to the past, and with Rozelyn and Nico managing her rescue—possible rescue—determining if there even needs to be one, there's no point in me continuing to call and text. What was a form of self-care now feels silly, since I don't even know if she has the same phone.

If she did, why wouldn't she call her sister, Rozelyn, and let her know she's all right?

Which means...she might not be all right.

"Yasmine, I'm worried about you. I'd do anything to know you're safe, but I think this might be it. I can't keep blowing up a phone you won't answer."

Reluctantly, I end the call and drop my phone between my legs on the lounge chair.

"Who are these messages to?" Erico's voice comes up behind me. His hand brushes the back of my neck as he takes a seat beside me, dressed in swim shorts, indicating he's come to hang out in the pool with me.

"Yasmine," I answer with a sigh, staring at the phone rather than him. "Yasmine De Falco."

"The same man who had your mother killed? Who caused all the drama with the Corsettis?" He jerks back.

"The very one. Yasmine's his youngest daughter. Rozelyn, his oldest, is dating Flynn, Nico's enforcer. Yasmine's her younger sister."

"Which would make her your ex-stepsister," he concludes, leaning forward, hands clenched between his open legs. "Nico mentioned you not having a positive relationship with them."

"He thinks so. Because that was the case for Della, and me too, once, but in the medical centre, on some random winter day, I got a visitor. Only two people were authorized to see me: Stefano and Della, though Stefano never did. Della only visited the week before, and it was unlike her to plan two trips back-to-back, so when it was Yasmine who walked through my door... well, surprise was too calm a term. I never even asked how she got in to see me." Her father's name, I suppose. "At first, it was weird. She literally sat in silence, staring at the floor. Obviously, I wasn't talking. Based on her behaviour, I actually thought something had happened with Della, but then finally, she spoke.

'I'm sorry for being a bitch,' she said. Then explained she was following her sister's orders. Then she left and I thought that was that until a week later, she returned holding a brand-new puzzle, which she gifted to me. And then mentioned her own dreams and nightmares. I think I became safety away from her father, but I didn't mind. If anything, I began looking forward to her visits. Started using the whiteboard I had to speak with her. She's actually the one who theorized why I stopped singing altogether."

"Oh, yeah?" He perks up at that. Erico's never hidden the fact he wants to hear me sing. And eventually, I will.

"Yeah." But I skip over what she told me. "That ended up being her last visit because Della got into the plot to capture Nico by that point, and her father probably locked her down. Then it all snowballed into more."

"You miss her," he correctly states. "She was company."

"For the past year, every few weeks, yeah."

He rolls his lips together, gaze lowering to my phone, like he's thinking hard. "So what's the story with her now then? Why's she not answering you?"

I huff, staring at the pool when I talk, focusing on the little ripples. "That's the grand question. When her father escaped Montreal, he left Rozelyn behind to stir shit while he went to British Columbia with Yasmine." Nico would probably be pissed with me admitting this to another organization's head when it's not their business, but at this rate, the past is the past. "That's where he's from. There's a whole thing there. A society of people he left her with. Basically, he pissed off the people he was working for, and they handed Stefano to Nico. Before his death, he gave two different answers regarding Yasmine's whereabouts and safety. Before you and I got married, Rozelyn was begging Nico to find her, but he won't risk a war with them. Della mentioned he has a plan, but even she's not too certain about it."

"But Yasmine's not answering her phone."

I reach forward to clutch that very device, waiting for the vibration of her response to come, even though it won't. "Yeah, which probably means it's not good."

We both fall silent, but my mind isn't. Rozelyn can't help her. Nico's hands are tied. But I...I glance at my husband. I have a Boss at my disposal, a mafia organization behind me the Seven isn't aware of. Or, at least don't realize is a player.

As fast as the idea comes to me, I'm backing down. It's all wishful thinking. Besides, we'd have to get *into* B.C. and find her. The searching is the impossible part.

Again, I look at my husband. Did he not say Caladin is his best tracker?

"Hey, you mentioned Caladin is good at hunting, right? Could he..."

Erico's eyes flash up, reading the rest of my question on my face. "Could he what? Find her? Probably. But with her in Canada, there's more to it. Like—" He cuts himself off. "I have an idea, but it might not work."

"Just like that? I barely convinced you."

His face scrunches in displeasure. "Like I need convincing where you're concerned. You ask, you shall receive. Would it make you happy to know she's alive and well, to have her brought back to her family?"

Hell, even if she didn't come home to Montreal or even to visit me, yeah, knowing she's okay would stop me from spamming her number, and would be a peace of mind to Rozelyn.

"Yeah, it would," I answer after a while. "I feel like, if we knew what was happening to her, it'd close the story. Like the final chapter we all need to put the De Falco drama behind us."

He nods. "Give me until tomorrow to determine how viable this is. But for now," he stands, linking his hand with mine to pull me up, "before I sit on a long phone call and have to convince Caladin he's heading to frosty Canada, I need something from you."

As he leads me around the bench, I roll my eyes. "You realize, it's August in Canada too? It's hot. No frostiness."

Erico completely ignores me and walks me straight into the pool, his arm banding around my waist as the water's buoyancy takes us. "Since the moment I found you in here, I had a fantasy that I'd like to play out."

I press my hand over his now-wet chest, over his gentle thumping heart and link my legs around his waist beneath the water. "What's that?"

With me in his hold, he swims us to the side of the pool, caging me in before spinning me entirely. His face is in the curve of my neck, his lips tracing a delicious line from my throat to the base of my ear, his nose nuzzling the skin.

"Bending *la mia sirena* over the side of the pool and fucking you until your throat is raw from screaming."

I shiver, peeking over my shoulder, right as he gently bends me forward. Before I hand over my submission though, I grasp his chin, angling his mouth against mine. "Only if you're good later and let me suck your cock."

He growls a delicious noise that makes my core tighten. "Too bad that's not a punishment."

I smile against his mouth. "It is when I don't let you come."

His pupils dilate, my own fantasy becoming his second one. "You win. You're truly a siren. Lured me in and now I'm yours to kill."

"Not kill," I murmur readjusting my chest against the cement pool siding, my hips arched for his pleasure. "Just keep. I chose you, Erico, because you're the man I want."

As he tugs my bikini bottoms aside and thrusts into me, I've never been more thankful for the single text message I sent to Nico that day, weeks ago, when he and Aurora were fighting over whether bringing Erico to Montreal to support taking down De Falco would be wise or not.

ME

I'll do it. I'm volunteering myself. You need someone to marry him, and I'll be that one.

From that message, I gained a husband.

My happily-ever-after.

Might not be perfect. Might still have challenges.

But it's mine. Erico is mine.

Best of all: Erico helped me uncover a piece of myself that was lost.

And reminded me how to make noise.

45

ERICO

"**T**hank you, Nico. I'll keep you updated, of course."

"When you find her, my only request is you keep her in New York for a while. Until I know she can be trusted, I don't want her around my family. It took a lot for me to see her sister isn't my enemy either, but with Yasmine wrapped up in the Seven, who knows what mind control shit they've done to her."

"Too easy," I reply. "Ariella will want to see her either way, and I can keep her with us until we decide how safe she is to go home."

"Thanks, Rossi. Damn," he grumbles, low enough I wonder if it's even for me, "I thought this De Falco bullshit was over, but it doesn't end. Honestly, actually, thank you. Rozelyn was asking me to go find her, but it's precarious between the Seven and us right now, so asking for favours right away isn't the smartest. With your plan, a lot of those concerns are negated."

My plan would only have the *Famiglia* come under fire if we were discovered. But we won't be because Caladin knows what he's doing.

Speaking of…his head pops into my doorway, so I mumble a goodbye to Nico, mention I'm finalizing the plans, and hang up right as Caladin crosses my office, dropping into one of the chairs. He hoists his legs up, crossed at the ankles, and plops them on my desk, much to my glaring annoyance.

"Finalizing what plan?" He nods toward my phone, indicating the final words I said to Nico.

"I have another person for you to find."

He groans, rolling his head to the back of the chair. "Fuck, man, who now?"

I slide over an image I printed earlier from Nico's email. It's of a woman, probably around Ariella's age, if I had to guess. She's sitting outside on the edge of a water fountain, staring at the ground in front of her. Long black hair is tied back in a braid and her skin is a deep tan, totally opposite from the pictures I've seen of her sister.

"Her."

He whistles, his mouth turned down appreciatively. "Damn. But you already have one gorgeous woman on your arm. Really need another?"

"Smartass. Her name is Yasmine De Falco."

His brows dive and he taps the picture, right over her face. "De Falco. Like the guy behind Ariella's mother's death."

"The very one. That's his daughter."

"Okay?"

"Ariella had a connection with her. When all the shit went down with the Corsettis, De Falco left Yasmine in White Rock, British Columbia, with his people. Her sister is dating the Corsetti enforcer. Both she and Ariella are worried about her."

"His people," he repeats, eyes narrowing. "Who's De Falco's people?"

Everything Nico told me on the phone, I relay to him.

Everything about the Seven, an extremely powerful society within Canada, and the academy Yasmine's trapped inside.

At the end, Caladin whistles again and tosses the picture at me. "No."

"Too bad." He'll do this, without an order too, because he's intrigued if the gaze he has locked on Yasmine's picture is any indicator. Plus, he can never avoid such a chase. He lives for the thrill shit like this brings.

"Erico," he groans, "you want me to find this girl in some random private university in *Canada*, and what...bring her back here?"

"That's exactly what you'll be doing."

"That's Nico's country."

"Technically he has no hold over British Columbia. Either way, he gave the green light for us to pass over the border. He's very supportive of this, considering her sister bothers him all the time."

"So why is this our issue?"

"Because Ariella asked me to ask you. You said so yourself, you like my wife, so consider this a favour to her rather than me. Your *Famiglia* queen gave you an order."

His eyes narrow into slits before he reaches for the picture again, grumbling, "For her. Asshole." He stands. "Guess I have a plane to catch to western Canada, huh."

"Yes."

When my cousin walks away, he glances at the picture again. Rather than boredom or disdain, there's a look I know all too well. A look I've caught on my own face when I'm with Ariella.

Interest.

Curiosity.

A few minutes after he leaves, the door opens again and Ariella strides in. She comes right to my side and climbs on my lap, reminding me of the time she stormed her way in here, dripping with pool water and dry humped me.

"Hey. Just saw Caladin leave."

"He say anything to you?"

"He promised to find her."

"And he will."

She purses her lips. "You really trust him. He kinda seems more like a brother than a cousin."

"Basically," I agree. "When he was ten, his parents were shot, orphaning him. Mine took him in, so he spent the second half of his life here with us. Neither of us had siblings so it was just us. Lived together, trained together. He's younger than me, so he had to wait longer to be inducted, but when he was, we were a power duo."

She smiles. "That's...sweet, despite the sad start."

"My aunt and uncle were wonderful people. They were so in love." The model for what the emotion looked like, rather than my own parents. "Caladin wasn't the same for a long time afterwards. Despite that, he became a man I think they'd be proud of. He saved my life once too."

"Really?"

"He knocked me to the ground in time, and a bullet narrowly missed my head. I'd be dead if it wasn't for him."

She frowns, like simply hearing it is too much. "Then I have faith he'll find and protect Yasmine."

"There's no one better," I agree, linking my arms around her centre. "For now, what brought you in here?"

She shrugs a shoulder playfully, biting down on her bottom lip, which does little to taper her grin. "Just wanted to see you." She lifts her hands and signs, *I love you.*

As much as I hate not touching her, I do, signing back, *I love you too.*

"If you do, you'll do one more thing for me."

"Anything," I reply with the complete truth. This woman can request anything from me, and I'd do it.

"Fuck me over your desk."

"Happily. Because you command it."

Her giggle is her final sound before I have her panties shoved down, dress hiked up, and my cock in her tight, wet core, making her moan.

La mia sirena is all-consuming, exactly like the water she adores.

Thank you for reading! Finish the series with The Obscurity in Wishing (Fractured Ever Afters #6), an Aladdin inspired romance between Yasmine & Caladin.

Please note: if you were upset by the lack of answers regarding Ariella's fertility, it's much too early to be getting a solution. By the end of the series, I *promise* there is an answer.

Shop signed books by scanning the code below:

Remember Vanessa Volkov? She too has her own book. Check out Merciless Queen (The Bravta's Elite #1) and experience her

rise to power after her father's death—and the man who nearly
tears her down.

ALSO BY M.L. PHILPITT

Fractured Ever Afters

A 6-book (& 2 novellas) mafia romance series of interconnected standalones based on fairytales, featuring the Montreal mafia and the New York Famiglia.

The Desire in Deception (Prequel Novella)

The Hunt in Elusion

The Craving in Slumber

The Beauty in Scars

The Freedom in Captivity

The Sound in Silence

The Obscurity in Wishing

The Bonds in Christmas (Epilogue Novella)

The Bratva's Elite

A 4-book mafia series of interconnected standalones featuring the Russian Bratva.

Merciless Queen

Deadly Knight

Defensive Rook

Violent Pawn

Captive Writings

A new adult suspenseful romance series that progressively gets darker with each book

Ruthless Letters

Obsessive Messages

Vicious Texts

Burning Notes

Twisted Holidays

A series of dark romance holiday novellas

Silent Night

Egg Hunt

Fright Night

Be Mine

Midnight Kiss

Lucky Clover

Black Magick

A 5-book paranormal romance series of interconnected standalones featuring witches, vampires, shifters, mortals, and demons.

Dark Flame

Dark Mist

Dark Storm

Standalones

A Vampire for Christmas

Audiobooks

Silent Night

ACKNOWLEDGMENTS

First and foremost, thank you to YOU - my readers. I can't believe we only have one more book to go of this series!

To my betas: Megan, Colleen, & Lee Jacquot - Thank you!

Thank you to my editor Rebecca Barney from Fairest Reviews Editing Services. Another book down!

To Megan, my PA, who keeps me on track.

Thank you to The Next Step PR. Colleen, Megan, Anna, and of course, Kiki - you're all amazing. Thank you for everything you do. You're the best team to have!

Thank you to Cat Imb of TRC Designs for making me choke on my spit when I got your message with this cover's mock-up. I just about died seeing what I think became my favourite cover.

Thank you to all the bloggers, booktokers, and bookstagrammers who helped with the release of this book. Your help doesn't go unnoticed!

ABOUT THE AUTHOR

USA Today Bestselling author M.L. Philpitt writes both dark romance and paranormal romance. When she's not writing made-up realities, she's reading them. She lives in Canada with her four pets and survives life with coffee and an obsession with fictional characters, especially the morally grey kind. By day, she masks as a therapist.

WARNINGS

- Explicit sexual content
- Depictions of trauma
- Depictions of depression
- Depictions of grief
- Suicidal ideation (brief mention)
- Orgasm denial
- Murder
- Physical violence
- Infertility
- Recollection of parental death
- Recollection of fatal accident

www.ingramcontent.com/pod-product-compliance
Lightning Source LLC
Chambersburg PA
CBHW020330010826

48973CB00005B/1206

REVENGE OF THE FORBIDDEN LANDS

Gryphon Press

Published by Gryphon Press
Waterloo, Ontario

Copyright © 2024 by Alice Hanov

First Edition

Paperback: 978-1-998835-18-8
Hardcover: 978-1-998835-19-5
Special Hardcover: 978-1-998835-20-1
Ebook: 978-1-998835-17-1

Edited by Sam Pollock, S.E. Fleenor and Jaime Powell
Cover design by The Book Designers

For my readers,
Thank you for believing in me.

Dear Reader,

This extended edition of The Head, the Heart, and the Heir was created because my readers wanted these extra scenes, and I was happy to oblige.

I now understand the importance of being prepared when you read a book. While this book deals with coming of age, and feeling different from everyone around you, there are themes or memories that could be hard for people to read.

If you'd like a list of what exactly this book will touch on, (both warnings and tropes) please see my website, AliceHanov.com, or scan the code below with your phone.

Happy reading, and take care of yourself.

Alice

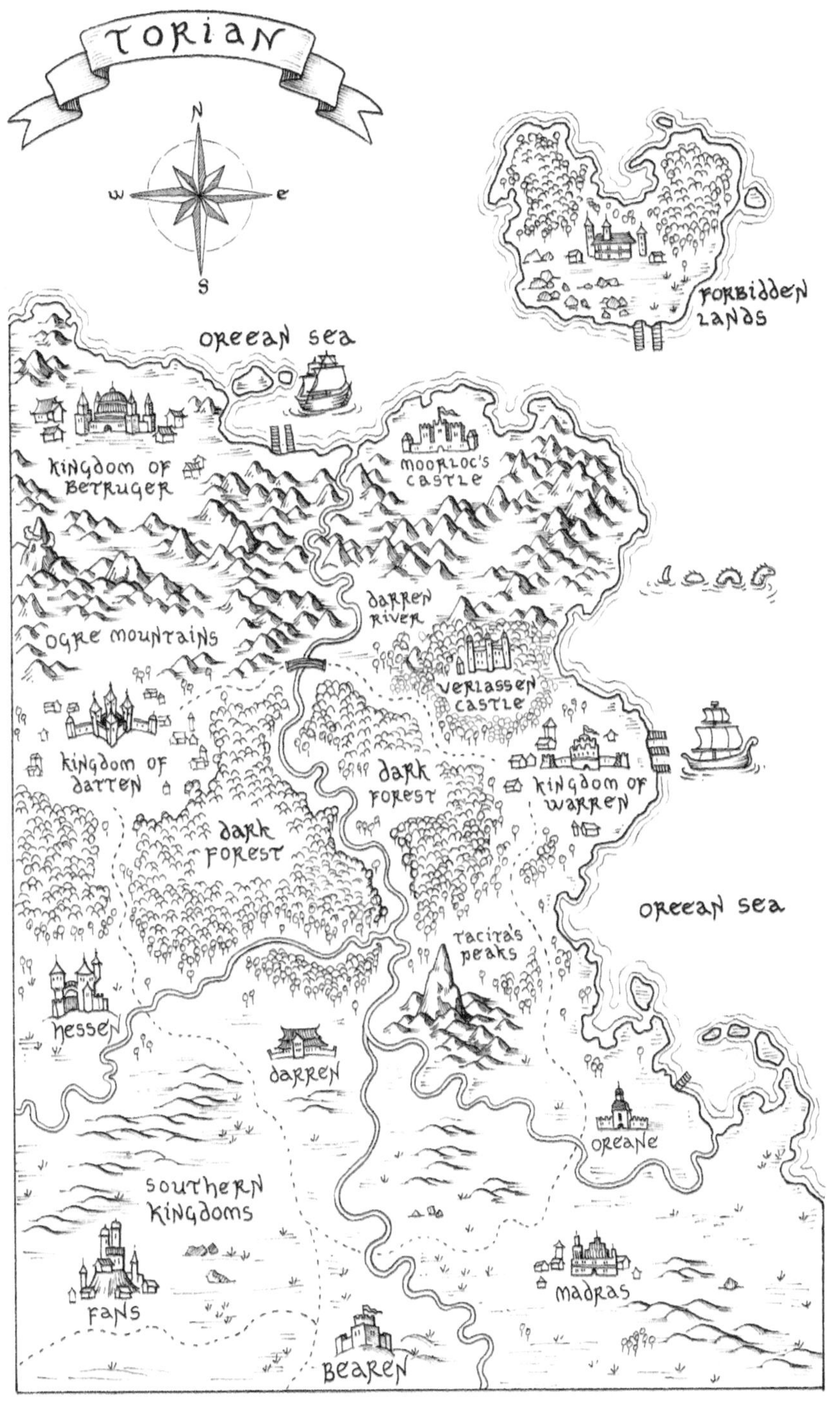

TORIAN
N
W E
S
OREEAN SEA
FORBIDDEN LANDS
KINGDOM OF BETRUGER
MOORLOC'S CASTLE
OGRE MOUNTAINS
DARREN RIVER
VERLASSEN CASTLE
KINGDOM OF DARREN
DARK FOREST
DARK FOREST
KINGDOM OF WARREN
HESSEN
TACITA'S PEAKS
OREEAN SEA
DARREN
OREANE
SOUTHERN KINGDOMS
FANS
BEAREN
MADRAS

Forbidden Lands
Salem
Cassandra
Merlin
Tiere
Ares
Celtics
Mire
Hades
Mystics
Poseidon
N

CHAPTER 1
ALEX

lex removed her braid, shaking out her long chestnut locks. They provided meager protection against the icy wind. During her childhood at the camp, the Ogre mountains had sent terrible storms, but those were nothing compared to what she and her companions faced on their journey to the labyrinth.

After ten days of traveling over mountains and through valleys, they had only traversed a paltry portion of the mountain range. The days were bitter, and the terrain was treacherous from all the ice, snow, and loose rocks. The nights were frigid and dark, and they struggled to keep their spirits up. They missed their loved ones, their beds, their lives. Each day, the Veremund map, was magically etched with green dashes tracing their path. It was in perfect condition, despite being passed through over thirty generations of Michael's family. It was both helpful and a stark reminder it would be a long time before they reached the labyrinth.

Edith and Michael had brought up the idea of Alex cracking them, but in this harsh landscape, the risk of ending up somewhere they shouldn't be or even inside the rocks was too great.

They remained on horseback, with Alex silently hating herself for failing them.

When they could ride no longer, they dismounted and hurried to make camp before they lost the light. Edith and Michael set up the tent and gathered wood for the fire Alex had already lit. Alex carefully surveyed the clearing. She twisted her hips forward, exhaled sharply, and brought her palms up, sprouting fully grown trees around their campsite. She'd been doing it every night to block the wind and provide shelter for the horses. As soon as the horses settled down, Alex set the fire roaring, threw blankets over the horses, and summoned water for them to drink. Edith had found a nice pile of wood for the fire and Michael had finished setting up their tent, leaving Alex in charge of food. She removed some dried venison and stale bread from their supplies. One of the trees she'd summoned was laden with apples. After giving some to the horses, she cut them into pieces and dropped them into the hot water simmering on the fire. It soon became fragrant, and she added some herbs and beat it with a spoon until it was thick like porridge.

They settled around the fire, warming themselves with cup after cup of the apple porridge Alex served to help take the chill off. Michael clutched the compass and peered at the map. His face had sprouted a bushy beard, and his thick black hair grew faster than the weeds in her garden back at Warren. She winced at the thought of home and then pushed it and the face of the man she loved from her mind.

Edith looked off into space, wrapped up in her cloak. The fire made her tan skin sparkle like the sand on Warren's beaches—all around them were reminders of what they'd left behind. Her sword leaned against the log next to her, illuminating the ground with its faint blue light.

Michael sighed and passed the book containing the map to

Alex. "It's taking longer than we hoped, but we are making progress."

Alex examined the book, twirling her hair absently. She had to be extra careful, as she'd developed the habit of using fire to warm her hands and didn't want to accidentally destroy the book holding the key to their quest. The green line that showed their progress only updated at night when they rested. Alex tried to determine the percentage of the trek they had made, but the way the line wound in and out and between rocks made it difficult.

Michael sneezed and Alex realized he was shivering. Edith was rocking and tightly clutching her blanket.

"You know I can make the fire hotter. You just have to ask."

"You were concentrating," Edith said, playing with her long, raven black hair. "We don't like to interrupt you when you focus that hard."

"What? How can you tell?"

Michael scooped more porridge into his bowl. "You scrunch your nose and sometimes stick out your tongue when you think too hard."

"I do not."

Edith laughed. "Sorry, but he's right."

"Stefan noticed it when you were around seven," Michael added.

Alex waved her hand, making the fire grow and warm the surrounding air. It had the added benefit of better illuminating the map and compass. She made an effort to keep her nose from scrunching. Tomorrow, they would reach a valley. The direction wasn't perfect, but it seemed to stretch a good distance. Alex leaned toward Michael and waved the map at him.

"What if we stick to this valley? It seems to have a river. Maybe the climate will be milder and the terrain easier on the horses."

"It's worth a shot," Edith said, taking a seat beside Alex. "I like the idea of not having to climb so high for a few days. I feel nause-ated being up here."

"Then we have a plan for tomorrow," Michael said. "Let's finish up our food and get some shuteye."

"Is it just me, or do you feel like Hestur is watching us?" Edith asked.

Alex looked back at the horses. Snow and Quiver were asleep on the ground, but Hestur remained standing.

"He's your betrothed's horse, and you took him," Michael said. "I think he's mad at you for leaving Harold behind." Michael stood up and brushed his pants off. "I'm ready for bed, so if you two want to change, I'd appreciate it if you could do it now."

"Alright, Michael," Alex teased. "We're going. When did you get so old that you need to go to bed so early?"

Edith snorted beside her. Michael opened his mouth to reply but Alex pointed her finger at him. "If you want any of your clothes washed and dried tomorrow morning, choose your words care-fully, Veremund."

"Playing the fresh clothes card! That's cruel." Michael clasped his chest, feigning injury. Edith and Alex laughed as they headed into the tent to get ready for bed.

THE THREE OF them shared one tent. Alex took the middle because of how long she'd known Michael. They weren't desperate for body heat, but they huddled together regardless.

Alex lay awake, squished between them, twirling her wedding ring. She didn't mind the sleeping arrangements. It was guilt keeping her awake. At night, it was impossible to keep Aaron's visage from her mind. She missed her husband so much it hurt. He'd been there for her when they learned about the labyrinth, and the existence of the scepter of the first king of Warren. He'd listened when she explained how Michael and her were taken to the Forbidden Lands, and learned what they'd need to do to save her from the fury.

And still she'd left him behind again. Guilt seeped into her soul, but she did not question her decision. There was no other way.

She hoped Jessica could explain her reasons well enough that he wouldn't be angry with her, or at least not for too long, and that Harold would forgive Edith. None of them had wanted to leave their loved ones, but the instructions in the Veremund's book were clear. The three of them–the heir to the throne of Warren and her Veremund and her Nial would have to enter the labyrinth. It was the only way she could get the king's scepter, which was supposed to hold a magical stone that would help her control the power of the fury—the goddess of revenge newly awakened inside of Alex fighting to gain control.

Deep inside, Alex knew she was losing to the fury, and this was her only hope. They all knew it, but she never spoke of it. She'd already committed two of the three crimes needed for the fury to take control of her: murder and spilling the blood of family. The fury wouldn't care her crimes were justified, or were out of her control. The only one that remained was betrayal. Whether the furies judged the kiss she'd shared with Gryphon to be a betrayal didn't matter, so long as Aaron never betrayed her.

Alex sighed and rolled over. *Aaron is too honorable to betray me.* Michael was snoring softly beside her, and the thought of him being away from Jessica in her condition brought on another wave of nauseating guilt. She stood and slipped out of the tent, letting the freezing night air punish her for the pain she always brought others. A different type of cold, gentler than the mountain air, engulfed her—*Daniel.* Aaron's late brother had protected her since the day he died. But ever since King Emmerich died, and Aaron became King of Datten, Daniel barely visited her. Alex guessed he had left the duty of her protection to his little brother.

"You know you aren't at fault for needing this scepter, so why are you punishing yourself?" Daniel asked.

Alex waved her hand, bringing the dying fire roaring back to life. The prince's blond hair caught the light of the dancing flames.

"Did you know Aaron's hair sparkles more than yours?" Alex asked.

Daniel narrowed his eyes.

"It does," she replied, crossing her arms. She kicked at the ground with her foot. The cold penetrated her nightclothes, even with the fire. "I know it's not my fault, but I have so much I still need to atone for: Reinhilde, lying to my father, losing the baby, failing the Betruger … and instead of doing that, I'm here looking for a magical scepter that my father thinks is a myth."

"Just because others cannot see what you do, doesn't make you wrong."

Alex chuckled. "You sound like your mother. I thought Aaron was supposed to take after her and you took after Emmerich."

"We each have our moments."

"Thank you, Daniel. I miss having Emmerich and Randal to talk to. Jerome is wonderful, but he doesn't hold on to guilt as much as I do, and Matthew only had sons. He doesn't understand the differences between us the way Randal does, and nobody understands the pressures of being born a royal destined for the throne the way Emmerich did."

"My father is happy to continue talking with you once he figures out how to come back to the world of the living."

"Ghosts have to learn that?"

"Of course we do. Why do you think it took me so long to come to you?" Daniel asked, giving her the smirk he shared with his brother. "You should go back to bed. I'll make sure everyone back home knows you three are alright."

"Thank you, Daniel," Alex whispered before she crept back into the tent to sleep.

CHAPTER 2
AARON

Aaron swirled the ale in his cup and stared into the roaring fire. He'd had the sitting room redecorated while they were in Warren for Edith and Harold's engagement party. His father had used this room to make his battle plans, but now, the walls that had once been lined with weapons and shields were covered with bookcases, and his father's war table was in storage. He'd styled the room after Alex's room in Warren, except the couches were the royal family's shade of red instead of gold. Moorloc had forced her to wear gold, the line color of Cassandra, every day, and Aaron didn't want her reminded of her time there.

He stood to refill his ale from the pitcher on the small writing table. He'd thrown tradition aside and brought the desk from Victoria's bedroom at the Verlassen Castle. That way, Alex would have something of her mother here, in Datten. With a full mug of ale, Aaron plopped down onto the couch and racked his brain, going over the events of the days before the party. *There must have been something, some warning I missed. Maybe if I'd paid more attention to her, or if I hadn't left her, or if I'd never gotten myself cursed and ruined our relationship.* Going to help his wife and friends was out of the question, so instead, he sat there worrying.

He took a gulp and his blond hair fell over his eyes. He needed a shave and a haircut, but he didn't care. The afternoon after she'd left—once they'd confirmed where she'd gone and with whom—he'd been ready to charge off after her. Jessica and Randal had put a stop to that.

He'd never felt so powerless. Harold sulked around the castle, wounded that his betrothed would leave him like this. Jessica kept busy helping Guinevere and making plans for the baby she and Michael were expecting. While it was still a long way off, Jessica was so excited she was preparing early, as any good Wafner would.

Aaron read Alex's letter over one more time, trying to calm himself. He played the part of the understanding, powerful king during the day, but at night, alone in the room, he'd set up specially for her; he felt every bit the unworthy husband, who couldn't do anything to protect his wife.

My dearest Aaron,

I know when you receive this letter, you will panic and everything will seem horrible, but please understand there was no other way. If I could've brought you, I would have, but everything we read said only one heir from the Nial, Warren, and Veremund line could travel to find the labyrinth. If any others came with us, we'd never find it.

I can feel the fury inside of me. I didn't know what it was before, but I've felt it since I returned from Moorloc's, since I ... well, since I did what I had to in order to survive there. If there is any chance we can get this under control, we have to do it, because I don't know if I'm strong enough to keep the monster at bay forever.

I am sorry I misled you. I promise to not be reckless, and to take every precaution.

Forever yours,

Alex

AARON SIGHED, refolded the letter, and returned it to the desk.

"I know you did what you had to, and that I couldn't come with you, but I wish I didn't blame myself for why you kept it from me. The cursed me was horrible, but the true me ... I would have let you go and I would have fought your father for you if we had to."

Aaron closed his eyes and pressed his knuckles against the desk. An icy chill surrounded him. He glanced around, but could find no source of the cold.

"Daniel?"

He turned around, but there was no one there. "Daniel or Father, if you're here and you know she's okay, give me a sign. Do anything you can. I just need to know she's safe."

There was a bang, and he spun back to the desk to see the chair had been thrown over and Alex's letter was on the floor in front of it. As he crept toward it, the entire room turned ice cold. When he picked up the letter and chair, the cold was immediately gone.

"Thank you," he whispered and headed up to bed.

. . .

THE RISING sun sent little streams of light through the windows, illuminating the stairwell. Determination drummed through Aaron as he stalked up the stairs to the third floor toward Harold's suite. With Edith gone, he didn't bother to knock and walked right into Harold's bedroom. Harold was staying in the most luxurious guest suite they had. The fireplace in the corner gave off a faint glow. When Aaron's eyes adjusted to the darkness, the giant King of the Betruger came into focus sprawled across the bed with one leg hanging off the side, his blankets a jumbled mess. Aaron chuckled. He, himself, had slept in the same position his whole life, and only when Alex joined him, did he stop his nightly roaming of the entire bed. He marched over to his sleeping friend and smacked his back before leaping out of harm's way.

Harold kicked his leg out and bolted upright, ready to fight. In the dim light, his violet eyes almost glowed, and his black hair all but vanished. He jerked his head, searching the room until his eyes locked onto Aaron. Aaron shot him a smirk from his place against the wall.

The Betruger king rubbed his eyes, presumably to make sure Aaron was actually there. "Why?"

"We have work to do, Your Royal Sleepiness," Aaron replied.

Harold dragged himself out of bed and stumbled to the balcony door, pulling back the curtains to see the early dawn light barely peeking over the horizon. "And what work do we have that couldn't wait for our sun to come up?"

"We've sulked enough. Today, you and I are going to act like the fearsome kings we are, and make our loves proud. Get dressed and meet me in the library. I'll have breakfast brought to us so we aren't interrupted."

"Fine," Harold groaned and Aaron hurried out of the room.

Aaron ran into Caleb on the stairs, and sent him off to retrieve Macht and Jerome, and then have breakfast brought to the library for all of them. In the library, Aaron wandered the shelves, grabbing books on Datten training techniques and the surviving Betruger books referencing training and warfare.

Soon enough, Jerome and Macht arrived carrying food. Jerome glanced at Aaron's piles of books and then at Aaron, a curious sparkle in his eyes. Aaron gave him only a mischievous grin in response.

The general groaned, helping himself to a crusty roll and dried venison. Aaron chuckled and grabbed a venison sausage off the platter of dried meats, fruit, and bread. The three men ate in silence until Harold arrived. He grunted a greeting and dropped himself onto a chair and took a sunflower roll. Aaron snorted at Harold. Like the rest of the men in the room, the two kings hadn't been in the mood for formalities. They both wore their simple sparring clothes.

Jerome was the first to speak up. "Alright, Aaron, you wanted us all here before the knights even started training. What is on your mind?"

Harold grumbled. "Besides having nothing better to do while missing his wife?"

Macht growled a warning at his king. Harold groaned and sat up properly to focus on Aaron. He reached across the table and pulled the Betruger books toward him.

Aaron shrugged. "Harold's right. I can't sleep while Alex is out there in the cold mountains searching for this labyrinth. Knowing I can't help her is infuriating, so instead, I've decided to be productive and start working on the things we wanted to do to make Datten more progressive."

Jerome and Harold shifted in their seats. "What did you have in mind?" Jerome asked.

"Alex and I have had a lot of conversations about what we'd like to do in Datten, but we wanted to give our people time to adjust to the Betruger being here and celebrate Harold and Edith's engagement. Now that everyone is settled and excited for the wedding, I want to move forward with our first plan, and I need your help."

"Aaron, I'm your general. I'll do anything you ask of me."

"If you give me your word that you won't wake me up as you did this morning ever again, Macht and I are at your disposal," Harold said.

"Right now, our men train together," Aaron said. "I want to go beyond that—complete integration of our guards and armies. Datten already has Warren men in our guard, and the Warrens have ours. Including Betruger men would be good for all of us, as the men will share skills and knowledge. It also would give your men something to do until we find a place to rebuild your kingdom."

Harold's brows furrowed as he looked from Aaron to Macht and back. "I think that's a great idea. Our men have adjusted well, but they grow restless. Allowing them into your guard and army will keep them fit until we can rebuild."

Aaron grinned. "I also want to bring Randal to Datten to organize the logistics. He'll be the Warren man. We'll also need one man each from Datten and Betruger. It wouldn't be fair unless a member from each guard has a say, and with three making decisions, there can't be a stalemate, which will speed up the process."

Jerome shifted in his chair.

Aaron narrowed his eyes. "To ensure this goes smoothly, I *insist* you all speak your mind."

Jerome grunted. "While I applaud your desire to help the former General Nial regain some of his honor after Edward removed his rank and title, I worry about giving him such an important role when your relationship with your godfather is already strained."

Aaron snorted. "Edward's going to hate me for the foreseeable future because of what happened between me and Alex when I was cursed."

"And afterward. You threw him out of Datten!"

"I had no choice. He struck Alex when she interfered with his one-sided fight with Randal."

"It was not an honorable match," Macht said.

"Exactly. But more importantly, I'm not afraid of Edward, because Alex agrees with me. She wants Randal to have a job that gives him purpose. She believes fate made him leave that day, and that without her mother's tragic death, she would not have the sorceress powers and skills she does today. So I will risk enraging the King of Warren, in order to keep the Queen of Datten and the future Queen of the Betruger happy."

"Edith misses her parents terribly when she's here," Harold said. "She'd be delighted for Randal to come to Datten."

"And in this role, he'll have rank in Datten. Eventually he'll be able to choose the kingdom he wishes to reside in. If that happens to be Betruger, Alex and I would allow it."

Harold dropped his elbows to the table and rubbed the sleep from his eyes. "You planned this!"

Aaron grinned. "Alex deserves the credit. We planned it as soon as we realized you were serious about pursuing Edith, though, at the time, I didn't know how I'd get Randal to give up the title of General of Warren."

"You're using this situation with Edward to get what you what," Macht said.

"Your father would be impressed," Jerome said. "He'd also be pleased to have the Betruger share their knowledge with our men. Our combined skills will make us all stronger."

Harold nodded. "Datten, Warren, or Betruger could easily handle an attack from any southern kingdoms without relying on the others. The bigger threat comes from these sorcerers. We have no way of knowing when they'll attack again. We need to train for *that*. There isn't enough red steel to equip every man."

"We'll ask Birch and Gryphon to provide insight into what we can do to stop them," Aaron said.

"Do you trust him?" Macht asked.

"I trust Gryphon will do everything he can to keep Alex safe and happy. And a safe kingdom to raise our family would make her very happy."

"Very well. When would you like to summon Megesti?" Jerome asked.

"Summon him? How does that work?" Harold asked.

"When my brother died, Megesti pledged an oath to always be there for me. If I'm in grave danger or need him, I can summon him by calling him. He still thinks I didn't know about it, but really, I knew better than to abuse the power."

"Your family is very tied to sorcerers," Macht said.

"I can't help who I love. My great-grandfather welcomed Merlock and Victoria here with open arms so it's in my blood to trust them."

Harold smiled. "After meeting Megesti and Alex, I have to agree with you. Merlock also seemed very competent before he gave himself up to save Alex."

"Alright. We'll make a list of men we think would be a great fit working with the other kingdom's men, and then I'll summon Megesti at a more reasonable hour," Aaron said. He laughed at the scowl Harold gave him.

CHAPTER 3

ALEX

Alex stopped her horse before a tree that looked familiar, much too familiar.

"What's wrong?" Edith asked as she and Michael moved their horses beside her.

"I've seen this tree."

"In a vision?" Michael asked.

"No. Yesterday," Alex said. "I feel like we're walking in circles."

"But we're following the map," Edith said.

"See, we're right here." Michael held the book out to Alex. She looked from it to Michael's face and then back to the book.

"Michael!" she groaned.

"What?"

"It's upside down." Alex covered her face with her hand and Edith burst out laughing.

Don't scream at Michael. You might set something on fire.

"No!" Michael flipped the book around to check and by the time Alex moved her hand his entire face was as red as a Datten tunic. "I'm sorry, Alex—"

"Michael, stop!" Alex shouted. Edith straightened on her horse, gripping the reins tighter, while Michael clutched the book to him. Alex took a deep breath before responding. "I'm not mad at you, just frustrated at the situation."

"You're allowed to be frustrated, Alex," Edith said. "It's been a long journey, and expressing your feelings is good for you."

"Edith's right. You can't keep things bottled up all the time. I know asking for help is hard for you, but you need to tell us what you need. We can't read your mind like Gryphon can."

"I do tell you, Michael."

"Exactly, you *only* tell Michael," Edith said. "You need to build that trust with the rest of us."

Especially Aaron. Alex exhaled and clutched her horse's reins. *How can I tell him what I need and what I'm comfortable with if I can't confide in him?*

Michael grinned. "If it makes you feel better you can push me off my horse."

"I'm not going to push you, Michael," Alex laughed. "I'm not ten anymore."

"So you'll just put a snake in my bed?"

"Of course not. We share a bed! So much for Veremund cleverness." Alex chuckled.

"I AM *NOT* WEARING a blue wedding dress." Edith giggled.

"Why not? Do the Betruger hate blue as much as Alex does?" Michael asked.

"No," Edith said, dismounting her horse. "Harold told me it's a tradition for brides to wear a purple or yellow gown. Yellow is more common while darker purple is reserved for royalty."

"So, you'll be in violet?" Alex asked, finally joining the conversation.

"Violet and yellow, since it's Harold's favorite color. Did you find a good place to make camp for the night?"

"I did. There is a cave ahead so we can get away from this nasty wind." Alex closed the book with the map and pointed a short walk away where a large rock stuck out of the mountain. When they arrived, Michael took the duty of brushing and feeding the horses while Alex and Edith set up the fire and laid out the sleeping mats.

"I'm glad we don't need the tent tonight," Edith said. "The wind has been freezing the last few nights."

"I know. Your chattering teeth woke me up," Alex said. "I wanted to make sure we were somewhere extra warm tonight."

Edith dropped her mat and hugged Alex. "Can you make the fire extra warm, too?" Alex nodded, making Edith smile even bigger. "For that you can have my share of bread!"

"Don't make promises you don't want to keep." Alex laughed.

They set up the fire and sleeping area together while Michael left to find food. He returned with a hare. Michael skinned it while Alex heated the water so they could make a stew. Having fresh food put them all in good spirits, even with Michael's map fiasco a few days before. A night with full bellies and a warm roof above their heads made things feel normal.

After they'd cleaned up and settled onto their mats, Edith asked for a story. "Tonight, I want to hear how you came to trust Michael in the camp."

"She found me covered in blood and brought me home," Michael said. "Typical child behavior."

Edith chuckled. "I know *how* she found you. I want to know what you did that made her trust you unconditionally. For Julius and myself, it was a night when I was nine. I had a fight with my sisters, and decided to run away from home. Taking nothing actually useful, I set out in the middle of the day while my mother had tea with Julius's mother. He noticed me sneaking out of the house and followed me. He didn't tell my parents, but came with me to make sure I was safe. By the time we got to his estate, he'd convinced me to stay, but to this day he's never told any of our parents."

"A knight who kept a secret from his general?" Michael smirked. "That is worth keeping."

"Graham," Alex said, groaning. "I trust Michael because of what he did to Graham."

Edith sat up straight and glanced back and forth between Alex and Michael.

"Do you want to start or should I?" Alex asked.

"When Alex was seven, I decided she needed to learn some more fighting skills."

"*You* thought this?" Edith narrowed her eyes at Michael.

"I was pretty scrawny when I was little," Alex said. "At that age, Stefan was more focused on my escaping skills."

"As I was saying … " Michael looked pointedly at Edith and Alex, making them still. "I wanted Alex to learn to protect herself better. So, I taught her to punch, and after that, we moved to the bow."

"Stefan thought he was wasting his time. I was terrible with a bow."

"So years of practice is what made you better?" Edith asked.

"That, and wind magic," Michael said, nudging Alex with his shoulder. "But Alex is right—her aim was terrible at the start. We practiced in the forest, well away from our friends to keep everyone safe, but Graham wouldn't listen to anyone, and worse—"

"Worse, he took pleasure in terrifying me!" Alex interjected. "He was sick in the head because he was never happy unless he was making someone else miserable!"

"Anyway, he snuck into the woods and jumped out to scare Alex—"

"I gave him an arrow in the thigh," Alex finished.

Edith gasped. "Oh no."

"And he was mad," Alex said. "He ripped the arrow out of his leg and came after me."

"I should mention Stefan was in town with Ian getting supplies. Usually he took Alex with him, but she'd begged to stay back and practice with me. He'd reluctantly agreed."

"What happened?" Edith asked. Eyes wide, she clutched her blanket closer.

"My scar is gone, but he took the bloody arrow and tried to stab me in the arm with it," Alex said. "The moment Michael saw my blood, something in him snapped and he became another person."

"A Veremund," Edith snickered.

Michael shrugged. "I went after Graham."

"He broke his nose!" Alex said. "Michael punched him in the face so hard, Graham's nose was never straight again. When he began to fight back, Michael slammed him into a tree and told him if he ever laid a finger on me, he wouldn't walk again."

"How old were you?" Edith asked Michael.

"Nine. But Stefan had been training me since I was seven."

"What did Stefan say?"

Alex turned to Michael, and he shrugged. "We never told Stefan," Alex replied. "Graham said he fell out of a tree and that's how he hurt his leg and broke his nose."

"Stefan suspected Alex or I pushed him out of the tree," Michael added.

"I did have a nasty habit of pushing people out of trees when I was young."

"But he couldn't prove anything, so in time everyone forgot."

"Everyone but Graham. He hated me until the day I left," Alex said. "Even before that day, Michael could sense things, like how Gryphon can read my emotions. We've always had that connection. Clearly it's because of who we are. Stefan always knew when I was upset, but it took him more work to figure out why, like Aaron. Graham's lucky that happened when I was seven. Once I got my powers, things that really bothered me were just set on fire."

"If that's true, then why haven't you set Wesley on fire yet?" Michael asked, making Edith giggle.

"He's not worth the magic. I can just punch him," Alex replied.

"You could use that on Stefan and Aaron, too," Edith said.

Alex snorted with laughter. "Hopefully, when I get back, Aaron and Stefan will be in a listening mood."

"And if not?" Michael asked.

"Then I'll use my plant magic to tie them to a chair and force them to listen."

Alex and Edith laughed, but Michael sighed, gazing into the fire. "I'm sorry I held the map wrong."

Alex threw her arms around Michael and hugged him.

"We already forgave you, Michael. Stop beating yourself up," Edith said.

"I know, but I added two days to our journey."

"It's fine." Alex squeezed him harder. "Without it, we wouldn't have found this cave, and I think we all needed a night in the warmth to lift our spirits."

"I know I did," Edith said.

"How are you feeling?" Michael asked.

Alex released him, bit her cheek, and let herself go quiet for a moment. Deep inside her, something unfamiliar stirred. A combination of heart break and the stomach ache she'd get when they were hungry in the woods. The times where even the thought of food made her ache. But this pain seemed to come from her soul. "The fury is getting restless, but I have her under control."

"Good," Michael said. Alex heard the relief in his voice.

"I think it's time for sleep. We should take advantage of this warm cave to get a nice long sleep," Edith said.

CHAPTER 4

GRYPHON

Gryphon stomped along the path beside the boxes of plants in Victoria's rooftop garden in the Verlassen Castle. He hadn't bothered to tie up his burnt orange robe, so it trailed behind him like an annoying tail, occasionally tangling on his leg. Scratching his head, he turned in a circle looking for the herb he'd come up for.

"How are they out of wormroot? It's a staple in so many potions."

"Well, you haven't stopped trying spells since Alex left, so that's probably why," Megesti said from across the roof. Holding up a jar, he crossed the garden and held it out to Gryphon. It was stuffed with wormroot.

Gryphon wasn't ready to admit it out loud yet, but he saw his adopted cousin as family. His own biological family were horrible monsters, and being tied to Birch and Megesti was the best gift Gryphon had ever received.

"You're not the only one who misses her," Megesti said, straightening his dull gray robe. He looked exhausted. His usually neat brown hair was in complete disarray and his emerald eyes had lost their shine. Like Alex's, their color dulled when he wasn't feeling his usual self.

"I know I'm not," Gryphon snapped.

"Well, you act as if you're the only one who cares about her. We're all scared for her, Aaron especially."

"I'm well aware of what Aaron thinks of Alex. Or have you forgotten that until recently, I had the unfortunate pleasure of reading his mind."

"You never did anything to stop it."

"I didn't know I could!" Gryphon replied. "Unlike you and Alex, I haven't read Merlin's journals repeatedly, and while we have historical records of a few powerful sorcerers bonding twice, the details were not written down."

Megesti stepped up to Gryphon. Despite being a few inches shorter, the power of his glare reminded Gryphon so much of Alex that he squirmed. "Aaron's my best friend," Megesti said, "and for a year, Alex was the only family I had. I will not let you come between them."

"I have no intention of causing any trouble for them. I just want to make sure she's safe."

Megesti narrowed his eyes and stared for a minute longer than Gryphon would have liked. "We should get to the lab. Birch is waiting for those." He turned and headed toward the stairs.

Gryphon summoned his courage. "Are you ever going to call her mother? Because she is, and I *know* it's hard for Alex to watch you push your mother away after being given another chance at getting to know her."

"I don't need your input on my relationships. If I ever decide to call Birch that, I shall. But right now, it's strange for me. I spent my entire life thinking she was dead."

"As someone who spent my life wishing my mother was dead because she was a monster, you're lucky you still have a mother, and an amazing one. The fact you didn't know about her isn't Birch's fault, so try not to take that out on her."

The two walked down the stairs in silence, neither one looking at the other. The lab was all the way in the basement. When they reached the second floor, Gryphon gave up and cracked himself there. *Let Megesti work on getting around. He needs the practice.*

Lynx looked up from the cauldron she was stirring. "What did you do? Lock him on the roof?"

"No." Gryphon placed the jar on the shelf near the fire. "I left him on the second floor."

"As long as you didn't hurt him. We're all worried about Alex, and fighting among ourselves won't help."

"I'd never hurt him. He's my family, too. Who would I pester if he was gone?"

Lynx shook her head and turned back to the potion. She usually left her flowing dirty blonde hair down to fly around her face. Working with spells was the only time she put her hair up. She was as wild as you'd expect the Titan of Tiere to be.

All of Gryphon's friends were now Titans. His aunt Birch was for Celtics, his old tutor Kharon was for Hades, Alex was Cassandra, and Megesti was for Merlin. Maybe growing up the Head's only son had something to do with it.

"How can I be surrounded by so many powerful and talented titans and yet Alex evades us for weeks?" Gryphon asked, raising his hands in frustration.

"Because she's not only a titan, but the Heart, and an exceptionally intelligent princess," Kharon said from the corner. Gryphon hadn't even noticed they were there, since their gray robes blended in with the stone walls.

Gryphon crossed his arms and smiled at his old instructor. "A fair assessment of Alex."

"Stefan would also add that she's incredibly sneaky," Lynx said.

"Must you bring him up in every conversation?"

"Yes." Lynx flicked the wooden spoon she'd been using to stir the potion at him.

The thick liquid sizzled when it struck his robe and arm. His Salem powers dissipated the heat before he could even register it. "Do you think it's ready?" Gryphon asked, peeking into the cauldron.

"Has it turned blue yet?" Birch asked, arriving with Megesti. "If you want to harness the power of a Mystics sorcerer without being one, it has to be cerulean or sapphire, like your robes."

"It's ... sort of blue," Lynx said.

Gryphon glanced at the sludge and groaned. "That is not blue. That's a grayish teal."

"So we try again," Lynx said.

"Seventh time's the charm," Kharon said from the corner.

Gryphon closed his eyes and roared in frustration, making the room fall silent. The bubbles popping in the cauldron and the fire crackling were the only sounds. He didn't even have to open his eyes to know he was glowing orange. His temper always brought out his Ares powers.

Birch pulled him into a hug and he immediately felt more grounded. "We're all worried, but I understand how truly terrifying this is for you. Your connection with Alex makes you feel everything surrounding her so much more intensely, and being a Mystics sorcerer who cannot see what's going on must feel like torture." Gryphon squeezed her back, and she kissed his cheek. "I think we should all get some sleep and start fresh tomorrow. We've been working on one potion or another since she left and we're all exhausted."

Gryphon reluctantly agreed to go to bed. Alone in his room, he stripped off his dirty robe and dropped it on the floor. Once he had his sleeping pants on, he sat on the edge of his bed, trying to reach into Alex, Michael, and Edith's minds one after another, repeatedly until his head pounded so hard he felt nauseated. Frustrated at his failure, he stood and paced the room, trying to decide what to do next, when an idea hit him. When the fireplace roared to life, he stopped pacing and leaned against the mantle.

"You were clever enough to keep me out of your head, but were you clever enough to keep me out of your dreams?"

Gryphon stared into the fire and opened his well just enough to feel his Mystics powers erupt. The blue light he emitted mixed with the fire's maroon glow, illuminating the floor in purple. At the window Gryphon focused on the moon and thought of Alex. Closing his eyes, he slowed his breathing and felt himself shift, as if part of him had left his body.

His eyes snapped open, and he found himself in a forest. Frustration and anger pooled in his stomach. *Why am I angry?* He spun at the sound of footsteps, only to see a familiar face glaring at him. The man was younger and not as muscular, but Stefan's scowl was unmistakable. Beside him was a scrawny, beardless Michael, and together they glanced up into the old oak tree beside them. Gryphon's gaze followed theirs, and even with his chaotic emotions, he couldn't help but smile.

Acorns flew at Stefan's head, but he batted them away. "Alex, stop that, and get down here, right now!"

"No." Despite being a tiny little thing, she was as defiant as ever.

"Alexandria, I am warning you," Stefan growled.

Another acorn flew at his head.

Michael sighed and looked cautiously at Stefan. "Go back to camp. Let me talk to her. You know she doesn't open up to you when she's upset."

Stefan didn't say anything for a long while before nodding. "Make sure you're both back for dinner," he said before shouting up into the tree, "or else you won't be eating tonight."

Stefan stormed away through the woods and Michael leaned

against the tree until he was gone. "It's okay. You can come down now."

Branches shook and a barrage of acorns and leaves fell. A moment later, Alex dropped out of the branches and landed on her feet. She brushed her hands against her pants and stood up.

"So, why are you hiding?" Michael asked.

"I wasn't hiding," Alex sniped. "Sometimes I want to be alone."

When Alex turned away from Michael and headed right for him, Gryphon's frustration intensified. *I'm feeling your emotions. That isn't normal for Mystics while dream walking. Could it be the bond?*

She couldn't have been more than eleven years old, but she was already fierce and beautiful. She brushed past him and Michael chased after her. Gryphon chuckled and followed them.

"If you aren't hiding, then where have you been disappearing to nearly every day for the last few months? You always tell Stefan you're with me, and I'm tired of covering for you when I don't know what's going on."

Alex stopped walking and her cheeks flushed. "I've been practicing."

"Practicing?" Michael asked.

"That's my little Heart." Gryphon laughed, knowing they couldn't hear him.

"So I don't ruin anything else," Alex whispered, and a sudden wind sent leaves flying. Gryphon covered his face, and when he looked back, they were in the Verlassen Castle's main room. It was a mess, and a vortex was spinning in the room.

Aaron, Stefan, Michael and a group of guards were on the outside of the vortex shouting. Gryphon crossed the room and entered the raging wind. Alex stood against her uncle, screaming at him, until power burst out of her. Wind threw her uncle backward, and Alex dropped to the ground before him. Her cry pierced through the chaos of the room, and she ripped away from Moorloc.

In her wake, Stefan was left slumped on the floor with a torch sticking out of his chest. The room vanished.

"This looks familiar," Gryphon said at the sight of the beach by Moorloc's castle materializing before him. Alex stood on the beach, trying to get her stance right. Gryphon watched himself examine her before he corrected her position and stepped back. The soft glow that had accompanied Alex those first days of learning to wield her magic made him smile. He watched the memory from her point of view, feeling the fear and frustration every time she failed, and the elation when she got it right.

He stayed in her dreams far longer than he'd intended, swept up in the wave of emotions he would have to sort through. When she dreamed about training with Megesti, working to master their spells, heartache and longing invaded every part of him. Soon, though, he felt guilty for having invaded this memory, and ended his time in her head.

Back in his room, he flicked his wrist to revive the fire. "When I was gone, you didn't just miss my teaching, you missed *me*. Seems like there's hope for us yet, Princess."

CHAPTER 5

ALEX

Taking the route through the valley proved to be a brilliant decision. It was easier on the horses, and when the sun peeked through the clouds, Alex could crack them ahead small distances, without fear of ending up in a tree or large rocks. It allowed them to gain ground during the day. Here, the nights were not as cold as up in the mountains, and they spent a little longer talking at the fire, enjoying their food and each other's company. In the weeks they'd been traveling, Alex and Michael regaled Edith with stories about their adventures in the camp, and she in turn told of the mischief she got into with Julius, and the aftermath of the trouble she witnessed when Aaron and Cameron got caught sneaking out of the stables when they were teens.

At the end of an exceptionally long day, Alex was fatigued. The sun had stayed out for hours allowing her to crack them often, and it had drained her. Even Edith and Michael noticed. They refused to eat more than one portion and demanded Alex eat the extra porridge. Smoked meat was delicious, but they'd run out of bread and Alex missed it. Despite her exhaustion, she'd quickly sprouted the trees and fire, so while Michael and Edith tended to the horses, she had a moment to sit by the fire with the map before her. *Twenty-two days of riding, and we're almost on top of it. I wonder if we'll find it tomorrow or the next day.*

"Acorn for your thoughts?" Michael asked from beside her.

"Acorn?" Edith asked, dropping on the ground beside Alex.

Alex smiled and explained. "We didn't have money in the camp, so we used acorns. They were Michael's and my currency of sorts. You could use them to trade chores, or get an extra piece of cheese and such. Basically, favors in physical form."

"That's adorable."

Michael cleared his throat, and Alex turned to find an acorn in front of her nose. She scoffed in shock and took it from Michael. "How do you have one? There are no oak trees here."

"I always keep one or two on me, just in case I need to strike a deal with you. So, what are you thinking?"

Alex twirled the acorn between her thumb and index finger. "We still have a long way to go to get to the labyrinth, and we don't even know how to find the entrance. The book says nothing about what it looks like."

"I assumed the compass would lead us," Edith said.

Michael dug through his satchel, removing random things: Stefan's knife, some handkerchiefs, bandages, extra hair ties, and a small painting of Jessica. Finally, he pulled the compass out and flipped the top open. Alex and Edith leaned over to watch the needle swing back and forth. Eventually it settled, pointing westward.

"Good to know it works," Edith said with a grin. "I wonder how far away we really are." She slid the book from Alex's lap into hers and examined it.

"I bet we'll find it within three days," Michael said. "And that Alex will be the one to find it."

"Oh, and why is that?" Alex asked. Edith scowled, and Alex tried not to laugh.

"It's magical, and you're magical. Won't you be drawn to it?"

"I never considered that," Alex said. "I know Gryphon is drawn to power. Maybe I need to try using my Ares powers the way he does. That's how he finds me sometimes, which is why I avoid using my powers too much here."

"We understand," Edith said, handing the book back and rubbing her hands together before the fire.

"We're so close now," Michael said. "The last thing we need is one of them showing up and keeping us from finding the labyrinth."

"It isn't as if Aaron listens or respects your boundaries," Edith said.

"He is trying. Part of the issue is I don't know how to tell him what they are." She paused for a few moments, scrunching her nose. "Or ... even what they are in the first place."

"Jessica and I simply discuss whatever bothers us and find a solution we are both happy with," Michael said.

"The sounds very ... Wafner." Edith giggled. "I'm a little more subtle with my family. I have spent years getting my mother and sisters to adhere to my requests for space without them even noticing they are doing it."

"I wish I knew what I needed from him. I don't know."

"And that's fine," Michael said. "The beauty of having someone who respects your boundaries is that it allows them to change as needed. You might not have very many today but that might change, and as long as you two are open and honest about what you need, you'll be fine."

Edith bumped Alex's shoulder with hers. "Did he believe you about the scepter being real?"

"When it comes to magic, Aaron always trusts me. But I'm still worried. We don't know what I'll become if we don't find it."

Edith wrapped her arms around Alex. "I don't care if you're a princess, a sorceress, a fury, or if you turn green and grow horns. You're my friend forever."

Michael nudged her. "And you're my family. As the oldest and wisest here, I suggest we go to bed. Who knows? We might find the labyrinth tomorrow, and we'll want all the energy we can gather to face whatever awaits us there."

ONCE AGAIN, Edith and Michael fell asleep quickly but Alex couldn't turn off her thoughts. All her regrets and fears were swirling together, making sleep impossible. Hoping for another visit from Daniel, she pulled on her pants, cloak, and boots and crept out of the tent. The wind whipped around the tent and burned icy against her cheeks, forcing her to bundle against it. She walked toward the trees surrounding the camp, her route taking her past the horses.

Snow raised his head and snorted, calling her to him. "I'll be careful," she said. She rubbed his face, and Snow laid his head back down. She slipped away between two trees.

Outside of their camp, it was pitch dark, so she summoned an orb of light and took her first step away from her friends. The wind was brutally cold, but she wouldn't be deterred and kept walking. Thinking of her mother, she closed her eyes and felt for her well. *Maybe Edith and Michael are right. Maybe my magic can find the labyrinth if I just let my power out.* Warmth covered her and an orange glow burst through the darkness of her closed eyes. Her Ares power swirled through her and Alex took a step forward, and then another, and another. Without opening her eyes, she journeyed onward, trusting her power to get her where she needed to go. She wandered for several minutes before she finally opened her eyes to find she'd lost track of where the camp was. Her stomach churned at the idea of being lost alone on this mountain. She clenched her fists and focused on her breathing to control the panic threatening to burst from her.

Something grabbed her.

Alex shrieked and spun on the balls of her feet, thrusting her arms before her. Fire erupted from her palms, illuminating Michael's face, but he knew enough to jump back. When he was a boy, he'd been thrown flat on his back enough times whenever he'd scared her. Back then, her wind powers had protected her from anything that frightened her.

"It's alright," he said. He held out his hands, and Alex closed hers, extinguishing the flames, and placed them into Michael's. The orange glow dimmed but Alex yanked her hands back before Michael could diminish all her power.

"I need some of it to help me find the labyrinth entrance."

Michael's lip curled into a small grin as he nodded. "You mean that?"

Alex sucked in a breath. Ahead of them was a mountain that would rival the height of any in Warren or Datten. Her fire orb illuminated the stone, revealing its deep red hue that reminded Alex of blood. A shiver trickled down her spine. She reached out to the rock, but before she could reach it, Michael touched her shoulder, steadying her hand. Finally, when she could force her lungs to work again, she took a deep breath and pulled back her hand.

The entrance was carved into the mountain itself. At first glance, it appeared to be nothing more than a crack or if she were being generous, a cave entrance. Alex flicked her wrist, sending her orb of light into the dark alcove before she and Michael stepped inside. After only a few steps they ended up at a dead end. The surrounding air was cold and damp, but all they could see was a large silver knocker protruding from the rock.

"Where's the door?" Michael asked.

Alex examined the knocker. It was carved into a sea dragon head, identical to the one on the Warren crest, with a large silver hoop in its mouth. She stroked the snout and felt a tingle blaze through her. She gasped and stepped back, bumping into Michael.

"What is it?"

"Magic," Alex replied. "This wall makes me feel the same way Gryphon's powers did when he found me on the beach at Moorloc's. It has my magic stirring and is sending a tingle through it."

"Then why is there no door?"

Alex exhaled. "Because we're missing someone."

Michael grinned. "Then I guess we should go wake our Nial."

ALEX AND MICHAEL let Edith sleep while they prepared breakfast and discussed what they should bring with them and what they should leave behind. They debated for a while but ultimately decided that once they'd entered the labyrinth, Alex would crack the horses back to Datten in order to keep them safe from whatever predators roamed the mountains. It also gave them a chance to send back letters to reassure everyone they were safe and were starting the next part of their journey. Michael worked on his letters to Jessica and Stefan while Alex finished cooking their porridge. She'd been cautious with the oats they'd carried to ensure the horses would be well fed, but if they were going to send their mounts home, it meant they could eat their fill. Alex delicately sliced the apple bits into the pot, and composed her letters to Aaron, her father, and Gryphon in her head.

"Alex?"

Startled, Alex dropped the spoon into the pot. *"Ferflucs!"*

Edith apologized and fished the spoon out. "I'll take over. You write your letters."

"Write yours, too."

"We're done," Michael said. "I'll pack up the tent while you do it." He held out the remaining paper to Alex, and she gulped as she took it from him.

"Take your time. We'll be ready when you are." Edith smiled and began stirring the food.

Alex took the supplies and walked toward the horses. Snow was lying on the ground. Alex sat down and leaned against her horse. She bit the pencil and tried to think of the right thing to say, but when the words didn't come, she started with Gryphon's letter. She apologized for locking him out completely and not warning him of her plans. Her letter to her father was similar, but she also noted that had he allowed Randal to explain everything, she wouldn't have needed to sneak around. She still hoped her father would yield to reason. Randal had simply done was he was destined to do.

Aaron's letter was the hardest. She didn't know if he was still angry or not. Part of her suspected he'd forgiven her because he loved her so much, but she also worried he wouldn't because of the cruelty he'd shown when he was cursed. By the time the sun came up on the mountain horizon, casting everything in a warm golden light, fear had wormed its way into Alex's mind and heart.

"Is it the fury that makes it so hard to believe you could forgive me?" Alex whispered when an icy wind engulfed her. Snow nickered beside her, so Alex stroked his face, knowing the cold wasn't anything to fear. When she looked up, she saw Daniel. Alex's stomach churned from the shame of having doubted Aaron's love and devotion to her, and she couldn't meet his eyes.

Daniel squatted before her and placed his hand on her knee. "He knows this weighs on you. He would have stood by you, even if he couldn't come."

Alex fought back guilty tears. "Is he angry?"

Daniel simply shook his head. The same blond hair Aaron had glittered in the firelight. "No tears. He has faith you'll succeed." Daniel winked at her.

Alex exhaled. Before she could ask anything else, he leaned down and kissed her forehead, then vanished, leaving a bit of frost on her skin. Alex breathed deeply and finished Aaron's letter before she lost her nerve. Knowing he wasn't upset with her helped her spill her thoughts and feelings onto the page, and in no time she was back at the fire with Edith and Michael.

"The porridge is extra nice today," Edith said, scooping herself another bowl. Michael pursed his lips and glanced nervously from Edith to Alex.

Alex smiled. "I'm alright, Michael. I got a dose of ghostly strength and I know Aaron understands. So once we're done here, we'll head to that cave."

"What did it look like?" Edith asked.

While they finished their breakfast, Alex went into detail about the strange blood colored mountain wall with a door knocker on it. Since they were so close, they took their time and ate in peace for the first time since leaving the inn in Kirsh.

"What did you say to Harold?" Alex asked. Michael dropped his bowl and wandered away to check their horses.

The ladies snickered as he left.

"Well, it was more of a love letter than anything else," Edith said.

"Oh no, is that what we were supposed to be doing?" Alex laughed.

"I did," Michael called from the horses, clearly eaves-dropping.

"Of course you both did," Alex said. "Edith is newly engaged, and Jessica already knows everything. I had to explain to Gryphon why he can't see us, and my father why I didn't tell the other living Warren what I was doing." Alex turned to Edith. "I also scolded him again for not hearing your father out. But Aaron, I mainly asked for forgiveness, and to make sure Stefan isn't angry when I get back."

"Stefan doesn't strike me as being a grudge holder," Edith said. "Jerome and Jessica aren't."

Alex and Michael burst into laughter together. "That's because they've never held a grudge against *you*," Michael said.

"If they did, you'd know," Alex added. "I'm more worried about Stefan being mad at me than I am Aaron."

"Of course you are. You can use your sorceress' wiles to make Aaron forgive you."

Alex ran over and shoved Michael, knocking him back on his butt, but he didn't stop laughing. Even Edith couldn't hold back her chuckles.

"On that note, I say we get to the cave," Alex said.

Alex walked in front, leading Snow by the bridle. There was enough nervous tension between them that no one said a word, and the only sound was the horses' hooves clopping on the ground. In the light, the landscape looked completely different. Gone were the creepy shadows and spikey little mounds of earth. They walked for about ten minutes before reaching a beautiful cobblestone path.

"It makes sense now why you found the cave so easily," Michael said.

Alex nodded. "My feet must have felt the stone and followed it."

Warmth and tingles spread through Alex, as they followed the path around a bend. Then, with no effort from Alex, flowers burst through the patches of snow on the ground. Michael tapped her shoulder. The mountain loomed before them. It was the one Alex had found that night before. In the sunlight, the mountain stones shimmered in hues of copper. Alex grew a tree for them to fasten the horses to while Edith grabbed some dead wood branches. Alex lit them on fire and the three of them crept to the cave entrance.

The opening was the same sliver cut from the mountain she'd seen the night before, so Alex swallowed hard and moved inside the crevasse. Edith and Michael followed, their small torches lighting the alcove enough for them to navigate toward the dead-end Michael and Alex had found. Alex stopped short when she found the wall, and Edith walked into her.

"Alex why did you sto—"

"Where did that come from?" Michael asked, his voice laced with fear and confusion.

Alex crept toward the wall with the large silver knocker, but what had been nothing more than a stone wall the night before now contained a door. The wall was made of carved blocks of stone, like the ones in Datten or Warren's castle, but these stones were as red as rust. The door was a solid slab of black obsidian, the same as the thrones of Datten and Warren were carved from. Alex could feel the magic humming from the door. She calmly strode toward it. Looking up at the silver dragon knocker, she gulped and glanced at Michael and Edith. Above the knocker, the words *the silver moon is rising* were etched in the stone and below it, the words *above the sea it's shining*. Michael nodded, so Alex grabbed the ring and banged it against the door. The deep clunking sound seemed to resonate down the door and deep into the earth beneath their feet. The rumbling grew and echoed around them, causing Michael and Edith to rush to Alex's side. Outside, the horses squealed. Alex was unsure of whether to rush to them or to stay here and see to the end of the chaos she'd unleashed.

The rumbles ceased and the cave fell as silent as a tomb. Three circles appeared carved on the front of the door where a moment before there was nothing. Alex held her torch up to them, and a glint caught her eye. Michael held out his own torch, revealing that each circle had a single letter etched into it.

"What are they?" Edith asked, joining them.

Michael moved Edith to his spot and took Alex's left. "Look at them now."

Alex ran her finger along the roughly carved 'W'. "Veremund, Warren, and Nial," she whispered.

"So, if we're to be the keys, how do we open the door?" Edith asked.

"Everything else that's precious in Warren is protected by blood. It could be a blood spell," Alex said.

"We should send the horses back. I don't want another rumble to scare them away," Edith said.

Alex took her time removing her items from her satchels to make sure Edith could properly calm both Quiver and Hester. Neither were fond of cracking, so Edith wanted to give them the best shot at arriving safely. Once they all had reduced their packs to the bare necessities, Alex patted Snow gently and sent the horses away.

The trio made their way back into the cavern. Alex planted her feet in the earth as her friends each took their place in front of their family's circle.

"Let's try the same code that gets us into the Warren treasure room."

Edith pulled out her sword and held it up to them, so each could pierce their finger enough to draw blood. Alex watched her blood bead on her index finger before she pressed her hand into the circle. "Warren the true."

"Veremund the wise."

"Nial the brave."

They stood side by side, and the earth around them grumbled as if enraged. Edith covered her ears. She cried out when Michael was violently knocked back.

Alex felt her hand grow hot and then it seemed to ... *melt* into the door. She dropped her torch, struggling to pull away.

"A Warren *and* a sorceress." The voice came from nowhere and everywhere at once, echoing from every wall in the cave.

Alex gulped. "I am. I come seeking the scepter of the first King of Warren."

"You, who broke the curse of old on the kingdoms, have come to claim your place as the true heir of your kind?"

A wind rushed through the cave, sending dirt flying into Alex's face. She still couldn't remove her hand. "I do," she said, choking on the dust filling her nose and mouth. "I need to hold the fury at bay and become the queen I was meant to be."

"Everything has a give and take, a push and pull. To achieve your ends will require sacrifice. Are you ready to give all that is asked of you? Are your Veremund and Nial prepared to give up what matters most to protect you?"

Alex's hand was released, and she fell back into Michael's arms.

Edith strode up to the door. "I'll sacrifice whatever I need in order to keep Alex safe. On my life as a Nial." Her lips curved into a serious scowl.

Michael finally let go of Alex, and shouted, "And I will die before I allow any harm to come to her."

With her friends around her, Alex held her head high. "I will do what you ask of me, so long as it is me alone who bears the burden of that sacrifice. I will not allow you to hurt another in my name."

"Then prepare yourselves, for you will be tested in turn, and should even one of you be found unworthy, then you all shall perish."

Alex gulped. Edith trembled beside her. Michael rubbed Alex's shoulder before he retrieved their torches from the ground.

"We will fear no one who's too much of a coward to show us his true face," Michael replied.

The echo of his angry words died away, and Alex's heart sped as her magic came to life. The surrounding mountain rumbled and before they could react, the stone walls shifted. The meager light coming from the crack where they'd entered faded and it slammed shut, trapping them inside. Edith's whimpers echoed around them. Chest heaving with fear, Alex grabbed Edith's hand. With her free hand, she grabbed her torch from Michael and set it ablaze. She held it out for Michael to light his own, but Edith's torch was nowhere to be found.

The dirt beneath them shifted, and they leaped back before the stone slab sank and was completely swallowed by the earth. They now stood before a long dark tunnel. The three of them glanced at each other before Edith drew her sword. It glowed blue as expected with Alex and Michael at her side.

"Try your compass," Alex said to Michael.

He dropped his bag and rummaged before he took it out. The needle spun a few times and then settled on north.

"At least one thing works," Alex muttered, holding her torch up. She dropped Edith's hand and gripped her necklace, taking the first step over the threshold. Inside the dark tunnel, the earth was also rust colored. An icy breeze made Alex shiver. *Is it the tunnel? Or is someone watching us?* She expected to find Daniel beside her, but only Edith and Michael accompanied her.

Alex swung her torch to light their way. The air was heavy and stale, and the rocky ground crunched beneath their boots. They walked for what could have been hours or minutes through the disorienting darkness until the passage narrowed and they were forced to continue single-file. The rust-colored dirt walls soon gave way to gray stones, similar to the Verlassen or Moorloc's castle. Alex gently grazed the stones with her fingers as they trudged along the snaking path.

"I think we're going downward. Do you feel that slope?" Alex asked.

"I do," Edith said.

"So far, there haven't been any forks," Michael said. "We're clearly being led somewhere. Guess we'll get to find out what's at the end of this creepy path. Why do all your sorcerer adventures involve being underground?"

Alex chuckled. "There is a whole sorcerer line dedicated to it, Michael, so what did you expect?" A sudden wave of magic hit Alex and she gasped.

"What's wrong?" Edith asked, grabbing her shoulder.

"I don't know." Alex held her chest and waited for her heart to stop pounding. "I feel like there is magic all around us, and I can't tell if it's the good kind or not."

"My sword is the same, so nothing bad is nearby," Edith said.

"You're probably just feeling claustrophobic. I know I am," Michael groaned from behind her.

Alex waved her hand and a breeze blew around them, bringing with it some fresher air.

Michael breathed deeply and exhaled loudly enough that Alex and Edith both giggled. "I'm glad that helped, Michael," Alex said. Ahead of them, she noticed something. She squinted and rubbed her eyes to make sure she wasn't imagining it, but a long way down the tunnel, she could see a faint orange or red light. She set off toward it so quickly that the others had to dash to catch her.

"Alex, slow down," Michael called from the back.

Alex couldn't, even if she wanted to. Something was pulling her toward that bright light. Soon, she arrived at the end of the tunnel and her mouth dropped.

A cavernous space opened before them. She had to crane her neck to see the ceiling. It was covered in stalactites that jutted down to meet the stalagmites on the floor.

"What is this place?" Edith asked as she caught up.

"The magic here ... it feels old and eerie. I'm not sure why, but it's making my entire body tremble."

"It's probably because it looks like the cave wants to eat you," Michael said.

"Like a dragon's mouth." Alex looked around the room with Michael.

"Michael, Alex!" Edith's voice quivered. "The tunnel's gone!"

Alex and Michael spun. Where the tunnel had been was now a solid wall. Alex rushed over and touched it, expecting a circle or a door to appear, but nothing happened. The wall remained solid, and her stomach dropped.

"No!" she screamed, trying to make the tunnel reappear, but her Mire powers were her weakest, and nothing happened. Not even a pebble fell out of place. Panic coursed through her and she fought to keep control over her emotions and her powers. Fear consumed her, and she pounded her fists into the wall and cried. *What if we die in here and it's all my fault?*

"We'll be alright, Alex," Michael pulled her away from the wall before she could hit it again and hurt herself. "Look at me." His voice was curt, and he sounded more like Stefan than himself. "You are not at fault here. We all knew this would be dangerous. We didn't expect a safe or easy passage here."

"He's right," Edith said, pushing Alex's braid off her shoulder. "And at least this room isn't as cramped or dark, though I *am* curious where the glow is coming from. It's lighting up this whole place."

"The hue makes me think it's a fire," Alex said, her curiosity overriding her fear. "But that would have to be a massive fire, and I don't smell anything burning."

"Then we'd better investigate," Edith said. She adjusted her backpack and heaved herself over the first stalagmite toward the open expanse.

Alex brushed away her tears and followed.

CHAPTER 6
ALEX

The trio continued to walk through the cave for ages. They found piles of various normal rocks and sometimes black and orange rocks. A few times they ended up at dead-ends, with thick gray stone walls and no way to go except backward, but it didn't discourage them. Alex was determined to find whatever was illuminating the room

To achieve your ends will require sacrifice.

The warning from the voice weighed heavy on her heart. When they stopped to eat, Alex examined the stalagmites on the ground. They had layers of white and red crystals. She knew they were ancient from the lines showing the passage of time since they first grew here.

Edith rubbed her shoulders, letting out a long, heavy breath. Her heavy backpack lay on the ground beside her. "It feels like we're going in circles," she said.

"Not full circles," Michael said. "But this compass is sending us on a rather interesting route."

"It hasn't led us astray yet, so I suggest we follow it," Alex said. She glanced over Michael's shoulder at the compass and veered right to follow the needle. Michael hurried to catch up with her and took the lead so they could continue in the right direction.

The farther they got from the tunnel, the heavier the air became. A shock went through Alex, like when she collected too much static in the air using her Poseidon powers. She felt Michael tug her backpack, and she stopped.

"What was that?" Michael asked.

"I don't know," Alex whispered. "Sometimes my magic does odd things, but this felt different."

As if on cue, the surrounding ground trembled. Edith stumbled but Michael grabbed her before she could fall.

"I really don't want this mountain to come down on us," Edith said.

"It won't," Alex said. Another shock went through her and her powers burst to life inside her. "It's magic doing this."

The light they had been pursuing was gone in a flash, like a candle being snuffed out. They were thrust into darkness, and Michael grabbed Alex's arm. Thankful to have him close, Alex rubbed her hands and sent an orb of light in front of them to lead their way. They trudged on.

Edith clutched her family's sword with both hands, wide-eyed. Michael squinted at the compass in the orb's dim light.

Alex's magic pulled her the same way it had the day she met Gryphon on the beach. She peered into the darkness, but could see nothing. She closed her eyes and opened her well to the surrounding magic and the pull strengthened. Keeping her eyes closed, she followed it. Michael's hurried footsteps followed closely while Edith's softer ones trailed behind. Something told Alex to throw her hands before her and she hit stone. She stopped so quickly that Michael ran into her, and she found herself face to face with another dead-end wall. The stone scratched against her palms.

"Why do we keep finding this castle wall in the middle of a mountain?" Edith asked.

"It's not a castle," Alex whispered. An icy wind whipped around them, freezing them to the bone. Then she heard something that chilled her heart.

"You heard the crying, too, right?" Edith asked.

Alex took the compass from Michael, and they followed the needle along the wall to the left. They walked for what could have been an hour, listening to only their footsteps pound on the stone, when a voice whispered to them.

"Child of Warren."

Edith shushed them and they all stood still.

"Child of Nial."

Alex and Edith turned to Michael, and he gulped.

"Child of Veremund. You have returned, and with you the lines remain unbroken."

"Is someone there?" Edith asked.

Michael threw his shoulders back. "Show yourself at once. We are armed and ready to fight if necessary. Don't make us hurt you."

"How could there be someone?" Alex whispered. "The cave was sealed shut until we arrived."

Another wind rushed past them, but Alex had enough and threw her hands up to stop it.

"A child of Warren and Cassandra. The one who broke the curse, who will either free them or burn them all to ash."

"Enough cryptic messages. We are here to find the scepter of the first King of Warren. Whoever you are, help us." Alex's heart beat so hard she could hear it drumming in her ears. "Please."

"Look!" Edith pointed down the wall where they'd come from. A torch appeared on the wall, lighting up a small section. They edged toward the flickering flames. There were two torches now, and a section of the wall between them had vanished, leaving a darkened opening. Alex stepped back to take in the expansive cavern ceiling. The wall before them stood at least four times Michael's height. Michael paused beneath the torch and beckoned Alex over. She knew what he wanted before she even lifted her foot.

After a few minutes, she was sitting on Michael's shoulders with their supplies strewn across the ground. Alex stretched her arm as far as she could without dislocating it. She wiggled her fingers, and Michael bounced her to adjust her again, almost dropping her. Alex grabbed his head and waited for him to stop squirming before she reached again. This time she grabbed the torch and Michael bent down to allow her to climb off.

"It looks as if you two have done that before," Edith laughed.

"More often than I will ever tell Aaron," Michael replied, slinging his pack on his back.

"Wait." Alex held the small torch up to the wall beside the new opening. Carved in the stone were the words *the golden sun is gone.* So many conflicting emotions swirled through her. *I don't know what is in store for us.* She didn't want Michael to know how terrified she was.

"It's okay to be scared," Edith told her.

"How did you know?"

"Because I'm terrified!" Edith answered.

"We all are," Michael said. "But do you know what scares me even more than a cryptic rhyme or that dark path into this creepy maze?"

Alex kicked a rock with her boot before looking at Michael. "I could probably guess."

"Well," he said, pulling her into a hug, "if you'd guess losing you to some curse—one that we could have stopped if we'd only been brave enough to try—you'd be right."

Alex wrapped her arms around his neck and squeezed him. Michael embraced her and squeezed her back just as hard. Edith used the new torch to light the two they had brought with them.

Alex took the smallest one, figuring her magic could relight it if needed, and together the three of them faced the dark entrance to the stone labyrinth.

"Do you think it's a maze or a labyrinth?" Michael asked.

"Aren't they the same thing?" Edith asked.

"No. A maze has a separate entrance and exit, and it has more twists and turns. A labyrinth leads you to the middle and then circles back to the same entrance."

Alex and Edith turned to Michael in surprise.

"I know, I know. I'm the funny one, so everyone thinks I don't know things."

Alex laughed. "I know you better than that, Michael. You are clever and you notice so many things other people miss."

They couldn't stall any longer. Alex took a deep breath and stepped across the threshold. When nothing terrible happened, she exhaled in relief. Edith and Michael joined her, and they continued their trek.

After only a few steps, they heard the rumbling of falling rocks. Alex whipped around, but it was too late. The entrance to the labyrinth had vanished and in its place was a solid stone wall.

Michael dashed to it. "No, no, no. This can't be happening," he said, desperately searching for an opening.

Alex's magic told her there wasn't one. Fear bled through her, and she couldn't breathe.

Edith stared at the wall for only a moment, then crossed the pathway to get to Michael, a determined look on her face. "Veremund, stand down!"

Michael stopped and slowly turned around to face Edith.

"We came here for this labyrinth, and we finally found it. Pull yourself together and we'll use your compass to see how to proceed."

Michael stared open-mouthed at Edith.

Finding herself comforted by her friend's newfound confidence, Alex snorted. "I think you just found your inner queen, Edith."

Edith grinned and playfully pushed Michael. "I thought you'd be used to women telling you what to do by now."

Michael laughed, and soon Edith and Alex were, too. Michael patted Edith's back, and they joined Alex. No longer nervous, Alex raised her torch and marched into the darkness.

With three lit torches, they illuminated the entire width of the path. Alex searched carefully for any clue about what awaited them. The brownish-red stones were carved from the mountain above them, but unlike the jagged stones that made up the walls of all the castles she'd seen, these were smooth. The glow of their torches reflected off the polished stone. There was no trace of moss or weeds. *I wouldn't expect a tree to survive down here, but to have no life is eerie.*

Michael ran his hand along the stone, rubbing his fingers together and frowning.

"The stones look wet," Edith said.

"But they're bone dry, and perfect, like a gem," Michael said.

Alex joined them at the wall and stared at her reflection. Her eyes were as dark as night, and her own reflection smirked back at her. The wicked grin made her stomach turn, but she couldn't let Michael sense her distress, so she quickly turned and feigned she simply intended to carry on.

"Alex, don't wander too far ahead," Michael called after her.

She held up her torch, illuminating a fork. She glanced back at her friends. "I'll be alright. We hit a break in the path. I'm just going to peek down a ways and be right back."

"Alex!" Michael's voice took on the commanding tone that usually only a Wafner could muster. "Just wait for us."

Alex turned back to see him round the corner and shouted. "I'm fine, Michael. See? Nothing happened—" was all she could utter before the wall closed up the space between them.

AARON

A young Betruger knight stood in the library's doorway. "King Aaron?"

While usually very good with names, it took Aaron a moment to recall his. All these new knights at once made for a challenge.

"Yes, Siegfried. What can I do for you?"

"Sir Reinhart, the senior one, asked that I let you know the training field is ready for you."

"Excellent." Aaron closed his book and stood. As part of their decision to include Betruger men in the guards and armies, Aaron and Harold wanted the men to train together to make things more fun for them. Aaron moved to grab his armor, but the young knight beat him to it.

"Allow me, Your Royal Highness," Siegfried said, hoisting Aaron's armor and sword. "The junior Reinhart is fetching King Harold as we speak."

"Wonderful. Did you place your bet yet? I don't mind if you bet on Harold."

"I actually bet on Macht, Your Royal Highness. Our king is skilled, but his general is better."

"My father always said you should surround yourself with men who are better than you," Aaron said.

They marched down the long stretch of the main Datten hallway and exited through the side door. The morning sun took some of the chill out of the air, but it was clear from the frosty ground that winter was coming. *I hope she brought warm clothes. And I hope I don't embarrass myself today, because even if she didn't witness it, she'll tease me about it for years.* He crossed the first set of smaller training fields where the squires and youngest knights were busy training.

"Boys!" Aaron shouted to them. "We're starting the demonstration, and you won't want to miss a minute. King's orders." The youngsters exchanged looks, their mouths agape. His crown was back in his bedroom, but his gold hair left no room for doubt. The group dropped their wooden swords and ran off as fast as their legs could carry them to the senior training field. Aaron chuckled and continued on his way.

Jerome was waiting for him when he arrived at the field. Aaron's general was standing in his favorite training circle, with Harold and Macht at his side. Aaron could still remember the day he'd realized Jerome had a favorite training spot. Naturally, he'd denied it, but they always went to the same circle, and it was not the closest one. Harold was still being suited up when Aaron reached them, but both generals were ready for their fights.

"Are you nervous?" Aaron teased Jerome while he finished fastening Aaron's armor to his chest.

"Not at all. Wafners have been training knights for centuries. I'm confident I can best a Betruger king. It is you who should be nervous, my king. You are fighting General Macht, after all."

"I fully expect to lose," Aaron said, tightening his arm guards.

"But then why agree to it?" Macht asked.

Aaron grinned. "It's simple, Macht. I can't very well ask my men to train with yours if I am not willing to do it myself and take a few hits."

"A noble sacrifice if I ever heard one," Harold laughed. "So who shall spar first?"

"I volunteer," Aaron said. Harold and Jerome nodded and moved aside, leaving Aaron and Macht in the ring together. Aaron exhaled sharply and glanced up at the Betruger general, who stood a full head above him.

A squire offered the general a shield, but he waved it away. "I shall try not to hurt you," Macht said.

Aaron laughed. "Alex would certainly appreciate that." He accepted the shield from the squire and turned toward the attentive knights. "Today we shall begin training as one: Datten, Betruger, and Warren. We will grow stronger by uniting all our combat knowledge. After centuries of warring against one another, we now have a common enemy and we will see to it that our kingdoms, our people, and our queens are safe from the sorcerers who mean us harm. Now watch closely and let's see how long I last against the most skilled swordsman in Torian."

The knights laughed heartily. Aaron smiled and turned to Macht. The pair bowed to each other while Jerome shouted the rules to everyone. Three strikes would win the match, and since helmets were not being worn, they were to avoid strikes higher than the shoulder. Aaron gripped the hilt of the sword Alex had gifted him. The weight and balance had clearly been made for him, and he could swing this sword with greater ease than any other he owned.

There was a loud pop, and Macht and Aaron circled one another. Aaron had been sparring with the Betruger ever since he'd convinced Harold to help him save Alex, so he had a good idea of how Macht would start. Keeping his sword low, Aaron slid his feet along the circle of dirt and waited for Macht to strike.

Macht stood unmoving, but when Aaron blinked, he was suddenly barreling down on him. Aaron spun and moved from Macht's attack at the last moment, barely keeping his shield from flying away. Macht reached the end of the circle and pivoted faster than should be possible for anyone of his size. Aaron gasped and leaped back, Macht's sword just missing him. A boyish grin spread across Macht's face, and it dawned on Aaron that he was being toyed with. Gripping his sword, Aaron swung at Macht. It only took a few strikes and a swift kick before Aaron was on his back looking up at the sky. He could hear Harold and Jerome's laughter as Macht extended his hand to help him up.

Aaron brushed himself off and smiled at his men. "Now that I've shown you what not to do, pay extra attention to Jerome and Harold's fight."

Harold and Jerome's match lasted longer than Aaron's had with Macht. This time, the Datten general came out victorious. In the end, it was Macht and Jerome who would fight for glory. Aaron stood beside Harold with his arms crossed as the generals took their places. Before they could begin, a stable boy came running over. "King Aaron, the queen's horse has just arrived in the stable."

"Snow's returned?" Aaron asked, trying to hide the excitement in his voice. "What of the queen?"

"I'm sorry, Your Royal Highness. Only horses appeared. Her Royal Highness's and two other Betruger horses. We believe they are Lady Nial's and King Harold's horses."

Harold grabbed Aaron's arm and turned to the young boy. "Do our horses look alright?"

"They arrived packed for travel and are perfectly fine."

"Then take us to them," Jerome instructed the boy.

Letting the stable boy do his duty and lead them to the correct stable stalls was excruciating for Aaron. All he wanted to do was run ahead and find Snow, but as king, he needed to allow his men to do their jobs.

They hurried past the guard and noble stables. Each was structurally the same, with horse pens and work areas, but the higher-ranking stables were constructed with finer materials. The royal stable had the best trained horsemen, most of whom were taught by Aaron's uncle Bernhard, and was built from silver pine wood. Like black pine, silver pine could only be found in the deepest parts of the Dark Forest, but silver pine trees were covered in a sap that could burn your skin if you weren't careful, and they had the largest thorns of any tree in Torian. It took great effort to harvest the wood, so it was only used by the wealthiest in Torian. It was prized for its odor. Even after decades, anything built from it would still have a woodsy smell. They walked through the ornately carved arc at the front of the stables, and Aaron noticed the unusual activity around them. Half a dozen stable boys rushed around holding bags and satchels full of odds and ends. Snow whinnied as soon as he saw Aaron.

Aaron grabbed a carrot from the barrel and hurried toward the colt, a beautiful white horse with black flecks on his face. Harold and Jerome headed to the other horses. He held the carrot out to Snow and pet the horse while he munched the treat. When the boys carried away the last of Snow's bags, he became agitated. Aaron called them back, and Snow head-butted the boy with Alex's satchel.

"I'll take that, Robin," Aaron said. He unlatched the bag, and a letter fell out. It was addressed to Gryphon. Pursing his lips, Aaron dug around and found another to Edward, and one to himself. Without waiting for the others, he ripped into Alex's letter.

"They found the labyrinth!" he shouted, feeling both pride at her progress, and fear that they were gone almost a month and had only now found for the entrance to the labyrinth.

"And they're all safe," Harold shouted, having found his own letter from Edith.

"They're heading into a cave. The labyrinth is inside the mountain?" Aaron asked Jerome. He didn't wait for an answer before continuing, "But they plan to crack back as soon as they find the scepter, so they sent the horses back now rather than risk their safety."

"At least we know they're safe," Harold said.

"And we have more letters to deliver," Aaron said. "Hunter!" Aaron called to his knight friend who was standing nearby. "Take these letters to be delivered by my birds."

"You don't want to summon Megesti and ask him to bring them, Your Royal Highness?" Jerome asked.

"And deprive everyone the opportunity of seeing you be beaten by Macht? Not a chance." Aaron pointed back to the training field, making Harold laugh.

CHAPTER 8
ALEX

Alex stared in shock at the spot where the path had been. "It's gone!"

She rushed to the wall and held out her hand, hoping the wall was imaginary like the one in Moorloc's kitchen to hide the food and servants, but it stood firm.

She could hear Michael calling to her from the other side of the wall, but his voice sounded far, far away. Alex muttered her unlocking spell, her spell to retrieve lost things, and all the other ones she could think of. Nothing worked. She focused on the wall until words appeared burned into the stones, the same ones she'd seen at the entrance. *Until the morning fires, and from the meadow rises.*

Alex closed her eyes and pressed her forehead against the stones. An image came to her mind, of herself frozen, unable to move and surrounded by ice. *Breathe. I have to stay calm, I can't panic.* She had entombed herself in ice to get away from Lygari, and years before that, she'd fallen through ice when she had ignored Michael's warning. She shook her head and pushed aside the memories.

"Child of Warren."

Alex straightened.

"Child of Warren and Cassandra. You are the first to be tested."

Over her shoulder, a hooded figure watched. Alex slowly picked up the torch she'd tossed aside in her panic to inspect the door.

The figure took a step toward her. He wore a long black robe, with the hood pulled over his head. The lining sparkled in the torchlight. *Silver?*

"Why are you testing me?" Alex asked.

"To ensure you are worthy," the figure said, raising his hands. "While anyone born to a Warren will carry on the Warren line, not all have been worthy of the name and the values it embodies."

"That's true," she whispered. "My grandfather shouldn't be considered the standard for the Warren name."

"Arthur put our name to shame. I must be sure you have not followed in his footsteps." The man pulled down his hood and Alex sucked in her breath. He had the same umber skin, thick raven-black hair, and warm sea-blue eyes as her father. It took a moment to register who Alex was looking at.

"Are you Arthur Warren? The first king?"

"The first king of Warren was my father. I'm Teon, the first Crown Prince of Warren, and it is I and the other first-borns of Nial and Veremund who have been tasked with testing you and your companions."

Alex gulped at the sight of the ghost before her. While not evil like her grandfather, Alex was clearly not the ideal Warren heir. She'd committed murder, and she struggled daily to live with everything she'd done to survive. "What if I fail your test? What happens if you find me unworthy?"

"Then you and your companions will never find your way out of here."

Bile rose from Alex's stomach. "You say that as though it means nothing to you."

"I have a duty to my parents to ensure the King's Scepter is not retrieved until it is time and not by anyone other than the worthy three. If that isn't you, then you shall perish, and I shall wait for them. We shall wait as long as necessary."

"We?"

"Each of you will be tested by the firstborn of your line. Are you ready, daughter of Warren?"

Alex exhaled slowly to buy a moment to compose herself. She pictured Aaron's face, and then her father's. She loved them dearly and needed to return to them. Looking up at the face before her, she sighed.

"I am," she said. "I accept your terms."

"Very well," Teon replied. "Choose a line."

"I'm sorry, I don't understand," Alex said.

"You are a daughter of Cassandra and a daughter of Warren. Only one of those may fight through the labyrinth, so you must choose. Your friends will not have this choice."

"What will that choice do exactly?"

"If you choose Warren, you will be stripped of your powers and be left to fight the dangers of the labyrinth as a mortal, but you'll have your Nial and Veremund."

"What if I choose my Cassandra side?" Alex asked.

"Then you will have your humanity stripped from you, and I cannot say what you will do to your friends without it as I am not a sorcerer."

"Would I be able to crack us to the end of the labyrinth?"

"If you wanted to, but whether or not you'd leave whole remains."

CHAPTER 9

GRYPHON

Gryphon's blood burned like acid. Pain ripped through every part of him as he lit up in white light. He grabbed his chest and dropped to the ground, writhing, trying desperately to catch enough breath to cry for help. The pain washed over him in endless waves. Across the lab, Megesti dropped to his knees, clutching his head. Gryphon's vision tunneled and orbs floated before him. He could hear his own blood racing through his skull. Megesti reached out, but before he could reach Gryphon, his eyes rolled up in his head and he screamed like a man possessed.

Magic. How did we get so much magic at once? It didn't even hurt this much when my Ares powers came in.

Gryphon struggled to crawl to the lab door. He heard a thump and saw Kharon shouting, but their voice sounded like a whisper. Birch appeared beside Kharon just before everything went dark.

Gryphon came to staring at the ceiling of the lab in the Verlassen castle. He tried to turn his head to the side and groaned. His entire body felt as if he'd been struck by lightning. Megesti was curled in the fetal position on the floor, glowing gold and whimpering.

Gold. Gryphon shot up. The room spun and he crawled across the floor toward Megesti and pressed his hand against his forehead.

He immediately collapsed onto the ground. "No. *No!*" he screamed.

"Gryphon! What's wrong?" Birch asked.

"Megesti ... he's the Titan of Cassandra."

"How is that possible?" Kharon asked.

"I don't know," Gryphon whimpered. "But he is."

Birch knelt between Megesti and Gryphon and stroked Megesti's hair out of his face. "The only way he'd become the Titan of Cassandra is if Alex died and her powers went to him."

"She's not dead," Gryphon spat.

"I'm sorry dear, but we don't know that," Birch said. "You and Megesti both dropped to the ground like stones, in severe pain. That's a normal reaction to a sudden death of a loved one. It happened to me when Merlock died."

Birch pursed her lips at Gryphon. "Do you feel up to trying to look through their eyes again? See what they can see?"

Gryphon pushed himself up, and once the room stopped spinning, slowly nodded. He took a deep breath, closed his eyes, opened his well, and searched for Alex or her companions. The feeling of rushing wind hit him, and then absolute terror flooded him. Screams filled his ears and searing heat enveloped every inch of him. When he opened his eyes, all he could see was flames. The pain and the smell of burning flesh invaded his nostrils. He quickly broke the connection. Gasping for breath, he rolled over and retched on the floor.

CHAPTER 10

ALEX

Alex thought of Michael and Edith. *We're here to stop the dark magic inside of me. I can't surrender my humanity. And I'd give up my powers to protect them in a heartbeat.*

"I choose Warren. My friends matter more than my powers and I shall not abandon them."

"Very well chosen, Warren, but know that not only will your powers be gone, but so will any spells you cast recently." He nodded to her bracelet. "But rest assured that once you leave this room, no one will help or hinder you until you three find your way out or die trying."

"Understood."

THE FLAMES SURROUNDED Alex but didn't even singe her skin. Instead, they burned her insides. The pain was unbearable—as if her blood was boiling out of her veins. A scream echoed through the room, and it took Alex a minute to realize it came from her. Flames covered her entire body and erupted into gold light that faded as quickly as it had appeared. She fell to her knees, gasping for breath. Hands clapped and the flames vanished. Slowly, she lifted her head to see Teon still standing there, watching her.

"Your magic has been stripped from you," he said. "and along with it, any spells you cast recently. Your powers will be held for you by the two sorcerers who have the closest ties to your family's magic lines and your generational gifts. You will have to navigate the labyrinth as a mortal and won't be able to heal any injuries you or your friends sustain along the way."

Alex slowly got to her feet.

"Alex! Are you okay?" Michael's voice came through the wall.

"You won't hurt them, right?"

"Your friends will be tested in their own way, just as you were. Whether they survive will be up to them."

"Wait," Alex said. "That was my test?"

Teon nodded. "You were willing to give up your powers for your friends. Truth and loyalty are what Warrens are known for. You proved you would put others above your own wants ... and needs."

Alex steeled herself and brushed a bit of ash off her clothes. *How did my clothes not burn? It must have been magical to just take my powers and not hurt me ... but how did a mortal ghost have magic to do that?*

When Alex looked up, he was gone. Another rumble echoed around her, but before she could even worry about it, Michael and Edith rushed over the rubble now scattered on the pathway. Alex stumbled toward them then threw her arms around Michael, clinging to him.

"Would you listen to me for once?" Michael scolded her before she burst into tears. Edith rubbed her back soothingly.

"I'm sorry," Alex whimpered. "I won't go ahead anymore. I'm so sorry."

Michael squeezed her tightly, while Edith picked up the supplies Alex lost during her time trapped in the stone chamber.

Alex tried to stop herself from trembling, but she couldn't, and Michael's tone switched from frustration to fear.

"What happened in here?" he asked.

"I lost my magic."

Edith dropped her bag with a loud thud. "Did you say you lost your magic?"

Alex just nodded, wiped her tears from her cheeks, and told them what happened with Teon. Then, to prove it to herself as much as them, she flicked her hand, and nothing happened. No wind, no water, no fire—nothing. She swallowed hard. *Without my magic, will I be of any use to them, or will I just be a burden?*

"I suppose we'll finally see how well Stefan and I trained you," Michael teased. He held up her pack for her to slip back on.

"You aren't angry?"

"Why in Torian would we be angry that you were willing to give up a part of you to make sure we'd have you with us through this?" Edith asked. She picked her sword and torch off the ground where she'd dropped them in her rush to help Alex.

"Because without my powers, we can't even light the torches or get water," Alex replied.

"Then we'll ration our water," Michael said. "You filled the water skins before we came in here, so we should be fine for a bit." He adjusted her back straps. "And we have three torches, so as long as one burns, we can light the others. We'll be alright."

"How are you so calm?" Alex whispered.

"Because I know what you're capable of. Not the sorceress, not the royal, but *you*. And you're amazing all on your own."

Alex couldn't help the smile that spread across her face.

Edith pinched Michael's cheek. "He's such a good big brother," she said, then stepped over the rubble from the wall and waved for them to follow.

Alex snickered at Michael's eye roll, but he lobbed his arm around her shoulder and led her back to the main pathway. The moment they were all out of the dead end, the wall reappeared. The three of them exchanged a look, knowing this would be much harder than they'd expected. Alex held her extinguished torch to Edith to be relit. With all three torches burning, the surrounding area was illuminated enough that Alex could see a few horse lengths ahead of her. She glanced back at her friends to make sure they were ready. When they nodded, she started again.

They talked about what happened to Alex and took guesses about what the trials of a Nial and Veremund would be based on their strengths of bravery and wisdom. Edith was the most nervous of the group.

"What if it's brute strength? My father trained me, but I'm not Julius or Cameron ... or even close to Stefan. That's why they taught me to use a bow and not a sword. I can barely carry this one." She tapped the sword on her belt that was almost touching the ground when worn on Edith's hilt. Michael clearly noticed as well. He removed his smaller sword and traded with Edith. She sighed loudly and slid his smaller guard sword into her belt.

"Here, you take the compass," Alex said, hoping it would make Edith feel better. "And remember, bravery doesn't require huge bouts of strength. Some of the bravest things Michael and Stefan have done for me required no physical strength."

Edith frowned. "Such as?"

"How about a twelve-year-old Stefan standing up to Ian and refusing to join the boys in the camp without me? Or a nine-year-old Michael going after Graham after he threatened me?"

"Stop bringing that up," Michael said.

"Or a scared princess defending a prince to his father," Alex whispered.

"We all heard about how furious Emmerich was after that," Edith said.

"Or a lovely lady shooting an arrow at a loud-mouthed sorcerer who was dishonoring her princess," Michael added.

Edith turned crimson as Michael beamed at her.

Alex laughed. "Is that when you hit Gryphon in the thigh with an arrow? He was furious when he came back."

"I knew nothing happened between you two," Edith said. "He was trying to make Aaron angry, and I'd had enough. No one lies about my Warren."

"Well, there's your proof that not all acts of bravery require extreme physical strength," Michael said.

Edith seemed to relax, and a smile lit up her face again.

They cautiously went along the dirt path. Alex monitored the rocks of the wall in case they shifted again, but they didn't—they remained as polished and stable as the stones outside. She noticed her reflection in the torchlight and did a double take.

"What's wrong?" Michael asked when she stumbled backward.

"Nothing." She shook her head and hurried ahead of him.

"Talk to us," he said.

She halted and turned around. "I still look the same. I still... look like *myself*."

"I don't understand," Edith said.

"I do," Michael said. "Alex, you didn't change the day your powers came to you, so why would you if you gave them up? I guess since it's such an integral part of you, like a limb, that losing it makes you feel incomplete. Right?"

Alex's eyes widened and her mouth hung open. "Yes ... that's exactly it."

"Wisdom. Remember?" Michael laughed and charged ahead, leaving Alex and Edith to chase after him.

THEY WALKED for what felt like hours. The stones were all the same, so it was impossible to tell how far they had gone. There were many dead ends along the path, but the compass kept them on the right track. When they needed a break, they'd find a corner to rest in. Alex didn't know if something was in here with them, so corners allowed them to keep watch in two directions.

Michael took stock of their remaining food. It wasn't much, but the dried meat and apples Alex had saved would last for a few days. Being unsure of how long they'd spend in this place, none of them were particularly eager to eat. Alex sliced an apple to share, and Michael did the same with the dried meat. Once they had something in their bellies, they discussed what they could do to ration their food, water, and how they might protect themselves if anything were in here with them. Despite her friends' reassurances, Alex couldn't help but feel useless with her powers gone. Michael suggested she take the lead with her bow, and she agreed. His confidence in her did little to change her mood—but little is not nothing and she held her head a little higher.

Once they were on their way, Alex and Edith peppered him with questions about the baby. They needed a distraction, and the more funny stories Edith told about her nephews, the more terrified Michael became about what a baby could get into. They didn't even notice the rising temperature.

Sweat pooled on Alex's neck. She raised a hand to stop her friends. "Is it just me, or did it suddenly get boiling hot in here?"

Edith stopped laughing at Michael's reaction to her story and stood still. "It does feel warmer."

Michael sniffed the air. "Do you smell burning?"

Alex felt the tingle in her nose of acrid smoke. She felt a wave of heat hit her and barely had time to turn around before a river of fire rounded the corner.

"Run!" she screamed. They ran back down the tunnel as fast as they could. Terror and adrenaline fueled them and they skidded around a corner and pushed themselves as hard as possible to find somewhere that would be safe.

"What do we do?" Edith screamed.

"I don't know!" Alex shouted back. *If I had my powers, this would have been nothing. This has to be a punishment, but for what?*

Just ahead, Michael turned a corner and cursed. They'd hit a dead end. With the heat baring down on them, Alex pushed Edith and Michael behind her. The river of flames rounded the corner. Edith screamed and fell silent. Alex spun in time to watch Michael vanish into the ground. With the fire surging toward her, Alex dashed to where her friends had been. The ground gave way beneath her, and then she was falling.

CHAPTER 11

GRYPHON

Birch and Kharon helped Gryphon to his feet. It had been a few minutes, and Megesti was now sitting at the table, sipping a mug, but the gold glow shone as bright as before. Birch handed Gryphon a drink, but he pushed it away. The magic pumping through him was enough to make him nauseated.

"Alex can't be dead," Megesti said.

"Kharon? What do the ghosts say?" Gryphon asked.

"They're silent, but I suspect she's alive. If she weren't she'd have come to us."

"Maybe she doesn't know how," Megesti said.

"How can she still be alive, Kharon? All I saw was Edith and Michael screaming and fire."

Lynx walked into the lab. "Why do you look like death Megesti?" The moment she spotted Gryphon, she rushed to his side and put her hand on his forehead.

"I'm fine, you overprotective she-cat," Gryphon growled, pushing her away. She immediately turned to Birch and Kharon who filled her in. Megesti had gone silent. His complexion was draining by the minute, and he seemed to be barely holding on.

Lynx smacked him with something making Gryphon turn to her. He snatched the letter from her and recognized his name and Alex's handwriting on the outside. "What is this?"

"Alex's horse arrived in Datten earlier this morning," Lynx explained. "A bird arrived to tell us, so I went to see what the others learned. Apparently, they found the labyrinth and are going inside today."

Gryphon ripped open his letter and cursed under his breath.

"What's wrong?" Megesti asked.

"She said her magic is acting up again. She's not sure why, but her powers are pulling her into this labyrinth."

"If she was that worried, why didn't she come back here to talk to us?" Birch asked.

"You don't understand how stubborn Alex can be," Megesti muttered.

"Stubborn enough to risk her own life?" Kharon asked.

The silence that followed was the only response.

"As much as I hate to say it, we need Aaron and the mortals." Gryphon pressed his hand to his forehead and closed his eyes to stop the spinning. He crumpled Alex's letter in his free hand and the new magic burned within him. "This power rushing through me is more than anything I've ever felt in my life. It's worse than when my powers first came in, and I thought *that* would kill me." Megesti was sitting on a lab chair with his head between his knees. Lynx handed him a bucket, and the sound of his retching was almost enough to make Gryphon sick.

"Can you sense her?" Birch asked.

"All I see when I try is fire. Kharon, do you know anything?" Gryphon asked.

Kharon went silent and illuminated in a faint gray light. Their eyes switched to gray, and they tilted their head to the side, staring at nothing.

"I hate when they get like that," Lynx whispered and Gryphon elbowed her to shush.

After a moment, Kharon blinked, and their eyes were blue again.

"Did they say anything?" Megesti whispered.

"Daniel couldn't go inside the cave. None of the ghosts know what's happening to them, but they know they're all alive," Kharon replied.

"That's a start," Lynx said. "What do we do now? Try another potion?"

"We need to go to Datten," Birch said. "Get Gryphon and Megesti their strength back and have them try the spell together. Merlins can sense kin, and so Megesti might help Gryphon pinpoint her location to get inside her head."

"Cassandras can also sense kin," Megesti said.

"You aren't a Cassandra, Megesti," Birch said. "Not fully. You never have been. Your father gave you Merlin, and I gave you the usurper ability. Unlike the Head or Heart, the usurper ability is a gift passed through our line. The Cassandra gifts you possess are from your Merlin side."

"Then how did I find Alex when we went hunting for her?" Megesti asked.

"Her Cassandra powers would have set off yours," Birch said. "You always detected Victoria when she arrived, but never your father. Your usurper gifts felt their magic."

Megesti groaned and held his stomach. "How do you do this?"

"Do what?" Birch asked.

"Gryphon," Megesti clarified, making Gryphon glance at him. "How do you and Alex hold this much power in you? It's making me ill."

"I don't know how she does it," Gryphon said. "Her burden is worse than mine."

"It must be her Returned One powers, and the lines her mother gave her," Birch said.

Lynx squeezed Gryphon's arm. "What do we need to do to help her?"

"I don't know, but what we are doing now is nothing," Gryphon said.

"Do you mean to find her or help her restore her powers?" Lynx asked.

"Both."

"Is there any way we can use the pearl to channel her?" Megesti asked. "Edward gave the white pearl to Harold. I'm sure he'd let us use it if it can help us get Edith back."

"So that's where the white pearl went."

Lynx glanced at Gryphon. "Did you know this?"

"Alex told me." Gryphon turned back to the cauldron. Another sharp pain burst through his head, and he dropped to the floor.

CHAPTER 12
ALEX

Alex slammed into freezing cold water so hard it knocked the air out of her lungs. She struggled to get to the surface before her body forced her to take another breath. When she broke through, she gasped and sucked in as much air as she could before a wave knocked her under again.

She was in an underground river, being dragged along by a current that would rival the Darren River after a rainfall in the mountains. A faint light illuminated the space down here. Her pack became soaked, and she struggled to stay afloat until it pulled her under again. *If I don't drop this pack, I'm doomed.* Alex took the deepest breath she could, reached back and grabbed her bow and quiver from the top of her pack before the water sucked her down. She held the bow in her mouth, and kicking her legs to keep herself near the surface, she slipped her arms free of the pack. The moment it was free, the current ripped it from her hands. She burst through the surface once more, clinging to her bow as the water carried her along.

She could see a growing light ahead. Michael and Edith were

screaming her name. With a powerful kick, she swam sideways against the current toward them. Near the bank, the current weakened, and Michael leaped into the water to drag her onto the barren ground. Alex lay on her back, gasping for breath. Michael collapsed beside her.

Edith paced around them. "We lost everything! What are we going to do?"

"We'll manage," Michael muttered, still catching his breath.

Alex patted his chest and sat up. "Thank you," she whispered. "Where are we?"

"How would we know?" Edith snapped. She was trembling, likely from the cold and fear.

Alex wrapped her arms around Edith, hugging her tightly. "It's going to be alright."

"How can you say that? You don't know."

"It's going to be alright," Alex repeated. She mustered the voice she only used when she spoke as Queen of Datten. Edith relented and leaned into her. "I will get you back to Harold. I promise." Michael joined them, throwing his arms around both of them and giving Alex the strength she needed to support Edith.

"Is anyone hurt?" Alex asked when Michael finally released them. Edith had a few scrapes and bruises from the water, and Michael had a mighty bump on his head. Alex had taken the most damage. When she'd hit the river rocks, they had torn through her shirt and left a gash on her bicep that was still bleeding. Michael cut a strip off the bottom of his shirt and wrapped it around her arm to stem the blood flow.

"I kept my pack. What did you manage to hold on to?" Michael asked.

Alex held up her bow and quiver. Edith held up the compass, her torch, and Michael's sword. Michael had the Nial sword and his pack, though the river had ripped it open and stolen much of his supplies. All the food except for one dried venison sausage had been washed away, but they had their water skins. Edith's face fell.

Alex grabbed her hand. "I know this looks bad, but you have to remember Michael and I grew up poor in the Dark Forest. We have survived longer on less."

Edith turned to Michael, a doubtful scowl on her face. "Is that really true?"

"Yes," Michael replied without looking up. "One time we got turned around in a storm with Oliver, and he was known to cry and panic if things looked bleak. Alex was only nine then, but she held it together while Oliver cried like we were going to die. I had to punch him to get him to catch his tongue."

Edith stared at Michael. "Does Jessica know about this secret temper?"

"I don't have a temper." Michael laughed. "I'm not Aaron. I do what's necessary to keep Alex safe, like Stefan taught me."

Alex shook her head and took in the beach they were standing on. The faint glow was coming from rocks at the top of the cave. They gave off a subtle turquoise light that made Alex smile. Even without her powers, she was convinced they were magical.

Edith shouted from the other side of the cave they were in. Alex and Michael rushed over to where Edith had found a small, dark tunnel leading away from the water. The three of them gathered their strewn supplies in silence before marching into the dark tunnel.

When they rounded the first corner, Alex gasped at the cave, composed entirely of the glowing turquoise stones. She quickly forgot her wet clothes and shivers and went to touch them. They looked jagged and sharp, but when her fingers grazed them, they felt smooth and warm.

"I suddenly have a lot more respect for what Mire sorcerers can do," she whispered, running her fingers along the glowing stones.

Edith and Michael continued down the tunnel, but Alex couldn't pull herself away from the glowing stones.

Michael came back for her and looped his arm around her shoulders to lead her on. They walked until they arrived in a cavern that glowed brighter than the moon in the sky. It was as vast as her father's throne room, reaching high above them. There was a dampness in the air, and like the entrance to the cave, it was filled with stalactites and stalagmites. Michael and Edith were in awe of the beauty of all the rocks. Alex examined one closely. It glowed in some parts, but not others. She weaved through them, exploring in circles when a breeze hit her. *Where did that come from?*

"Hello," Edith shouted. Her voice echoed through the space.

Alex looked back at her friends. Michael was poking at one of the glowing rocks that stuck out of the cave wall. It was larger than his head. Edith's head was thrown back, and she was staring at the ceiling. It reminded Alex of when she first saw the ceiling fires in Moorloc's castle. The walls were rough in here, so she was extra careful with her steps to avoid another injury. When she felt the breeze again, she headed toward it. The smell of a fire surrounded her. She crept along the edge of the wall and found a hole in the ceiling in one of the far back corners. Through it, she could barely make out a large gray stone.

"Could that be the labyrinth wall?" Alex asked herself. It was large enough for them to fit through. She examined the wall it was attached to and noticed rocks jutting out of it.

"Michael! Edith! I think I found a way out!" Alex shouted.

Michael stared at the hole without saying a word. After a full minute, Edith was losing her patience even faster than Alex was.

She crossed her arms. "I think Alex is right. We can climb these rocks and get out."

"I'm not risking you two getting hurt," Michael finally said. "Just let me think."

"Edith's right, Michael. We can't stand here and stare at that hole forever. I think we can make it. We just need to try." Alex walked over to Michael, in case she needed to knock some sense into him.

Edith grabbed hold of the closest rock and pulled herself up against the wall. Michael and Alex rushed toward her, but she was too quick, scrambling up the wall like a Warren squirrel on a castle tree. Alex couldn't help but be impressed with Edith's bravery and skill. She made it all the way to the top before her left foot slipped, sending a chunk of rock flying at them. Alex pulled Michael out of its path before it struck the cave floor, shattering into a thousand shards of rock and crystal.

"Sorry!" Edith called down, but when Alex looked up to respond, she was gone.

"Edith?"

Her face appeared in the hole and smiled back at them. "You were right, Alex. I'm back in the labyrinth, and the burning smell is from a bit of fire up here on a wall. At least we can relight the torch."

Alex smiled at Michael. "Your turn."

Michael begged Alex to go next so he could catch her if she fell, but after she reminded him he'd fallen out of more trees than her, he relented and climbed up next. He was not nearly as fast as Edith, but he found the footholds she had used easily enough. He slipped at the same place Edith had, but Alex was out of harm's way this time.

When he was safe, Alex began her climb. Her boots struggled to find the footing on the jagged, slippery crystal rocks. *I wish I had my powers right now.* When she neared the dangerous step, she noticed one rock was glowing brighter than the others. It was the size of a bush mushroom cap. She grasped it, and after two good yanks, she was examining it in her palm.

"Stop playing on the wall, and get up here," Michael shouted.

He startled Alex, and she nearly dropped the stone, but caught it at the last second. She slipped down and cut her gripping hand. Heart pounding in her chest, she clung to the wall, wincing at the pain her grip was causing. She slipped the rock into her pocket so she could use both hands to climb. By the time she was at the slippery rock again, Michael and Edith were reaching for her, to help her get up, so she accepted their hands and was pulled up the hole to safety.

She wiped her hands on her pants. The air smelled like a dying campfire, with a hint of ash. Burn marks covered the labyrinth walls, and in a few places, fire was still burning some long dead plant matter on the walls.

The walls here were three times Michael's height, so climbing them was impossible. Edith was trying to light her torch at one of the small fires, but the wood, still wet from the river, wouldn't catch.

"Alex?"

Michael was a way ahead. "What did you find?" Alex asked, heading over to him.

He was standing near two small torches jutting from the wall. "Do you think it's a trap?" he asked.

"Maybe. But we don't really have a choice, do we?" Alex reached for them, but Michael grabbed her arm and yanked her back. "What are you doing?"

"Go back to Edith. If anyone is risking themselves for this, it's me."

Alex opened her mouth to object, but Michael glared down at her like a stern older brother. He rarely used this look on her anymore, so she nodded and took a few steps away.

"Alex—" Michael growled.

She held her hand out to him and beckoned him closer. "Just give me your pack. In case you need to run."

Michael nodded and handed her his pack. She and Edith moved to the fork in the labyrinth to give themselves multiple escape routes. When Alex checked, the compass was pointing toward the right fork, so they moved to that side. Michael watched them and when they nodded, he reached toward the torches. Edith and Alex positioned themselves to run if needed.

Almost as soon as he'd placed it there, Michael ripped his hand away from the wall.

CHAPTER 13
ΛARON

Aaron silently picked at his breakfast in the dining hall with Harold, Jessica, Stefan, Macht, and Jerome. He finally understood why Alex ate little when she was worried or upset. Everything felt like iron in his stomach or went sour the moment he swallowed it. But he would need his energy. He still had to train with Jerome and their men, and meet with his mother about the new committee he wanted her and Jessica to run, not to mention all his regular duties as king.

It had been weeks since Alex had ventured off, but in his heart, a lifetime had passed, and he struggled to eat anything decent. *Absconded in the night. That's what Jerome called it, and it has a nice ring to it.* He eyed his men carefully to see who was watching him while they ate their breakfast.

"Aaron, they're fine," Stefan said, and stuffed another thick slice of venison into his mouth. "I trained both Alex and Michael. They're smart, and honestly, they're much better when they're together in situations like this. They work off of one another."

"But their horses returned with their supplies on them." Macht had more concern in his voice than Aaron had ever heard from him.

"According to their letters, they reached what they believed was the cave," Jerome said. "Horses wouldn't have been much use to them there. Alexandria returned them for the animals' safety."

"Won't they need them to get back?" Jessica asked.

"No. Alex will just bring everyone back when they're done," Stefan replied. "When they survive this ordeal, I'll give the both of them so much extra training that they won't get into anything for at least a month."

"Aren't you a ray of sunshine this morning?" Harold teased.

"Why should I be?" Stefan asked. "She left us all behind. She never even gave us the chance to help."

Aaron flung his fork down, and it clattered on his plate. "Regardless, she's your queen and you would do well to remember that. I'm tired of reminding you, and I won't be this kind the next time I have to."

"Have you ever really been kind to me?" Stefan seemed ready to jump up.

"Stefan," Jessica snapped at her brother while Jerome squeezed his shoulder.

Aaron forced his lips into a smile. "You and I have had our differences, but I thought we moved past that, what with our mutual dislike of Gryphon."

Stefan grumbled. "It isn't that I dislike him. I'm suspicious of him. But as Alex needs him to manage her magic, we're stuck with him."

Jerome turned toward his son, but Jessica spoke up first. "If you think I'm going to sit here and let you judge my queen, then you are sadly mistaken, Stefan. Yes, Alex is known for making rash decisions and not always thinking everything through. But do you know what else she is? An imperfect eighteen-year-old girl who grew up away from all our rules and formalities, where she learned how to survive. She is one of the most resilient people I know. She will survive this."

Aaron couldn't help but smile. "Jessica's right."

Stefan still grumbled, but Jessica smacked his arm. "If you're this cranky, summon Lynx. I'm sure *she* can fix your mood."

Stefan dropped his mug and choked on his food. Macht slapped him behind the back until the bread dislodged and he panted for breath. There was true terror on his face when he glanced at his father.

A vicious smirk spread across Jerome's lips. "If you thought you could keep the fact you're in love from your sister and I, you forget your place, son."

"So … you approve?" Stefan said, looking from his father to Jessica.

"If she makes you happy, that's all that matters to us," Jessica said.

"Though as the queen's head guard, it is up to Alexandria and Aaron to approve your bride or else you must forfeit your position," Jerome said.

"What an absurd rule," Harold said. "Why should Aaron have a say over who Stefan weds?"

"It's Alex more than Aaron," Jerome said. "As her personal guard, Stefan needs to be available to Alex day and night. The job is for life, or so long as *she* wishes. That strain is a lot for a marriage, and if the royal dislikes the spouse, it can be difficult, if not impossible."

Aaron couldn't help but chuckle. "Alex loves Lynx. And from what I've seen, Lynx is as protective of Alex as you are."

Perking up, Stefan grinned. "Well, that's wonderful, because I've already proposed to her."

"That deserves a drink," Harold said, and called the servants to bring them some celebratory ale.

Breakfast went longer than expected after Stefan's announcement. Jessica wanted all the details, but her brother said little. He shot down every elaborate plan she suggested, explaining that he and Lynx wanted to get married privately with only their closest friends there, exactly how their mother and father had married. They did however intend to perform both human and sorcerer wedding ceremonies.

Aaron was thrilled. Lynx had accompanied Alex after Aaron's curse, so he knew that Alex not only trusted Lynx but adored her, and Lynx was certainly aware of Stefan's duties as Alex's guard. After growing up surrounded by men, having a sorceress friend who behaved like an older sister to her was Alex's dream come true.

After breakfast, Aaron and Harold headed to the stables with Macht and Jerome in tow.

"Have you decided what to do about your cousin?" Harold asked.

"I think so," Aaron said. "My father begged me not to exile the Rassgats, but after Kruft, and seeing Wesley's attitude, I can't for the life of me figure out why. He clearly knew something I don't."

"And what of their demands?"

"I'm giving Wesley what he wants. He wanted land for people to farm, so he'll have it. But he'll have it my way. It will be far away from the other nobles, even farther from me, and he won't have a say who works it. I've assigned Jerome to pick another noble to be in charge of who will work the land. It shall be someone respected enough that even Wesley won't dare cross him."

"A well thought through plan," Harold said.

"It should keep Wesley out of trouble and keep him away from me and Alex. There is no love lost between us, but Alex might actually set him on fire, so it's better they stay far apart."

A voice rang out. "Stop!"

"Aaron, you can't leave!" shouted another.

Aaron and Harold stopped short of the stable and spun. Hunter and Lucas were running toward them as if the castle was on fire. Aaron's breakfast soured in his stomach, and he pressed his hand against himself to keep from being sick.

"What is the matter with you two?" Jerome scolded. "You both know better than to address Aaron so informally."

"Gryphon and Megesti cracked here with the other sorcerers, and they're in terrible shape," Lucas explained between hurried breaths.

"Who's in terrible shape?" Aaron asked, feeling his fear move up his throat.

"Gryphon and Megesti," Hunter said.

Aaron glanced from his friends to the generals beside them. "Where?"

Moments later, Aaron threw open the door to the Datten sorcerers' lab and found Megesti leaning against the table. Gryphon was sitting with his head in a bucket. Both of them were pale as ghosts and sweating profusely. "What happened to you?" Aaron asked, rushing to Megesti's side. Harold and Jessica followed him into the room.

"Something's wrong with Alex," Lynx said. She told the Dattenites about what had been going on with Gryphon and Megesti, and what they suspected it meant.

"There must have been some magic shielding them from me, because I couldn't sense anything until recently," Gryphon said.

"Perhaps this cave has magic," Harold said.

"It's not the cave," Jessica said. "Alex found a spell that allowed her to enchant things, such as rings and leather straps, to keep you from reading their minds. All of them are wearing leather bands."

Gryphon's eyes narrowed and flashed orange for a moment. "You knew this the entire time?"

Aaron leaped from Megesti's side to stand between Gryphon and Jessica. "I knew, too, so if you want to take your anger out on someone, you can fight me."

"When did you find out?" Jessica asked.

"Alex enchanted my wedding ring before she left, so Gryphon wouldn't be able to read my mind. She did it because apparently he and I are … connected. Through her."

Gryphon growled and flicked his hands, lighting his arms on fire and extinguishing them just as fast. His sinister scowl wandered from Aaron to Jessica and back. Slowly, the orange glow in his eyes dimmed and then turned back to blue. Wordlessly, he strode over to Aaron and exhaled.

"Give me your ring," he said.

Aaron had barely slipped off his ring before Gryphon snatched it from his fingers. He flicked his hand and fire erupted from it. The ring floated there, suspended inside the flame.

"What are you doing? Don't damage it!" Aaron charged toward him.

Lynx stopped him. "He won't. Just give him a moment."

Gryphon squinted and moved his face closer to the flames. "The ring turns violet in the fire, so it must be one of Merlin's spells. I'm tiring of that sorcerer causing so much trouble." He extinguished the flames and tossed the ring back to Aaron.

Aaron clutched it in his palm, and stared at Gryphon, defiantly keeping himself from wincing as it cooled.

"Does it help if you know who wrote the spell?" Jessica asked.

"Only if the spell was authored by someone from one of my lines. When it's from one of Alex's, then I'm at a loss," Gryphon admitted. "Merlock and Victoria took their books with them when they fled, so we aren't as well versed in them."

Lynx addressed Harold. "We were told you have the white pearl. Gryphon might be able to use it to channel Alex."

"Why would our pearl help?" Harold asked, scratching his biceps.

"Because it was made by a Cassandra," Gryphon said.

Megesti suddenly gripped Gryphon's shoulder. "Try it again."

"What?" Aaron asked.

"Gryphon, try to read her again."

"Why? We've just tried that. I'm tired," Gryphon told him.

"Just do it!" Megesti snapped.

Megesti rarely raised his voice, so hearing him snap at Gryphon made Aaron step back. The two sorcerers stared at one another before Gryphon relented and rolled his eyes. His body glowed a soft blue. A moment later, he turned to Aaron, eyes wide. "I can see through her eyes again," he said.

"What do you see?" Lynx asked.

"A dark tunnel. Edith is beside her, and Michael is a distance away from them. But ... she's different."

"Different? How?" Aaron asked.

"Kharon!" Gryphon shouted into the air.

The sorcerous cracked into the room, arms filled with books. "You told me to keep looking for spells, Gryphon, so why are you interrupting me?"

Gryphon gulped at the older sorcerous. "I need to know if I'm right. I need you to summon Victoria. Or Merlin."

"You can't just summon a line founder like that, Gryphon," Birch said. "It's dangerous and exhausting for anyone who tries."

"I know that," Gryphon said. "But with Megesti here, Kharon should be able to do it more safely. And we have to know!"

"Know what?" Aaron asked.

Gryphon gave him a look that sent chills through him.

CHAPTER 14
ALEX

The ground beneath their feet rumbled as Michael rushed toward them. The area where he'd been standing was gone, and a chasm formed just at his heels, the ground collapsing into the cave below. Alex gasped when he stumbled and then caught himself. With a sudden burst of energy, he raced up to them and thrust the torches into the fire on the wall.

"Run!" he screamed.

Edith grabbed a torch and took the lead, following the compass desperately clutched in her other hand. Alex and Michael chased her toward the right as fast as they could. Michael stopped to cough and the sinking ground almost caught up with them. They frantically raced to get ahead of the collapsing path. The compass led them around a corner and they slammed into another dead end. The three of them spun to see the chasm had stopped growing. They were now trapped between three stone walls and a hole large enough to swallow all three of them.

"There are more words here," Michael said. He held up his torch, and the letters in the stone glistened. *"The magic mists of dawn. The forest starts to frighten,"* he read aloud.

"It might not make any sense, but maybe this is what the path was trying to show us," Alex whispered.

Edith started creeping toward the chasm with Alex a step behind. As they approached it, the hole filled in and vanished.

Edith extended her toe and tapped the ground. "Do you think it's safe?" she asked.

"Only one way to find out." Michael handed her the torches, removed his pack, and tossed it over the spot the hole had been. It landed with a solid thud and spilled a few items onto the pathway.

Alex crept toward his bag, and before Michael could stop her, she was standing next to it. When nothing happened, she picked it up, slung it on her back, and turned to Edith. "Lead the way."

They only had two torches to light the front and back of their group. Each time they got to a corner, they bunched together and peeked around the wall to see what awaited them. Alex refused to give Michael the pack and kept it strapped to her body. Despite being utterly exhausted, she would not be the one to force them to stop and rest.

Michael stepped up and took her arm. "I think we should rest," he said. "I'm not sure how long we've been walking since it's dark down here, but it feels like days."

"Are you sure?" Alex asked, trying to hide her exhaustion. *Please let us rest. I've never been this tired in my life. Is that what mortals feel like? It's horrible.*

"Please," Edith replied, leaning against the wall facing another corner. "I'm so tired I can barely stand, but I didn't want to be the one to make us stop."

Relief flooded Alex. "I think a rest sounds wonderful." She slipped her arms out of the pack, and Michael snatched it off her back.

"What did we lose?" Edith asked.

Michael dug through the bag and pulled out his wet blanket.

He dropped it on the ground with a thwap and the drops splashed the group. Edith sighed.

"So, no pillows then," Alex said, taking the bag from Michael and digging through it. She pulled out one of the few remaining dried sausages. "At least there is a bit of food. We should eat it before it goes bad from the water."

"Agreed," Michael said. He was already digging a small hole to hold up the torches.

"Should we blow one out to preserve it?" Edith asked.

Alex picked one up and examined where the fire hit the wood. It didn't look different from any of the torches in Datten or Warren. "I wish I had my powers so I could see if they were enchanted."

"Don't let it upset you," Michael said. "We'll leave one on so we can be sure."

Alex nodded her agreement nervously and Michael blew out the larger torch, plunging them into near darkness. Michael lazily dropped to the ground and shuffled into the corner. He stretched his legs out and beckoned Alex and Edith over. Alex leaned against the stones beside him and let herself slide down until she lay next to him. He wrapped his arm around her, pulling her close as he hummed the Veremund lullaby—the song they shared as children that Michael knew always calmed Alex. His loving grip on her immediately released the tension she had in her body, and she melted against him, despite the ache in her shoulder.

Edith chuckled.

"What?" Michael asked.

"Nothing."

"Tell us, Nial," Alex teased, narrowing her eyes at Edith.

Edith laughed and plopped herself on the ground beside Alex, squeezing her against Michael. "You two make me laugh, because I suspect how I see you two is how people see Julius and me."

Alex smiled at Michael. He nodded back to her, and she turned to Edith. "According to Jessica and Aaron, it is."

"Too bad a Bishop wasn't part of this spell, too. It would have been nice to have some extra help," Michael said.

"When magic is involved, the extra help usually ends up being another person to save," Alex said.

Edith wrapped her arms around Alex's neck and hugged her. "Not this time, Princess."

Alex grabbed Edith's arm and squeezed it back.

"Alright ladies, you sleep and I'll keep watch," Michael said. Alex was going to object, but then he grunted at her, making it clear he wasn't taking no for an answer. She sighed, nuzzled against his shoulder, and let sleep overtake her.

ALEX'S MOUTH felt as dry as the Warren beaches midsummer. She moaned as she pushed herself away from Michael and rolled her stiff neck, setting off a cacophony of cracks. Thrusting her arms above her head, she stretched and loosened her back. Now it hurt from sleeping sitting up against Michael for so long.

Edith is gone.

"Edith?" Alex screamed, waking Michael so suddenly he fell over and scrambled to his feet.

"Why are you screaming?" he asked.

"I can't find Edith!" Alex leaped to her feet and looked around the corner. Her heart beat so hard she thought it might break her ribs, and the little food they'd eaten was trying to come back up. Michael reached out and touched her. Even without her magic, he calmed her panic. Still shaking with fear, Alex grabbed the lit torch off the ground and headed down the path.

Michael grabbed her arm. "Oh no. You're not getting lost in this labyrinth."

"Michael, let me go. I have to find her."

"We'll call her. Despite all the scary things that have happened in here, so far only we and the ground rumbling have made any noise. If we scream loud enough, she'll hear us."

"What if she doesn't?" Alex crossed her arms.

"If she doesn't respond when I think she should have, then we pack up and go look for her."

Alex scowled. "When *you* think we should?"

"I'm terrified for her. But she *is* a general's child, the same as Jessica and Stefan. She's trained to take care of herself, and you have to learn to let us take care of ourselves. Especially since you never let *us* help *you*."

Alex was going to shout at Michael, but nothing came out, and she just stared at him.

"And you know I'm right. You only lose your words when you realize you're wrong and you're mad about it."

Alex clenched her jaw before she huffed at him.

"More proof!" Michael held out his hand to her. "Now let's go find Edith."

"Edith!" Alex's voice echoed off the stones before being swallowed by the darkness.

Michael held the torch up to see if they could find any trace of where she might have gone. "There are footprints here!" He dropped to the ground, holding the torch above himself. "They're much smaller than mine, so they must be Edith's."

Alex examined them. "But they're headed to where we slept. Shouldn't we have passed her coming back?"

Michael frowned at something ahead. Alex followed his line of sight and spotted what was amiss. Everywhere else, the walls were lined with loose stones and dust. At this one spot, there weren't any. It was as if the stone had moved and pushed the pile away. Alex and Michael crept toward the wall and exchanged a quick look. His pursed lips, wide eyes, and quick breaths told her everything she needed to know. Without a word, they felt along the stones for some kind of lever or switch to move the wall.

"It's useless. There isn't anything here." Michael sighed and leaned against the wall. Suddenly his eyes lit up. "Hey, there are more footprints."

They followed them down into a darker area where the walls changed. *Are the stones darker, or do they absorb the light?* An icy wind swept past them.

Michael stopped and offered his hand to her. Swallowing hard, Alex accepted it, and they went side-by-side down the new passage. Alex's breath hitched, and she squeezed his hand.

"It's okay, Alex. I'm here. We're going to find Edith, and I won't abandon you."

"I know," Alex croaked back. As the icy wind swirled around them, the memory of falling through the ice overtook her. She could feel the endless cold and darkness of the Darren River water, and it made her shiver.

Michael clenched her hand, tugged her along.

"You can drop the act, Michael. I know you too well for it."

He looked over his shoulder at her.

"You may look confident, but I know your tells. You're just as scared as I am." Alex pulled her hand from his and patted his shoulder.

"What tells?"

"Your ears turn red." Alex almost smiled at him.

"They do not turn red." Michael grabbed his ears.

"Red, maroon ... same thing."

"Let's focus on finding Edith and not on debating if my ears change color."

"No debate needed, since they do." Alex smirked and stole the torch from him. She slunk down the path, keeping a careful eye out for any disturbances along the bottom of the wall that would indicate a section had moved.

Soon, Alex's throat hurt from calling Edith's name, and her voice was hoarse, so they walked in silence. She listened intently, but all she could make out was Michael's breathing beside her. The dirt floor absorbed their footsteps. *We wouldn't hear if anyone was around the corner.*

"How long ago did she leave? I didn't expect her to have gotten this far," Michael groaned.

"Me neither. I noticed she was gone when I was waking up, but I stupidly assumed she'd wandered off to relieve herself."

"Could the labyrinth be testing her? Or us?"

"I don't know," Alex said, looking around. She breathed deeply and shouted. "Edith! Please, Edith, if you can hear me then answer."

After a long pause, they heard a faint voice call back. It was Edith.

"Edith! We're here. Where are you?" Alex screamed.

"Follow our voice if you can hear us," Michael said. "We'll stay put, so you come to us."

Alex's heart cantered in her chest, ready to burst out if some terrible creature came around the corner, but it was Edith. Alex raced for her and hugged her neck. The two clung to each other and sobbed until Michael caught up to them and threw his arms around them both.

"You scared us, Edith," he said. "When we woke up, and you were gone, it was terrifying."

Edith sounded confused when she spoke. "But I didn't leave. I woke up on the ground and you were both gone. You left me."

"Edith, we didn't go anywhere, I swear," Michael said with raised shoulders.

"Then how did we get separated?" Edith asked.

Alex's voice was soft when she said, "I don't know."

"Now that we know someone or something is in here with us, we won't go to sleep without posting a guard," Michael said.

Alex and Edith nodded.

"Does anyone know how to get back to our things?" Alex asked. "I can't remember what direction we came from."

"I lost track once we started following the walls where the dirt was shifted," Michael said.

"I don't think we should waste any more time hunting for it," Edith said, "because I have something to show you."

"More words?" Alex asked.

"Not just words." Edith hurried off in the direction she'd come, so Alex and Michael followed her. She led them a long way, weaving around corners and into new passages until a light appeared ahead.

"Is that path lit?" Alex asked, squinting.

"It is, but that's not what you need to see. Come on." Edith raised her torch and headed toward the light.

CHAPTER 15

GRYPHON

Gryphon crossed his arms while Megesti paced the throne room, muttering to himself.

"I heard madness runs in your line, but I assumed it was an exaggeration." Gryphon smirked at his cousin.

Megesti scowled. "We failed to summon Merlin, so can you behave yourself for ten minutes while we wait for Harold to bring the pearl?"

"Why on earth they gave it to him in the first place, I'll never understand."

Megesti growled and thrust his hands down his sides. "We've been over this. Edward told Aaron to bring the pearl to the Betruger to prove he loved Alex and was entering their kingdom with pure intentions."

"I know that," Gryphon snapped. "But why does Harold still have it? Once he learned it was Alex's, he should have returned it."

Megesti scoffed. "You clearly don't know her as well as you think you do. She insisted Harold keep it. It was a gift, after all."

"No Cassandra would part with such an important object," Gryphon said.

A crash echoed through the deserted hall, and Kharon brushed themselves off and headed toward them.

"They would if they were powerful enough to not need it," they said. "The others will be here momentarily."

"Did you explain to the mortals how dangerous this spell is?"

"Stop referring to Alex and my friends as *the mortals*; they have names."

"So does your mother," Gryphon snapped and stepped up to Megesti, glaring down at him. "But there are too many mortals to list them by name."

"Down, boy," Lynx scolded Gryphon. She was standing at the doorway holding a jar. Birch was with her and gave them a quieting look.

Gryphon stepped back from Megesti, but continued glaring. *If she weren't here, I'd teach you just why sorcerers don't anger the next Head, or an Ares.*

"I don't care what you're thinking right now," Megesti said. "I'm not afraid of you, and I never will be. My mother helped raise you, and my cousin—my *real* cousin—is your other half. If you ever lay a finger on me, they'd deal with you."

"Letting others fight your battles. How very mortal of you."

"Enough," Birch snapped. "You're acting like children."

The doors to the throne room opened, revealing Aaron, Harold, and Stefan.

"We told you to come alone." Gryphon's head was pounding from the building tension. Unconsciously, he lit his hands on fire. Sighing loudly, he extinguished himself and turned back toward the men.

"I'm the King of Datten," Aaron said. "I do nothing alone."

"We really need to keep it sparse for your safety," Birch said, a forced smile crossing her lips.

"Do you have the pearl?" Megesti asked.

"I do," Harold responded and offered the velvet bag to Megesti.

The sorcerer crept toward Harold and nodded, accepting the bag. "It would seem I owe Birch my appreciation," Harold continued. "It was in my library when she removed our books."

Birch smiled. "I took everything as a precaution."

Lynx skipped to Stefan's side and looped her arm through his. Gryphon held back a snort. *I'm glad you're finally happy, after years of idiot sorcerers mistreating you, never giving you back the love you gave them—you deserve to be. But of all the mortals, him?* As if Lynx sensed his thoughts, she winked at him and kissed Stefan's cheek.

"I wasn't sure you'd ever settle down, Stefan," Megesti said, smiling.

Aaron chuckled. "Apparently he was waiting for his own sorceress."

Stefan, normally stoic, almost grinned before his face returned to its usual coldness. "You have the pearl. Now what do we do?" he asked.

"You do nothing," Gryphon said. "Megesti and I will combine our powers with those of the pearl to see if we can break through the spell protecting the cave. Then we'll be able to see what those three are up to."

"Will it hurt?" Megesti asked.

"Excruciatingly," Gryphon replied, as he removed his robe and handed it to Kharon.

He glanced at Megesti. The sorcerer rarely wore his robes, opting instead for pants, boots, and a Datten shirt. Alex had mentioned to Gryphon that after Merlock's death, Megesti couldn't stand wearing anything his father had picked out. Emmerich and Edward had gifted him an entirely new wardrobe that he chose for himself. *Soon enough, Birch and I will have you back into your proper clothes, but that is another day's battle.*

"The shirt, too," Birch said.

"My shirt?" Megesti asked.

"Mixing magic is dangerous, and while Gryphon rarely catches on fire from his Salem powers, we aren't taking any chances," Birch said. She held out her hand until Megesti tossed her his shirt.

Gryphon snorted at Megesti's scowl as he stripped off his Mystics colored shirt. Locking his fingers together, he extended his arms upward and stretched. He could sense Harold and Aaron watching him. Unlike Aaron, who never seemed to tan regardless of how much time he spent outside, Gryphon's skin had taken on a bronze tint similar to Harold's. Despite using his powers to make much of his day to day effortless, wielding magic had toned his body and given him a strength that rivaled Aaron's and Michael's. He adjusted the position of his pants, letting them settle on his hips, and scratched the scar on his shoulder where his father had burned him. Alex had healed the pain, but Aaron had interrupted her, and the scar had stayed.

When Stefan strode over to Megesti to grab the bag, he gawked at Gryphon's back. "Why do you have the same mark on your shoulder that Alex does?"

"It's their sorcerer bond mark, darling," Lynx answered from across the room. "I'd wager Aaron has the same mark. Occasionally, sorcerers with a deep connection will bond as youngsters, and they can bond again after their powers come in if they wish."

"Does that mean we'll have one after we're married?" Stefan asked.

"Yes, because of what Lynx is," Gryphon answered. Megesti followed Gryphon into the middle of the room. "Everyone should stand back. I've never cast this spell before, so I'm not sure how dangerous it is, especially for non-sorcerers."

For once, the mortals all moved away. Alex's memories from the day she hurt Aaron and Stefan crossed Gryphon's mind. He looked at Megesti and realized the Titan of Merlin was shaking.

"Cold or afraid?" Gryphon whispered to him.

"Can I be both?"

"Yes." Kharon took the bag from Gryphon and waited for him

to face Megesti. "Remember, Gryphon, the pearl will try to control you, but you must control it. Only then can we use the power in it to channel Alex, Michael, or Edith." Kharon set the bag upside-down on Gryphon's outstretched hands.

The velvet slipped away, and the moment the fist-sized pearl landed in Gryphon's palm, memories erupted out of him. The more he tried to stop them, the more came out. He heard his father, mother, and hexa's voices shouting at him, scolding and threatening him. He heard Phobos laughing at him when he failed to wield his Ares powers as a boy.

"Focus on Alexandria," Birch commanded.

Gryphon held the pearl to Megesti but the moment his thoughts switched to Alex, his memories of her roared out and into the room for everyone to see: their first meeting, Alex successfully parting the sea, her exploding rocks, even killing Kruft's men. Stefan's laughter surrounded them when Gryphon kissed Alex and she clocked him without hesitation, but silence filled the room when their fight on the beach played out before everyone. Megesti's eyes filled with tears when the ghostly memory of Alex dropped to her knees and sobbed. He grabbed the pearl, clutching it between his hand and Gryphon's, and a rush of power flew through the room. The memories faded, replaced with dirt flying past.

Gryphon couldn't even breathe. The spell whipped his consciousness across all of Torian. Finally, he was looking through Alex's eyes and Michael's face appeared in the room. Gryphon squeezed his hands around the pearl, despite its searing heat. His burned, but he ignored the feeling and shifted from Alex's mind to Michael's. Alex's face filled the fog before them. It was full of worry as she argued with Michael about which direction to go to find Edith. Aside from losing Edith, they both seemed to be in decent shape, but the moment Alex turned to walk down the pathway, everything changed.

"Who is that?" Kharon asked.

"What do you mean, Kharon?" Lynx asked.

"The man beside her," they replied.

"There isn't anyone beside her," Aaron replied.

Kharon ripped their robe off and dropped it on the floor, lighting up in a gray. Before Gryphon could protest, their hands were on the pearl, and in that instant, a man appeared beside Alex. Raven-black hair covered his head and chin, forming a thick beard. His sea-blue eyes sparkled against his umber skin.

"Who is that?" Gryphon asked, pointing at the apparition a step behind Alex.

"It's Arthur," Aaron said.

ALEX

Alex followed Edith around the corner and down the illuminated path. After all the darkness, she squinted in the light.

"How is this area so bright?" Michael asked behind them.

"There are torches all along the top. This is the only area I found that's lit."

Alex rubbed her eyes and forced herself to take in her surroundings anew. Edith was right. A torch was mounted every few feet along the top of the wall. Alex reached out and gently caressed the stones. These were smoother than any of the others and felt closer to glass than rocks. She caught her reflection in the smooth stone. Her face was covered in dirt, and her braid was a wild tangle of hair, but her eyes didn't have any hint of the darkness she'd seen so often lately.

"Alex? What I wanted to show you is over here." Edith was pointing down the long corridor where a dark shadow fell across the path. When they got closer, Alex found it wasn't a shadow, but a giant hole. She shuffled to the edge and peered over the side. The hole seemed to go on forever, with no end in sight.

"Michael, grab a torch," Alex said.

He was already at the wall grabbing one. Edith came to Alex's other side, and the two of them watched Michael lean as far as he dared and drop the torch into the pit. All three of them sat deathly still as the lit torch shrank and then vanished without ever hitting the bottom.

Alex gulped. The hole was wider across than her and Michael would be tall if she stood on his shoulders. *We can't jump across since we don't have any rope or boards.* "We'll need to find another way around," she said.

"I tried while I was looking for you. There isn't one," Edith said. "And we have to go through here." She held the compass out to Alex. The needle was pointing right at the pit.

Alex threw her arms up in frustration. "This makes no sense. How are we supposed to get across there without my magic?"

Michael was lost in thought. He scratched his thickening beard and leaned against the wall. Edith walked around the edge of the pit when another rumble hit.

Alex grabbed Edith's shirt and yanked her away from the pit edge just in time. The ground beneath them shook violently, sending both of them to the ground. Michael let out a startled cry and vanished.

In her panicked state, it took a moment for Alex to realize it wasn't only Michael who had vanished, but the entire wall was gone. "Michael?"

There was a loud groan followed by coughing. Alex and Edith sprang to their feet and hurried through the now open passage to where they found Michael on the ground. He was uninjured, but had clearly gotten the wind knocked out of him.

"What happened?" Edith asked.

"I don't know," Michael said. Alex helped him to his feet, and he brushed off as much dirt as he could. "I leaned against this wall and then it was gone."

"Our bag!" Alex brushed past Michael to the corner, only a few steps behind him. Their supplies were all sitting there, but instead of just one bag, there were now two. Alex picked up her pack and turned toward her friends.

"Did you find the other bag while I was gone?" Edith asked.

Michael shook his head. "At least we have an idea how you ended up away from us in the middle of the night. Could you have sleep-walked?"

"It's possible," Edith said. "I did it often as a child."

Alex dug through the new pack. "These aren't our things," she said.

"What's inside it?" Michael asked, picking up his pack.

Alex scrunched up her nose and scowled. "Rope, cloth, a small pickaxe—everything you'd want if you were trying to cross an open pit."

"That's not suspicious at all," Michael grumbled.

"Well, not as suspicious as sticks and boards," Edith said. She'd wandered a short distance ahead.

"What?" Alex tightened her bag and slung it over her shoulder as she hurried toward Edith. Leaning against the wall around another corner was a collection of long boards and wooden poles. Alex cautiously touched them. "They're real," she said.

"Can we trust them? What if they were placed here for us to use, only to have them break so we'd fall to our deaths?" Michael asked.

Alex and Edith both turned toward him, mouths open. "Why would you say that?" Edith asked.

"This is not the time to lose your optimism, Michael," Alex replied.

"One of us needs to think critically," he said.

Alex and Edith looked at each other. "Well, we might as well get started," Alex said and grabbed the wooden poles, dragging them toward the pit.

Soon, they had a pile of supplies at the edge of the pit. Alex took stock of them. "We have five long poles, four boards, a few suitable lengths of thick rope, and our water satchels," she said.

"How are the water bottles going to help get us across?" Michael asked.

"They aren't. I'm just thirsty," Alex said, and took a big swig of water. Edith snorted and shook her head. Michael playfully pushed Alex then walked to the pit. He squatted at the edge and rubbed his chin.

"Edith, you said there were words here, too," Alex said.

"Over here." Edith led Alex to the wall opposite where Michael had fallen through.

"'*While mountains show their violence, the evening wind grows cold.*'" Alex wrinkled her nose at Edith. "They get stranger each time."

"Any idea what it means?" Edith asked.

She heard Michael grunt as he got to his feet. "We can't slink around the edge. It looks wide enough to stand on, but with how slippery the rocks are on this side of the pit, we can't risk it."

"What if we tied the wooden boards together?" Edith asked. "We could put one across in the middle to attach them there."

"That won't work," Alex said. "As soon as one of us got to the middle, the whole thing would collapse. You'd need a board that goes all the way across to hold up the central part."

"How do you know?" Edith asked.

"She knows from experience," Michael said.

"Don't look at me like that," Alex said. "I bet you're thrilled right now that my makeshift childhood bridge across the Darren River collapsed."

"I wouldn't say *thrilled*."

"We could use the poles and leap over the pit," Edith said.

Alex and Michael both cocked their heads toward her. "Do what?" Michael asked.

"Vault. You use the pole and throw yourself over it. Did you not do that as children?" Edith asked.

"No," Alex said. She tried to picture Edith in a dress like the ones Alex wore, throwing herself across a fence or puddle. "Though I'm honestly not surprised you did. Was it with Julius and his brothers?"

Edith grinned and nodded.

"I have an idea," Michael said. "We could use the poles to make a sort of cross to span the hole. If we overlap them a foot or so and bind them together, then the four ends should all be able to reach the edges. Then we could tie the boards together like Edith suggested and put them in the middle. The center of the poles should hold long enough for us to get across, if we're quick about it."

"That's the best plan we have so far," Alex said, and the three of them got to work tying and binding the wood. Soon the makeshift cross brace lay across the pit and Michael carefully slid the heavy bound boards onto the middle of the poles.

Edith frowned at the rickety wooden structure. "We made it, but now how do we test it?" she asked.

Michael held out his pack to Alex and took a step toward the pit. "I'll go," he said.

"Absolutely not," Alex grabbed his arm to pull him back.

"Alex, I'm not risking you," Michael snapped.

"I'll be fine. I have magic—" The words caught in Alex's throat as she glanced at her hands, closing them into fists.

"Exactly." Michael grabbed her arms and rubbed them. "You're Queen of Datten, and Edith is going to be Queen of Betruger. I may be an Earl, but I'm the lowest ranking in this cave, and more importantly, if anything went wrong, I couldn't live with myself."

"But you expect me to?" Alex whispered. Her lip trembled, and she looked down to hide her tears. *I never should have given up my magic.*

Michael pressed his forehead against hers until she could meet his eye. "You're stronger than anyone I've ever met. You'd survive anything, given enough time."

"But Jessica—"

"She'd have the baby."

"Your son."

Michael smiled softly. "Yes our son. But also, her brother, father, you. She'd be fine."

Alex took the bag from Michael and gulped.

"Good luck," Edith said.

Michael took a deep breath and put his first foot on the board. With every step, the boards creaked and bounced. Alex held her breath while he took each slow and perilous step, until he made it to the other side. Victorious, he cheered and spun around to the ladies. "Toss the bags over. No one needs to carry them."

Alex and Edith tossed their two supply bags across the pit, and Michael caught them effortlessly. When all their supplies were safe Alex turned to Edith. "You go next. I'll go last."

"No. You're still my queen, too," Edith said. "You're going next."

"Edith—"

"No arguing, Alex," Michael shouted from the other side.

"You two planned this!" Alex muttered.

Edith gave Alex a quick hug before pushing her ahead. "I'll hold the boards on this side, and Michael will hold the other. Now go, Warren."

Alex rolled her eyes and marched to the pit. When she looked into it, her confidence vanished. She closed her eyes to calm her pounding heart. *Michael made it. You will, too. You're a Warren—and we are not quitters.*

Michael was squatting down to hold the board, his eyes fixed on her face. "Just look at me. Nothing scary here. You and I, playing in the woods by the camp, like we did hundreds of times."

Alex gently placed her boot onto the board. After a few steps, it creaked, and she froze, too scared to move.

"You can do it, Alex," Edith urged. "A few more steps is all."

"I can't," Alex stuttered, and her entire body trembled.

A loud roar echoed around them. Alex's scream was drowned out by a gale force wind burst from below, rattling the structure that was barely supporting her.

"Alex, run!" Michael shouted. Alex tried to take another step, but the boards shifted, and she missed landing on the pole. It snapped from her weight.

CHAPTER 17

GRYPHON

"Arthur? As in Alex's grandfather? The mortal who killed Victoria?" Gryphon asked.

"It looks like him," Aaron said. "The hair is a little different, but I'd know those eyes anywhere."

"I don't think it's Arthur," Megesti said, squinting at the figure. "I knew him a long time, and that face doesn't look evil the way Arthur's did. He was always angry, from the day Edward was born until he died."

"How can you not know your former King?" Gryphon scoffed in exasperation. "Is there any way we can be sure who it is?"

"Kharon and I will collect General Randal and King Edward. They'd know," Lynx said.

"Agreed," Aaron said, and the two cracked away.

Gryphon nodded to Megesti, and they released the pearl together. Megesti slumped to his knees. Gryphon stepped back, feeling the pearl's power drain from him. Alex's magic made his chest and fingers itch as the room filled with nervous energy. *It's no wonder Alex can't control her magic. Just holding it, I feel as if I'll burst into flames. She's not even old enough to properly wield it.* Megesti groaned, diverting his attention. *Wait—I'm not even holding all of it!*

"What if it is Arthur?" Aaron asked Birch.

"Let's not worry until we know for certain," she said, smiling sweetly.

"Easy for you to say," Megesti said. "You weren't here. You didn't have to deal with him or watch what he did to everyone around him."

"Watch your mouth when you speak to your mother," Gryphon warned. "Usurper or not, if you disrespect Birch, you'll deal with me."

Megesti scrambled to his feet. "I'm not afraid of you. You act like a complete ass to everyone. We've been nothing but kind to you, but because we have something you don't, you throw a temper tantrum."

Gryphon cackled and stalked closer to Megesti. Alex's magic swirled with his own, making it harder to hold back his Ares powers, but he managed to stop himself inches from Megesti's face. "You have nothing I want."

"Except Alex's unconditional love and complete trust," Megesti spat back, his eyes flashing violet. "She doesn't trust you ... she tolerates you, because she needs you to teach her to control this immeasurable amount of power she carries around. She loves Aaron, and has proved it over and over, but you still follow her like a pathetic lap dog."

Gryphon lunged for him, and the mortals in the room rushed over. Gryphon felt his Ares powers overtake him and erupted into orange and violet light. Megesti pulled and Gryphon's powers flowed out of him. Megesti was stealing them. A fist collided with his face, sending warmth running down his cheeks. He ignored the pain and threw himself forward, pinning Megesti to the ground. Blood pouring from his nose, he growled at the sorcerer below him.

Something slammed into him from the side, taking him to the stone floor with brutal force. Birch grabbed his face and burst into a beautiful deep green glow that reminded him of her cottage garden in the evening light. Gryphon's rage vanished, and the orange glow with it. She hurried over to Megesti and repeated the process. Stefan climbed off Gryphon and held his hand out to him. Thinking of Alex and Lynx, Gryphon allowed Stefan to pull him to his feet.

"Did you have to hit me so hard?" Gryphon grumbled as Stefan slapped his back.

"You're lucky he did." Aaron crossed his arms. "Alex is attached to Megesti. She'd never have forgiven you if you'd hurt him."

"Gryphon, I'm sorry," Megesti said, rubbing his arms. "I don't know what came over me, or why I said those things. I didn't mean them."

"It's alright, Megesti," Gryphon said. "Alex can barely manage her Ares powers. I should have expected that you wouldn't be able to handle taking mine while you're holding hers."

"What is going on here?" Edward demanded.

Gryphon and the others fell silent upon the arrival of Lynx and the Warren King. "Can't I leave you alone for five minutes?"

"Where's Kharon?" Birch asked.

"Finding Randal. He'll be here in a minute," Lynx said.

Edward narrowed his eyes. "You failed to mention he was going to be here."

"Naturally," Lynx said without even glancing back. "If I had, you wouldn't have come." She tossed her hair and looped her arm through Stefan's. "Thank you for keeping Gryphon in line for me."

"I apologize for the deception, Your Royal Highness," Birch said. "But we need your help, in order to assist both your daughters. I expect you can be civilized for a short while."

"Of course I can." Edward glanced at Aaron but turned away quickly, frowning.

"You're still holding a grudge against Aaron? What is happening to Warren?" Gryphon asked.

"Who I am on good footing with is none of your concern," Edward snapped.

"It is, when your childish actions put Alex in danger," Gryphon replied.

"I am a king, not a child, so you will address me as—"

"You conveniently forget I'll be a king in my own right one day," Gryphon replied. "And just because you're older than Alex, doesn't make you older or wiser than me."

"What did we miss?" Kharon asked loudly from behind Aaron and Megesti.

"Kharon informed me you need help to identify someone." Randal said. "Apologies I took so long. I was in a meeting with Macht and Jerome."

"No apologies needed, Randal," Aaron said, smiling. "New recruits always take a lot of time."

"You'd know," Megesti replied.

"So who are we supposed to identify?" Edward asked, glaring at Randal from across the hall.

"There is an apparition following Alex," Kharon said. "None of the spirits here would tell me who he is, and Aaron and Megesti are unsure whether it's Arthur Warren."

Edward's umber skin went gray. "You believe my father is stalking Alexandria in the labyrinth? What do we do? How do we stop him?"

"First, we need to make sure it is your father," Birch said. "That's why you're both here. Gryphon, Megesti, please?"

Once again, they collected the pearl and focused their magic as hard as they could. A fog washed over them all, revealing Alex and Edith at the edge of a large pit, and beside Alex was the same regal apparition they'd seen. He stood proudly beside her with a slight grin on his face.

"It can't be," Randal said.

"That's not our Arthur Warren, but another," Edward said. "That's the first-born son of the Arthur Warren who founded Warren with Patrick Nial and George Veremund."

"So Alex is being followed by the first Prince of Warren?" Aaron asked.

"Yes," Edward said. "Though for what purpose, I'm not sure."

Randal scoffed. "She passed her test."

Everyone turned to Randal, questioning.

"The legend says those who venture to the labyrinth will demonstrate the skills of those who founded their lines. That means Alex proved herself honorable and loyal, and so now the first Warren heir is at her side for the rest of the trail. I would hope that eventually Edith and Michael would have apparitions at their sides, too."

Megesti and Gryphon released the pearl, and it dropped between them. The amount of magic it took to get into Alex, Edith, and Michael's minds was draining. Megesti dropped to his knees and sighed. Gryphon rubbed his face, trying to settle his nerves.

"At least we know they aren't in danger from the ghost," Lynx said, clearly trying to lighten the mood.

Randal and Edward stared at one another a moment. Finally, Edward turned toward Aaron and Harold. "I see you went through with your plan to allow my disgraced general to lead your new counsel. You couldn't get anyone in Datten to take the job?" His tone was curt, and his body stood cold and stiff.

"Your *daughter* and I decided it was the right thing to do," Aaron replied.

Edward scoffed and turned back to Birch and Gryphon. "If that is all I was needed for, you may return me to Warren."

Gryphon was about to reply when the sound of bells echoed through the hall.

"What now?" Aaron groaned. He motioned to Stefan and the younger Wafner nodded and headed toward the doors.

With a loud crack, a new sorcerer appeared.

"Hello, cousin." Lygari chortled and strutted toward Megesti. The Titan of Merlin went ashen as his blood cousin moved closer. "Where's our youngest cousin?"

"How did you get in?" Aaron shouted, drawing his sword.

Gryphon noticed the blade's red sheen and cringed. It appeared Alex wasn't the only one who possessed red steel. He snapped his finger, sending Randal from the room to summon help.

Lygari laughed. "Your protection spells all use Merlin and Cassandra magic—*my* magic. I've been watching you for some time now, though the witch has a nasty habit of sensing me, even when she's asleep."

"You're the one the men have been seeing out of the corner of their eyes," Jerome accused.

"And you're the coward who tried to break into the king's suite while Alex was sleeping," Stefan said.

"Guilty," Lygari smirked. "Your little spell keeps out all the other sorcerers, but not me. Now that I'm here, all I have to do is invite them in." With a snap of his fingers, a dark oak staff appeared in his hand, and he struck the stone floor with it. The sound of glass shattering echoed through the hall. Lygari smirked, turning to Megesti. "Our dear little cousin isn't the only one who can break protection spells."

CHAPTER 18

ΛARON

Aaron was momentarily stunned. *Lygari is the one causing Alex's night terrors and making her feel watched all the time in our home. This ends today.* Aaron rushed to intervene, but before he could reach Lygari and Megesti, a ring of fire surged to life around him, stopping him in his tracks. The flames threatened to lick his chest.

"Not so fast, mortals," Ember said. She thrust out her arm, sending more flames racing across the stone floor to trap Edward and Harold in their own rings of fire.

Out of the corner of his eye, Aaron spotted Stefan creeping toward the sorceress, but an old woman cracked behind him before he could do anything. With a flick of her wrist, she sent Stefan flying into the wall. He slammed into the Wafner family portrait so hard it teetered on its hooks. Stefan writhed against the invisible hands holding him into place high above the floor.

"Is this the one she gutted?" the woman asked Lygari, and he grunted in reply.

"And the one who helped her escape us," Ember sneered.

Lynx cracked behind them and snarled, revealing her oversized canine teeth. "Eris, put him down."

Eris spun on Lynx, lighting up in orange. "You know better than to command me, kitten." She clenched her fist and Lynx grasped at her throat, fighting for breath. Gryphon cracked between them and slapped the old woman's arm away, sending her stumbling back in surprise. Lynx sucked in a breath and dropped to her knees.

"Put him down!" Gryphon ordered.

"Or what, Gryphon? You'll murder your own hexa? Or will you have one of them do your dirty work for you, like you did with your mother?"

"My mother deserved what she got," Gryphon said, bursting into the same orange glow as Eris. "She knew better than to go after Alex. I will personally kill anyone who tries to hurt her."

The throne room doors burst open. Jerome rushed in with Macht, Randal, and Aaron's guards at their sides. Eris curled her hand in, sending Stefan to the ground in a heap.

The sound of him striking the stones was the distraction Aaron needed. He pulled his shirt over his head and ran through the flames. The silken fabric lit up in flames immediately, and he tossed it to the floor, leaving only his gold tunic.

Lygari threw Megesti into the guards and charged toward Aaron but stumbled when the ground rumbled beneath them. The power was coming from Gryphon and Eris. Both of them were almost blinding in their orange light staring each other down.

"Ember, go!" Eris shouted.

Smirking, Ember set the entire floor between them and the guards on fire before she vanished.

The guards frantically tried to find a path through the blazing inferno that separated them from their king. Lygari had regained his balance and advanced toward Aaron with murder in his eyes. He halted abruptly, and Aaron followed his gaze to where Harold and Edward were trapped by the fire. Birch was with them, using her magic to create a safe passage for them. Aaron reached for his sword, but a sudden blast of wind knocked it out of his grasp. Lygari stalked toward Aaron, his eyes violet and his hands ablaze.

Aaron inhaled and clenched his fists, ready to face Lygari with nothing but his bare hands, but before Lygari could reach him, a golden figure appeared between them. It took Aaron a moment to recognize Megesti. He was radiating the same light that Alex did when she used her power. Lygari didn't even have time to react before Megesti slammed his fist into his face. Lygari fell to the ground with a thud, and vines sprouted from the cracks in the stones, wrapping around him and pinning him down.

Birch joined them, standing over Lygari with a fierce expression. "Do not touch my son." She spat the words with venom, and her vines tightened around Lygari, squeezing the breath out of him.

A loud bang made them all look up. The guards had ripped some decorative tapestries off the wall and were beating back the flames, but that wasn't what caused the noise. A stone hit Aaron in the hip, making him gasp in pain. Another one hit Megesti in the shoulder, making his golden glow rush to the wound. Unconcerned with who else they hit, Gryphon and Eris hurled stones at each other with their magic, tearing apart the wall in their duel.

Harold staggered over to Aaron's side, fixing his hatred-filled eyes on Lygari. The sorcerer was still trapped by Birch's vines, but Harold was clearly not satisfied. "Don't think I've forgotten what you did. When this is over, it's you and me, *witch*." He spat the last word as if it tasted foul in his mouth.

Aaron barely had time to nod at Harold before another rock whizzed past his ear. He turned to see Jerome rushing toward him, holding up a Datten shield to deflect the rocks.

"We need to get you out of here," Jerome said urgently, grabbing Aaron's arm.

"I would have removed him if it got too dangerous," Birch said calmly, gesturing at Aaron with her free hand. She was still holding Lygari in place with her vines, which tightened around him every time he tried to struggle. "But I agree, we should leave now."

"Macht and Hunter are getting Stefan and Edward, but we need to vacate the castle." Jerome searched for an exit, but they were blocked by the fire and smoke.

"Why?" Harold asked, confused. "What's going on?"

Before Jerome could answer, a loud and ominous sound filled the air. The Datten alarm bells rang, signaling a dire emergency. Aaron felt a surge of fear in his chest.

"Jerome, what's happening?" he demanded.

"The castle's on fire." Jerome's voice was grim. "And we're trapped inside."

CHAPTER 19

ALEX

One moment Alex was upright, and the next she was falling onto the board before her. The only thing that kept her from flying off the structure was the wind still surging against her. Her knee slammed down and there was another crack. Before she even had time to cry out, Michael stepped out onto the precarious edge of the plank, grabbed her shirt in his fist, and yanked her off the boards.

When she slammed into the ground beside him, the air left her lungs. She spun in time to see their makeshift bridge slipping off the side of the edge. The three of them scrambled to the edge. The boards crash into the side of the pit and disappeared into the abyss.

Trembling, Alex looked across the pit at Edith. The youngest Nial was sitting on her knees staring into the pit, but where Alex expected fear, she found anger.

"Edith, I'm so sorry," Alex began.

Edith held up her hand. "This wasn't your fault. This place is trying to break us, but I will not let it." She stood and began searching near her.

Michael rushed to his feet. "Edith, what are you doing?" Alex followed him and soon they were both standing at the edge across the pit from Edith. After a moment, she returned holding the last and largest pole in her hands. They hadn't used it in the structure, and now Alex questioned whether it would have made the difference for them. Edith carefully pressed the pole against the ground and tried to bend it.

When she realized what her friend was going to do, Alex watched in rising panic. "Edith!" she shouted.

Edith finally looked up at them. "I'm going to vault over the pit."

"No," Alex said. "You could fall! We'll think of another way!"

"There is no other way, Alex. The bridge and supplies are gone. You and Michael are on the other side and the only way we are going to finish this ridiculous journey is if we do it together. Now move back so I have room to land."

"You cannot be serious," Michael said, stepping aside.

Alex's leg was still throbbing where the pole had scratched her when she'd broken through the bridge. She stood there in disbelief, looking back and forth between her two friends. Michael's face was ashen and clearly full of worry. Edith was stoic and determined, a mirror of her father.

"Alex, I can do this," Edith said. "Have faith in me, the same way I always do in you."

Alex stilled for a long moment, before she exhaled, and nodded to Edith. *Please don't get hurt.*

Edith held the pole pointed at the ground behind her, its tip raised above her shoulder toward the labyrinth ceiling. Alex clenched her hands into fists, and bit her cheek. Edith ground her feet into the dirt and positioned herself to run. With her pole raised like a lance at a tournament, she charged forward. Edith plunged the pole into the ground just before the edge. It quivered and Alex sucked in her breath, then the force of the strike lifted her off the ground and flung her above the pit, feet first. Alex held her breath as Edith released the pole and it dropped into the pit. The same wind and roar Alex had experienced burst up from the pit, sending Edith flying to the left.

Michael pushed Alex aside and ran toward Edith, but he was too slow to catch her before she hit the ground with a gut-wrenching crack.

Alex followed Michael. Although they reached Edith in seconds, each step felt like an hour. She was sitting up and cradling her ankle.

Alex dropped to her side. Struggling to hold back her tears, she asked, "Are you alright?"

"I'm rusty but it's fine. I'll walk it off." Edith winced trying to stand.

"Rusty?" Michael asked. "That was amazing. I've never seen anything like it."

Edith grinned. "You'll have to ask Julius and his brothers to teach you when you get back. In Warren, we've used poles for centuries, but mostly to get around streams and creeks in the fields. The Bishop family are the ones who made a sport out of it."

Alex yanked her pack across the ground toward her so she could use it to elevate Edith's ankle.

"How bad is it?" Edith asked.

"You're lucky it's not broken. I wish you could stay off it. But we need to keep going. Let me wrap it and we'll see if you can stand on it." Alex grabbed her spare shirt that survived the river and had settled in the bottom of her pack. Tearing it with her teeth, she ripped the cloth into long strips and wrapped them around Edith's ankle. After she'd done all she could, Michael held his hands out to Edith and helped her up.

Edith winced, and said through clenched teeth, "It's fine. I'll walk it off."

"Liar." Michael spun around and squatted in front of Edith.

"Get on. I'll carry you. We'll have to walk slower, but we can't risk you hurting yourself worse."

"Michael that's not neccess—"

"Don't argue with him," Alex said, shoving her remaining supplies into Michael's bag, along with the cold extinguished torches. "Michael is as stubborn about health matters as Stefan is about everything else."

Edith exhaled and smiled weakly at Michael. "Thank you." She wrapped her arms around Michael's neck and her legs around his hips as he bounced her up onto his back.

"Ready, Alex?" Michael asked.

Alex tied up the bag, slipped it on her back, and slid the sword of Nial through her belt sheath. She examined the compass, and an icy stiff wind made her shiver. "Let's go," she said, and they started again, though more slowly this time.

THEY FOLLOWED the compass along the torch-lined pathways. There weren't many, but they cast enough light that Alex didn't need to hold one, and Michael could easily see while he carried Edith. Alex glanced around every corner to be sure it was safe. None of them felt especially chatty, so they moved in silence, with only the thumping of Alex or Michael's boots and their own heartbeats to spur them on.

Soon, Alex noticed Michael's boots were scraping against the rocky floor, so she suggested they rest. Once again, they leaned against the wall in a corner so they could get a view of both directions of the pathway.

They finished the last of their food in silence. *What can I say to apologize for getting us into this mess?* Alex avoided looking at them, drawing in the dirt.

"Stop that," Michael scolded, lips pursed and head cocked to the side.

"We're out of food, and low on water ..." Alex began. "What if we—"

"Don't," Edith interjected. "I just leaped over a giant pit, and I will not let you come apart because of water." She grabbed Alex's hands and looked at her so sternly Alex couldn't help but laugh.

"We should keep going," Michael said. They quickly packed their things and set off.

The compass took them left, then right and then left again. This part of the maze kept winding back on itself, and Alex couldn't tell if they were making any progress. After at least a dozen sharp turns, they finally reached a straight stretch. Edith's legs were sore from clinging to Michael, so he let her down and she hobbled along using Alex's shoulder and the wall for support.

Near the end of the path Alex spotted more words etched into the wall.

"We're at a dead end," Michael said.

A loud rumble shook the ground, and Edith hung on to Alex. Alex dropped the bag she was carrying so they wouldn't both fall. When the rumbling stopped, they found the way they'd come down was blocked by a new wall.

"Alex," Edith asked with a gulp. "Is that wall still moving?"

Alex's voice caught in her throat. The surrounding stones rattled as the gigantic wall moved toward them. It was moving at a glacial pace, but that wouldn't help them if they couldn't find a way out.

"Try pushing the stones," Michael said. "Maybe we can get another wall to move, like we did by the hole."

Edith pushed against the wall that she was leaning on. Alex and Michael rushed to work on the other two walls.

"What about the words here?" Alex asked, pointing at her wall.

"As all the beasts go rest, dear children, we behest, you let your dreams now take hold."

"Why do they all rhyme?" Edith asked.

"I don't know," Alex said, feeling herself begin to panic.

"Could it be a poem or a children's story?" Michael asked.

"Why would that be in the maze?" Alex snapped. "It's mad!"

"I don't know. You come up with an explanation then," Michael said.

"Fighting won't help right now," Edith said.

"She's right. I'm going to stop the wall." Alex sprinted to the far wall. Unlike the smooth and shiny stones that made up the path, the stones on the wall were rough and dark gray like the Warren castle. She threw her weight against the wall, but it did nothing. When she pushed against it, the wall moved a little faster. Next Alex tried to scale the wall. She'd made it halfway when the entire thing rumbled as if it were trying to throw her off. She desperately squeezed the rock, trying to hang on, but the cuts on her hand and shoulder shot a wave of pain through her, and she fell into Michael's arms.

"Breaking your neck won't solve anything," he whispered to her.

Edith was still pushing against the stones, occasionally wincing in pain from her ankle, searching for a switch or a way out. Alex glanced up at Michael, trying to find the words to thank him for everything he'd done, but nothing was enough to properly say goodbye.

"We are not giving up yet, Alex," Michael said and pressed his forehead to hers. "I've never given up on you, so don't you dare give up on me. I promised to bring you home safe, and I *ferflucsing* intend to keep that promise."

Alex swallowed back the emotion gathering in her throat and nodded at Michael. "I'll go help Edith."

Alex dashed over to Edith. Together, they completed a second sweep of the stones, pushing each one with their hands, hoping to trigger some mechanism that would open a door, but nothing happened. The stones were cold and silent.

"Edith, please, let's take a break," Alex pleaded. She could see the sweat on her forehead and the grimace on her face. "You need to rest your ankle."

Edith sighed as she settled onto the ground and leaned against Alex for a moment. Alex wrapped her arm around Edith and felt her lean on her while Michael pushed against the wall.

Soon, she began to hum a tune to soothe them and hold back her panic. Soft music filled the air, soothing them, until Michael stopped and faced Alex.

"What?" she asked, making Edith sit up.

"It's not a poem," Michael replied, running to catch up to them. "It's a lullaby."

Alex scrambled to her feet and helped Edith up. They joined Michael at the etching. "Michael—"

Michael held his arm out and shushed her. He traced his fingers over the words and sang them aloud. Recognizing it as their song, the Veremund lullaby, Alex joined him. After they finished, he sang.

> *"The silver moon is rising,*
> *Above the sea it's shining,*
> *The golden sun is gone.*
> *Until the morning fires,*
> *And from the meadow rises,*
> *The magic mists of dawn.*
> *The forest starts to frighten,*
> *While mountains show their violence,*
> *The evening wind grows cold.*
> *As all the beasts go rest,*
> *Dear children, we behest,*

You let your dreams now take hold."

When he'd finished, they heard complete silence.

"The wall stopped! Michael, sing it again," Edith pleaded. Michael sang it twice more. After the first time, the wall completely disappeared, and after the second, the wall with the etchings rumbled and a door appeared. It was a solid piece of polished obsidian. It sparkled in the dim torchlights and had a large handle made of silver. Michael gulped and stepped up to it. Like the one that had appeared at the entrance to the cave, this one had a 'W', 'V' and 'N' carved into the stone. He clenched his teeth as he held his hand out to Alex.

She pulled out the sword of Nial, and they took turns slicing a finger to put their blood against the door. Then, they waited.

Nothing happened.

"Try the words from Warren," Michael said. "Veremund the wise."

"Nial the brave," Edith whispered.

"Warren the true," Alex announced, and the door swung open.

CHAPTER 20

AARON

Aaron fought a wave of nausea trying to focus on Jerome's words. His mouth was dry and his heart pounding when he asked, "What did you say?"

Jerome adjusted his grip on the shield above their heads and stepped closer to Aaron. His face was grim and his voice low. "The red-haired sorceress. She set fire to both towers, and the stables." Out the window, flames and smoke billowed from the castle. Focusing on the outside, Aaron could hear the screams of people and horses, along with the thud of rocks hitting the shield. Jerome continued. "Randal and Avery are getting your mother and Jessica out. But I need to get both of you to safety. The guards will deal with the rest."

"I'm not leaving our people behind, and that includes the sorcerers." Aaron turned to Birch. "Take Lynx, Megesti, and Harold to the old stables. We'll get Gryphon and be right behind you."

Birch nodded and cracked the requested people out of the room. As soon as Birch vanished, Lygari broke free from his restraints and cracked away.

"Coward," Jerome muttered, moving in front of Aaron and

lowering the shield to block their heads better. The Datten knights had put out the fire in the room. Gryphon and Eris were so focused on each other and their battle that they didn't seem to notice anything around them.

Aaron grabbed a rock from the ground and lowered Jerome's shield slightly. He took aim and threw the rock at Eris, hitting her in the shoulder. She let out a horrible shriek, as if he'd stabbed her with a knife, and whipped her head toward him, eyes narrowing with hatred. She raised her hand to unleash a blast of fire at him, but before she could do so, a flash of orange light blinded him, and Gryphon appeared between Aaron and Eris.

"You would defend this mortal whelp?" Eris shouted. "Why not let me finish him and his guard? You could tell the Heart it was an accident. I'll even knock you unconscious." She stalked toward the group.

"Gryphon, we have to go," Aaron said, shaking Gryphon's arm. Gryphon slowly turned to Aaron. His eyes were glowing as brightly as the moon in the night sky. Aaron gulped and stepped back.

"Gryphon," Jerome growled, but Gryphon snapped his fingers and the general vanished, leaving Aaron alone with Eris and Gryphon. Determined not to show any fear, Aaron puffed out his chest and stared Gryphon down.

Submit. Gryphon's voice echoed in his head.

"I'm not afraid of you," Aaron spat.

Back down, so I can get rid of her. Finally understanding, Aaron stepped back from Gryphon letting his fear show on his face. "You can't hurt me. You might not want to wait a few decades, but if you lay a finger on me, she'd never forgive you, and you know it." Aaron reached down for his sword, a rock, or anything he could use as a weapon.

Eris joined Gryphon's side. "He doesn't *need* her to forgive him. He just needs to set their bond, and she'll give into her sorceress nature and forget all about you."

"I would say it's been nice knowing you, Princeling, but we both know I'd be lying." Gryphon rubbed his hands together, forming a swirling fireball. The glow illuminated his face, making his eyes glow red.

Aaron gulped. *What if he really kills me?*

Gryphon smirked at Aaron, then raised the fireball, took aim, and at the last second, spun and plunged it into Eris's chest. The sorceress was sent flying across the hall. Aaron's skin sizzled when Gryphon grabbed his wrist and cracked them away.

They were in the courtyard at the Verlassen Castle, and birds were singing around them.

"Have you lost your mind?" Aaron shouted. "Why did you bring us here?"

"To save your life, Princeling."

"Lygari and Moorloc attacked us here before. Take me back to Datten now. Our kings do not flee."

"Just catch your tongue so I can think," Gryphon snapped. "I am not about to let you get yourself killed. The last thing I need is Alex blaming me because you have a hero complex."

Aaron's stomach roiled with rage. "I do not have hero issues. I'm a king." He stormed over to Gryphon and shoved the sorcerer. "Take me back."

Gryphon reeled and whipped around with orange glowing eyes. "Keep your hands off me."

"Or what?" Aaron stepped up to Gryphon and glared.

Gryphon scoffed. His orange cloak billowed in the wind, a brazen smirk painted across his lips.

Something inside Aaron snapped, and he shoved Gryphon away again. The sorcerer growled and swung the first punch. Aaron threw his arm up easily, diverting Gryphon's unskilled blow, and sent his fist into the sorcerer's smug face.

Gryphon's nose erupted with blood. The fire in his eyes made Aaron pause and Gryphon took full advantage and gestured at the ground, making it shake beneath them. Aaron steadied himself while he unsheathed his sword and thrust the blade toward Gryphon. The sorcerer leaped backward, and Aaron saw a flicker of fear in his face.

Don't kill the cocky sorcerer. Just scare him enough to keep him in line, until his dangerous temper fizzles out.

Eyes switching to blue, Gryphon thrust his hands out and his whole body became a pillar of fire. A whirling finger of flame shot out and licked the blade. In seconds, Aaron smelled burning flesh. The skin on his hand sizzled, making him drop the sword.

Gryphon stalked toward him. Vines erupted from the ground forcefully and coiled around his legs, locking him in place. Aaron smirked, when he felt hands wrap around him and yank him away.

"Can't we leave you alone for two minutes?" Lynx roared, stepping between them.

It was Harold who had grabbed Aaron. His friend glared at him, and Aaron let out a ragged breath. He'd be getting an earful later. *For someone who doesn't want to interfere with how I run my kingdom, you certainly have a lot of opinions.*

Gryphon growled, but Lynx slapped him upside the head. "Don't you dare growl at Aaron," she said, "Or any other mortal who Alex cares about."

The scowl left Gryphon's face, and his orange glow abated.

"That's better. Now, why did you come here?"

"With what happened to his brother," Gryphon said. "I didn't think Alex would want Aaron near another stable fire. Especially with Lygari on the loose."

"I tried to explain to him that this is where Lygari and Moorloc attacked Alex and caused the vortex that nearly killed me and Stefan," Aaron said. "If Alex put the same protection spell on this place as Datten, then we can't be here."

Lynx sighed, then nodded. "Then, back to Datten with you."

"I have to agree with Gryphon," Harold said. "*You* stay away from anything on fire."

AARON FELT an icy knot in his stomach striding through the gates of Datten. The sorcerers had completed their mission of devastation and vanished. The towers where he and Megesti had grown up were still standing, but the roofs had been burned off and the stone walls were scorched.

"We won't know the extent of the damage until we go in, Your Royal Highness," one of his master builders said. "The stables are gone completely, but the boys got the horses out. They can move into the barns with the cows until we build a new one. I suspect it'll take a few weeks, maybe a month …"

The builder's voice faded away as Aaron looked at what remained of his home. Both towers were as black as Thunder's hair. Everything his brother had owned in the world was now gone. *How will I tell mother?* The stench of burned wood filled the air, and bits of ash floated around them. Aaron's eyes shifted to the enormous wooden drawbridge used to get supplies into and out of the castle. It had been burned beyond repair, too. "The drawbridge needs to be replaced first," Aaron said.

"Of course, my king," the builder said. He bowed and joined the other royal builders gathered by the door into the castle.

Aaron turned to see a grim-looking Jerome walking toward him. "I've spoken with General Avery, Caleb, and Lucas," Jerome said. "The bird coop was also burned, but the birds got out, so Lucas and Hunter will track them down."

"Send Lucas's brother with them," Aaron said. His voice had no expression, or emotion to it. He couldn't let himself feel the pain for what had happened right now. He needed to be strong and fix this. "What else was damaged? I'm sure there's more you aren't telling me."

Jerome exhaled loudly. "They destroyed the royal sorcerer lab. All the tools, ingredients, Merlock's journals."

"No." Aaron felt a jolt of pain in his chest. He ran his hand through his hair. "That was everything Megesti had left of his father."

"War is rarely fair," Jerome said.

Aaron groaned. "I know, but I wish it wasn't my friends and family who suffered. I made the choice to keep Alex safe *here*, so I should bear the consequences of that choice."

"If she heard you say something so foolish, she'd push you in the moat again," Jessica said. She and Stefan had climbed the steps from the castle basement.

"She's right. Alex would have soaked you for trying to take the blame for her choices," Stefan said. "Nothing else on the third floor or the basement was damaged."

"I'll finish inspecting the dungeons and treasure room," Jerome said. He nodded to Aaron, kissed Jessica's cheek, and headed toward the castle.

"We're lucky they didn't go after the library." Aaron said. "I couldn't stomach Alex losing her favorite place in my home after everything she's been through."

"It's her home, too," Stefan said.

Jessica and Aaron shook their heads before Aaron spoke. "Warren will always be her home, and Datten mine. I try to make this one bearable for her."

Stefan sighed. "Ask her."

Aaron glared at Stefan.

"She didn't care when we lived in a tiny hut in the woods. So long as she's with the people she loves, that's home. Datten is her home because *you* are here."

Aaron exhaled as the shame of how he'd ignored his friends

and punished his wife for simply being herself overwhelmed him. *After everything I put her through, I don't deserve her. I don't know if my people know how lucky they are to have her as their queen, after everything she's endured.* Promising himself he'd do better Aaron pushed down the guilt of the pain he'd caused her during his curse. "Thank you, Stefan. I needed to hear that, because Datten won't be the same when she gets back, and she's gone through enough with me this year."

"We should focus on rebuilding what we can, in the time we have," Jessica said.

"I see this as an opportunity," Harold said, joining the group.

"Opportunity?" Stefan asked.

"These damaged areas were weak points. Now you can repair and strengthen them. And you have both Datten and Betruger's best builders at your disposal."

Aaron chuckled at the Wafners. "You're not wrong, Harold. What do you think we should rebuild first?"

Harold smiled and pointed across the way. "After your drawbridge, I would suggest your stables, and then your towers. Damage inside your castle needs a finer set of skills to repair, so two groups can work at once."

Aaron took in his home with a new hope. "You're right. I'll look at this as an opportunity to fortify and rebuild my home along with my kingdom and to make it into something all of Datten can be proud of."

He didn't say it aloud, but Aaron hoped Alex, most of all, would be proud. *I'll do everything I can to make that happen.*

CHAPTER 21

ALEX

Inside the door, a narrow tunnel stretched into the darkness. Alex winced at the sight of it. *Another closed space in this death trap.*

"Why did it have to be dark again?" Michael complained.

"At least it's narrow. I can lean on the wall, and you won't have to carry me," Edith said. Alex and Michael exchanged a quick look. When Edith saw their faces, she threw up her hands in surrender. "Alright, you can carry me."

Alex secured the last supply bag to her back and grabbed a torch from the wall. Michael squatted down, and once Edith had a good grip on him, they set off down the tunnel.

After only a few steps, the door slammed shut behind them, making Edith scream. The rush of air from the door almost extinguished the torch.

"Sorry," Edith said. "I should expect doors to slam by now."

They continued cautiously. Anxiety tied knots in Alex's stomach, and her heart was racing. She reached for her necklace, but she'd removed it and Michael had fastened it inside the bag for safekeeping. Instead, she found the rock she'd plucked from the cave wall in her pocket. She squeezed it, letting its firmness heat her palm before she pulled it out and twirled it between her fingers as she walked.

To keep track of time, Alex counted the heavy breaths coming from Michael. He'd refused to put Edith down for even a few minutes and was clearly worn out.

Alex stopped abruptly. "Do you hear that?" She cupped her ear to amplify the sound.

"Hear what?" Michael asked. His ragged breaths were so loud, it was no wonder he couldn't hear anything. He let Edith down and Alex shushed them.

Edith hobbled beside Alex. "I hear it, too. It sounds like water."

Alex lifted the torch. They'd reached a fork, so Edith pulled the compass from Alex's pack and they followed it. The further they went, the louder the rushing sound. Despite everything, the sound of water boosted their moods. Edith limped along as they turned corner after corner.

When she saw a light beyond the next corner, Alex held her arm out to stop Edith, intending to go on by herself, but Michael pulled her back. He took the torch from her, crept to the edge and peeked around.

With a gasp, he dropped their only remaining torch, and it went out. Alex rushed over to him and stared. Before them was a cavernous room. The stone walls sparkled, and in the middle, a fountain was carved from the rocks. It was even larger than the one in her father's garden.

"This certainly is an improvement," Edith said, joining them. Michael carried her into the room and set her down on the ledge that surrounded the fountain.

Alex slowly turned around, taking in the space. There were no windows, yet the room was exceptionally well lit with only a handful of scattered torches. After the stale air of the maze, the freshness of the deep breath she took lifted her spirits. There were carvings on the stone wall. When she ran her fingers along them, the line marks burned on her neck began to tingle.

"There's only one entrance or exit," Michael said. "We must be meant to do something here."

"I assumed the hole and song were our tests," Edith said. She lifted her swollen ankle onto the ledge and removed her boot.

Alex moved closer to the fountain. It was made of various rocks stacked on top of one another until they met and vanished into the ceiling. Clean water ran down along the rocks into the large pool of water at the base. Alex trudged around it, keeping Edith and Michael in her sights all the while. At three breaking points the water was diverted to a specific part of the pool, and the circle seemed to break into three areas. The first was near Edith and seemed to be made of black onyx rocks. The next was made of the same glowing blue moonstone that Alex had found in the cave and brought with her in her pocket, though these were very rough compared to the one she carried. The final one was made of gray granite.

"Alex, there's a letter on this side." Michael was standing beside Edith examining the onyx part.

Alex hurried over. If she squinted, she could make out the letter 'N'. The other parts were the same. The moonstone had a 'W' and the granite a 'V'.

"Warren, Nial, and Veremund." Edith sighed. "I suppose we knew this room wouldn't be easy, but what are we supposed to do with a fountain?"

"I don't know," Alex said, running her fingers along the cold water at her section of the fountain. "If I had my magic, I could try to figure it out."

"I think that was the point of the test, Alex," Edith said. "For you to live as a mortal and learn how scary and complicated things are without magic."

"Alex is an expert at scary and complicated things," Michael chuckled, and Alex leaned over to splash him.

"I surrender!" Michael cried out after only a few splashes.

Alex turned to Edith, but she was sitting on the ledge with her feet in the fountain staring at the water, and not moving.

"Edith?" Alex leaped from the fountain and rushed to her friend. Michael was already shaking her shoulder, but Edith's eyes never left the water.

"What do you think is happening?" Michael asked.

"I don't know, but since we both have a side, I think this part of whatever it is we're supposed to do."

Michael gulped. "Are you scared?" When Alex nodded, he grabbed her into a hug. He kissed the top of her head the way her father would. "Whatever happens when we look into that fountain, we'll come out of it. I know you, the real you, and you'll be fine."

Alex nodded and walked to her part of the fountain. After removing her boots, and rolling up her pants, Alex exhaled loudly and gazed into the water.

The whoosh of air was so sudden she had to close her eyes. It felt like falling. When she felt the ground against her feet again, her eyes snapped open. She was in a room with stone walls. *A castle. But which one?* A cry echoed down the hall, and she ran toward it, turning down halls and following the sound. She threw open a heavy set of doors and froze. *The Warren throne room.* Across the dimly lit hall, a body lay on the ground, and a little girl was shaking it, sobbing.

Nausea filled Alex's throat, a sickening sensation that seemed to grow with every step. She crept across the hall, ignoring the inner voice that screamed at her to run. Finally, she reached the dais. The blood had spread here in a crimson pool. Alex forced herself to look at the toddler version of herself, sobbing over her mother's body. Her hands flew to her mouth, to lock in the scream trying to free itself from her.

"Why did you do it?"

Alex screamed and spun. Before her stood a small boy with golden blond hair and sky-blue eyes. "Aaron?" Alex whispered, taking in the childhood version of her husband. When she glanced back, her mother's body was gone.

"Why did you kill my brother?"

"I didn't!" Alex squeaked. Aaron vanished, and Alex headed for the door, but stumbled. Somehow, she was now wearing a heavy gown. She lifted the oversized skirt and headed to the hallway.

"He's right, you know. You're the reason I'm dead." It was Daniel, but instead of the smiling prince who had protected her, his face was raw and blistered, the haunted boy who'd burned alive. The sight of his wounds made Alex want to retch, and she covered her mouth and reeled backward.

"Difficult to stomach the consequences of your failings, is it?"

"It wasn't my fault," she whispered. "I was a child." Alex bumped into someone and turned to find the familiar eyes of a woman she once knew. Her eyes, normally kind, were accusatory.

"You weren't a child when you killed me." Reinhilde's voice was soft, but curt. "Have you even told my family that you found me there? That I loved them? Missed them?"

Alex shook her head.

"You're a coward. You don't deserve the name Warren." Reinhilde spat and faded away.

"Will you leave me like your mother left you?"

Trembling Alex at the sight of a small boy. She squatted before him and brushed his bushy golden hair from his face. His sea-blue eyes gave Alex pause. The hair was right, but the eyes weren't Aaron's. They were her father's.

"When my father betrays you, will you leave us to be raised by someone else, the way you were?"

Our son. You're Aaron's and my son.

"I'll never leave you, Daniel." The name came out naturally, and the boy looked her up and down.

"Liar." And he vanished.

Alex covered her face with her hands and tried to calm her pounding heart. Now, she was in a crypt, in front of a row of burial statues bearing the stone faces of Edward, Aaron, Stefan, Michael, along with all her friends and loved ones. Slumping over the closest statue—Aaron's—Alex caught the sight of her hands, and though she expected them to be old and wrinkled in this future, was surprised to find herself still young. Aaron's visage carved in stone made her heart ache and tears roll down her cheeks. *I don't want to live centuries without you. If I could make you a sorcerer, I would, even if I had to give up half my life.*

"Clearly, our kind are worthless to you," Gryphon growled behind her.

Alex sighed back. "I didn't say that. It's just not the same."

"What's not the same? Me, or the sorcerers?"

"It's complicated," Alex whispered.

"No, it's not. It's simple in your mind—I'm not him." Orange light raced up Gryphon's arms and Alex's core heated.

"Aaron's my soulmate," Alex snapped. She walked up to him. "He's the man I *chose*, and you're the sorcerer I'm bonded to by magic."

"By destiny."

"So you say."

"And that means nothing to you?"

"I had no say in the matter."

"Answer the question. Does our bond mean nothing to you?" Gryphon's eyes flashed orange.

"I didn't say that. You're putting words into my mouth." Alex felt uncomfortably hot under his gaze and struggled when he grabbed her waist and pulled her against his body. Then, he *sniffed* her.

"What are yo—" Gryphon's mouth slammed into hers, and a heat she'd never felt before crashed through her. She felt her hands snake around Gryphon's neck and head, and her lips kissed him back as fiercely as she'd ever kissed Aaron. Something inside her awakened, filling her with a heat and lust she didn't even know herself capable of.

"Seems there is a sorceress in you after all," Gryphon chuckled before pulling away from her. "I look forward to making you mine." He turned and walked down the hallway.

Panting for breath, Alex touched her lips, trying to temper the raging want that was flooding her body. "Gryphon, wait." She chased him down the hallway and out to the courtyard, but instead of the familiar sights of Datten or Warren, there was only an expansive barren field. With growing horror, she walked further and further into the open, finding a field of dead bodies. She stopped in her tracks and stifled a scream. A lone woman stood amongst the bodies. Her hair was silver and straight as an arrow. She wore a flowing black dress and a crown of glistening black gems, and when she turned around Alex's breath caught in her throat.

The woman was her and yet wasn't. It was as if she were peering into a distorted mirror, seeing an alternate version of herself. A wicked smirk spread across the other version's face, and her emerald eyes sparkled with mischief. Alex peeked down and realized the surrounding bodies were sorcerers. Line marks of every kind were burned into their skin and splotched with blood. The sorceress's unending gaze bore into Alex's soul.

"To remake something properly, you must burn the old one to the ground." Then she raised her arm and pointed toward a pile of bodies at the edge of the field. "Getting vengeance makes it exceptionally delightful."

Alex made herself move toward the bodies. Aaron, Cameron, Stefan, Wesley, her father, Graham, and every other person who'd ever hurt or wronged her.

Retching, she stumbled backward to get away from the stench of the dead. The sorceress appeared right in front of her.

"You and I are one, Cassandra. You are the weakness, and I am the strength. I shall avenge us, and right the wrongs."

"No," Alex panted.

"We will face this future and remake this world."

Alex shook her head. "I can't hurt people like this. I won't."

"I will." The sorceress' eyes flashed black. "You will surrender control to me, and I'll destroy them all."

Alex dropped her arms. "No, you won't." Cold black eyes narrowed at Alex who stepped up to her other half. "Alone, I'm weak, scared, and broken. But *with* them, I'm strong, confident—whole." The image of the bodies faded away. "If walking my path alone leads to this ... then I will never walk it alone again."

"What if they won't follow you?"

"Then I will listen to them and decide what is right." Alex stared up at the black eyes, of the fury buried deep inside her.

"You're too stubborn to ever truly let them in. You will give into me one day, little one."

"I will not become you! I will let them help me, as much as they love me. I pledge to myself a blood oath that I will not push them away ever again."

A wind rustled Alex's hair, and she threw her hand to cover her eyes. Now, she was staring at the fountain. Drawing a ragged breath, she came back into herself, finding both Michael and Edith still staring into their respective sides of the fountain. Her palm stung and blood dribbled off it. *My oath was real.* Curling her hand into a fist, she reached into the fountain and washed her hands, her blood swirling in the water. Then she took a seat between Edith and Michael to wait for them to win their own battles.

CHAPTER 22

ALEX

Edith's scream pierced the silence, causing Alex to topple from her slumber against the wall. She scrambled to her feet and dashed to Edith, who threw her arms around Alex's neck and burst into tears.

"I could never betray them. How is my loyalty to my family a weakness? I don't understand." Her sobs echoed through the room.

"If you're meant to marry Harold and become Queen of the Betruger, a loyal tie to Warren could be a problem," Alex said to her friend gently. "You'll need to learn to put him above your father, and above Warren."

"But Warren is my home," she sobbed.

"Not for much longer," Alex said, squeezing her in a tight hug. "And that's okay. You'll be my friend regardless of where your loyalties lie, or where you live."

"Promise? I've struggled with having lady friends because of who my father is, and with my sister going around telling people things about me ..."

Alex laughed. "If you haven't noticed, I'm not the best with ladies either."

"I guess that's why we both have Jessica."

"And now, Lynx. I suspect she'll be staying with us for the future."

"I hope so," Edith said. She turned her sleeve inside out and used the cleanest part to wipe the tears from her eyes. "What did you have to face?"

Alex motioned for Edith to sit back on her bench. They took in the room for a moment before Alex answered softly. "I swore to stop leaving everyone behind, and actually let those around me help."

"Do you think you can actually do that?" Edith asked, twirling her hair and looking at Alex with doubt.

Alex held her hands up, revealing the bloody markings. "I'll have to. I made a blood oath with myself."

Edith grabbed Alex's hands. "Let me help you with those."

They washed her hands and then Edith ripped the bottom of her tunic off to wrap Alex's hands. As she was doing so, they both heard a loud thump followed by a moan.

"Are you alright, Michael?" Edith asked. She tried to get up but winced as she stood on her sore ankle. Alex hurried over to help Michael up.

Michael's face was forlorn, and his eyes were filled with painful sadness. "I'd rather fall on the ground than go through what I saw in there. It was terrible."

"What did you see?" Edith asked.

"I lost everyone," Michael whispered.

"You mean Jessica and the baby?" Alex asked.

Michael shook his head. "Everyone. Jessica, Stefan, Aaron … you. I couldn't live with myself if I let something like that happen to you." Michael grabbed Alex and locked her into a tight hug like he'd always done when they were young. Alex gave in. Ages ago, she'd learned that he needed the connection and support more than her in moments like this. *I wish I had my Celtics magic to help him.* All she could do was hold him.

Alex stood on her tippy toes to press her forehead against his, just as they always had as children. "I'm not going anywhere, and my dream made me promise to ask for help, so you have less to worry about."

"I will hold you to that," he replied.

"As will I," Edith said.

They joined Edith at the fountain. Michael's eyes kept darting around the room with trepidation. "We did what we were supposed to, didn't we?" he asked. "Why are we still trapped in here?"

A deep voice came from behind the fountain. "It's good to know the inquisitive Veremund nature is alive and well, even if you never learned patience."

Alex and Michael were back on their feet in seconds. They couldn't see anyone behind the fountain. Edith gulped loudly and wrenched Alex's arm, making her cry out in pain. But her cry died in her throat when three men appeared out of nowhere and stepped toward them.

Alex recognized the man in the middle as Teon, the first Prince of Warren who'd presented her the challenge at the start of the maze. His blue eyes sparked even in the dim light. All three were dressed in the fine clothes of Torian noblemen, though the style was outdated. Alex took in the other two men and terror drummed through her. They were at least as tall as Michael. The slimmer of them had brown hair that hung messily down to his shoulders, framing his light brown features and blue eyes. On Teon's other side, the larger man had brown eyes as dark as Alex's hair, and his skin had the same pinkish hue her own did.

"Who are you and what do you want?" Michael demanded, pulling Edith's sword from his belt and wielding it at the men.

"Such savagery. Do not shame those who came before you with

violence," said the slimmest of the men. At this, Teon scowled at him, and he looked to the ground.

"Apologies, Princess," Teon said. "Percius forgets to think before he speaks."

"A common trait in Veremunds," the larger man said, looking Michael over. "I'm Verndari Nial, oldest son of Patrick Nial, the–"

"The founding Nial of Warren," Edith finished.

Verndari nodded. "And the son from which your family is descended, Edith. The remaining Nial line all came from me. It was my duty to guard him." Verndari nodded toward Teon, who scoffed.

"I'll introduce myself to your companions. I'm Teon Warren, the first Crown Prince of Warren. It was our fathers who founded Warren all those centuries ago. Percius is the only son of George Veremund, the royal advisor and a close friend of my father's."

"If you're all dead, how can we see you?" Edith asked. She grabbed Alex's hand excitedly. "Did you get your powers back?"

Alex shook her head as Percius spoke. "No. We have been waiting here for you since our deaths. It was our duty to guard this maze for the last true heirs of our lines. Those who would solve the puzzles to find their way here, and then return with the knowledge and gifts needed to stop the fury that threatens to destroy Torian."

"How did you know what to do?" Michael asked.

"Cassandra told us," Percius replied. "She lived in Warren after fleeing the Forbidden Lands and warned us of the consequences for granting her sanctuary. Before her gifts were taken from her, she used her magic to create this place, and the magical items that brought you here. She also tied us to it so upon our deaths, we were drawn here to wait."

"So you've been here for over fifteen centuries?" Alex asked.

"Has it been that long since our fathers founded Warren?" Verndari asked and Edith nodded in reply. "Then indeed we have."

"But if you gave us the supplies to get over the pit, why didn't you save us from the fire, or falling into the river?" Michael asked.

"We were not to interfere with your tests. The boards were needed to give you options to get across, but no other assistance was allowed. We needed to know if the lines were as strong as they were when we led them," Percius said.

"And to our delight, they were," Verndari added.

"Now that you have proved yourself," Teon began. "You will pass into the next room where Cassandra will give you each a gift to help you contain the fury and save both the world and you, Alexandria. These gifts come with a price, and it is necessary to know you would pay it before being offered them."

"If there is a price to pay, then I shall pay it," Alex said. "You will not put that burden on—"

"That decision isn't yours to make," Michael said.

"We decide what we can bear," Edith added.

Alex's throat went bone dry, making it impossible to swallow. She turned to her friends. "You're right. I said I'd trust you and so I will."

"Then allow us to show you the way," Teon replied and the three men moved quickly around the startled friends to take their places before the three sections of the fountain. Each man stood before the part that had been intended for their line. Alex and Michael followed Teon and Percius, leaving Verndari with Edith. Once they were all before their own part of the fountain, the men placed their hands into the water. Teon motioned for Alex to copy him, so she leaned down and put her hand into the cold water. Without being told to, all of them spoke their family's mottos. As the words filled the room, there was a loud rumbling sound, and an arch appeared on the wall. Beyond it, a long hallway glowed with a golden light.

"Don't be frightened," Verndari said. "She's waiting for you."

Michael came over to Edith and dropped low so he could carry her on his back again. After Alex grabbed their bag, the three of them waved goodbye to their relations and headed into the tunnel.

GRYPHON

The salty sea sprinkled Gryphon's face as he looked out across the Oreean Sea toward the Forbidden Lands. He tossed his shoes aside and stomped into the shallow edge of the water. The frigid waters did nothing to temper his seething rage. He thrust out his arms and threw open his well, letting power erupt from him.

"I've had enough of weak, useless mortal boys who don't know how to protect her from the dangers of our kind. They cower from the immense power she wields. They are unworthy of her!"

With a loud crack, a part of the sea was sucked beneath the waves. A heartbeat later, a mountain burst from the water. Water coursed from the jagged rocks shooting toward the sky. Heat bubbled up from Gryphon's core and flowed down his arms until the mountain erupted in fire. Because of the distance, it was several seconds before the wave of heat blasted his skin. He took a deep breath, letting the searing heat fill his lungs, calming him in a way only pure natural violence could do.

"Someone's clearly in a mood."

Gryphon's jaw clenched. He dropped his arms, sending the

volcano crashing back into the depth of the Oreean Sea before turning to Lynx. Despite the playful tone, she stood with her arms crossed, and her face was pinched. He rarely saw her like this.

"I'm blowing off some steam. Isn't that what you and Birch always tell me to do when I'm upset?"

"Upset, yes. Dangerously close to losing control? No."

"What could you possibly know about losing control?" Gryphon snapped.

Lynx dropped her arms and softened her expression, stepping closer to him. "Just because I don't explode if I hold my feelings inside doesn't mean I don't lose control of my magic from time to time, especially when someone I care about is in danger."

"You speak as though you have a lot of experience with that."

Lynx grabbed his hands and squeezed them despite the heat he knew was still radiating off him.

"You don't think Birch and I struggled to leave you with them? Your father is a beast, your mother only cared for herself, and your hexa is probably the most evil creature alive. It killed us to leave you there." Lynx's voice went higher as she spoke. "Every time I left you, I worried it might be the last time I saw you, or that they would do horrible things to you. With all the scars you have from them—physical and mental—it's a wonder you haven't gone mad."

"I didn't go mad because I knew I had you and Birch." His heat cooled and the weight of Lynx's in his made him feel calmer. "Now why are you here?"

"To check on you. I know how you get when you're angry. I wanted to make sure you didn't do anything you'd regret."

"I'm tired of having to listen to mortals. They don't understand our ways. They don't have a clue of what we are truly capable of, especially Alex and I." Gryphon squeezed Lynx's hands. "I had no idea how much power she carries."

"None of us did. We knew she was strong, but watching you

and Megesti struggle to control only half of her gifts has made it clear how heavy her burden is."

He scoffed and shook his head. "Both their burdens. Our young Usurper has so much more to him than they'll ever know. Merlock held him back, and Alex will never learn to harness her full powers if I have to follow their rules."

"Then don't."

Gryphon pulled his hands back and looked Lynx over slowly.

She smiled. "I haven't lost my mind, thank you. I just know there are *some* mortals who believe you are doing the right thing. They know Alex needs to be pushed."

Gryphon tilted his head toward Lynx. "You've been spending too much time with the little Wafner."

"Give him a proper chance. I know Alex and I are why you're so hard on him."

"Lynx—"

"He loves us both. He's risked his life protecting Alex more than anyone. Don't use me as an excuse to let your Ares out."

Gryphon pulled his hands away from Lynx and paced the rocky shore.

"Stefan is your ally here. He agrees with your methods for helping Alex, even if Aaron doesn't."

"I can't just do what I want to. Not without their support." Even if Alex's opinion was the only one that mattered to him, *she* would care what Aaron thought.

"What about her father? He's another mortal she'll listen to."

"After the argument that ended violently, he seems to stay quiet."

"Then perhaps we need to have a conversation with His Royal Highness. If we can get him and Stefan on our side, we might have a chance at getting permission for you to train Alex properly."

With Datten in chaos, it wasn't hard to speak with Edward or Stefan in private. It seemed they were all in agreement that Alex needed to be trained harder than Aaron was allowing. After learning how many people were on his side, Gryphon returned to the Verlassen Castle with Megesti and Stefan to come up with a proper training plan for Alex. Victoria's old lab was a convenient meeting place where they wouldn't be interrupted.

Months ago, Megesti and Alex had found a spell to allow all of them to access her mother's lab without spilling blood. Together, their power was more capable than either of them had ever thought possible.

"Did we have to go behind Aaron's back?" Megesti asked.

"We aren't going behind his back," Stefan said, leafing through one of the spell books. "We're simply coming up with a plan that will have Alex learning her magic more efficiently. Whether she and Aaron approve is up to them."

"Though if he tries to stop us, he might find himself on the receiving end of another nasty curse."

"Gryphon ..." Stefan's voice was more feral than Lynx's Tiere voice.

"I was joking ... mostly."

Stefan glared at him with narrowed eyes.

"Enough of that, Little Wafner. I'm not afraid of mortals, even if they are physically larger than me." Gryphon wiggled his fingers at Stefan and the scowl dropped instantly.

"Stefan, you've trained her more than anybody," Megesti said, clearly trying to break the tension. "How do you know when you're pushing her too hard?"

"She has tells. Physically, her posture shifts, and her shoulders drop. Her voice goes up ever so slightly, and her eyes lose their sparkle. If you look closely at her face when she's tired, the sparkle isn't there."

"That helps," Gryphon said. "While taxing in another way,

magic training will drain her physically, too. If we can tell she's draining herself, it'll help keep accidents to a minimum when we work on the more dangerous magic."

"Where are we supposed to train her?" Megesti asked. "We can't be training her Ares magic inside the castle."

"There are a few large clearings in the forest nearby. You can use those," Stefan said. "And the old Wafner estate will work for some things, too."

"Thank you. Now we just need to decide *what* to teach her. Any suggestions on which powers? I was hoping to work with two or three abilities," Gryphon said.

"Something deadly."

"Stefan," Megesti said, slamming another book shut. "Magic doesn't have to be violent."

Stefan's eyes narrowed. "I've had enough of sorcerers injuring her. We need her to defend herself for a change."

"I agree with Stefan," Gryphon said. "She cares far too much about protecting all of you. She needs to be able to manage herself."

"On that lovely note," Stefan said, sliding a spell book toward Gryphon. "What about this?"

ALEX

The tunnel was lit in a golden glow. When Alex crossed the threshold, the passage narrowed, forcing the three of them to turn sideways. Alex couldn't tell if the light was reflecting from somewhere or if the stones themselves were glowing. The further down the tunnel they crept, the brighter the light grew.

After a few minutes, they entered a vast room. It was as if a sphere had been cut from the brass-colored stone of the mountain. At the apex of the rounded ceiling was a mark of Cassandra bigger than Alex was. Rays of sunlight ran down the curved ceiling and walls, reflecting off the intricate carvings to illuminate the entire room. Alex wrapped her arm around Edith's waist and helped her toward the center of the room. Wherever their boots struck, individual stones illuminated. It reminded Alex of playing in the throne room the day her mother was killed. But as they approached the center of the room, a golden light spread from the sunbeams and snaked across the floor toward them. It hit Alex first, flowing up her leg, filling her with warmth and making each step feel lighter. After the light left Edith, she pulled away from Alex and took a tentative step forward.

"Careful, Edith," Michael said. He moved to steady her, but Edith held out her hand to stop him.

"My ankle ... it's fine."

"So is my leg," Alex said, running her finger along the spot on her calf that had been cut when she'd fallen on the planks of wood.

"Did you get your powers back?" Michael asked.

There was a soft chuckle from across the room, and a golden figure glided over to them. "Hello, my last true heirs."

"Cassandra?" Edith mouthed at Alex.

"Who else would be waiting for us here," Alex replied, stepping toward the ghost of the sorceress who was responsible for her line and her very existence. Cassandra cupped Alex's face in her cool hands and pressed her forehead to Alex's. The icy chill that spread through her made Alex shiver until Cassandra released her and stepped back. "I'm so proud. If I could have chosen any of my line to be the strongest of us, I would have chosen you. Your power is twice that of any before you. You broke the curse that was placed on your kingdom, and with love, I know you'll break the curse placed on our line through hatred so many centuries ago."

"Do you mean the fury?" Edith asked.

Cassandra held one hand out to Edith and the other to Michael. When they placed their hands in hers, a rumble echoed through the room, and a magnificent stone mantle rose from the ground. In awe, they watched a sparkling scepter ascend from the obsidian stone. Gold and gems covered it, but Alex focused on the glint of red steel at its base.

Cassandra led them to the mantel and carefully picked up the scepter to present it to them. The three of them moved in unison toward it and stopped in front of the stand. The scepter sparkled with emerald, sapphire, and ruby gems along the top, bottom, and grip.

"How will it protect her if it's made of red steel?" Michael asked Cassandra.

Edith examined the scepter closely. "It's missing something."

"You are correct, young Nial. It is missing the stone of protection, but luckily your Warren followed her intuition and chose wisely."

Alex gulped and slid her hand into her pocket where she kept the strange glowing rock she'd collected in the cave. She rubbed it with her thumb, considering its smoothness.

"Why would you make it from red steel if it's deadly to sorcerers?" Michael asked, gesturing toward Alex's belt, where her dagger would normally hang. His eyes widened. "Wait, your mother had red steel, too! It doesn't affect Alex the way it does other sorcerers, does it?"

A smile spread across Cassandra's lips. "The Veremunds were always intuitive. You're correct, Michael. In the Forbidden Lands, my daughter and my former lover slayed several dragons. When the beasts' blood soaked the ground, they extracted the ore and used it to create weapons. My daughter twisted her healing gifts with a chaos potion, so it would be impossible to heal a red steel wound, even by the most powerful Cassandra, but in doing so, they made Cassandras immune to it. Sorcerers are rarely hurt by their own powers."

"That's why Gryphon never hides from my fire powers," Alex said to Michael.

Cassandra nodded. She pointed the scepter's tip at Alex.

Alex held up the stone, but there was nothing for it to attach to. Cassandra merely smiled. Trusting herself, Alex held the stone against the top of the scepter and in seconds, prongs broke from the top and clamped onto the stone, holding it in place.

"Wow," Edith whispered, leaning over Alex's shoulder.

Finally, Cassandra handed Alex the scepter. The moment her hands touched it, an overwhelming sense of calm flooded her entire being, reminding her of playing in the castle gardens as a girl.

"Now you all have your physical line gifts," Cassandra said.

"Physical gifts?" Michael asked and Alex handed him the scepter. "Does that mean you have other gifts for Alex?"

Cassandra chuckled and placed her hand on Michael. "Alex received the scepter and will be given a choice, but as she was born a sorceress of my line, she needs nothing else. However, you and Edith will both receive gifts of magic."

Michael stepped back from Cassandra, while Edith pressed into Alex, trying to get closer. "What kind of magic?"

"You each were born with a special ability that may or may not have awakened already. I will strengthen those gifts, so they will affect more than just yourselves."

"Do you mean Michael's power to calm me?" Alex asked and Cassandra nodded. She held her hand out to Michael waiting for him to take it. Once he did, a gold light left her and flitted across him until it shone brightly over his heart and vanished.

"After today, he will not only calm you when you are in chaos but also know the chaos that exists inside you."

"What does that mean exactly?" Michael asked, glancing at Alex quickly.

"That is for you to figure out," Cassandra replied. She turned and held her hands out to Edith, who lifted her chin bravely and took the sorceress' hands with a determination only the Nials or Wafners could muster. "You, dear Edith, have the gift to tell kindness from wickedness, a talent that will be most handy when you rule as queen."

Edith's glance had wandered to the ground—she was lost in thought. When she understood what Cassandra was implying, she gasped. "Do you mean how I can tell when someone lies?"

Cassandra nodded.

"Your father is an exceptional judge of character," Alex said, but Edith's mouth was still hanging open.

"Will you return Alex's powers now?" Michael asked.

"If she wishes it."

"If I wish it?" Alex asked.

"Your powers were taken from you as a part of the test to prove your worth as a child of Warren. In your life, they have taken a great deal from you, and I will not force them upon you. If you do not want them, then you shall remain mortal."

"Mortal?"

"Just as I did, you would live your mortal life, and your gifts would pass to the next in your line."

Not having to deal with all this chaotic magic would be heaven. I could actually be normal. But what about my children with Gryphon? What would happen to them? Alex bit her lip.

"No matter what you decide, I'll be at your side," Michael said.

"What are you going to do?" Edith asked.

CHAPTER 25
ALEX

Alex exhaled and looked down at the ground for what felt like an eternity. *I don't know.* When she gathered the courage to look to her friends, they were frozen. Teon's voice whispered in her head.

"This decision cannot be rushed. Cassandra has made them still, but they will be fine. Only once you've made your choice will they awaken."

The smell of flowers rushed at her, as a giggle echoed off the area behind her. Alex turned to find a wall, and when she glanced back, Michael and Edith had vanished. Before her the room filled with fog. *Oh no. Another underworld visit?* Alex stepped into it, trying hard to hold back the panic, but warmth filled her the moment she heard a child's laugh. Turning to her right, Alex saw a ghostly image of two small boys-one blond and one with familiar fiery red hair—running across the meadow, leading two horses. Aaron appeared behind them carrying a pair of small lances and shields.

A warm breeze surrounded Alex and she found herself in the meadow.

"Aaron! We only have an hour!" Alex shouted. "If you make me late for the celebration of peace that *you* agreed to, I'll push you in the moat!"

Cooing sounded and she looked down to find a baby strapped to her. *I'm sorry, Your Royal Highnesses, we couldn't stop the bleeding without removing everything. You won't be able to have any more children.* The voice of Datten's physician echoed in her mind, making her heart heavy. A cool breeze rushed past her face and Alex turned to see the apparitions of three young sorcerers looking at her. They never made a sound, but their features made it clear they were the children she should have had with Gryphon.

A strong hand squeezed her shoulder, filling her with warmth.

"Are you seeing them again?"

Alex nodded. Stefan shrugged sympathetically and took his place at her side. Adjusting the sleeping baby in her wrap, Alex took in her dear friend. He'd aged. He stood stiffer, his expression more stoic than normal, and the bags under his eyes told her he wasn't sleeping.

"Why did we have to have this 'five year of peace' celebration in Datten?" he complained, moving his hands to his back.

"Because the Betruger already needed a month to get here. Going to Warren would have added another week or ten days," Alex replied without even thinking.

"Times like this I miss your cracking."

"I do, too. It's hard only seeing our friends once or twice a year because it takes forever to travel anywhere, and Megesti doesn't have it in him to crack so many people."

"Well, he is the only sorcerer left in the mortal world. The three kingdoms keep him busy enough that he's always tired."

Alex turned back to the field where Aaron chased the boys around. With years of peace, he was more relaxed and happier than she'd ever seen him. "Aaron! Don't you dare let the boys get in that mud. Jessica will have my head if Jerome comes back filthy again."

"It's fine," Aaron called back. "I'll just put him in Daniel's clothes. She'll never notice."

"She'll notice," Stefan said.

A sharp pain hit her pelvis, and her hand moved to rub it until the pain lessened. Stefan reached into the satchel he had on his side that Alex didn't even notice. He pulled out a handkerchief and unwrapped a root and held it out to her. "You keep forgetting to take it, so Aaron insisted I carry extra around at all times. You won't heal if you don't listen to the physician. You can't self-heal anymore."

"I know." Alex grabbed the root from him. "Thank you." She chewed it for a moment, when little shouts took their attention.

"Mommy, look at me. I'm a knight!" Daniel was on Thunder holding up the short lance, and a shield.

"Me, too. Uncle Stefan, look! I'm just like you!"

"Great form, Jerome." Stefan shouted at Jessica and Michael's son. The boy grinned at him and pulled his helmet down.

"Stefan."

"Nope."

"You don't know what I was going to say."

He turned toward her and glanced down at the baby attached to her. "I'm not settling down. My duty is to you, your children, and my sister's children."

"That doesn't mean you have to live alone." Alex rubbed the baby's back and looked up at him. "I miss her, too. But just because Lynx is living in the Forbidden Lands with Gryphon doesn't—"

"Alex," he growled at her.

"I'm just saying you could find someone else. Someone to fill your off days with love and happiness."

"You keep me busy enough. I don't need to add anyone else."

Alex opened her mouth to argue, when a loud whinny sounded, followed by a scream.

"Daniel!" Aaron's cry felt like knife in her heart.

No, no, no, no! Gryphon!

"Megesti, we need you!" Stefan shouted and ran for Aaron and the boys. Thunder bolted, and Aaron and Jerome dropped to the ground beside Daniel. Panic seized Alex, locking her in place for a moment as nausea overwhelmed her. Alex supported her baby and lifted her skirt to rush toward them, but moving through the long grass in her dress was tedious.

Gryphon, I'm serious. I need you! Stupid dresses that keep my mortal body from going fast enough.

Megesti arrived beside her son.

He's not coming. She realized. *Gryphon's never coming again because he can't hear me. He's gone ...*

The fog swallowed up her children and Alex covered her mouth. Her hand grew wet, and she realized she'd been crying. Wiping her tears away, she considered the two versions of her future—a simple mortal life with love and peace and all the struggles mortals endure, or a magical one where she'd suffer the eventual heartache but her loved ones would live fulfilling lives and become who they were meant to be.

After some time, Alex whispered. "I've made my choice." The fog vanished, leaving Edith and Michael staring at her.

CHAPTER 26
ALEX

The trio arrived in Datten's courtyard amid a bustle of people. Men in Datten and Betruger colors were hauling stones, hammering nails, and shouting orders. It was clear to Alex they'd replaced the drawbridge door. Emmerich had been intending to replace it for the last year but never got around to it, and now a gigantic wooden door that could hold over twenty horses stood gleaming in the sun. Within moments the men noticed them and stopped working. A younger man in a Datten uniform scrambled inside to announce their arrival. It wasn't until General Avery Reinhard came running toward them with fear in his eyes that Alex glanced down at herself.

She laughed and hurried to greet Avery. "Despite what my clothes would suggest, I assure you I'm fine."

A smile spread across Avery's lips, and he held out his arms to embrace Alex. "Welcome home, Your Royal Highness."

"Thank you, Avery."

"What's going on here?" Michael asked.

Avery cleared his throat. "I will allow our king or a Wafner to explain that."

"Where's Aaron?" Alex asked.

"Dealing with the lords on the outskirts of town. They've been causing him headaches since you left."

"And Harold?" Edith asked, nudging Alex with her hip. She had a hopeful look on her face.

"King Harold is in the library and Lady Jessica is in her suite," Avery said, glancing at them with a knowing smile. "Might I suggest you all freshen up before seeing them?"

Alex bit her lip at Michael's shocked expression. "General Reinhard, are you implying we are not up to standards for Datten nobility?"

Before the poor general could reply, Alex and Edith burst into laughter. Alex patted Michael on the shoulder and scrunched her nose at his rank smell. She hadn't noticed it until they were out of the maze. "I think you make a good point. Avery, please let the others know we'll meet in the library to discuss everything after Aaron returns."

"As you wish." He nodded and headed toward the men working across the field.

Alex followed Michael and Edith into the castle. Edith left to head to her suite, and Michael escorted Alex to hers before heading to his own. Alex softly closed the door to her suite and leaned against it, sighing loudly. She took a moment to breathe and let the smells of home wash over her. The room she shared with Aaron smelled like pine, cedar, and books.

She opened her eyes, stepped away from the door, and froze.

Bookcases lined every wall, filled with books of all kinds: Datten History and Culture, Lore and Legends of Torian, and journals of former kings and queens, including her mother's. Her favorite childhood painting hung above the fireplace, the last one made of her mother, father, and her as a little girl. Beneath it, on the mantel, were her and Aaron's matching crowns.

Grinning, Alex picked up hers and turned to take in the rest of the room. She recognized some of the furniture from Verlassen Castle: a chair and a table. On her way to the bookshelf, she was so lost in thought, she tripped over the head of her bear rug.

"Beowulf," Alex said to her bear rug. "It seems my husband has been busy in my absence."

Alex headed into their bathing suite to clean up before anyone else had to contend with her stench. It took more rounds of fresh water than when she'd first arrived from Kirsh, a secret she'd take to the grave with her. Finally dressed in clean clothes, and feeling like herself, she opened the door to her room and was struck with the heavenly scent of fresh baked bread.

"Based on experience, I expected you to be a lot dirtier... and smellier," Stefan said, getting up from a chair.

Alex couldn't contain the squeal that left her as she rushed him and threw herself into his embrace. Stefan snatched her up in his arms midair and squeezed her tightly.

"I missed you, too, Alex."

When he was finally ready to put her down, they sat together on the couch and Stefan held the gold serving platter of food out to her. Alex grabbed it and ate with gusto, savoring every morsel of sunflower loaf, hard cheese, and dried boar before taking the larger apple and tossing Stefan the small one.

"Glad to see your appetite is as strong as ever."

Alex ignored the tease in favor of taking a huge bite of her apple, sending juice running down her chin and causing her to moan with delight. "So, are you here to keep me company until your father returns with my husband?"

Stefan laughed. "That's one reason. I'm also here to update you on everything that happened ... and to talk to you about something before you hear it from someone else."

"That doesn't sound good."

"We were attacked by sorcerers again, and they did a great deal of damage to the castle. The worst of which was—"

"That isn't what I was referring to," Alex interjected. "I want to know what you're concerned about me learning from someone else."

Stefan flushed, making Alex sit up straight. *How bad is this if you're embarrassed? You never get embarrassed.* "Tell me you didn't get into another fight with Aaron! You promised to work things out with him."

"Nothing like that," Stefan said.

Alex noticed him scratching his thighs, one of his few tells. "Stefan, you're scaring me."

"I'm engaged."

Alex's mind went completely blank, and she stared at him for what felt like hours. Sweat appeared on Stefan's forehead, and he pursed his lips. "Alex, say something."

"No," Alex croaked. "You wouldn't."

"Alex, you said Lynx and I were meant to be."

"How could you?"

Stefan's face went gray. "How could I what? I didn't see a need to wait."

"I wasn't here!" Alex shouted. A loud rumble came from the walls of her room as Stefan's eyes fixed onto hers.

"Alex—"

Her lip trembled and she glared at him. "I missed Michael's proposal. I didn't get to help him pick the ring or be there to congratulate him. I didn't even hear Edith's story until the next day."

Stefan moved closer to her until their knees bumped. When he grabbed her hands, she felt her powers mix with the emotions swirling inside her. "I'm sorry, Alex. I thought you knew my intentions."

"Thinking and knowing are different. You should have told me."

"You're right." Stefan pulled her into a hug. "With all your visions, I forget you need help to figure out which are real and which are dreams. Are you at least happy for me?"

Alex shoved him, but he was too strong and didn't move despite her efforts.

"Well?"

"Of course I am!" She tried to shove him again.

Stefan grabbed her into another hug. "Well, you still get to pick her ring."

"You proposed without a ring?"

"Apparently, sorcerers don't use them, so I need you, as her Heart, to convince her to take one."

Alex smiled into his chest. "I think if we find the right one, she'll happily accept it." She pulled away. "Now tell me about this attack. Was anyone hurt or just the building?"

"Only sticks and stones," Gryphon replied from behind her, making Alex turn to see him. She couldn't help the smile that spread across her mouth when Gryphon grinned at her. "Though I gave your husband quite the scare."

"What did you do?"

"My father was convinced he'd sided with the enemy," Stefan replied.

"You wouldn't have doubted me, Little Wafner. Not with our agreement." Gryphon smirked at Stefan.

"This, I need to hear." Alex dropped her elbows on the back of the couch, rested her chin on hands, and stared patiently at Gryphon.

Gryphon just smiled. "There's nothing to tell, Princess."

"Gryphon and I have simply come to an understanding," Stefan replied.

Alex raised her eyebrows at him, demanding more.

"I'm marrying Lynx. She sees Gryphon as a brother, the way I see you as a sister."

"She also reminded him that I am one of the few people who

actually listens to you when you talk, and who doesn't force you into the box that mortals have made for you."

"We don't force her into a box," Stefan snapped.

"Sometimes it feels that way," Alex whispered. "Michael and Gryphon are the two people who always hear me. My father used to, but now he's changed."

"I hear you," Stefan grunted.

"Yes, but you don't *listen*. You hear what I say but still do whatever you think will keep me safe, regardless of what I want."

Stefan sucked in a breath. "Your father will come around."

"Do we know how he's doing?" Alex asked, looking at the two men.

"Sadly, no." Aaron's voice came down the stairs, followed by his footsteps. "Edward still isn't speaking to me, but I asked my mother to send word that you've returned. I hope my mother and news about you will get him to reply."

"And that's our sign to leave," Stefan said. Gryphon simply winked at Alex and cracked away. Stefan gave her one last squeeze and stood. Alex was so focused on Aaron she didn't even hear him leave.

"You look surprised to see me," Aaron said. "Almost as if you didn't expect me to drop everything and rush back once I heard you were home." He sauntered across the room and cautiously sat beside her. His golden thread sparkled in the firelight.

Alex's breathing sped. "I didn't want to interrupt your work."

"After months apart, you are more important."

"I missed you."

"That's good news," Aaron smiled and leaned down to gently kiss her. "I was worried you'd forget me after that adventure."

Alex smirked. "I was only gone for a month. I didn't forget you after twelve years in the woods."

"You were gone for nearly three months."

"Three months? But we were only in the maze for a few days, and it only took one month to get there."

"Three months. Though it felt far longer to me." Aaron cupped her cheek with his hand and softly caressed it with his thumb, examining her face. "I expected more dirt, and a few scrapes and bumps."

"I bathed while you were playing king, and Cassandra healed my wounds at the center of the maze. As much as I know you need to know what happened, I'd prefer to talk about that later, with everyone. I don't want to tell the entire story multiple times."

"Good."

"Good?" Alex frowned at Aaron, but he just gave her his most mischievous smile.

"You've been gone for months. Talking about your trip is the last thing I want to do with you right now."

Heat flooded Alex's insides as she stared back at Aaron. *Maybe you will listen to me when I show you what I need.* She moved a hand to Aaron's neck and kissed him fiercely. She felt his arms snake around her back and force her down, closer to him, until she was straddling him, with her chest flush against his. She smiled. "Is this more what you had in mind?"

"To be completely correct," Aaron said. "There would be no clothing."

"Well, if you take me upstairs," Alex whispered, peppering kisses on Aaron's neck and chin, "we can easily remedy that."

"That's too far."

Alex lifted her hands from Aaron's chest, and he took advantage to pull his shirt over his head. He moved to grip her shirt, but she grabbed his hand to stop him.

"What's this?" The skin on his hand was mottled and scarred.

"I was burned during the attack by the sorcerers. It's fine now. I scarcely notice it anymore."

Alex turned his hand to look at the palm. Concentrating, she gently ran her thumbs along the scar, brought his palm to her lips, and kissed it. A gold light left her and spread across the scars, making them disappear. Aaron pulled his hand from her, and they watched the gold light vanish into his hand.

"Thank you." He moved his finger under her chin and tilted it up.

Alex let him kiss her for a few moments before she pressed her entire body against him, desperate for more. His hands moved around her back until they found the hem of her shirt, and she pulled away from him long enough for him to pull her shirt over her head. A shiver raced down Alex's back when her still-damp hair tumbled down her back and onto her breasts. Aaron gazed at her and slowly tucked a wayward curl behind her ear. His hands found her rear, and gripping her roughly, he ground himself into her. He crashed his mouth onto hers. Alex moaned and locked her arms around his neck, pressing her breasts against him. He pulled his lips from hers and nipped her neck. He bit harder and Alex's moans grew louder.

Aaron shifted his weight to lay her down on the couch. She fumbled with his pants to untie them, but finally gave up and ripped them open. Aaron laughed and pulled them off before kissing her again. The night air was crisp and when Alex wriggled out of her pants, her skin broke into goose bumps. She squeaked when Aaron quickly grasped and pulled them down over her knees in one smooth stroke. It didn't matter how many times she'd made love to Aaron. He still made her heart hammer in her chest whenever he looked at her naked. A mischievous grin graced Aaron's face, and he climbed over her and kissed her. Alex reached down for him, and he snatched her wrist.

"Naughty queen," he said, still gripping her wrist.

Alex moaned in desperation as he grabbed her hip and pulled her down onto the couch. He grabbed her other hand and plunged them both into the soft velvet fabric above her head before he kissed her neck up to her ear. "For three months, I spent every night dreaming of what I would do to you once I got you back. I won't have you rushing me."

He nibbled her ear and neck, and she felt her whole body arch toward him. Still, he restrained her hands. Her nipples pebbled, and he picked his favorite one and alternated between gently scraping his teeth and swirling his tongue around it.

Alex could scarcely contain herself. "Please," she begged.

Looking into her eyes, he slid his free hand down her abdomen to her thigh. His fingers traced lazy circles near the apex of her thighs, and she groaned in frustration.

"Patience, Princess," he said.

Alex narrowed her eyes. *My turn.* "No," she said, and cracked.

They arrived in their bed, but with Alex on top of him. She smiled mischievously and lowered herself onto him. The moan that left Aaron was animalistic. He grabbed her hips and slammed her down onto him.

"Hang on," Aaron growled into her ear. He shifted them to the edge of their massive bed, and Alex clamped her arms and legs around him. He stood swiftly and brought her to the wall. An image of the cursed Aaron flashed into her thoughts, as this was the spot where he'd hurt her before. Sensing her hesitation, he whispered. "I have many things to make up for, starting with this … but only if you approve."

Alex nodded, and Aaron pressed her against the wall with such force that she gasped. Aaron kissed her roughly, playfully biting her lower lip, as he began driving into her. Trapped between the wall and Aaron's muscular body, Alex forced the cursed image from her mind, and clung to this version of him—the true version, until she found her rhythm, and matched Aaron's thrusts with her own. She'd missed Aaron more than she'd ever be able to explain to him, and being with him made her whole body heat as if it were on fire. In their year together, Aaron had mastered precisely how to make her scream, a talent he enjoyed using on her. Nothing in the Nial sisters' conversation had prepared her for the pleasure Aaron took from coaxing various sounds out of her.

Alex clung to him, and her body shuddered with waves of pleasure. He'd slowed his rhythm and sweetly kissed her while she struggled to steady her breathing. "I love you," she panted, but her emotions overwhelmed her. It was impossible to express the love she held for him. He grinned triumphantly, then swiftly spun her and laid her back on their bed.

The moment he left, loneliness flooded her. She reached out for him, but he had gone to throw wood on the fire.

"I'm not leaving," he whispered. He fell back into bed beside her, ran his hand up her arm, cupped her chin, and kissed her. "I know you need physical love and closeness when we're intimate, but especially after being apart for a few days. As it's been months, I don't plan to go anywhere until you're ready for me to."

Alex wrapped her arms around him tightly, and let his body warm hers as she settled into the soft bedding.

CHAPTER 27
AARON

Aaron tucked his shirt into his pants and fastened his winter riding cape around his shoulders. He leaned over and kissed Alex's forehead. She sighed and snuggled against his abandoned pillow. He pulled their blanket over her bare back to keep her warm, then opened their bedroom door where Hunter was waiting.

"Hunter, have Jerome meet me in the stables, and summon Stefan to take over watching Alex for the rest of the night."

"Right away." Hunter hurried off, and Aaron headed down to their sitting area to wait.

A few minutes later, Stefan walked in, half asleep. "Is there a reason you don't trust your own guards to watch Alex?" he asked.

"I trust them, but you and I both know what happens when Alex has a nightmare and wakes up scared or confused. She's been gone for months, we don't know what her sleep is like, and I care more about her being comforted than offending my friends."

Stefan dropped onto the couch and took out the book he'd brought. "Alex is going to be pleasantly surprised how far you've come since she left," he said.

Aaron scoffed and scratched his head to hide his nervous tick of rubbing his hair. "I have a list of things to make up for, even if she doesn't feel that way."

Stefan sat up and fixed his eyes on Aaron. "I need you to really listen to me, Aaron. The curse used your weaknesses to hurt her. But it would have done the same to me. We both have blind spots when it comes to Alex."

"But you've never actually hurt her. I'm terrified she'll never feel safe with me again. I was raised to value honor above every-thing—protect my people ... my wife. And then I ..."

"You're working to prove it wasn't you, one action at a time. It won't happen tomorrow but one day it will. Now go. My father's waiting, and I'll be here if she wakes up."

Aaron nodded. He avoided looking back at Stefan as he left.

Jerome, Harold, Macht, and Gryphon were waiting in the stable when Aaron arrived. The horses were already saddled. The night was black and cold as they traversed the narrow trail that ran along the back of the castle. Although the moon was full, it was behind a dark cloud. Gryphon provided fire orbs to light the way.

The path widened, and Harold came up to ride beside Aaron. "So, everyone is on board now?" he asked.

Aaron smirked. "The Rassgats were difficult, but in the end, they were most inclined to accept my offer."

"Tell me you didn't give into that sniveling coward," Macht scoffed.

"You better not have," Gryphon snapped.

"Nothing like that," Jerome said. "Aaron merely reminded them that blood or not, it's the right of the king to assign and *remove* titles as he sees fit."

"You threatened him," Harold chuckled.

"I didn't think you had it in you, Princeling," Gryphon said. "Maybe that curse woke something up inside you."

Aaron stopped Thunder and spun on his horse to face

Gryphon. Don't you ever suggest that the curse *your family* put on me was anything but torture. I hide it well, but do not think for a second I don't carry what it put me through every day. I lost time, memories, control over my body, and now I wake up every morning, knowing what I did to the woman I love because I was too weak and stupid to listen to my friends when they tried to tell me I wasn't acting like myself."

Gryphon's usually cocky demeanor vanished; he looked almost *nervous*, but he pushed his shoulders back. "It was from my line, and was enacted by my hexa, but I had nothing to do with it."

"That doesn't give you the right to judge me for it," Aaron snapped.

"I wasn't judging you. I let my excitement about Alex being back distract me."

Harold patted his shoulder and Aaron's anger seeped away.

"We're all excited to have them home safe," Harold said. "We should complete our mission so we can return to our wives."

"You aren't even married yet," Jerome said, chuckling.

"Our people consider a couple married once a betrothal is accepted," Macht said. "In our kingdom, a couple would then live together to ensure they are compatible, and only then would they wed."

"Can we get going now?" Gryphon asked. "The sooner we get to the Ratsass estate, the sooner I can enchant the border and the sooner I can go back to bed."

Aaron choked back a laugh, as Jerome narrowed his eyes at Gryphon.

"Unless you don't want the warning if anything magical sets foot in Datten," Gryphon added, smirking at them.

"How far does your spell reach?" Macht asked.

"Only to the largest estates. But I'll skillfully hide it, so they shouldn't sense it until they've already set it off."

"And it will detect sorcerers and magical creatures?"

"Of course," Gryphon said, losing patience. "Both Tiere sorcerers in their beast form, and the magical beasts that still roam the lands."

"There are no monsters in *our* mountains," Harold said confidently, elbowing Aaron.

"None you've seen," Gryphon corrected, and moved his horse ahead of them down the trail, muttering to himself.

Aaron groaned and pushed Thunder to follow. The Rassgat estate was one of the largest in the Datten nobility. On his Warren side, Aaron's uncle Bernhard held a comparable estate, but had put his land to good use. He used a portion to raise horses. The rest, he rented to families who were trying to better their station, and charged them a pittance. All he asked in return was that they assist him if he should ever ask, and that they share their good fortune with others when they could.

The Rassgats couldn't be more different. They overcharged their tenants and refused to make any improvements or even basic repairs. Since becoming king, Aaron had learned that his father had employed three men to handle the lands the Rassgats should have been managing. Aaron hated letting them keep the privileges of their title while they shirked their responsibility, but he'd decided against making any drastic change without Alex. Now that she had returned, he planned for them to have a discussion with Harold, Jerome, and Randal to see how they would handle a family like the Rassgats in their kingdoms.

Gryphon had stopped and was squatting beside a large obsidian rock. He laid his hand against the weathered stone, and a bright blue light left him and flowed into the stone and then along the ground.

"If he's Ares, why's his hand blue?" Jerome whispered to Aaron. "Merlock only ever glowed violet."

"It's a peculiarity of the Head and Heart," Gryphon responded. He stood and brushed his hands on his pants. "Alex can glow other colors too, but only if she needs to harness more power than you'd normally see her use. I've seen it many times."

"When will you start her lessons again?" Aaron asked.

Gryphon flinched and turned to Aaron. "Tomorrow, if you're agreeable, and she feels up to it. Megesti's had a few months to work with me on his own, and I'd like to see how he handles channeling her powers for a change."

Aaron nodded. "Good. I don't want to push her into it, but also, I don't want her waiting needlessly."

"Michael and Stefan will see that she is back to training as soon as possible," Jerome said, smiling for the briefest moment.

Gryphon waved his hands, wriggled his fingers, and sniffed the air. "The spell is cast. We can head back now, if you'd like."

"Let's go," Aaron said, but before he could say anything else, Gryphon snapped his fingers, and they were cracked back to the stables. "Gryphon, I—"

Gryphon was gone, having left his horse behind for them.

Jerome shook his head. He and Macht offered to handle the horses, and Aaron headed into the castle with Harold. The hallway to the library was lit with torches. Aaron rubbed his hands together to warm them. "How are you never cold?" he asked standing before the roaring fire in the library.

"The mountains have harsher winters. It snows for nearly half our year."

Aaron shivered, remembering his journey across the Ogre Mountains to find Moorloc's castle and get Alex back. "It was a little over a year ago we met."

"And you begged me to help you save Alex."

Aaron chuckled.

The Betruger king settled onto the golden hued couch while Aaron tried to thaw his frozen legs. "If you freeze so easily, I can have some Betruger clothing sent. Our pants are exceptionally warm."

"Alex wasn't shy about wearing Edith's new clothing to go into the mountains. Clearly, there is something to them, and I suppose I should finally accept your offer."

"I'll ask my tailor to visit you this week." Harold shifted in his seat, bringing his locked hands to his knees. "How much do you plan to tell Alexandria?"

"About what happened while she was gone? Everything. After what we went through, I need her to trust me, and keeping anything from her won't help with that." A slight groan escaped his lips when he said, "I'm not looking forward to telling her how much Gryphon and I have been arguing. I know it will upset her."

Harold frowned. "She'll always be between you two. You both love her, and she will love you both, in your own times and ways."

"Is it too much to want *my* time with her to not include *him?*"

"No. But she needs his help."

"I know." Aaron sighed, and finally removed his cloak. "Shall we go see if our ladies are awake yet?"

"Yours might be. Alex rises before our sun most days, but Edith enjoys sleeping," Harold said.

"And how would you know that?" Aaron teased.

Harold wouldn't take the bait. "She refuses to agree to any meeting before ten."

"Alex is a fan of early morning adventures. I think it's leftover from her time in the camp where they were always up at dawn."

"Are you warm yet?" Harold asked.

"I am. We should get some food for our ladies before waking them."

Harold nodded, and they headed into the hallway toward the kitchen, but halted when they heard laughter echoing down the main hall. They hurried toward the throne room, but aside from the usual guards, it was empty. A younger guard nodded his head toward the dining hall. Inside, Aaron and Harold found Alex and Edith sitting at one of the knights' tables with their friends. The table was spread with the traditional Datten pre-hunt feast of hard-cooked eggs, buns stuffed with cheese and venison, dried fruit mixed with nuts, and hot porridge. Edith, Lynx, and Jessica were trying hard to hide their laughter while Alex and Michael argued across the table. Judging from the size of Alex's exaggerated arm movements, it was clear to Aaron she would win.

Stefan called the newcomers to join them. Harold dropped beside Edith and gave her a peck on the cheek. She placed an empty plate before him and put his favorites on it. Alex and Megesti scooched apart on the bench to make room for Aaron between them. He patted Megesti's back and sat.

"Did you all have a good rest?" Harold asked the group, but everyone knew he meant the trio who'd returned to them.

"I did," Edith said. "My parents were thrilled to have me back. My mother tried to make me come home, but my father insisted I stay at the castle. He knew we wouldn't be able to get away with not telling everyone every detail today."

Michael flashed a smile at Jessica. "It was so nice to be back in my bed. I don't think I moved the whole night," he said.

"You didn't." Jessica rubbed her growing belly. "This little one already wakes me up a few times a night, and each time, you were dead to the world."

"How about you, Alex?" Lynx asked, picking at her nuts and fruit. "Did you *sleep* well?"

"I did, thank you." She winked at Aaron and stuffed an entire egg in her mouth. Aaron knew she did it to avoid answering anymore.

"What time will we be meeting with everyone today?" Michael asked.

"I honestly expected you all to be more exhausted, so I asked the generals to arrive later this morning, but we can move it sooner," Aaron said.

Alex shook her head. "We're in no rush, and we won't forget anything in that extra hour or two."

The group finished their meals. As they headed back to their room, Aaron watched Alex's face for signs of sadness, exhaustion, or stress, but she seemed to be in a daze. When the door closed behind them, Aaron touched her arm, and she startled. Her flinch broke his heart.

"Sorry, I was lost in thought."

"Clearly." Aaron took her hand. "Anything you want to discuss alone before we talk with everyone?"

"Actually, yes." Alex gripped his hand and pulled him to their seats. She moved a few books from the couch to the table and motioned for Aaron to sit.

Aaron took a deep breath and nestled beside her, holding on to as much of her as he comfortably could. The last time she had left him, she—*No. Let her speak.* "Whatever you have to say, I love you, and won't think less of you."

"It isn't anything like that. I made a choice, and swore an oath in the labyrinth, and I need you to know." Alex replayed her conversation with Prince Teon and how she lost her powers.

"That explains the pain that hit Gryphon and Megesti suddenly."

Alex nodded. "My powers were stored within them until I made the choice to take them back."

"Why them?" Aaron asked. "Megesti, I can understand. But Gryphon?"

"Megesti took the powers of our family's lines—Cassandra and Merlin. Gryphon took the powers I have from being the Heart. Honestly, when I felt them leave, it was more of a relief."

"I thought you liked your magic now?"

"I do, but it's also a burden. Like being royal. I was born into it, and am proud of who I am, but worry whether I'm doing enough with it, or if someone else could do it better."

Aaron leaned down and kissed the top of Alex's head, making her turn to face him. "I can understand that feeling."

"I know." Alex nodded, scrunching her nose and biting her cheek. His hand moved to her face.

"Anything else you need me to know? I know you only do this when you are nervous."

"I'm not nervous. I'm just not sure how to explain this."

"Try. If I'm confused, I'll ask questions."

"In the last room, we had to look into a fountain and face our worst fears. Only then could we leave. That's one place where I don't know how long it took... maybe that's where the lost time went."

"What did you see?"

"Failure. Trying to do everything alone."

Aaron shifted and pulled Alex against him. She nuzzled against his chest and took a few deep breaths before continuing. "I saw your brother, you, and everyone accusing me of failing because I abandoned them and left them behind. So I ... I took a blood oath to never do it again."

Aaron's heart hammered in his chest. "A blood oath? To whom, and why?"

"Because it was the only way to force me to do it."

"Alex, those are dangerous. Now someone can hold that over your head!"

Alex held her palm out to Aaron. A few small crescent-shaped scars lingered there.

"I gave the oath to myself."

"Is that even possible?"

"I don't actually know, but I'm going to live my life assuming it is. I swore to never leave you all behind, to let the people who love me help me—and I will keep to that oath."

Aaron hugged her tightly. They sat in silence for a long time.

"How are you feeling now?" he finally asked. "Do you feel more in control after getting the scepter?"

"I'm not sure." Alex looked ready to say more, but there was a soft knock at the door. She kissed his cheek. "Come in, Guinevere."

Aaron's mother entered the room as gracefully as deer walking through a meadow. She held her arms out, and Alex was already hurrying to accept her embrace.

Aaron beamed at his mother. She'd loved Alex since the day she was born, but ever since the lost princess had been found, she'd taken on a motherly role, helping Alex adjust to royal life. Guinevere knew first-hand how challenging it was to adjust to the Datten court life.

"Welcome home, dear," Guinevere said, giving Alex a long squeeze.

"I'm sorry for leaving so stealthily," Alex said.

"We're just thankful you told Jessica."

"I had to. I couldn't have her worrying in her condition."

"You're as thoughtful as my son." Guinevere released Alex and turned to Aaron.

He stepped up and kissed her cheek. "Morning, mother. I trust you slept well."

"I did, after the noise died down. The entire castle was celebrating your return, Alexandria."

"Have you heard from my father?" Alex asked. Aaron heard desperation in her voice.

"I have." She turned back to Aaron. "He's asking to be allowed to come to Datten to see you."

"Of course," Aaron said. "I'll have Megesti fetch him."

Alex stiffened. "Megesti can crack people now?"

Guinevere chuckled. "He's had private lessons with Gryphon every day for almost three months. He's become as powerful as his father was."

A mischievous little grin spread across Alex's lips. "I can't wait for our first lesson together. This should be fun."

"Wicked queen," Aaron whispered to her, making her giggle.

"You two continue to catch up. I'll ask Megesti or Birch to summon Edward."

"Make sure they warn him that Randal will be in attendance and I expect him to be civil," Aaron said.

Guinevere nodded and gave Alex another big hug before leaving.

"She was worried," Aaron said.

"I told Jessica she could tell her where we'd gone as soon as we were out of reach."

"She did. But mother and I can't help it. We've lost Daniel, Victoria, and my father, and now Edward is ..."

"Being stubborn?"

"Yes. Guess we know where you get it from."

Alex slammed her hip into Aaron, throwing him off balance. "So, where were you this morning?"

Aaron explained how Gryphon and Kharon had developed a spell that would set off an alarm of sorts if anything magical were to arrive in Datten. It was so complex that Gryphon had to put it down one small area at a time, but now that they'd finished, they could rest more easily.

"How will he know if someone comes?"

"He wears a chain with an obsidian stone. If anything magical arrives, it will glow the color of the line, and if it's a creature, white."

"That's amazing. Where did they find that spell?"

"They found a smaller version in a Merlin book, and then Gryphon and Kharon spent a month expanding on it. We'll do the Verlassen Castle next."

"I hope it works."

"Gryphon has faith, so you should, too."

Alex stuck her tongue out. "Let me go change. Then we can grab the scepter and go to the library."

Aaron looked her up and down. Dressed in her usual sparring attire, she appeared clean and kempt. "Why do you need to change?"

"The queen has returned, and you want me to show up for my first official royal duty in sparring clothes?"

Aaron pulled her hands into his. "I don't care what you wear, and neither do our friends, but if you want to present yourself in a manner befitting a royal, then by all means, do so."

"Thank you."

CHAPTER 28

ALEX

When they arrived in the library, Edward was already there. Despite the awkwardness between him and Aaron, they greeted each other respectfully before Edward threw his arms around Alex. He squeezed her so hard, she almost dropped the scepter. Aaron slipped it from her hand so she could hug her father with both arms. She could feel him shaking.

"I'm fine. Really," Alex whispered to him. "I'm sorry I worried you."

Edward released her but grabbed her shoulder so hard Alex winced. "I know," he said. "I've played that night over in my mind every day since you left. Regardless of what happened, I should not have lost my temper with you." He turned to Aaron. "And I shouldn't have treated you as disrespectfully as I did for stepping in."

"I understand how you felt," Aaron said. "I wanted to strangle Stefan for keeping Alex from me after I came back from the curse, but ... he was right."

"And so were you," Edward turned to Alex. He cupped her

cheek, and warmth spread across her face. "I'm so sorry I struck you. I never thought I'd become my father."

"One mistake doesn't make you him," Alex said, wrapping her arms around his middle and hugging him tightly. She glanced at Aaron who was rubbing the back of his neck, watching the door. *Aaron clearly hasn't forgiven you yet.*

Soon, the entire Wafner family entered. Michael placed his compass on the table beside Alex's scepter. "I asked Jessica to join us, if you don't mind," he said.

"Of course. I don't want to tell this story twice, so why would you?" Alex replied.

Aaron motioned to the table, and everyone took a seat. Alex pulled Aaron to sit with Michael and Jessica, ensuring that Randal and Edward would be as far apart as possible. Soon, everyone else wandered in. Harold and Macht arrived with Edith and Randal, while Lynx, Birch, Gryphon, and Megesti arrived last. Everyone looked at Alex, Edith, and Michael expectantly.

The trio began by apologizing for keeping everyone in the dark about their plans. Gryphon demanded to know how Alex figured out how to keep him out of her head, and Alex confirmed what they'd suspected about her losing her powers in the maze, though she kept her choice to take them back to herself. Stefan almost fell off his seat when Alex and Michael told them about fleeing from the fire and ending up in the raging river. Harold and Randal beamed when they heard about Edith vaulting over the pit.

Alex watched Aaron and Gryphon closely while they spoke about their various trials and figuring out the Veremund lullaby unlocked the last door. The room went silent as the three of them talked about their final trial, facing their worst qualities, and having to push through that pain to free themselves. Finally, they told of their visit with Cassandra and the gifts she'd bestowed on them.

"So you can tell when someone is lying?" Stefan asked Edith.

"Apparently, but no one has lied to me yet, so I'll have to wait and see what—"

"Your dress is ugly," Jessica exclaimed.

Edith's head snapped toward her, but her eyes widened, and she gasped.

"What did you see?" Randal asked.

"The air turned gray. It was like how Alex glows gold when she uses too much magic."

"So, you have to be looking at them to tell," Macht said.

"I don't know how mine works either," Michael said, looking at Alex. She just shrugged at him. "But hopefully we'll never find out."

Gryphon picked up the scepter, but cried out and dropped it the instant the metal touched his flesh. "What the Ares?"

"The base is red steel," Michael explained. He snatched it and handed it to Alex, explaining what they had learned from Cassandra about red steel and Cassandra sorcerers.

"Now I understand how your mother could walk around with a red steel dagger," Birch said.

"Did any of you know this?" Alex asked, but the sorcerers all shook their heads.

"While we know much of the founders of our lines, we only know what they and their children recorded," Kharon said. "It seems the Cassandras' immunity to red steel was not something they wanted widely known."

"And now the real work starts," Stefan said. Everyone turned to him, and his father nodded. "Alex is invincible to red steel, so Michael and I will train her with it. It will be an extra defense for her, against any sorcerer who comes after her."

Jerome cleared his throat. "I think you should leave the sword training to Randal and me. We're the most experienced in teaching a lady to wield a sword."

Edith and Jessica snickered.

"True, but I'm the most experienced in training Alex," Stefan replied.

"Macht can help," Harold added. "Alex would learn a great deal from our methods."

Stefan nodded to Harold. "While we train her with her red steel swords, Michael can work on sensing the finer points of Alex's emotions. He already understands her moods better than Aaron and I do, so keeping him at her side will be crucial. In the meantime, Edith should try to see how small of a lie she can detect."

"I'd also like to resume my magic training," Alex said.

Gryphon and Aaron exchanged a look.

"I think that's a splendid idea," Aaron said. "If you truly lost your powers for the two months you were inside of the cave, I'm sure you're rusty."

Are you? Gryphon asked inside her head. His intense gaze made her squirm in her seat.

A little. I had to try three times last night to get the fireplace to light, and it's a good thing no one was in front of it when it finally happened.

"A refresher would be helpful," Alex said, adjusting her skirt to avoid looking at anyone.

"Is there anything we can do to help with repairing the castle?" Edith asked.

"You all have specific tasks that will need to be done," Aaron said. "Edith, you'll be working with Harold and the builders. Michael, your estates still need finishing, so you need to contact both your grandmother and my uncle to arrange things. And Alex, my mother believes it's time to let our new queen handle more of the queen's duties."

"Estates?" Michael asked. "As in, more than one?"

Jessica smiled. "Your grandmother and my father are having a new estate built for us on the land that held the old Wafner home. It'll be a fresh start, since it was that fire that brought you, Stefan, and Alex together."

Michael squeezed her hand. "If that's what you want, I'm fully on board."

"It is. I want a home beside my father. In Datten, we will live on Wafner land, and in Warren, the Veremund."

Harold turned to Edith. "Would you like additional homes as well?"

Edith shook her head. "We won't need them. If we visit Warren or Datten, we would be royal guests and thus be expected to stay in the castle."

"And if you wished to visit quietly, you could simply stay with us," Randal added.

Harold nodded. "I need your opinions on our castle. We've just begun rebuilding the Betruger houses, and when that's done, we'll need our design ready. My people deserve to have their homes back before we start a castle."

Edith kissed Harold's cheek. "And that is why I love you."

"If we're all up to speed, then I think we can start the day," Jerome said. "Alexandria, would you prefer to do swords in the morning, afternoon, or evening?"

"I would prefer to study magic in the morning, before my other duties."

Michael laughed. "That way, you can take out your frustrations on the generals."

"He really knows you," Aaron replied. "Now if you're all going to start your days, Harold and I would like a word with Edward, alone."

ALEX WANTED to hear what Aaron had to say to her father, but Aaron playfully shooed her from the room, promising to tell her later. She went back to her room and found the Betruger training clothes that Aaron asked Harold to make for her. They were as comfortable as her normal sparring clothes but had an extra layer of soft fur for warmth. Alex ran her hand along the sleeve, trying to figure out what made it so soft, when she heard Megesti and Gryphon waiting for her on the main floor of her suite.

"Where's Stefan?" Alex asked, coming downstairs.

Gryphon smirked. "Are you that scared of us?"

Alex snorted. "Hardly. I just thought that …"

"Aaron has come to his senses about many things while you were away," Megesti said. "Trusting you unconditionally, being a big one."

"What else has he been up to?" Alex crossed her arms.

"You'll have to ask him that," Megesti replied. "I won't take that away from him."

Gryphon held his hand out to Alex. "Don't worry. He's been on a never-ending mission to earn your forgiveness for all his failings."

"Despite knowing you already gave it," Megesti added. "But enough about Aaron. I want to show off my new abilities to our Heart."

Alex frowned, but before she could argue with Megesti, Gryphon cracked them into a vast open field. Despite the winter months, wildflowers, shrubs, and clovers poked through the snow dusted soil. Scanning the tree-lined perimeter, Alex could identify at least a dozen unique varieties and a few she couldn't name. She shivered against the icy wind, her winter clothing doing little to warm her.

Megesti caught her attention, flicked his wrist, and the wind vanished.

"Not bad," Alex said, grinning.

"It took a lot of work to get the area to remain in spring despite the harsh winter around it, but with Birch's help, I've channeled Celtic powers to do it."

"He has a knack for the powers his parents possessed,"

Gryphon said. "That's why you are here. Merlock was a Merlin, and although he possessed various powers from several lines, they are more of a match with your powers than mine."

"What do we do? Hurt you and see if Megesti can heal you?" Alex and Megesti both chuckled.

Gryphon rolled his eyes. "Not quite, Princess."

"Poseidon, then?" Alex asked, straightening her back. Gryphon and Megesti nodded.

Gryphon explained that they would start with her trying to let Megesti take her powers. Once they'd learned to allow her powers to pass easily between them, Alex would then try to prevent Megesti from taking them.

Alex nodded and took her position, catching Gryphon grimacing. *Clearly I'm rusty. You can fix me.*

After Gryphon adjusted her stance, Alex pulled the water from the air and rained it down on the surrounding ground. Megesti took his position beside her, and as soon as he touched her, heat filled her back where he made contact. The rain slowed to a drizzle, and a puddle formed. Megesti's eyes glow violet as the water flowed from his free hand to the ground.

She was suddenly dizzy and stumbled. Gryphon dove and caught her before she lost her footing. Megesti ambled backward, shaking his head until the violet left his eyes.

"You're not supposed to take so much magic, Megesti," Gryphon scolded. Alex held onto him, waiting for the dizziness to pass.

"I didn't mean to," Megesti said, rubbing his face. "Her powers came to me more easily than anyone else's have."

"Why is that?" Alex asked.

"You two are the closest relation and he held your line powers while you were in the labyrinth," Gryphon replied. "Birch is his mother, but he didn't get her Celtics powers. He got the usurper gift. We'll need to be more careful with how we handle this."

"Could it also be because I'm out of practice?"

"All the more reason to practice resisting him."

Alex wanted to argue, but Megesti had drained her, and her usual fire was gone. She huffed, and when she looked at Gryphon, the stone hanging around his neck was glowing white.

"Gryphon." Alex stepped back and pointed at his necklace.

"*Ferflucs!* Go back to the castle. I have to deal with this."

CHAPTER 29

GRYPHON

Gryphon tried to grab Alex to send her back, but she jumped out of his reach.

"I'm not letting you handle this alone," she said.

"Alex, I appreciate you wanting to help, but you're drained. I'll take Lynx and Megesti."

"But—"

"No!" Gryphon snapped his fingers and Alex vanished.

Megesti raised his eyebrows. "You know you're going to pay for that later, right?"

"I'd rather she be furious and safe." Gryphon looked up. "Lynx. Birch. We need you, *now*."

The sorceresses arrived in the field in seconds. "What happened?" Birch asked, rushing to Megesti.

Lynx sniffed the air and snarled. "Something's here."

"Take us there," Megesti said.

Gryphon closed his eyes and opened his well. His Mystic powers raced along the boundary he'd set up, feeling for the hotspot. He found it close to them, coming down from the Ogre

Mountains. Without warning, he cracked them all to the border of Datten in the Dark Forest.

"It figures they'd come in through the forest," Megesti said.

Birch groaned. She placed her hand on a tree, and it burst to life, sprouting fresh green foliage. The wind rustling through the leaves sounded like whispers, and Birch whispered back. Gryphon paced, listening as best he could while Birch asked the forest what had been here.

"It's gone now," she said, rubbing her hands together.

"Do they know what it was?" Megesti asked, but Birch shook her head.

Lynx turned around and howled into the forest. Soon, a fox scurried up to her. The others gave her space to bark back and forth with the fox. After a brief exchange, it hurried back into the woods, and Lynx turned around.

"Cerberus was here," she said. "Your father's using Cerberus to spy on us. He must have sensed your barrier and taken off."

"Good thing you didn't bring Kharon," Megesti said.

Birch sighed. "They're going to be livid about this. It's bad enough your father parades that poor beast around as a body-guard, but now he's forcing it to do his dirty work, too."

Gryphon wove his hands and cracked them back to the partially repaired lab in the Datten castle. Megesti had insisted they not finish without Alex's input, since it would be her lab as much as his. Kharon was sitting at the worktable reading a book while Alex paced back and forth with a murderous expression on her face. Kharon finished the page before glancing up at the sorcerers.

"Where did you all vanish off to?" they asked, placing a bookmark into the Merlin text before closing it.

Alex had stopped pacing and was now glaring at them all.

"Don't look at me like that," Megesti said, throwing his hands before him. "I didn't leave you behind. I had no say in the matter."

"Cerberus triggered the barrier alarm," Lynx said.

Kharon turned red with rage.

Alex's pale complexion went ashen. "Cerberus?" She swallowed. "That monster that attacked us in the Forbidden Lands?"

"He's not a monster," Kharon and Lynx replied in unison.

"He was birthed for the founder of the Hades line," Kharon explained. "His job was to protect the mortal underworld with the previous Titan of Hades. Our last duty as Titans is to sit at the entrance of the mortal underworld and judge the souls of those who died. Cerberus' job was to stop any from escaping. That is, until four or five generations ago. At that time, the upcoming Head was an Ares, and he got it into his head that he needed the most ferocious beast to be his guard. Dragons were extinct, so he murdered the current Titan of Hades, forcing the changeover to take place. While everyone was distracted, he stole Cerberus."

"He's unpredictable and looks terrifying," Lynx added. "But his poor behavior is because he's not doing the job he's meant to. It's no different from a horse becoming anxious for not being tended to, or a hunting dog becoming aggressive because it isn't run enough."

"That makes me feel sorry for him," Alex said.

"We all do," Gryphon said. "At least when he's not chewing on me."

"Is there anything we can do to help him?" Alex asked.

"Nothing at the moment," Kharon said. "It's impossible for a sorcerer to enter the human underworld. We'd be trapped there forever."

"I've already promised Kharon if he passes on while I'm Head, he can take Cerberus home," Gryphon said.

Alex dropped onto the stool beside Kharon and rubbed her temples.

"Are you alright, Petal?" Birch asked.

"Megesti took too much of her magic," Gryphon said. He rolled up his sleeve and ran his hand softly along her spine, releasing his magic into her. Her back lit up, and she arched and moaned loudly before jerking away from him and leaping from the stool. When she turned to him, her normally pale cheeks were as red as Datten's crest.

"Nice to know I can still influence you after your time away." Gryphon winked at her and shook his hand, sending his magic away. Lynx's laughter broke the silence.

"What just happened?" Megesti asked.

Uh oh. Have you and Megesti never had a euphoric magic moment?

"It's very simple," Birch said, smiling at Alex. "When two sorcerers share a special bond, sometimes—"

"No!" Alex pointed at Birch and cracked away.

Lynx, Gryphon, and Birch turned toward Megesti.

"I'm still waiting for that explanation," Megesti said.

"You don't know what a magic rush is?" Lynx asked.

Megesti shook his head. Lynx's eyes went wide with panic. "Where is she? I need to explain to her what just happened."

"I can go," Birch offered. "It might be easier coming from a more experienced sorceress."

"I'll go," Lynx said. "She won't want to hear this from you."

Gryphon sighed, closed his eyes, and felt for Alex. In her panicked state, she was much easier to find. He slipped into her mind and saw Stefan arguing with her about what was wrong, while she shoved a saddle at him.

"She's in the stable. You'd better hurry, though. She's making a run for it with your betrothed," Gryphon said.

"He won't be happy with you if she explains what happened," Lynx said.

"I don't think she'll want to tell anyone this," Megesti said, and Lynx cracked away.

"So, who do we tell?" Kharon asked.

"Tell? I'm not telling anyone. I made Alex moan by giving her some magic. Her husband only recently stopped trying to stab me."

"I meant about Cerberus breaching the border."

"Oh, that," Gryphon said, scratching his head. He hoped his face wasn't as red as the heat coming from his cheeks made him suspect. "I suppose we go to the generals."

CHAPTER 30
ALEX

"It's normal," Lynx said.

"Nothing about that was normal!" Alex snapped. Her face was overheating, and she wished she could crawl into the hay around them and hide.

Stefan leaned against the wall of the stable, arms crossed, trying to hold back his obvious amusement.

Alex grabbed a handful of hay off the ground and threw it at him. "And it isn't funny."

"I think it's funny."

"You're not helping, Stefan," Lynx scolded.

"I can, though." Stefan walked over, grabbed her hands, and tugged on her until she relented and looked at him. "Remember when Oliver had feelings for the miller's daughter, and turned into a bumbling idiot every time he went near the mill? It's like that."

"No, it isn't. Oliver had feelings for Robyn. I have no feelings for Gryphon."

"But you do. You can't help it. Even if you just see him as a friend, the Alex I know cares *deeply* about her friends. Once you let someone into your heart, they stay there."

"And you have a bond with Gryphon," Lynx added. "You can resist it, but a nature bond isn't something you can ignore forever. It is called *'nature'* for a reason. It's because you are supposed to achieve something evolutionary together. Even if your heart doesn't yet love him, the magic inside of you does."

"But … I moaned!"

"I know," Lynx said, rubbing Alex's shoulder.

"You know you moan in your sleep, right?" Stefan asked.

Alex froze and glanced at Lynx. She quickly threw her hands out toward Stefan, soaking him with a wave of Poseidon powers, and fled the stable as fast as her legs could carry her. She could hear Stefan shouting after her. Alex raced through the castle toward the safety of her suite.

Once inside her room, she stripped off her training clothes and threw on the simple red Datten dress Aaron had given her. She was trying to tie the back when there was a knock at the door.

It was Jessica. "Her Majesty went with your father to Warren to visit her brother. She asked me to take you to the council. You'll be sitting on it in her stead."

"Which council, exactly?" Alex asked.

Jessica finished tying her dress and smiled. "I'm not allowed to say. Aaron wants it to be a surprise when you arrive," she said, holding up Alex's necklace.

Alex took it and turned her back to Jessica. When she touched the three different gemstones, she remembered how much she'd cried when Aaron had given it to her for their wedding. A sudden warmth rushed up her arm, jerking her from her reverie.

"Are you alright?" Jessica asked, squeezing her arm.

"Yes, thank you," Alex said. "I'm just tired. It was a strange lesson this morning with Megesti and Gryphon."

"Understandable. Shall we go?" Jessica motioned to the door, and Alex followed her into the hallway. As they walked, Jessica explained that when rebuilding sections of the castle damaged during the attack, Aaron had made changes. They ended up in a room Alex had never seen before. It was in the center region of the castle on the second floor. The space was nearly the size of the throne room and had some people sitting in rows of benches. They were facing a large row of tables at the front. Alex recognized a few of the people, but not many. It resembled her father's council chambers.

"What is this?" Alex asked.

"Datten's answer to your father's labor council," Jessica replied. "Aaron and my father collected the best people in each industry in Datten, regardless of station and gender, and put them on this council."

"Why?" Alex asked.

"Because we've let the rich make choices for everyone for too long," Aaron said, arriving in the room. He'd dressed simply and had left his crown behind. "You're free to go, Jessica." She nodded and greeted an older woman before leaving. Alex recognized her as the royal seamstress.

Aaron offered her his arm, and she took it. "How does this work?" she asked.

"Well, here I'm Aaron, and you're Alexandria. We will listen more than we talk, and we will learn what struggles our people face in completing the work that feeds their families. If there is anything we can do or provide them to help, we will. We'll also use the council to settle disputes that come up between different industries. This way, everyone who is impacted can have a say."

"How did you choose who would represent each industry?"

"I didn't. My mother and Jerome did. They know better than me who excels at particular skills. I could tell you who the best squires or equestrians are, but beyond that, I'm not as knowledgeable as I should be."

Alex squeezed his arm closer. "In your defense, you spent the last two years finding and winning your kingdom's queen. I hope they found that of value."

Aaron beamed and leaned down to kiss her. Alex flinched instinctually, but relaxed when clanking *didn't* accompany his affections. A quick glance around the room showed several knights on guard. Aaron noticed her confusion and whispered, "It wasn't me or Jerome. Apparently, I needed my mother to scold the knights. All the castle guards have been told not to react when we kiss. I hope you'll forgive a few of the older ones who are slow to give it up, but the sound should be much better now."

Alex sighed happily. "Thank you."

"Come on. I'll introduce you to everyone, and then we can hear about the lives of our people. You're also the head of the women's council, with my mother and Jessica. The three of you will provide assistance to any Torian lady, not just Datten, who wants to leave an abusive situation."

Alex stopped and stared at Aaron.

"That can mean husband, father, sister ... anyone with power or authority over her—real or imagined. I wanted to make sure any lady in your situation had someone to help them, like you had Jerome, Michael, and Stefan."

Alex squeezed Aaron's hand. "Aaron." He looked down and turned red. *Alright, I won't push you about this here. But I do want to hear more about this idea.*

Alex kissed his cheek quickly, bringing his attention back to her. "And tomorrow, we'll be meeting with the newly expanded advisory council. I retired the oldest members and replaced them with the most forward thinking member of their family, regardless of age or gender."

"Which Rassgat did you pick?" Alex asked.

"Wesley, but only because I know he hates council meetings and won't come."

Alex giggled, and they went to greet the first group of Dattenites.

Alex stood on her balcony wrapped in Aaron's cloak, watching the moon rise across the sky. Aaron had stepped out to meet with Harold and the master builders about the supplies they needed for the next day's work on the Betruger village. Enjoying the crisp air, Alex took another bite of her apple.

"I missed you when I was in the maze," she said to Daniel. "As much as you annoy me when you get overprotective, having you around is a comfort for me."

The ghost winked at her.

"Can't you look older?" Alex asked.

"Why?"

"It's disconcerting that you look younger than your little brother."

Daniel chuckled. "I can understand that. Would you prefer the version who came to your rescue at Moorloc's castle?"

"If that's how you see yourself, then yes."

"What if I see myself as a boy?" he teased.

"You're as difficult as your brother."

"Who is?" Gryphon asked, stepping onto the balcony.

"You're supposed to knock," Daniel said.

"I did. No one answered. Why are you older?" Gryphon asked.

"Because she prefers me this way," Daniel replied.

So now you like older men. Gryphon thought at her.

Alex rolled her eyes at Gryphon. "Don't put words in my mouth. I just feel strange that my husband's older brother looks ten years younger than him."

"Fair," Gryphon said. "Daniel, would you excuse us? I need to discuss something with Alexandria in private."

Daniel shot Gryphon an icy glare.

"It's alright, Daniel. Thank you."

Daniel held the glare as he vanished.

"Aaron and Stefan are both fine with me, but now your ghostly guard has it out for me?"

"Someone has to watch you," Alex teased. She pulled the cloak tighter. "I know why you're here. I'm embarrassed and I'd rather not discuss it."

"You mean the moaning?" Gryphon smirked slightly.

Alex groaned and covered her face with her hands. Gryphon pulled her hands away from her face and a gentle warmth ran up her arms. *I'm sorry. That wasn't what I wanted to talk about.*

"Then what?" Alex asked.

"I want to go cast the spell on the Verlassen castle as soon as possible. Cerberus snooping around means we're being watched, and your mother's castle needs to be protected. It has a great deal of magical items inside it—things that could be used against you."

"No," Alex snapped before she could stop herself.

"No?"

She pushed past Gryphon and stormed back into her bedroom. "I haven't even been home a day. I want a few days of peace, of getting to just live, before the next disaster and danger strikes."

Gryphon pursed his lips and stepped up to her. Tingles ran through her as he caressed her arms. "I know, and I'm sorry. But we are being hunted by my family, and they don't care that you're tired. They won't quit."

Alex rubbed her eyes, trying to hold back her frustrated tears. A door closed behind them.

"Are you crying?" Aaron asked, rushing over.

"I'm fine," Alex lied.

"Alex—"

"She's upset that I think we need to protect the Verlassen Castle now," Gryphon said.

Alex buried her face in her husband's chest to hide. Aaron stroked her back to soothe her while he and Gryphon discussed the best way to protect the remaining castles. It quickly became clear the Verlassen Castle would likely be the next target because of the sentimental value it held for Alex and the lingering magic from Victoria that filled every stone in the place.

"Thank you, Gryphon. Alex and I will discuss it."

Gryphon rolled his eyes but nodded before he cracked away.

"Why don't you want to go?" Aaron asked.

Alex was still clinging to him. "I just got home. I don't want to leave already."

"You consider Datten home now?"

Not a place.

"Home is where you are," Alex said, and squeezed him tighter. Aaron kissed the top of her head.

"Then a compromise. You leave in the morning with whomever Gryphon thinks you need. Have your magic lesson there and spend the day working on the barrier. Then come home for dinner. That way, you'll sleep in our bed, and still have time for yourself if you need it."

"I don't want time to myself." Alex looked up at Aaron and gripped his tunic. "I just want to be alone with you."

"I like the sound of that." He nuzzled her head.

"Aaron ... Do I moan in my sleep?"

"That's a strange question."

"Answer it."

Aaron leaned over, gently kissed her neck, and whispered, "Sometimes, but more often on nights when neither of us are sleeping."

ALEX

"Alex, stop pushing so hard," Megesti scolded.

"You can't tell if I'm pushing hard."

"I can when you turn red from exertion."

"It's freezing. I'm red from the cold," Alex snapped.

"Liar."

Alex stood and turned toward her cousin. His powers had grown more in the months she'd been gone than in all the years alone with his father. It seemed all he needed to come into his own was to be surrounded by sorcerers. He stood tall and crossed his arms, studying her. The resemblance between him and his late father wasn't as striking as Alex's to her mother, but the way he glared down at her made her feel like Merlock was watching her. Alex deliberately rubbed her hands on her pants before placing them on her hips.

"So I'm a liar?" she snapped. "Can you read my thoughts now, too?"

"It doesn't take a mystic to notice how tired and cranky you've been the last week."

Alex *was* tired, but life had been a whirlwind since she'd

returned from the maze. "We've been working on these protection spells non-stop for two months. We finished the Verlassen Castle, and then Moorloc's old place, but Warren is huge, and is taking longer than expected."

"That isn't why you've been biting everyone's heads off."

"I have not." Alex turned and stormed out of the woods toward the fields and the manor. They'd been working on the borders of the old family estates. So far, they'd finished the Nials, Bishops, and Strobels. Today they were on Michael's land. As Alex stormed through the footpath between the trees, Megesti cracked in front of her.

"You're doing it again," he said. "The whole 'avoiding talking about something that makes you uncomfortable' thing."

"Maybe I'd rather talk to someone who understands, or even better, get this whole charade over with and never think of it again." Alex swerved around Megesti and increased her pace.

"An official death compensation trial is not a charade."

"It is, when your father and husband are both kings. No one wants to hold a princess or queen accountable."

"Alex, please!"

She whipped around and faced him. His shoulders drooped, and his brows were twisted in loving concern for her.

"We're here for you. All of us. You just need to let us in."

Bug off.

"There is nothing you can say unless you've had to face the family of someone you killed." Alex turned her back on him and cracked herself to the castle.

She stalked into her room, where Jessica and Edith were waiting for her. They worked in silence as Jessica tied up Alex's blue dress, and Edith fixed her hair. Her father had suggested that she'd attend under the title of Crown Princess of Warren, since the Vinur family was Warren nobility. Alex couldn't even look at herself in the mirror as her ladies turned the wild sorceress into a proper Warren Princess.

"It'll be alright." Edith squeezed Alex's hand once they'd finished.

"You don't have to attend," Jessica whispered. "Your father said he'd handle this with General Bishop."

"I would have thought you of all people would understand why I have to do this," Alex whispered.

Jessica ran her hand across her bump. "I didn't at first, but then my father explained it to me."

Edith scoffed but tried to hide it by coughing.

"You can speak openly, Edith," Alex said.

Edith sighed. "It feels like you're torturing yourself for no reason."

Alex stopped fidgeting and grabbed Edith's hands. "You're going to be a queen, too. Facing your mistakes and setting the right example is crucial, even if it hurts."

Edith pulled her hands back and grabbed Alex in a tight hug. "We'll be here when you're done."

There was a knock at the door.

Julius Bishop nodded to her ladies before turning to Alex. "Our fathers asked me to escort you to the meeting, if you still wish to attend."

"I do."

Julius bowed slightly and held his arm out, but Alex shook her head. Pushing her shoulders back and raising her chin, she locked her hands in a ball at her waist and began the long walk to the spare hall. Their footsteps echoed against the polished stone of the empty hallway. When they rounded the last corner, Alex saw Daniel standing beside the door. He appeared as the older version of himself and smiled weakly at Alex. Saying nothing. She shook her head twice, and he slowly vanished as Julius opened the door for her.

You can do this. After today, this will be over, and you can move on.

Entering the room, a chill crept up Alex's spine. Julius closed the door behind her, and chairs scraped as the men present all rose. The spare hall was used for various royal events, but court cases always made it feel cold. Today, the room was arranged differently than usual. Two long tables ran the length of the room in parallel. Behind one sat her father, along with Harold and Aaron, while Macht and Matthew stood at either end. Across from them sat the Vinur family: Reinhilde's son Germund, and her grandsons Felix, Archibald, and Henry. All were dressed in the darker blue tunics signifying their position as Warren nobility, but the three sons all wore the uniforms of average knights.

Alex felt like retching but swallowed hard. The last time she'd seen them, they'd been in her royal guard. They were removed after Stefan learned they were gossiping about her personal life with people in the kingdom. Although Felix and Henry had brought their discharge upon themselves, Alex still felt guilt. Remembering everything Jessica and Guinevere had taught her, she held her breath and marched toward her father. She rounded the table and Harold pulled her chair out. When she sat, everyone besides her father did, too. Harold held his hand out to her, and she grabbed it.

Edward cleared his throat. "As King of Warren, I accept the case brought before us by the Vinur family. You are seeking compensation for the accidental death of your matriarch, Reinhilde Vinur, at the hand of my daughter Alexandria, Crown Princess of Warren, and Queen of Datten. Is this accurate, Germund?"

The Baron stood. "It is, Your Royal Highnesses. We accept the princess held no ill will against my mother, and while we are devastated by her loss, we understand her death was caused by an unfortunate magic training accident during the time she was imprisoned by the princess's uncle."

"And you agree to the Torian terms?" Aaron asked from his seat.

Germund exhaled. "Yes. In order to move on from this, we will allow the case to proceed following the standard knight rules."

Edward finally settled into his chair. "Then proceed with your request for compensation."

ALEX BARELY MADE it out of the room before retching. Thankfully, someone had thought ahead and left a bucket outside every door to the spare hall. Bile burned her throat and nose as she tried to rid herself of the memory of the smell of burned flesh. Germund had demanded Alex describe his mother's death in intricate detail before Edward and Aaron could reply to his demands. Tears rolled down Alex's face. She slumped to the ground and lost what remained in her stomach.

"Here." A handkerchief and mug appeared beside her face. She took them with her shaky hands, and Harold dropped on the ground beside her. "Drink. It'll help settle your stomach. Your throat must be on fire."

Alex took a large swig and swished the cool water around her mouth to remove the taste that lingered there. After another few drinks, and wiping her lips, her mouth no longer tasted so foul, though her throat still ached.

"You aren't alone in this, Alex. Aaron and your father will handle these Vinurs. You understand they aren't hurting, don't you?"

Alex stared at him. "What do you mean?"

"When I was a young man, I killed my friend Gunther Schmit in a sparring match. We both moved incorrectly, and I cut him on his leg in a bad place. He bled to death before we could do anything."

"Harold, I'm so sorry."

"I'm not telling you this so you feel bad. I want you to see how it should be." Harold shifted closer and nudged her in the way Stefan would. Alex dropped her head on his shoulder and he continued. "Gunther's family forgave me. Matthias, my blacksmith, is Gunther's older brother. We still talk about Gunther and remember him. I mourned with his family and was there to bury him."

"So his entire family forgave you?" Alex glanced up at Harold.

"Nearly. His sister has not spoken to me since that day. It is her pain I carry."

She nodded and returned her head to his shoulder.

"But Gunther's family didn't want money from me. They wanted their son to be remembered. These Vinurs ... they only want money."

"It seems that way, but it isn't."

"How so?"

"By accepting the Torian rules, Gunther waved his right to speak about the pain I caused him. That law was enacted by Datten over a millennia ago to simplify the process of giving compensation to a family when their loved one was killed in a training accident." Alex tugged on her dress for a moment before adding. "Aaron practically memorized that book when he was trying to prove his father wrong."

"If her son can hide his love so easily, then I still believe they didn't love Reinhilde how you did. You mourn her, but they shed no tears, especially the young men. They only have eyes for what her death can get them."

Alex scoffed. "That's because they're angry. Stefan removed them from my royal guard when he learned they were gossiping about my sharing a bed with Aaron before we were wed."

"I see." Harold patted Alex's leg. "After today, you must forget them, but find a way to honor *her*. A way that will make things better for people like her."

Alex sat quietly and thought. "I'd like to use my Cassandra and Celtic gifts to provide medicine for the poorer people of Torian, not just Warren and Datten. Reinhilde trained with my mother, and was exceptional at helping people, and it was Germund falling deathly ill that sent her to Moorloc. If she'd had other options ... things would have turned out differently."

"I think she'd appreciate that. If you'd like help to do this, I'm here. My healers are at your disposal."

Alex let out a breath and pressed her head against the cold stone behind her. "Right now, I'd rather you help with another problem."

"Aaron?"

Alex nodded. "He never talks about being cursed other than to apologize over and over again. I'm worried about him. Does he open up to you at all?"

"He has," Harold said. "He doesn't speak to you about it because his dark side scares him, and he wants to be brave and strong for you."

Alex frowned. "I don't need Aaron to protect me. I have Stefan and an army for that. What I need is for him to be my husband, and let me into his pain, the same way he expects to be allowed into mine."

"So tell him that," Harold said. "He'll want to talk with you after today."

Alex nodded. "Are you going back in? I wanted to stay the whole time, but after hearing their stories and sharing mine, I can't be in there anymore."

Harold stood and helped Alex up. "Where will you go?"

"To find Gryphon and manage these feelings productively."

Harold smiled. "Are you going to grow some plants?"

Alex shook her head. "No. I'm going to burn something."

CHAPTER 32

GRYPHON

"Good job. Your stance is almost perfect." Gryphon smiled, but she didn't even glance back.

I was being nice.

"I don't need *nice*," Alex snapped. "I need you to *work* me."

"You're going to regret that in a few minutes."

"Just do it, *Sunset*."

Gryphon smirked, stepped behind Alex, and gripped her hips. He twisted her forward, then drove his thumbs into her tailbone so hard it sent her entire back arching forward with a grunt.

"Palms up. Arms out. I need you to master Poseidon with Salem."

Alex grunted and her eyes and skin erupted in a blazing golden glow. She locked her gaze out over the sea.

They could go anywhere, but both preferred to train at the same beach where they'd first met. Gryphon glanced down the narrow part of the beach and shuddered. It was here he'd found Alex's goodbye letter. It was here he'd nearly lost her, and here that he'd been forever changed. After decades of cruelty at the hands of his parents, he'd thought he could handle anything, but a sorceress's broken heart had proved him wrong. Alex was his breaking point, and he'd burn the world to the ground and kill everyone in it before he let any more harm befall her.

Gryphon moved to her side, checked her stance one more time, and satisfied it was correct, ordered, "Raise it."

The sand between them rumbled. Gryphon smiled at Alex's tongue poking out of her mouth. It happened when she focused intently. Her glow darkened as her magic poured into the sea, but this time, the water was unaffected. Gryphon pursed his lips and was about to stop her when the waves tripled in size. He waded into the surf and squinted at a small mound of earth that had broken through the sea. He nodded and turned back to Alex. Her skin was pale all over, but her face was glistening with sweat.

"Okay, that's enough," he said, but she furrowed her brow and stretched her arms out as far as she could. The mound grew until a mountain lifted out of the water.

"Stop!" Gryphon shouted, but she ignored him.

I said enough! Gryphon cracked to where Alex was standing and grabbed her arm. The earth plummeted back into the Oreean Sea, and the waves violently crashed into the beach, pulling them both into the roiling current. Gryphon tried to scream as the icy sea froze him to the core, but only managed to suck in freezing water. His lungs felt like they would burst from the pain. A warm hand gripped his, and then he was on the beach. He doubled over, coughing up seawater. Alex dropped onto her back beside him.

"You coward," she panted. "Why did you stop me?"

You were draining yourself, Gryphon thought back, still unable to speak. *Ferflucs! I hate being cold. It's the worst feeling in the world.*

Her face contorted in sadness and anger. "No, it isn't. The worst feeling is having no one believe in you. I'll see you at home."

When she cracked away, Gryphon roared in frustration. A flock of birds that had been resting on a nearby tree fled in terror.

"I do believe in you, Alex, but I won't risk you to let you prove it to yourself, especially now that I know how much power you carry."

A soft breeze hit Gryphon, enveloping him in the smell of spring. "Hello Birch."

"What did you do, Sprout?"

"You're bringing out my childhood pet name?" He sat up, resting on his elbows.

"You're clearly upset."

"Not as upset as Alex is," Lynx said from over Birch's shoulder.

"Uh. The double lecture." He lay down on his back and burst into flames to dry his clothes. After he stood and beat the sand off himself. "What did she say?"

"She said nothing, Gryphon. We're Titans. When you two fight like this, we feel it," Lynx said. "Hopefully, nobody else did. You're lucky it was only a moment."

"We aren't fighting, per se," Gryphon said. "She was already angry about the trial, and I wasn't willing to let her punish herself."

"Good," Lynx said. "Stefan told me what the Vinurs demanded. They're going to benefit from her friend's death, both in station and financially."

Birch frowned. "That poor girl. She carries that death on her soul, and they are using it to line their pockets."

"Which is why I thought training would help," Gryphon said. "She's too raw, though. She won't listen to her body when her emotions are out of control, which means she can't control her magic."

"I thought you'd have an easier time helping her after holding her magic," Birch said.

"So did I, but her magic is wild compared to mine. I don't know if it's the combination of being a returned one, or if that's how Merlin powers feel."

"Let her sleep her frustrations off. Tomorrow you can work on the barrier some more. Stefan and I can come with you," Lynx said. "Stefan can help keep her in check, or at least be another target for her."

They all cracked back to the Verlassen Castle. Gryphon headed to his room, stripped off his sandy clothes, and tossed them into a pile in the corner. He paused at the large mirror on the door of his wardrobe. The scar no longer hurt, but after Aaron interrupted Alex's attempt to remove it, the faint outline of his father's hand-print remained permanently etched on his shoulder. He turned his head to the side. Most days, he barely noticed the bond mark on his neck. Today it had darkened and burned painfully.

What is going on in your mind, Princess, that this keeps happening? It seems to only hurt when we're fighting, but nothing I've read about bonds talks about the mark hurting.

Gryphon traced the tender skin around the mark of the Head and Heart, with a sword through it. He shut his eyes, shaking away the memories of a sword with an identical hilt. "Are you trying to reject our bond, Alex? Or is Aaron's connection to us destroying it?"

He continued muttering to himself as he headed into the bathing chamber.

GRYPHON GAVE up trying to sleep. With his bond mark burning, he couldn't get comfortable in his normal position. His mind kept wandering back to Alex's lesson. *I wish you would have just done what I told you.* Wandering through the Verlassen Castle, he paused in the main hall to look at the paintings. The one of Birch was especially beautiful, and he'd never seen her so happy. Her smile had a hint of mischief behind it, and she wore a crown she'd made from ivy, wildflowers, and dragon's heart. Gryphon leaned in closer. The leaves had a crimson hue and serrated edges that resembled the beast's vital organ.

"Where did you find dragon's heart? I thought it was extinct."

Bile erupted from his stomach, sending rage coursing through his veins. He burst into an orange glow. Glancing around the room to make sure no one saw, he cracked out of the castle to the woods just outside of the protective border. The thick canopy blocked the moon above him, and his orange glow only lit a few paces in front of him. He heard leaves rustling in the trees above him, and a small rodent scurry away to his right.

"Who's here?" Gryphon demanded. He flicked his fingers, sending out a spray of small fireballs to illuminate the space. A stick snapped behind him. He summoned flames to his palms, ready to pounce. When he turned, chaos engulfed him, and a dark figure sent Gryphon to his knees in terror.

"Ares ..."

The founder of Gryphon's line towered over him. Even in death, the god of war was a sight to behold. His golden armor, forever splattered with blood, fit him like a second skin. Unlike mortal armor, it merely covered his chest, and the flaps off the main piece covered his groin and thighs. Beneath the gold, his body was bare and emitted the same orange aura Gryphon's did. He stepped toward Gryphon and removed his helmet—a solid piece of gold, shaped like an acorn, with terrifying dragon scales protruding from the top and back. His eyes gleamed with the same golden hue as Gryphon's line, but when he fixed on Gryphon, they flashed darkly and became orange. He held a halberd, the curve of which perfectly matched the Ares ax line mark.

Gryphon lowered his head, in both reverence and submission to the god of war and chaos approaching him. Terrified to even breathe in his presence, Gryphon stared at the ground.

"Do not cower from me, Gryphon, son of Garrick, son of Aeron, heir to my line."

Gryphon slowly got to his feet and finally raised his eyes toward the god. Ares opened his hands, releasing both his helmet and halberd. They vanished before they hit the ground, along with their orange auras.

"What have I done to deserve a visit from you, oh mighty Titan of Chaos?"

"Nothing. You required a reminder, boy." Ares' voice boomed into Gryphon's mind without the god ever opening his mouth. "A lesson in how an Ares is to conduct himself. Two decades ago, you allowed a Cassandra to deter your duty to your line and disobeyed a direct order from your Head and line titan. Now another Cassandra, a younger one, consumes your every thought and action. She weakens you."

"Alex doesn't weaken me. She—"

"Do not interrupt me!" Ares roared, sending all the woodland creatures fleeing.

"Apologies," Gryphon whimpered.

"Cassandras are devious and have a natural siren power over Ares males. Their gifts of premonition allow them to predict our behaviors and understand our desires. They use them to manipulate us. To control your lesser half, you will need to be stronger than her in both power and will. You must dominate her and remove *all* male rivals for her attention. If you fail, she will control you, and our line, as we know it, will end with you."

Gryphon swallowed.

"Should you fail to bring your Cassandra to heed, I will intervene, as your father and hexa should have twenty years ago, when you failed your test."

Gryphon's stomach revolted against him. He had never been more afraid in his life. "If I had followed through with my test, Alexandria would never have been born. Victoria told me if I killed him, she'd never bear children."

"More Cassandra lies! She would not have allowed her line to end with her. She knew the true value of her line just as I do. You fell for her lies. All because of the hope that the daughter, who would look exactly like the girl in your dreams, would love you. Love makes you weak. If you want her, you *take* her. Had you done your duty, you wouldn't have to fight for her now."

"What would you have me do?"

"Simple, finish the task you failed all those years ago."

Gryphon fell to his knees, ready to beg. "There has to be another way. Anything else. If I kill him, she'd never forgive me."

Ares erupted in orange and rocks, sticks, and everything else in close proximity rose from the ground, circling them. "Do not test me. You will prove yourself a true Ares, and kill the King of Datten, or I will kill you."

CHAPTER 33

AARON

"That was a colossal waste of time!" Alex said, ripping her crown off her head and throwing it on their bed in her Warren suite. She failed to undo her dress, then became frustrated and shook with rage.

Aaron set his own crown on his bedside table. He approached her from behind and grabbed her in his muscular arms, holding her body against his chest to sooth her.

Her shaking wilted into trembles, and she struggled to slow her breathing. "I can't keep doing this."

"Doing what exactly?"

"Being royal. I'm useless at it."

"You're amazing."

"I'm a mess."

Aaron turned her around. Cupping her face, he brushed away the tears on her cheeks with his thumbs. "You are young, and were never prepared for this life or your role in it. I'm honored you agreed to stand by my side, and I would never ask for a different partner."

Alex half laughed and half cried. Aaron held her as she cried, muttering incoherent things about the Vinurs, gold, her father's cold shoulder, and a mountain that wouldn't breathe fire. At last, she was sharing things with him, even if he didn't understand her. He kept holding her, saying nothing, until all her fears and frustrations were expressed. Then he tilted her head up to him, kissed her, then rested his forehead against hers.

"I'm sorry your father and I are not mending bridges as fast as you'd like. I'm trying but I'm struggling to forgive him for hurting you, when I can't even forgive myself for hurting you. The Vinurs received much more than anyone would have asked for as compensation, but the one thing Edward and I did agree on recently was to end this swiftly in order to avoid causing *you* additional pain. Hopefully, you can find peace now."

Alex nodded against Aaron. "I have ideas on how we can commemorate her."

"I'll help however you want me to, even if it's staying out of it."

Alex pushed away from Aaron and gazed at him. "Are you still having nightmares about the curse? About being trapped in the room?"

Aaron nodded. "I'm afraid to go to sleep. I keep expecting to wake up back in there. Part of me worries that getting out was just a dream."

Alex stroked his face and smiled at him. "What can I do?"

"Alex, I'm fine. Let's just focus on you." She scowled at him, and he sighed. "You being away was more difficult for me than you know," he said reluctantly. "I would prefer you to stay with me in Datten at night. Wherever you go, whatever you do, come home at night, so I don't have to sleep alone. Holding you in my arms as I fall asleep grounds me to this world."

Alex kissed him. "I promise." She turned so he could loosen the straps on her corset.

"I don't think I can help with the mountain that won't … breathe fire?"

Alex sighed. "I'm trying to raise a volcano from the seabed. It's a lot harder than I expected, and Gryphon wouldn't let me push myself."

"Considering everything that happened today, that might be a good idea."

"I don't appreciate having limits forced on me. After giving up my power in the labyrinth, I'm more aware of just how strong I am."

"I know, but sometimes you need reminding that even you have limits."

At that, she turned and groaned. But he smiled at her, and she couldn't keep her scowl. With a huff, she dropped the gown on the floor, stepped out of it, then headed downstairs.

Aaron grabbed Alex's crown from the bed to put it away. Seeing the familiar nick on one prong, he chuckled. She'd accidentally worn his today. *I won't tease her this time. She's been through enough today.* Suddenly, he had an idea.

"Put on some pants, not a nightgown," he shouted down the stairs. He grabbed his cloak, lit a torch, and then rushed down to join her. It took a bit of convincing, but he got Alex into some sparring clothes, and before she could protest, he grabbed her hand and pulled her up to the painting with the secret entrance. She looked at him with a wrinkle in her nose but allowed him to pull her through the opening he made.

As soon as the wind hit them, the torch flickered out. Alex squeezed his hand and the torch burst back to life. Locking their hands together, he led her through the paths and secret entrances until they ended up at a drainage tunnel. It was here where they'd spent the night talking after their birthday party.

Alex pulled her hand from his. Aaron glanced around, saw the scorch marks on the ground, and remembered. "Alex, I'm sorry. I forgot about Ember. I didn't mean—"

"Don't apologize." Alex kicked the scorch mark on the ground and grabbed his hand again. "The same as the throne room. You give me strength."

He could almost hear her heart racing. Aaron nodded and slowly led her down the tunnel.

When they reached the edge of the rock face, Aaron placed the torch in the dirt and wrapped his arms around Alex's belly. Pulling her flush against him, he leaned down to rest his chin in the crook of her neck. He could feel the tension drain from her looking at the moon reflecting on the Oreean Sea.

"I brought my cloak in case you wanted to sit and watch the waves."

Alex kissed his cheek. "I'd like that." With a wave of her hand, their small torch became a warm fire.

Aaron pulled his cloak off his shoulders. Once Alex was comfortably seated, he joined her on the ground. She leaned back against him, and he wrapped his cloak around them.

She grabbed his hand and wrapped it around her waist. "Why didn't you kiss me the night you brought me here?" she asked.

Aaron felt his cheeks warm. *Getting right to embarrassing me, are we?* "I wanted to. Desperately. But after the attack, and Wesley, I didn't want to be yet another man forcing my attention upon you."

Alex went silent for a moment and that's when it dawned on him.

"Did you want me to kiss you?"

Alex smiled wickedly. "Desperately," she whispered.

"Ah!" Aaron groaned, making Alex giggle. "Why didn't you kiss me then?"

"You had told me you weren't a suitor."

"I was trying to forget that."

"I will never let you forget it. But truthfully, I was scared you didn't feel the same."

"You? Scared?" Aaron teased and playfully nipped her ear.

She laughed and tried to get away, but Aaron held on tight. When she finally turned back to him, Aaron smiled.

"Allow me to fix what I should have done that night." He took his hands off her waist and cupped her face. Alex leaned into him, and he kissed her with all the love he could muster.

Aaron woke up leaning on the tunnel wall. They'd spent the night there, hiding from the world and their responsibilities. The sun was just rising over the Oreean Sea, and the waves sent sparkles of light throughout the tunnel entrance. Alex had fallen asleep on his shoulder, but now she was gazing at him.

"Morning," she whispered.

"Were you watching me sleep?"

"I was."

"Why?"

Alex smiled at him before quickly kissing him. "So you wouldn't get taken away." She stood and stretched her arms over her head before dropping water on their fire. "Ready to go? As much as I'd love to hide here with you, I have lessons."

"And I promised Harold and Edith I'd go to the Warren builders to order some supplies. For anything Edith wants, Harold doesn't trust anyone else to do it." As he spoke, Alex snaked her arm around his and locked their fingers together. "Do you have time for breakfast with me before you start lessons?" Aaron asked.

"If we get back soon enough. Shall I crack us?"

Aaron nodded, and they arrived in the main hallway outside the dining room. Alex playfully tugged Aaron toward the hall when Julius and Stefan came barreling around the corner.

"We found you!" Stefan said.

"Can this wait?" Aaron asked, not even bothering to hide the frustration in his voice.

"Aaron." Alex pinched him, but her knights didn't laugh.

"I'm sorry to have to bother you, Aaron, but there's been a fire at the Verlassen Castle."

"A fire!" Alex exclaimed. "When?"

"Just now."

Lynx appeared beside them. "Oh, they found you. I came to fetch you, but we couldn't find you."

"Sorry. We were just catching up," Alex said, looking at the floor.

Lynx smiled. "Don't be embarrassed for spending time with your husband. But we should go."

"One second." Aaron turned to Julius. "Go find Harold and let him know what's going on. Tell him I'll be back as soon as I can."

Julius nodded and Lynx cracked the rest of them to the courtyard of the Verlassen Castle. Guards were scurrying back and forth with buckets of water. Alex started after one, but Stefan grabbed her arm, pulling her another direction. He let go when Lynx scowled at him.

"Lynx, where's the fire?" Aaron asked. He grabbed Alex's hand.

"At the far stables. The horses cried out and alerted me. Gryphon, Megesti, Birch, and Kharon helped the mortals while I was looking for you."

Megesti jogged across the courtyard and spotted them. "We put out the fire, but I don't think we can save the stable. I'm sorry, Alex."

Aaron took in his friend. His face was streaked with ash, and he gave off a strong odor of campfire. "Are you okay, Megesti?" Aaron scrunched his nose. He smelled like Gryphon.

"I'm exhausted. That wasn't a normal fire. It didn't matter how much water or earth we threw on it, the flames would not die."

"Was anyone hurt?" Stefan asked.

When Megesti nodded, Aaron felt Alex tense, so he moved a hand to her back to reassure her.

"Some minor burns, and a broken bone from a very determined stable boy who refused to leave until all the animals were out," Megesti said.

"Is it safe to examine the damage?" Alex asked.

"If you're careful," Gryphon replied, joining the group alongside Birch.

"Tell me it wasn't Nathaniel's boy who got hurt," Aaron said. "My uncle is going to be livid if the stable boy we got from him was injured."

Megesti tugged on his collar. "It was."

"Go with Stefan to see him," Alex said. "I'll go with Megesti and Gryphon to examine the damage."

"You sure?" Aaron asked.

"If you know the boy, it's best you go. I don't want to risk healing him until I know more about this fire."

"You think the injury could be magical?" Stefan asked.

"Let's not jump to conclusions," Gryphon said.

"I'll bring you to the lad," Birch said to Aaron. "After you're done, I'll bring you to the stable."

CHAPTER 34

ALEX

"Why are you so pale, Gryphon?"

"Why are you so short?" he asked, glaring at Alex. "I mean, Megesti's covered in ash, but you're as white as a ghost."

"You know I get dirty easily," Megesti teased.

"I'm a fire sorcerer," Gryphon replied. "Megesti had to fight fire with water, but I just took the fire into me."

"So you're both alright."

"I don't think I'll ever get the stench out of these clothes." Megesti sighed.

"I'm fine, Princess," Gryphon said. "Though I appreciate your concern for my wellbeing."

Alex rolled her eyes and brushed past them toward the stables. A strange tingle rushed through her. She glanced behind her but Gryphon and Megesti showed no sign of having noticed it. It felt as if it were coming from the ground, so Alex squatted to get a closer feel.

"Do you sense it?" Megesti asked.

"I feel something." Alex slid her palm along the ground, tracing the invisible line where they had put up the protection spells. "They're testing the barrier, aren't they?"

"I believe so." Gryphon joined Alex and brushed the ground she'd touched. "What else do you feel here?"

Alex put her hands flat on the ground. *What do you mean?*

"Don't ask. Just feel. Anything?"

"The dirt is warmer outside the boundary. Is that even possible?"

"Yes. What else?"

"Something feels wrong. I can't explain it beyond that, but I feel it in my bones. What is that?"

"I think the mortals call it a gut tell." He stood and held his hand out to Alex.

"The burned stable is over there," said Megesti, motioning further down the path.

Alex wiped her hands on her dusty pants. As they walked, she pulled the ribbon out of her braid and shook her hair out.

"How does a Poseidon sorceress have so much dirt in her hair?" Gryphon teased. "Why do you do that?"

She stuck her tongue out at him and re-braided her hair. "It's not that it's dirty. I hate when my braid comes out because I end up with hair in my face and you can't fight when you can't see."

Alex became more and more uneasy the farther they walked. She called to Megesti to stop. "What if it's a trap?" she asked.

"How is a burned stable a trap?" Gryphon asked.

"I didn't think of that," Megesti said exhaling loudly. "We should stay inside the barrier."

Alex tried to hide her rising fear. "We don't have the best track record with stable fires."

That's why I'm here, Alex. To make sure you're safe.

That you didn't call me Princess is concerning.

Forgive me for trying to be serious, Princess.

Alex nodded at Gryphon, and they continued on their way.

When the smell of smoke filled her nostrils, Gryphon brushed past her and shoved her behind him. *I won't fight you this time.* Although they'd extinguished the fire in one of the stables, another had caught on fire.

"This is the strangest fire I've ever seen," Megesti said. "Gryphon, have you ever experienced this before?"

"No. I wish I had, so we'd know what it is. Our protection spell goes through the stable."

The searing flames licked the wood beams, but only on one half the building. The other half had fresh hay that was completely unscathed.

Alex moved between the sorcerers and shifted her stance. "Well, at least we can see what my powers do to it." She extended her hands. Droplets of water brushed her cheek as they spiraled around her. In moments, a large stream of water swirled in the air. Alex took a step over the protective barrier and thrust out her arms, sending the water exploding out over the entire fire at once. It hissed and popped, and at once they were engulfed in an impenetrable fog of smoke and steam. Taking a shallow breath, she turned her head toward where the sky should be. She raised her arm and spun her wrist, bringing storm clouds over them, and in seconds it rained on the stable, quenching the smoke.

"Just in case," she said.

"Better safe than sorry." Megesti stepped past her to head into the half-burned entrance of the stable.

"It looks safe to go inside, if that's what you're waiting for," Gryphon said.

Alex looked back over the forest, scanning the trees. Her rain clouds had made it harder to see and her stomach felt as if it were filled with rocks.

"Nothing's here," Gryphon whispered. "But I can double check. I am the son of a powerful Tiere."

Alex heard Megesti curse, and she rushed into the building

without answering. He was crouching on the ground rubbing his knee. "Sorry. I slipped on your puddle and bashed my knee."

Gryphon slowly looked him up and down before glancing at Alex. *Didn't he train with Aaron and Emmerich?*

Alex bit her lip to keep herself from laughing and nodded at Gryphon.

What happened?

Alex covered her mouth and slunk away to examine the wall. There was a perfect line down the center, where half was blackened and charred, and half remained as perfect as the day it had been built. Alex brushed her fingers against the burned boards. Bravery filled her as she placed her palm against the wall, but they felt completely cool.

"Gryphon, I know you can make a fire burn for light without damaging the space—"

"Like Moorloc had?"

"Yes, but is there any way to make a fire burn cold?"

Megesti joined her and touched the wall with her before touching the other side.

"Maybe the heat is at the back." Alex went over to the most burned area of the stable. When she touched the wall there, it crumbled beneath her palm. It didn't feel like any burned wood she'd ever felt before. Rubbing the strange black substance between her fingertips, ice crept up her spine. *Daniel, what is it now?* Alex turned to her side and screamed.

Most of the ghosts who came to see Alex were clean and presented themselves as their best self, but Moorloc was pale as death and drenched in his own blood, the way Alex had left him that day on the battlefield. Her hands flew over her mouth, and she reeled backward, slamming into one of the stable's support beams.

QUIET! Gryphon's voice was desperate and full of terror inside her head.

Gryphon and Megesti were shaking their heads at her from the end of the stable. She turned back to find Moorloc gone. Her heart was pounding so hard she could barely hear anything besides her blood pumping through her ears, but from the other side of the wall came a loud, distinctive growl.

Alex pressed her hands over her mouth to keep herself from crying out. She clenched her jaw and locked eyes with Gryphon. He just shook his head at her. *I can't crack when I'm this upset. I'll end up getting myself killed.*

Megesti was shouting something, trying to help her, but Gryphon shoved him to the protected half of the stable and warned him to stay back. Gryphon crept toward her to retrieve her. Alex closed her eyes and begged Daniel to come, but when she opened them again, her scream rattled the entire stable.

Imelda's ghost howled at her, and the ground rumbled beneath her. Gryphon dove for her and there was a deafening crash. An enormous tail smashed through the stable as if it were matchsticks and slammed into his body. The force sent him flying into Megesti and was enough to send them both flying back to the unburned side of the stable. Alex covered her head, expecting the entire structure to come down. When she looked up, the tail was gone.

Gryphon … Gryphon! Are you both alright?

Alex backed away from the wall just as a gigantic claw burst through it. Shaking, she reeled backward and tripped over something on the ground. Falling onto her side, she cursed, and pain surged through her. The claw soon reduced the entire back wall to kindling. Alex tried to drag herself farther away. Now, three sets of eyes fixed on her. *Cerberus.* The beast had been huge when she met him in the Forbidden Lands, but now he had somehow tripled in size. The hound poked his enormous central head into the building and snorted. Alex felt a blast of putrid, wet air slam into her face.

CHAPTER 35

AARON

"How young is too young for a knight to retire?" Aaron asked.

"What do you mean?" Stefan asked.

"Sir Christian has the worst luck on guard duty."

"I admire his determination to continue guarding Alex and her home, despite everything that's happened," Stefan said, "But maybe Edward can convince him to take a safer assignment."

They had just left the young knight's room and were standing in the hallway. His injuries were mostly from the smoke, and miraculously, what they thought had been burns turned out to be simply minor scrapes.

"Some people refuse to give up on their responsibilities," Lynx said, grinning at Stefan.

"Being a Wafner is different, though."

"That doesn't mean *you* have to," Aaron said.

Stefan scoffed and hurried ahead, and Aaron had to rush to catch up. "I'm serious, Stefan. Just because your family has guarded mine for generations doesn't mean you must adopt that life."

Stefan kept walking. "I have already broken with enough tradition," he said.

Lynx hurried after him. "Which traditions?"

"I'm guarding Warren royalty, not Datten."

Lynx chuckled and looped her arm through his. "I suspect you're the only Wafner to be bonded to a sorceress, too." Stefan nodded and kissed her cheek.

They heard shouting coming from down the hall, and Stefan's expression went stoic. They rushed forward and into the main hall where Birch tried to calm down a panicking Megesti so he could tell them what happened, but he was so distraught she couldn't understand what he was saying.

Aaron marched over to his friend. "Megesti, what's wrong? The last time you acted like this was when Alex went with Moorloc."

"I need Lynx and Kharon!"

"I'm here," Lynx said, stepping out from behind Stefan.

"Gryphon and Alex are in trouble. The sorcerers sent that three-headed dog here to test the castle, and as we speak, it has them cornered in the stable."

"Why are we standing here?" Aaron shouted. "Crack us there!"

"No," Lynx said. "If we spook Cerberus, he'll become more aggressive. Our best shot at helping them is to get me there quickly and calmly."

Stefan grabbed Lynx's hand and pulled her toward the entrance of the hall.

"Where are we going?" Aaron asked.

"The front door," Stefan shouted. "The sorcerers will expect us to out-think them, so we'll do the opposite and take the easiest route to the stables."

"What if that's what they're expecting?" Megesti asked.

"Garrick isn't one to expect the obvious," Birch said. "It's worth a try."

The group slipped through the bushes around the moat. With

luck, the running water would drown out their footsteps. Aaron reluctantly let himself be pushed to the middle of the group so Stefan and Lynx could lead the way. He knew Lynx's magic would be more helpful than his sword. Megesti was at his side. His face looked brave, but Aaron knew his friend. Megesti's shirt was crooked from him tugging on his collar. Alex played with her shirt hem, and Megesti, the collar. Despite having such wildly distinct personalities, anyone who really knew the last Merlin sorcerers could spot their family connections.

"It'll be alright," Birch chirped from behind them. The sorceress of plants and peace was always the first to look on the bright side.

"I hope you're right—" Aaron was cut off by a loud scream.

"Alex!" Stefan and Lynx gave up trying to be quiet and charged ahead. Lynx threw her magic ahead of them, clearing a path through the brush and sending the critters scurrying to safety. When they reached the clearing, Aaron's heart dropped into his stomach.

Alex had described the monster to him before, but he was unprepared for the size. The hound was the height of the stable. Aaron moved up beside Lynx and Stefan. "Now what?" he asked.

"Kharon, we need you," Lynx called softly, so that the beast wouldn't notice them.

"You summoned me?" Kharon arrived with a grin, but it quickly vanished. "Cerberus? What have they done to you, boy?"

"Boy?" Megesti whispered to Aaron. Kharon seemed to look at the monster with affection.

Stefan drew his sword, but Lynx grabbed his arm and shook her head. "Not everything needs a sword, love."

"Let us try first," Kharon said. "I won't allow you to hurt him. He may look ferocious, but Cerberus is not inherently vicious. The Ares line made him that way over the generations. I hope we can reach him."

CHAPTER 36

GRYPHON

Gryphon stood frozen. Never in his life had he been so terrified, especially not of Cerberus. His mother's faithful pet had spent his entire childhood stalking him and using him as a chew toy. Birch had healed his scars, and Lynx had taught him how to sense the beast coming. Now he stood so close to Alex, Gryphon was sure she'd be able to smell what the mutt ate for breakfast.

Alex, stay calm. Just take a few deep breaths and run.

I'm scared.

I know, but I won't let anything happen to you. Well, nothing you can't heal.

Alex whimpered, and Gryphon couldn't tell if it was in his head or out loud. He held his breath, trying not to make a sound as he crept toward Cerberus. The beast was entirely focused on Alex, who stood ready to run. Gryphon suddenly got a terrible feeling in his gut. The instant she twisted to go, Cerberus pounced.

The hellhound burst through the remaining bits of the charred stable with speed Gryphon had never witnessed in his life. He snatched Alex's leg in his tremendous jaws, and Gryphon heard a sickening thud. Her scream echoed through the stable when she hit the ground and was dragged from the building. By the time Gryphon caught his breath, she was gone. A heartbeat later, the rest of the stable collapsed. The force of it smashing to the ground sent him flying and a thick cloud of dust and ash blocked his vision.

Gryphon had the wind knocked from him and sucked in a lungful of ash. Coughing uncontrollably, he stumbled out of the ruins. *We're in trouble.* Someone had given Cerberus a growing potion, and he was mad. Gryphon scanned the rubble and found Alex pinned under a giant paw. The dominant middle head snarled as she struggled to free herself from his hold. Gryphon moved toward her, but another head shot toward him. Ears back and teeth bared, the head growled at Gryphon. The last head was sniffing toward the wooded area.

Alex, stay calm. I won't leave you. Can you breathe?

A little, but it hurts.

Okay. Hang on, Princess.

Sunset ... I'm sorry.

Don't start that. You're too valuable for anyone to let Cerberus eat you.

Not helping.

Gryphon cracked away from the burned stable and dropped himself before Cerberus. The third head that had been watching the woods lurched toward him. Alex cried out when the beast shifted its weight toward its attacker. Gryphon opened his well and erupted in a blinding orange light.

Cerberus winced and sat back on his haunches but shook it off. Bits of fire rained down onto Gryphon, Alex, and the ground. The hound bared his teeth down at them once again.

Alex coughed, struggling to breathe. Rage filled Gryphon and his Ares temper frothed out of his well. His blood boiled. A moment later, fur and feathers ripped through his skin. Each felt like a thorn piercing him, thousands of jabs sending pain radiating over every inch of his body. Gryphon fixed his eyes on Cerberus and dropped to all fours. His limbs transformed and his beast side took over.

CHAPTER 37
ALEX

Cerberus's claw had gone right through Alex's shoulder. The pain was excruciating, and each time the beast moved it tugged on the wound. Alex had blacked out from the pain twice. The wound was mortal, but she couldn't heal it—she'd drained herself too much the last few days practicing with Megesti and working on the border spells. She only managed a faint glow to keep herself from bleeding out.

Breathe. Megesti will get help. Trust him.

Gryphon's scream made Alex flinch, but his cry after that truly terrified her. She clenched her jaw to hold back her own scream. If Cerberus shifted his weight again, she'd be finished.

Cerberus' paw lifted slightly, and Alex wriggled enough that when he pressed his weight back down, his weight was supported by his heel rather than her body. While the crushing weight made it hard to breathe, it was holding her wound shut.

There was another cry. Alex couldn't see anything, so she closed her eyes and waited for death.

CHAPTER 38

AARON

The entire structure came crashing to the ground as Aaron watched in terror. Cerberus tossed something across the ground and then pounced on it. When they crept closer, it became horribly clear that the bundle was Alex.

I'll gut that mutt myself if he so much as leaves a scratch on her.

A scream rang out from the burned stable, and Gryphon emerged from the rubble. Despite their distance, Aaron could see the sorcerer of chaos was as furious as he. Gryphon opened his mouth and emitted an animalistic cry. His body fell away and transformed into the terrifying beast that was his namesake. Aaron couldn't help but stare at the gryphon roaring at the three-headed hound.

"That's bad," Lynx groaned. "Stefan, keep everyone back while Kharon and I deal with Cerberus. Birch—"

"I'll handle Gryphon," Birch said. She rubbed her hands together and frowned at the sight before her.

Megesti slipped past Aaron to join Birch at her side. Despite the surrounding chaos, Aaron was glad to see his best friend finally connecting with his mother.

Lynx turned to Stefan, grabbed his tunic, and pulled him down to kiss her. After she released him, she gestured toward Aaron. "Keep this one in line. We don't need him getting himself injured while we save Alex. He has a hero complex."

"You say that as if it's a bad thing!" Aaron said, but Lynx and Kharon were already gone. He crossed his arms at Stefan. "You're as bad as I am with Alex, but no one's criticizing you for it."

Birch cracked herself over to Gryphon. She stayed a few steps behind him and sent a faint green fog across the ground. When it enveloped Gryphon, he stopped growling and sat back on his haunches.

While Gryphon's presence clearly angered Cerberus, Lynx and Kharon were having the opposite effect. Lynx held both palms out and crept toward the dog, glowing a green as deep as the Dark Forest in the summer. The main head fixed on her and roared as it drew close, but the Titan of Tiere didn't even flinch. Instead, she barked back at it, and Cerberus cocked that head to the side. Kharon held their hands up, emitting a gray glow and approached Lynx. They caught the attention of the other two heads and herded them toward the first.

The three heads looked at each other and then at the sorcerers. Finally, the head closest to Kharon leaned down and sniffed them. The dog's tension vanished, and it licked them. A moment later the other head licked Lynx, and she laughed. The three of them closed in, but as they neared, the dog shifted into a defensive posture and Alex screamed in pain. Lynx howled at him, and he froze and sat back down. He dropped a head and whimpered.

"Stefan, come here." Lynx motioned for him to join her, and they walked under the dog to Alex. Stefan squatted beside her, and Lynx patted Cerberus's leg. "Let her up," she said.

The main head swung toward Stefan, but Lynx raised her hand and it stopped. "No. He's with me. It is your job to keep mortals in their place, and his place is with the sorceress you're hurting and me, so behave."

Cerberus whimpered again. He cautiously sniffed Stefan, and once satisfied, stepped back, finally removing his paw from Alex.

"Move slowly, Stefan," Kharon said, positioning themself between Cerberus and the others. "Pick her up, and slowly carry her to Aaron and Megesti. Once you're safe, we'll send you all into the protective barrier."

Stefan did as he was told and scooped Alex into his arms. Without a word, he walked back and handed her off to Aaron. The moment her arms were around his neck, Aaron could have sobbed for joy, but he held himself together while they were cracked to the Verlassen courtyard.

Alex was soaked in blood, and more was pouring from the gaping wound in her shoulder.

Megesti gently touched her face. "She's passed out from the pain and losing so much blood. She'll need food once I've healed her."

"Have food sent to the library," Aaron said.

Stefan nodded and ran into the castle.

Megesti cracked his knuckles and smiled weakly at Aaron. "Hold her tight, alright?"

"I have no intention of letting her go," Aaron said, clutching Alex tighter in his arms.

Birch had arrived. When she placed her hand on Aaron's shoulder, warmth and love flooded him, keeping his growing rage at bay. Megesti placed his hand on Alex, and she immediately lit up in golden light. Aaron watched with relief as the light rushed into her and the wound became smaller and smaller until it closed over with new skin.

Relief hit him harder than he expected, and he clutched her tighter.

"Don't hold your tears in," Birch whispered. "You love her dearly and have no reason to hide that."

"Especially not from your friends," Megesti said, patting Aaron's back. "Let's get her into the library."

"I'm going to help the others," Birch said. "We need to figure out how to get Gryphon back to normal. Oh, and he'll need some new clothes …"

"Megesti can crack you some of mine when we're in the castle," Aaron said.

"Thank you." Birch nodded, and the next moment they were in the library. Megesti hurried through the bookcase door that led into Alex's bedroom.

Aaron laid Alex down on her favorite couch and kneeled before her. He brushed a loose curl out of her face. She was pale from the blood loss. "How is it that after all that, you don't have a scratch on you outside of the shoulder?"

"Has she woken up yet?" asked Megesti, returning from the other room.

"No. You're sure she's just passed out?"

As he set down a tray of bread and cheese, Stefan said, "She's faking to hear what you'll say about her."

Megesti glared at him, but Stefan was proven right moments later when Alex's head moved. Her gaze landed on Aaron, and she reached up for his face. "You came. I knew you would."

Aaron snatched her hand and kissed it. "We'll always come for you."

"Can you eat?" Megesti asked. "You lost a lot of blood, and that's beyond my skills. You'll need energy to heal yourself."

Alex swung her legs over the couch, but as soon as she tried to stand, she wobbled and went down.

Aaron had her in his arms before she had fully crumpled. "Let me help," he said.

"Alright."

"Did someone place a curse on our Alex on the field out there?" Stefan asked with a smirk. "Because this Alex is listening far too much to be ours."

Alex scrunched her nose and stuck her tongue out at Stefan.

"Seems fine to me," Aaron said.

"You complain I don't listen, and now you complain I am. Brothers!" Alex rolled her eyes.

Stefan pulled out her chair, and Aaron lowered her onto it. "Right now I need to know you're alright," Aaron said.

"A little shaken, but I'm okay," Alex said. She grabbed a sunflower loaf. "Where's Gryphon?"

"He's with Lynx, Kharon, and Birch. They're trying to figure out what to do about Cerberus," Stefan said.

Alex took a huge bite. As she chewed, her eyes widened, and she turned to Megesti.

"You felt that, too?" he asked.

"Felt what?" Stefan asked.

Megesti tugged on his collar. "Someone powerful is here."

CHAPTER 39

GRYPHON

Lynx giggled, and Gryphon looked down. He'd always thought Aaron wasn't that much shorter than him, but these pants said otherwise. The amount of his bare shin sticking out was ridiculous. Luckily, fire sorcerers ran hot, so even in the chilly spring air, he was comfortable in Aaron's training clothes. Gryphon gave Lynx a push with his shoulder, and Cerberus growled at him.

"Stop it," Kharon scolded, making the dog whimper.

Birch patted his large fuzzy leg, and he lay down before her, lowering his main head so Birch could reach his ears.

"How do we get him back to normal?" Lynx asked.

"I'm not sure," Birch said. "Hopefully, the spell they used is temporary and will wear off in due time. Kharon, is there any reason to believe this is Cerberus' doing?"

"Cerberus guards the mortal underworld. He can shift his size as needed to do his job, but nothing I read said he could get this large or that he'd remain large for this long." Kharon joined Birch and scratched the dog's other ear.

Gryphon was keeping a healthy distance. Now that Alex was

out of danger, he had no interest in hurting the dog. His family had done that enough over the last few generations. Cerberus' heads all moved up at once, and his ears dropped back, and he bared his teeth. A heat spread through Gryphon, warning him magic was near.

"Someone's here."

"Why am I not surprised that they used the witch to calm the mutt," came a voice from behind them. Ember wore the maroon-colored robe of the Salem Titan, and it hugged the curves of her body. "Then again, she sleeps with a mortal, so clearly she can manage beasts."

Gryphon cracked beside Lynx. He wouldn't fight her battles for her, but he wanted her to know he was there if she needed him.

"You were best friends with my sister for a century, Ember," Birch said calmly. "Have you already forgotten that she was a Tiere?"

"Have you forgotten that it was the Heart and her pets that caused your sister's death? We may not know who ended her with certainty, but we know they are standing in front of me now. Garrick is heartbroken."

Gryphon laughed. "My father barely tolerated my mother being in the same castle as him. You can't expect me to believe he misses her in the slightest. The only people who would actually mourn her are also those standing before you."

"Is that how you speak of your mother? Disgraceful."

"Disgraceful is certainly fitting of my mother," Gryphon snapped. "But I'll still mourn her. Not for the mother she was, but the one I hoped she'd become."

"I hope she haunts your little witch friends," Ember said, smirking. "I see you've come up with a cute little plan to keep us out. We'll get through soon enough. You always forget we have sorcerers of the Merlin line, too, and the Head on our side." She strolled toward them, rubbing her hands together. "So if you'll hand over Garrick's dear pet, I'll be on my way and no one has to get hurt."

"You're not taking him," Kharon said. "And he's not a pet. He belongs with the Hades line."

"I'm sorry, do you expect me to care what you think?" Ember cackled, throwing flames at Kharon. They jumped and just missed being burned. "If I'm not listening to the next Head, I'm certainly not going to listen to a useless Hades."

"Then you'll have to contend with all of us," Alex said, appearing beside Lynx with Megesti, with Stefan and Aaron behind her. Stefan looked unhappy to be out here, but regardless his stance was the protective one Gryphon would expect.

"Lynx!" Gryphon shouted. *Alex, what are you doing here? You are supposed to be recuperating after being stabbed.*

Since when has an injury stopped anyone here from doing their part to help? Besides, I'm fine and probably don't even need to fight. I'm hoping our presence here will be enough to get rid of her.

"Hello, little witch." Ember crossed her arms and looked Alex up and down before scoffing. "You're either very brave or idiotic coming out here now. Probably both. Titans can tell when a young sorcerer is drained, Princess. It helps us protect the young in our lines, and since you're still a child, you're clearly out of your depths."

Megesti and Stefan moved at once to block Alex from Ember.

Ember chuckled. "I admire your loyalty, but you really should pick better friends." A loud snap made her look away. Lynx took that moment to crack to Alex's side.

Gryphon's terror eased. Lynx could whisk Alex away if things got out of hand. But now he couldn't find Kharon. A quick sweep showed him Cerberus was crouched low, stalking Ember.

"Are we finished then?" Gryphon shouted in the cocky tone he knew Ember despised. Scowling, she erupted in flames, pulling fire toward herself from the surrounding air. *Good, she's distracted. But she's going to be hard to match.* Gryphon dug deep into his own well, but he'd already used much of his reserves to protect the mortal castles. He glowed dimly and tried to summon his own flames. Birch was using her magic to send vines after Ember.

Thunder cracked above, and a moment later rain drenched them all. *Alex.* Gryphon spun and saw her holding Megesti's hand.

At least you're getting help. He wondered if she could sense his snippiness.

I made a promise.

I thought it was an oath.

Same thing.

Ember's flames sputtered amid Alex and Megesti's monsoon and she screamed in rage. "Two can play at this game," she shrieked. A moment later, Lygari and three younger sorcerers appeared around her. Gryphon groaned as he recognized Kit, Hanish, and Glenn, the next in line to be Titans of Tiere, Poseidon, and Celtics. All were his age, and exhibited exceptional talent and power, but like many talented young sorcerers, their arrogance overshadowed their talents.

Hanish thrust their hand into the sky, and the rain stopped. Ember wasted no time in relighting her fire, and then she and Lygari launched fireballs at Alex and Megesti. They dodged them, and Birch cracked into the group to whisper something to Stefan and Aaron. Alex's scream rang out through the field when Stefan threw her over his shoulder and ran back toward the castle with Aaron a step behind. Lygari shot a giant fireball at them, but it vanished a mere foot from hitting them.

"I can help!" Alex shouted and Stefan grudgingly plopped her down.

"You can help from inside that border," Lynx shouted back, and leaped into the air. She transformed in mid-air and landed as a lynx. Immediately, she pounced at Lygari.

Megesti cracked to Gryphon's side and held out his hand.

"You're drained, too. I guess it's time for that lesson in taking powers from an unwilling sorcerer."

Gryphon smiled and turned toward the newcomers. Kit had trained with Lynx and Gryphon's mother, and he knew Lynx would enjoy taking him down. It had to be one of the other two. "I would suggest we go for your horrible cousin. The family tie will make it easier to drain him."

Megesti nodded and fixed his gaze on Lygari. Violet color burst from him and Lygari dropped to his knees, glowing a pale shade of violet.

Gryphon checked on how the others were doing. Kit had turned into an oversized fox, but he was too slow for Lynx. She charged him, knocked him back and viciously bit into his back. Ember was screaming at Hanish and Glenn to do something and seemed to have forgotten about Kharon and Cerberus, who were now right behind her. Cerberus attacked, sending the younger two flying. When Ember turned in surprise, he swatted her, slicing open her shoulder and sending blood running down her chest. She burst into flames to seal her wounds, and with a cry of anguish and frustration, she cracked away. The others looked at each other and vanished.

Birch came over and rubbed Megesti's shoulder, calming him.

"Nice job," Gryphon said, making the usurper grin broadly.

Alex cracked over to them, having abandoned Stefan and Aaron. She threw her arms around Megesti. "You were amazing. But next time, why don't you *start* by stealing Lygari's energy? He deserves it."

"Stefan dear, you'll want to help Lynx," Birch called as Lynx shifted back from her feline form. Stefan removed his shirt and hurried to Lynx. When she put it on, it hung to her knees.

"Now the hard question," Lynx said.

"What is it?" Alex asked.

Lynx gestured toward Cerberus. He was sitting beside Kharon and towered over the sorcerer. "Can I keep him?" she asked.

"I promised Kharon we'd return him to the mortal underworld one day," Gryphon said. "But we still have to figure out how to do that without Kharon needing to die," Gryphon said.

"He's not supposed to be this large either. We'll figure out what's wrong with him, so he can get back to normal," Lynx said with hope in her eyes.

Aaron had joined them and ran his hands through his hair. "It's fine with me, as long as I don't have to clean up after him."

CHAPTER 40

AARON

"You'll let her keep him?" Alex asked.

"Of course," Aaron said. After all, he'd married a sorceress. He had to expect a few oddities to come along with that. "Lynx, I'd like you to keep him here until we get him back to normal size. It'll be a lot easier to explain to our guards in Verlassen why there's a giant three-headed dog roaming around then it would be in Datten."

"I've taught these knights not to attack anything odd until they know for certain it's an enemy," Stefan said.

"That's fine," Lynx said.

"One of us will stay here with him," Kharon said. "This poor boy needs some love and a gentle hand right now."

"Stefan, are you ready for training?" Alex asked.

"There will be no training today," Stefan said.

"Why not?" Alex demanded.

"Because Jerome has a very strict rule about training after blood loss," Aaron replied. "I've used it to my advantage more than once." *Dozens of times, actually.*

"Then what am I supposed to do? I refuse to sit around."

Lynx smiled. "Practice your Tiere magic. Go for a ride with Aaron and see who can control their horse better. The king, who's riding a horse picked for him, or the sorceress who can talk to her horse."

Aaron felt a sheepish grin spread across his face. "It has been a while since we took the horses out. I'm not due back in Datten until the day after tomorrow."

"It would give you a chance to clear your head after the last few days," Stefan said. "And if you promise to leave the bracelet that locks Gryphon out of your head with me, you two can go alone."

Aaron was staring at Alex when she looked up from her book and caught him. She smiled and blushed, then hid behind her book again. They needed the rest after the ride through the Dark Forest back to Warren, and what happened afterward.

They'd returned in time for a late dinner and had expected to be alone, so they hadn't changed out of their riding clothes. But their friends had all been waiting for them, and Alex had difficulty explaining why there were leaves in her hair after they'd gone off alone. Aaron had kept his mouth shut as she dug herself into a deeper hole trying to explain away the leaves. It was Lynx who finally saved her by warning everyone that sorceresses were very graphic when discussing their love lives so unless they wanted to hear about her and Stefan, they'd better stop asking Alex about what she and Aaron got up to when alone.

In the two months since she returned from the maze, he'd worked so hard to show Alex he'd changed from the Aaron who'd been cursed and hurt her. She hadn't flinched at him in weeks, and even sought him out when she hadn't seen him all day. Still, a part of him was terrified she was pretending.

"Alex?"

She looked up from her book. "Yes?"

"Are you happy?"

She closed the book on her lap nervously. "Yes. I would have thought this afternoon in the woods made that clear. Aren't you?"

"I am." Aaron went over to her and kneeled, taking her hands into his. He struggled to find the words.

Alex pulled her hands out to grasp his instead. "I'm here, and I'm listening. It doesn't have to be perfect. Just get it out."

Aaron exhaled. "I'm worried you'll never get over the things that happened while I was cursed. That you'll always fear me or doubt my love for you."

Alex squeezed his hands. "I already am over it, Aaron. Truly. I might get nervous if you shout or drink too much because it makes me remember those nights, but I love you and I know that wasn't really you. What can I do to convince you?"

"I don't think you can," Aaron replied. "My fears you'll leave are mixed up with my frustration at myself for not listening to Megesti and Harold when they tried to tell me. I should have trusted them."

She simply held his hand and he let his fears pour out. He told her of his fears of losing her and the anger he felt at Gryphon and sorcerers over the curse. "I don't understand how I can be so angry at all sorcerers, but still love you so intensely," he said.

Alex tugged on his hands and pulled him onto the couch beside her. "I understand how you feel. Sometimes I hate sorcerers, too, and I am one. It's alright to be scared and angry. A curse took control of your body and made you do terrible things you'd never do on your own. I understand that. For most of my life, my powers took control of me and would wreak havoc around me. If there is anything I can do to help you, tell me. I will be at your side every night to fight off the nightmares and ground you to this world, but if you need anything else from me, then ask."

Aaron grabbed Alex and kissed her. Alex wrapped her arms around his neck and kissed him back. He pressed his forehead against hers. "How will I ever be worthy of you?"

"You don't have to be anything but yourself. I knew who you'd become. I picked you when we were children, and I've never regretted my choice."

Aaron narrowed his eyes. "Never?"

"Never while you were in your right mind."

"I appreciate your honesty."

"We promised honesty." Alex's smile turned wicked. "I also remember you promising me other things."

Aaron stood and scooped Alex in his arms, making her squeal. "After everything today, you have enough energy for this again?"

"I always have energy for you."

Aaron woke up in a cold sweat. It had been weeks since he'd dreamed about being trapped in that horrible stone room. He rolled over and looked at Alex sleeping beside him. Her hand rested lazily across her belly, and it was glowing. Aaron sat up and picked up her hand. Beneath it, he found the entire area around her belly button glowing gold, the way it did when she was healing. *That's odd. She and Megesti must have missed healing something earlier.*

Aaron snuggled up to Alex and reached across her belly to interlock their fingers. Soon, he was asleep.

CHAPTER 41

ALEX

Alex woke up stiff and sore all over. Aaron was gone, and a small whimper left her before she could stop it. "I have to stop being so needy. I'm married to a king. He has important work to do." Alex climbed out of bed and rubbed the head of her bear rug before she stretched. "What do you think, Callisto? Do you think Gryphon and Stefan will let me have lessons today?"

"We agreed on light exercises, if you are up for it."

"Michael? Why are you hiding?"

"Because you sleep naked."

A robe came flying up the stairs and landed on the floor in front of her.

"Men." Alex slipped into her favorite green training clothes and hurried downstairs. "So what *light* training are we going to do?"

"Everyone else is occupied this morning, it'll just be us. Since we're in Warren, I thought we could try out my archery range at the estate."

"We haven't done that in forever! I'd love to."

"I expected you to say that, so I had the kitchen prepare a picnic." Michael held up a basket and Alex squealed with delight.

"Do you have bows there or should we get ours?"

"I have dozens for you to pick from, so you can just crack us there."

"Perfect!" Alex flicked her wrist, and they were on the grounds of the Veremund estate. It took them a minute to figure out where exactly on the estate Alex had brought them, but once they spotted the oversized weeping willow tree, they knew where they were and hurried off to the archery range.

Alex gasped at the sight of it. The field was large enough for twelve people to practice at one time, or for one to set up targets at twelve different distances. A row of saplings lined one side, and what looked like a stable marked the bounds of the other side.

"It's a sitting area," Michael said. "So Jessica and the baby can join me when they want to."

"Michael, it's amazing. Back when we were in Kirsh, did you ever think that one day you'd have all this?"

"I never even dreamed it." He grinned down at her. "Any chance you want to help with those tiny trees? They won't really help block the wind."

"Of course," Alex chuckled. She squatted and counted them, before touching the earth and sending her Celtic gifts over to them. One by one, the trees popped out of the ground and rose into the sky. At the end of the row, a new tree grew from the ground. Michael just shook his head when he saw apple blossoms burst from the branches.

"In case you get hungry," Alex laughed. "I also told the grass to never grow higher than the heel of your boot."

"That's very helpful. Thank you."

"Happy to. Now where are these bows, and who gets first pick?"

"Over here, and of course, ladies first." Michael motioned for

Alex to follow him into the structure. To the left was a luxurious seating area with a table, benches, and beautiful silk cushions. The other side had a door, and when Michael opened it, Alex's heart jumped for joy. The entire room was filled with bows, quivers, and barrels of arrows.

"You have almost as much in here as my father does!"

"Funny story about that. I couldn't decide what I wanted, so your father told the archer to just give me the same as the castle had. Feast your eyes upon the bounties of indecision."

"Caleb will be so jealous! I can't wait to make him escort me here."

Michael laughed. "That'll be mean."

"Please, he's the son of Datten's general of archers, and close friends with the king. He gets whatever he wants in Datten. But he doesn't have a barrel of Warren arrows."

"Or a Warren bow."

"He has a bow. I had one custom made for him on his birthday."

"Such a good queen," Michael teased.

"Hush. I'm supposed to be a terrifying sorceress."

"I'll keep your secret for you." Michael grabbed a bow off the wall and handed it to her. "This is the same as the one you use in the castle."

They headed into the field and debated for a while about which targets to aim for. They tried them all by taking turns. Since they'd each picked a different color arrow, they could see who won at the end. Michael insisted Alex go first, so she lined up with the target and let her three arrows fly, before releasing the shooting line to Michael.

After they shot at all twelve distances, they walked along the field to retrieve their arrows. "Are you nervous?" Alex asked.

"Nervous for what?"

"The baby, of course. Jessica told Edith and I that she only has a few weeks left before the baby arrives. Are you nervous about becoming a father?"

"If I answer, do you swear to keep it a secret?"

"Of course."

"Even from Aaron?"

"If it's personal, and not a danger to me, then yes."

"I'm terrified." Michael stuffed his arrows back into their quiver. "Everyone is so excited about this baby, but Alex, I don't know what I'm doing! I don't remember my father, and we grew up feral in the woods. What do I know about taking care of a child?" Michael's chest heaved and he struggled to regain control of his breathing.

"Breathe, Michael. It's okay."

"No, it isn't. Jessica has a wonderful father, and grew up in the castle, surrounded by love and everything she needed. We fought for everything we had, and even then it often wasn't enough. And it isn't just supporting them with food and love, it's making sure the baby has everything they need—an education, skills to find a job, friends. Alex, what if my baby is weird, or stupid?"

Alex dropped their supplies and pulled Michael into the seating area. She sat him down, fetched him a mug from the basket and poured wine into it. "Drink and listen."

"But—"

"Don't make me order you, Veremund."

"Yes, Alex." He drank his wine in a huge gulp. Alex snorted and poured him another cup before setting the bottle down.

"He *will* be weird, but no more than you are. He will have many friends, including siblings, cousins, other knight children, and, of course, royalty. Your first born will be kind, patient, and all the best parts of his mother, and father, which he will need for his future."

Michael chugged the second cup and looked at Alex as he wiped his mouth and set it down. "You've seen his future?"

"I have. He'll make you so proud, and you'll worry you didn't do enough or give him enough or teach him enough, but it *will have been* enough. At least in her eyes."

"Her eyes?"

"My daughter's." Alex beamed. "It takes the combined wisdom of a Wafner and Veremund to control the sorceress daughter of Aaron and me. We'll have many sons, but only one daughter, and she will be the child who gives Aaron gray hair and keeps him up at night with worry. It will be worse than anything I ever put you and Stefan through. But your son will calm her, in the same way you can calm me. He'll grow up learning with our sons, because if he's expected to marry the future Queen of Datten, he'll need to know how to rule."

"He'll be a king?"

"Aaron and I have plans for Datten, but they can only be pushed so far in one generation, and if I expect my daughter to be queen, having a Wafner for a husband makes things much easier."

"I can see that. So I won't fail him?"

Alex had seen something she wished she hadn't, but turned away from it, focusing on his children. "No, Michael. You worry losing your parents will make you a bad one, but it's the opposite. Having grown up without them, you'll give all your children everything you dreamed of having, and so much more."

Michael rubbed his face with his hands. "Thank you—for listening, and for telling me everything you know. Even if it's not all true, I feel better."

"I'm glad, but it is all true. My daughter will be living chaos. You'd think she was an Ares."

Michael laughed. "I'm not surprised. I grew up with you and have the scars to prove it." He played with his mug for a moment, then asked, "How are you handling things?"

"Handling what, exactly?" Alex playfully narrowed her eyes at Michael.

"I'm serious, Alex. In less than a year, you got your memories back, married Aaron, lost Emmerich and became Queen of Datten, only to have Aaron cursed. That doesn't even include Gryphon and friends being thrown into the mix while you're under threat of death all the time. Any one or two of those would be enough to break someone, and yet you push through every day with all of them."

"You forgot about my husband and father not speaking to each other."

"Alex—"

"I know. I decided to forgive Aaron and my father a long time ago, but I get anxious whenever they're in the same room. I never know where my loyalty should lie."

"Aaron had better never hurt you again."

"He won't."

"I don't just mean hitting you," Michael whispered, and despite them being all alone, he looked around and still turned red. "I mean if he forces you to do anything you don't want."

Alex looked down, trying hard not to blush.

"If that's a confession, Alex, I swear I'll—"

"No. Aaron is very respectful of that. He'd never. Once when he was cursed he became violent, but I punched him, like you taught me. And now we've had a talk."

"What does that mean?"

"If, for any reason, Aaron is ever not in control of himself, he has ordered me—in his sound mind—to use whatever magic necessary to protect myself."

"Was that one of your boundaries?" Michael asked, nudging her with his shoulder.

"Yes."

"What else?"

"I asked him to really listen to me, like you do. I'm fine if he disagrees, but I prefer to feel as if he is deciding things with me, and not as a king ordering me around. And I needed him to be nicer to Gryphon and Stefan. I think he wanted pairing them together as my guards to bother Stefan more than it does."

"But with Lynx in the mix, Stefan and Gryphon have become friends."

"You see it, too?" Alex asked, excited to have another person on her side.

"They act mean to each other, but it doesn't bother Lynx at all. It's strange."

"Perhaps Stefan is calming down because of Lynx. Stefan and Aaron have also found a peaceful co-existence."

"That's because Stefan protected you," Michael said. "Aaron was livid when Stefan kept him away from you, but after seeing how bad the curse was, Aaron gained more respect for Stefan. Especially after Her Majesty set him straight."

"I thought it was Harold who set him straight."

"Not this time."

"Huh. I hope he eventually finds the same peace with Gryphon. I know that's a lot to ask considering Gryphon and I have a future together, after Aaron is gone, and it was Gryphon's grandmother who cursed him, but it's not just me Gryphon has to help. He's done wonders for Megesti, and I'm going to have sorcerer children. I was never properly taught about my magic as a child. If we don't want our kingdoms destroyed, I'll need help to teach them."

Michael smirked.

"What?"

"You were a bit of a menace once your magic came in."

Alex playfully shoved Michael. As she did so, she spotted someone walking over to them. "We have company," she whispered.

"It's probably Stefan or my wife." Michael turned and squinted.

"Neither. No red hair."

The figure moved closer until it was obvious. "Morning."

Alex waved. "I thought you had wedding preparations, Edith."

Edith sighed. "Weddings are so much work. I am leaving it to my mother, sisters, Jessica, and a few Betruger advisors. They all love this sort of thing, but I can't stand it, so I came to find you."

"How'd you find us?" Michael asked. "Is there some secret connection that tells us where the others are?"

Alex and Edith burst out laughing and Edith joined them at the table. "I asked Julius. Now what were you two talking about before I interrupted?"

"What a wonderful father Michael will make," Alex said.

"Obviously! Just make sure you give your daughters' freedom like my father did, especially if you want them to be good with a bow. What else?"

"Michael asked if Aaron was taking care of me in the bedroom," Alex said and Michael choked on his bread. "I assured him Aaron is very respectful and things are more than fine there."

Edith laughed so hard she snorted. "Clearly Michael and Jessica know what they're doing." Poor Michael turned bright red, and Alex burst in laughter.

"We're teasing you, Michael." Alex reached over and hugged him. "I really appreciate you asking. Stefan just growls at Aaron, and that doesn't really accomplish much."

"The same protection extends to you, Edith," Michael said. "If Harold is ever rough with you, just say the word, and Stefan, Julius, and I will have words with him."

"Plus her father, brother-in-laws, not to mention me, and by extension Aaron," Alex said. "Harold knows if he ever hurts Edith, the kingdoms of Warren and Datten will be on his doorstep."

"Along with the most powerful sorcerers in Torian," Edith said, grabbing a roll and picking it apart.

"Of course."

"Would you like to try my new archery range, Edith? Alex and I had a blast, and we had planned another round."

Edith squealed with delight. "I'd love to."

After spending most of the day with Edith and Michael at his new estate, Alex returned to the castle to search for Gryphon. She closed her eyes and slowly exhaled, trying to sense him. He wasn't in Warren or the Verlassen Castle. *Perhaps he went to Moorloc's beach.* She cracked herself there. The Oreean Sea was rough, sending salty spray toward her. She protected her face with her hand and glanced up and down the beach, before sighing in frustration.

"Are you avoiding me, Gryphon?" she asked out loud and waited for him to appear and contradict her. A heavy feeling took over as the waves crashed into each other. She wrapped her arms around herself. After a few minutes, the feeling became nauseating, and she cracked back to Warren.

Night fell over the kingdom while Alex searched for Aaron, finding he and Harold in another meeting with her father. As much as she wanted to know whether her father and Aaron were behaving themselves, she felt drained and headed to the library to find something to read.

Alex slipped inside the library. It was dark and deserted. Part of her had hoped Gryphon would be there. "What did I do?" she shouted when she found the room empty.

"Nothing."

Alex turned around to find Gryphon standing across the library from her. His shirt was splattered with dirt and grass, and his arms were crossed. His usually gold eyes had a hint of blue around them, as if he'd been using a great deal of magic only a moment ago.

"Then why are you acting weird?" she asked him.

"I'm not. I'm just not replying to your summons like one of your lackeys."

Alex stepped back. His tone was cruel, and his words stung, but Alex sensed he was trying to be cruel to keep her out. "I don't have 'lackeys'."

"Then what do you call your knights who follow you around and obey your every whim?"

"My friends and royal guards. I'm obligated to have protection with me."

"Of course. You are oh-so-precious." There was malice in his voice.

"Stop it," Alex said, marching across the room to stand in front of him. "What is wrong with you? You never speak to me like that."

"The last time I checked, I was the Head, meaning I can do whatever I want. You certainly do." He turned to leave but Alex grabbed his shoulder, and he ended up cracking them both to the forest by Datten. "Go home, Alex," he snapped.

Alex shoved him, sending him stumbling forward away from her. "Not until you tell me why you're being cruel. I've done nothing to deserve this."

"You don't have to *do* anything," he shouted. "Just being around you is enough to make me mad. I have to watch you with him every day. Yes, Aaron has honor. Yes, he's kind, and yes, he loves you, but so do I, and with me you would never have to hold back any part of yourself. So, forgive me if I don't feel like playing pretend today."

"Pretend?"

"Pretending I'm okay with the sorceress—the sorceress I'm *destined to be with*—spending the next three decades with some worthless mortal."

"Aaron is not worthless!" Alex screamed in Gryphon's face.

"To mortals, perhaps, but sorcerers haven't concerned

ourselves with mortals in over a thousand years. If you gave him up, I'd never give this part of the world a second thought."

"No. This isn't you." Alex turned to leave but Gryphon grabbed her arm, pulled her back and grabbed her other arm bringing her face to his.

"This is *me*, Princess. The Ares side of me I've worked so hard to keep from you—the part of me that's possessive, violent, and that everyone's terrified of. The monster."

"You are *not* a monster!" Alex shouted, breaking Gryphon's hold on her.

"I have done things that would make you hate me. I was sent to the mortal world twenty years ago to do an unforgivable thing and the only reason I didn't was because—"

"Because you aren't a monster. If you were, then nothing would have stopped you."

"You don't understand. You could never understand."

"I refuse to accept that you could be a monster."

"Why?"

"Because I didn't sacrifice the normal life—the life I've always wanted—in exchange for *our* future together, only to watch you turn into a monster."

Gryphon's anger evaporated. "What do you mean?"

Alex's stomach dropped. "Nothing. Forget it." She broke away from him and turned to leave, but he cracked in front of her.

"Tell me."

Alex's lip quivered. He stared at her as if he were trying to look into her soul. "No."

"Alex … please." Gryphon's eyes were searching her face for something she couldn't sense.

She swallowed. "Cassandra gave me a choice. I could have given up my powers and lived a single, mortal life with Aaron."

Gryphon's chest heaved when she closed the space between them. Softly, he touched her face.

"It's just … I've seen our future … our children." Alex stumbled over her words. "You're becoming more than a friend to me. It's selfish, but I couldn't give up what we're supposed to have. So whatever you did all those years ago, forget it. It didn't happen. One day I'll ask for the truth, but today I can't … I can't regret the decision I made in that labyrinth."

He opened his mouth but closed it again.

"It's getting late. I have to go."

"No. You can't say that and run."

"It changes nothing. I'm still Aaron's wife, and as long as he's alive, I will always be his. But one day, in the future, I'll be yours … *only* yours. I know it isn't fair to ask you to wait for that, but—"

Gryphon grabbed her face and looked into her eyes. "I'd wait a hundred lifetimes for you, if I had to." Softly, he kissed her forehead.

"Good night, Gryphon," Alex said and cracked away.

GRYPHON

The smell of sea air and wildflowers lingered in the air where she'd been. Gryphon stood there, heart pounding so hard in his chest he couldn't breathe. The images that the pearl had shown him swirled in his mind. He closed his eyes and watched them play out—meeting her on the beach at Moorloc's; holding hands in their throne room; standing on stone tiles with their line marks etches in them; Alex chasing a little girl with his black hair and a chestnut brown streak starting above her emerald eyes. But his favorite was Alex kissing him and meaning it. In a flash, those beautiful images were replaced by Ares threatening him.

His pain and rage overwhelmed him, and he exploded, sending out a torrent of flames. He let out a powerful roar that shook the forest. When it was over, he took in the surrounding carnage. He'd decimated the area as badly as when his powers had arrived when he was nineteen. The closest trees had exploded from the force of his rage, and the ground was charred to the bare dirt. Gryphon dropped to his knees and hung his head.

"She wants our future ... wants to be with me. She's seen what we become, and she actually wants it. But how do I keep her from changing her mind when Ares is trying to ruin everything?"

There has to be a way around this. But not with the truth. She can never find out. Never know what my father and hexa sent me to do. If Victoria hadn't been there, hadn't stopped me—. Gryphon stood and brushed ash off his shirt.

But it wasn't her who stopped me.

The trees beyond the charred circle reminded Gryphon of the forest Alex created around Morlooc's castle. Where he caused destruction, she brought life to a desolate mountain rock.

"Alex is right. I wouldn't have done it. I was cruel then because I was angry. But Birch and Lynx would have sensed the change in me if I'd even tried to sink that low." He reached up and scratched his bond mark. After her confession, it burned, but he accepted the pain. It was proof every word she'd said was true.

He spun in place. The forest was watching him—judging him for his youthful crimes.

"I didn't do it," he shouted into the trees, sending the animals fleeing. He clenched and opened his fists, sending flames flicking at his pants. "Who am I trying to convince? Victoria was the excuse I gave my father and hexa. I couldn't do what they wanted. I knew when I left I would fail. But if I couldn't ... then I let my heart dictate my actions. I always let my heart rule me where Alex is concerned, and Victoria used hers to bring me to heel."

Gryphon closed his eyes and remembered how grateful she'd been after she'd discovered her Ares powers. He could still feel her lips on his. The need coming off her had been insatiable. *I could have claimed her then. I could have made her mine, but I resisted because she'd have hated herself. She's accomplished so much at her young age—twice returned, holding her own against sorcerers centuries her senior, and she made it out of the underworld when Lygari opened it onto the battlefield. None of us should be able to do what she can do.*

A blue light lit up the surrounding ground, as his Mystics

powers filled him. *Even Aaron believes she'd sacrifice herself in a heart-beat for her people: Warren, Datten, or sorcerers.*

"I obey my heart, while she follows her own logic, even when it's mistaken ... *ferflucs!*"

Gryphon cracked himself to the Verlassen Castle and ran across the main hall and down the stairs to the lab. His hurried footsteps echoed through the room as he headed to the wall and pulled out an armful of books. An icy chill surrounded him, and he glanced over his shoulder. It was just Daniel, albeit the new older version. Gryphon didn't turn around. "Go away, Princeling. I need Victoria."

Daniel crossed his arms. "I'm not your errand boy."

"Then why are you bothering me?"

"She'll never leave him. It doesn't matter what you say or what she admits. She loves Aaron, and that's all that matters."

Gryphon slammed a book shut and turned toward Daniel. "You had no right to eavesdrop on our private conversation. And you conveniently forget that sorcerers can love more than one person. Unlike mortals, we don't believe love is finite. Loving me does not change or take away her feelings for Aaron. Her love for her father, her friends, and even you won't change how much your brother means to her, so why would I?"

"That's different. They aren't trying to take her from him."

"I don't have time for your paranoid delusions. I need Victoria, so either summon her or leave."

Daniel scowled at Gryphon but didn't move.

With a grunt, Gryphon went back to his reading. "You're lucky I don't send Kharon to remove you from Alex's side. You're just a stubborn, useless former mortal."

"Don't speak to him like that," Victoria scolded.

Gryphon dropped the book he was holding and narrowed his eyes at the ghost of Alex's mother.

"Did you know?"

"Know what?"

"That Alex is the Head?"

Victoria's mouth dropped open and her eyes widened.

"So you didn't know."

"No, that's impossible. She can't be the Head. I've seen her future. She's the Heart—loving, kind ... she's going to be a mother, for Merlin's sake!"

"What does being a mother have to do with being the Head? Do you honestly think she can't think logically and be immensely powerful, and also gentle and loving to her children?"

"There's never been a sorceress Head."

Gryphon began nervously pacing around the room.

Victoria followed him. "What makes you think she's the Head?"

"Everything. She does what's best for the kingdom or mortals, while I always do what's best for *her*. I don't care who dies, as long as it's not her."

"Heads are logical and—"

"And they will do whatever is necessary, no matter the consequences. I, on the other hand, couldn't even kill Aaron when my hexa and father sent me to do it."

"He was a helpless infant!"

"Do you think that would have mattered, if I were actually the future Head?"

"My daughter couldn't have killed someone."

"She has, many times. If you'd put her in front of infant Kruft or Moorloc, they'd be dead. I didn't have it in me. All you had to do was threaten my future with Alex, and I gave in. I didn't care about the consequences for my family."

Victoria went silent again.

"How is she so powerful?" Gryphon asked.

"She was destined to be. *She* is the one they warned Warren about—the one who can bring down the entire mortal world. But her fury is the monster, not her."

"That's not all of it. It can't be. I held her power while she was in the maze. I nearly died from receiving it, and I only got half!"

Victoria shook her head. "She is not the Head. She is merely twice returned and inherited the power from our lines, and … Edward."

"Edward? How would she get magic from a mortal?"

"Cassandra gifted it to his line."

"That makes no sense. Sorcerers can't gift their power—we're born with it."

"It was needed to break the curse," Victoria whispered. "Perhaps her exceptional power *is* tied to her fury. Cassandra came to me after Alex was born, and warned me about which fury lives in her, and what terror she would raise if she were to escape."

"Which is it, then?"

"Alecto. Her vengeance will never be satisfied until the entire world is burned to ash."

Gryphon went pale. "I still don't understand how her mortal father gave her magic?"

Victoria looked at him. "Mortal sons of Cassandra can't inherit her power."

Gryphon stared at Victoria as it hit him. "Cassandra was the first Queen of Warren?"

Victoria nodded. "Her sons passed her power through thirty-six generations, until my daughter claimed it."

CHAPTER 43
AARON

Aaron stood up so fast he knocked his chair back. "I am *not* trying to become my father," he snapped. He'd spent the last hour speaking with Edward in the King of Warren's meeting room, but they weren't getting anywhere.

"You're acting like a boy trying to fit into his father's armor," Edward said. He was clearly still holding onto his anger about how Aaron had treated Alex while cursed, and also because Aaron had him forcibly removed from Datten after the incident with Randal.

"That's because I am! I was supposed to have peace after we settled things with the Betruger, but since becoming king I've faced one problem after another."

"Welcome to being a king, Aaron. Did you believe it would be easy? That you would figure it out overnight?"

"Of course not, but I never expected to be fighting with *you*. You were my father's best friend. You treated me like a son growing up. I thought I would have you to advise me, but now ... I'm handling things while you act like a child, throwing a tantrum."

Edward got to his feet. "You will not insult me in my home. This isn't Datten, where you can say as you please. This is Warren

—my home, and your wife's home. You will show me the respect that is due."

"I respect you, Edward, more than almost every person in Torian. But I will not let your behavior impact Alex. Yes, I hurt her, but you hurt her, too, and I won't let you add to her burdens. I'm here because she's not up to it."

"My daughter is not afraid of me. You're the one keeping her from me."

"That's a lie and you know it. No one makes Alex do anything she doesn't want to. You cannot stand there and tell me I'm not enough for her because I hurt her when I was cursed and not in my right mind. You did the same thing while supposedly in full control of yourself."

Edward pounded his fist on the table, knocking over his ale mug. "I lost my temper because I learned my best friend let my father murder my wife!"

"I understand why you lost control in that room and lashed out at Randal, but you *struck Alex*. And the violence you showed is exactly how Arthur would have handled it!" Aaron ran his hands through his hair. "I always admired you. I wanted to be a king like you. But I don't know who this man before me is anymore."

"We're finished here. You're turning into your father, especially when it comes to sticking your nose where it doesn't belong."

Aaron turned to the door and stalled before turning back to Edward. "I'd rather become my father than yours. I'll summon Megesti and we'll be out of your hair."

"My daughter is welcome to stay. This is her home, after all."

"It isn't."

"Oh, and you think Datten is?"

"No," Aaron said, shaking his head. "It's been made very clear to me that Alex's home is the people she loves."

Aaron slammed the door behind him and entered his and Alex's Warren suite, pinching the bridge of his nose. "How am I supposed to tell her that talking to Edward just made things worse?"

"With honesty."

Aaron opened his eyes to see Alex, Michael, and Jessica standing before him. There were two large chests open on the floor. Michael and Alex were putting books into one of them while Jessica folded a blanket on the couch.

"How much did you hear?"

"Everything. As you know my father's yelling carries." Alex dropped the book she was holding into the chest and turned to Michael and Jessica. "Would you give us a minute?"

"Of course," Michael said.

"We'll see how Stefan is doing with his packing," Jessica said. She gave Aaron a slight nod before leaving the room.

Aaron ran his hand through his hair and groaned. "Alex, I'm sorry—"

Alex's kiss cut him off and she wrapped her arms around his waist. "You were nearly right. My home is wherever *you* are. If my father is going to be stubborn and unreasonable, then we'll go to Datten."

"I can't be responsible for you not speaking with your father."

"You aren't. He is. He'll come around eventually." Alex went back to dropping books into the chest.

"How do you know?" Aaron asked nervously.

Alex smirked. "We are trying to make an heir. I can't see my father holding a grudge against you once a grandchild is in the picture."

"Are you saying you intend to use our baby to manipulate your father?"

"'Manipulate' is such a harsh word. I prefer 'persuade'." She finished packing the last book and stood. "I can send you to Datten now and I'll come in a bit, once we've packed the rest of the things

I want to take." She put her hand over her heart. "I promise to stay with Michael and Stefan as soon as I find them."

"Wouldn't you like some help?"

Alex chuckled. "I suspect you have more important king responsibilities to do than help me decide on what dresses and books absolutely have to come with me."

"Bring your simple red and green dresses. They're my favorites."

"I've already packed them."

"What did I do to deserve you?"

"Nothing, other than being you." Alex kissed him and whispered, "Go, and be my king."

Aaron arrived in the king's suite in Datten. He headed up to the wardrobe to change into his more formal attire. He was just finishing when he heard a knock at the door. It came from the seating area he shared with Alex. *It's probably mother. She would actually be a good person to ask about handling Edward, or I could ask Kharon to let me speak to my father.* He knew Kharon's line could easily summon a ghost, but he didn't want to ask for favors. Aaron returned to the main floor and found the secret door that connected the queen's suite to his own ajar. But when he opened it, no one was there. He stepped inside to see the room transformed.

Someone had stripped the suite of his mother's things. In their place were blue and silver banners, a large painting of the seashore, and a painting of a smiling royal family—typical Warren décor. The painting, with the beaming faces of the king and queen and their two sons, reminded him of the last portrait that had been taken of his family. The king resembled Edward, with auburn skin and piercing blue eyes. It was likely one of the earlier kings, if not the first. The queen was beautiful, with blonde hair, delicate features, and emerald eyes. The oldest boy resembled his father, while the youngest resembled his mother. A normal Torian family.

Aaron stepped back to get a better look and bumped into something. When he saw what it was, he knew why his mother had given up her room. "Never one for subtleties, are we, mother?"

"I hoped it would encourage you," Guinevere said, coming down the stairs from the bedroom with a vase of fresh flowers. "Not all of us have the scent of flowers surrounding us all the time."

"You didn't have to do this, mother. We would have figured things out."

"Nonsense." The former queen smiled down at the wooden crib before them. "You slept in this very crib, in this suite, and when the time is right, so will the next Prince of Datten."

"And where will you go?"

Guinevere positioned the vase on a small table and softly brushed Aaron's cheek. "I intend to have a nice long visit with my brother and dear sister-in-law. My things are packed, and Bernhard has prepared a room for me. I hoped Alexandria could send me there. Has she returned yet?"

"She's still in Warren, packing her favorite things."

"Is Edward still being stubborn?"

"Very."

"Bernhard and I will work on him. I'll see if I can find Birch or Megesti to send me then." Guinevere kissed Aaron's cheek and turned to leave when he called after her.

"Who are the royals in the painting?"

She paused in the doorway. "The first King and Queen of Warren. It's the only surviving painting. It was a gift to Datten upon the betrothal of their younger son Daniel to our last Princess Elfrieda."

"So, he's to blame for my hair?"

Guinevere left the room, chuckling. The door had just closed when Gryphon cracked in front of Aaron. "We need to talk, now."

CHAPTER 44
AARON

Aaron crossed his arms and huffed at the arrogant sorcerer. "Gryphon, I'm busy. What do you want?"

"We have a problem," Gryphon said, but froze when he spotted the crib. "Why is that thing in here?"

"My mother brought it out. Now what do you want?"

"I need your help." Gryphon twitched, seemingly unable to turn away from the crib. "Can we go into the other room?"

"You're acting stranger than usual. Do you hate all babies, or just the idea of Alex having one with me? So much for your next evolution of sorcerers if you can't even look at a crib." Aaron snickered and pulled the book on the shelf that opened the door and motioned for Gryphon to go in.

Gryphon straightened and marched through the opening. "Sorcerer babies don't need to be caged."

Aaron scoffed as the door closed. "Now what could you possibly need my help with?"

"Before you say something stupid, it's for Alex, but involves both of us. I need you to let me kill you."

Aaron stepped back and bumped into the fireplace. Gryphon

motioned for them to sit, and reiterated the entire conversation with Ares. Crossing his arms, Aaron listened intently and held his tongue when he wanted to snap that Ares should just kill Gryphon.

After he'd finished, they sat in silence. "Say something," Gryphon said.

"I don't love you in my castle, or around Alex, but I've seen the effect having you here has on her. She has control of her magic, her confidence is better, but most important? She's happy, and despite how I feel about you, I would never wish her to be alone after I die."

"I hoped you'd see reason."

"There is a cavern between seeing your reasoning and letting you kill me, even if Alex could bring me back. Have you told her any of this?"

"No." Gryphon shook his head.

"I don't know if we should keep this from her. She's trying so hard to let us all help her. It feels wrong to not give her the same respect."

"You know she'd only insist on getting involved, and I'll die before I let Ares anywhere near her."

"He's dead. How dangerous can he be?"

"He's a god of war, and the founder of my chaos line. We need to act soon. I doubt Ares is the patient type."

"But can a ghost actually hurt you?"

"Mortal ghosts may be weak, but your brother can touch Alex to save her. Sorcerer ghosts? That would depend on how much power they had in life, but a god? Absolutely."

CHAPTER 45

ALEX

Alex rushed through the castle. Aaron wasn't in the kitchen, throne room, stables, or library. The only room she hadn't searched yet was theirs, so she ran down the side hall and threw open the door to their suite. Aaron and Gryphon were inside, sitting on the couches and chatting. Shock overtook her excitement as she eyed them suspiciously. "What is going on in here?"

"Sorry. I didn't realize I needed the queen's permission to address the king." Gryphon winked at her.

Alex stuck out her tongue at him and turned to Aaron. "Is he bothering you?"

"No," Aaron replied.

"Then is he asking for wild and unreasonable things?"

"Yes," Aaron said.

Gryphon shrugged. "The Betruger are getting an entire kingdom. I didn't think a training cabin in the woods was that big of an ask."

Aaron sighed. "You can have your lab. But I'm only building it once. If Megesti or Alex sets it on fire, you're fixing it."

"Wonderful." Alex clapped her hands loudly. "In other exciting news, Harold has asked us to move up the wedding."

"What for?" Gryphon asked.

Alex dropped onto the couch beside Aaron. "They really want Jessica there, and she's growing more tired each day. The doctor thinks she could have the baby as early as a few weeks from now. Harold and Edith want to ensure she can attend."

"If that's what Harold and Edith want, I won't argue."

"I hoped you'd say that." Alex turned toward Gryphon and smiled sweetly. "I'll need your help tomorrow. I'm planning a present for the second day's celebration."

"The second day?" Aaron asked.

"Betruger weddings last three days. The first day is the private ceremony with only the families and close friends. The larger public ceremony is on the second day, and in this case, Edith will be crowned. The all-day celebration with food and entertainment is on the last day." Alex grinned at Gryphon. "And hopefully some magic."

Gryphon chuckled. "What do you have in mind, Princess?"

"So many things." Alex couldn't contain her excitement and grabbed Aaron's knee, shaking his leg while talking at Gryphon. "I'm hoping all of us can use our specific powers to show off something amazing. Birch can grow things. Lynx can ask animals to do things. You and I can fight fire with water."

"What about me? I don't have any powers," Aaron said.

Gryphon raised an eyebrow. "Aren't you supposed to be good on your horse? You could challenge Harold to a joust." He looked at Aaron pointedly.

"Aaron doesn't joust anymore," Alex said. "He gave it up after we became betrothed, and now, as King of Datten, he wouldn't be allowed to take part."

"I'm sure a friendly match wouldn't be too much for him," Gryphon said, narrowing his eyes at Aaron briefly before looking back at Alex. "Especially if you're there. Your healing magic can handle anything."

Alex tugged on her necklace chain and glanced between Aaron and Gryphon. *You're up to something and I don't like it.*

You always think I'm up to something.

That's because you usually are.

Aaron squeezed her knee. "I thought we agreed on no more silent conversations."

"Sorry. I was just telling him I know he's up to something, and I'm going to find out what it is."

"And I told her to stop being so suspicious. It isn't as if I told you the big secret she's been keeping about what went on between us in the lab."

Alex's face erupted in heat. Her hands flew to her cheeks, trying to hide the evidence, but Aaron was staring at her.

"What secret?" he asked.

Her heart beat so hard it made her chest hurt. *He can't tell Aaron what I confessed to him. What is he thinking?* Terror made her stomach lurch.

"If you give Alex too much magic at once when she's drained, she moans. It's a rather naughty sound."

The relief that filled Alex nearly made her pass out. Her head bobbed forward for a moment, but Aaron grabbed her. "Are you alright?"

"Maybe she needs some magic now. Care for a demonstration for the delightful little sound? Though, as her husband, I certainly hope you'd be familiar with it."

"And you crossed the line," Aaron snapped. "Alex, is that why you asked me if you moan in your sleep?"

"Yes," Alex replied through clenched teeth. "Stefan said I did, and I didn't believe him."

Gryphon stood and adjusted his tunic. "And before you throw a tantrum over nothing, Kingling, you should know that this happened in the lab, with Megesti, Lynx, Kharon, and Birch present. It's actually a common reaction to getting magic when you desperately need it. I've also heard her moan that loudly while eating bread."

Catch your tongue.

"You're going to have a fun lesson tomorrow, Gryphon." Aaron smirked. "She's going to burn you."

Gryphon laughed. "That was the plan. She tries harder when she's mad."

Alex grabbed a book off the couch and threw it at him, but he was too fast and cracked away. Flopping back onto the couch, she huffed and crossed her arms. Aaron watched her for a long minute before he broke out in laughter.

"It's not funny." Alex moved her hands to cover her face. "He wasn't wrong about it being the same as …" She peeked between her fingers. Aaron picked up the book she'd thrown and returned it to the bookshelf.

A wicked smile spread across his face. "I still think it's funny." He walked to Alex, held his hands out to her, and pulled her to her feet.

"I don't. It was humiliating. Lynx had to explain to me how our bond makes getting power from him feel different from if I take it from someone else. Megesti didn't know either, so at least I wasn't the only one surprised."

"Well, I'm glad he told me. I don't like secrets, and this one really isn't a big deal."

"You say that now, but—" Alex gasped and clamped her mouth shut.

"But?"

"Nothing."

"Alex, say it. We can't get past this, not really, if you can't speak openly."

"I don't want to intentionally hurt you."

"For this, you have to." He took her hands and pressed his forehead to hers.

"I was going to say … cursed Aaron would have been furious."

"Which is why I'm not upset you were afraid to tell me. So please take my laughing at the situation as the proper reaction to a funny and embarrassing story."

"There is one other thing."

"Oh?"

"Sometimes I have dreams," Alex gulped. "That wouldn't be considered appropriate in mortal circles." Aaron raised his eyebrows and grinned.

"You can't control your dreams, and as long as I get to be in them—"

"You are! Often." Alex's cheeks heated and Aaron released her hands to cup her face.

"Then don't let it bother you. I will never be angry for what your beautiful imagination does after you go to sleep."

"Thank you," Alex sighed with relief.

"Time for bed. You need to be rested for your magic lessons tomorrow if you're going to try to get revenge on Gryphon."

"Do I have court or anything?"

"Not until the day after. It's late spring, so many of the farmers, hunters, and trappers are busy. We'll meet less often when they are planting and harvesting. And your queen's committee only meets as needed."

"Alright."

ALEX LAID AWAKE IN BED, thinking over the last few days. Cerberus' attack on her had made her realize how unprepared they were if she were the one seriously injured. *I should go through my mother's healing journals and see what potions I can make in advance, just in case. If I make them, Megesti should be able to use them to help me if I'm injured. At least I don't need to be so careful around red steel. Would that be true for Megesti as well? Maybe it didn't work for the sons of the line.*

She soon gave up trying to sleep and put on her training clothes. She paused and looked down at her sleeping husband. Whenever she'd leave, he'd turn onto his stomach and gradually move to her side of the bed. She leaned down and kissed his cheek, but he didn't even stir. Alex grabbed a cloak off a hook and cracked herself onto the beach. She sat on the sand and breathed in the sea air, the waves of the Oreean Sea soothing her busy mind. After some time, she picked up a stick and absently drew on the wet sand.

"This is new for you," Gryphon said, plopping onto the sand beside her.

"I come here to think. It's where I keep all my biggest failures."

Gryphon winced. "Nothing that happened here was a failure on your part. We lost the castle but saved the people. Harold has told you that repeatedly. And if you mean your baby, that wasn't your fault. It was Ridge and Pearl's."

"Logically, I know that, but my heart disagrees."

"You're very calm considering how badly I teased you in front of Aaron. Tell me what you're holding in. If you'd like, I can fetch someone else—Michael? You're comfortable baring your soul to him, right? Or I can just poke around in your head."

Alex flicked her wrist and sent a wave right for Gryphon. He cracked away just before it reached him. Now he was standing on her opposite side. "I'll go get Michael, then. Or is this a sorceress issue? Would you rather have Edith?"

"Is something wrong with my magic?"

"Which magic are you referring to? Because your Poseidon is clearly on point."

"Having children," Alex said. She knew this would make him uncomfortable. "I thought sorcerers were supposed to have control over these matters. But it isn't working." His mouth dropped open. "We don't have to talk about this if it's too hard for you."

He regained himself, and crouched down beside her, so she could look into his eyes. "I'm not sure why it wouldn't be working. We have so few children; miscarriages are incredibly rare."

"Really?"

Gryphon nodded. "I only know of one, and that's because my parents talked about it at a council meeting."

Alex dug her stick into the sand, flicking it toward the waves. "Could I have damaged myself somehow? By giving up my magic in the labyrinth, or when I was injured here?"

"No."

Alex was about to snap at him for how sure he sounded, but his expression was a combination of anguish and pain.

"But you are young," he said.

"I'm eighteen, Gryphon. I'm the right age—"

He grabbed her hand. "You're young for a sorceress. Most of our kind don't consider children until well past our first century. Your mother had you at eighty, and even that would have been early. Your issues are likely because of your age."

"Oh."

"Consider this. Yes, you're eighteen. Yes, you have been given the powers of your line. But you cannot yet fully control them. Most sorceresses have been in full control of all their powers by the time they use them to conceive. If your powers are not stable yet, and you're constantly being drained, it would make sense that you're struggling."

Alex let out a frustrated cry and dropped back onto the sand, covering her face with her fists.

"Give it a year or two. If it doesn't work by then, Birch can teach you the ritual we use to choose line powers in our children."

"Thank you, Gryphon."

"Is that why you came here? To mourn and be miserable?"

"No!" Alex bolted upright and shoved him, sending him toppling onto the damp sand. "Not that it's any of your business."

"So why are you sitting here in the moonlight staring at the cold water?" Gryphon shivered looking at the sea.

"I told you. I'm thinking."

"About what?"

"Magic," Alex said, grinning at Gryphon. He scoffed and rolled his eyes, making her laugh. "I'm thinking about what we can do for the wedding. So far, most of the magic people have witnessed has been about death and destruction. I want people to see how amazing our powers are rather than only the ways they can be used against them."

"Do you ever have selfish thoughts?"

"I'm sorry?"

"You always consider the greater good or kingdoms. Don't you ever just want something for yourself?"

"I did." Alex grinned. "And now I have him."

Gryphon groaned, making Alex giggle.

"You asked," she said. She stood, brushed the wet sand off herself and walked into the water, letting it lap the remaining sand from her toes. Then she spun to face him. "If you and I put our powers together, and Megesti helps, exactly how powerful would we be?"

"Incredibly so. Why, what are you thinking?"

"Megesti, I know you're tired, but that's no excuse for the attitude," Alex said.

Megesti rolled his eyes. "*Your* insomniac cousins didn't drag *you* out of bed in the middle of the night."

Gryphon laughed. "He's not wrong."

Megesti rolled his neck, emitting a crack so loud Alex winced.

"He's fine," Gryphon teased. "He's just getting old."

"I'm barely five years older than you!"

"That's still older," Gryphon said.

"Gryphon, behave," Alex said. "Or else we'll soak you."

Gryphon shivered and stepped away from them.

"So what did you want to try?" Megesti asked.

"I'd like Gryphon to create a fire ring around the whole ceremony area. Then, you and I can put it out by raining on it, without making any guests wet."

"How large is the celebration area going to be?" Gryphon asked.

Megesti smirked. "Why? Worried you won't be able to cut it?"

He's getting as lippy as your husband.

I won't warn you again, Sunset.

Megesti seemed to wait for them to let him in on their conversation. When they didn't, he narrowed his eyes at Gryphon. "You never explained how you found this area in the woods."

For an instant only Alex noticed, Gryphon stiffened before crossing his arms and resuming his ambivalent expression. "I was bored and went exploring. I don't know what else to tell you," he said. "We should get started. Megesti, you're up first."

The clearing was devoid of plant life, and they were standing on bare rock and earth. That wasn't unusual for late spring in the Dark Forest, but it's perfectly circular boundary was unnatural.

This can't be natural. Did a fire do it? Alex looked at Gryphon, hoping he'd give something away in his face. His eyes locked onto hers, and Alex swallowed. *Did he do this after I told him I—?*

Alex's stomach dropped. *He did ... this happened because I told him why I couldn't give up my powers.*

"Megesti, your stance is crooked again," Gryphon shouted and moved to adjust his legs. His path took him past Alex and she felt him softly caress her back. "Why is it every time we train with Alex, you revert to old habits?"

"Because I like her more than I like you. You may be family, too, but she's blood." Megesti rested his elbow on Alex's shoulder and smiled at her.

Gryphon looked aghast. "Are you saying you used me? What would your mother say?"

Alex laughed. "She'd probably say it serves you right for teasing everyone."

Gryphon clomped over to Megesti and playfully nudged him. The Merlin Titan laughed out loud, and Alex couldn't help but giggle at them. When he'd first arrived in Datten, Gryphon had been brash and cold toward everyone besides her but seeing him getting along with Megesti warmed her heart. Megesti needed more sorcerer friends in his life. But Gryphon and Stefan had also been getting on better, and even though that would make Lynx's life easier, it made her nervous. The two men could read her like a book. Certainly, Aaron could sense her mood, but Stefan could often guess with a single look what she was thinking, and Gryphon could literally read her mind. He could read Aaron's, too, but at least Aaron had his ring to keep him out of his head. After the scare she'd given them all while in the maze, they'd all agreed he could wear his, but Alex had to leave her connection with Gryphon open for safety. If Aaron were ever in danger, either Megesti's protection oath or her connection with him would let them find him.

Sensing her trepidation, Gryphon gave her a wink before adjusting Megesti's stance. "Stand up straight and stop twitching your knees so much." He sighed and walked around Megesti again. "At least you don't drop your elbows like some sorcerers."

Megesti had a gleam in his eye. "I want to try taking your power, Gryphon. See if Alex can put out a fire made by our combined powers."

Gryphon frowned. "That would be a lot of fire."

"So you don't think I can handle it?" Alex crossed her arms.

"I didn't say that," Gryphon retorted. "I think it's *safer* to master the water part before we grow the fire larger than life. I'm not one for playing it safe, but considering who I'm working with, I'd rather not get stabbed for putting you at risk."

"If you're going to plan every lesson around the fear that Aaron will stab you, then we won't get very far," Megesti said.

"Megesti's right. Give us a chance and let me deal with Aaron. I can be rather persuasive."

Megesti made a face. "I don't need to know how my cousin convinces my best friend to do things."

"I wouldn't mind the details," Gryphon said, smirking.

"Stop thinking about that and focus," Alex said.

"Spoil sport." Gryphon turned back to Megesti. "You remember the process, right?"

Megesti nodded and stepped toward Gryphon. He closed his eyes and exhaled. Gryphon backed up a few paces so they wouldn't be touching. Megesti raised his hands and slowly wiggled his fingers. He instantly found Gryphon's magic, and his hands lit up in flames. Megesti looked at his hands and turned the palms upward so that the random flames shifted to his palms. In moments, they formed into a pair of burning fire spheres in his hands.

"How do I send it into a circle?" Megesti asked weakly. But his hands trembled, and the fire vanished. *"Ferflucs!"*

"It's alright, Megesti," Gryphon said. "Salem and Ares are hard to control for long. Try again, and this time when you feel the spheres, flick your fingers out and picture a circle of flames around us." Gryphon demonstrated the hand movement, and Megesti shook out his arms and tried again. This time, the flames made it to the ground before sputtering, and on the next try, they all landed in a tree. Alex used her Poseidon powers to quench the blaze.

"I want you to ramp it up. Take more to start off with, but not so much that you lose control."

Alex strolled toward the edge of the clearing and sat on a fallen log to watch the sorcerers work. This time, the fire was larger and when he threw it down, it popped loudly and sent a shower of flames raining around them. The birds and critters on the edge of the clearing fled. Alex twirled her fingers to make sure there was enough moisture in the air that the flames wouldn't take to the dry plants.

"Next, I want you to make the flames larger," Gryphon said. "And try not to take the explosive part of Salem if you can avoid it. Alex, are you ready, just in case?"

"I am," Alex called across the ground from her seat.

"Alright, Megesti. Try it." Gryphon cracked beside Alex and watched Megesti extend his hands. His fingers wiggled around the air until he caught hold of Gryphon's powers and his palm lit up.

Alex felt a tugging and gasped sharply.

Gryphon turned to her. "Alex?"

Alex shook her head, but the strange sensation of being pulled hit her again. Her hand slammed into her chest, taking her breath away.

Gryphon grabbed her and looked at her face intensely. "Megesti, stop now. You're taking from Alex and not me."

Megesti's flames grew larger and his violet glow intensified. Gryphon groaned and burst into his mystic blue color. Alex felt the pull lessen, but another yank pulled her off balance and she fell forward. Gryphon lunged to catch her. The surrounding air became heavy, and Alex could feel the crackles of power all around them.

"Gryphon, what's happening?"

Gryphon's face was tight, and his jaw clenched. "Megesti is losing control. He's taking too much power, and he can't channel it. The ability to control explosive powers becomes exponentially harder the larger it grows."

"Megesti, stop!" Alex shouted, but the flames on Megesti's hands continued to grow larger as he drew out more of Alex's powers. The force made her stumble, but she caught herself on Gryphon. The heat of Megesti's flames slammed into them across the barren field.

"How can he stand it?" Alex asked.

"Megesti! Release the fire into the sky," Gryphon screamed and shoved Alex behind himself. "It's out of control. You cannot explode it!"

Megesti must have finally heard them, because he slammed his hands together. Alex recognized the move Gryphon had taught them to extinguish a Salem flame, but these were clearly too large for that, since the slapping did nothing to quell them. Alex pulled water from the air, but Gryphon touched her arm. "If you splash him now, the temperature change will set off an explosion for sure."

"Then what do we do?"

"We do nothing. You are going back to Datten and I'm going to take his fire from him."

"Gryphon, don't you—" A gale force wind of heat slammed into them and threw them backward. Expecting the ground, Alex slammed into something but it was soft. She opened her eyes and saw red hair. Jerome stood and helped her to her feet. Alex spun around in confusion. She was in the Datten throne room with Kharon, Randal, and Jerome.

"Alex, what is going on?" Randal asked.

"Kharon came running in here shouting that Daniel needed us to catch you—" The Datten alarm bells drowned out Jerome's voice.

Alex bolted from the throne room without uttering a word. With the generals on her heels, she dashed up the stairs to the third floor and up to the tallest spire. She leaned over the precipice gasping for breath as she looked out the watchtower. Far off in the distance, the Dark Forest was on fire. The sun had not yet risen, but the fire was large enough that she could see the flames and smoke billowing out of the woods.

"Alex, what happened?" Randal asked.

"Megesti lost control of his Salem powers because he took from me and Gryphon. Kharon, we need Lynx and Birch. Megesti and Gryphon are still out there. We have to go find them."

"I'll bring them to the lab." Kharon cracked away and Alex hurried back down the tower steps.

"Alexandria, you can't go after them," Jerome called to her, but Alex barely listened. She was too focused on finding Megesti and Gryphon.

The lab was empty. It still smelled of cedar and black pine from the renovations instead of the usual scent of exotic herbs. She paced the room until she heard the door swing open. She whipped around, expecting to see Lynx or Birch, but Jerome was standing there glaring with his arms crossed instead. His massive build took up the entire door frame.

Alex glared back. "I'm going, Jerome. They're my friends, and my magic can help."

"You are Queen of Datten. You don't run into danger—you send your men. That's why you have a guard."

"Our men can't help with this, and I won't risk them."

She heard Aaron's kingly voice coming from the hallway. "Jerome? Where are you? I don't expect to have to search for my general when there is an emergency and your queen is missing!"

"I'm not missing," Alex shouted. "I'm with Jerome in the lab." Footsteps rushed down the hallway toward them. Aaron burst through the door, wearing only his sleeping pants, and headed right for Alex. She wrapped her arms around his chest, letting him hold her as tightly as he needed. "I'm alright, but I need to go back to get Megesti and Gryphon."

"What happened to Gryphon?" Stefan asked, arriving with

Lynx, Randal, and the other sorcerers. Alex filled everyone in as fast as she could, even though she was desperate to get back out there and find them.

"We'll get the men suited up and head out," Aaron said.

"That'll take too long. I've already been here too long," Alex said.

"Alex, you are not going alone," Stefan said.

"I'm not. I'm taking Kharon, Lynx, and Birch. Gryphon sent me back here to protect me, but we don't know how bad it is there. I can see the fire from here."

"Which is precisely why you cannot go," Jerome said.

"That's actually why she should go," Lynx said. "If it's still burning, we'll need Alex's Poseidon powers. She is the only one who can put it out and clear the smoke."

"I'll go with her," Stefan said. He looked down at Alex. It was clear from his Wafner glare it was nonnegotiable.

"Agreed. Can we go now?"

Aaron kissed her quickly. "Be safe and bring my best friend back to me."

"I will." With that, Alex cracked the group away.

GRYPHON

Gryphon had been on fire before, but this was different. The flesh on every part of his body was burning. The instant he'd cracked Alex away, Megesti had lost control. He'd sent fire and explosions everywhere, turning the open field into a raging inferno. They were both thrown into the surrounding woods which were erupting in flames. Plumes of smoke rose around Gryphon, making it almost impossible to breathe. The fire crackled loudly and his skin seared. He tried to roll on the ground and screamed in pain.

He looked down in shock at a broken tree limb protruding from his shoulder. The wood was red with his blood. A coppery taste filled his mouth, and he spat out a mouthful of blood. He tried to crack, but with his injuries, he couldn't focus enough to separate himself from the tree.

"Megesti!" Gryphon shouted as the smoke thickened and settled around him. He waved his hand in front of his face, trying to get some fresh air, but it only pulled on his wound and made him regret the choice. Each breath was a struggle. A bright orange glow appeared beside him. Gryphon didn't have to move to know Ares had returned.

"How are you an Ares? Pathetic, disgrace to my line," Ares said. "You could have saved yourself, but you wasted your time saving her. The Cassandra really has her talons in you." Ares walked up to Gryphon and grinned menacingly down at him. "If you fail to dispense with the mortal and I have to kill you, I'll pay her a visit. See how well she cowers."

"She won't cower before you. She's not afraid of our kind."

"We'll see about that. Maybe she won't fear me, but I'm certain she'll fear losing you. Taking away what someone loves is far worse than anything you could do to them." Thunder cracked above their heads, and a moment later, water drops fell all around them. A strong wind blew away the smoke. "It seems she is desperate to get you and her cousin back, even at the risk of draining herself after he took too much from her. What else would she do to protect you?"

The rain fell harder and Ares glared at him. "Remember what I said before: It's him or you. And I'm not patient, Gryphon." Ares's light grew brighter before he vanished.

I can't let him get his hands on Alex. How do I stop this? I have to get up.

The rain had soaked him to the bone. Teeth chattering, he closed his eyes. He needed to find Alex and get her out of here in case Ares returned. Reaching deeply, he found his well was dangerously low, but that wouldn't stop him from saving her. All he could see was smoke and burned trees. His eyes grew heavy and everything went dark.

"Stefan, he's over here!"

Gryphon snapped open his eyes and clenched his teeth against the pain when he turned his head. A gold light brightened as it hurried toward him. The rain was pounding on his face, but he didn't dare blink, in case she vanished.

"Thank Merlin we found you!" Alex's face appeared above his. Her eyes were red, and her cheeks streaked with tears.

"I told you we'd find him," Stefan said.

"We're getting you out of here, and you'll be right as rain in no time," Alex said.

Gryphon tried to smile at her but coughed, and pain shot through his upper body. "Don't make me laugh," he said. His deep breaths made his vision tunnel from the pain. He raised his hand to Alex's cheek and caressed it weakly. She stopped examining him and put her hand over his. "If your face is the last thing I see, then I'll die a happy sorcerer," he whispered to her.

You don't get to die on me, Sunset. I told you: I didn't keep my powers so that I would spend centuries alone. You're stuck with me.

"Promise?"

Alex nodded and quickly turned to Stefan. "How do we get him off the branch?"

Stefan squatted and spent a long time examining Gryphon's injury before speaking. "I'm going to pull you off this branch, Gryphon. It's going to hurt like nothing you've ever felt, at least until Alex cauterizes the wound to stave off infection. After we get you back to the castle, it'll be up to her to heal the rest."

"I have all the time in the world," Gryphon said, which started him coughing again.

"Smart-ass sorcerer," Stefan grumbled.

"Be nice to me, Little Wafner. I'm hurt and you'll make Lynx sad."

"I'm well aware of that fact, Gryphon." Stefan said. "It seems my life is to be spent keeping you and Aaron out of harm's way for the sorceresses in my life."

Alex grabbed the branch, and her hands glowed, but Gryphon knew it wouldn't work. "Celtic powers won't affect it because it's dead," he said.

Alex let go. "We'll have to cut it back then."

"Just pull me off," Gryphon whispered.

"Are you sure?" Alex asked. "It could damage you more."

"Are you afraid you can't heal me, Princess?"

"No, I'm worried about causing you more pain."

"I can take it, but I need you out of here ... *now*."

Alex turned and muttered something to Stefan. Gryphon couldn't see her face, but the clenched jaw Stefan responded with made it clear she was scared. Finally, she took a deep breath and turned back to Gryphon. She squeezed his arm, and a warmth trickled through him. It was only when Stefan motioned for her to go that she released Gryphon's hand and stepped back.

Stefan leaned down over Gryphon with his back to Alex. "Don't you die on me, Gryphon. Lynx has her heart set on a sorcerer bonding ceremony, and she expects you and Birch to be there in place of her family. She doesn't have much family left, so you matter, to all of us." Stefan held out a stick. "Put this in your mouth so you don't break a tooth when I lift you up."

Gryphon did as he was told, and then Stefan reached under his injured shoulder. Alex came and took hold of his good side. They counted to three and lifted him off the branch.

Gryphon turned his head and moaned. Electric pain shot through the entire left side of his body. He carefully twisted his neck to look at the oversized bandage wrapped around his shoulder. The cloth was mostly brown from the blood soaking it. He clenched his jaw until the pain passed and then took in the unfamiliar room.

He was in a large bed. The four poles were carved with little knight shields and Datten's motto. The bedding was the softest he'd ever felt, and its golden sheen was blinding. The stone walls were bare except for the burning torches, and there was a large balcony to the side letting moonlight shine into the room. Stefan was snoring in the middle of a couch facing the bed, with Lynx and Alex asleep on either shoulder. Birch and Megesti were passed out on a second couch.

Gryphon heard footsteps and then Aaron came up the stairs, startled to see him awake. He mustered his strength and held up his hand to stop Aaron from waking everyone.

Aaron quietly padded across the room, picked up a mug from the side of the bed and held it up to Gryphon's mouth.

The smell of mint meant it was one of Birch's pain remedies. Gryphon took a swig and lay back against the pillows.

"When did you wake up?" Aaron asked softly.

"A minute ago. How long have I been asleep?"

"A day and a half. Stefan and Alex got you back here, but she was too weak to heal you all at once. She had to split her powers between healing you and Megesti." Aaron explained that Megesti had been covered in burns, and it had taken a lot out of her to make sure he didn't get infected. For Gryphon, she'd managed to stop the bleeding and clean the wound, but that had been as far as she could get before Birch and Lynx made her stop and recover.

"Was she hurt?" Gryphon asked.

Aaron shook his head. "You sent her back before anything happened. Jerome even caught her."

"No wonder you keep those Wafners around."

"You gave us a pretty good scare." Aaron motioned at everyone behind him. "They refused to leave your side until you woke up. Kharon was here, too, but now they're finding potions to help Birch and Alex heal you."

"They love their books. I would expect nothing else from them. Where am I?"

"The Queen's suite. My mother's gone to Warren to visit my uncle."

"And to convince Edward to forgive you?"

"Hopefully." Aaron rolled his eyes.

"We have more in common than you'd like to admit, Aaron." Gryphon smiled.

Aaron crossed his arms and glared. "Loving Alex does not mean we have more in common."

"We both grew up with fathers who wanted us to be what we aren't, and with people who thought we weren't good enough. We have a few friends who see the real us, but we wear a mask for everyone else—a mask that was forced on us to make us fit the role we were born into but never wanted."

Aaron's eyes softened, and he uncrossed his arms.

"And we both became who we were destined to when Alex came into our lives," Gryphon said.

Aaron ran his hand through his bushy hair and looked behind him at their sleeping friends before turning back to Gryphon.

"Thank you for saving her. I know it's your job and you do it because you love her, too, but ... I can't do this without her."

"Aaron—"

"Let me say this. I know you all went into the woods to work on their powers, and something went wrong. Megesti came back covered in burns, and you came back with a hole in your body I could see through. But Alex—she didn't have a scratch on her. She'll feel guilty for that, but I'll never stop thanking you for it."

"I'd do it again in a heartbeat."

"I know," Aaron said.

Gryphon glanced at the others, all still sleeping. "We have to talk about Ares again, but not now. Not here."

Aaron nodded and a rustling sound made them both turn toward Alex's couch. She was sitting up and rubbing her neck.

"Morning, sleepy," Aaron said.

Alex gasped. "You're awake!" She leaped off the couch and rushed to Gryphon's other side. "How do you feel? Are you alright?"

"I'm thirsty and sore," Gryphon replied. "But I'll live."

Alex leaned over him, trembling as she unwrapped his shoulder.

"Gryphon?" Lynx bolted up and hurried over to help with the bandage. Aaron stepped away from the bed when Birch and Megesti woke up and hurried to his other side.

"You two can stop fussing over me," Gryphon said, but Alex and Lynx ignored him and kept unwrapping his wound. Once the bandages were off, Alex covered it with her hand and sent a warm gold light into the wound. All the pain immediately vanished, and Gryphon heard himself moan as he sunk into the pillows.

"Feel better?" Stefan asked.

"Immensely," Gryphon said, closing his eyes and letting the healing magic do its job.

"Not too much, Alex," Birch warned. "We talked about this, dear. You can't heal him all at once."

"I know." Alex frowned looking Gryphon over. *I'm sorry.*

No apologies, Princess. You just need a few days and I'll be right as rain.

Alex smiled weakly and squeezed his hand.

Gryphon turned slightly to face Stefan. "I'm alive and fine. You can all go to bed now. I'm sure Birch has a vile concoction waiting for me to knock me out so I can heal better and we can all get some rest."

"Are you sure?" Alex asked. Gryphon nodded back to her, and she sighed loudly. "Alright."

Gryphon grabbed Lynx's hand, smiling weakly as the others left the room. "I approve."

"Of what?" Lynx asked.

"Of Stefan. He may not live more than a few decades, but he'd go to the end of the world to make you happy, and that's all I ever wanted for you."

Lynx leaned down and kissed Gryphon's cheek. "Thank you."

CHAPTER 47

AARON

"Why do you insist we travel by horse?" Gryphon asked.

Aaron chuckled as he dismounted Thunder. He took Harold's reins and tied them to a large oak tree beside the stream. Harold held out his hand and Gryphon tossed him his horse's reins before sliding awkwardly to the ground.

Harold grinned. "You should have complained your shoulder hurt. Then Aaron would have let you crack us."

Gryphon tried to cross his arms but seemed to wince in pain. "We didn't have to do this today. If we waited another day, Alex could have finished healing me."

"You said she needed a week to rest before she could finish." Aaron took the saddles off their horses. "Besides, after everything that's happened in the last few months, I won't postpone handling a threat, even by a day."

"I need it known that I think not telling Alexandria is a mistake," Harold said. "When she learns what's going on, and she will, you are both going to regret it."

Gryphon pursed his lips and glared at Aaron. "You had to bring him?"

"It was Harold or Jerome. I needed a neutral party's input."

Gryphon rubbed his shoulder and muttered, "Neither one of them are neutral." He raised his arm above his head and the ground rumbled. A trio of oversized rocks lifted out of the earth, and he hopped on top of one. Aaron and Harold took a seat on the other rocks.

"Harold, I will tell Alex, but not until we have a plan. After everything that's happened, I need to be able to protect her," Aaron said. "Now Gryphon, tell us exactly what Ares told you when he appeared."

"The gist of it is he doesn't even consider me a true Ares, because of my respect for Alex. He's demanding I kill you to prove I'm Ares enough or he'll kill me."

"Why Aaron, though? If he wants to punish you, wouldn't killing Alex be worse?" Harold asked.

"We can't kill Alex," Gryphon said. "She's too important for the next generation of sorcerers. He knows that if the choice were me or her, I'd kill myself in an instant, taking away the torture."

"But killing me means hurting Alex," Aaron said.

Gryphon nodded. "And ruining any chance of me having a meaningful future with her—one where she actually likes me."

"I see," Harold said. "Sorcerers are a rather devious bunch, aren't you?"

"Devious? By mortal standards, maybe. That's just how my line gets things done. So ... ideas?"

"So far, we only have the one," Aaron said. "An accident, where I'm killed—but not completely—and Alex brings me back. She's done it before, when her vortex impaled me."

"That would be risky without her knowing our plan," Harold said.

"Especially if we need her fully rested so we know she'd be able to heal you."

"Gryphon, it was me or you, right? If Ares comes for you, is there any chance Alex could bring you back instead?" Aaron asked, and Gryphon shook his head.

"This is why we should talk to Alex," Harold said.

Aaron ignored him. "We don't have to kill me. What if we just *said* you did?"

Gryphon gave him a look. "Ares is a sorcerer god. He's also dead, which means he'll know if you are, too."

"Could we have my brother pretend to be me?"

"He'd know."

"What if you hide from him?" Harold asked.

"You want Aaron to hide for the next thirty years?" Gryphon rolled his eyes. "That's an even worse idea than pretending to be dead."

"Then you come up with some ideas, if you're so smart," Aaron snapped.

"Negotiate. Offer him something else," Harold said. "What about that dog we took from your father?"

"The only reason Ares would want Cerberus would be to upset Hades," Gryphon said. "But that isn't a terrible idea."

They continued to toss ideas around. Soon, Aaron noticed an eerie silence around them. As soon as he brought it to Harold and Gryphon's attention, an icy breeze surrounded them, and the grass turned brown.

"He's here," Gryphon whispered. He scrambled up his rock and peered into the forest, his face ashen.

Aaron's heart pounded in his chest as they all stared at the woods. The weeds and young trees swayed. The moment stretched into eternity, until Gryphon's expression changed from fear to shock.

"What are you doing here?" he asked.

"That's what I want to know," Alex said, appearing between the rocks occupied by Aaron and Gryphon. Her presence startled Aaron so much he slipped off his rock. Megesti and Stefan appeared at her sides.

Aaron stood and brushed the leaves off his pants, then looked at his wife. Her eyes, normally emerald, were blazing gold as she took in the scene.

"You have *one* chance to tell me what is going on out here," Alex said. Stefan crossed his arms behind her and gave Aaron the Wafner scowl.

Alex waited, then frowned. "Do I have to count down, as if you're children? Fine. Five … four … three—"

Harold cleared his throat loudly. "Ares threatened Gryphon," he said. "He was told to kill Aaron or else Ares would kill him. Apparently Gryphon's not Ares enough to be Titan of Ares."

A smirk spread across Alex's face, and she glanced up at Stefan. "I told you he'd crack first. I get to pick training for the next week."

Megesti looked confused. "Crack first?"

"Sorry, Megesti. You are the only one here who doesn't know what's going on," Stefan said.

"What?" Aaron asked.

"It's simple," Stefan said. "Each of you already told Alex about Ares's threat, but none of you would admit to the others that you confessed."

Gryphon groaned and dropped his head into his hands.

"The only one who actually kept it secret was Jerome. But Stefan overheard Aaron ordering him to do so," Alex said.

"If you knew all along, why did you let them sneak around and meet in secret?" Megesti asked.

"For the lesson," Alex replied. She snapped her fingers and their horses vanished. "You're all going to walk home and think about why don't lie or withhold important information, both from me, but also from our allies." She turned her face to Gryphon and smiled wickedly at him. "If you crack them back, I'll know and I'll have Stefan tie you up before I crack you into the Oreean Sea. Understood?"

The three of them nodded.

"Very good. Do you feel like some dinner, Alex?" Stefan asked.

"Yes please. I'm starving," she said.

"And afterward we can see what Kharon's come up with," Megesti said. "We asked them for help since they have access to all the dead sorcerers in existence."

"Have a delightful walk, boys." Alex giggled before cracking away with Stefan and Megesti.

Aaron scratched his head and slowly laughed. "I did not see that coming."

"I like it when she takes charge." Gryphon smirked.

"I stand by my earlier comment," Harold said. "Sorcerers are devious."

CHAPTER 48

ALEX

Alex grabbed a sunflower roll and slathered it in butter, then dropped a thick slice of cheese on it for good measure. Edith topped up everyone's goblets with more Warren wine. Lynx stalked the table and kept changing her mind about what she wanted to eat, before finally deciding on a sweet bun with apple chunks. Jessica sat back on the couch and sighed happily. Michael's and her estate in Datten was nearly finished, and their sitting room was a perfect place to have some time with the soon-to-be bride. Alex laughed at the plate Jessica had balanced on her pregnant belly.

"Jessica!" Edith squealed. "I never thought I'd see you using your baby as a table."

"What else am I supposed to do?" She feigned trying to sit up in the overly plush red velvet couch. "I can't reach the table over it."

Edith took Jessica's order and filled her plate again. She set it back on her belly, making everyone burst into giggles again.

There was a soft knock on the door, and Michael peeked into the room. "Everything fine in here?"

"Yes, you busybody." Edith threw a pillow embroidered with flowers at him. "If we want anything else, Lynx or Alex will get it."

"If you need something to do, you can take Stefan and bring some horses to Aaron, Harold, and Gryphon. Perhaps walking for three hours is enough thinking," Alex said.

"Three hours thinking is more than Gryphon has done in his whole life," Lynx said, sending the ladies into more laughter.

"As you wish," Michael said, and softly closed the door.

"Alright, Edith," Alex said and settled into the pile of cushions on the floor. "This is our version of your Warren tea. We're here to answer all your questions about your upcoming wedding. No subject is off limits, so ask whatever you want to know."

"Have you ever seen a naked man?" Lynx asked before bringing her wine to her lips.

Jessica groaned and covered her face with her hand. "In the first five minutes."

"I have," Edith said, sipping her wine, clearly trying to hide her blush. "Both in real life and in paintings at Alex's Warren tea with my sisters."

Alex didn't reflect fondly on her tea with the Nial sisters—rather than put her at ease, they'd made her so nervous she and Aaron had been caught by her father *before* their wedding night. Everything had turned out alright ... for a while. Alex's stomach turned at the thought of the unease between Aaron and her father.

Jessica sat up so quickly she almost knocked the plate off her belly, bringing Alex back to the conversation at hand. "Who did you see naked?" Jessica asked.

"Julius, but it was when we were young."

"None of this 'when you were young' nonsense," Alex said. "We're your friends, and we've all been in your shoes at one time, so we're here to ease your anxiety."

"I'm honestly not worried about the wedding night," Edith said. "Harold is a Betruger, and he knows what he's doing. He's older, and unlike your partners, he's been with other women." Edith motioned to the surrounding ladies, and they all nodded or shrugged in agreement. "What I'm terrified of is after we're married."

"Childbirth?" Jessica asked.

"—or other expectations he may have?" Lynx winked.

Alex leaned toward Edith. "Being queen?"

Edith nodded at Alex and stuffed a chunk of cheese into her mouth.

"You're a noblewoman, Edith, with many talents and skills, not to mention your exceptional beauty. You'll be a fine queen," Jessica said.

"I agree with Jessica," Lynx said. "You have a good head on your shoulders, and Harold clearly adores you. His people will, too."

Alex sat silently while Jessica and Lynx took turns listing all the qualities Edith possessed that would make her a wonderful queen. When they ran out of ideas, she finally spoke. "I'll give you the same advice Emmerich and Guinevere gave me when I was nervous about marrying Aaron. Being a good queen happens when you *want* to be a good queen. It's easy to be a queen who smiles and waves and looks beautiful the way her people expect. But an exceptional queen will fight for her people when they aren't looking, and when no one is around to give her credit. Edith, I know you possess the desire to be a great queen."

Edith teared up. "You really think so?"

Alex nodded and held her arms out to Edith. She embraced Alex so hard she almost choked her. "You will be amazing, and you'll do it without the expectation of praise or admiration from the Betruger people, because that's who you are." Alex held onto her until she was ready to let go.

"So there's nothing sexual you want help with?" Lynx asked.

"Ew," Jessica shouted. "Lynx, you're marrying my brother!"

"I know. Getting him into bed is why he wants to marry me so quickly. It's some nonsense about honor. Is that a mortal thing, Alex?" Lynx asked. She stuffed the last bite of her sweet bun into her mouth.

Edith took another swig of her wine, avoiding looking at Jessica. Alex turned to her friend to see her mouth open and her face beat red.

"Jessica, before you say anything negative about sorceresses, I would like to remind you I am also a sorceress, and that I did the same thing to Aaron."

"Drink?" Lynx offered Jessica a gold goblet with rubies around the rim. "Birch made this one for you. It has herbs that are good for the baby."

Jessica took the drink and nodded to Lynx before chugging the entire goblet. Everyone burst into laughter, and Jessica wiped her mouth with her hand.

"I have one serious question," Edith said.

"Anything," Alex said.

"How many babies am I going to have?" Edith asked.

Alex burst into laughter. "More than your own mother. But you will have some boys in there, too."

Edith's mouth dropped open. "How many more?"

Alex was sitting on the edge of her bed brushing her hair when she heard the door to her main room close.

"Alex?" came Aaron's voice.

"I'm upstairs," she called down.

Footsteps echoed up the stairs. Aaron stopped in his tracks

when he spotted her. She was wearing the same gold nightdress she'd worn on their wedding night.

"Is that dress your apology for making me walk home?"

"Maybe. Though honestly, I don't think I owe you an apology. We agreed to be honest with each other and you were going to withhold something this important from me."

"Uh-uh," Aaron said, leaning down to her so they were eye to eye. "I didn't lie to you. I lied to Gryphon. You are the one who said you wouldn't tell him you knew."

"And I kept that promise. I was very convincing when he told me about the threat."

Aaron exhaled and ran his hand along her thigh, watching the fabric sparkle in the firelight. "You're right. I shouldn't have asked you to keep it a secret from him, too."

"Gryphon is my guard, and if there is a threat that impacts me, we all need to know about it."

"But this threat is to me and Gryphon," Aaron said.

"And it only exists because of me."

"You can't say that every threat and danger is your fault. You may be the future Heart of sorcerers, but in Datten you are the queen, and threats against the king will not all be your fault."

Alex sighed and moved to kiss him. "I know. But I will end any threat against you."

It wasn't an actual blood oath, but Alex meant her promise just as sincerely.

ALEX

Alex's smile was so broad her cheeks hurt. Getting ready for a royal wedding that wasn't her own was a lot less nerve wracking and she enjoyed soaking in the moment. Edith looked amazing in her traditional Betruger wedding dress. Harold had suggested she wear a Warren style, even if only for the private ceremony, but she wanted to embrace her new people and had decided to follow their traditions instead.

The royal guest suite Edith was staying in, had been decorated in the colors of the Betruger kingdom—yellow and green with hints of brown. Alex had made sure they included purple as well, as it was the color only worn by the nobility and on special occasions. Before they arrived to get ready, Birch and Lynx had covered the room with bouquets of various yellow and purple flowers filling the space with a sweet and calming aroma.

Edith had chosen plum purple for her gown and given Alex an emerald-green dress and Jessica a sunflower yellow one. The neckline cut across her lower collarbone, providing the coverage Alex always longed for. Alex and Jessica's were typical for Datten ladies, but Edith's was a sight to behold. The material circled around her bust, and the sleeves hung from her shoulders, leaving them bare. All three gowns had long sleeves, but Edith's were fitted to her arms and dyed a few shades lighter than the gown itself. It went almost to the floor, allowing her to move with ease, and her waist was cinched with a thick jewel-encrusted leather belt. In accordance with Betruger tradition, Harold had made the belt himself. The complexity of the pattern of the jewels indicated her rank in the kingdom, and their quantity showed the time the groom had to put into the piece. Lastly, a flowing cape, woven from a shimmering purple thread that was darker than the rest, was strung from her shoulders. Unlike the thick, fur-lined capes worn by the royal males of Torian, Edith's was of a thinner material. It worked as a train on the dress, following her as she moved.

The door closed behind the Nial ladies who left to take their seats. Jessica was standing next to Edith, finishing her hair. A short distance away, Randal watched them, clutching a small tiara that Edith's mother and sisters had all worn to their weddings. He looked down at the tiara and back at Edith's elaborate gown, and Alex sensed his hesitation.

"Is that Lady Judith's tiara that Edith has been talking about?" Alex snatched it from him and left him standing in shock while she brought it over to them.

Edith's eyes lit up. "Thank you, daddy. I've been dreaming of wearing this my whole life."

Her smile seemed to warm his heart. "My father had it made for your mother on our wedding day," he told her.

Alex placed the tiara into Edith's hair, and then reluctantly fetched her own crown from a small table. She'd argued with Edward and Aaron to be allowed to go crownless so Edith could shine, but everyone insisted that as a born royal, she had to wear one. In the end, they'd compromised on a smaller emerald-green Warren crown that matched her dress.

With her tiara in place, Edith was giddy with excitement.

Tonight, the first small ceremony for the family would be held in Warren at the Nial estate. It would officially make her and Harold husband and wife. Tomorrow's wedding would be much larger and held before the Betruger people in Datten. There, Harold would crown Edith. The feast and entertainment were reserved for the third day.

Alex and Jessica whispered encouragement to Edith and left her with her father. They headed down the hallway to the back door to find their seats.

The tent Edward had bought for the wedding was almost the size of a throne room. Michael and Stefan were sitting with the Nial ladies and Bishop family. Jessica left Alex to join them, and Alex took her seat with Aaron on the other side of the aisle, near the Betruger knights Harold was closest with.

Betruger weddings were short. Randal only walked Edith part of the way down the aisle. In Alex's own wedding, Edward had given her to Aaron, but today, Edith's father left her to make the choice to take Harold on her own. She walked the last bit of the aisle alone. Macht had explained it symbolized her leaving her parents' home to start her own. Once she freely took Harold's hand, they shifted their grasp, so they each held the other's forearm. Then a Betruger elder from Harold's mother's family pulled out a leather strap. With it, he bound their arms together, making them one from this day forward. Harold agreed to put Edith above all other duties and vows, including being king, and Edith agreed to provide a home for him to come back to and a legacy to carry on his name. Once they agreed, the elder removed the binding, and they were officially married.

There was no traditional banquet for the private ceremony, but in true Warren fashion the Nials had arranged for a feast of Edith's favorite foods. Everyone enjoyed the food and laughed at Edith's family's tales of her wild streak as a young girl.

As the meal was finishing, Randal raised a glass of wine. "Welcome to the family, Harold," he said.

"We aren't perfect," Lady Judith added. "But we are full of love, and we welcome you with open arms, and hope you'll come to Randal and me with issues you wish your parents were around to help with."

"I can say from experience they are very good at listening without overreacting too terribly," Edith's brother-in-law Aiden Bishop said looking at his own father and then Randal. Edith's oldest sister, Abigail, turned bright red and covered her face with her hands.

"Still, Abigail?" Edith laughed.

Aaron leaned over to Macht and relayed the tale of how Matthew caught Abigail in Aiden's bed, resulting in the speedy wedding of the children of Warren's two generals. "But honestly, the entire kingdom wanted a Nial daughter to marry a Bishop son, so everyone ignores how it came to be."

"The way everyone ignores how you and Alex began?" Edith asked, grinning at Aaron.

"Yes," Aaron replied without an ounce of embarrassment. "Everyone wanted us together even more. There are benefits to going along with what everyone wants of you." Alex playfully smacked him, but he just smiled, leaned down, and whispered, "You should try it sometime, Princess."

CHAPTER 50

AARON

The second wedding was held in Datten's castle and was as lovely as the first. This time, the celebration was held in the Betruger language so Aaron and their friends didn't know what was being said. It didn't matter. Edith's smile was all they needed to see to know everything was perfect. It wasn't until Harold crowned Edith that she showed any sign of nervousness. Aaron knew she'd be a wonderful queen, as long as she stayed true to herself. Alex cried during the ceremony and Aaron held her. She'd been sensitive since Gryphon and Megesti's accident, so Aaron was doing his best to be supportive and give her extra time despite his duties.

The second wedding combined elements of both Betruger and Warren traditions. Once the ceremony was complete, the hall doors were swung open to reveal a traditional Warren feast for the guests. Aaron had snuck his favorite Datten foods into the feast as well, but he was most excited for the sword fighting and other displays that accompanied the final wedding. It was a chance for his men to show off their skills and bravery, and after so many months of training together at Moorloc's old castle they would be in top form.

Alex squeezed his thigh. "Any guesses what the special entertainment Edith and Harold have planned for tomorrow will be?"

"All I know is that Gryphon is in on it, too."

"It's unfair that they asked him and not me." Alex pouted as she bit into her sweet bun with apple chunks.

"They probably did it because he isn't as closely tied to the couple like you are."

Alex sighed. "I'm sure whatever they come up with will be lovely, but it won't be better than what I have planned."

"Care to share?"

"No. The sorcerer's gift is from the sorcerers."

Aaron leaned down and stole the last bite of her bun, stuffing it in his mouth. Alex kissed his nose and smiled.

"I'm going to sneak off now to prepare. I'll be back once I've changed."

"Promise?"

Alex chuckled. "Yes. Lynx is waiting to help me. Birch, Kharon, and Megesti are already setting up."

As soon as Alex left, Aaron turned his attention back to the wedding party. Harold and Edith were seated at the head table which was flanked by two large tables. Aaron and Alex were on Harold's side with Macht, while the Nials were seated on Edith's side.

A few minutes later, the room rumbled loudly, and two hooded figures appeared in front of the tables. Harold flung his arm in front of Edith to protect her, but Aaron stood and motioned for him to wait. The crowd chattered nervously. The sorcerers were dressed in black robes that resembled the Titan's robes, except they had the addition of the heart and crown stitched on the front. In unison, Alex and Gryphon removed their hoods and smiled.

"King Harold and Queen Edith of the Betruger," Gryphon

began. "My Heart and I come before you as the future rulers of the Forbidden Lands to ask you for peace between our lands."

Edith stood and grinned. "What do you propose, Gryphon?"

Harold joined her and took her hand in his. "I agree with my wife. We would love a formal peace with future leaders of Torian Sorcerers," Harold said.

"Yes, tell us your terms," Aaron added, smiling at his wife. In the short time she'd been gone, she'd not only changed out of her formal gown and into a Titan robe, but also taken down her hair, a task that Aaron knew would have taken an hour if Jessica had insisted on a formal updo.

Alex stepped beside Gryphon. "We have no terms, but we wish to return something our kind took from you."

"A sign of goodwill. May I?" Gryphon opened his palms and motioned to the room full of people. Edith and Harold exchanged a brief look before nodding to Gryphon.

A wind hit them, and when Aaron blinked, only the married couple, himself, and Macht stood in the Ogre mountains overlooking the sea. Kharon waited for them near the edge of a cliff.

"Where are we?" Edith asked, clinging to Harold.

"This is where the Betruger kingdom used to be, Your Majesty," Kharon said. "Now if you'll step closer, they can begin."

"Begin what?" Aaron asked, but when he reached the cliff face, he spotted the sorcerers down on the beach. Lit up in their line colors, it was obvious who was who. Dark and light green stepped forward first. Lynx and Birch waved their arms, and soon the barren earth surrounding them erupted in grass, flowers and new trees. After the plants returned, it only took a minute before they could hear birds in the trees.

Harold smiled and pulled Edith closer. "I haven't seen it this green up here since I was a boy."

They watched in awe as the gold figure stepped away from the group. Alex thrust out her hands and the sea rushed away from the beach. After a few more motions, she could walk out onto the seabed. Megesti and Gryphon followed closely. They stood so close, their orange and violet blended into a rusty brown, and the earth beneath their feet trembled.

"Get back," Aaron cried, and they hurried away from the cliff face as the force strengthened and started knocking some of the larger boulders from the edge loose. But just when the mountain stopped shaking, there was a deafening roar. Aaron turned back to the sea and rubbed his eyes in disbelief—a spire was rising out of the sea.

It appeared as if Alex were lowering the water level.

"They're raising our castle," Harold shouted over the wind.

"How?" Edith asked.

"I don't know," Aaron said.

"Alex wanted to return something to you that sorcerers took from you," Kharon said. "She's been training for this since she returned from the maze."

When the other spires broke through the sea's surface, hushed exclamations of disbelief and awe rippled through the group. Slowly the entire castle became visible, and water poured from the windows. Aaron noticed Alex's glow was lightening in color. "Kharon, can you send me down there?" Aaron asked anxiously.

"Let them be, Aaron," Edith said. "Look."

Aaron followed Edith's gaze and found Lynx and Birch making their way over to Alex. As soon as they stood next to her, Alex's light brightened again, and the castle rose faster.

It must have been half an hour before the earth stopped rumbling and the castle stopped moving. Gryphon burst into flames and a giant ball of fire the size of a horse flew from him and burst out of every window and door of the castle. The mortals all looked at Kharon but he simply grinned. "Gryphon's drying it for you."

With a soft crack, the five sorcerers appeared before them. They were all more disheveled than usual, with Alex and Megesti weariest of all.

Edith ran and threw her arms around Alex so hard she would have knocked her over if Gryphon hadn't caught them. "Thank you so much," she said.

Alex squeezed Edith and sighed. It was the sound she made when someone thanked her for something she thought was a failing on her part. "I'm sorry it took me so long to learn to do it."

"Don't do that," Edith replied. "The maze taught you to let us help you. That's not a weakness, and your struggle to do it before was not failure."

"Edith's right," Harold said. "It doesn't matter how you did it, or how long it took. You gave me back my family's home; one we've lived in for generations. I appreciate this more than I can ever say." Harold squeezed Edith's shoulder, and she released Alex so Harold could hug her, too. He then turned to Lynx, Megesti, and Birch and hugged them too. "Thank you, all of you."

Edith hugged the others, and Gryphon shook Harold's hand. "It was all her idea."

"I didn't realize you wanted to get rid of me so badly," Edith teased.

"Kharon, Gryphon, any luck figuring out how to make a blue pearl so Edith can visit Datten or Warren whenever she wants?"

"We have a few options for spells but you need to be well rested first," Kharon said. "And we need to figure out exactly where she'd arrive so nothing is left in that spot that could hurt her."

"The garden!" Alex and Edith replied in unison, making them laugh.

"Tell me," Alex pleaded. She was kneeling on their bed in her nightdress, trying to find out what their friends had planned for the last wedding day's entertainment.

Aaron dropped his gold shirt on the couch before the fireplace and turned back to his wife. "I know that look. You can beg all you want, but you didn't tell me about your big show today, so I don't have to tell you anything, Your Royal Highness."

"Oh, you think so?"

"Yes. And don't think you can use those feminine wiles to convince me to tell you."

"I would never," Alex said, a mischievous smile spreading across her face. She swung her legs over the side of the bed and toyed with the hem of her nightgown.

"That will not work on me tonight, so you can just give up."

Alex pulled off her gown and threw it at him. He caught it and the smell of flowers engulfed him. Aaron groaned internally. *They taught me to be strong, and never yield even under torture ... but you ... how do you have such power over me?*

"Good night, Your Royal Highness," she said. She'd crawled into their giant bed and covered herself up in their quilt. He could see her body shake as she fought back her wicked giggles. Aaron hurried across the room and jumped onto the bed, making her scream.

There were three loud knocks at the door and then Jerome's face appeared, checking on them.

"Still?" Aaron groaned, rolling over on the bed.

Alex sat up, covering herself with the quilt. "At ease, General. I'm fine."

Jerome nodded and closed the door.

"I know it bothers you, but I appreciate that they care this—" Alex abruptly stopped and emitted a terrible croak. Her hand was on her throat and she was wheezing. Aaron dove for her, but she erupted in orange light.

"Alex what's going on?"

"I don't know," she croaked.

"Help! Gryphon!" Aaron shouted.

Jerome burst through their door just as Gryphon cracked into the room. "I'm busy right now," Gryphon snapped.

"I don't care, Alex is glowing—" Aaron froze. Gryphon was glowing orange, too.

"Ferflucs," Gryphon muttered. His eyes lingered on her body for longer than Aaron liked.

"Stop ogling my wife and help us."

"Get her dressed," Gryphon said. "We're being summoned."

"By who?" Jerome asked.

"Ares."

CHAPTER 51

ALEX

An icy shiver rushed down her spine, but a hot hand found hers and squeezed it. It helped to control her choppy breaths. When the smell of pine and campfire enveloped her, Alex closed her eyes and pictured Cassandra, trying to recall everything she'd learned from her line's founder. Cassandra was a lovely, benevolent founder. Ares couldn't be as bad as Gryphon made him out to be. She knew he liked to exaggerate, but never when her safety was at risk. Though technically, it was her happiness, not her life, that was on the line.

"Alex?" Aaron's hand caressed her lower back, and his voice startled her out of her thoughts.

"Yes?"

"You stopped walking. Are you alright?"

"Yes," Alex answered. She swallowed the lump in her throat and hurried ahead of him to catch up with Gryphon. "Where exactly are we going?" she asked the sorcerer.

"I don't know. Last time, he just appeared."

"What does he want?" Aaron asked.

"How would I know?" Gryphon muttered, pushing aside

another low branch to make room for them. "I'm not privy to the plans of a crazed god."

Thunder cracked behind them, and Gryphon spun and shoved Alex behind him so quickly she barely registered what was happening. When she regained her footing, a giant of a man was standing before them. His armor was splattered red with blood, and his piercing stare reminded Alex of her grandfather's. He pulled off his helmet, freeing his head of thick wavy chestnut hair. His eyes fixed on Gryphon, but then shifted to Alex. Mustering everything Stefan, Jerome, and Emmerich had taught her about facing her fears, Alex resisted the urge to run, and instead stuck her chest out and lifted her chin up.

"Well, well. Who do we have here?" Ares only made it two steps before Aaron jumped between him and Alex. He brandished his red steel sword, clearly trying to keep Ares as far away from Alex as possible.

"Foolish mortal. Setting aside that I'm dead, it was my pure chaos that twisted the young Cassandra's healing powers to create red steel. So while you could kill those of my line, the poison wouldn't have affected me even in my time." Ares ripped the sword out of Aaron's hands and stabbed it into the ground beside him.

"You're dead. How can you touch things?" Aaron asked.

"The same way your dead brother touches your wife to save her whenever you fail to protect her. Ghosts are capable of many things when the need arises, and sorcerers even more so." Ares turned to Gryphon and with a wave of his hand, the orange glow from him and Alex ceased. The god of chaos pointed at Gryphon and when he curled his finger up, Gryphon was dragged across the ground as if pulled by invisible hands.

Alex shuddered, remembering Moorloc's spell that had taken control of her. Gryphon came to a halt and dropped to his knees before Ares.

"I gave you the chance to finish what you failed to do decades ago—to prove to me that you aren't the disgrace your father always said you were. I was clear, was I not?" Ares grabbed Gryphon's face and dug his fingers into the sorcerer's face. The sizzling sound of Ares scorching his skin was sickening, and Aaron grabbed Alex's arms to keep her with him.

"You had a choice—him or you. So which is it?"

"I haven't formed a decision. You didn't give us enough time," Gryphon argued, trying to break free, but Alex pulled away from Aaron and diverted Ares' attention. He shoved Gryphon away and turned to face Alex. Ares towered over her even more than Harold and Stefan did, but Alex refused to show any weakness as she faced down the god of war.

"I've decided," Alex said.

"Figures the worthless Ares would make a woman decide. Do tell, Princess."

Alex scowled at his use of Gryphon's nickname for her. "Neither. You will take no one I love from me."

Ares started to laugh, but Alex stood taller and closed the distance between them. "I've had enough of self-righteous males taking what's mine. Those two are bonded to me, so they belong to me, and you cannot have either of them."

"You are exceptionally brave, little Cassandra." With lighting speed, Ares was in front of Alex and his hand was around her neck. He stank of rotten earth, death and stale blood. "It has been a millennium since anyone dared to speak to me with that tone."

"You're free to leave if you don't like it," Alex snapped, trying to pry his hand off her neck. His grip wasn't painful but the meaning behind it was clear. If he wanted to, he could hurt her. Alex refused to back down and glared up at him the same way she would when disagreeing with Stefan.

Alex, this is a bad idea.

Don't interfere, Gryphon. He won't hurt me.

We don't know that, and he's not going to hesitate to hurt Aaron or me.

Ares scrutinized her face. He released her neck only to grab her chin and turned her face from side to side, seeming to take his time to go over every detail. "You really are identical to her. Over the centuries I'd heard it was so, but never thought it was possible."

"Why do you care if I look like the first daughter of Cassandra?"

"You're lucky, little Heart, that you resemble the daughter and not the mother."

"Why's that?"

"Because if you looked like Cassandra, I'd have killed you already." Ares raised his hand toward Alex's face, but she moved to slap it away. Ares was faster and grabbed her wrist.

Alex gulped at the orange flames in his eyes.

Behave. Ares' voice shouted in her head.

His lips scowled, and he thrust his free hand out at Aaron, who'd been trying to get to his sword again. Orange light hit Aaron, throwing him back until he slammed into a tree trunk with a loud thump followed by a pained groan. She struggled to slow her breathing and trembled when he caressed her cheek with his thumb. His eyes seemed to take in every detail of her face, ending on her eyes. He brought his face down to Alex's until it was so close they shared breath.

"There she is," he whispered, focusing on her eyes. "Lies and murder are finished, plus half of betrayal. Seems our young Ares is not as useless as I thought. He's complicated things for you and will push you all toward the final betrayal."

Ares released Alex's face, and she brought her hands up to rub her sore chin.

"Alright, daughter of Cassandra, I will take neither from you. Consider it a belated coronation gift from me."

"A gift ... from you?"

"Are you in the habit of questioning gifts?" he snapped.

"Only when they come from someone who threatened to kill someone I love."

Ares tilted his head to the side and looked her up and down. "Why would I kill you when I'm the one who asked Hades to put the fury in you?"

Alex stared, waiting for him to say more. She bit her cheek so hard it drew blood.

"Why did you do that?"

"To punish Cassandra. She abandoned our daughter. With the fury, no one would ever hurt her or her descendants again without suffering a brutal death."

"Your daughter?"

"That's right. The daughters of Cassandra were fathered by me, the first Head, and most terrifying founder of any line."

"I have no intention of killing anyone or letting them kill each other," Alex whispered.

"Perhaps you don't, but your fury will, and you only need a betrayal *against* you to set her free. Has Gryphon confessed *what* he failed to accomplish all those years ago?"

"Ares, please no," Gryphon begged.

"Silence!" the god shouted, making the ground around them shake and Gryphon turn away in fear. Then Ares slowly turned back to Alex. "Well then, let me enlighten you. Twenty-three years ago, his father and hexa sent him to the mortal world—this very kingdom, in fact—to remove an obstacle to his future reign as Head."

"I'm so sorry, Alex," Gryphon whimpered.

"He came here, in the dead of the night, slinking through the castle like a serpent in the grass, intending to kill an infant. But not any infant. He was sent after the newborn prince of Datten. The prince who now stands as your husband."

Alex gasped and stumbled back, covering her mouth. "You lie."

"He would have killed the child, had your mother not interfered. She predicted the threat, knew he'd come, and so stayed in Aaron's nursery night after night to catch him in the act. Her threat to never bear a child kept Gryphon from completing his duty. He'd seen your face already and knew who you were and what you'd be to him. The anger your mother and brother-in-law's ghosts have toward Gryphon stems from that night. Had Victoria not been watching over Aaron, he'd be dead, and you would either never have been born or would have ended up in the sorcerer world under the control of his family when your mother died."

"Why should we believe you?" Aaron asked. He stumbled up to Alex and squeezed her shoulders.

"She doesn't need to believe me. She can feel the guilt radiating off my little Ares now. And if she had any remaining doubts, one quick peek would prove me right."

"No. NO!" she screamed. Alex lunged for Ares, but he grabbed her wrists and threw her to the ground.

"Do not turn on me, little Cassandra. I have more patience for you than any other, but it isn't infinite."

"Alex, I can explain," Gryphon said, crawling on the ground to her. "I'm not that heartless sorcerer anymore."

Alex turned and glared at him. "Leave. I never want to see you again."

"I'm sorry. You changed me. I didn't know any better back then!" He moved for her, but Alex slapped him across the face hard enough to leave her handprint.

"On the beach at Moorloc's I asked you how you knew my mother. You lied to me! Worse, you tried to murder the man I love. Leave now or I'll crack you into the middle of the Oreean Sea and freeze you there."

Gryphon slunk back from her, holding his cheek. Without a word, he cracked away, and Aaron pulled Alex to her feet. Alex turned to Ares. "You did what you came here for. Now leave us alone."

Ares looked down at her. "I'll see you again soon, my little one. That fury inside you is going to come out. I'll stop by for a visit when she's released. We have so much to catch up on. Take my word—a mortal you love will betray you. Men always do. He'll break your heart, and that will break you." Ares vanished, leaving Alex with her fists clenched at her sides and her heart pounding in her chest.

"Alex?" Aaron turned her to face him and Alex fell into his arms. Wordlessly, he wrapped his arms around her, and she let the tears fall. The harder she cried, the harder he held her. "I can't believe I'm going to defend him, but the Gryphon who wanted to kill me years ago isn't *your* Gryphon. I'm sure he wishes I wasn't in your life, but he respects your wants, and he would burn the world to protect you. He's the one I trust to guard you with his life. That Gryphon is the one we need to forgive."

Alex sniffled and hugged him. "I know. I just need a minute. He met my mother and never told me, Aaron. And he would have killed you if she hadn't been there."

"None of us are perfect, especially not as stupid youngsters. I wasn't. My father wasn't. You weren't—according to Stefan, at least."

Alex kissed him.

"Send me home and talk to Gryphon. We can't have a heartbroken titan on the loose."

Alex nodded. As soon as she'd cracked him away, she cracked to the Verlassen Castle, Moorloc's beach and all the labs. *Where are you? I'm sorry. I didn't mean it.* Dejected, she went back to her mother's lab. She was gazing at the books on her shelf when it hit her.

It was nightfall, but the clearing where Megesti had lost control was utterly silent. *This is where he keeps his failures.* She lit an orb. "Gryphon? Please come out." Her voice wavered.

The orb shot ahead of her into the woods. Alex raced to keep up with it until it finally stopped.

Gryphon was sitting on an old log. He turned back toward her, mouth open in shock. "Alex? What are you doing here?"

"To bring you home. Ares wouldn't have left until he won. I didn't mean what I said."

"Really?" His face was red and he scowled at her. "You expect me to believe Aaron will tolerate me being around now? After he learned I was going to kill him?"

"He's not thrilled, but he's the one who told me to come get you." Alex stepped toward Gryphon. She grabbed his hand so he couldn't crack away and sat beside him on the log. "Datten's history is nothing but war kings. Emmerich did some terrible things on the battlefield. Even before he was cursed, Aaron understood what people are capable of. We also know the sorcerer you were twenty years ago is not who you are today."

"You actually want me to come back?" Gryphon glanced at her sheepishly.

"Yes. Though I'm still furious that you met my mother and never told me."

"You're more upset about that than almost killing your husband?"

"I don't believe you would have gone through with it. My mother was just an easy excuse for you." They sat in silence for what felt like forever before Alex asked. "Why didn't you tell me you met her when she was alive?"

"It was more her shouting and threatening me than a proper meeting. She was furious when she realized who I was and why I was there. Apparently, she knew Aaron was in danger, but not from who."

"I'm not surprised she was angry."

Gryphon squeezed her hand. His eyes were fixed on her face with the same intensity Ares had used. "I can't believe you stood up to Ares like that. I'm terrified of him."

"He's a bit intimidating, but I've stood up to so many pompous men that one more didn't scare me."

"No wonder you're such a good queen."

"Well, you could thank me by telling me what the entertainment is tomorrow."

"Really?" Gryphon laughed, interlocking their fingers and pulling Alex off the log along the path back to the Datten castle. "After standing up to the most terrifying sorcerer ever born, you still remember to figure out what Edith has planned tomorrow."

"I have an exceptional memory. Besides, you can't say for sure Ares was the most intimidating sorcerer ever, because we never met Merlin."

CHAPTER 52

ALEX

Alex couldn't sleep. She tossed and turned for what little was left of the night until it was reasonable for her to get up. She headed down to her bathing suite to wash off the stench from the night before. By now, her maids had learned to keep the tub full, and Alex would heat the water herself to her preferred temperature. When she finished washing herself and her hair, she bundled herself in her robe and cracked upstairs. Aaron was still asleep, but there was a large gold box on her bed.

Alex searched the room, but no one was there apart from Aaron. She went over and tugged his blanket off. "Aaron, if you—" she began, but he just snored and rolled over.

Returning her attention to the box, Alex pulled on the black ribbon and pulled apart the tissue paper. Inside was a beautiful gold dress. It was simple, like her favorite gown, but had intricate embroidery along the trim of the sleeves, waist, skirt, and neckline. Alex squinted until it came into focus. Someone had stitched small line marks in a darker shade of gold around the entire trim.

"What is this?" she whispered.

"Your dress for the entertainment," Stefan replied. He had gently opened the door and now entered.

"So I have a specific dress for this event, but no one will tell me what it is."

"I promise you're going to love it. Just go with this."

"Alright. I trust you."

Stefan gave Alex a big hug. "I'm sorry about yesterday. Gryphon told me after you went to bed."

Alex looked up at him. "About everything?"

"Yes, everything." Stefan squeezed her harder. "I thought we talked about you not running into danger anymore."

"I brought Gryphon and Aaron with me."

"You went after a sorcerer god—the one who founded the strongest and most destructive line!"

"And apparently fathered my line," Alex muttered.

"What did you say?"

"I protected what's mine." Alex crossed her arms. "You taught me that."

"I think I taught you too well." Stefan sighed and pulled Alex back into another hug. "Let Aaron sleep. You get dressed and we'll go find something to eat before this big celebration begins."

"Alright, but I have to have a quick conversation with someone after we eat."

EVERYONE WAS HURRYING to prepare for the large celebration, leaving Alex alone She rushed down the quiet second-floor hall, clutching the bag of sleeping tea she'd received from Aaron's physician. *Well, my physician now, too.* The tea was supposed to help her sleep better and not feel so nauseous all the time. If it didn't work, she'd ask Birch for something stronger.

Alex slipped into her empty room. *Good, he's not here. My news can wait one more day. I don't want to take any attention off Edith and*

Harold's celebration. Alex hurried across the space and tucked the bag of dried peppermint leaves mixed with ginger into her drawer on their writing table. Then she grabbed her queen's journal and placed it on top to hide it. When she heard the door click open behind her, she slammed the drawer shut just in time. Alex spun around and leaned against the desk to find Aaron grinning at her from the door frame.

"Here you are." Aaron closed the door and crossed the room, taking her in. "You look enchanting."

"You don't think it's too much?" Alex looked down at the ornate Titan's robe Stefan had left for her. "I feel like I'm glowing."

"You are, but I love that." Aaron tucked a loose little curl behind her ear and kissed her quickly. "I love when you glow because it makes it easier for me to find you."

Alex gave him a playful pinch, and he jumped back, laughing. He was wearing one of his simpler royal shirts, with black pants and boots. The gold stitching on the black shirt matched his hair. "I thought you'd be dressed more formally," she said.

"Harold told me to wear this. He's going to wear the same thing. Neither of us wants to make this celebration about us, so we're trying to hide in plain sight."

"But the celebration is for Harold's marriage," Alex said.

"He wants today to be about celebrating Edith becoming part of the Betruger."

"That, I understand." Alex grabbed his hand and pulled him toward the door. "In that case, we don't want to be late."

Aaron interlaced their fingers, and they strolled through the courtyard and listed off all the exciting things that would take place on that day. The feast would be in the main hall and throne room, allowing for food to be changed throughout the day. The smaller events would be in the courtyard, mainly things for children such as squire demonstrations, puppet shows, and a reading from Alex's favorite book, *Legends of Torian*. For those in the town,

Aaron was paying for the taverns and other food establishments to feed everyone today and send him the bill. He'd also paid the theater to bring a group from the southern kingdoms to perform a popular play from down there. They would perform three times today, and all the tickets were free.

"Why a play from the southern kingdom? Aren't there any Datten ones?"

"Of course there are, but ours are often about war, and the one coming is a love story."

"How romantic of you." Alex hugged his arm. They nodded to the men setting up the puppet theater and headed out of the castle grounds.

"But the largest events will take place on the Datten training fields." Aaron excitedly pulled Alex toward the large protective wall. "There will be sword fights, jousting, archers—pretty much everything you'd find at a tournament."

"So there will be prizes?"

"Of course there are prizes. What tournament doesn't have prizes?" Aaron laughed.

"What's that?" Alex pointed across the field. Birch was standing there growing an arch out of plants.

"I don't know. We could ask."

"Lead the way," Alex said, and Aaron marched them over to Birch.

"Is that a bonding arch?" Alex asked, tilting her head at the floral structure.

Birch smiled. "Yes, Petal. When sorcerers bond, they often want something from their line to be present. So Lynx asked me to build her an arch like the one I had when I bonded with Merlock. How she convinced Stefan to have a proper bonding ceremony, I'll never know, but Lynx gets what she wants."

A bonding ceremony?

Birch wore a robe very similar to hers, except it was light green, like the vines she was twisting into an arch.

"Didn't they tell you?" Birch asked.

"No," Alex said.

"Harold and Edith offered to hold their sorcerer wedding during the celebrations today. Stefan was shy and wanted a quiet event, but Lynx loves a celebration. I suspect they'll have a quiet mortal wedding at some point, but today they're going to get a proper sorcerer bonding ceremony, presided over by you and Gryphon."

"Alex and Gryphon? Shouldn't it be Kharon or you?" Aaron asked.

Birch paused her work to respond. "Why?"

"An elder normally marries mortals," Alex explained.

Birch smiled. "Not for sorcerers. Bonding can be done anywhere, alone in nature, or in front of hundreds. There are no rules because once the couple commits, they cannot undo it."

"So why me and Gryphon? Because we're the Head and the Heart?" Alex asked.

"No, dear," Birch replied.

"We picked you because of how much you mean to us," Lynx said. "Having two people perform the bonding is common. One is chosen by each of the sorcerers. I chose Gryphon, since he's practically my brother, and Stefan chose you. You're family to him even more than Michael or his own sister some days."

Alex felt warmth on her belly as Aaron's arms wrapped around her waist and he hugged her closely. "Is that why we have these new robes?" she asked.

"Stefan had them made by the royal seamstress. We started with yours to get the style just right," Lynx said.

"I know you're not a huge fan of gold, but it suits you," Birch said.

Alex felt heat on her cheeks. They smiled kindly with nothing but love on their faces. She ran her hand along her sleeve, feeling the soft, luxurious fabric, and the amazing embroidery on her sleeve.

"My sister did your embroidery," Stefan said, arriving with Michael.

"Jessica wouldn't trust anyone else to adorn your robe," Michael added.

Alex hugged her robe closer. "I could get used to *this* gold outfit. It looks nothing like what I wore at Moorloc's, and it has a wonderful meaning behind it."

"What time is the ceremony?" Aaron asked.

"Harold and Edith suggested we do it before lunch. We figured everyone could watch us … *wed* as you call it, and then enjoy the feast," Lynx said.

"Sounds perfect," Aaron said.

Stefan held his arm out to Lynx. "You promised you'd leave Birch to set things up, and not be a bother."

"I'm not being a bother. I'm explaining our traditions to Alex."

"It's true," Alex said. "I don't know how any of this works."

"And that's why it's you and Gryphon." Birch rubbed her hands together and flicked them at the arch, sending leaves and flowers bursting out of it.

"That was incredible," Stefan said.

"It's perfect. Thank you." Lynx hugged Birch.

"What do you wear to a sorcerer bonding?" Alex asked. Lynx was still in her training clothes.

"Each sorcerer is different. My parents were naked, but I'll wear my Titan robe. It's the same as yours, but forest green. Gryphon and Kharon enchanted it so my line marks glow."

"And which kingdom are you wearing, Stefan?" Aaron asked. "Datten or Warren?"

"You'd better say Datten," Alex teased.

"Why?" Michael asked.

Alex rolled her eyes and listed the points on her fingers. "He was born here, his family is from here, the town we grew up in is in Datten, he's head of the Queen's Guard ..."

"I'm wearing Datten," Stefan said.

"Good."

Aaron pecked Alex on the cheek. "Since you're clearly in excellent hands, I'm going to find Harold and run through our jousting plan one more time." He went through the arch toward the jousting field.

"Now what?" Alex asked. "It's still too early for anything to officially start."

"Gryphon's looking for you," Lynx said. "There are a few things about your role you need to know."

CHAPTER 53
ALEX

Alex listened intently as Gryphon went over all the things that would happen during the bonding ceremony. Several were unlikely to occur, with Stefan being a mortal, but Gryphon said it was better for Alex to be fully prepared.

Lynx poked her head into the library. Her dirty blonde hair was braided and twisted up on her head like a crown of flowers, and the Tiere line marks on her robe were glowing a beautiful yellow.

"Are you finished? I was hoping we could look at the entertainment together."

"We just finished," Gryphon said. He turned back to Alex. "Do you feel ready for the ceremony?"

"I do," Alex said, and rushed over to Lynx. "Can we start in the dining hall?"

The three sorcerers grabbed a bite to eat to settle Alex's nerves and then headed into the courtyard. Neither Gryphon nor Lynx had ever seen a puppet show before, so Alex made them stay and watch. Despite trying to maintain his intimidating stance, Gryphon laughed out loud more than the others.

Lynx's face lit up anytime the children ran around them.

"Oh no," Gryphon muttered, after Lynx stepped away for a moment to help a scared little rabbit that had wandered into the courtyard.

"What?" Alex asked.

"The look Lynx is giving the children. I'm expecting there will be little Wafners sooner than I'd like." Alex punched Gryphon in the shoulder. "What was that for?"

"Don't you dare say anything to either of them. They're allowed to be happy, and I know from experience that Stefan will be an amazing father. He spent twelve years raising me."

Alex turned and hurried after Lynx. She was crouching beside the poor little rabbit, which she had coaxed out of its hiding spot under some logs. She gingerly picked it up and cradled it in her arms. "Alex, do you know a good place to bring it?"

"I do." Alex cracked them into the forest.

Lynx let the rabbit go, and it hopped away. Then she gently grabbed Alex's arm. "Are you alright, Alex?"

"Of course. I'm excited about your wedding."

"That's not what I mean," Lynx said.

"Oh?"

"You smell different."

Alex sighed. "We talked about this. Mortals don't like being sniffed."

"You're not a mortal, so I didn't think it applied to you."

Alex laughed and hugged her. "I'm fine. But thank you for your concern. I appreciate it."

"Let's go find Gryphon before he gets into trouble," Lynx said, and they cracked back to the courtyard, but Gryphon was still watching the puppet show. When it was over, they wandered out to the tournament grounds for some more exciting entertainment. Gryphon dragged them to the sword fights where they found Stefan.

"Don't you look handsome," Lynx teased, looping her arm

through his. Stefan was dressed in his finest uniform. Alex recognized it as the one she had given him for her wedding to Aaron. He caught her gaze and shot her a warning look, but Alex giggled anyway.

"You really do look handsome, Stefan," she said. "Who'd have thought you'd clean up so well."

Stefan dove for Alex, but she squealed and felt arms pull her away from him. The smell of a campfire engulfed her, and Gryphon appeared between her and Stefan. "Playing or not, it's my job to protect her from everyone, and today that includes guarding her golden robe."

Alex bit her lip as a wicked smirk spread across her face. She raised her arms and summoned a flood of water over Gryphon, soaking him to the bone, and sending her and Lynx into a fit of laughter. Stefan couldn't help but chuckle, though he tried to cover it with a cough.

Gryphon shrugged. "Go ahead and laugh, Stefan." He turned his piercing gold eyes to Alex. "We both know what Alex is capable of."

"We think we do," Stefan corrected, and Alex smiled. He took a deep breath and extended his arm to Lynx. "Are you ready to get married?"

"I thought you'd never ask." Lynx accepted his arm and winked at them. "See you at the arch." She cracked herself and Stefan away.

"I suppose we'd better find the others," Alex said to Gryphon.

ALEX FOUND the royals watching a group of archers. Caleb kept challenging Edith, but she just laughed and shook her head, holding her new crown so it wouldn't slip off. Today, she wore the simplest of the wedding dresses. It was a common style for Warren, but made with purple Betruger velvet. The belt was emerald green, and the dress' trim was sunflower yellow. Harold matched her with a purple tunic that was embroidered with the Betruger crest—two black wolves holding a shield and a boar on top with an ax. The yellow and green of the crest were the same colors as Edith's dress.

Aaron slipped his hand into Alex's as the archers finish their round. Every time Harold and Edith looked at each other, they couldn't help but smile. Alex noticed they hadn't let the other out of their sight since the first wedding. Her heart felt heavy so she squeezed Aaron's hand. *I hope they don't have the struggles Aaron and I did, and that they never have to be apart the way we were.*

"Is it time for the sorcerer wedding?" Edith asked.

"I think they call it a bonding," Harold said. Alex nodded and motioned for them to join her. They strolled and collected the others on their way. Stefan, Lynx, and a crowd of people were waiting for them. They left Aaron with his friends, and Gryphon led Alex to the arch. When Gryphon and Alex passed through the arch together, the area fell silent. Gryphon stood stoically and looked over the crowd of mortals before them. Alex glanced at Aaron and Michael. Both beamed at her, knowing the fear she had of crowds. Aaron nodded toward her and before she could determine what it meant, warmth flooded her back.

Alex shot Gryphon a look but he was focused on Aaron. *Oh. Playing nice, are we, boys? Figures. I scold you both for keeping secrets, and you suddenly decide to be friends.*

Birch winked at them and ran her fingers along the arch, sending all the flowers into bloom. The space was filled with the scent of spring and the awed sounds of the Betruger audience. Alex noticed shade creeping over the space so she waved her hand and sent away the clouds. Birds chirped and then sang as the crowd parted. Lynx held Stefan's arm and smiled from the edge of the crowd. The Tiere line marks on her emerald robe glowed gold, and on Stefan's shirt, the golden thread that stitched the crest of

Datten glowed with the same intensity. They walked in unison toward Alex and Gryphon, stopping beneath the arch.

Alex took a deep breath, locked her hands together, and took a small step forward. "As the future Head and Heart, Gryphon and I approve of this union. We wish you many years of joy, and many children. You may proceed." She stepped back until she bumped into Gryphon's hand.

Lynx turned to Stefan and held out her hands. Stefan took them without taking his eyes off Lynx's face. "Your quiet charm, determination, and handsome face stole my heart the moment I set foot in this world," she began, "And as long as you live, you will be the only man, sorcerer or mortal, to whom I give my love and attention." A dark green glow flared from her line marks and spread through her before jumping into Stefan and making him glow too. She reached into her robe, pulled out a ring, and slid it onto Stefan's finger.

Ignoring the light, Stefan breathed deeply. "I never expected to marry, because I never expected to find someone who understands my duty to Alex. But you're as protective of her as I am. You slipped into my family as if you'd always been there and won the affection of my father and sister with ease. I love how carefree you are and how you embrace the world around you. Seeing things through your eyes has changed me for the better, and I can't wait to see what other magic you bring into our lives." Stefan then produced the wedding band Alex had given him. The band was cut from an emerald she'd found in the Warren treasure room, and on it was etched the Tiere line mark. Lynx stared at the ring open-mouthed while Stefan slid it onto her finger.

Alex caught Harold's eye and winked at him. It was his jeweler who'd achieved what Alex had envisioned. After missing out on Jessica and Edith's rings, Alex had made up for it with Lynx's. When the green light faded, Lynx grabbed her robe and looked down at her shoulder.

"Are you alright?" Stefan asked and Alex rushed to them.

"Of course!" Lynx laughed. "I just want to see what our bond mark looks like."

Stefan turned to Alex. "Will I have one?"

"I do," Aaron said, joining them at the front. Lynx pulled her robe aside and there was a shield with a Tiere line mark in the middle of it.

"How come Aaron got a sword, and I got a shield?" Stefan asked.

"Each bond mark is unique, and combines the sorcerers' line marks," Birch explained. "Merlock and I have a leaf, where the stem rounds into the second half of an infinity symbol."

"I think it's because you're protective," Michael said.

"You have always guarded us," Alex said, hugging Stefan. "Congratulations to both of you." She turned and hugged Lynx.

Jessica hugged Stefan and Lynx before rubbing her swollen belly. "I'm off to lie down. Michael?"

"I'll be back in a bit," Michael said, slapping Stefan's back before glancing at Harold and Aaron. "You two should go get ready for your joust. The people will want something exciting after a wedding."

Aaron kissed Alex's cheek and turned back to Harold, who was holding Edith's hand. "Shall we find your father?"

"Yes please," Edith smiled back and the three of them headed off, leaving Stefan with the sorcerers. He was still staring at his bond mark under his shirt.

"It's not going to go away, Stefan," Alex said.

"He'll get used to it," Lynx said. She looked up at the arch and tweeted at the birds watching them. They took flight and vanished.

There was a quiet growl from somewhere, and they searched in vain until Stefan chuckled.

"Lynx, did you summon a badger?"

"A badger?" The badger snapped at his leg and Stefan jumped back. "Can you ask it to not bite me?" Stefan asked.

Lynx's face went ashen. "Stefan, that's not a badger. Get away from it."

There was a deep growl from behind them, and Alex spun to see a huge, sandy colored wolf stalking toward them.

CHAPTER 54

GRYPHON

"Fenrir!" Gryphon heard Birch shout. She pushed Lynx behind her. "Orion! What are you doing here?"

The sandy wolf lowered itself to the ground and snarled at her. Unfazed, she erupted in green and held her hands out toward the creature. That seemed to hold it at bay while the vicious little badger kept trying to bite Stefan's leg.

Gryphon cracked himself between Birch and the wolf. He lit up in orange and began growling back at it while closing the distance between them. "You're not welcome here, Fenrir. Leave," he ordered.

The wolf eyed him and snarled. In the blink of an eye, it leaped between Stefan and Lynx and transformed back into a sorcerer. "Are you trying to tell me I'm unwelcome at my only daughter's bonding ceremony?" The sorcerer looked down at Lynx and the family resemblance was clear. They shared the same rich brown eyes, sandy colored skin, and dirty blonde hair, but where Lynx was petite and feminine, Fenrir was tall and built for battle.

"He's saying you weren't wanted," Lynx snapped.

Fenrir raised his hand and struck her across the face. Rage filled

Gryphon, and he lunged for the sorcerer, knocking him to the ground. Stefan shouted in rage. He reached down and grabbed the screaming badger by the scruff of its neck and hurled it as far as he could before he rushed to Lynx and Gryphon.

"You knew I'd never approve of you bonding with a filthy mortal. You may be a Titan, but that doesn't give you the right to bring shame to our family," Fenrir shouted as Gryphon and Stefan helped Lynx up from the ground.

"The only person who shames our family is you," Lynx shouted back.

Her father smirked wickedly at her. "You are just like your mother. A talented sorceress who doesn't know her place."

There was a high-pitched shriek behind them. The badger was now snapping at Megesti. "What is wrong with it? I don't want to hurt it," Megesti shouted, trying to shake it off his leg.

"Set it on fire," Gryphon shouted. "It's a sorcerer, not an animal. You don't have to worry."

Megesti landed a kick, sending it flying back. It transformed, and an old sorcerer hit the ground. Gray speckled his black hair, and his eyes were acorn brown. He was shorter than Fenrir and Stefan, but still muscular. He stalked toward Megesti.

Alex cracked over and grabbed her cousin, then she sent Orion flying back with a gust of wind. "Gryphon, Birch, who are these sorcerers?" she asked.

"More friends of my father," Gryphon replied.

"Why are they here?" Megesti asked.

"To ruin Lynx's bonding, apparently," Birch said. She threw her hand in the air and grew a large vine that grabbed both sorcerers and held them in place. She marched up to Fenrir and glared at him. "What are you doing in the mortal world?"

"I'm here to stop my daughter from bonding with that mutt."

"You're too late," Alex snapped. "The ceremony is over and was presided over by the future Head and Heart, so there is nothing you can do anymore."

"I can kill her," Fenrir said curtly. His stoic face moved from Alex toward Lynx. "Better dead than married to a mortal."

"Don't you dare touch her!" Stefan marched past Gryphon right up to the bound sorcerer. "She is my wife, and if you so much as look at her wrong, I will gut you, and before you think you don't need to be afraid of mortals, know that the mortals who surround the *Heart*, as you call her, are all armed with red steel."

"All of you? Well, that's an interesting development. I'm sure Garrick will be happy to learn this. What do you think, Orion?"

"I know Eris will want to know as well. She has plans for our little Heart, considering Gryphon has turned out to be such a disappointment."

Stefan stepped back from them and exchanged a nervous glance with Gryphon.

Alex stood taller. "I'm not scared of Eris. She may be powerful for an Ares and an experienced sorceress, but I'm already powerful for a Heart, and I'm not even finished getting my powers yet."

"And that, little witch, is why she wants you," Orion said. He lit up in orange light, and the vines holding him in place all snapped. Alex gasped and jerked back, bumping into Gryphon.

Orion smiled. "Don't worry, Gryphon. Even though you're a disappointment, she'll let you stick around. You're destined to be the father of the greatest sorcerer ever born, so you're needed for that part at least."

Gryphon walked up to Orion, malice in his voice when he said, "Leave now, or I'll make you regret it."

"See you soon," Fenrir said, and the two of them vanished.

Stefan rushed to Lynx and turned her face to see where she'd been struck. "Are you alright?"

"I'll be fine," she whispered.

"Let me help you," Alex said. Gryphon moved aside to let her heal Lynx's bruising face, and the badger bite on Stefan's hand.

Stefan seemed distracted by something, then finally remarked, "I couldn't help noticing they transformed with clothes on." He looked at his wife pointedly.

"I'm not experienced enough to do it," Gryphon replied. "Lynx just can't be bothered."

She scoffed. "No, it's because I usually get what I want if I'm naked afterward. And blood really stains."

Alex let out a chuckle when Stefan's mouth dropped open in shock.

"Stefan ... bugs," Alex said, making Lynx laugh, too.

Edith arrived with Randal at her side, and Lynx looked up at her, mortified. "Edith, I need to apologize! My father disrupted your special day."

"You have nothing to apologize for," she said. "I just need to know you're all unharmed."

"We're fine," Stefan said. "Confused by how quickly that was over, but fine."

"I suspect there was more to that," Alex said. She searched and found Gryphon and then Stefan, and Edith. "Where's Aaron? Where are Jessica and Michael? What if this was a distraction? What if they took them?"

"Michael took Jessica to lie down. She was tired," Edith said.

"What if they didn't make it?" Alex asked.

Gryphon held his hand out. "Come on. We'll go check on them."

"I'll come, too," Stefan said.

"No. You stay with Lynx. It's your wedding, too, Stefan," Alex said.

"We won't be long," Gryphon said.

The first place they cracked was Michael and Jessica's Datten estate. Alex burst through the door and ran from room to room calling their names. She was on the verge of panic when Michael came out of one of the upstairs bedrooms.

"What is going on?"

Alex ran down the hall and threw her arms around him and Gryphon brought him up to speed.

"Jessica's asleep. We're both fine," Michael said as Alex clung to him harder. "I was going to stay with her, but if you need me at the castle, I can come back."

"No, you stay with Jessica," Alex said.

"We have the Wafners and the sorcerers," Gryphon added.

"You sure?" Michael asked Alex when she finally released him. Alex nodded and rubbed her eyes quickly.

"Yes. Now we just have to find Aaron," Gryphon said.

"The field was full of people. He wanted to blend in, so he's probably just mixed up in there," Michael said. "He can take care of himself."

"I know."

Michael playfully pushed Alex before Gryphon cracked them to the lab.

CHAPTER 55
ALEX

"What are we doing here?" Alex asked.

"I need to find that spell—the one that finds lost things. If we adjust it, I'm sure we can get Aaron to light up."

Alex snickered. "We can get Aaron to glow?"

"Yes." Gryphon scanned the bookshelves and grabbed a book. He smirked up at Alex. "Do you have a color preference?"

"Gold, so he matches me."

"Done." Gryphon dropped the book on the table and flipped through it until he found the spell. He spun the book around to face Alex. "This is a simple one that doesn't require any ingredients. But you should be the one to cast it."

"But ... how will we get him to *stop* glowing?"

"That's why you'll do it. It's allowing *you* to find Aaron. That way, when you touch him, the spell will complete, and he'll return to normal."

"Alright." Alex took a deep breath and read the incantation. After a few unsuccessful tries, Gryphon reached over and grabbed her hand.

"Go slower. And try not to be so anxious."

Alex nodded and recited the words as carefully and clearly as she could. "Let's see if it worked."

They arrived in the field where a small crowd had gathered around a glowing figure. Alex ran as hard as she could toward it and found Megesti and Harold trying to calm Aaron. He was dressed in his armor so his gold light was reflecting off it. *Your armor. You were getting ready for the joust. No wonder you weren't here.* When Gryphon appeared, Alex whispered her gratitude.

She cleared her throat loudly and then pushed past the knights crowded around Aaron. She grasped the top of his chest plate and pulled him down to her. The moment she kissed him, his light vanished.

"What happened?" Harold asked.

"I was scared the sorcerers were a distraction and that something terrible had happened, so Gryphon helped me find him."

Aaron still looked confused, so Gryphon clarified.

"I take it you missed the excitement because you were getting ready for jousting?"

"We did," Harold replied. "Edith and Stefan were giving us the news when he started glowing. They went off to find you."

"I'm so sorry, Harold. This whole thing is a mess," Alex said.

"It's making for a unique wedding celebration," Harold smiled. "No one will ever best us."

"I'm glad you're in such good spirits about the whole thing," Alex said.

Alex felt Gryphon rub her back. "I'm going to go check on Lynx and the other sorcerers," he said. "See if they have any idea what really brought Fenrir and Orion here."

"You don't think it was to stop Lynx's wedding?" Aaron asked.

"If it were, only Fenrir would have come. Orion is my hexa's friend, but not Fenrir's. He's always been jealous of my hexa's friendship with him. When they were younger, they both wanted my grandmother. She indulged them, but it went no further, and they both blame the other to this day. So, when they show up together, it's never a good thing."

"Let us know if you learn anything," Aaron said, and Gryphon vanished. When he put his hand on her, she grabbed his arm and pulled it around her collarbone, like a protective cloak.

"We should set up for our joust," Harold said.

"You're still going to joust?" Alex asked, turning to face Aaron.

"Of course. If we let nasty sorcerers ruin our day, then they win," Harold said. "Besides, our people deserve some fun after all they've endured."

"Harold, you're a wonderful king," Alex said.

"Thank you. You're both doing wonderfully, too," he replied.

Alex kissed Aaron's cheek. "I'll have the younger knights spread the word that your joust will start shortly. The guests inside the hall likely don't even know anything happened out here."

"An advantage of having so many things happening," Harold said.

Aaron grabbed Alex's face and kissed her. "See you at the field. I brought your handkerchief." He nodded for Harold to follow him, and the two kings headed off to the match.

Alex spotted Caleb in the crowd and told him the news. He found Edith, Jerome, and Stefan. The news that the kings would joust spread quickly, and most of the guests started filing out to the jousting field. The Betruger people loved jousting as much as the Dattens did. Alex sent Edith ahead with Jerome to find seats.

"Why are we not going?" Stefan asked.

"Are you waiting for me?" Lynx asked. She grabbed Stefan's arm and kissed him on the lips.

"How does it feel to be the new Lady Wafner?" Alex asked.

Lynx wrinkled her nose. "What's that?"

"That is the title you now hold as Stefan's wife," Alex said, snickering. "Stefan, you explained the importance of rings to her, but not how titles work?"

"I covered the important parts."

"I think Jessica would disagree with you," Alex said.

"In the sorcerer world," Lynx said, "Bonding changes neither a sorcerer's name nor line. It simply allows us to have a child with that sorcerer. Until we bond, we can't have children, so it's really just for procreation."

"How practical," Stefan said.

Lynx shrugged. "We love whom we love and that doesn't change when we bond. Though in our situation, I also promise to abstain from taking any other lovers so long as we're married."

"Thank you," Stefan said. He glanced at Alex, and she had to cover her mouth to hide her laugh. On the other side of the field, the guests were getting excited about the jousting match.

"Is Aaron actually good?" Lynx asked.

"Before me, he was undefeated," Alex replied. A chill ran up her spine, and she stiffened. Alex turned to look for Daniel but gasped. "Mother?"

Victoria was standing there, wide eyed and trembling. Her chest was heaving as she fought to speak to Alex.

"Mother, what's wrong?"

"Your mother's here?" Stefan asked, but Alex waved her hand in his face to shush him.

Victoria spoke. "It was a distraction, but they weren't after Michael or Aaron."

Alex's heart stopped and the world around her ground to a halt. *Father? They went after my father!*

"Go, before it's too late!" Victoria vanished, and time caught up with Alex. Her heart made up the lost beats and she thought it would burst or maybe she'd pass out.

Stefan grabbed her shoulders, shaking her. "Alex! Look at me."

Her eyes locked onto his, and staring back at her was a terror she'd seen only a handful of times. "Get your father. Get Randal, Gryphon, and everyone. They're going after my father," she said.

"They wouldn't!" Lynx said.

Alex barely heard her. "I have to go."

"Alex, don't you dare—" Stefan's voice vanished when Alex cracked to Warren.

She missed the throne room, landing instead in the courtyard. The usually loud and busy area was silent as a grave. Filled with terror, she ran across the grass to the door that led to her and Edward's suites. She tore past her own room and threw open the door to her father's.

It was empty.

"Father!" Alex rushed to his guard's room, but it was empty, too.

"Father! Answer me!" Alex screamed, racing up the stairs to his changing area and then his bedroom. Nothing was out of place, but it felt wrong. Alex spun around the room, trying to contain her panic and not set anything on fire. The smell of fire hit her, anyway.

"Gryphon?" Alex whispered, but he didn't reply. "Daniel? What is that?"

Her ghostly guard wasn't answering her either, so she rolled up her sleeves and threw open her well just in case and ran back into the hallway. She rounded the corner to the second floor and rushed to the throne room. Her feet slammed onto the stones, filling the eerie silence with her pounding steps. Alex pushed open a door that led to the rarely used balcony that ran above the throne room and was blown back by the force of the flames.

"Gryphon!" Alex screamed, throwing her arm across her face to stop the heat from burning her face. This time he heard her and appeared beside her. His usual smirk vanished the moment arrived.

"Get your water ready," was all he said. He burst into the

maroon glow of Salem and threw open the doors. Flames shot out at them and Alex thrust her hands out, sending a wave of water into the throne room, while Gryphon spun his arms in large circles, bringing the flames escaping the room all to him. The more fire Gryphon siphoned into himself, the more Alex could move into the room. When she made it to the balcony, she screamed. The entire throne room was ablaze. The paintings of long ago were crumbling to nothing, and the tapestries that told their history had been turned to charred bits. Alex scanned the room for her father, but he wasn't there. *Where is he?* A shrill laugh echoed off the bare walls. Alex looked at Gryphon, but he was still struggling with the fire.

"Alex, no!" Gryphon shouted. Alex ignored him and cracked herself into the middle of the throne room. There, Ember stood in the blazing inferno that used to be Alex's family's most important room.

"You're too late, witch. He's ours now. It was high time your father and Garrick worked out their differences, since they both have such a vested interest in your future."

"Give me back my father," Alex said through clenched teeth. Her control was waning by the second, and Ember's wicked giggle told Alex she knew it too.

"Now why would we do that? We finally found a way to get to you and turn you into the obedient sorceress we want you to be. He'll be our *guest* as long as necessary."

"What do you want, you heartless witch?" Alex screamed.

"Temper, temper, little one. We want you to be in the Forbidden Lands using those wonderful gifts to improve our lives, not wasting them here on worthless mortals. And Gryphon's family would love to see him, too." Ember strutted through the flames to Alex. "You understand the value of family, don't you, witch? Well, now you have to choose which family matters more to you—the new one with your husband, or the old one with your father."

"I can't pick between the people I love," Alex sobbed.

"You have three days, or we'll decide for you, and you'll never see your father again. We'll see to it that even his ghost never sets foot in this world."

Alex dropped to her knees. Her heart was pounding so fast she couldn't breathe.

"Three days, Alexandria." Ember grinned and vanished.

Alex dropped her head onto the scalding hot stones that made up the throne room floor. She was filled with more rage than she could take. The walls shook so much that the few remaining portrait frames broke free and crashed to the ground in splinters. Alex pushed up her body, threw her head back and screamed so loudly that the entire roof of the hall exploded and rained down on her. Gryphon made it to her side just in time to shield her from the falling debris. Alex trembled so violently she thought her teeth would shatter. Without a word, she cracked out of the room, leaving Gryphon behind to deal with the mess. *Let him tell everyone what happened.*

Alex landed on the beach at Moorloc's castle. She dropped to her knees and screamed again. All around her, the water receded into the sea, as if the Oreean Sea was trying to protect itself from her. Her tumultuous emotions sent dark clouds across the sky and her entire body continued to glow orange, lighting up the beach around her. She closed her eyes and slammed her fists into the wet sand over and over, as if she could pound the rage she was feeling out of herself and into the earth so she could focus.

"If they do anything to him, I'll burn them to ash and make sure they feel it into the afterlife."

Need More of Torian?

If you enjoyed the book be sure to leave a review since they are a huge help to indie authors like me! They can even just be a few words that you enjoyed the book!

Join the Facebook Fan group to engage with other fans and get fun updates from Alice!
    https://www.facebook.com/groups/theheadheartandheir/

Sign up for the monthly newsletter via my website!
    alicehanov.com

Support Alice on Patreon and get early or exclusive access to things.
    patreon.com/AliceHanov

TORIAN TIMELINE

Sorcerers Arrive	No one Knows
Founding of Datten	year 0
Founding of Warren	50
Founding of six Southern Kingdoms	50-100
Merlock & Victoria arrive in Datten	1469
Megesti is born	1483
Arthur of Warren is born	1484
Gryphon is born	1488
Emmerich of Datten is born	1503
Edward of Warren is born	1510
King Emmerich is crowned King of Datten	1516
Prince Daniel of Datten is born	1522
Prince Aaron of Datten is born	1530
Princess Elizabeth of Warren (Alex) is born	1533
Princess Elizabeth vanishes	
Princess Victoria is murdered	
Prince Daniel is killed	1538
Princess Alex returns to Warren	1552
Princess Alex is taken by Moorloc	1552
Datten brings Princess Alex home	1552
Present day story	1553

KINGDOMS

DATTEN

HONOR ABODE ACC

Motto: Honor above All

Royal Family
King Emmerich (1503–)
Queen Guinevere (1504–)
Dead Prince Daniel (1521–1538)
Prince Aaron (1530–)

House of Wafner
Jerome (General of Datten) and dead Lady Gwendalin
Seven children: Patrick (Stefan), Jessica, dead Ryan, Arthur,
Samuel, Olivia, and David

House of Merlock
Merlock: royal sorcerer and king's advisor
Megesti: sorcerer apprentice and Merlock's son

DATTEN

THE FIRST KING
OF DATTEN
THE FIRST QUEEN
OF DATTEN
PRINCE DANIEL
OF WARREN
PRINCESS ELFRIEDA
32 Generations
KING DANIEL
KING ALARIC
EMMERICH
GUINEVERE
BERNHARD
STROBEL
ELFRIEDA
BISHOP
CAMERON
DANIEL
First born
AARON
Second born

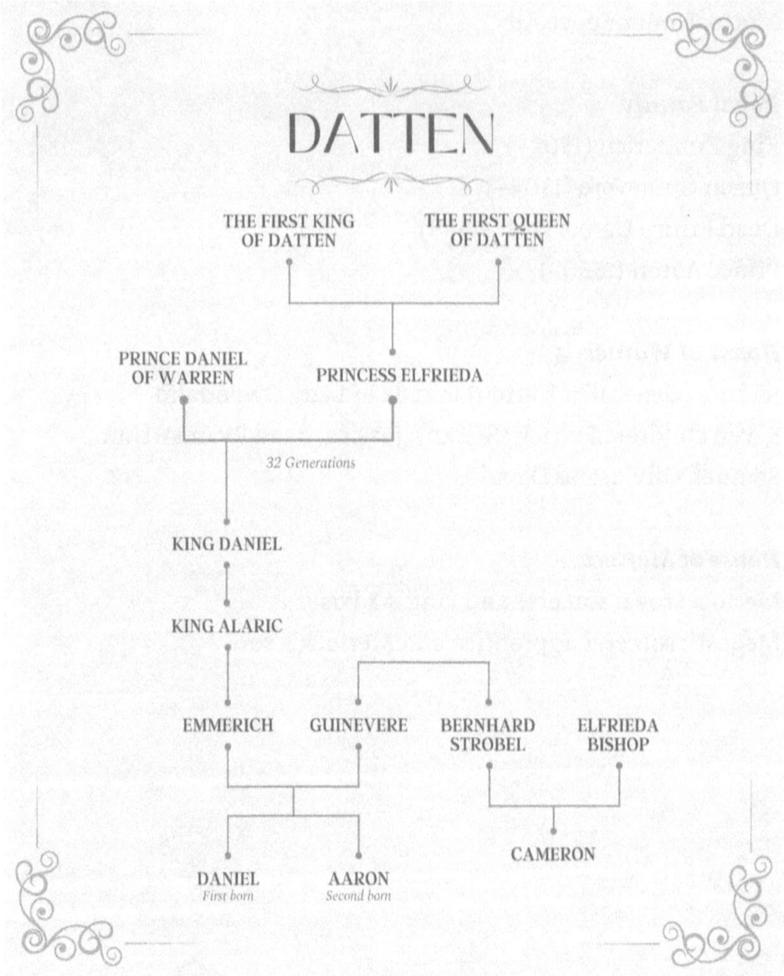

KINGDOMS
WARREN

Motto: Prosperity through Courage

Royal Family
King Edward (1509–)
Dead Princess Victoria (1451–1538)
Princess Elizabeth aka Alex (1533–)

House of Nial
Randal (General of Warren) and Lady Judith
Three daughters: Abigail, Diana, and Edith

House of Bishop
Matthew (retired general) and Lady Lillian
Three sons: Marco, Aiden, and Julius

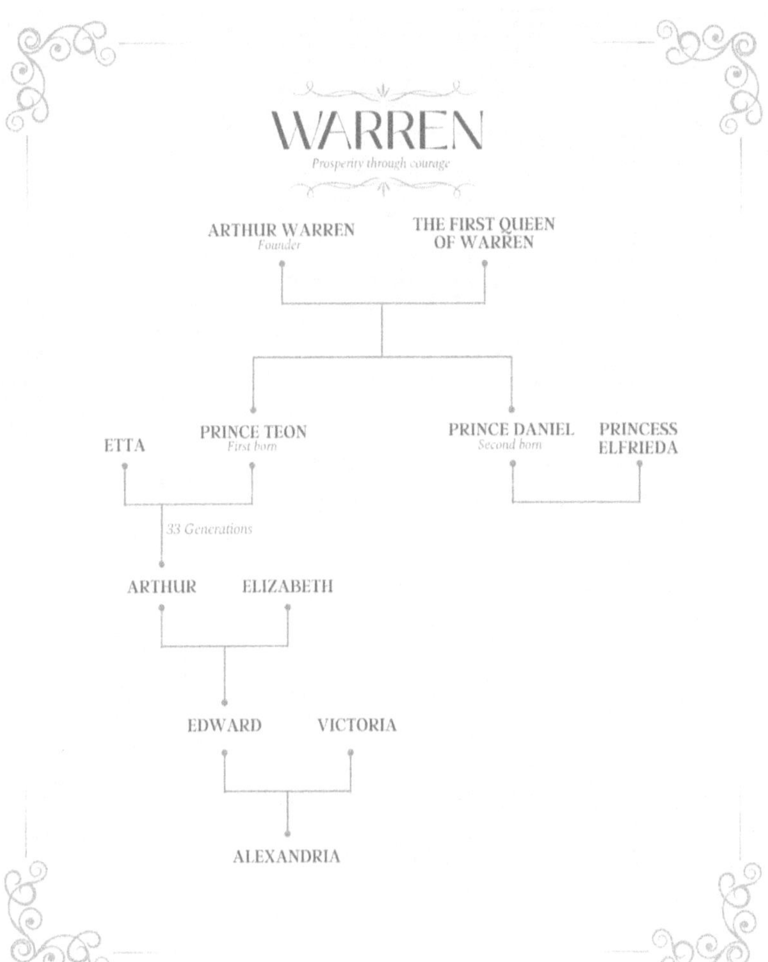

WARREN
Prosperity through courage
ARTHUR WARREN
Founder
THE FIRST QUEEN
OF WARREN
ETTA
PRINCE TEON
First born
PRINCE DANIEL
Second born
PRINCESS
ELFRIEDA
33 Generations
ARTHUR
ELIZABETH
EDWARD
VICTORIA
ALEXANDRIA

KINGDOMS
BETRUGER

LEGACY NEVER DIES

Motto: Legacy Never Dies

Royal Family
King Harold (1525–)

House of Macht
Bruno (Head Guard of Betruger)

SORCERERS OF TORIAN

TORIAN SORCERERS

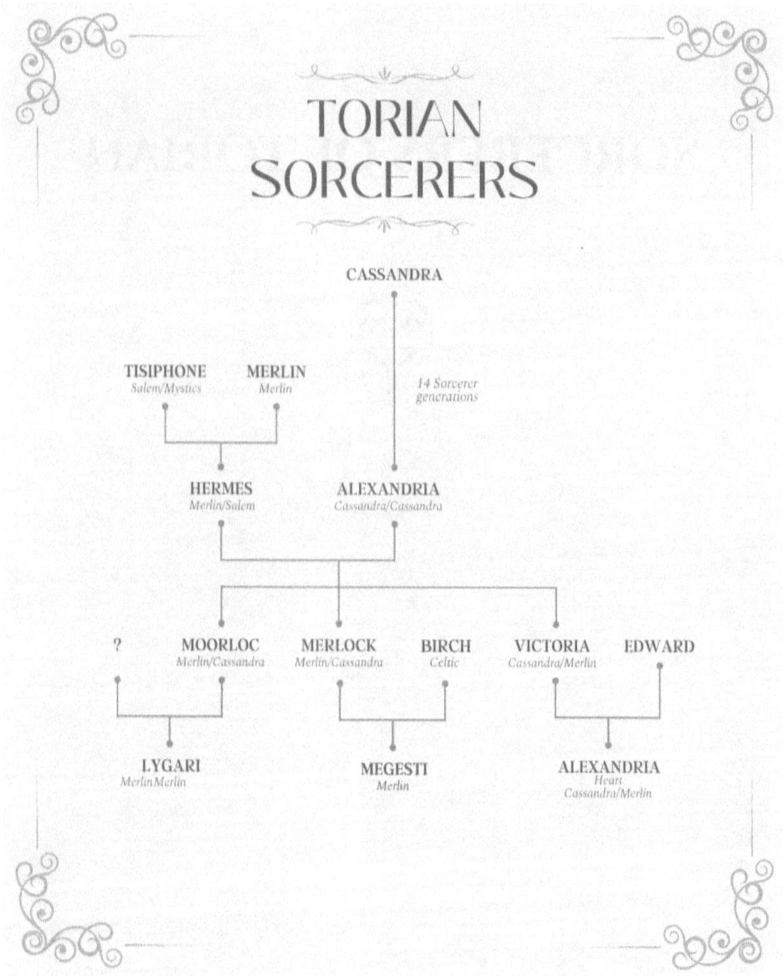

FORBIDDEN LANDS

ARES

- orange
- chaos and violence

CASSANDRA

- gold
- healing and premonitions

CELTICS

- light green
- plants and peace

HADES

- grey
- death related

MERLIN

- violet
- varies

MIRE

- brown
- earth powers

MYSTICS

- royal blue
- mind control

POSEIDON

- dark blue
- water and weather

SALEM

- maroon
- fire and explosions

TIERE

- dark green
- animal powers

HEAD

- one of two strongest born in a generation
- logic ruled

HEART

- other strongest born in a generation
- emotional ruled

PRONUNCIATION GUIDE

Ares: Air-ease

Bernhard: Burn-hart

Betruger: Beh-True-Grrrr

Cassandra: Cas-an-draw

Celtic: Kel-tick

Datten: Day-ten

Ferflucs: Fair-f-looks

Hades: Hay-dees

Lygari: Le-garh-ee

Kirsh: K-ear-sh

Kruft: K-ruff-t

Merlin: Mer-lin

Merlock: Mer-lock

Mire: Mirr-ah

Moorloc: More-lock

Mystics: Myst-ics

Nial: N-aisle

Ogre: O-grah

Oreean: Or-ian

Poseidon: Poe-sigh-done

Rassgat: Ras-gat

Salem: Say-lem

Tiere: Teer-rah

Torian: Tore-Ian

Warren: War-en

GLOSSARY

Betrayer: term used for a sorcerer who tries to kill or severely wound their own family. Appears as three x's stacked on top of each other on the left inner forearm.

Bond marks: a mark that a mated pair of sorcerers share. Each is unique, made up of their line marks, and can appear on the back of either shoulder or neck.

Hexa: sorcerer grandmother.

Hexen: sorcerer grandfather.

Line marks: images used to show the ten sorcerer lines.

Magician: insult that implies a person has no power as all human "magicians" were frauds.

Pearls: magical spheres that show the past (clear), present (white), and future (black).

Returned one: a sorcerer who dies but is brought back.

Sorcerer line: also known as a line, this is the legacy of sorcerers born from a founding sorcerer. For example, the line of Merlin includes all Merlin sorcerers born from him with Merlin powers.

Sorcerer awakening: a time in a sorcerer's life when they go through puberty and subsequently receive their powers and learn which line they are.

Sorcerer: sorcerer who identifies as male.

Sorceress: sorcerer who identifies as female.

Sorcerous: sorcerer who identifies as neither male nor female, nonbinary.

Titan: strongest sorcerer of a particular line.

Usurper: a special sorcerer born every two or three generations who can borrow or siphon the power of sorcerers around them. Only one can ever be alive at a time.

Witch: insult that implies a person has no power as all human "witches" were frauds.

SERIES LIST

The Spare Who Became the Heir and Other Stories

The Head, the Heart, and the Heir

Broken Sons

The Heir Rises

The Last True Heirs

Revenge of the Forbidden Lands

Book 6 - coming 2025

Book 7 - coming 2025/2026

Extended Omnibus Kickstarter

Volume 1 - May 2024

Volume 2 - February 2025

Volume 3 - late 2025/early 2026

A Note from the Author

When I started writing this series, I was intending to write a YA epic fantasy, but my characters had other ideas.

The themes and tropes that are developing as the story carries on, especially book 3 and on are of a much more adult level than originally expected. So in order to be true to the characters and meet reader expectations I'm aging everyone up 2 years.

So if you read this before March 15, 2024 the characters would have been younger than they are in this edition. A detailed breakdown is on my website if you need to visually see what happened.

Thank you for your understanding.

Acknowledgments

ALWAYS first. Thank you to my husband, Steve, and my children, Lillian, Katrina, and Zack. They believe in me, love my characters, and give up time with me to write my books.

To my mom, Elke, and stepdad, Al, thank you for supporting all my crazy dreams.

My amazing friend **Andrea** who is always there for me and gives me the best ideas and lets me ramble at her until I figure things out. I love you more than you know! And her cat is a lovely purrball.

To my amazeball friend **Brittany** you are AMAZING and I can't thank you enough for taking on my crazy.

To my amazing online BookTok and Bookstagram friends, thank you for bringing a smile to my face and giving me a safe place to vent and talk books and cry when I needed. To my fantastic author friends I found online—you are shining lights in my dark days. Killian, Nikki, Sonja, Rosalyn, Laura, Bekah, and countless more—you all make writing so much more enjoyable!

To my ferflucsing photographer, and FRIEND **Brittany Nosal** —I hate the way I look in photos, but you made the entire process painless and, more importantly, made me feel beautiful and gave me photos I love and can use knowing they captured the real me in all my happy, loving craziness! You are the best.

My editors are the bomb! **Sam,** my amazing developmental editor! You love my characters a much as I do and I know they are always safe in your hands! **S. E.,** I can't thank you enough for keeping me on track and keeping things rolling. You are so easy to talk to you and I value you so much. **Jaime** my amazing copy editor! Thank you for helping me keep things consistent and making sure people can read my words.

To my cover designers, **Alan and Ian**—I cannot thank you enough for making magic again! I love my covers.

ABOUT THE AUTHOR

Photo by Brittany Jean Photography

Alice Hanov was born in Germany and then raised on Pelee Island in the middle of one of the Great Lakes, spending her days imagining grand adventures in the woods around the island. She has never stopped writing and has a degree in rhetoric and professional writing from the University of Waterloo. Alice lives in Ontario with her hubby and three kids, various pets, and many, many books.

You can visit her online at alicehanov.com.

www.ingramcontent.com/pod-product-compliance
Lightning Source LLC
Chambersburg PA
CBHW020345010826
48973CB00005B/1283